HAZARDING

❧ HEARTS ❧

by

J.D. HARRISON

Cover Photography copyright © 2019 Magnus Hargis
Cover Design copyright © 2019 Shoshanah Holl
The Fell Types used on the cover and interior
are digitally reproduced by Igino Marini
www.iginomarini.com

Author may be contacted at: j.d.harrison.author@gmail.com

ISBN: 9781081739904

Self Published via
Amazon Direct Publishing

To Dreams

May they be big and small, wild and tame,
achievable and unlikely. May they never, ever stop.

Risks must be taken because the greatest hazard in life is to risk nothing."
— Leo Buscaglia

Aaron

I usually loved to fly. Taking off in an airplane hit my nervous system with the same tingling anticipation that came from launching into the jousting lyst or flooring the gas pedal in a muscle car. Gravity pulls on your body, your muscles strive to hold still against the intensity, and there's that wild moment where your life or death seems to hang on the edge of a razor blade. One breath later, everything smoothes out like glass, and the world falls away.

But not this time. For once in my life, I was too tired and too fixed on my destination to immerse myself in the experience. Nervous excitement over who waited on the other end of this flight did a great job dividing my attention from the physical discomfort left after three days of tournament level jousting.

The first leg of my journey, I nodded off, trying to make up for the lack of rest over the weekend. After two nights back at Bart's family's ranch, Haven, the bruises and strains had only settled in deeper. Nor had I slept as much as I should have. Hell, I'd hardly been able to close my eyes the night before, so sleeping had definitely been the best way to pass the time from San Francisco to Denver.

After the adrenaline rush of running through the huge terminal to catch my next flight, I couldn't rest anymore. With hours of sitting still to go, and little to occupy myself except for thoughts of where I was headed, I could hardly keep still. My leg bounced restlessly beneath the tray table, jiggling my empty beer bottle. That earned a glare from the well-heeled businessman beside me. I attempted to quell it. Again.

A few seats back, someone wore an ungodly amount of perfume, which made the close confines of the plane seem even tighter. Pressing the overhead button to call for a flight attendant, I closed my eyes, trying to relax.

"May I help you sir?" The woman leaned over me with warm concern and if I were to guess, a bit of awareness. Leggy, and busty, with a clean lined frame I typically enjoyed in my sexual partners. And I felt not a damn thing for her aside from gratitude for her prompt response.

"Yes ma'am, may I have another beer?" I gave her a warm smile and my credit card, watching her sashay back up the aisle just to test my disinterest. Nope, not so much as a twitch, above or below the belt.

I nursed that beer for another hour, looking at my phone for the hundredth time. Jaqueline Sauveterre's picture filled the screen. Her sweet smile, the happiness in her eyes, and even the feathery edge of black and purple hair brushing her cheek started a warmth that wrapped around my heart. Memories played behind my eyes, a better buffer for my restlessness than any alcohol I'd ever had.

For two years, she and I barely spoke beyond our business arrangement for her carriage company to lease the spare draft horses that belonged to my younger brother and I's jousting troupe. But watching said younger brother, Bart, fall in love, seeing him so fulfilled and content, created an itch no amount of random hookups could touch. It didn't help that Bart and his now fiancée Josephine, shared an apartment with me. That Jo was also a jouster, who traveled with us on the road, only rubbed salt in the wound left by my dissatisfaction.

When Jaque picked up the horses shortly before Thanksgiving this year, I had been antsy, which I attributed to all the changes going on with Bart and Jo. As a creature of habit, the risks involved in their relationship left me mentally chewing holes in everything. But halfway through the holiday season, the truck Jaque used to haul for her commercial carriage jobs broke down, and I offered to help fix it. One late night drive to pick up her trailer and get everything home, then a few days in her yard, replacing the water pump, revealed much more to Jaque than met the eye.

Usually, I didn't like company while I worked, but she provided a quiet source of calm. And I still smiled every time I thought of catching her in fleece pajamas and a pair of muck boots as she headed out to feed that first morning. She hadn't expected me to pop out from under her truck, and the defiant lift of her chin even as she blushed and kept walking had been both charming and sexy as hell. Jaque's sassy, determined march, her curvy hips covered in cartoon figures, beat out the flight attendant's practiced slink a thousand to one.

Just after Christmas, when she returned the borrowed horses and tried to pay me for the labor on the truck, I refused. Hell, even if I hadn't harbored a curious awareness of her as a woman, I would have turned it down. I'd been in similar shoes enough times as the jousting company experienced growing pains, and the kindness of friends and strangers had seen me through. The least I could do was pay that goodwill forward. Instead, I sucked up my courage and asked her to dinner, sure she would turn me down. After all, she'd gotten what she needed from me, and had no reason to speak to me again until the next holiday season.

She agreed, not understanding how badly I needed a friend that night. Fresh from the holiday at my mother's house, my emotions were in shambles. With Bart and Jo off at her parents' place for another few days, I didn't want to be alone. It had been difficult to know how to treat her when we'd always just been acquaintances, but I hadn't expected to pick my jaw up off the floor when she answered her door either.

In a deep purple dress that made her black hair look even darker, she had transformed entirely from the working woman I had always known. The strappy heels she wore made her legs look miles long and put her sweet chocolate brown eyes close enough to my own that I could see flecks of honey. I went from zero to horny in less than a breath, but I respected her too much to hand her one of my usual canned compliments. She deserved far better.

We went to dinner at my favorite barbeque joint, and I had fumbled conversation, pointedly avoiding stupid come-ons and meaningless flirtations. I barely remembered what we ate, I'd been so disconnected from my own body, too emotionally exhausted and physically overwhelmed. But somehow, she read me like a book, and after dinner, she suggested we try putt-putt golf. I worried about the cold night with her dressed so nicely, but she laughed it off.

"Being from Canada, I am quite cold tolerant," She slanted a grin at me that I could not leave unanswered. "Though if you would like to use it as an excuse to put your arm around me, I would enjoy it a good deal."

She played in her bare feet, giving off a refreshing innocence that wasn't the least contrived. The laughter as we worked our way around the fairy tale themed track healed the fissures left from the holidays. My sense of humor creaked with disuse, but by the final hole I laughed wholeheartedly and scooped her up in a hug of congratulations. We fit against each other seamlessly, and when I set her back down it felt like peeling away a layer of myself.

On the drive back to her place, I'd never been more scared or more at peace. I didn't want our time to end, but I also didn't want to just take her to bed either. Okay, that was a lie. I wanted to take her to bed so badly that my whole body throbbed. But I couldn't cheapen her that way.

I handed her down from the truck, listening to her little Sheltie dog bark its head off as if I were an axe murderer, and thanked her for a marvelous evening. Then, my arms were full of warm, glorious woman, as she leaned against me and tugged me down for a kiss. Jaqueline obliterated me where I stood from the first touch of her lips on mine. My hands buried themselves in her hair, anchoring me from blowing away in a hurricane of desire.

The ding of the seat belt light broke into my memories and the pilot's voice informed us we were making our approach into Charleston. Politely thanking the attendant as I handed her my empties, I put my tray table up and ignored the guy next to me as he started shoving things in his bag to get ready to land. I was too busy remembering the way Jaque whispered my name as I settled her back on her feet. I missed the way it rolled off her tongue like some exotic flavor, and I hoped I'd hear it again soon. Her being gone for two months had been too long. Listening to her say my name over the phone could never substitute for feeling her breathe it across my lips.

Jaque

This was foolish. So very foolish. But that did not stop me from pressing fingers against my tingling lips, smiling as I slowly paced back and forth beside the baggage claim. Aaron texted as soon as the plane landed, and my heart buzzed like I had consumed ten espresso shots instead of the two in my mocha. Only three minutes had passed, not even enough time for them to taxi to the gate, but it felt like twenty. For all I knew, my expectations of his visit were set too high. He might not wish to renew his acquaintance with my lips, after all. The singular time we even mentioned our kisses, he apologized for them. Despite the wound left on my confidence from that needless apology, I mentally shook myself. Kissing him had been glorious, and I could not wait to obliterate his regret with a fresh memory of how good we were together.

He had earned my kisses and then some over the last several months. Despite the several hour time difference, he had taken time to call every day. Listening to me vent about the Dutch trainer who had insulted my mare, Lyric, and sharing his recent travels had closed the distance between us. Nothing had ever felt so intimate as lying in the darkness, listening to him speak.

Anyone with a pulse would consider Aaron handsome, but from the first time I spoke to him on the phone, I had been wooed by the sound of his voice. He spoke clearly, precisely, with surprisingly clipped diction for a traveling entertainer. I had been impressed, not just by his high drive in business, but by the quality of his horses. They were very trainable, adaptable, and friendly, which made it even easier to appreciate their owner. But I never entertained more than a fancy for him over the years. A man of his quality had too many women to choose from to even see me. Even with the purple highlights in my hair, I was easy to overlook. I simply did not put myself out there. I played the part of invisible on purpose.

Something had been different this last season though. His behaviour seemed sharp edged with worry, and I struggled with the urge to soothe it, as I never coped well with other people's pain. And Josephine, Bart's girlfriend, had been so warm with him, letting me see the other side of his carefulness. While he repaired my truck, I teetered on the edge of asking him out, but the pajama incident pricked a hole in my pride. Then, just as I began preparations for heading south, he asked me. My practical side said no, but a yes leapt from my mouth like a racehorse leaving the starting gate.

After the soul-wrenching kiss at the end of our date, stepping back proved difficult. My body screamed that I should drag him inside and have my way with him. Repeatedly. But I needed to be honest, if only for myself.

"Aaron, I must tell you, I leave next week for Florida, to train and compete. Lyric and I are aiming for the Championships, and I must give this my full attention." Still, nothing could stop my fingers tracing his muscular torso, my hands sliding inside his open jacket. Who knew when I would be able to take such liberties again? "I pray you will forgive me. I do not mean to lead you on."

Though he made every effort to remain polite and kind, I felt the passion between us shift. The tension in him no longer strained closer but prepared to leap away. "No, I understand." His smile appeared forced and I wanted so badly to kiss his lips back to softness. "That's usually my line, you know. Thanks, I had a nice time, but I'm leaving tomorrow."

His honesty about how he lived was meant to push me away, I could tell, but his body language said otherwise. The hand settled on my waist remained firm and held me still. The one that stroked my cheek almost brought me to tears. When it fell away, I snatched it with my own, sandwiching it between my palms before pressing the threaded weight to my sternum. "Then allow me to follow in that line. I ask no commitments of you, but should you care to try this again when I return, I would be delighted."

We parted company with a much more chaste kiss, and for the first time in years, a shadow of regret marked my departure for Florida. His first text shortly after I arrived in Ocala, no more than a generic hope that my trip had gone well, prompted me to brighter hopes. Before long, texting him became a daily habit, and soon we were calling each other, even if just to say goodnight.

Once, we stayed up all night, watching the sun set and rise together. I shared my competitive dreams with him, told him of my family in Quebec, the Percherons I grew up with. He revealed a hundred memories of his own, though any family beyond his brother were absent from most of them. In saying nothing, he said enough, and while I would never press for more, I prayed that someday he would share everything.

Rubbing the goosebumps moving over my arms, I frowned as the baggage carousel began to divulge bags, though Aaron had yet to appear. But my worry melted away at the sound of his voice behind me, a raw silk texture reaching through my ears to caress my heart.

"Jaqueline." Any hope I might have had of behaving like a grown woman disappeared, and I swung around to drink in the sight of him like I might die of thirst. As he studied me in return, I needlessly tugged on the hem of my blouse. He smiled at the small fidget, a sign of humour that I welcomed like a drought-stricken crop eager for rain. But he looked as nervous as I felt, shifting from one foot to the other as if he did not know how to proceed. "It's good to see you."

"You as well." Something in the quirk of his lips made me risk a little more, taking a step closer. "Though if you do not mind, I should rather feel you."

He dropped his small bag to the ground in answer, and opened his arms, a longing in his dark sapphire eyes that echoed the deepest parts of my heart. Throwing caution to the wind, much as I the last time I saw him, I flung myself against him with a less than attractive desperation. Despite that, he gathered me close, and I buried my nose in his sweater. The fine wool felt warm with the heat of his body, and I breathed deeply, greedy for more proof that he truly stood in my arms. He smelled of fresh laundry, with a woody undertone of cologne and the faintest hint of the horses he left behind in California. Perfectly lovely.

"Is it foolish to have missed you so much when I've only held you once, Jaqueline?" His thumb and forefinger stroked my shoulder blade, soothing and invigorating all at once.

"Yes, completely. But then, we are both fools, perhaps, and good company for each other."

His silent chuckle felt like another sort of embrace, and I tightened my arms around his waist despite the inner voice that complained my actions were too forward. The need to be close, to touch, had ended most of my relationships and we barely knew each other. This was too soon. I stepped back, not wanting to chase him away by clinging, and distracted myself with something safer.

"Come, surely you have a bag to grab? I should like to hurry as the parking fees here are steep."

Shadows I wished I understood clouded his eyes, something much lonelier than the connection that I longed for.

"Yes, sorry, I don't mean to inconvenience you." He hastily shouldered his messenger bag, creating a barrier against further closeness, and I deemed it for the best. Already he withdrew from my touch. The baggage from his flight had arrived while we greeted each other, and he quickly scooped a large duffel from the carousel before turning toward me with a brittle smile. "Lead on, my lady."

We fell in beside each other, his casual strides easy to match though my legs were shorter. My hands itched to thread themselves through his arm, to be close again, but I restrained the urge. Maybe in time. I would not rush, too afraid I might push him away by drawing him closer. As I once told Jo, my relationships in the past had all been fraught with passion but burned out too quickly. With Aaron, I would prefer to linger in the warmth as long as he would let me.

Once we were in the truck, he offered to pay my parking fees, but I denied him the opportunity. The few dollars were a small price to pay for his company, not when he had come so far. Surely, he had better things to do than rerouting his travels to see me. We felt too far apart as I wound my way through traffic, so I attempted to close the distance with conversation. "Tell me, how are Bart and Jo? And the horses? Are they traveling well?"

"Mmm, yes, Jo texted while I was on the plane. They're making good time, probably about two hours outside of their layover spot. It helps, being able to swap out drivers." He ruffled his wild hair for the fourth time since climbing in the truck, and I wanted to steal that hand, keep it still. The nervous energy made me worry. "If you ever need help driving cross country, I'd be happy to help."

My heart stuttered, and I marveled again at the good fortune to have found an experienced horseman. So many of my boyfriends had been intimidated by or jealous of the horses, leaving me caught between two different loves. Aaron left me undivided for only the second time, and I smiled through the welcome sensation of wholeness. "We shall see. After all, it is one thing to trust you with me, and another thing entirely to trust you with my Lyric."

He smirked, a cocky tilt to his mouth that made my stomach flip erratically. "Well, it's nice to know you trust me at least that much. I'll have to see what I can do about the second part."

Despite the flush on my face, I kept my eyes on the traffic—most people felt the need to cut off a large truck, as if we were able to stop on a dime, and it was always worse around cities. "Time, I think, would serve that best. I am grateful you could take time to come see me at all."

"It is enough to have earned me another kiss?" he asked, the husky rasp in the words rubbing over my heart like a caress.

Suddenly flushed all over, I felt tempted to swerve the truck into the median and climb across the console to answer him. But I needed to get back to the showgrounds so Lyric could get out of her stall for a nice walk. "If you can be patient, yes. Much as I wish I could give you my undivided attention, I must be a competitor first. I appreciate you coming to see me, but..."

A quick shake of his head in my peripheral vision stopped the nervous flow of words. "Jaqueline, please, I know I'm nothing but an inconvenience this weekend. But I'm determined to be helpful if you will allow it. I'm a good stall mucker and can fetch and carry with the best of them. All I wanted was to see you, and the chance to watch you perform. Anything else is icing on the cake."

Oh, my heavens. He was setting himself up for far more than he bargained for. "No, you are a guest, I cannot take advantage. As well, I have no desire to run you off with my bossiness. I am a far different creature when it comes to my work, and I do not wish to risk these new feelings between us to such high pressure."

"Jaque," The soft treatment he gave my name imparted a feminine flare that had my foot easing up on the gas pedal, so I had enough time to look over at him. The emotions in his eyes were deep enough to swim in, and I regretted having to look away. "Don't spare me. I'm relieved to hear you feel this too. But I'd rather risk those feelings now, than to wait until later, when they'll be ingrained." Then he chuckled again, a plush velvet sound that tempted me to dark and warm imaginings. "Besides, as crass as it sounds, I'm hoping someday you'll take advantage of me in more ways than one."

The urge to close my eyes and let my forehead rest on the steering wheel was intense, and I forced myself to settle for a sigh. "Sooner, rather than later, if I have anything to say about it." I answered, the muscles of my stomach tight with the weight of want. He went still, like a falcon on a cliff studying his prey at a distance, and I swallowed my foolishness. "I am sorry; I do not mean to tease."

"Don't apologize." There was an air of command in the tone that helped my heart relax, even as my body wound tighter. "I should apologize for being so forward."

But then anger ribboned through the warmth I basked in, and I frowned. "You must not apologize either. I spent months thinking you regretted our kiss, that I came on too strongly, all because you apologized. I will tell you if you are unwelcome, if what you say or do bothers me." I curled my hands around the steering wheel, then willed my body to relax as traffic thickened for the afternoon commute. With miles to go before our turn off, it would not do to let my emotions affect my driving. "Be yourself, Aaron. I too would rather know if this thing between us is made of spun sugar, sweet but quickly consumed."

Quiet lingered for quite some time. Had I already done the work of pushing him away? My temper, while difficult to raise, tended to burn too hot. I had not meant to blister him. Still, the busy commuters around us took away the leisure to look over at him, and not until we were exiting the freeway did he break the silence.

"How far away is the hotel?"

I glanced at the GPS, concerned that he wanted to get away from me. Already, I had ruined things. "Ten miles, I believe. Why?"

"Because I'm an impatient bastard, and I don't know if I can wait to kiss you until tonight. Maybe I can sneak one in after I get my bags dropped off."

Relief made my bones watery at the same time heat cascaded down my spine, and I hunted the road ahead for a place to pull off, not certain I could resist temptation that long. A wide shoulder appeared, and I carefully parked the truck, purposefully setting the brake so I could give him my full attention. Traffic zoomed by, but I could not hear any of it around the sound of my own pulse, the way it galloped beneath my skin as our eyes met. "I think it best to give me that kiss now, before I expire of wanting and cause a wreck."

He leaned over the centre console and I moved in to meet him. "Smart woman, safety first." Careful fingertips traced my jaw as his gaze dropped to my lips. Reflexively, I licked the bottom one, as it burned so hungrily for his touch.

"And bossy. Do not forget bossy." Melting with desire for one singular kiss, I impatiently tangled a hand in his wild hair, intending to haul him the last inch closer. But his slow smile caressed me as he did the same with my hair, palm cupping the back of my skull.

"No, I couldn't forget, Jaqueline. In fact, I'm looking forward to you telling me exactly how to please you."

Panting at the coruscating whirlwind he caused in my chest, I forced out the next words. "Then stop speaking and kiss me, Aaron, before I change my mind."

A flare of light in his eyes blinded me even before my lashes fell closed. He stole everything from me but the ability to feel. His lips were soft yet demanding, and I answered every command, my fist tight in his hair. The kiss felt like everything, yet not enough, satisfying one hunger and setting off a thousand more. Our lips parted at almost the same moment, and we tasted each other's mouths, desire roiling like a storm cloud heavy with rain.

Aaron

Base instinct set its claws in me, eviscerating reason without mercy. Every soft whimper or throaty groan I swallowed fed the desire to lose myself in her, with an intensity I couldn't see my way around. All from a kiss, from the most luscious lips I'd ever tasted. As I drew a breath, hoping for control, I got lost again. Beyond the earthy scent of horses, she smelled like the caress of a warm wind and the silver of clouds, like a flower that bloomed at midnight. I'd have kissed her forever, relishing her grip in my hair, if not for a car that zoomed past, blaring its horn. Only the knowledge I cheapened her, kept her from her responsibilities, made me soften, begin to pull away.

"Now that was worth waiting months for," I murmured, stroking her cheek with my knuckles, intrigued by the storm in her dark eyes as she smiled.

"If you would give me three hours, perhaps we can resume that train of thought after dinner? Provided you are willing?"

I blinked several times to hold back the want rearing and bucking in my gut like Byzantine with a full head of steam. "If I'm willing? Jaque, I've never been more willing in all my life."

She rewarded my confession with another kiss, though wisely, this one landed on my cheek, a spark of lightning less likely to consume me. "Then let us get on with our responsibilities, Aaron. The needs of my mare shall have to come before my own desires."

Once settled back on the opposite side of the truck, she secured her safety belt with a girlish smile that I found as alluring as her more stormy expressions. As she piloted the big diesel back onto the road, I stared into the distance, for once content to let silence fill the air.

At the hotel, not wanting to delay Jaque anymore than I already had, I ran in the office just long enough to check in and get a room key. When I reemerged, she was typing furiously on her phone, a scowl darkening her expression.

"Something wrong?" As I climbed back in the truck, she looked up, the drawn lines between her brows shallowing as she mustered a smile.

"Hmm, a minor inconvenience. My usual assistant is delayed in her travels. Work difficulties. Are you ready to go?"

I clicked my belt back into place and turned to face her. "I'm all yours."

Good Lord, the play of emotions on her face fascinated me. A cat-like smile of mystery overtook her lips as her lashes slowly fell and her throat flushed, but I found nothing shy about the way she met my eyes.

"I surely hope so." Smoky and dark, her voice reached right inside my chest and squeezed my heart, tightening its fist around my innards. She could gut me with a few words, and the sensation was hellishly frightening. After a lifetime of having to be strong, vulnerability wasn't something I did well with.

At the showgrounds, she led me into a huge tent set up as a temporary barn, the inside lined with stalls. Horses of all shapes and colors filled them, from a pair of pinto miniature horses only slightly taller than my knee to a sun faded black Percheron that could rival my own in size. Near the middle of the tent Jaque slowed and whistled one note, answered by a guttural nicker from the other end of the aisle that made her smile.

"Ah, she is awake then. Lovely. Sometimes she naps in the afternoons."

The stall she stopped in front of contained a glossy black mare I'd only met once before when Jaque had given me the nickel tour of her farm in Kentucky. Her neatly trimmed mane lay closely along her muscular neck, unlike the naturally kept jousting horses, though her thick forelock half concealed a crescent shaped white mark. She greeted Jaque with enthusiasm, snuffling as if to inspect her human, and Jaque melted into her in a way I wish I understood. Even my old jousting horse, Argo, never would have welcomed such affection.

"How is *ma fille*? I see you took a nap."

Jaque brushed shavings from the thin cotton sheet the mare wore before unbuckling it and sliding it off over the haunches. Though the jousting horses were all slick with good health, Lyric outshone them, her short coat displaying faint dapples that I knew would catch light in the sun. When Jaque turned back toward the door, she startled, a hand flying up to cover the surprised O of her mouth.

"Oh, Aaron, I did not make you comfortable. My apologies. Lyric makes me forget myself."

"No apologies, remember?" I took the sheet from her fingers and lifted a halter from the hook by the door to offer instead. "Take care of your horse. I'm a big boy, I'll be okay."

She fidgeted with the buckle of the halter after accepting it, her eyes flitting between the mare and I. Wishing I knew how to calm her nervousness, I waited, smiling when the mare bumped her elbow as if to hurry her along.

"Yes, *mon tresor*, give me a moment." Jaqueline absently stroked the mare's withers as she sorted me out, pointing to a neighboring stall. "That area is also mine. There are chairs, and water in the cooler, if you would like to wait? We shall not take long."

While I had no intention of sitting around, I nodded and smiled reassuringly. "I'll be fine. But don't rush on my account. You're worth waiting for."

In a blink, she stepped in close, the eyes lifted to mine glittering with promise. "I believe we have waited long enough, Aaron."

Pulling me down by my collar, she pressed a fierce kiss to my lips that tested my self-control, but just as quickly, she returned her attention to the mare. The two of them sashayed down the aisle moments later, their shadows burned into my eyes by the sunshine outside, and I had to shake myself to get moving again. Needing something to do, anything to drown out the storm in my gut, I folded the sheet and then located the tools to clean the stall. While not my favored chore, the familiarity let me relax, even as my brain reminded me that I couldn't trust her not to hurt me. My heart argued the risk would be worth it.

Jaque

Lyric and I walked the length and breadth of the stabling area, stopping occasionally so she could crop the grass. As we wandered further away from the hustle and bustle of the barns, I found Sue, a lovely woman I knew from numerous clinics and shows. Blonde and tan, she employed a ready smile that invited friendship from the first moment we met. We were both independent women who loved their mares, her Rhapsody an elegant Morgan with doe-like eyes, and my Lyric, a graceful Canadien with demure power.

Neither Sue nor I would ever be on the cover of a fashion magazine, our bodies shaped by our work, our skin marked by sun and weather. But passion came through in everything we did, which made for a deeper beauty than any makeup could impart. Besides, how could I not be friends with a woman who also had a mare with a musical name?

"Ladies, how are you this afternoon?"

"Doing well, though Rhapsody is making the Dutch stallion the next aisle over a little crazy. Flirt," Sue answered, though she patted the mare's mahogany neck with unmistakable fondness.

I gave Lyric an extra pet, grateful for her usual disinterest in the male of her species. But with hope flaring in my heart that Aaron and I might make a lasting connection, I found myself dreaming of the day we would find a stallion befitting my mare. Just as I had welcomed Lyric into the world, I once dreamed the same for her foals. Other goals distracted me from that vision for many years, but now, my heart panged with longing for that future.

Still, as Sue and I discussed the coming competition, sharing strategies and encouragements, I felt no rush to turn my lovely partner into a mama just yet. The polished black pearl of her coat stretched over strong joints, muscles curving in arcs of potential power. She and I had challenges yet to face in the competitive arena.

Sue lingered for a few more minutes before saying goodbye, which tempted me to forego the rest of the time I allotted to Lyric. Usually, I stayed out for over an hour, but I wanted to jog all the way back to the barn and kiss Aaron again. Which made it absolutely imperative that I take my time, to linger with my mare as we stood in the golden glow that hinted at the coming of spring. I wanted to rush, which meant I needed to slow down.

We meandered purposefully, killing an hour of time, though it hardly made up for Lyric being deprived of the freedom of actual turnout. At home, she lived in the pasture most of the time, and even in Florida, I made sure she went out all night. Only the heat of midday chased us inside, the sunshine a threat to her black coat, the heat more intense than either of us enjoyed.

When we finally turned toward the barn, my preoccupation with Aaron showed itself most clearly, otherwise I might have noticed our route carried me past enemy territory.

"Careful, pet, don't get close to such a common workhorse." Maarten van den Berg's thick Dutch accent grated on me, but I refused to look his way.

Still, the way his student stepped back as if Lyric might sully the warmblood he led made my ears burn. The monstrously sized chestnut snorted as if alarmed, and I tried not to judge the creature for his behaviour. Most of it could be laid at the feet of his trainer, after all. Horses mirrored their drivers, and this driver appeared to mirror the former world champion's superior attitude. Not a reflection you would think anyone would want to emulate.

At my ex-boyfriend's endorsement, I had paid good money to attend a clinic of van den Berg's shortly after my arrival in January. When van den Berg patronized my choice of horse, and talked down to me for it, I immediately raised a complaint over the discrimination and received my money back. But since then, all of van den Berg's coattail hangers disparaged me at every available opportunity.

I had built up quite the head of steam by the time we reached our own stall. When I stomped in to let Lyric go it took several deep breaths before my brain could register anything past the frustration clouding my senses.

More than anything in the world, I hated people who judged others based on their exterior. As a Canadian Horse, or Le Cheval Canadien, Lyric did not have the long limbs or springy loft of most horses competing in Advanced level combined driving. But in people and horses, the one thing I valued more than anything else remained the quality of their heart. She possessed more heart than a thousand finely limbed horses and had proven it to me time and again.

"Jaqueline," I spun on my heel, putting a hand on Lyric's shoulder to steady myself as adrenaline made my head swim. Aaron stood in the doorway, concern in his ocean dark eyes and sweat making his long sleeve t-shirt stick to his well-defined pectorals. "You okay?"

Oh, I would be, if only he could hold me for a few moments. Yet, I could not be that needy, not so soon. Wanting this to last as long as possible, I knew being clingy would end things before they barely began. So, I struggled to smile, and patted my mare on the neck as she picked at her hay net—which had been empty when we left and was now full. Eyes wide, I looked around, taking in the cleaned bedding. Her water buckets had been scrubbed and filled. Her sheet lay folded neatly over the stall wall. When I looked back to the man responsible, I hardly knew what to say. In the end, I went with what seemed simplest.

"I am now. Thank you for this."

His arms folded across his magnificent chest and he smiled, though I detected a bit of hesitation. "Hopefully I did everything up to snuff. If anything is wrong, let me know how you'd like it done in the future. I catch on fast."

My eyes betrayed me, flickering over everything, double checking the work. He even hung the hay net the same way I had, tightly attached to the corner so it could not get underfoot. I often used the dense mesh to make up balls of hay the horses could eat from the ground, but when horses wore shoes for competition, they could easily become tangled. The only thing that still needed to be done was adding a new bag of shavings. When I finally looked to him again, he seemed to have shrunk in on himself.

"This is perfect. And completely unexpected. That you would even think to do this for me, I hardly know how to thank you."

His eyes lit, an innocent sort of wonder filling them. The dichotomy both fascinated and horrified me. What could put such doubt in a man who seemed so outwardly confident? A man not only gorgeous, but courageous in the way he chased his dreams and shook hands with Fear. But then his eyes hooded, and I lost my thoughts as he stepped closer to run his hands down my arms. "In your case, I could be persuaded to work for kisses."

"Then take whatever you think your efforts are worth, Aaron," Tipping my chin up to welcome the kiss, I finally allowed myself to touch him. Muscles in his stomach clenched beneath my fingertips, even as he leaned in closer. "Because that is a price I will gladly pay."

I expected him to envelop me, to sweep me off my feet, but what I received made me dizzy with emotion. The kiss he gave moved slowly, gently trapping my lower lip as he slicked his tongue over it. A needy moan escaped as he skated his teeth over the sensitized skin, our bodies still too far apart to satisfy me, but I felt a chuckle that vibrated through us both.

"Greedy woman," he teased, whispering into my mouth, and God help me, I froze. Had I already slipped too far? "Jaqueline, I don't want you to take this the wrong way, but I want to kiss you until I can't breathe. Perhaps we'd better negotiate a trade when we don't have an audience."

"What?" The words he uttered muddled my brain, but when they registered, I spun around, expecting to find a barn full of people. Instead, I found Lyric, studying us with an awareness one rarely saw in horses. I apologized to her with a maple candy from my pocket, and once I had her sheet back on, I turned back to my incredibly attractive companion. "I apologize, it is unlike me to forget myself so easily."

His smirk of satisfaction raised goosebumps on my shoulders that quickly raced over the rest of my body. "I'll take that as a compliment. Now, how about we get your girlfriend settled so we can go get dinner. The sandwich I ate in Chicago is wearing thin."

Pretending I did not want to press him up against a wall and slide my hands under his shirt, I answered casually. "If you could

retrieve a bale of shavings from the tack room, I will show you
how I like to make her bed at night."

When he turned to do as I asked, the sight of his denim-clad
behind turned my thoughts to how I would like to unmake my bed
with him.

↬ 2 ↫

Aaron

We stopped at Jaque's trailer to pick up her dog, the sweat I'd
worked up quickly chilling as the sun went down. The little puff of
a creature surveyed me with suspicion as she did her business, but
once in the truck, collapsed on a tiny dog bed tucked behind the
driver's seat. When Jaque caught me staring at the animal, she
grinned indulgently.

"Forgive her, she is wary of men in general. But in the truck
she knows the best thing is sleep."

I shook my head, having zero experience with little things.
Growing up, my family had a hundred-pound Great Dane mix, and
my horses were sizeable as well. "What possessed you to get such
a miniature dog? I'd think she'd be in danger around the horses."

"I found her at a shelter and thought the same. The life she had
before me is unknown, but clearly, circumstances had left her ill
equipped for much. I could not leave her huddled in that cage, even
when fear made her snap at me." She reached back to gently stroke
the pointy muzzle that lay conveniently close before putting the
vehicle in drive. "But she unfolded into the best companion,
willing to spend hours on the carriage or in the truck with me. And
the small size makes her quick, so she darts out of the way when
needed. She is a survivor, is my sweet Soleil."

So Jaque liked to rescue things. Was it stupid to hope she might
save me too? Yet, I could barely keep control of my baser instincts
where she was concerned, and I knew she deserved better. No, I'd
take what I could get and be satisfied.

We drove into town, stopping at a little cafe near the hotel to
grab a bite to eat. While I ordered a pesto chicken sandwich with a
side of fries, Jaque ordered a salad, casting shade on my decision
to take her for barbeque on our first date. But I shook off the worry
as the waitress left to put in our orders. We'd been on the move

since I arrived, and now I took the leisure to drink up the sight of her.

Pictures and memories of Jaque fell flat compared to the reality. In person, her energy filled the space between us with calm warmth. I wanted to lean in closer, as much to feel that glow as to touch her. Watching her black hair sway around her shoulders, the dense strands flashing purple highlights as she moved added dimension to our quiet conversation. Her lips were a fabulous barometer of her emotions, pursing with consideration, twisting in frustration and softening in a way that intensified my hunger to kiss her again.

When our food arrived she ate efficiently, small bites that were thoroughly chewed, and I got hung up on watching her swallow. The motion brought too much attention to the delicate pulse at the base of her throat, and my mouth watered in a way that had nothing to do with my food. When she caught me staring, she swallowed harder, chasing the bite down with water. "I have been eating alone for so long now, I nearly forgot myself. How is your sandwich?"

I cleared my throat, not wanting to growl at her. "Quite good. I hope your salad is enjoyable."

Her nose wrinkled as she stirred the plate of mixed greens with her fork. "Good enough, as salads go. I would prefer to eat your french fries but I refuse risk such indulgence during competition."

When I frowned, she continued. "Weight adds up for marathon on Saturday. I will not make Lyric haul a pound more than necessary, when I ask her to give so much. The least I can do is watch what I eat."

Since women could be quite touchy when it came to their weight, I hesitated to give my opinion. The numbers on the scale were a constant source of complaint growing up with three sisters and a mother who put so much stock in looks. But I took a risk and stuck my neck out anyway. "You can't weigh that much, Jaque. Surely you don't have to starve yourself."

She grew sharp, but not in anger. I recognized the expression as one I often wore inside my helm when I jousted, the serious mien of a competitor. "No, Lyric and I already suffer enough handicaps. If all I asked was for her to pull the carriage straight, my weight would be of little concern. Shifting a well-built carriage is hardly an effort. But add in the tight turns, and the way the weight slings itself from side to side, I cannot subject her to extra torque if it can be helped."

Thinking back to the videos she'd shared, the way the horse practically bent the carriage double to make a turn, I winced. The more I came to care for Jaque, the more I worried about her being at risk for injury. How the hell Bart managed with Jo, I didn't know. "Okay, I can understand that. But I don't think you've got anything to worry about weight wise. You feel perfect to me."

The words came out thoughtlessly, but her fork hit the plate with a loud clatter as she stared in disbelief.

"Oh, you..." she trailed off, lifting her napkin to dab a bit of dressing from her lips. "I always knew you would be a charmer." Yet, that didn't sound like she meant it as a compliment.

"What?" I asked immediately, worried I'd done something wrong again. I really was at a loss without my usual canned compliments and platitudes.

"Do you think you can just throw pretty words around and I shall fall into your arms with a sigh?" She crossed her arms and sat back, leveling the driest stare on me. The Sahara at midday in summer probably felt more temperate. "Surely that is all it usually takes."

Dammit, the one-eighty threw me. Not wanting to sink myself any further, I held my hands out in defeat. "I'm sorry if anything I said upset you. I meant it. You fit perfectly in my arms, Jaque, but I totally understand your commitment to your sport. Hell, I worked out twice as hard as usual leading up to the tourney, but in my case I was trying to gain, not lose. Whatever weight you need or want to be, I'm perfectly happy to have you in my arms as long as you want to be there."

"Oh," One word, made incredibly small by her sad tone. Her brown eyes, usually warm and lively, dimmed considerably. "I am sorry."

I wanted to scoop her up and hold her until the sadness faded. But something told me she wouldn't welcome the liberty just yet. Instead, I set a hand on the tabletop, palm upward to invite a connection. Unfortunately, she curled further in on herself, shoulders drawn together.

"Don't be sorry Jaque. I'm so far out of my depth, I'm sure I'm screwing this up." Words tumbled out recklessly fast, with little thought behind them other than desperation to repair the rift. "Usually, I'd have this checklist of compliments and pick up lines to work through, but I don't want things to be like that between us. We've spent all this time becoming friends, and I respect you too much to cheapen our time together. But I promise you, any compliments I offer are heartfelt."

Wide eyes lifted to mine, and much as I usually shied away from emotions, I rejoiced to see them. Jaque closing herself up reminded me too much of the way Rowan looked when Bart first brought him to the farm, the lifelessness a travesty. Not that I had room to talk, since I'd been trying to do the same thing to my own horse, however unintentional it had been. I needed to be especially careful not to let such things happen again, with both Jaqueline and Byzantine, now that I understood my part in it.

"Lines? Whatever for?"

I might have accused her of playing coy, were she any other woman, But the question was forthright, and she genuinely looked like the mere idea confused her. Heated base instinct and a surprising amount of embarrassment colored my reply.

"So I could get a woman out of her pants and in bed as quickly as possible."

Heavy lashes blinked several times until a slow smile developed on her lips, as if I weren't the only one having those thoughts. Her elbows came to rest on the cloth covered table and she leaned toward me, closing the distance so our conversation would remain private. When I leaned in to match, I had to shift in my chair to alleviate the pressure in my jeans.

"You need not use lines, Aaron Drew. Not with me. Nor do I think you need them with other women. Simply being yourself would do."

I winced again, wondering if it was going to turn into a facial tick.

"That's the thing, Jaque. I'm not myself when I offer up canned compliments and flattery." Carefully, afraid she might deny me even with the warmth back in her eyes, I reached out and cupped her elbow. "But you make me want to be myself."

"Oh," This time, that tiny word came across completely different, warm with delight. "Please, do."

I grinned. "I'm trying, but I'm rusty. It's only going to work if you can cut me some slack. I don't do it very often, and I'm afraid I'll make a few mistakes along the way."

Her hand closed around my wrist, keeping me in place right where I cupped her arm. "We are only human, and fallible. Pardon my mistake in assuming your intent." Then her fingers tightened and the storm wrapped around us again. "Though I do hope your intent is to get me out of my pants at some point."

Heat rolled up my back and moved over my shoulders as I struggled to stay calm. "Rest assured, it's on my to-do list. But don't think I'm in a rush. You've been worth waiting for the last two months."

She blushed prettily, her fingers lightening, then playing over the bones in my wrist. Each stroke across the hairs there vibrated through me on a gut deep level. "I dreamt of us often, you should know."

Swallowing hard, I prepared to divulge the same, but she suddenly sat up and away from me. The withdrawal made my stomach drop to my feet, but as she stared at something behind me, her sweet eyes grew hard in a way that tightened every muscle in my back.

"We should ask for the check." The ice in her voice didn't sting, being directed at something else, but I hated it just as much as the earlier distance. It was not a natural state for her, and she wore it poorly, fidgeting with her plate as she hunted for our waiter.

I waved at the girl who'd been serving us, smiling encouragement when she headed our way. Before Jaque could shake her mood, I fished out my wallet and paid for the meal, asking to have the leftovers boxed up. She'd barely touched her salad, and weight concerns aside, she still needed to fuel her body to get through the weekend ahead.

As we walked through the restaurant, I watched the way she angled her body away from a particular table. Among the large group sitting there were several good-looking dudes, in a superiorly European way. When the guy furthest from us smiled snidely at Jaque's retreating form, I put my hand on her back and glared until he noticed. He had the balls to lean over and say something to one of the other men, then they both laughed. The sound made Jaque's body tense beneath my touch, and I hated them for it, whoever they were.

Outside, her strides stretched longer, and I stepped up the pace to match her. Not hard, since my legs were longer, but I'd grown comfortable with slowing myself down, with taking my time. She made it easy.

"Jaque, what's going on?" I asked as we reached the truck and she clicked the locks open. Before she could get there, I used my free hand to open the door, and it startled her enough that she finally looked up at me.

"Do you recall my frustration with the man who insulted Lyric?" When I nodded, she relaxed slightly. "That was him, with a group of his hangers-on. And while I expected to see him this weekend, I hoped to get through one day without running into him." Damp eyes met mine, and her smile trembled slightly. "Foolish of me to want time to focus on you."

Well, short of walking back inside and laying the guy out, I could only think of one thing that might reassure her. When I set the bag of leftovers on the ground, her head cocked to the side, but as I stepped in close the confusion burned away.

"Rest assured, Jaque, whatever happens this weekend, the focus is not on me, but you." She shivered as I slipped a hand along her full cheek and slid around to grasp the back of her head. The weight of her hair caressed my knuckles, catching slightly on a rough spot left by my armor. As I leaned down to kiss the lips she tipped up in offer, she moved in the last inch, putting us thigh to thigh, belly to belly.

That kiss, illuminated only by the cab light, superseded all the ones from before. I tasted the desperation in her hunger, the need to be consumed by something other than hurt, and I answered with a ravenous exploration of her mouth. Her hands clutched my sweater, as if trying to get closer, so I hitched her into my arms. She went one better and wrapped her legs around my hips, and control threatened to escape my grasp. Panic and need pulled hard enough in opposite directions that I thought she might unravel me completely.

I tore away from her lips and panted against her throat, "Jaqueline, please."

Immediately, her legs dropped down and she pulled back, real and absolute fear in her wide eyes. "Oh, no, I am so sorry!"

Still breathing hard, I followed when she stepped away, wedging her in the open door of the truck. "Don't apologize. Not for being so damn delicious I nearly lost it."

Risking a tiny smile, I kissed her gently and gathered her too-still frame against my chest. It took a minute of stroking up and down her back, of soaking in her scent, for my breathing and heart rate to recover. Just in time for her to relax into the embrace, her nose burrowing into my chest. "Let's go back to the hotel, okay? We can talk this out before we're too far gone to manage words."

She nodded against me, then gasped when I put my hands around her waist and lifted her onto the seat. A growl from the backseat reminded me weren't alone, and I smiled. "See, even our chaperone thinks we need to slow down."

Jaque grasped my chin with her thumb and forefinger and leaned out for a lingering press of lips onto mine. "Happily, I am a grown woman and can choose my own fate." Then she started the truck and looked at me pointedly until I caught on and closed her door. I was halfway in the passenger side when I groaned and climbed back out to grab the leftovers I'd forgotten on the ground. Blood loss to the brain will do that to a guy.

Jaque

I did not want to talk. We had talked for months. Not about anything to do with the feelings ricocheting through my chest, but he was finally with me, and words were the last thing I wanted more of. Words could wait until he went back to Kentucky and we had to be apart again.

Yet, as he followed me from the truck to my room with his fingers lightly pressed to my lower back, I realized slowing down was wise. If I pushed too hard, I could chase him away like I had the others. My relationships tended to burn white hot, then fizzle out quickly, everything of substance consumed in the heat of passion until nothing remained to keep us connected. To have that happen with Aaron would be a tragedy.

As soon the door of my room opened and I flicked on a light, he moved past me, but the way he did it thrilled me. His fingers traced a path over my hip, then down my arm as he pulled away, as if he wanted to touch as much as possible. I followed in his wake, pausing beside the bed to call Soleil.

"Here, *ma petit chou*." She leapt onto the variegated coverlet and sat nicely to have her leash removed. Holding her sweet face in both hands, my thumbs ran along her narrow muzzle, and the love in her eyes regrounded me.

When the door opened again I looked up to find Aaron stepping out, the ice bucket in his hand. "I'll be right back, going to see if they have any utensils in the lobby so you can eat, and to get this filled. Then we won't have to venture out for a while."

Pleasure coiled in my gut at the thought of spending time alone with him and also at his thoughtfulness. When had a man last done so many simple kindnesses for me? Not that I had any reason to complain. None had been truly unkind either, unless you counted Maarten and his disciples.

Once the door closed, I hurried to feed Soleil. She was a fussy eater, requiring tiny kibble and a leisurely amount of time to consume even the smallest portions. I feared she might not eat once Aaron returned, as she was put off by the slightest changes in her environment. When my father came to visit last year she had staged a hunger strike until I tempted her with canned food.

A knock sounded as I shed my sweater against the warmth of the room, and when I glimpsed Aaron through the peephole, I pressed my hand against the heat welling in my belly. Though I was accustomed to running a trifle passionate with my lovers, this was altogether more intense. If I had any sense, I would be cautious, but craving edged out concern where Aaron became involved. My fingers itched to be buried in his wild hair again, so they opened the door and I welcomed him in.

He strode through the doorway like a conquering hero, waving a plastic packet of utensils on his way to the table. I smiled even as I latched the door behind him. Such a tiny victory, but he won it for me. "Alright, my lady, let's get you fed so you're ready for competition tomorrow."

Soleil cast a hopeful eye our direction as we sat down to finish our meals, but when nothing proved forthcoming, she curled up in her bed with a sigh. A bit of guilt shadowed my appetite as I noticed Aaron left his french fries alone now that they were cold. Shame, really, as I had hoped to steal a few before Maarten and company put me off my food. Fries truly were my one weakness, from a dietary standpoint, though I would trade them all for another taste of the man across the table.

I felt a little bereft as he never looked up from his food. At the cafe, his eyes touched me constantly, tightening the distance between us. Now, I wondered if he might be avoiding the contact. Yet I muddled through my salad, limp as it was, because he was correct—I needed to take care of myself if I wanted to be prepared for tomorrow.

Once my tray was picked clean he rose to take care of our trash and my spirits fell when he returned to the chair without so much as an errant brush of his fingers. He leaned deeply back into the seat, eyes hooded and his smile dim. Some way or another, I had pushed him too far. The distance between us suddenly felt even harder to gulf than when he was in California.

"So, what's on the agenda tomorrow?"

At least I could muster some enthusiasm. "We will have dressage in the afternoon. You might find it boring, to be frank, but it is very busy beforehand." Ticking off the items on my fingers, I watched his eyes widen. "I must groom her extensively, as some of our score will be based on appearances, and her harness must be impeccable. The carriage too, will require a going over. Even my own attire needs careful attention to detail. I find the preparations much more stressful than the actual test, to be honest."

"Wow, no wonder you said you're tired after a show. And that's just Friday, right?"

More settled now that he was looking at me again, I smiled. "Indeed. As well, before and after dressage, I shall go out and walk the marathon course."

He frowned slightly as he leaned back in his chair, eyes now steady on mine. The hawkish attention bore the mien of a serious competitor, and I knew I could rely upon his understanding, in that at least. "You walk a marathon? Twice?"

The question startled me to laughter. "Oh, no, I have rented a golf cart, much of it will be traveled that way. The true walking happens in the obstacles, or hazards as they are also called, so I can memorize my routes. Hopefully, my navigator will be here in time for the evening walk. She was the one I texted with earlier, her arrival has been delayed slightly."

"Navigator?" The quizzical slant of his brows was delightful. This is what I wanted so much, all those dark nights on the phone with him. The conversation playing out on his features. I had been as hungry for that as I had his touch.

"Yes, though you will hear many call them 'gators for short. They help us keep on track with our course and time, so we can focus on our horses. And in the obstacles, they provide counterbalance through the fast turns."

The wrinkles left his forehead and deepened around his eyes as he smiled sharply. "Now that part of the job looks damn fun."

I grinned back at him. "Oh, it is. I have taken the back step for many friends over the years and even now, I occasionally step in to help when there is need. You see, most carriages must have a second person on board, to assist in case of accident or hold up. Unless you have very small equines, like little ponies or miniatures."

"Ah, so like a squire in jousting?"

"Yes, much like." Though I loved sharing my passion with him, I did not want to bore him with the details. The minutia could glaze over the eyes of the most dedicated student if one spoke too long. Tomorrow, he would see for himself. "When I return to Kentucky I would be pleased to let you try your hand at it. With your athleticism, you would likely be a natural."

Energy seemed to gather under his skin at the suggestion, and I wished we were close enough to touch, to see if I could feel it crackling under my fingertips.

"I'd like that, very much. Speed is my one real vice, I think. Not ridiculous or unsafe, mind you, but the rush of power, the stretch of the comfort zone." He flashed a rakish smile, showing off a bit of the bad boy I saw in some of the pictures Jo shared online. The ones that made you wish you could be one of his vices. "Someday, I want to get a muscle car and fix it up, drive it across the country."

Oh, this was a step in the right direction! Something more personal. "Why have you not? Clearly, you have the skills to work on a vehicle."

All that crackling energy dampened slightly, and I missed it. "The Company, mostly. I've been holding it together on my own for a while now." Then he shook his head slightly, untidy hair sweeping across his forehead. "Though Bart's back now. Might be time to start working on that particular dream again."

No longer able to bear the distance, I scooted my chair closer and leaned forward to touch his knee. The jeans he wore were slightly thin there, allowing me to feel his warmth, and the contours of the joint. His eyes darted down to where I touched him, then moved slowly up, causing my skin to tighten. Yet, I did not say a word until our eyes met, longing for the link.

"Should you get that car, I would be happy to play navigator for you as well."

He sucked in a breath, as if I had surprised him, and stared into my eyes as if he might read the contents of my soul. It felt more intimate than a million kisses and while my insides tumbled about like leaves in an updraft, I had no desire to look away. No one had ever reached so deeply inside of me with a look.

"Where did you come from, Jaqueline? How did I not know you were right in front of me?" Awe and fear both laced those questions, and I could not be sure he wanted me to answer them. But I could offer him something else.

"Foolish though it may be, I have had a childish crush on you since the first time we spoke." I shrugged away my own discomfort over the admission, committed to the course. "Perhaps neither of us were ready for each other? You were so intense and distracted, and I was focused on making a go of my decision to come to the States for training."

His hair flipped across his forehead again, and my empty hand itched to straighten it. Yet, he maintained the distance, and I would not push my way into anything with him, however much I desired it. "I worry I still might not be ready."

The thready confession erased my will power, and I slid from my chair until I knelt between his knees. I took one of his hands in mine to keep them from roving up his body, then tugged him forward. "And yet, you are here. This gives me hope. Or should I hold back?"

He leaned in finally, our lips mere inches away, and cupped my chin. The friction of his thumb caressing my jaw made my limbs heavy, but I kept my attention firmly on his eyes. "No, please, don't hold back. Though, I'm going to ask if we can take things slowly for now."

Sighing heavily, I closed my eyes to hide the disappointment I felt. "I know, I am sorry for pushing so hard."

His chuckle smoothed over the rough ache in my chest and I opened my eyes to see a world of dark promise looking back at me. "No, lady, don't ever apologize for how quickly your blood runs, or how fast you get me wound up. But this intense a connection is unfamiliar territory for me, and I won't be reckless with either of us. You make me want to savor the time we have."

How was one even supposed to respond to such passionate sweetness? But he saved me an answer and swooped in to steal a gentle kiss. Every argument or objection I might have to taking things slowly, he stole away with my breath. By the time he pulled back, my body went weak and I swayed toward him. When he went to his knees to catch me up, my heart jumped as if it were trying to give itself to him, and I curled myself around his strength.

"I should go, Jaqueline. You need to rest up for tomorrow." Whispering the words softly against my hair, he stroked my back. The languorous attention had me nodding against his chest, unable to manage so much as a tiny disagreement. I barely found the wherewithal to appreciate the flex of his body beneath my hands as he rose to his feet with me still in his arms. But then he slowly pulled away, mindful of my unsteady legs.

"No," I managed as he made a step toward the door. My feet moved automatically to follow, though I planted my hand on the dresser to keep my balance. "Aaron, we are finally together. Please, do not go."

Immediately, he returned, putting his hands on my upper arms and tenderly kissing my cheek. "My lady, much as I want to, if I stay rest will be the last thing on my mind. But I can promise you this. If you call, I'll answer. If you text, I'll respond. I'm never too far away." When he leaned back and tightened his grip, an adorably playful smile lifted one side of his mouth. "After all, I'm right next door."

Then he left in earnest, closing the door softly behind him. I stared at the knob for several seconds, contemplating chasing him down, when I heard the door open for the neighbouring room. Many times over the course of my life I had known cause for hating the thin walls in budget motels, but for once, as I slowly prepared for bed and listened to him do the same, I rejoiced. No, we were not together. Yet. But we were certainly closer than we had ever been before.

Aaron

Ridiculously, I did have to bridge the gap I made between us before I fell asleep. I'd never been more grateful for being forgetful, in several instances. Absent-minded had never been one of my failings, yet somehow, knowing Jaque could get so far under my skin made me smile as I typed a short text.

'What time do I need to be ready to leave in the morning?'

'6 AM, if you don't mind?' quickly flashed across the screen and I wondered what she looked like, just on the other side of the wall. Did she curl under the covers or lay out flat? Would she sprawl over my chest or tangle our limbs together? Not thoughts I needed to entertain if I wanted to keep things slow, but my imagination didn't listen to logic. Particularly not after the sips I'd taken of her luscious mouth. Nor after seeing her lean forward to touch me, unaware that her camisole fell open and gave a spectacular view of her cleavage. This time, her bra was dark purple, and it set off the cream of her skin so well my mouth watered to taste it. I never would have considered purple a good color before Jaque, but now, every time I saw it, she jumped to the front of my thoughts.

The phone buzzed in my hand and I shook my head to clear it. *'Aaron, is that okay?'*

See? Forgetful. Though I doubted I'd ever forget a single thing about Jaque.

'Yes, 6 is fine. fais de beaux rêves, Jaqueline.' I sent back, laughing a little when my phone predicted the text the instant I began to type it. She was leaving her mark in my life in the most unexpected ways.

'My dreams will be sweet, as I shall find you in them.'

My heart and other parts of my body throbbed their approval of the idea. *'Then I hope to see you there, my lady.'*

No reply came back, so I put on my earbuds and opened the music app on my phone to start the familiar sounds of rainfall that would soothe me to sleep. A few finger flicks later, I had my alarm set, and the charger plugged in. When I closed my eyes and laid back into the pillows, my imagination carried me into the next room and wrapped itself around the sweetest woman I'd ever known. Even in dreams, I kept things slow, content to cuddle and kiss. Because Jaque was like nothing I'd known before, and I wanted to cherish it for however long it lasted.

3

Aaron

I wasn't a morning person, not even by a tiny margin. The Company often dictated the need for me to pretend, because the work wouldn't wait, but I didn't like it. Yet, for the second day in a row, I found myself up while the sun still slept, and I managed to smile about it. Spending time with Jaqueline gave me something to look forward to, in supporting her work and discovering what else might link us.

My body felt sluggish as I forced myself to move, like trying to swim in mud. Which meant a hot shower was the first thing on my agenda if I wanted to pass for fully human. Halfway through a vigorous scrub, hoping to get the blood moving, something else did the job for me. I heard Jaque's shower start.

Knowing she was just on the other side of the tile wall was like being slammed back in the seat of a drag racing car, the adrenaline dump working better than a full pot of coffee. Before my imagination could start putting together specific details, I shoved my head under the spray to get the shampoo out of my hair and practically jumped out of the tub to get some distance. Otherwise, I was going to tell my noble intentions to take a flying leap.

My eyes flinched away when I caught a look at myself in the mirror. They were slightly bloodshot, as if I'd been on a beer bender the night before, and I had an impressive amount of scruff on my jaw. Not that Jaque had said a word about it last night, but I didn't want people to think she'd picked up a homeless guy on her way to the show. So, I dug up my razor and tidied my appearance as best I could, including trying to tame my hair. Fruitless, really, as long as I kept it. Too short to put in a tail, too long to properly style, the best I could do was comb it back behind my ears before it dried and hope it would behave.

When a knock sounded at the door, I finished buttoning up my jeans and turned to answer it, not really thinking things through.

Again, not a morning person. As the door swung open Jaque morphed from a soft smile to a pleased grin as she shamelessly checked me out. No lie, the attention put a little swagger in my stride as I stepped over to the dresser to dig through my suitcase.

"Oh my, should this be the way you greet me every morning, I might never need coffee again." The teasing lilt of her voice made me grin as I hastily pulled a t-shirt on, pleased beyond explanation that she didn't seem at all put off by the bruises littering my torso.

"While I'd be glad to be of assistance to you, Jaqueline, I'm still going to need a stop to get caffeine. It's three in the morning where I came from."

Whip fast, her expression shifted, worry lines marring her forehead. "My apologies, Aaron, I do not mean to make light. I will go down and get the truck warmed up while you finish getting ready."

Before she could turn away, I shot back to the door and reached for her hand. Her little dog growled at me again, though I thought it was more from the startle than any real consideration of threat.

"No, I'm sorry." Her rich eyes were shaded, emotions hidden. "Mornings really aren't my strong suit, but I can think of one thing that might make it easier to bear."

Her fingers tightened in mine, earnest curiosity making an appearance as I slowly stepped closer. "Anything I can do to help, you shall have it."

When I moved her hand to my waist and leaned in, words were no longer necessary. She lifted her chin to offer her lips, and I kissed her. Intent had been just a soft brush, but she sighed, giving me a taste of mint and something else worth exploring. God, she felt so soft and welcoming, like my bed at the end of a long day, and I wanted to linger. Inhaling deeply to find my self-control, I felt it slipping further away with her flowery scent fresh from the shower, and the still damp curls at the base of her skull where my hand found purchase.

"Okay, you were right," I murmured as I finally pulled back and stared into the now languid depths of her eyes. "Greetings like this might make coffee unnecessary."

She chuckled softly, fingers slowly unraveling from her grip on my shirt. "Unnecessary, perhaps, but still desired. Shall we go?"

That she made a question of it, and not a demand, made me smile as I turned away to get my jacket and phone. Knowing how important her mare was to her, that she could even be slightly swayed to stay longer was quite the compliment.

We made a quick jaunt through a drive-up coffee kiosk for her mocha and my dark roast with three sugars. I would have given my second-best socket wrench for a good blueberry spinach smoothie, but having no such option available, I leaned heavily on caffeine and sugar instead. When we pulled into the showgrounds in the pre-dawn light the place was busier than a beehive, people zipping in every direction. We parked her truck in front of her trailer, then walked the short distance to the barn, staying well to the side so golf carts and ATVs could pass. Lyric waited quietly for her breakfast, despite the animals around her raising a fuss. Truthfully, the mare had an uncannily aware gaze, studying everything around her as if there would be a test later.

I did my best to be useful, refilling the hay net while Jaque fixed up her grain, a much lengthier process than the one we used for the jousting horses. Though she already had the ration in a plastic baggie, it had to be soaked and stirred before consumption. When she caught me looking, she straightened from her task and leveled a questioning gaze my way.

"What?" I asked when she shifted restlessly, clearly undecided on something.

"I find myself in unfamiliar territory," She smiled, then continued, "And now more empathetic to your phrasing last night. I cannot tell if I should explain what I am doing. Your expression conveys curiosity, yet I do not want you to think me condescending of your own knowledge. After all, there are many ways to care for a horse."

To which I shrugged. "Incredibly true, and I'm unfamiliar with most of them. Bart is more educated than I am in just about anything to do with horses."

She put her hands on her hips and frowned. "I find that difficult to believe, Aaron. You clearly have some experience, to do the work you do. And they are all healthy, well cared for."

I denied her, much as it pained me. "Sadly, I'm a good athlete at best. My father, while a rodeo cowboy, kept care to a basic minimum when it came to horses." And anything else, for that matter, but that was a subject for a later date. "At the theatrical tournament in Vegas the horses were cared for mostly by staff. I just had to do my stunts and go home."

Her eyes blinked repeatedly before she could muster a response, arms falling against her sides. "Then why do it? I cannot imagine why one would have a life with horses if their heart was not fully invested in it."

I cinched the hay net closed and tied it off the way she preferred as I considered the question. "I think my heart is in it." Then I grinned a little sheepishly, hoping I wasn't getting ahead of myself. "Just like it's invested in whatever this is with us. In both cases, I've got some gaps in my experience. But that won't stop me from trying."

Soft hope colored Jaque's expression, and I'd have loved nothing more than to gather her close for a moment. But then a girl let herself into the stall next to us, clearly intent on her chores, which made us both straighten purposefully. Jaque grabbed the feed bucket, I snatched up the net and we made our way to Lyric's stall.

The mare remained polite as we doled out her food, completely unlike Byzantine's aggressiveness at mealtimes, and I made a note to ask Jaque for pointers later. Surely, there had to be a way to address the matter. But we had no time, at that moment, as Jaque led the way back out to the trailer. I helped her set up several pop up sunshades, and she opened the back ramp of the trailer to wheel out an elegant, clean lined carriage. When she began to wipe it down, I stopped her long enough to ask for my own rag, and we spent an equitable half hour polishing every glossy black surface free of dust. From the patent leather dash to the silver hubs of the wheels, it reminded me of a classic European sports car, except for one tiny discrepancy. The pin striping, thin and tastefully outlining the carriage body, was purple. I was beginning to detect a theme.

Thinking back, I recalled various details over the years I'd known her. The purple wasn't all encompassing or loud, just a hint of it always about her. From the streaks in her hair, to the purple flowers on her top hat when I'd gone to see her drive over Christmas, and even a big mixer on her kitchen counter. Little flashes of individuality in an otherwise traditional look. And damn if it didn't make her even more attractive to me. Refreshing as hell after over a decade of my mother throwing her beauty pageant friends my way. I wanted none of their homogenized perfection.

Jaque pulled out an oversized wooden sawhorse and set up her harness on it, then handed me a clean rag when I joined her. "Would you go over all the metal fittings for me? I will tend the patent leather, but it will simplify things if you follow after me to do the stainless and chrome."

I nodded, taking the time to study her more as she turned her attention to the saddle of the harness. Every moment was practiced and smooth, buffing out fingerprints like my mother always did on her silver and crystal. That memory, I wrenched away from immediately. While I understood Jaque worked to present a pretty picture to the judges, this held none of the vanity that wreathed my mother like the stench of the cigarettes she swore she no longer smoked.

Speaking of pretty pictures. Jaque tended to stick her lower lip out as she concentrated, her dark brows knit together hard enough that she wore a pair of wrinkles between them. She pushed up the sleeves on her fleece jacket, exposing the fine bones in her wrists and the shapely muscles of her forearms. All of her was art in motion, purposeful grace.

We made short work of the harness between the two of us, and she covered the whole thing with a soft sheet of cotton before we returned to the barn. In a pattern that already felt familiar, she took the mare out for a walk and I cleaned the stall. But just as I worked to open another bag of shavings, she returned.

"Oh, no, Aaron, a new bag at nighttime only." Her brusque tone might have rankled if not for the softness around her eyes. "I shall explain."

Turning the mare loose to continue with her hay, she held out her hand for the manure rake. "Look, if we push most of the shavings to the back of the stall, they will remain cleaner." Suiting deed to words, she piled them all along the rear wall, keeping barely an inch on the rest of the dirt floor. "During the day, when I do not want her to lay down, I leave only enough to be absorbent. Then, at night, I will lay a thick bed, to encourage her to rest."

Hmm, learn something new every day, though it irked me to be so far behind the curve. Didn't help that my whole life felt that way lately. Yet, that wasn't Jaque's fault. "Makes sense. I'll remember tomorrow."

I didn't have much to do when Jaque set about grooming. To my eye, the glossy animal needed no improvement, but then again, I'd never been in a show ring. So, I settled in a folding camp chair beside the stall door and watched as she went over the blue-black coat with a soft brush, slicking away every trace of sawdust from last night's sleep. She'd just climbed up on a stepstool to begin braiding the mare's mane when I caught the unmistakable growl of her stomach.

"Jesus, Jaque, we never got any food. Do you have anything to eat?"

Confusion laced her brows together as she stepped off the stool. "Oh, again, my apologies. I often forget to eat until after I show. If you are hungry there is a food vendor down by the main arena."

As I stood she fished in her jacket pocket for her wallet. "No, I've got this one. What would you like?"

"I believe they make crepes. Should they have them, I would prefer one with hazelnut spread."

My lips thinned in disapproval. "Jaqueline, you really should have some protein if you're going to get through the day in good shape."

Her lips thinned right back and a glimmer of anger lit her flashing eyes. "Do not presume too much, Aaron. I cannot eat heavily before I compete, and tend to survive the morning on sugar and caffeine. While I appreciate your very welcome help, I have done this many years on my own."

Up went my hands again, warding off any further chastisement as I took a step backward. "My turn to apologize, I'll be back shortly."

I fumed all the way to the food truck, itching to do more for Jaque, yet chafing against the limitations. Yes, she was a grown woman, and clearly had been doing just fine without my help. She didn't need me...but I wanted her to.

As I waited in line, I watched a couple competitors go, zoning out as they traced patterns in the grass arena. No fence kept the horses contained, just a low white railing to define the limits, while big boxes with flowers spilling out the tops sat evenly spaced around the area, marked with singular letters for the drivers to aim for.

Shortly after a single horse and carriage exited the arena, a pair of horses entered at a dynamic high-stepping trot. The animals had long, arched necks, elegant frames and energetic movement, turning the boring patterns into something more artistic. But I was glad to turn away when the line moved forward, impatience to be back with Jaque already rearing its head.

I ate my chicken Florentine crepe on the way back to the barn, my stomach settling gratefully as I swallowed the first bite. The reminder that I needed to take care of myself came through loud and clear. I'd put my body through the wringer for several days and was still in recovery. Not to mention I wouldn't be much use to Jaque if I flagged.

Her reaction to her own crepe erased any objection I might have raised over the dubious nutritional value. She sank down on the step stool she'd been using and held it reverently in both hands as she took a bite. Eyelashes fluttered down and a soft groan filled the quiet between us. The sound made me inhale as I turned away to disguise the effect on my body. Dropping back into the chair by the door, I rearranged my jacket so no one passing by would get an eyeful.

"Aaron, did you not get food for yourself?"

Cracking my eyes open to look over at her, I flashed a reassuring smile. "Ate on the way back. No need to worry over me."

Knowing eyes bored into mine as she swallowed the bite she'd taken. "I might say the same to you about me."

"Fair enough, my lady. And I'm trying. I'm used to taking care of everyone on my team, so it might take a bit of time to find my way."

A hint of heat shimmered between us as she raked her gaze downward to land on the portion of my anatomy I'd recently covered up. My jeans suddenly shrank a size, and when she came back to my eyes, the flash of power in that stare said she knew exactly what affect she had on me. "I do need you, Aaron. Only perhaps not in a way we can indulge in public."

My fingers curled around the arm rests on the chair, needing the restraint. Somehow, I found the strength to angle toward her, closing some of the distance between us. "Jaque, going slow is for more than just my benefit." I pressed a finger to the edge of her smile to catch a slight bit of the chocolate and hazelnut spread, then brought it to my own mouth to lick it off while she gave a stuttering inhale. "When I take you to bed, I want your mind on nothing but us. Not the competition, not your horse. Just us."

A man came up the aisle just then, breaking the connection, but not before I caught sight of the flush on her neck and the quickening of her pulse. Pleased to have made my point, I settled back in the chair and smiled up at the striped vinyl roof of the tent as Jaque finished her food. Somehow, knowing I wasn't the only one eager and a little overwhelmed eased the tension in my chest and the tightness in my jeans.

Jaque

Braiding Lyric did not require much of my attention, as I had done it countless times over our fourteen years together. In one way, it reminded me of watching my grandmother crochet, how her hands could keep moving with perfect tension and rhythm even as she held conversations or watched her game shows. Perhaps the knack ran in my blood, a gift I was grateful for as I daydreamed about Aaron.

The way he answered the door that morning warmed me from head to toe. A few old scars and fading bruises randomly littered his muscular frame, making curiosity as potent in my veins as passion. Where his brother was built like the draft horses they rode, Aaron remained a bit more refined, a correlation I could draw with the Canadien Horses I loved. Strong, capable of immense power, but with a natural athleticism and subtle elegance. My fingers slowed as I imagined tracing the lines of his muscles, and I was reminded of my work by an impatient shake of Lyric's head.

"Ah, yes, only three more to go," I murmured as I tied off the end of another braid and sewed it into a tight button along her arched neck. Much like myself, Lyric was no wilting flower, muscles adding to her feminine curves. We both tended toward plump if we did not maintain a regular workout schedule, but I preferred to think of us as more baroque. Our beauty would not grace the covers of magazines, but our looks would endure the test of time.

Once her braids were finished, I checked the clock on my phone. We were perfectly on time. I unclipped the lead from Lyric's halter, admonishing her to not roll and giving her our customary kiss before leaving her to her hay. Aaron fiddled on his phone as I closed the stall door behind me, though he quickly wound things up and straightened.

"What's next, my lady?"

The pet name tickled the constant warmth in my belly, mostly for the implication that I was his lady. More practical parts of my brain complained that surely he used the term of endearment with all the women he met on his travels, but I refused to listen to it. The smile he offered felt too special to sully with petty jealousies.

"To the office to pick up a golf cart, and on to the marathon course. Unless you would rather stay here?" I gestured to his phone and he hastily shoved it in his pocket as he stood up.

"No, just checking in with Bart. They're almost home now, so that'll be a load off my mind."

As I led the way out of the barn, he kept a respectful distance. But once outside where we could walk next to each other, his fingers landed lightly on the small of my back. One more thing to give me hope that things could work between us. In every case before, I had been the one to initiate touch, yet despite his wish to keep things slow, he sought ways to stay close.

We stopped at the trailer to pick up Soleil, who then boldly pranced ahead of us as we headed for the show office. The portable building sat near the main arena, and we arrived just as a few other people left. Happily, this meant we had no wait, and I stepped up to the counter to greet Joyce Benton, the main organizer for the show.

"Any need for flying monkeys today, Mrs. Joyce?"

The silver-haired woman waved a hand at the old joke. She had attended one of the competitor's parties as the Wicked Witch of the West, since she often played the bad guy when competitors could not have what they wanted, and the nickname stuck. "Not yet, though I'm definitely not in Kansas anymore. What can I help you with, oh politest of my charges? And did you bring your adorable dog? I have cookies, you know!"

At the word cookies Soleil pulled on her leash, and I let it go so she could charm the lady out of a few biscuits. Owing to the size of her tiny mouth, she could not enjoy most treats that people carried, but Joyce always made sure to have miniature-sized tidbits on hand. "Once you are finished bribing Soleil, perhaps I could bother you for the keys to my golf cart?"

She giggled as Soleil sat down and offered her paw, doling out a cookie before returning her attention to me. "Of course, always happy to help." But then her eyes flickered past me, stuttering on the handsome man who stood at my back, a blush tickling her tan cheeks. Much like most horse folk, she spent most of her days outside, lending her a wealth of storied wrinkles. "Though it would be rude not to introduce your charming companion."

"Aaron Drew, ma'am, at your service." He took the hand she offered and bowed over it like a storybook knight, making me wonder how much I missed out on by not going to see him joust. "I'm here to watch Jaqueline compete this weekend, so I hope to see you about."

She ran assessing eyes over him, her lips thinning as the wheels began to turn in her head. "Well, with pretty turns of phrase like that, you are likely to be wrangled into helping with cones on Sunday. But I'm sure we will be seeing you at tonight's supper, and tomorrow's awards. Do you dance, young man?"

I struggled not to lay a claiming hand on him, though I had nothing to worry about in Joyce's specific case. She was happily married over twenty years to the gentleman who owned the farm we stood on. But owing to her reputation as the hub of all gossip I knew Aaron would be the afternoon topic *du jour*.

All the chaos in my gut quieted as he took my hand in his. "Very little, though I'll be saving most of it for Jaqueline. We've been apart for two months while she's been in Florida for the season, and I'm eager for an excuse to hold her close."

My eyes widened at such a public declaration, and I managed a smile as Joyce stared at me.

"Well, look at you, Miss Sauveterre. Here I thought you'd be too busy for romance, with your rigorous schedule." I held my breath, unsure if her words were positive or negative as she dug beneath the counter for my paperwork. But when she slid the forms and a set of keys onto the laminate surface, her hand fell on mine as I reached for a pen. Real, genuine warmth shone in her sweet eyes. "Good for you!"

My smile grew as Joyce pulled away to answer a radio call, and Aaron squeezed my fingers before letting me go so I could fill out the liability contract. Soleil finagled a few more cookies and then we were back outside. While Aaron volunteered to drive so I could concentrate on the course, I shook my head to the negative as I stepped into the little car and placed Soleil on the seat.

"No, it truly helps for me to drive it, so I can treat it just as if I were in the carriage. Though I appreciate the offer." He slid into the passenger seat, earning a dirty look from my little companion, though I soothed her with a quick pet.

"Makes absolute sense. Though tell me if I can be of any help."

"Perhaps this afternoon, we will take notes. But for this first trip, we will simply commit our eyes to the markers." As we pulled up to the starting area, several sets of people were departing, and I paused to let them get ahead so I could look at a sketched-out map. "We have a bit over thirteen kilometres to cover, or ten miles to your American sensibilities. And just as it is here at the start gate, the white flag must go on the right, red on the left. For the Advanced level, we must search for the triangles with blue."

Aaron proved adept at spotting the markers, well before I might have seen them myself. This enabled me to drive as if I already had my navigator in place, and we were through the endurance portion of the course much faster than usual. He did not initiate conversation often, even as we worked through the hazards, content to walk through the gates by my side. Yet, I sensed a weighty awareness from him, an energy that reminded me of Lyric, as if he were paying attention to the smallest details.

While he did not follow me through the water obstacle, lacking waterproof footwear, he stood on the bank and watched me. The hawk like gaze missed not a thing, yet never felt controlling or superior. Just there, like the comforting weight of a blanket.

At the last obstacle, a grouping of massive flowerpots that surrounded a ribbon wrapped maypole, he finally spoke as I walked through the third gate. "Jaque, why take the longer route? Couldn't you just cut through here?" He pointed to the left of us, a wrinkle appearing on his brow when I shook my head.

"No, I cannot. That is my last gate, and I cannot use a gate out of order. They are only usable to reach another gate once I have passed through it in correct order." I held out my paper map and used a finger to trace the pattern I meant to use as he stepped in close enough to watch. "The course designer does these to test our ability to recall our route and the athleticism of our horses. In the instance of this gate, I could have gone left to get here, but it would have meant an even tighter turn in Lyric's tougher direction, with the slope of the ground creating the possibility of upsetting the carriage if I did not manage it perfectly."

I watched his jaw jut forward as he looked up and found the turn I meant. His eyes drew the lines so firmly in the air, I would have been unsurprised to see them show up visibly. "Wouldn't that save you time?"

There, I sighed, chafing slightly to see his competitiveness outweigh thoughts for my horse. Perhaps he might never understand. "It could. But we would have to slow down to turn that tightly, and I feel I can make up some of the time with speed. But more than that, I will not risk Lyric. This is her first season at the Advanced level. Successful trips will lend her more bravery than winning ones."

The vehemence of my reply brought his studious gaze back to me, and he gently touched my elbow. "A lesson I'm learning, thanks to you."

To that, I did not even know what to say. Did he feel gratitude or irritation for my interference? But I had no time to puzzle things out, which was reinforced by the quiet beep from my phone to keep me on track. So I flashed him a smile and finished my walk, pacing out distances with hurried strides.

Once back in the cart, I headed for the finish line, determined to make up time. Show schedules were unforgiving, and I hated to rush my warmup. Lyric liked to walk for a bit, slowly loosening up the muscles, and I would not fail her. Aaron remained blessedly silent, nodding his agreement when I asked him to wait at the trailer while I went to get my partner. Yet, when I returned, my heart puddled into my feet. He had gotten Soleil off her seat in the cart and was walking her along the periphery of my little camp so she could stretch her legs and sniff. Not an ounce of rush marked his stride as she moved from scent to scent in fits and starts.

"Thank you."

He smiled, though it carried an edgy quality. "I almost left her. She sounded pretty upset with me when I reached for her. But once I picked up her leash, she was very polite."

I clipped Lyric's lead into the quick release snap on the side of the trailer and began to undo all the straps on her mesh sheet. The smooth fabric kept most of the dust off of her, and the white colour helped her stay cooler than her black coat allowed. "Soleil does not care for the course walk. I am too focused to allow her much relaxing. She is often shortchanged at shows, with Lyric's needs coming before hers."

He attached her leash to one of the chairs, and thoughtfully retrieved her water bowl from the trailer. "Well then, barring any help you might require, I'll try to make sure she gets out more."

As I ran an extra-soft goat hair brush over Lyric's coal black coat to put the final shine on, he came to lean against the side of the trailer to watch me. He never got in the way, or pestered, simply lingered nearby, as if he wanted to be close. When I put on cotton gloves and began to harness, the hyper awareness returned, this time with an edginess. Lyric pushed her head through the oval of her formal driving collar the instant I unsnapped her lead—she loved her work more than any horse I had ever known.

But Aaron's edge continued to sharpen as I retrieved the traces, and I could not bear it any longer. Turning toward him, I planted my hands on my hips, as much to convey my impatience as to keep from reaching for him. His eyes followed my hands as if drawn there by magnets.

"Are you well, Aaron? I feel as though something is wrong."

"It's the gloves. Not you," he grumbled, quickly looking away. "Old memories, sorry. I know you're on the clock, I'll stop bothering you." Then he quit his post beside the trailer, heading for the chairs under the shade.

Baffled by how the white cotton could be attached to something negative, I returned to my work. The thin fabric kept me from marking the patent leather and now shiny metal fittings with fingerprints. Yet, the ten feet between us felt much greater than the distance he created, and it put a hitch in my movements. Fingers that had fastened a thousand buckles now fumbled, and I grew increasingly impatient with myself, which compounded the problem.

When I finished smoothing Lyric's thick tail so the hairs lay flat through the crupper, I went back to her head and offered her a maple candy from my pocket. She crunched it happily and lifted her nose up for our habitual kiss, the scent of her sweet breath calming the anxiety crawling around under my skin. The tiny little white arrow mark brushed against my lips and brought the world right-side up again.

Aaron

Jaque's agitation created a pit in my stomach, guilt gnawing holes in the happiness we'd been enjoying. I ruined it, all over a stupid childhood memory. Why did everything about my family have to feel like poison? Not that I had no good memories...but they were in the minority.

She headed my direction once the mare was harnessed, and I reached out. Pausing just before my fingers came in contact with hers, she looked down at my hand, a barrier up in her usually open expression. "I do not have time to fix whatever this is, Aaron. As I explained, Lyric must come first."

I closed that last inch, carefully lifting her hand up to press a kiss to her fingertips, even with the wretched gloves present. "Later then. But my intent is definitely to explain myself. I didn't mean to cause a problem."

When she pulled her hand away my stomach dropped, but then she peeled off the gloves and put both hands on my cheeks. The warm contact soothed, even as her eyes softened. "Later then. And thank you, that takes a great deal of worry off of my heart."

Then she stood on her toes and I met her halfway for a brief kiss that stole away the last of my guilt. I wondered at the easy forgiveness, as I always expected to pay handsomely for my mistakes. Absurdly, without the pressure to do so, the need to make amends felt much stronger.

My lips still tingled as she stepped away and let herself into the dressing room of the trailer, the door softly clicking shut. Yes, in a very physical way, Jaque undid me, but it hardly held a candle to the effect she had on my heart.

Looking into the distance, I took a deep breath, exhaling as a four-in-hand of horses trotted past as if in a hurry. The burnt orange color of the horse's coats were offset by splashy white markings and incredibly high stepping legs. For how close they were, they made remarkably little noise, hooves landing lightly before pushing them back into flight. They gave the impression that they shunned the earth, preferring to fly.

While Lyric turned her head to watch, she didn't move a hoof, content to wait for her mistress's return. That calm pulled at me, and before I knew it, I had stepped up to the mare's shoulder. A limpid brown eye turned my way, the color as rich as Jaque's, and with an awareness that matched. As I lifted a hand up to let her sniff, she lowered her muzzle, meeting me part way. The warm breath offered to wash away my troubles, and I wondered once more how much I had missed out on with the horses in my life. Why had I always seen them as tools when they clearly offered much more? Even with Argo, the one horse I got on truly well with, I'd shortchanged us both.

The mare did not cuddle like Rowan did with Jo, or offer her ears to be rubbed like Eros did with Bart. She simply rested the softness of her muzzle against my wrist and breathed with me. Time ceased to exist, noise from the distant announcer faded back, and everything in me quieted.

At any other time in my life, the sensation of a pair of arms circling my waist might have startled me. Yet, that touch too served as an anchor as Jaque pressed herself against my back and sighed deeply. My body echoed it instinctively, and my free hand came up to touch hers where they rested on my abs. I never wanted to leave that moment of total acceptance, yet my drive to take care of Jaque won out, and I turned away from the mare to address the woman who tore my reservations down with so little effort.

"Come on, let's get you ladies ready to roll." The end of the sentence drawled out slowly as I finally caught sight of the classy transformation of Jaqueline. Eye makeup made her best feature stand out, even beneath the brim of her fancy dark gray hat with its deep purple flowers and she wore a matching fitted charcoal wool jacket that accentuated her glorious figure. An abundance of buttons down the front made me think of nothing more than undoing every last one of them. Though none of it could compare to the gentle peace in the smile she bestowed on me. "Wow, just when I think you can't surprise me anymore. You look amazing."

No girlish blush for Jaque, though she still blinked a few times as if testing the sincerity of the compliment. "Thank you. I am pleased to see you had a moment to bond with Lyric. Being my closest friend, her good opinion of you is incredibly reassuring."

I carefully touched her cheek with my knuckles, not wanting to muss her makeup. Life with my mother and sisters made me far more cognizant of such things than most men. "She feels like you. Peaceful and powerful all at the same time." There, the blush warmed her skin, making the sentimental words infinitely easier to have said.

"I can think of no sweeter compliment, Aaron." Yet, the pleased flush she favored me with could not hide her concern, and I knew she worried over the time. So I lifted up her hand again, this time pressing a kiss to the bare skin of her wrist, just above the cuff of her brown leather gloves.

"Now, what can I do to see the two of you off?"

She launched into motion the moment I released her, threading fine leather reins through metal loops in the harness before bridling the mare. Just as with the collar, Lyric dropped her head and reached for the bit, allowing Jaque to carefully slide the thick leather of the blinders over the orbits of her eyes. A few moments of careful fussing saw the reins attached to the bit, then Jaque turned to me.

"Would you hold her?"

When I stepped up, she took my hands and deliberately placed them on the cheeks of the bridle. "Here, unless she takes off. The reins should be kept clear, so the driver still holds influence."

I nodded my understanding, letting questions pile up behind my teeth for later. I'd already delayed her enough. Faster than I could clearly follow, Jaque rolled her carriage around and slid the curved shafts into leather loops along the sides of the harness, then unwound long straps to attach them to the carriage. More straps and buckles than I could possibly name were wrapped and secured, but I itched to know what each piece did, how it all functioned. Not because I anticipated carriage driving, but because I wanted to be part of Jaque's world.

After a thorough inspection of her work, she turned back to the trailer to kick off her knee-high boots and slide on a pair of patent leather shoes. The sight of her pale ankles brought up the memory of helping her out of her high heels, a surprisingly potent distraction. Jesus, I'd stepped into a freaking period romance, to be so enchanted by the tiny show of skin. Again, much as I'd cursed it as a kid, my sisters were responsible for my even knowing about such things. Sure, I got priority to watch baseball or football, but my sisters outnumbered me three to one. I'd caught enough Masterpiece Theatre to know where this was headed. Suddenly, I very much wanted her to drop a handkerchief for me, as several ladies had done over the years I'd played a knight. But I wouldn't be returning it if she did.

Jaque hitched her fitted skirt up a bit higher, flashing knees as she clambered up the side of the carriage and onto the driver's box. Reins in hand, she shimmied the skirt back into place and spared me a harried look. "A moment more, Aaron."

I smiled and felt privileged when she took a second to return it, despite the ticking clock. Yet, time waited for no man or woman, which prompted her to hurry into the apron that covered her lap. The plush dark purple wool covered her from just above her waist to her ankles, draping over her knees as she sat down in the slanted driver's seat and took up her whip. "I have her, thank you."

As I stepped away, I grinned at the mimic from my own work, where a squire would hold my horse as I donned my helmet, then turn them loose when requested. Jaque's armor was a bit softer than mine, but she prepared herself for competition just as thoroughly. And now, I would finally get to see that side of her for myself.

"Soleil and I will see you at the arena," I offered when she remained in place, her eyes darting around as if mentally double checking everything.

"Yes, good. See you there." Then she gave the mare her full attention, and a change came over the horse's body, a gathering of energy before a word had been said or a rein so much as moved. "Lyric, walk on."

The mare immediately stepped forward and to the left, though I didn't see a rein tighten. I moved out ahead of them to make sure the way was clear, then watched as they smoothly turned into the lane, following the countless wheel and hoof marks of those who had gone before. Jaque made a glorious silhouette, spine straight and shoulders back enough to make my beauty pageant mother happy. But while the overlaps continued to throw me, the softness of her movements made her real, and kept bringing me back for more.

Jaque

Many times people mistook Lyric's watchful nature for quietness. They judged her behavior as too still or unresponsive, her blood running too cool to truly succeed as a performance horse. And one-by-one, we proved them wrong, showing them that powerful currents can run under an unrippled calm. Today, we would do it again.

As she walked along on a loose rein, her head moved from side to side, taking in the goings-on around us. From barking dogs to the scents coming from the food vendors, and the faint breeze that brushed my face with the warmth of the afternoon sun, she missed nothing. Hyperawareness and hyperreactivity were two very different things, and when one of the horses alongside the path spooked at a paper coffee cup that rolled along the ground, I could almost hear her dismissal. What foolishness and such a waste of energy as far as she was concerned.

Her tail swayed as she moved, displaying her utter relaxation as readily as the undulation in her spine. A lovely bodywork specialist helped me find every point of resistance in her and then showed me how to alleviate them. The therapy had lengthened her stride and improved our dressage score by quite a few points.

I did not turn straight for the warmup arena, content to skirt the edges of activity so Lyric could walk as long as she needed. In the time it took for us to circuit the area a couple times, the rest of my fellow competitors joined the fray. Here, toward the end of the day, our smaller numbers allowed plenty of room for everyone to put their horses through their paces.

Susie and her mare were diligent, working through some trot transitions, while a pair of drivers created big circles around their coach, Maarten van den Berg. Circles were an integral part of all dressage work, yet rather than the perfect roundness of the shape, all I could see were two horses completely overbent. Their noses were behind the vertical, nearly curled into their chests for a few strides before being pushed forward into that hard contact.

My stomach clenched in objection to such treatment of one's partner. I had seen many different types of drivers over the years, from those who handled the reins more lightly than one might manoeuvre silk threads, to others who hung on their reins as if they were boat anchors. Horses, bless them, often adapted. Yet this erratic treatment from van den Berg's students never allowed the horses to find the right way, creating tension and frustration. A shame, as both animals were bred for quality movement, which would cover for a multitude of flaws. Yet, I saw it in the irritated switch of one's tail, and the other's neck muscles braced against the contact. For not the first, nor the last time, I thanked the heavens for my intuition in pulling Lyric from that fateful clinic.

I stopped once by the ring steward to be sure we were running on time, and for the cursory safety inspection that assured my equipment was in order. Aaron had taken up a station between the two arenas and waved a water bottle at me as I passed. *I'll be back*, I mouthed, and he nodded his understanding.

A quick glance at my watch barely preceded the careful reach Lyric made of the reins, telling me regardless of the clock that she was ready to begin her real warmup. I took up the contact, watching her neck and ears rise up before me, the latter flickering in my direction in readiness for her instructions.

"Trr-ot," I said sharply, rewarded with an immediate lift into the steady metronome count of her favourite gait. I steered her away from the dirt ring used by everyone else, wanting a bit of solitude. We had the neighbouring field to ourselves, so I could let her settle in without too much fussing of the reins. I took ten minutes to block out everything else in the world and focus solely on my horse.

We did changes of direction and serpentines to get her focused on my cues, hind legs driving further under her body, her mouth growing lighter in my hands by the moment. A few transitions within the trot had her sharp off of my voice, and her ears were completely aimed at me, ready for the last big ask before we returned to the arena.

"Can-ter," I asked quietly as I bent her slightly to the right and she rolled up into a smooth departure that felt lighter than a horse of her build looked to be capable of. Therein lay our secret, even now that most people on the circuit knew us. We flew under the radar with our understated elegance and drama free performances, never drawing attention until the moment we entered the ring.

After a large oval to let her work the kinks out, I trilled softly, bringing her down to a walk so we could go wait for our turn. As we approached, Aaron uncapped the water bottle and held it up, a very serious expression on his face.

"Hey, a girl ran by here a few minutes ago and said she couldn't stay to help you. Penny, I think. Is there something I can do?"

I took a few gulps of water before answering, disappointment flooding my limbs with weight. Lyric responded to the change in my demeanor by turning her head to look back at me, a wrinkle of concern over her nose. "I am well, *mon coeur*, do not trouble yourself."

When she turned to face front again, I gently feathered her side with the long lash of the whip. "Be at ease."

"Huh," Aaron's soft sound of surprise reminded me that he was there. I still could not comprehend what had possessed him to come watch me compete, or that he would throw himself so wholeheartedly into being helpful.

"What is so surprising, then?" I inquired as I handed him back the bottle.

"I suppose I thought the whip was meant more as a gas pedal or a correction." He waved toward Lyric as she intently studied one of the horses in the arena who seemed to be tense. "But you just used it to pet her."

I grinned down at him, appreciative of not just his perception but of the glimmer of awareness in his eyes. To have him see me after so many years of acquaintance still felt miraculous. "Oh, yes, it is also for forward. But I do not want her to fear it. As I have no legs against her body to cue her, nor hands to stroke her, I use the whip to touch her. It can be used for good or ill, just as any other tool."

Watching him think gave new depths to the silences I experienced while speaking to him on the phone. "Fair enough. But you aren't here to answer twenty questions. What can I do to help you?"

"My needs are slight. I set a bucket in the golf cart, if you would retrieve it."

The words barely escaped before he turned to do as I asked. Soleil regarded him suspiciously still, for all his care with her, but did not move from her station on the passenger seat as he picked up the pail from the floorboards. He looked inside the bucket as he made the few steps back to our side, and I thanked heaven for his ever-curious mind. Teaching was so much easier when your student came with the hunger to learn.

"Just before we go in, I would like you to take the damp cloth and go over her eyes and nose. Try not to touch the patent leather, if possible." He nodded sharply, touching the cloth as if to attach the thought to it. "The dry cloth can be used on harness and carriage, if there are any dirty places, and the soft brush can take the dust from her legs. Once we do a few laps of the warmup arena, we will likely need it."

"I've got it, bossy lady." He accompanied the moniker with a playful wink that I relished. Aaron wore his responsibilities like a heavy weight on his back, and to see that lighten was a blessing.

My eye caught on the glossy length of a Morgan neck as Sue trotted past us on her way to the dressage arena. She lifted her whip hand in a greeting I returned. "Have a lovely drive!"

She smiled for mere seconds before her concentration turned completely to her mare, and I watched as they trotted boldly down the centerline to halt and salute the judges.

But then, I knew the time had come to put my own game face on. "We will return shortly."

My erstwhile groom and more than capable eye candy bowed slightly from the hips. "I shall await your return with bated breath."

Ah, there was the playfulness again, which allowed me to walk away with a smile on my lips. Lyric and I merged into the flow of traffic with practised ease, though the big ring was now amply filled by several larger turnouts. The pairs and tandems would follow the singles, then the four-in-hands would finish up the competition day with their jaunty carriages and formal attire. Theirs was a level I never even hoped to aspire to, being reliant on other people to assist you with the care of so many horses. Not to mention the costs involved in such an endeavor. My own kit had barely begun to come together correctly after three years of serious competition. Caring for and outfitting a larger string remained out of the question.

Lyric and I made quick work of our final warmup, finishing in time to watch the woman before us enter the ring with her flashy pinto. Aaron wasted no time, handing up my water as soon as

Lyric stopped, then setting to work on the tasks appointed to him. Quickly, he dusted the carriage, removing a film of red clay from the glossy black paint and chrome hubs. But when it came time to do Lyric, he moved with caution, deliberate in his intent to do everything correctly.

"Eyes, then nose," I directed as he traded the brush for the rag, delicately stroking between her eyes and the blinkers that partially obscured them. Watching his care with her softened my heart as surely as her early care with him. Just as well, as he would have to share that heart with her if he wanted the keeping of it.

But I had no more time to reflect on the romantic feelings, as the driver before me finished their test with a crisp salute, and the ring steward called my name. Now, all I had room for in my heart and mind was Lyric, and the dance we must do for the judges.

Aaron

"Now entering the arena is number 131, Jaqueline Sauveterre, driving her own Bonterre Regal Lyric, a fourteen-year-old Cheval Canadien mare." The announcer had an incredibly smooth voice, but too dry for my tastes. To be honest, it came off a little stuck up, which I'd had more than enough of over the years.

Watching Jaque work was a wonder. As the mare crisply stepped into a trot, she gave another cluck of encouragement, gaining a longer stride. Yet, as they entered the ring, they gained substance and spirit, damn near radiant with power as they headed toward their fate. When the mare halted no movement from the reins marred the tranquility of the moment, still with anticipation. Though I couldn't be certain it was intended, as Jaque raised her whip to salute the judge at the opposite end of the arena, the mare too seemed to dip her head respectfully.

They launched right back into that dynamic trot, making an arcing turn to the left. I wished, not for the first time, that I were a little less ignorant. Much like watching Bart and Eros together, all I knew was it looked impressive. I had walk, trot, lope and run at my disposal, but Jaque asked for different speeds and movements within those gaits. The fact that she accomplished the task with little more than her reins, voice, and a few discrete touches from the whip made it even more remarkable.

Jesus, she managed perfect figure eights with the reins held in one hand. Her whip was held in the other, lifted clearly out to the side. I'd have been impressed to see someone make such even turns on horseback, but in that case you could lay the reins against the horse's neck to steer. Not so here, where the circles were inscribed by the smallest movements of hand and body.

When they rolled up into a canter a crackle of energy ran across my shoulders. The mare looked every bit a war horse, arching her neck and throwing her forelegs out to eat up the turf. I couldn't hear a word Jaque said over the music playing on the loudspeakers, but every time I saw her face, her lips were moving.

I was confused when they halted in the middle...were they done? Should I applaud? Yet, the small audience remained as still as the horse and carriage, so I waited, watched as they walked a half circle to stop again, facing the other direction. This time, the mare leaned her weight into her haunches and pushed the carriage backward several steps, still with very little pressure on the reins.

I wish I could say I spent the whole test admiring them. After all, while they weren't as airy or elegant as the leggy, high-headed animals that had gone before, they did have an unmatched tranquility. And, not that I was biased, I thought they looked ten times classier. Yet, somewhere in the midst of the display of horsemanship, a punch landed square in my ego. Between that, and the chill in the air as the clouds blocked the sun, I hunched around my discomfort and shoved my hands in the pockets of my jacket.

Jesus, I was so far out of my league it wasn't even funny. These people performed at a level I could hardly imagine, some of them with horses that looked much more sensitive than Byzantine. When Jaque asked me to wipe off Lyric's face, I'd been terrified I might do something wrong, my movements careful lest I upset the mare or make a mess. I'd offered Jaque a water bottle simply because it was the one thing I could correlate from my own experiences. So many times, I'd been up on my horse desperate for a drink. And getting up on the carriage was as much a production as clambering onto Byzantine in full plate.

Applause pulled me from my inner reflection, and I hastily joined them as I noticed Jaque saluting the judges once again. Then they were trotting toward the exit, and I mustered a smile, though the effort in it disappeared as her eyes latched onto mine. Her smile was so gloriously genuine, so full of joy, it lit up all the shadowed corners of my heart and gave my doubts no place to hide. God, that smile! I could be forgiven for not noticing how beautiful a figure Jaque cut, considering I'd only ever seen her in jeans and jackets. But damn, how had I missed that smile?

"You both looked beautiful," I commented as Jaque halted the mare beside me. "May I offer her a treat?"

Confusion made her smile flicker, but then it returned, twice as bright. "I would be delighted. She has earned it, and a hundred more. Truly, that was our best test, ever."

So I fished out one of the tiny cookies that Byz preferred, a leftover from when I'd loaded him on the trailer in California, and stepped toward the mare's head. The instant I came into view around her blinders, she turned a polite muzzle toward me, a quiver in her lips that quieted her breathing as I lifted a flattened palm. Delicately, as if she were plucking down off a dandelion, she accepted the proffered treat. My neck relaxed slightly to know she liked them too, and I shared a small smile with Jaque before returning my attention to the horse.

After rolling it around in her mouth a few times, most likely to work it past the bit, she contentedly crunched the little cookie and looked at me hopefully, even as her nostrils continued to flare and relax as she recovered from her efforts in the ring.

Jaque laughed brightly as she stroked the mare's haunch with the tip of the whip. "No, *ma petit*, one for now, but more after you are out of harness. Let us walk to cool you." Then her eyes fell to me, and her gracious smile made me wish I could offer more than a cookie. Given little prompting, I felt sure I'd be offering her my heart on a platter. The idea was much less terrifying than I thought it might have been. "We shall be just a short while. Thank you."

As they walked away I headed back to the golf cart, wondering how in hell I'd fallen so far so fast. But there, as I thoughtlessly reached over to pet Soleil in greeting, I was reminded that not everything would be easy. The little Sheltie leaned away and growled, eyes narrowing suspiciously. Though she did not bare her teeth, I pulled back respectfully.

"Duly noted, little girl."

As I put both hands on the wheel and pressed on the accelerator, I found cause to chuckle. Because while Soleil clearly wasn't ready to be friends, judging by the way she lay down and imperiously crossed her front paws, she certainly found me to be a more than adequate chauffeur.

Jaque

With Aaron's help, we made short work of unhitching. I quickly shed my show clothes once my marvellous mare was unharnessed, pleased to find he had offered her a bucket of water while I changed. As I worked to remove the meticulous braids in Lyric's mane he asked for something to do, so I set him to the task of pulling out the marathon carriage. Though I heard a few muffled sounds of frustration from inside the trailer, he stuck with the task, easing the stainless-steel war wagon down the ramp right as I smoothed out the last plait.

"Holy hell, this thing is a piece of work!" The admiration in his voice carried enthusiasm, but my capacity for speech momentarily derailed. He had shed his jacket while getting the tie downs undone, and I felt compelled to openly admire his arms as he controlled the descent. Some women were into biceps, and his were clearly admirable, but for myself, I looked to the forearm. I loved to watch the play of muscles as they rotated and flexed. The dexterity involved was delicious, and in Aaron's case, I wanted little more than to feel them wrapped around me again. Yet, the needs of the moment would not allow such a liberty.

"We have only taken it on a course once so far this season. The marketing work Jo did gained me an additional sponsor, and between the three sponsors, I was able to upgrade." Once he had it parked beside the presentation carriage, I stepped closer and ran a hand along one of the swooping fenders. "We have been playing with hand me downs and now, we are of a level with our peers, equipment wise. I believe, now that I have a better idea of how to drive it, this marathon will be very enlightening."

He studied it with a critical eye, and now that I knew his affinity for fast cars, I recognized the look. My Papa had worn it often over the years while looking at airplanes.

"While I have no idea what I'm really looking at, I can appreciate the short turning radius, and low center of gravity. The suspension looks automotive grade!"

"You have an excellent eye."

At the praise, those eagle eyes turned on me, and my temperature instantly rose. "I like to think so. But somehow I missed seeing you for years."

I took a step toward him, Lyric content to ignore us in favour of her hay bag. We were in a small pocket of privacy for the moment, most people having gone down to watch the four-in-hand drivers perform. "I am grateful you see me now."

He did not just match my step, but took several, coming around the corner of the carriage to stand toe to toe with me. A knotted knuckle gently brushed my jaw, leaving behind a fiery trail of awareness. "Right now, you're all I see."

Surely, I would have been kissed, if not for the athletic blonde who rounded the end of the trailer, whistling lowly when she caught sight of us. "Whoa, Jaque, if I'd known you had company..." The brusque yet amused tone wore a Midwestern sensibility to it, as she stepped over to Lyric to give Aaron and I a moment to ourselves. "Hey big miss, are ya ready to give it the gusto tomorrow?"

Thankfully, Aaron's blue eyes colored with amusement as his hand fell back to his side. Immediately, I wanted to pull it back up, missing the touch. "Later."

"You may be sure." I promised quietly, before leading him over to meet the other member of my team. "Cardinal Collins, this is Aaron Drew, he has come to see us compete this weekend. Aaron, this is my navigator, Cardi."

Cardi turned toward us, smiling mischievously as she studied him. "Oh, don't think you're fooling me, Jaque. I heard from Joyce you were harbouring a looker. You know all the ladies will be aflutter at supper tonight."

Lifting my chin to hide my discomfort over her honest assessment of the situation, I purposely redirected the conversation. "At the moment, it is of little matter to me. If we hurry, we can beat most of the crowd out to the course. Give me a moment to return Lyric to her stall, and we can go."

Before I could reach for the lead rope Aaron's hand closed on my shoulder, turning me toward him.

"If you'll trust me, Jaqueline, I'll take care of her. You go do what you need to do." Though I caught the echo of my statement the day before, more than his words spoke to me. The quiet reassurance in his steady gaze, and the firm stroke of his thumb along my arm both told me I could believe him.

Before I could overthink it, I went to my toes and pulled him down so I could kiss his cheek. "Thank you for taking care of us." Then I turned to Cardi, endeavoring to ignore her pleased smirk as I gestured toward the waiting golf cart. We climbed aboard, Soleil immediately setting her front paws on my thigh, her tail wagging in anticipation of what lay ahead. "Don't forget to put her sheet on, Aaron! I will be back soon."

Turning my mind to business even as I turned the golf cart toward the woods, I ignored the pang in my heart that worried over what I left behind. Whether my concern was for the man, or for Lyric, who I trusted to so few, I could not have rightly said.

Cardi and I got on well for one very important reason—once we were in the zone, our focus never wavered. There were plenty of silences where she might have teased or questioned me over Aaron, yet she kept her eyes on the track as we cruised through Section A.

Once on course that focus tightened further as we worked through the hazards one at a time. We discussed the routes I intended, Cardi sketching them into the provided maps and scribbling notes in the margins. But on the last obstacle, my conviction wavered, as I recalled my earlier discussion with Aaron. I stood in the D gate, hands on hips, and studied my options one more time. To the right, I took a longer, safer route, but a hard left could gain precious seconds if we executed it correctly.

"Cardi, what do you think? Should I be careful or competitive?"

She gave the question due consideration as I showed her my options, but when I offered the second route she began to grin. "Praise be, Jaque, you're finally stepping up your game! Lyric is ready, and with the new carriage, we should ace this."

Though I smiled at her excitement, my stomach performed a brief somersault. Lyric might be in her best shape ever, but the question never lay with her...was I ready? Could I take such a risk with my very best friend? I never feared for myself half as much as I did for my Lyric, who trusted me implicitly with her wellbeing. Failing her once, oh so long ago, had been too much.

So, we traced both routes on the map, and I vowed to consider the tighter turn should Lyric come through the rest of the course in good form. This gave me an out, easing my apprehension, and we finished the course with a thorough plan of attack. Perhaps I could at last prove my intent toward the Championships, silencing the doubters. For our first run at the pinnacle I did not expect to come home with the grand prize, but we deserved our shot at it. Without fighting the detractions of Maarten and his followers.

On the way back toward the barn we dropped by the office to check the scoreboard and retrieve my dressage test. It was that sheet of paper that I truly craved, much more than my placings. The notes in the margins were my barometer for improvement, so I could ferret out my weaknesses and strive to do better. Our limits were not Lyric's, but my own alone. She could only rise if I elevated myself.

As I studiously devoured the comments, I found them exceedingly fair from both judges. Yes, our second extended trot could have used a cleaner transition, and one of my departures to canter had come a bit late. But in the end, comments like "a pleasure to watch", "beautiful connection between driver and horse" meant as much to me as the best score we had achieved at Advanced so far.

Cardi dove into the bodies around the scoreboard with her endless enthusiasm, and when she re-emerged, it had multiplied. Bouncing on her toes, she set her hands on mine in a crushing grip, wrinkling the paper I still held. "Jaque, you're in second!"

I felt the blood leave my face even as Cardi's brows pulled down in concern. If not for her grip on my hands, I might have swayed unsteadily. "Second," I whispered around the cotton in my mouth as Cardi pulled the test papers from my fingers and began to fan my face. "I did not imagine..."

"Come on, let's sit down." No nonsense and practical, she deftly steered us back to the golf cart and pushed me onto the seat. Immediately, Soleil jumped up, her tiny feet pressed to my chest so she could reach my face. The frantic lick of her tongue against my chin helped to pull me from the shock as my hands reflexively soothed her. "Sucre, I am well, thank you."

Managing a smile for both Soleil and Cardi, I drew a deep breath as I turned toward the front of the cart. "Truly, well earned.

Lyric gave me her all today, and I think it best to praise her for the effort. What say you, *mademoiselles*?"

Soleil answered my more cheerful tone with a wagging tail and a rare bark, and I responded to a few congratulations from fellow competitors as Cardi moved around to take her own seat. The woman's smile held mischief as I turned the key and set us in motion.

"I don't know, I'm thinking you should do some praising of that delicious specimen taking care of your horse. Heck, it took you months to let me hand walk her, and you might have taken even longer if you hadn't sprained your ankle." The sharp poke of her finger against my arm pulled my eyes to hers for a moment, allowing me to see her amusement.

"I have known Aaron for years," I responded perversely, not wanting her to feel slighted. Yet, the fading light as the sun went down lent me the courage to share greater truths. "Besides, I knew so few people back then. Lyric was my only friend."

"So, this Aaron, is he your friend or something more?"

I considered the question. Our mutual attraction said more, but months of late-night phone calls had created a strong fabric of friendship. Risking my hopes, I gave them a voice. "Both, I believe. Though we have had little time to explore something more, the possibilities are breathtaking."

"You've known him for years, and haven't made a move on him? Good Lord, woman, what are you, a nun?" Her baffled disbelief made me laugh.

"No, I can assure you, the thoughts I have harboured over him have been anything but pure. Yet, we were embroiled in our own lives, not ready for whatever this is between us." Then my voice grew smaller as we drew close to the stabling area, unwilling to share my vulnerability with passersby when I could barely speak it aloud to begin with. "I hope we are ready for it now. It is terribly powerful, as capable of ruin as it is of reward."

As I put the golf cart into park beside several others at the end of the aisle way, Cardi proved her generous heart to a fault, clasping my shoulder so I could not escape. "Well, much like this placing today, I'd say you've earned a reward. If you'll give me the hotel key, I'll go get settled in with a good book rather than facing the competitors party. This week's been rough, and I need the rest if I'm going to give you my best tomorrow. We'll go over routes and times again in the morning."

A trifle numb at the unexpected gift, and still reeling over my score, I told her where to find the key card I had left in the truck. She disappeared into the twilight with a wave and I took up Soleil's leash with chilled fingertips that I curled into my palms to warm. The aisle was peaceful, as many people had either gone into town to get cleaned up for the party or were still coming in from their course walks. Which was perhaps why I found Aaron asleep, his head lolling back against the wall beside Lyric's door. The mare herself stood over him, deep breaths ruffling his wild hair, quietly watchful as I approached. The serenity in her eyes spoke as loudly as her deeply bedded stall, all of her needs already attended to by the man quickly laying waste to my reservations.

Soleil still did not want to approach him, so I tucked her into the tack stall with her supper. After playing with several of her doggie friends during the course walk, she happily curled up on her little bed, which is where I would find her even after the party wore down. Not that I meant to stay long tonight. I had far more appealing options for a change.

As I approached Aaron again, I took advantage of the time to truly study him. Sleep stole years from his face, smoothing the worry lines that I had always known. Now that I knew him better, understood that those lines were because of his care for others, I appreciated them more. His blade-straight nose and noble brow brought to mind childhood fairytales, while his full lips awakened much more adult fantasies. Already, stubble shadowed his jaw, though he had shaved just that morning.

Foolish as the notion may have been, I wanted to crawl into his lap and rest with him. Instead, I stood, frozen with indecision as Lyric stared at me.

Taking matters into her own hooves, she cleared her nose loudly. Aaron startled awake, hands clutching the arms of the chair, pushing himself away from the explosion of air. "Christ, mare, way to kill a good dream."

My amusement at his affronted expression escaped in a choked giggle that brought his eyes to mine. They quickly morphed from wild surprise to heavy lidded pleasure, thickening the blood in my veins.

"Wow, dream of an angel and she appears."

I giggled again, this time allowing it to escape. "Is that one of your lines, Aaron? Because that was ridiculous." Still, I stepped closer to the heat between us, smiling as I leaned down over him. His eyes shifted with his thoughts, though a playful smile appeared immediately.

"I guess it could be, Jaque, though I've never dreamed of any woman as much as you."

My fingers closed on his rough chin, leaving me unaccountably turned on by the way he yielded to the touch. Though I heard people approaching and their horses beginning to fuss for their dinner, I risked a quick taste of his lips before pulling away.

"Give me a few moments to fix Lyric's supplements, then perhaps you would be willing to assist with putting away my presentation carriage before the party?"

He grinned as I stepped away, slouching even deeper into the chair. "Whatever you desire, Jaqueline."

That open-ended statement caused a moment's dizziness as I stepped into my equipment stall, and I frowned despite my pleasure at his words. That was twice in one afternoon, and I could afford no weaknesses. Yet, the haze faded back as I stirred water into the pellets, and I took a moment to pet Soleil while the feed soaked.

Aaron stood and folded his chair as I reentered the aisle. Intent on my goal, I unclipped the stall guard and stepped in next to Lyric, grateful for her grounding solidity as I served her food. While she ate I traced her body with my hands, checking for unusual tightness or heat. She stood hipshot for the inspection, lifting her tail up so I could scratch around her tail head as I moved to her other side. Satisfied by her condition, I switched out her sheet for a thin blanket, smoothing it over her muscular frame. With a last pat, I left the stall, securing the door before turning toward Aaron. Only to find him gone.

Perhaps he had needed to use the restroom? So, I tidied the tack room and filled the spare hay net for later, until my phone chimed in my back pocket. Brows drawn down, I pulled it out, only to smile as I read the message.

'Waiting for you at the trailer. Come find me.'

Oh that man. A short jaunt in the golf cart found my camp empty, my carriage no longer where I had left it, and the trailer ramp already closed. But then, I caught the faintest groan from the trailer shocks, cluing me in to his hiding place. When I walked around the opposite side of the trailer, I saw the small walk through door open by a crack. A dark chuckle eased through the air as I stepped inside.

"Beautiful and clever. A lethal combo."

I kept my phone flashlight pointed at the ground, not wanting to blind either of us. The light reflected enough off the pale walls to show him perched on the back of the carriage where the wicker basket usually sat. Long, denim clad legs swung in the air as he held out his hand to beckon me closer. I took the time to turn off the light as I stepped between his knees. "I did not mean for you to put the carriage away on your own, Aaron."

Hands closed on my upper arms, one sliding upward until he reached my throat. A breath later, I felt him lean in and down, his lips landing beside his thumb as I drew an excited breath. My hands landed on his thighs, the muscles bunching as I found my balance.

"I am at your service, Jaqueline." He whispered the oath against the edge of my jaw before moving his mouth up beside my ear. "Much as I look forward to the moments I can have your undivided attention, I knew going in that your focus would not be on me. And I love seeing this side of you, so sharp and intent."

There in the darkness, with such beautiful praise caressing my ears and surrounded by the familiar scents of my life with Lyric, he swept in and captured my mouth. Hungry, yet gentle, he stole my breath and even more of my heart. But my body proved the weakest link, knees giving way as the lightheaded sensation returned. Before I could so much as brace myself against it, his arms closed around my waist, keeping me upright.

"Jaque, are you okay?" The worry in his voice pushed back the threatening blackness as he moved to his feet and scooped me up to set me in his place. Hands cupped my face, the warmth in them clearing my head even more. "What's wrong?"

I pressed my hands over his and closed my eyes, hating that I had ruined the passionate moment. "I do not know. This is the third time it has happened since Cardi and I did our course walk."

He pulled his hands from under mine, and a moment later, light bloomed beside us from his phone. Concern deepened his worry wrinkles, and his kissable lips had all but disappeared into a thin slash.

"Jaque, did you eat anything after your dressage test?"

Mute with frustration, I shook my head.

"Dammit, I knew I forgot something." His frown seemed entirely self-directed, but before I could address it, he pulled me down from my perch and turned us toward the door. "Come on, let's go get you some dinner before you pass out in earnest. While I like you weak in the knees, I'd rather it be because you were starving for my kisses, not because you were actually starving."

Much as I hated my weakness, I will admit that being hauled up against his side and so devotedly attended to almost made it worth it. Yet, as he stepped toward the truck, I found some resistance still in me. Setting my chin, I slowed my feet until he stopped trying to herd me. A frown of grim determination stretched his lips taut when he looked down, and I glared back with some of my own stubbornness.

"No, Aaron, we have the competitor's dinner to attend. There will be plenty of food there, I promise you."

"Jaque, you need to rest, not socialize, particularly with your marathon tomorrow. Don't be ridiculous."

Ah, no, that wouldn't do at all! I stomped my foot, a childish gesture perhaps, but it made him straighten and step back. "Aaron Drew, you will not dictate my life, well-meaning or no!"

"Dammit, Jaque, that's not what I meant!" His hands flew up between us as if to ward me off as he shifted his weight backward. "I'm just trying to fix my mistake."

"Your mistake?" I asked incredulously, setting my fists on my hips to keep from shaking him. "What mistake would that be? Maybe your mistake was coming out here in the first place."

At that, he truly took a step back, his jaw rigid and outthrust. "Do you really believe that? Even for a moment? Because if so, I should go."

The very idea drove a spike of despair into my chest, puncturing my ego. All the pride that had straightened my spine suddenly puddled in my feet as my hands fell to my sides. "Perhaps you should." I said the words softly, hating each syllable as it fell.

"Then you would not have to see me at my worst. Then I could concentrate on my work, and you would not be reduced to playing helper."

"This is you at your worst?" The flat inflection stung, making it clear how much damage I had just done, and I could no longer meet his eyes. But he called me out immediately. "Jaqueline, don't quit on me now. I'm trying here."

I had to dash away a tear before I could raise my head, and I caught his shocked inhale as he lifted a hand toward me. Desperate to bridge the gap, I took it, grateful for the tightening of his grip. "I am sorry. I have been on my own for so long that I do not know how to accept help graciously."

His cheeks softened and he cracked a sheepish smile. "And I'm too used to giving orders, even to people I care about. But I'd like to think we both can learn."

When I managed to return his smile, he pulled me to him by the fingertips and turned toward the golf cart.

"What say you, my lady, shall we hunt down sustenance and face the inquisition of your peers?"

To which I groaned and acquiesced, grateful to have him pilot us toward the big tent down by the arena. Perhaps I had not received the kisses I desired, but something about the way he kept me close to him as he drove, even after our misunderstanding, felt equally as important.

Aaron

The competitor's party was already well underway as I parked the golf cart beside countless others. Inside, they had an open bar, which held not even the slightest appeal, even with the stress of our recent disagreement. Usually after getting into it with my mother or sisters I dove for the solace found in a couple beers. Instead, I steered us for the huge buffet table stretching along the back of the space, the surface covered in a wide assortment of southern favorites. The fried chicken wafted like perfume in the air, and my own stomach joined Jaque's in a hearty chorus as we picked up plates and began to dish.

Once Jaque ate a little something the color began to return to her face and I could smile as she introduced me to the curious folk who approached to congratulate her. Finding out she was in second place brought a swell of pride, particularly when one of the judges sought her out for a handshake and a hearty well done. This woman that I wanted so badly to call mine was as fierce a competitor as any of the knights in Gallant Company, however different her goals may be.

Her graciousness never flagged as she introduced me to countless faces, knowing the names of all the drivers, their grooms, and families. She asked after their horses, chatting about the course for the next day and faultlessly redirected praise onto her own horse.

A clearing throat pulled everyone's attention to the small stage, and Joyce waved at the room at large. "Good evening, carriage driving enthusiasts. It's Harv and I's great privilege to have you all here at our home." One of the gentlemen in the band stood up from his chair and tipped his hat genially. He looked placid as a pond on a still day, a trait that likely came in handy when married to a motivated woman like Joyce. "You've all put in some amazing efforts today, and I'd like to welcome our dressage judges up to pass out the awards for this first phase."

The woman who had shaken Jaque's hand earlier took the microphone from our host, and slowly went through a long list of awards, beginning with the youth competitors. Jaque clapped with each one, her enthusiasm never waning.

When the Advanced competitors were announced, she cheered quite loudly for a blonde gal named Sue, which perhaps made it more notable when the applause faded over a man I recognized from the restaurant the night before. Grady Malone made his way to the stage with a condescending grin that made me want to throw down a gauntlet for fun. It was nice to put a name to the slick looking asshole.

Jaque was called up after another woman and accepted her red ribbon with a thank you to both the judges and the organizers as she joined the lineup. Yet, the next was another of the pricks from the night before, Paul Scott. The instant he joined the group, I watched Jaque's body grow rigid, though she still shook his hand in congratulations. After a few pictures, they dispersed, and Joyce reclaimed the microphone to admonish us all to stay for dancing.

Jaque took her chair, smoothing her ribbon against the tablecloth with a quivering smile. "It will look beautiful against her black coat, I think."

I scooted closer so I could set my hand on her knee, ignoring the smirk from Paul as he and Grady walked past. "I think the color of the ribbon doesn't matter that much to you, Jaque."

Her smile steadied as she touched my cheek, fingertips dragging along the rough stubble. My mother would have had a conniption to see me at a dinner out with a five o'clock shadow already sprouting, but Jaque didn't seem to mind at all. "No, not in the least. Though, you know, in Canada, a red ribbon goes to the winner. Receiving a blue still seems a bit surreal, to my mind."

I held that hand to my cheek for a second, letting the world fade back even as the band began to warm up in the background. Storm of emotions or no, the peace I felt with Jaque was second to none.

Joyce found us as the first song began to play, a sly smile on her painted lips that made me straighten. My feet itched with the urge to run as she raked her eyes over where our linked hands lay on the table. "Ah, there you two are! Can I rely on you to set an example for the others, and get the dancing started?"

I looked to Jaque, willing to follow her lead. Yet, she surprised me, turning toward Joyce with an expression of regret. "Would you forgive me if I bow out tonight, Miss Joyce? I overdid a bit today, and if I am to perform well tomorrow, I need to recharge."

Though Joyce's painted lips pursed with disappointment, motherly concern colored her eyes. "Oh, goodness, by all means! You go tend to your pretty mare, then get some rest, Jaqueline. But tomorrow night, I expect you to grace the arms of your gentleman friend."

Jaque looked to me for an answer, which I quickly provided, throwing in an extra measure of charm to win her friend over. "Miss Joyce, it would be my pleasure. Please tell your husband he's a fine hand on the guitar and thank you so much for your hospitality."

Her cheeks pinked, and she fanned herself with a hand. "My, such pretty manners. Young man, you make sure she actually rests tonight, if you take my meaning."

Though I smiled and assured her I would, the instant we quit the tent, Jaque began to test my resolve. She scooted close to me on the seat, smiling in the half-light when I lifted an arm to allow her even closer. Her hand fell on my thigh, moving over the denim with featherlight strokes as I drove us back to the barn.

As we checked on Lyric, she brushed against me at every opportunity. A breast against my arm as I hung the new hay net, her fingers over my abs as I let myself back out of the stall. Once she said goodnight to the mare and took up Soleil's leash, I sought to slow things down by taking her free hand as we walked to her truck. Yet, even that contact felt heady, the soft skin on my bare palm making me feel three beers into a bender.

"Would you drive us?" She asked as we approached her camp, and I answered by leading her around to the passenger side. Soleil jumped in the instant I opened the door, but Jaque seemed in no hurry as she turned toward me. "I can see the care you are taking with me, Aaron, and I am grateful for it, even if I react poorly sometimes." Her hand slid up my arm, slithering over the thin fleece jacket I wore until her fingers feathered into the hair around my ears. "Please accept my apology."

"Accepted, though it's not necessary all the time, Jaque. I'm sure we will both fumble much more as we figure each other out." I pulled her hand down and pressed a kiss to her palm, despite the lingering scent of horse. Her fingers curled over it as soon as I released her, and her opposite hand blazed a fiery path down the side of my torso to catch a finger in my front pocket.

"Then perhaps you will allow me to apologize more physically." She reeled me in slowly, her lips already parted on a soft sigh as she lifted them up. "Perhaps in those kisses I promised to pay you in."

"Just kisses, Jaque," I qualified as I pressed her back into the open doorway in a distinct echo of the night before, though the strain in my voice no doubt gave away my weakness. "You really do need to rest for tomorrow."

Her throaty chuckle as she pulled me down made me worry for a moment, but then, she was kissing me. I lost myself in the first taste, my objections not even a memory as she bloomed beneath my mouth. Dammit, the feel of her hands in my hair was like an off switch for rational thought. This time, when her legs wound around my hips, I groaned into her and yielded. There was little danger of things going much further, not so publicly, but feeling her heat pressed against the most insistent part of me sure threatened my intentions. I ground against her, a low growl escaping when she arched her belly against mine. Yes, more!

If she hadn't pulled back I might have spent hours exploring her mouth alone, the hot depths as delicious as her passionate embrace. But I let her go as she scooted up onto the seat, sure I'd taken things a step too far. Her lips were swollen with the force of our kisses, and her eyes looked nearly black in the overhead lights as she reached for her seatbelt.

"My turn to apologize." I sighed and began to turn away, but Jaque wasn't done with me. Her fist knotted around the fabric of my jacket, tugging me back toward her.

"No apologies needed, though I would appreciate it if you could get us back to the hotel quickly. Though you seem determined to take things slow, the way those kisses were escalating is not something I wish to share with the general public." Her nose wrinkled with amusement as her fingers brushed my lips, and I kissed them when she lingered. "After all, I have a reputation to maintain."

Then she shoved me away and reached for the door, but I was determined to land my own blows. When I stepped back into her space and pulled her down just enough to plant a rough kiss on her lips, she yielded easily. Her lashes fluttered charmingly as she sighed her pleasure into the air between us.

"Yes, as easily the most beautiful and bossy woman I know. Good thing I happen to like it."

Then I shut the door on her and marched around to the driver's side, ignoring the insistent throb in my jeans. I had little regret as we pulled out the gate of the showgrounds and merged onto the little two-lane highway that would take us back to town. Yet, by the time we walked upstairs to our rooms, sense had returned. When she waited for me to open the door to my room, her hand drawing circles on my lower back, I had to address my concerns. Once we were alone in the room together, I highly doubted either of us would be in a talking mood.

"Jaque, I meant what I said, though I think I need to make myself clear." Her frown had me bending down to kiss the corner, trying to soften it. "I didn't come out here to get laid, and I mean to wait until your attentions aren't divided. Maybe that'll be Sunday night, maybe it'll be when you get home, but I think we'll be worth waiting for."

"Oh," That quiet syllable held a wealth of pain, and I hated that I'd caused it. When I reached out to hold her, she stepped back. "I did not realize my attentions were unwelcome."

"Not unwelcome, Jaqueline." I rushed to explain, stepping to block her door as she fished in a pocket for her key card. "I'm happy to kiss you until neither of us can breathe and to test the limits of my resolve, if you like. But I want you to know how much I respect you, and that your goals this weekend are important to me."

She froze, hand still in her pocket, Soleil looking between us with narrow eyes. I felt two seconds from getting my ankle bitten.

"You truly mean that." A statement, not a question, though I thought I heard confusion in her voice. When she looked up again her cheeks were taut, but her eyes relaxed. "I should rest, but I must admit, I slept poorly last night. My mind was on you rather than my work, a situation I am unfamiliar with."

Concern for her wellbeing argued with a hefty boost to my ego, knowing I hadn't been the only one thinking of the person in the other room. "Is there anything I can do to help?"

She shifted her weight onto one leg, studying me as if I held all the answers. Sadly, I was so lost I could barely find my own ass with both hands.

"Would you be averse to cuddling? I know most men do not enjoy such things, yet, I wanted so very much to curl up with you when I found you asleep."

Relief made my legs feel watery. "Jaque, I can think of nothing I'd like more."

Her hand came to rest on the center of my chest, grounding me again, and she smiled as if I'd given her diamonds. "Then let me change into my pajamas and get Soleil settled. I should not be long."

"You can bring her with you, you know." I offered, knowing I still had some ways to go before the little creature would accept me. When Jaque stared at me for a beat too long, her eyebrows knitting together, I thought I'd done something wrong again.

"You do not have to try so hard, Aaron. I am already yours for the taking."

To which I smiled and stepped toward my own door. "But this isn't about taking, Jaque. It's about giving." A quick slide of the key card popped the catch on my door, and I opened it with one hand while holding the card out toward her. "Let yourself in whenever you like."

My inner compass lurched toward the soft wonder in her eyes. As soon as her fingers plucked the card from mine, I stepped inside my room to give us both a little space. Yet, the effort was futile, because no matter how much distance lay between us, I would always feel her pulling me closer.

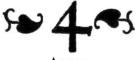

Aaron

I woke the next morning to a decided emptiness in my arms. Jaque had spent the night pressed to my chest, barely more than a few passionate kisses exchanged before she yawned, giving away her exhaustion. I'd held her as she fell asleep, slow breaths puffing against my sternum. For the first time in a long time, I dozed off with no music or television show as background noise, content to listen to the silence between the slowing beats of my heart.

Then I bolted upright, scrabbling for my phone as I noticed the sunlight sneaking in around the curtains. Dammit! Eight AM! Not only had Jaque snuck out without waking me, I'd overslept! Why hadn't she come pounding on my door yet?

The lock screen on my phone showed several missed messages, all from Jaque. I flicked them open on the move, already headed for the shower, when the contents slowed my steps.

'Aaron, thank you for last night. I have never enjoyed anyone's companionship more.'

'I did not have the heart to wake you, you looked so peaceful. Though I would have wished for some kisses to start my day, I look forward to the ones we might enjoy at the end of it.'

'Do not worry, Cardi and I are taking her vehicle to the show grounds. I left the keys to my truck on your dresser, join us when you are ready.'

I cranked on the hot water in the shower, allowing the room to steam up as I typed a reply.

'Feel free to wake me anytime you like for more kisses. Last night was my pleasure, and I hope to repeat it. I'll be there shortly.'

Then I set the phone by the sink and threw my sleep clothes on top of it before diving into the scalding spray. The heat stung, yet I breathed through the pain as I leaned against the slick tiles of the wall. Much as I had thoroughly enjoyed sleeping with Jaque, my body wasn't used to maintaining a single position all night. My muscles were stiff and I needed to get the blood flowing again.

Not until I was freshly shaved and fully dressed did I pick up the phone again, finding a new message waiting.

'Do not rush, we do not start on course until 1:20pm. Cardi and I have things well in hand.'

After making sure the room door latched behind me, I jogged down the stairs toward Jaque's truck, smiling at the memories surrounding it. If not for a problem with the water pump, I don't know that I'd have ever slowed down enough to notice Jaque as more than a business acquaintance.

The older model diesel hummed as the starter coils warmed up, then reliably rumbled to life. Once Jaque returned to Kentucky I wanted to give it a thorough going over. No sense having it break down on her if it could be prevented. I let it warm up while I texted Jaque, the heater intensifying the phantom traces of her perfume.

'I'm going to grab a quick breakfast, see you in a bit.'

The town was too small to expect a decent smoothie, but I did need a more substantial breakfast. While not my first choice, I found a bigger coffee shop than the drive up we visited the day before and put down a decent breakfast burrito along with several cups of dark roast. In the same shopping center was a supermarket, so I cruised the aisles to make sure Jaque had food to see her through the day. A few pre-made salads with plenty of chicken, some fruit, a case of water, a handful of protein bars and a couple bags of ice would do the trick, I hoped. A cheap Styrofoam cooler kept it all corralled, but as I loaded it all in the back seat, one more idea occurred to me.

Another trip into the coffee shop, and I was back on the road, hoping my offerings wouldn't be taken amiss. With Jaque, I walked a fine line between pleasing her and upsetting her...but unlike dealing with my mother, the line didn't seem to move. Figuring out the boundaries felt possible in this case. I hoped.

On the driveway into the grounds, I slowed at the now familiar sight of Jaque, her mare grazing in the short grass along the fence line. The highlights in her hair were brought out by the matching dark purple of her polo shirt, her full hips filling out a pair of dark jeans, finished off by the same waterproof leather and canvas boots from yesterday. A quick look at the rear-view mirror showed no one behind me, so I stopped and rolled down the window. She headed my way with a hurried stride, Lyric falling in next to her with little resistance. If it had been Byz, I'd have had to haul him away from the grass by force.

"Good morning, ladies."

Jaque smiled, though it seemed edgy, so I offered her the paper coffee cup in lieu of further words. She snatched it so quickly I almost feared pulling back a bloody stump, but after a sniff of the contents, her expression softened.

"You are a paragon among men, Aaron." The gratitude laced into that statement made the expression of praise into something more meaningful than many a warm compliment from hundreds of other women I had flirted with. "The coffee shop had not opened yet when we drove past."

"Hopefully, this redeems me for not waking up to see you off," I teased carefully, earning a lopsided and much more real smile.

"No, I could not bear to wake you. Though you were reluctant to release me, once I moved, you pulled the blanket over your face." Her eyes went round with softness, making me wish we had time to linger. "You needed the sleep after last weekend's efforts at the tournament."

"My thanks. I slept like a rock for a change. Most of the time I tend to toss and turn."

Inside my chest, I felt memories stir, thick and sticky like old motor oil. My father stumbling into the house in the middle of the night, drunk off his ass, hollering at my mother for some stupid thing or another. The screeching replies and the reverberation through the wall as she threw objects and invectives at his head. Then Jaque's hand folded around my arm, and the memories vanished like a wisp of smoke in a gale force wind. I met her gaze and found myself in the eerie stillness of the eye of the same storm.

"Then I am glad we both found solace with each other. I have not shared a bed with anyone in several years and feared we might not be compatible."

I dropped my chin and directed a bit of heat her way, gratified when she shook her head and pursed her lips in what I took for mock disapproval. "Well, not that way. Though I look forward to testing our partnering as lovers as well. But companionably we certainly seem a match."

When I caught sight of another truck coming up the drive behind me, I knew our time was at an end. "And I look forward to a repeat tonight. But for now, take care of your mare, and I'll see you back at the barn."

The mare in question chose that moment to nod her head emphatically, and Jaque stepped back with a velvet laugh. She raised her cup in salute as I took my foot off the brake. "Thank you again, good sir."

"A pleasure, my lady." I shot back, before turning my attention to the traffic ahead.

The lanes around the barns and trailers looked much busier than the day before, an edge in the air as carriages trotted past. The horses were a little more up-headed, looking into the distance as their drivers sent them down the road. Flashing legs were wrapped in protective boots, and the metal carriages gleamed in the sunlight. Everyone wore much more casual clothing, and some of them looked downright gaudy, in neon colors that I'm sure could be seen for miles.

When I arrived at Jaque's trailer I found Cardi setting a large tote beside the carriage, while Soleil watched from her vantage on a camp chair. The dog monitored my activities with narrowed eyes as I unloaded the cooler I'd brought, despite the fact that I had given her a bit of cheese before Jaque and I wound ourselves together the night before. Apparently, I still had some wooing to do, but I'd brought a secret weapon. Crouching in front of the fox-faced creature I slowly opened the wrapper on a string cheese. Her button nose wiggled madly as I peeled off a thin section. Though she did not unbend enough to take the treat from my hand, she delicately consumed the proffered morsel once I placed it on the seat in front of her, and I accepted the little victory with a huff of amusement. But the feeling was short lived as I turned around to face another set of narrowed eyes from Cardi.

"What, do you want some too?" I asked, reflexively going on the offensive, though the woman had done nothing to deserve it.

She rolled her eyes and lifted her chin in clear disdain, but my mother had the market on that look, so it hardly touched me. "This knight in shining armor shit might work on a tender heart like Jaqueline, but you aren't fooling me with the chiseled jaw and charming manners. What's your angle here? Shit, I figured now that you'd gotten her into your bed, you'd be outta here like yesterday's news."

I wanted to lash out, to defend myself, but what happened between Jaque and I wasn't any of the woman's business unless Jaque chose to share it with her friend. Obviously, she had not. While I frowned at Cardi's vehemence, I managed to keep my voice calm. "No, I'm here for Jaque as long as she wants me. I don't know much about what needs doing in order to help her, but I take instruction well, if you point me in the right direction."

Her eyes squinted further and she crossed her arms, the defensive posture rankling. I hadn't done anything to deserve it, which made me wonder who had done Jaque wrong in the past. Cardi was right. Jaque did have a tender heart, which made me want to pummel whoever had taken advantage of it.

"Alright, Prince Charming, I'll take you at your word. We could always use the extra hands."

Then her grin went mercenary and my scalp tightened with dread. "First things first. I need these bushel buckets filled with water. Sadly, the tap is over by the barn. Would you mind?"

My mind did the math as I took in the three large tubs, and the two smaller buckets beside them. But my body, honed by exercise and the fortitude required by jousting, was already in motion. Shedding my jacket, I picked up the smaller buckets as I headed for the barn.

"Consider it done." I tossed over my shoulder without looking back, my arms already flexing with anticipation over the Herculean task ahead. After all, faint heart never won fair lady, and I'd never met one more worthy of the effort.

Jaque

Dismay and appreciation argued with each other as I approached the camp, following in Aaron's wake. Little could improve the view afforded, his shoulders rippling with muscle as he stabilized the buckets in his hands. Lyric tugged lightly on the lead to speed my steps—she knew what lay ahead of us today and had met me at her stall door with her game face firmly in place. We did not have time for this distraction.

When we reached the camp, he emptied the water into one of the bushel buckets sitting under the shade and spun around. His wrinkled brow immediately smoothed as our eyes met and he flashed me a grin. "Ladies, nice to see you again. Be back in a few."

Before I could stay him, he was off once more, determined purpose in his strides. That left me to turn to Cardi for answers, but my narrow-eyed glare yielded only an unrepentant grin as she worked to remove Lyric's sheet.

"Would you care to explain why my guest is currently toiling in this heat, when he could have used the golf cart to drive the big buckets to the spigot?" I asked calmly as I tied Lyric's lead to the trailer and crouched to run my hands over her lower legs. Only the old thickness over her left knee slowed my touch, but I pushed away the memories attached to that scar in favour of more immediate concerns. The tendons and muscles were tight and cool, ready for the action to come.

Cardi snickered as she tossed the sheet over the back of a chair and handed me the first of the boots Lyric would wear to protect her legs. "Because I wanted to know he was more than just arm candy. If he's going to have his way with you, then he should earn the privilege."

To which I grumbled indelicately, "Perhaps it is me that seeks to have my way, my friend?"

No, I would not share Aaron's hesitancy to come together intimately. Much as it chafed my nerves, my heart understood it to be a rare and precious thing. I felt cherished, not a sensation I had often experienced at the hands of my lovers. Wanted, needed, even appreciated? Certainly. Yet Aaron made me feel all those things and more, all without removing a stitch of clothing.

Cardi cleared her throat, recalling me to the present, where I had frozen in place. Even Lyric, who had thus far been understanding of my distraction over the man, turned a questioning eye upon me. So I carefully and hurriedly finished securing the Velcro on the boots, and stood to take the next set.

Though only one of my girlfriends could give voice, she seemed to convey enough doubt for the both of them. "Are you sure your head is in the game, Jaque? Now isn't the time to be distracted, no matter how delicious the temptation."

Laughing, though it held little humour, I quickly applied the boots to Lyric's hind legs, tracing the familiar joints and taut skin with knowing hands. You could blind me, and I would know Lyric by touch alone. "Cardinal Collins, I cannot believe you would even consider such a question. You have seen me through several break ups and upheavals, and never once have I let a single tear interfere with Lyric."

When I stood, Cardi levelled a firm stare at me, as if rifling through the contents of my brain. "No, you never have, and you're a stronger woman than me. I've fallen apart over far less. But this is new, so I want to be sure we're still on the same page." Her hand gripped my shoulder with implacable resolve, turning me toward where Aaron had dumped the last two pails of water out and grabbed the hem of his shirt to mop the sweat off his face. My brain went to pudding at the sight of his well-defined abdomen, and my hands twitched, wanting to trace every line until I knew him by touch as well as I knew my mare. Cardi's shoulder bumped mine and she chuckled, no doubt amused by my weakness, though not maliciously. "All I'm saying, Jaqueline, is if you're gonna have a weakness, damn, you picked some fine kryptonite."

To that I offered a rare giggle, leaning against her in camaraderie. Aaron looked up at the sound, dropping his shirt and grinning with a boyish innocence that quite belied the heat in his eyes.

"Indeed, I did." I replied quietly, lingering in the intimate gaze before bumping Cardi roughly to the side. "Now, how about we get to our work? I too must earn the privilege of such a weakness."

Cardi shoved back before stepping away to fetch the first bit of harness. "And there's the difference between us, Jaque. I feel like I have to fight to be strong, and only you feel like you have to earn the right to be vulnerable."

To which I said nothing, storing that profound truth away for a time when I could afford to reflect on it. I broke away from the temptation of Aaron and lost myself in more necessary endeavors. As we harnessed Lyric, the synthetic straps laying against her like a second skin, I reviewed obstacles in my head. The challenging mazes played on a loop in my memory, meant to test not just courage, but forgiveness and tenacity. Each one was the combination on a lock, this much left, then a hard twist right to a second right, circling around wide left to a sharp left and out to the right at a gallop. Every one we conquered would take us that much closer to our prize, which contrary to some competitor's beliefs, were not the ribbons. My prize was ever stronger faith between Lyric and I, a validation that the training we had done, the partnership we had created, was perfect for us. I could not say that what we had accomplished would ever be replicated with another horse, nor did I care. Combined driving had not been my goal until Lyric showed an eagerness for it during her rehab. With another horse my goals might change entirely, to suit them, not myself.

Of course, one hour later, as we worked our way through the steady booming trot work of Section A, I had cause to doubt that thought. Lyric's muscular haunches pistoned before me, a sight I doubted I would ever tire of. Could I give up the sweaty exhilaration? Would anything taste as sweet to me as the briny flavour of effort? The way Lyric's ears flickered out to take in her surroundings, then back to me at each inflection of my voice? Somehow, I doubted I could be content to return to the oval of the show ring, where looks alone seemed to account for so much. No, I wanted this proving ground, to be tested to our limits.

I poured my heart entirely into my mare, encouraging her to soldier onward even as the sweat began to lather between her hind legs. I focused on the relaxed sway of her braided-up tail, allowed her to pull strongly up a hill and slowed her slightly as we went through an intersection. Cardi faithfully kept us on track, calling out times as we passed the kilometre markers, and we took some of the quieter stretches of road to discuss the greater test ahead. Never once during that time did the thought of Aaron distract me from my goal.

Yet, as we pulled into the ten-minute rest area where Aaron waited with a pail for Lyric and bottles of water for Cardi and I, I had to admit to myself that he had been with me. Perhaps not in thought, but in spirit. For in him too, I saw a challenge, a test in partnership that all other relationships had merely been preparation for. And much like the trial that waited for Lyric and I, I felt a thrill as fear skittered along my skin that I could not wait to experience again.

We walked out of the mandatory ten-minute rest after a smile and nod from the veterinarian doing pulse and temperature checks. Though Lyric had grown warm from effort, the overcast day had kept her from overheating. Being muscular and black, she occasionally took a bit longer to cool down, but the weather favoured us for a change. I tipped my chin in acknowledgement as Aaron waved goodbye, giddy for the attention, but all of my earlier worry slid away as I turned us toward the truest test of horsemanship I had ever known.

We timed our departure near perfectly, approaching the start flags at a relaxed walk, though I felt Lyric's eagerness through the reins. She would never be so rude as to pull, but more a rolling sensation from one rein to the other as she sucked the bit higher in her mouth, looking for the moment she could take up more contact.

"131," Cardi called out as we grew closer, so the volunteers knew who we were on their clipboards.

The lady in charge replied, "54 seconds!"

I turned Lyric away, inscribing a small circle rather than slowing our momentum. Starting a vehicle from a complete stop would be a more taxing effort, creating impatience where none was needed. Any horse at the Advanced level well knew what the start flags were, though Lyric had figured out the game after our very first driving trial. It had taken over a year to teach her to maintain relaxation as we approached, wasting energy better saved for the real game.

As we came around straight on the track again the timer waved us onward, and I clucked needlessly to my mare as she lifted into a trot. Instantly, the reins hummed with an expectant electricity, power flowing from her to me, then back again in an ever-building loop.

"Have a great drive!" The starter called out as we passed her.

"Thank you!" Cardi and I both responded as I lifted my whip in salute. Events like this would never work without the hundreds of people that gave up their time to make this happen. I had done my time in their ranks, learning the ins and outs before I ever competed. Even still, I volunteered at local lower level shows, when my schedule allowed.

"Time!" Cardi said as we passed the start flags, letting me know she had started the first stopwatch. From now on, she would provide time checks as we passed the quarter marks in our distance, so I knew our pacing. With the cloudy day in our favour I felt confident we would finish in the allotted time, but with Cardi keeping track, I would know when I could walk Lyric to save her speed for the obstacles themselves.

The wheels of the carriage hummed lowly as we hustled down the road, Lyric's strides steady and powerful. The breeching around her hind quarters moved loosely against her skin as she strove into the wide breast collar, and the faint bump of the singletree swinging back and forth added another rhythm to the sound of her hoof beats. The numbered gates fell by the wayside like rungs on a ladder, climbing to the next objective with steady strides.

As the first hazard came into view around a corner, I checked in with my mare, making sure I could bend her head slightly right or left without losing momentum and tightening my core to ask for balance. When she responded, lifting her head to look where we were going at the same time her hindquarters lowered, I could not help a grin of excitement.

She and I had built toward this moment since her birth, still wet and blinking at the brand-new world as I toweled her dry. I held her head in my hands and kissed the tiny bit of white on her lip as she lay in my lap, and ever since that day, we belonged to each other. We had challenged each other, learned to find a balance between work and play, and finally reached the pinnacle of our chosen sport.

My eyes narrowed as they latched onto the first letter, and I barely kissed my lips before Lyric threw herself into the harness, ears pointed where my gaze landed. Cardi's announcement of our number as we flew through the entrance was muffled to my ears, my nervous system now hardwired to Lyric's. We swung around on a curving line to slot ourselves into A, and I hollered "Hard!" as I gave her some of the left rein and closed my hand on the right. Her canter barely stuttered as she wheeled tightly through two uprights to reach B.

As I relaxed, she straightened and picked up momentum again as we took a wider right swoop to find C. I had replayed these obstacles so many times in my mind I knew them by heart, but now I no longer saw anything beyond the white and red markers with their bold letters. D came up three turns to the right, Lyric dropping to the trot to balance herself as the ground sloped away.

"Hup, hup!" I shouted, pitching my voice high with excitement so she would gain speed coming out of the last turn, and I caught

Cardi's excited yip as we slung around straight. Grinning madly as we shot back outside the obstacle, I braced my feet against the footboard as we hand galloped around to the E gate. As soon as I tightened my stomach and purled softly, Lyric came back into my hands, sitting on her haunches as we dropped back into the middle of the tangle of uprights. F lay in the middle of the warren, and I made a slight left into an even tighter right that had the carriage scraping against a corner. Lyric slowed at the additional friction, unsure of the noise, but I kept her aimed for the gate and urged her on. "That's my girl!"

Faithful and bold, she answered my surety with a stronger stride, the wheels on the carriage chittering as we made the final gate and I turned her toward the exit. "Get out, mare!"

She knew those words and flattened out, her ears aimed directly at the flags. There was no need to tap her with the whip as we galloped. I barely managed a giddy "Thank you!" for the volunteers, and I heard one of the women laugh as we flew by her. Once we were clear, I purled my tongue again, and Lyric dropped back to a trot, a jaunty lift in her tail.

"Such a glorious mare!" I praised, softly stroking the top of her haunches with the short lash on the whip.

"Glorious!" Cardi echoed, dissolving into a muffled giggle that made Lyric tip her head slightly, wondering what we were up to behind her. "So help me, woman, if this is how you drive after getting well laid, then I firmly declare it on the approved list for marathon preparation!"

I couldn't help giggling back, though I kept my words for Lyric as I fed her a little extra rein and she reached down into the contact, straightening in the process. "Do not listen to the silly gator, *mon coeur*, this is all girl power!"

"Go, glorious girl power!" Cardi crowed, and I giggled some more even as her hand came up just ahead of my left arm to point us at the next numbered gate. We had made a grand start to the course, but as Lyric curved her body into the turn with a toss of her head, I sobered slightly. One hazard down, several more to go, and a mare who deserved my complete and total commitment to every stride she took.

Aaron

Cardi had been kind enough to direct me to the best places to watch the competition, and I hustled from the holding box with Soleil in tow, hoping to get to obstacle three before Jaque did. This particular one had been built to resemble a marina, the shallow water broken up with small docks and posts painted to look like buoys. Someone had even gone to the trouble of adding fake seagulls and a plush toy seal.

A horse and driver were splashing back out of the obstacle as I arrived, and I took up a station nearest the entry where I could see everything clearly. Not that I had long to wait as the black mare came around a clump of trees at a booming trot, then smoothly upshifted to a bouncy looking canter. Jaque was captivating, so completely in the moment, practically vibrating with energy as she directed the mare with unerring accuracy.

The mare did not hesitate as they aimed for the bridge, her hooves thundering across the wood planks, nostrils stretched wide to draw in the air. Once back on the ground, a hard left had Cardi leaning out over the side to keep the wheels on the ground, but then she agilely jumped up onto a higher step as they dove into the water. The mare's big feet sprayed water in every direction, but she never so much as flinched, cantering around one of the buoys with a total disregard for the stuffed seal.

Even though I had walked the hazards with Jaque the day before, I was instantly lost, wondering how she managed to keep everything straight at such a rate of speed. Lyric rarely dropped to a trot, threading through turns at the canter, several of them alarmingly tight. In one, the carriage scraped against the rope wrapped corner post with a zip of friction that tightened every muscle in my back, but Cardi kept it upright and Lyric threw herself into the harness to get clear.

Through it all, Jaque maintained a symphony of motion and sound, body leaned forward to encourage, or back to balance. Her hands danced lightly on the reins, the whip still and quiet but for the lash being pushed by the wind. Her voice too, changed to suit the moment, from excited yipping noises to a strange musical sort of purr that I might not have heard if she wasn't passing close by. But for all of that, the true wildness appeared at the very end, as they took one last turn and she pointed the mare for the exit.

"Get out, mare!" she shouted harshly, the whip lightly touching the mare's back. Lyric curled her body before exploding forward, galloping flat out for the finish flags that would mark their time, Cardi throwing in her own excited crowing to spur their speed.

I barely saw them drop back to a trot before the trees swallowed them again, and I stood in stunned silence for nearly a minute before Soleil's warning growl pulled me back into my own skin. An older man approached with an elderly Labrador at his heels, the calm creature gray in the face, and surely no threat to the smaller dog. When I tugged carefully on her lead, Soleil looked up at me in narrow-eyed disgust and sat primly before deigning to ignore me.

"Hmm, I've seen that look before." The gentleman said, his voice pleasantly raspy as he held out a hand for me.

"What look?" I shook his hand, reassured by his steady grip and the steadier eyes that looked out from under his straw fedora. Sure, my Dad had proven you could have a good handshake and still be an asshole, but I'd learned to read people better over the years. Product of working so closely with the public meant I could now see the calm light in someone's eyes, just as much as the sharpness that would set me on alert.

"The shocked wonder of watching your woman turn into a speed-crazed Amazon right in front of you." He chuckled when I straightened and schooled my face. "No worries there, you're in good company. I've worn it myself, as have most of the other fellows you'll meet on the circuit. I'm Harvey Benton, the farm owner. Joyce told me all about you yesterday, and I figured I'd roll out the welcome wagon in case you were feeling a little adrift."

"Aaron Drew. And thank you sir, so far everyone seems very friendly."

Harvey grinned widely, deepening every sun-worn wrinkle on his face. "That's carriage driving folk for you. We're a social lot, aside from a few stuffed shirts who think this is a status symbol. This sport isn't exactly mainstream athletics, and it costs too damn much to do it if you don't love it."

I couldn't help a huff of amusement. "I think I've got your lot beat, Harvey. I'm a jouster. We're just a speck in the bucket when it comes to horse sports."

While he went a little wide eyed at my profession, his smile quickly reappeared as he turned away, gesturing me to follow.

"Here, let's get you to the next hazard before you miss out. And I've got news for you, Aaron. Judging by the looks you've been giving Jaque, you're gonna be one of our number soon enough. She'll have you on the back step before you know it, mucking stalls and grooming too."

Grateful for Harvey's lead, I walked along beside him, my amusement continuing to grow. "Ha, I'm already in on the last two. I imagine I'll be navigating as soon as she has time to teach me the job."

Laughing outright as we dropped down a slight hill into another small valley, this one holding a warren of rainbow-colored squares, Harvey led me over to a ridge where we had the best view. "Then, my good man, you're already one of our number, and a fine addition by my estimation. You should be plenty tough, and clearly, you're in good enough shape to be useful at the Advanced level."

I barely had time to thank him for the compliment when I heard Cardi yelling out their number. Lyric burst through the timer flags with all the fire of any war horse I'd ever known, her mistress as focused and determined as any knight. As they tore through the gates at a dizzying rate of speed, my heart kept time with the mare's hooves, enjoying a vicarious thrill from their courage.

Then they were gone again, and I found Harvey had walked down the hill to speak with one of the volunteers, leaving me to my own devices. Wandering in the direction of the next obstacle, I took a few moments to wonder over the woman I was quickly falling for. Everything about her spoke to me, calling on my own courage and stirring the depths of a heart that had been stagnant for too long. I only hoped that when I finally yielded to the pull of love that I wouldn't find myself alone.

Jaque

We came out of the sixth hazard on wings, Lyric still high-headed and light in the bridle despite the exertion she had to be feeling. Mind you, she went right to a trot once we were through the flags, telling me she could use a rest.

"Cardi, what's our time?" I threw back over my shoulder, keeping my eyes ahead where they belonged.

"Smokin', Jaque. We're ahead of the curve by about a minute, so we can save a little gas for the next run, if you want."

"Easy, *fille merveilleuse*," I murmured, Lyric's ears flicking back to hear me clearly. Reinforcing the idea, I sighed deeply and settled against the back of my seat, letting my legs soften where they braced against the footboard.

She readily dropped to a softer trot, letting the hill we were going down aid us as I lightly applied the brakes so the carriage would not chase her too badly. The reins slid through my lax fingers as she stretched downward, loosening her whole topline in the process. Once we reached level ground again, she shook her whole body, a trick I had never seen another horse manage while at the trot. Her harness shifted all around her at the violent motion, but once the moment had passed, she sighed happily and lifted her head again. Clearly, my beautiful partner was as eager for our work as I.

As I readjusted my rein length to maintain good contact we reached our last flag before the final obstacle. Taking a deep breath, I committed myself to the faster route, knowing my mare had it in her. Now, I simply had to get her around safely.

Cardi patted me on the back when I informed her. "You've got this, Jaqueline. You're both ready, and I'm glad to be along for the ride."

Listening to the wheels hum, and the muffled thump of Lyric's hooves on the dry grass-stubbled path, I soaked up the reassurance. "Thank you, my friend. We would not be so far without you."

Then I shook off the last shadows of my old fears and threw my heart down the lines. Lyric did not need my cluck of encouragement as we started up the slight incline that led toward the Buffalo Encampment hazard. She could feel my resolve, knew me better than I often knew myself. And while my brain understood that as a horse, she would rather be standing in a field eating grass, I also knew her faithfulness was true. Whatever I asked for, she would give, down to the very last breath she owned. She had proved it, once before, and I prayed she would never have to again.

A familiar bark rang in the air as we leveled back out, and I looked to the right to find Soleil leaping along beside Aaron as they ran through the woods. Though he did not notice me, I grinned widely to see my tiny dog unbending enough to show her excitement. Her emotions were not easily revealed. Cardi even laughed a bit, though we did not have time to linger on the fine sight of the man.

"There's your prize, Jaque, whatever happens this weekend."

Though I said nothing, my cheeks ached with happiness as I turned my attention ahead again. She was so right. Lyric could stop in her tracks and refuse to take one more step, and I would still love her. She owed me nothing, and the ribbons mattered not at all. Aaron was working himself steadily into that rare company, and love grew more inevitable by the day.

I felt the carriage bounce slightly as Cardi lifted onto her toes a few times, stretching her legs so she would be ready for the effort ahead. One more, one more, repeated over and over in my heart as my mind focused on the route we would take. Then the hazard came into view, and I checked in with my mare, making sure she would answer my reins.

"131!" Cardi yelled like it was a war cry, and three Amazons hurtled through the time flags, determined to conquer our foe.

A soft bend around a pot of pale rhododendrons brought us to A, Lyric shortening her stride as I took up more rein for the turn to B. We wove diagonally between the maypole at the center and a pot of bright yellow marigolds, then she strove up a slight incline to reach C between a tree and a container overflowing with pink petunias. Slowing as we rounded the mark, the carriage dropped back down the hill with all the stomach pitching adrenaline of a roller coaster.

Then we were on to D, and the challenge we had set for ourselves. Pushing out a breath, I made sure of my feet, bracing them widely on the perforated metal of the footboard. The belt across my waist tightened as Cardi shifted, throwing a bit of her weight into the strap that kept me secure. My eyes were dead on the mark, Lyric completely in the moment as we went back between the rhododendrons and the maypole to reach our goal.

"Come, Lyric, come hard!" With rein and voice, we slung around the turn, slipping between the white and red markers by mere inches, but that was nothing compared to the next. I changed directions even as Lyric strove forward, heeling around to the right.

"Come, come, come!"

A touch of the whip on her left side reinforced the words, and while her limbs looked for purchase, she bent as asked. The deep bow of her body grew tense, hesitating for the merest of moments as one of the posts loomed in front of her.

"Hup, hup!" I encouraged, letting her know she was correct, and she threw herself sideways, pushing against the shaft with all her might. The carriage whipped through the turn with a slip of the wheels that made my heart lurch, the rear wheels chittering as they spun at different speeds. With Cardi's expert ballast and the speed we had, it quickly came straight.

Barely three strides later, we made one last right turn, this one a bit less extreme, and the timer flags came into view. Lyric's haunches bunched in anticipation, legs digging deep beneath her body as I hollered. "Get out, mare!"

Then we were through, and as I sat up to slow her for the trot toward the finish line, I felt not the least bit of shame over the tears of gratitude that leaked from my eyes. My throat was thick as I murmured nonsense to my mare, and I knew in my heart of hearts that the foe we had conquered was not the obstacle. We had overcome ourselves, which would always be our greatest challenge.

Aaron

The afternoon disappeared in a flurry of activity. I helped cool Lyric off after they crossed the finish line, sloshing ice cold water onto the mare's heavily veined muscles while Cardi followed behind to scrape it off. Jaque grinned the whole time, damn near effervescent with joy, pleasure making her glow from within as she sat on the carriage and provided a litany of praise for her mare.

I learned a lot in a very short space of time, about recovery rates in athletic horses, temperatures and heart rates. We pulled off the protective boots, sponging beneath the wide breast collar and between the hind legs to get rid of sweat. Unlike the patent leather of the day before, this harness was made of synthetic material, light, strong, and able to be rinsed clean along with the mare. Lyric took small sips of water in between short walking laps to prevent her muscles from stiffening, and Cardi toweled her head off in order to keep the water from trapping heat. Hell, I didn't even know that was a thing. I thought you just wet a horse down to cool them off, but apparently, once the water warmed with their body, it kept them from being able to dissipate the heat unless you scraped it off.

The vet cleared us to head back to the barn, and while I got there ahead of them with the golf cart, I barely had time to get a drink before they arrived. Jaque had me head the mare while they unhooked from the carriage, but as soon as the shafts were clear, she took my position. A quiet communion occurred after Jaque took off the bridle and slid on the halter, the intimacy prompting me to step away. Much as I wanted to hug the hell out of the woman and congratulate her on a job well done, I obviously needed to wait my turn.

I suppose it would be natural for me to feel jealous, or even neglected, but strangely, I felt neither. Everything about Jaque drew me in, and her relationship with her horse was too intertwined with the fabric of her for me to be so selfish. Instead, as I made myself useful pushing the carriage out of the way and dipping out a fresh bucket of water for Lyric to drink from, I soaked in the beauty of their relationship.

It would take a jaded heart to not feel the love they exuded, the mare bending to press her forehead into Jaque's stomach and Jaque carefully embracing the trusting animal. Not that I fancied I'd ever enjoy such a moment with Byz. Both of us were a little too macho to share that sort of sweetness. But damn, it sure would be nice to have him welcome my touch again.

Once the mare was completely stripped of her harness Jaque led her away, and I immediately turned to Cardi. I wanted to be useful in some way, even if Jaque didn't need me at the moment. "Well, what's next?"

Cardi swiveled slowly toward me as if she'd forgotten I was there, a frown maring her usually cheerful face. "Hmm, I guess you could go get us some food? Once Jaque winds down a bit, she's gonna hit a wall."

"Already done. Cooler is full of stuff, even for you."

Her forehead turned into deep furrows as her eyes went wide with surprise. "I might have to be a little impressed, if that's the case. Good job, Prince Charming. Though I'm not as easy as the dog. Hope you brought more than string cheese."

Barking a laugh, I opened the cooler and tossed her a water bottle. Her quick reflexes were impressive as she snatched it out of the air and twisted off the top in one smooth motion. She grinned at my respectful nod, then gave me one in return.

"Alright then, if you're game, let's get things clean. We've got a lot to tidy up so we're ready for tomorrow."

I followed her lead as we washed off the harness and all the boots, hanging them in the sun to dry. The carriage I took as my own little project while Cardi worked on straightening the camp. No surprise that the stainless steel and glossy paint appealed to me, and after seeing the machine in action, I had even more appreciation for the design.

Rolling it out into the sunshine, I dipped out a bucket of water and washed off all the grit and dust. I was buffing it dry when Jaque came around the corner of the trailer, absent the mare. Her hair had transformed into a fuzzy halo around her head after all that sweaty effort, and hours in her helmet, a situation I well understood. She had a ring of dirt around her neck and her lips were chapped. Yet, contentment glowed from within, and she still looked like the most beautiful woman in the world to me.

"You ready to take care of yourself?" I asked, making sure to preface it with a broad smile in hopes she'd hear the tease in it.

She smiled tiredly, but the peaceful light in her eyes held only happiness. "Yes, I suppose I should. Would you mind driving me up to the food vendors?"

From behind me, Cardi spoke up. "No need, Jaque. Prince Charming here brought in our sustenance."

I turned around just in time to see Cardi shove another forkful of salad into her mouth, but the urge to laugh disappeared as Jaque's arms circled my waist from behind. Her hands spread possessively over my belly as she pressed her body into my back, and I breathed deeply as she delivered a kiss to my shoulder blade.

"You are going to spoil me." The muffled words humbled me as much as the loving touches, and I took one of her hands to pull her around in front of me.

"You deserve it," I replied honestly, dipping down to kiss her forehead despite our audience. "Now, go sit down and eat. I didn't get anything too heavy, since we have a dinner tonight, but we all need to take care of ourselves if you're going to be at your best tomorrow."

Her fingers tightened briefly on mine before she stepped away. I frowned slightly at Cardi, noticing she'd taken the middle chair. Jaque saved me the bother of irritation, grabbing one of the empty chairs and dropping it beside the other before plopping into one of them and waving me to join them.

Cardi's eyes danced with humor as I took my seat and handed Jaque her salad, and I nodded shortly when she met my eye. While I didn't understand the woman's aim, I got the impression she was warming to me, and I hoped the trend would continue. In any relationship, I had enough stacked against me without opposition from outside sources.

After our late lunch, I watched Jaque sponge liniment onto the tendons of Lyric's legs. Then she wrapped the sturdy limbs in bandages, special ones that she said would promote good blood flow overnight. She took the mare through a series of stretches that she said she would repeat later, and in the morning, to keep her from stiffening up. To my inexperienced eyes, Jaque's care didn't just soften the mare's body, but Lyric's whole demeanor. I caught them echoing each other's sighs and spending minutes at a time in quiet unity.

Cardi returned from her trip to the office with a squeal of delight that preceded her down the aisle way, drawing both Jaque and I out of the stall where we had been laying a thick bed for the mare. "Jaqueline! Your score held! You're still in second place!"

Confusion drew my brows together when Jaque was suddenly in my arms, though I instinctively held her. After all, I'd wanted this for hours, and would take advantage of it while I could. But I couldn't understand the tears that I felt soaking into my shirt, or the way she shook, unsure of how to fix whatever bothered her. Aiding my confusion was the widening of Cardi's grin as she went to Lyric and offered her a maple candy from her pocket.

"Jaque, what's wrong?" I murmured quietly as I stroked her hair back from her forehead and pressed a kiss to her scalp.

"Absolutely nothing," She sniffled, her fingers tightening along my spine to pull me even closer. "Happy tears, I assure you."

While the notion confused the hell out of me, I closed my eyes, smiling where my lips touched her head. Tears weren't something I coped well with, after a lifetime of my mother's manipulations or my sisters' real heartaches. But for Jaque, I'd learn to deal with it.

We broke apart after a couple minutes, and I listened to the women chatter over penalty points and other technicalities I didn't understand as they did one more check on the mare. Lyric paid them little mind, perfectly comfortable with the many hands running over her. Then we all loaded up in the truck to head for the hotel, needing to get ready for the competitor's party.

When I heard it was a costume party, dread had crept in. But as I took a quick shower and pulled out my kit, I grinned, grateful to whatever imp of the perverse decided the theme would be Camelot. Because while much of the weekend lay completely outside my comfort zone, in this, I now owned the advantage.

Jaque

As Aaron escorted Cardi and I into the big tent for the competitor's party, I barely noticed the décor around the dizzy haze that had overtaken my senses. The man had knocked on the door of our room at the appointed time, and I quickly discovered that photos of Aaron in armour were nothing compared to in person. Not that it was necessarily the armour that hit me so hard, as much as the completely confident air that possessed him. He wore the articulated metal with the same grace another man might don a tailored three-piece suit, and his courtly manner even reduced Cardi to girlish titters when he presented each of us with a single white rose.

Nor were we the only ones so affected. Once we arrived at the party and received our table assignments, a palpable wave of awareness moved over the sea of people. Joyce parted that ocean like a great galleon, the silly conical hat and veil she wore billowing behind her like a sail as she approached.

"Well! Had I known Lancelot and Guinevere themselves would be visiting our humble feast, I might have laid on a better spread." She ran her eyes over us, lingering noticeably on Aaron. Nor could I blame her. While I wore a rented a costume that did not quite fit, he sported a rich tabard in dark blue and gold, accented with bits of armour that bore scars from his work. Devastating did not begin to touch on the effect.

"Who would that make you, oh loveliest of maids?" he teased, bowing low over her hand, and I swear to heaven, I feared Joyce might faint. Luckily, Harv moved in beside her, a hand on her back to steady her when a blush moved up her décolletage.

"I told you, Joyce, he's as real as they come," Harv boomed, tipping the plastic crown on his head the same way he might his usual fedora. "Aaron, good to see you again. I did a bit of research on you after our little meeting this afternoon. Maybe we should have hired you and your crew for entertainment."

Aaron laughed easily, his hand moving to cover mine where it lay on his arm, the weighted touch welcome and reassuring. "Thanks, but no, Harv. I'd rather keep the focus on Jaque this weekend. Though I do hope you can make it to one of the faires where we work, if scheduling permits. We're due near Aiken soon."

"We'd be delighted, if the show schedule permits. Joyce likes to drive in the Hitchcock Woods there, so we could make a productive trip out of it in more ways than one."

My brain feverishly jumped ahead. When would they be in Aiken? Would I be returning home while they were gone? It would be a shame to miss him, if that were the case. But before I could worry the thought too much Cardi swooped in on my other side and pulled me away from Aaron. We were immediately swallowed by our peers, the giddy throng at least one drink ahead of me and eager for information on my companion.

"What great arm candy!" One of the four-in-hand drivers enthused, while a woman with an entirely too hungry expression stared across the tent at Aaron. My hands fisted instinctively, but I fought the urge to bare my claws. However long he and I lasted, I still held no ownership of him. And had I not looked at him with such yearning not too long ago?

In fact, to be entirely honest, he drew the eye. While Joyce and her team of volunteers had turned the big white tent into a feast hall fit for royalty, with hanging banners and a band of minstrels for atmosphere during dinner, Aaron was easily more striking. Compared to the plastic breastplates and polyester tabards several people wore, he had no equal. Even among a bevy of gorgeous women in a wide variety of dresses, he was the most stunning jewel. Nor would I say that just because I was partial to his good looks. As the most genuine thing in the room he made all the gaudy décor feel a little more real. He made you want to believe in things like fairy tales and knights in shining armour. Or, at least he made *me* want to believe, more desperately than I ever expected to feel about a man.

A jester rousted the minstrels for a resounding roll of the drums to get our attention, so I broke away from the questions peppering me from every direction. Dinner was about to be served, and I fled for my table, eager for the calming companionship of my friends. Aaron waited, gesturing me into a chair he had pulled out before taking his own seat.

Despite the chivalry, something felt off as plates were set before us. Aaron engaged with the entire table, telling jovial tales of his jousting life and the horses involved. He sipped judiciously at his beer, so I knew alcohol was no issue, but he never once looked to me. The lack of connection chafed terribly, and while the prime rib they served was perfectly prepared, every bite I took felt as though I were swallowing a knot of burlap, dry and unpleasant. Still, I ate it all, ravenous after the day's efforts. Now that the marathon was done weight no longer concerned me.

Twice, Cardi touched my elbow, leaning in to see if I felt okay. I smiled, of course. What could be wrong? I had reached new heights in my partnership with Lyric, she was sound and happy, and I wanted for nothing. And yet...

When dessert arrived, I could no longer keep still, and excused myself to go to the bar. Perhaps a bit of champagne would lift my mood? A shame, since the crème brulee looked divine, but it would wait for me to return. Though the way Cardi dove into hers, I should probably hurry. The woman was a dessert fiend.

Aaron

I watched Jaque weave through the crowd, a thread in my chest pulling taut the further away she moved. Graceful and elegant in her purple cotehardie, I wanted nothing more than to chase her down, to keep her close. Yet, with the crowd to play to, I stayed, not wanting to be rude. After all, these were her friends, and I wanted so badly to be part of her world.

As I listened to one of the women expound on her own experiences with draft horses, a sharp jab landed on my foot, as hard and unforgiving as any time Byz had done it to get my attention. My head swiveled sideways, powered by an unuttered expletive, but I came up short against the implacably fierce glare Cardi delivered.

"What the hell, Cardi?" I asked lowly, itching for a fight. She'd been needling me all day, and I was about sick of it.

Her caustic growl could have taken paint off a tractor at twenty paces. "Have you lost your mind? I thought you were all about Jaque?"

"I am! I've been trying to prove that to you all damn day, so get off my back."

She sat back like I'd slapped her, eyes narrowing dangerously before she leaned in close so no one would hear us. "None of that was for you. That was for her. I wanted her to see how much effort you are willing to put out. But you're blowing it."

Frustration swelled like a cloud bank filled with rolling lightning, but I breathed carefully through my nose, trying to cut to the chase. "What're you talking about, Cardi? I'm at a loss here."

Her lips thinned, and she regarded me with a look I recognized from Jo's repertoire of expressions. The one that said I might be stupider than I appeared. "Clearly, you've fallen off your horse one too many times. You haven't said a word to Jaque since we sat down, dumbass, and she's not taking it well."

I wanted to snap at her, to bleed off some of the sudden worry raging through my veins, but she was right. In my efforts to win over her friends, I'd neglected the lady herself. Christ, I was an idiot. Cardi's eyes softened into a rounder shape when I straightened and touched her shoulder. "Thanks. You're a good friend, Cardi."

But then I was out of my chair, not even excusing myself, an action that brought on a phantom chastisement that screeched far too much like my mother. I ignored it, dodging wait staff and the odd party goer, my singular focus back where it needed to be. Just to the side of the bar, a flash of purple caught my eye as it ducked between tent flaps. Determined to catch her, I picked up speed.

She spun around as I broke out into the dark pocket of quiet she'd found, eyes catching the light behind me. In fact, were I any judge, they were a little bright with tears that I wanted to kick myself for. Still, she managed a smile.

"Aaron, what are you doing out here?"

"You tell me," I demanded firmly as I closed the distance, noticing the way the empty champagne flute she held trembled. "Once you left, my whole reason for being at that table went with you."

"Nonsense, you appeared to be having a good time. I only needed to clear my head. This costume is quite warm, and the tent is stuffy."

"Appearances can be deceiving. And when you walked away, I felt several degrees colder." Barely touching her, my fingers landed on her shoulder, slowly skating their way down the wool velvet sleeve until I found her hand. Her skin felt cool against mine, and I wanted little more than to hold her until we were both warm again. Yet, the armor I wore wouldn't make for the most comfortable embrace. "When I put on the costume, I put on a personality to go with it. But it's not who I am, really. Not who I want to be."

"Why, Aaron? Why do you try so hard? There is no expectation from me. I like all the parts of you, whether you are in or out of your armor." Her smile warmed by several degrees, her hand turning until our fingers were interwoven and the thread in my chest tugged mercilessly with a welcome ache. "You are devastatingly handsome in it, mind you. But your looks, your skill, your charm, they mean little to me compared to the contents of your heart."

I pulled her in with the grip I had on her hand and tipped my head down until our foreheads touched. "Jaque, you've no idea how badly I want to hold you right now, but armor isn't very forgiving."

She lifted her chin, putting our lips ever closer together. A frisson of absolute lust ran through my body as she pointedly dropped her glass and ran her fingers into my hair. "Hold me all the same, Aaron. I will not break."

So, I scooped her up, turning my nose into the soft hairs along the edge of her neck, completely disregarding the way my gorget dug into my throat. Small price to pay for the way she molded herself against me, despite the steel seams of my armor that pressed into her back. She turned her head, kissing my temple as her fingers combed through my hair, and I swallowed hard as her acceptance washed over me again.

"Where did you lovebirds get to?" Joyce queried far too loudly for it not to be completely deliberate, and while I appreciated the warning, I mumbled an unintelligible curse into the shoulder of Jaque's costume. God bless her, she wrapped her arms a bit tighter and muffled a giggle against my head before releasing me. I had just set her down when Joyce appeared around a bunch of crates.

"Ah, there you are, you naughty things! I insist you come back in this instant. You promised to dance tonight, and I know both of you are too honorable to disappoint me." Her mischievous smile would have looked just as at home on my five-year-old niece when I caught her with her hand in the cookie jar. And just like with Nessie, I couldn't stay mad at her.

"Mistress Joyce, I assure you, I'd love nothing more than to spend the evening with Jaqueline in my arms." What I left unsaid was that I wished we could be alone. The day felt like it had stretched on for far too long, and I wanted little more than the quiet of my hotel room, where I could listen to Jaque breathe in the darkness. As if she knew what was on my mind, Jaque's arms tightened around my waist and she sighed.

"Then come on, darlings! The band should be taking the stage any moment!" Joyce chivied us back into the tent like a proper chaperone, though I kept Jaque close as we emerged into the light.

Several sets of eyes tracked on us, some out of simple curiosity, and for those, I smiled. But a few narrow-eyed stares I met with detached disdain, particularly those of the men who'd riled up Jaque. Her success this weekend would be a serious threat to their claims about her horse being inferior, and judging by their sneers, they weren't taking it well.

But then, as I got a clear look at them through a gap in the crowd, I had to smile at them too. The three of them were dressed up in cheap rented costumes, as King Arthur and two of his knights. Which might have been alright, except clearly these were from the Monty Python skit, and I had a strong inkling from the superior way they held themselves that they had no idea. The urge to walk up and demand a shrubbery nearly overwhelmed me, laughter pushing at my throat.

I swallowed it down as my eyes moved past them, finding Cardi leaning back in her chair with cat-like satisfaction in her expression. There was barely a moment to return her nod of approval before we were through the throng of tables and emerging onto the hardwood dance floor. Worse still, a spotlight found us, making sure everyone's attention swung our way. My arms tightened with real fear as Jaque swung around in front of me with a practiced curtsy. Sweat broke out on the back of my neck as I bowed low in return. God, please don't let me screw this up, I prayed, as we moved into the only formal dance pose I knew.

For the third time in ten minutes, I swallowed hard, but Jaque made me teeter even closer to falling for her completely when her hand tightened in mine. "Aaron, this is like when we played golf," Her smile caressed the panic squeezing my heart, and I grinned at the happy memory. "We will have fun, no matter what anyone else thinks."

Thus, when the band struck up some peppy jazz number that I had never heard before, we moved into the only dance I could do reasonably well. Somehow, the fact that it was a basic waltz didn't seem to matter at all, and as Joyce invited everyone to join us on the floor, everything faded away except for the woman in my arms.

Jaque

Heaven help me, as much as I enjoyed Aaron the bold and brave, Aaron the awkward and fumbling was easily as charming. How he could go from one extreme to the other completely baffled me, but I shook away the confusion and took my own advice. We had fun, enjoying the time to focus on each other to the exclusion of all else. Though concern for Lyric continued to swirl in my mind, I let it fade away from the forefront, smiling at the handsome man who had such depths of feeling in his eyes.

My favourites were the slow dances. In school, I had only attended one dance with my best girlfriends, having been painfully shy and insecure about my looks. Boys had been a delicious mystery, mostly unexplored until I graduated secondary school. My adult discoveries had been a bit injudicious in my naiveté, grateful for any attention, and it had taken some time to grow out of making poor choices. Not that I regretted the experiences in the least, as that self-knowledge was priceless, but when Aaron held me close, our feet shuffling in time to the wordless music, those years seemed to fall away. For all that we were two grown adults who were attracted to each other, an innocent shade of softness made the sharp edge of physical need much easier to bear.

The brushed cotton of his tabard pressed soft against my cheek, his heartbeat a relaxed throb that soothed, a contrast to the armour that covered his shoulders, arms and legs. My heavy skirts muffled the rub of the steel against my knees as we swayed, and every once and awhile, he would press his lips to the top of my head.

Would that it could have lasted, but a rough shove from someone's elbow knocked me out of the peaceful cocoon, and I looked up into the cold, disdainful eyes of one of van den Berg's students, Paul Scott. While we had competed in the same circles for years, even dated for a time, all it had taken was his coach's censure to bring out an animosity I had done nothing to earn.

"My apologies, Miss Sauveterre. I should have expected to find you in the slow lane, owing to your comfort there."

My stomach soured and a flush rose up on my skin in response, but before I could say a word, Aaron beat me to it.

"I don't know, Mr. Scott, judging by the scores I saw, she fired past you in more than half of the obstacles today." His smile filled with condescending pity, cutting far more deeply than he could possibly understand. "Maybe you should take a page from her book and learn when to pace yourself so you don't fall short when it counts."

Paul's lips curled nastily as he stopped in place, and I felt sure he would come up with something meaner to say, but Aaron spun us away, putting several couples between us. I was caught between mortification at the confrontation and undeniable pride in Aaron for handling things so smoothly. He had delivered a stinging blow to the man's pride and it was liberating to have him so clearly in my corner.

We were able to head back to the table after that song ended, as Joyce took over the microphone to announce the placing for the obstacles. As they worked their way through the divisions, I slowly savoured my crème brulee, grateful to Cardi for saving it. Not only had she not eaten it, she had protected it from the efforts of the wait staff to clear the tables. Tomorrow, I owed her the biggest bar of chocolate I could find for such faithful friendship. However much I appreciated Aaron being in my corner, Cardi had been by my side for much longer.

When they called out the Advanced single horse competitors, I accepted the proffered accolades, my friends shoring me up against sharing the stage with Paul and Grady. I came in first in three out of seven obstacles, though my overall time kept me from winning outright. For our first season at Advanced, I would have been content with much less.

Sue had blasted all of us in the first obstacle, her mare agile and fast, though she stayed right on everyone's heels for the rest. Grady won two, and Paul took the remaining. For winning the most obstacles, I received much more than a ribbon. They handed me a check that would cover the cost of my entries. No small amount when you looked at my dwindling bank account. I had enough to get me through the remainder of my stay in Florida, as well as a chunk of savings meant for emergencies, but this little windfall would be a boon.

The band struck up again once the multiples received their awards, but the long day caught up with me, and I wanted nothing more than to tuck Lyric in for the evening. Aaron remained at my elbow as I said goodnight to our hosts and my friends, Cardi begging off as soon as we cleared the exit. I hugged her a little tighter than normal, so thankful for her efforts and her friendship. She would be headed to the airport tomorrow evening, needing to get back to Kentucky so she could be at work on Monday. Not to mention a husband at home who would be eager to see her.

Back at the truck, Aaron began to unbuckle his armour, and I moved to stay him. "You do not need to take that off. We should be done with Lyric rather quickly if she is feeling well."

He shook his head, unruly hair flopping across his brow. "Most horses don't take kindly to the sound it makes, and I wouldn't want to disturb Lyric, or any of the others for that matter."

To that, I smiled, and helped as I could. For all his limited equine education, his heart truly was in the right place to be thinking not only of my horse, but ones that he didn't even know. Lyric herself lay curled up the deep bedding, every breath making the pine shavings puff up a little under her nose. We woke her as we opened the door to my equipment area, but she did little more than lift her head to blink sleepily at the goings on. The contentment of her expression reassured me that she felt well, despite the day's exertions. Aaron topped off her water and I gave her some loose hay to supplement what remained in the net, then we left her to her well-deserved rest.

We picked up Soleil, since I could not leave her unattended at the hotel, then we were on the highway toward town, little traffic moving about at such a late hour. At the hotel, I ducked in to my own room long enough to grab my pyjamas and my tooth brush before heading back to his room, which provided a delicious view of Aaron's muscles as I let myself back in. The way his shoulders bunched and flexed as he shed his white under tunic would have tempted a nun to sin, every line tapering down to a trim waist. Better still, as he wore close fitting riding breeches, I could memorize the glorious curve of his *derrière* with little to interfere.

Clearing my throat to draw his attention, I could be forgiven for being distracted by the front view when he turned around. But his smile of welcome reeled me in more surely than the shape of his body.

"Jaque, I figured I'd let you have the shower, if you'd like one. That wool has to be warm in all this humidity."

Ah, such a giving heart! Which made mine teeter ever so much closer toward falling madly in love with him. Who would have thought a weekend together would be enough for such strong feelings? But as I moved past him with an unexpectedly shy smile and closed the door on the sound of him kicking off his tall leather boots, I admitted, if only to myself, that I had been on the cusp for a long time. This weekend was merely the tipping point.

As I went through the tedious process of undoing all the tiny buttons on my dress, I thought back to the various times I fancied myself in love. Those men, however beautiful or charming, paled in comparison to Aaron. They gave so little of themselves, held so much back, and I gave more and more of myself, hoping for reciprocation. That if I perhaps proved my love to them, they would trust me enough to love me in return.

Stepping into the shower to rinse the sweat from my skin, I closed my eyes, replaying everything Aaron had done since he arrived, with no expectation of reward. He asked for nothing but my company, and in fact, demanded the focus remain on me for the weekend, despite my efforts to the contrary. He was a gift I was not sure how to accept, and I prayed he would let me return the favour in the future. No one in the world had earned my undivided attention more than this man who would not ask for it.

Once in my pyjamas, I stepped back into the room, greeted by the softest of snores. Aaron had propped himself up against the headboard while waiting for me, but sleep had stolen him away, all unwitting. He wore loose knit pants and a thin t-shirt, both faded by time and use. Unguarded like this, he looked remarkably innocent for his age, and I wondered what he looked like as a child. Had he always been so serious, so worried about everything and everyone?

Folding my dress over a chair, I then went around the room, dousing all the lights but one. Soleil accepted a caress of her pointy little muzzle when I bent down to check on her. Once assured of her comfort, I moved onto the bed on my knees, getting close enough so I could lean over and kiss Aaron's brow. He roused at the touch of my lips, inhaling sharply as he straightened, the edge of panic in his eyes caching me by surprise.

"Jaque?"

"Shhh, my champion, I am right here." His thick hair swallowed my fingers as I brushed it back from his ear, and he focused on me, calming quickly. "Let us get settled for the night."

His tall frame slid down, but he tugged me toward him until I fell against his chest, lips close enough that I felt his huff of breath at the impact. "I'm so glad you let me come see you, Jaque. You're amazing."

Then he kissed me, a soft, sweet exploration that held no urgency, and I lingered in the gentle haze that came with it. He made me feel as if we had forever for only this kiss. Not that I felt any less desired because of it, mind you. One could not mistake the strength of his hands as he pressed me closer, or his heart pounding hard enough that I could feel it in my own chest.

Time ceased to matter for those magical moments, even as want coiled ever thicker in my belly. Yet, it remained content to lay quiet when I finally pulled back from our kiss to regain the intimacy of his eyes. The dark blue orbs met my gaze so fully, hiding nothing, a gift I appreciated more than any other. And though I had a million questions to ask, I also understood now was not the time. The inevitability of sleep tugged at both of us, and I muffled a yawn behind my hand, earning a chuckle that warmed me as surely as his kisses.

"Let's get some rest while you can. You've got another big day tomorrow." He kissed my forehead, then reached over to flick off the remaining lamp. I curled against his side, smiling as the dark and his warmth stole my consciousness. Truly, however I finished this weekend at the competition, my real prizes would be the ever-stronger bond I found with my mare and the growing possibility of love I found with this man.

Aaron

Owing to waking up with Jaque in my bed, I couldn't even object to the early hour we needed to roll out on Sunday morning. Never in my life had I been kissed awake, her minty mouth refreshing and sweet as she coaxed me to consciousness. I revisited the thought that kissing her might make coffee unnecessary. When I rolled over and pinned her down, her eyes dancing with the same contentment I felt.

"Good morning, my champion." Jaque's voice, husky with passion, finished the job of waking me. The hand I hadn't captured found the hem of my shirt, and I pressed my hips closer to hers as she explored the bare skin along my ribs. "I do hope we can find ourselves in this position tonight, once I have the time to focus on you."

My body answered for me, the blood running out of my brain to fulfill baser concerns. Her eyelashes fluttered when she felt the result, and she worked a leg out from under my weight to wrap it around my hip. I dove for her lips, achingly desperate for some sort of anchor in the storm threatening to envelop my reason, and she kissed me with a hunger that spun us even higher.

"Jaque," I groaned roughly as I pulled away, but she stole my ability to form words when her hand slid past the waist of my sleep pants and found purchase on my ass. Grinding against the heat between her legs, I pressed an open-mouthed kiss against the tender skin of her shoulder, ravenous for more of the wild potential swelling between us.

"Aaron," she whimpered, body arching up to meet my touch as I moved to test the weight of her breast.

Who knows how much further we would have allowed ourselves to go if not for the emphatic pounding on the wall. I froze in horror as Cardi yelled through the thin walls, barely hearable as Soleil began barking like a rabid attack dog.

"Save that shit for tonight, love birds! I don't want to have to listen in!"

Burying a giggle against my shoulder, Jaque slowly withdrew her exploring hand, and I rolled to the side to free her. She followed the motion, kissing me soundly as she briefly straddled my hips before dismounting the bed entirely. Every part of me missed her touch, and I sat up to drink in the sight of her as she crouched down to quiet her dog.

"Shush, *sucre*, all is well."

Soleil settled back onto her bed, though she still kept her eyes on the offending wall, growling lowly. I agreed completely with the sentiment, because however much I didn't want to distract Jaque from her goals for the weekend, I'd have given a good deal for just a few more minutes in her tumultuous embrace.

We shared a chaste kiss before she gathered up her things then ducked through the darkness outside to get to her own room. I rushed through a rather cold shower, both to calm my raging hormones and rouse my still sleepy brain. As I pulled on my jeans, I had a thought that sent me after my phone, and I typed quickly before I could overthink things.

'With Cardi leaving, do you want to move in here? No expectations or pressure.'

I'd finished dressing by the time she replied, and I grinned foolishly as I read. *'I would be delighted. But what if I have expectations?'*

'Expect away' I shot back, then turned to tidy the room while I waited for the ladies to be ready. Fifteen minutes later, Soleil preceded her mistress back through the door as if she owned the place. Jaque dropped her luggage beside mine, then slipped the dog's leash off her wrist before flinging herself back into my arms. Her joy spilled out like sunshine, warming me all over.

"Cardi is loading up her car and will go get coffee for us. That gives us a few minutes before I have to drag you downstairs so we can get on with the day. Would you care to resume our earlier activities?"

Smiling even as I struggled against the hunger that clawed at my guts, I kissed her cheek. "No, because if I get you back in my bed, I won't be letting you back out for a while. Even fooling around, I tend to get lost in you. But I promise to make it up to you tonight."

"May I at least have another kiss to tide me over? The taste of you is becoming more necessary than coffee, I think."

Delighted to find our thoughts so closely aligned, I obliged, and we stole a few minutes of passion that stirred the blood more thoroughly than any caffeine ever had. But time waited for no man or woman, and afterward, I was grateful for the drive to the show grounds so I could compose myself. Once there, we settled into familiar roles, Jaque and Lyric heading out for their morning constitutional. Even if stall cleaning wasn't my favorite thing to do, it gave me plenty of time to get my head back in the game.

When the ladies returned I sat down by the stall door and watched as Jaque repeated Lyric's stretching. She manipulated the mare's thick limbs with remarkable ease, lifting them up or pulling them forward and back to effect certain muscle groups. The mare yawned and her head dropped lower and lower as her body relaxed. I wondered if something similar could be done with Byz, who carried tension just as badly as I did. Maybe Jaque could show me how to do such things once we were both back in Kentucky?

Which reminded me that I would be returning home tomorrow, by myself. A week alone seemed like an eternity to go without her particular touch, or the grace she so readily gave me. But if we made a real relationship out of the foundation we built this weekend, then this would not be the last time we had to be apart. Our respective jobs kept us on the road constantly, often in different directions, and I'd best learn to suck it up now. But that didn't mean I had to like it.

Cardi arrived with our breakfast and coffee just as Jaque finished with Lyric, and we all settled onto an assortment of buckets and bales to enjoy croissants with ham, egg and cheese. Surprisingly, Jaque ate the sandwich without an ounce of hesitation, a welcome change after the last several mornings. I barely finished the last bite when Cardi brushed the crumbs from her lap and shot to her feet.

"Well, come on, Prince Charming, we've got stuff to do. Jaque doesn't need you mooning over her while she gets Lyric braided up."

While I grumbled for effect, I stood up to comply. "Alright, you slave driver, I'm coming." Then, regardless of an audience, I leaned down and dropped a kiss on Jaque's cheek. "See you in a bit, my lady."

A rare blush warmed her skin, but she met my eyes as I pulled away, delight easily read in her upturned lips. A pretty picture to take with me as I followed Cardi out to the golf cart, and I kept smiling even as we set to work. The fancy harness came back out, and when the presentation carriage had been dusted off, Cardi handed me some tools and set me to the task of bolting a seat onto the rear where the basket had been.

By the time I finished tightening the last bolt a fine sheen of sweat had popped up on my skin, but I kept my jacket on as a breeze picked up, shifting the clouds overhead into something potentially unfriendly. Hopefully, anything it threw down would wait until after the show finished.

To be safe, we pushed the carriage back into the trailer and set the harness on its stand right inside the door, both covered in sheets. Wheeling them back out again would be the work of a moment, much simpler than having to clean them again. Working with Cardi had gained some ease after clearing the air the night before, so I hardly thought much of it when she dropped into a chair and gestured me to the one beside her. I fell into it with a grunt of satisfaction after fetching us some water, and she grinned her thanks when I handed her the dripping bottle, fresh from the ice chest.

"You know, Aaron, I'm not going to know what to do with myself at the next show. I'm getting used to having the extra hands."

I made a scoffing noise in the back of my throat. "Cardi, I'm well aware you could run circles around me. But I'm glad to be of some kind of help. I didn't want to get in the way."

She flicked a bit of water at me with her fingertips, but I didn't give her the satisfaction of a flinch, meeting her straightforward gaze without blinking. "Well, I'm glad you came. It's rare to see Jaque this relaxed, and she deserves some happiness for a change."

I narrowed my eyes, thinking back to Cardi's earlier hints at Jaque being hurt and how Jaque herself often expected the worst. My hand tightened around the water bottle I held, until the crinkle of plastic reminded me to ease up. But it wasn't just anger for Jaque that drove my response. My own frustrations at the conditional affection within my family made my stomach clench with bitter memories of guilt trips and manipulative pressure. Not to say I wasn't selfish about some things, but the family I'd built with Gallant Company had given me a taste for something much more pure. In Jaque, I seemed to have discovered a bottomless well of unconditional fondness, even when she grew upset or disagreed with me.

"She deserves all the happiness she can stand," I agreed, leaving it at that. Much as I wanted to know where Jaque's doubts were rooted, I didn't want to go digging.

My curiosity needed to be shelved anyway, as a golf cart pulled up with a rather harried looking Harv at the wheel. His ever-present fedora looked creased with as much worry as his forehead. "Aaron, any chance you're free to help out at the arena? Three volunteers called in with stomach flu, and Joyce is fit to be tied. We'll keep you fed and watered for your trouble."

I swallowed a hefty dose of sympathy for the afflicted at the same time I looked to Cardi. "You need anything from me?"

She shook her head emphatically. "No, you head on over. If we don't have enough volunteers then cones will take all damn day to get through, and I need to be on time for my plane tonight."

Pushing to my feet, I looked in the direction of the barns, but Cardi shoved me toward Harv. "Don't worry, I'll let Jaque know, and we'll see you just after lunch for our round. You'll have a front row seat after all."

Harv barely let my butt hit the seat before he slammed on the gas and dang near peeled out on the damp grass. He whipped a U-turn that made me clutch the roof, and then floored it back toward the arena, getting up enough speed that I worried we might tip through a couple of the turns. When we got to the office, he buried the brake pedal in the floorboards, causing the poor cart to skid and shimmy as it came to a halt. Took serious effort to push out a relaxed breath and unwrap my now claw-shaped fingers from the grip I'd taken.

Joyce popped her head out the door and beckoned me inside, a manic smile plastered on her gently weathered face. I barely dismounted before Harv tore off again, probably on the hunt for more unsuspecting victims. Shaking my head, I climbed the stairs, resigned to whatever fate awaited me at the hands of Mrs. Joyce. After all, I hit people with sticks for a living, and made good money for falling off my horse. It certainly couldn't be any harder than that.

Jaque

Rain began as we started toward the trailer, a mere sprinkle of foreboding that speckled the dust kicked up over two days of horses and carriages tearing up the grass. Lyric's head lifted up, nostrils wide to catch the scent of the storm, a sparkle of delight in her eye. She loved weather of all kinds, everything but intense heat, and I laughed softly as she took a few prancing steps when the droplets hit her back.

Canadian Horses were a product of survival in an unforgiving country, tougher by far than many more finely bred animals. A snowstorm was Lyric's favourite playground, something she hadn't been able to enjoy in years thanks to our winters in Florida, but rain was her second favourite. She loved to cavort in the wet, splashing in puddles while her coat turned to shimmering jet.

As for the show, well, it would go on regardless of the weather, unless lightning made an appearance. No one wanted to risk being struck, after all. And I, knowing my mare's penchant for weather, had amassed a collection of gear to keep myself comfortable. We would enjoy our day, regardless of the conditions.

Cardi waved at me from the open door on the side of the trailer, and I led Lyric straight up the ramp, taking shelter in the area that the mare usually traveled in. We had barely clipped her lead to the wall before the tempo of the rain increased, and I looked back outside as the world went to watercolours under the silvery influence of the storm.

"Well, this should make things interesting." I said, swiveling back toward my two best girlfriends with a sharp, toothy grin. But the grin faded as I noticed a marked absence, and I wondered at how Aaron become so ingrained in my little team so quickly. "Where is Aaron?"

"Ah, he volunteered to help out with cones when Harv came recruiting," Cardi answered, even as she bent to place a protective boot on Lyric's lower leg.

The sound of the Velcro abraded my nerves as I moved to do the same on the opposite leg, struggling with both disappointment and pride. His big heart meant Aaron would try to fill a need wherever he found one, but selfishly, my need for him was all I could feel. As I stood up to retrieve the hind boots Cardi stepped in front of me, her expression remarkably kind.

"If it's any help, his eyes looked just as conflicted as yours when he left. Whatever is going on between you, I'd say the feeling is entirely mutual."

To which I sighed dreamily, drawn back to our early morning tumble on the bed. This earned me an eye roll and a grunt of disgust, Cardi tossing me the boot I'd been after. I caught it reflexively, surprised at the force behind the throw. "My apologies, Cardi, if having Aaron here is bothering you. I shall work to rein myself in."

"Oh no, you keep on galloping, girlfriend. Charming is much better for you than any of your exes have ever been." She frowned even as she crouched, hand smoothing down Lyric's leg before she strapped the boot in place. I followed suit, working quickly so I could give my full attention to Cardi. While she never condemned my poor choices in men, she gave no such grace to those she thought had done me wrong. Every woman should be so lucky to have a girlfriend so steadfast, and I did my best to return that loyalty in full.

Butterfly quick, she stood back up, and her mood shifted faster than a rollback turn going down an incline during marathon. But much like then, she leaned into the turn with everything she had, keeping the wheels on the ground. Her grin held an edge that could have cut someone who did not know her moods. "Helping you kick some ass has been the best. Watching van den Berg's cronies eat crow is absolutely delicious." Then she smiled, a gentle softness filling her eyes that made my heart feel too full. "And seeing you fall in love would be worth a thousand unspoken worries. You're like a sister to me, and your happiness is my happiness."

At that, I moved around Lyric and crushed Cardi into a hug that warmed me to my very soul. We were hidden from the world by the storm, united in the spirit of mutual admiration, and our passion for driving competition. One might have been tempted to linger there, but my watch beeped, reminding me of the time. Though the show would likely experience some delays with the weather, it would still soldier on, and I would not be the one to make it run any later.

As I stepped back, I clutched my friend's steady hands, grateful beyond expression for her abundant faith. "Then let us get to our work, dear sister. We have a storm ahead, one way or another, and I should like to face it well prepared."

In a blink, she returned to Lyric, and I moved to the door behind the mare that led to my dressing room. Soleil wagged her tail in delight as I entered, rising from her little nest of fleece blankets to greet me. I pet her petite ears, grateful for her love as well. A hug from Aaron would have been a delightful way to round out the feeling of acceptance, but that would have to wait until later.

The ritual of donning my show clothes helped put my mind on the task ahead. Owing to the weather, a pair of sleek grey wool slacks promised some warmth no matter how damp they grew. A tailored coat of plush lavender tweed wrapped around me, the tall velvet collar soft on my neck. Even whimsical purple pinstripes in my trouser socks added to my layers of preparation, a lighthearted defiance to proper appearance that made me grin. By the time I donned my waxed cotton hat with its wild profusion of artificial lilac flowers, I felt much more equipped for the challenges ahead, whatever they were.

Aaron

Though I wore a waterproof jacket, after hours of steady rain I felt damp all the way to my bones. The temperature might have been pleasant without the moisture, but combined, they tested my resolve. Not that I ever contemplated quitting, regardless of my feelings for Jaque. The other volunteers were hanging in there, and after spending the morning in their company I'd completely committed to seeing the day out, even if I felt like a drowned rat. From the fiery eyed older woman who measured the incoming rigs, to the pair of teenagers that had shown me how to reset downed obstacles, we were all soldiers in this battle with endurance, and I would not be the first one to flag.

Harv and Joyce made sure we had a pop-up tent to hide under in between rounds, and they provided a steady supply of hot beverages, as well as a surprisingly hearty lunch. Normally, I'd have eaten lightly at mid-day, but the constant movement and chill seeping into my core demanded feeding. I'd just run in from resetting a cone that had been taken out by an enthusiastic four-in-hand of ponies when Harv waved me over. I had to step in close so I could hear him over the patter of raindrops on our shelter.

"What?" I repeated, as I peered into the dreary distance that he had gestured toward. Though I could see carriages moving around in the mist, they remained indistinct and vague.

He leaned closer, clapping a firm hand onto my shoulder to steer me in the right direction. "I said, isn't that your girlfriend?"

I squinted and pushed my hood back as if it might help me pick out the drivers, but they all remained a blur. The only way I spotted her at all was the glossy black horse dancing through a puddle in the warmup, neck arched like some sort of renaissance sculpture. The grin that stretched my face warmed my cheeks at least, as I realized exactly how alike mare and mistress truly were. Apparently, both were perfectly at home in the midst of a storm, as well as able to calm the one that constantly swirled inside me.

As they swooped closer, the elegant carriage cutting through a thin puddle fast enough to throw up arcs of water, Jaque's grin reflected the mare's joy, which brought a twist of emotions to my gut. A warm thread of happiness to be connected to that much beauty, and an icy thread of self-recrimination over my relationship with Byzantine. However much I enjoyed the chance to focus on the growing connection with this amazing woman, I also felt a strong tug toward home. The drive to fix the damage I'd done felt like the itch I got in my palms when I needed to work on an engine, as if the vibrations of a running motor were moving through my nervous system.

"Go see her, Aaron," Harv urged, grinning sympathetically when I looked toward him for confirmation. After all, we had work to do, resetting the course for the Advanced drivers. "We've got this, I promise."

As if I needed encouragement, the rain slackened, and I took the omen in earnest, stepping out from under the shelter to blaze a path toward my goal. Jaque had steered her horse outside the arena, taking up a solitary post on the outskirts of all the activity, though I had to weave my way between a few competitors on the move in order to reach them. Her attention was on the steward checking

Lyric's bit, but Cardi waved as I approached, smiling a welcome from her seat on the back of the carriage. She wore a waxed jacket and a wool bowler, both dripping with moisture.

"Hey, Prince Charming, how's it going? You're just in time to lend a hand here."

"You know I'm here to serve," I shot back, the banter coming easily now that I understood it better. "How can I help?"

"Once the course is set Jaque will go walk it one more time. I'll be taking the reins for a few minutes, and it's easier to manage things if we have a header."

Nodding my understanding, I moved up to the mare's head, which put me directly in Jaque's line of sight. Though she listened intently to the steward, her smile grew as Lyric snuffled my pockets with interest. Clearly, the black mare's spirit was not dampened by the steady drizzle. I showed her my hands, enjoying the warm breath against my cool skin. "I'm all out, war-mare. But I'll make it up to you later."

"Aaron!" Cardi barked to get my attention, and I carefully placed my hands on the bridle as I'd been taught as she clambered from her seat to Jaque's. Once the reins were safely passed over, Jaque dropped down to the ground, her boots squelching in the wet grass. I let Lyric go and reached for her mistress instead, pleased when she reached right back. Her arms wrapped around my waist, and even though my jacket hung heavy with rain, she snuggled in close, pressing a quick kiss to the edge of my jaw.

"I missed you. A silly thing to say after so few hours. But there you have it."

The words and the kiss warmed me from the inside out and I tucked my chin down against her neck so I could answer her in the relative privacy afforded by the brim of her hat. "We'll make it up to each other later."

The crackle of a loudspeaker intruded on the moment, and she lifted her head to listen to the call for the Advanced drivers to walk their course. I could practically hear an apology in the air as she began to step away, but I shook my head in denial. "Go, Jaqueline. You've got a challenge to prepare for, and I'll be right here when you get back."

Her gloved hand found mine, then pulled it up to the rounded warmth of her cheek. When I cupped the fullness, stroking carefully along the faint hollow beneath my thumb, her eyes went soft with emotion. "Thank you, Aaron."

Then she pulled away entirely, and I watched her change, going from the soft lover I cherished to the fierce competitor I admired in less than three strides. Neck stretched long, and shoulders pulled back, she joined the other drivers filing into the grassy field, completely at home in the pressure cooker of competition.

The rain let up as the drivers walked their course, and while I kept half my attention on Lyric, just in case, my eyes followed Jaque. Her focus was total, weaving through the course with her chin up and eyes looking through the turns. Well, at least until she caught up with the guys who had been needling her all weekend.

They were standing just off to the side of one of the trickier combinations, which I only knew because Harv had explained it to me. As Jaque made her approach, one of them leaned in toward the others to speak. The three of them threw their heads back and laughed loudly enough to garner the attention of the other people in the ring, and Jaque's stride stuttered as her body tensed. My hands fisted as I struggled with the urge to pummel the lot of them, which only strengthened when Cardi spoke up behind me.

"Jesus, I don't hate often, but those butt waffles sure make it easy."

I nodded my agreement, though my eyes never left Jaque. *Come on, you've got this*, I thought at her, pride blooming in my chest as she straightened her shoulders and moved past them without giving them the satisfaction of a response.

Another woman caught up with her near the bridge obstacle, and some of the tightness in her back bled off as they spoke. The knot under my sternum loosened in response, and I fought the urge to rub at it, conditioned by my father not to show my emotions too readily, particularly in public. By the time she walked out of the ring the knot had disappeared, but a different tangle had taken up residence in my head. That pain at the root of my chest felt familiar, though this was the first time I'd experienced it with a woman outside of those related to me. I'd felt it for my mother, though not in a long time, and for my sisters even now, which included Jo. But Jaque was the first lover to have ever caused it, which baffled and frightened me. Neither lessened my delight when Jaque walked back out of the ring, her smile warm as she closed in on us.

Cardi didn't even bother to hide her laughter when Jaque went right past me to love on her mare. Nor did it bother me much, aside from a superficial sting to my ego. Jaque's happiness truly meant that much to me, and if I wanted a chance with her heart, then I'd have to share it with the mare. Jaque did spare me an apologetic squeeze of the arm before she turned back to the carriage, resuming the high-set, slanted seat which would keep her secure in the tight turns.

"You've got this, ladies," I encouraged as Lyric moved off again, smoothly merging into the traffic around the arena. Jaque lifted her whip in salute as she passed, and I blew her a kiss, garnering a rare blush. When I turned to make my way back toward the volunteer tent, I fetched up short as another carriage halted in my path. My frown of frustration deepened to outright disdain as I met the driver's eyes, finding none other than the douchebag, Paul.

"No wonder you've fallen back in the placings, Mr. Scott. Your driving clearly leaves something to be desired."

His eyes narrowed and the sneer he employed the night before made its return. "As if you'd know anything about driving? Clearly, your fucking leaves something to be desired, if you're stooping to volunteer work to win Jaque's favor. I never worked that hard when we were together."

Twenty thoughts at once ran through my head, though the one that screamed the loudest wanted me to put my fists to his face. I struggled past it though, puzzle pieces clicking into place as I considered his behavior over the last several days. Not that I understood the flawed logic that made this guy think he had any claim on Jaque, or what prompted such ugliness. But I did understand Jaque's reactions a little better, and I took a great deal of pleasure in returning his insult with interest.

"Hmm, well, there's the flaw then. Because you clearly weren't good enough in bed for her to ignore the deficit in your personality. You might want to look into that."

While he sputtered indignantly, his groom clapped a hand over her mouth to muffle her amusement, though her wide eyes held enough laughter to let me know I'd aimed correctly. Before the man could muster a reply, I moved around them, eager to rejoin my fellow volunteers. At least in their company I'd be too busy to dwell on how much it bugged me that Paul Scott had so much as touched Jaqueline, let alone been in a relationship with her. Yes, jealousy raised its voice, but confusion clamored loudest. Why would Jaque bother with someone so egotistical and stupid? I was no saint, but she outclassed Paul on every level, and deserved better than his self-serving attentions.

"Aaron!" Harv barked, waving his arm when I looked up from my determined march. I broke into a jog, ready for a distraction. But my feet slowed immediately when a wolf whistle sharpened the air. I turned in time to see Lyric blowing past at a strong trot, Jaque pointedly looking away from me, though she couldn't hide her smug smile. If not for Cardi pointing at Jaque while she laughed her ass off in the rumble seat, I might have doubted the source.

Shaking my head, I turned toward Harv at a more sedate pace, though my footsteps were lighter. Whatever storm clouds rolled in Jaque could handle them with the level of seriousness they required. In this case, Paul Scott could be blown off with one well timed whistle and a playful grin.

Jaque

I did not dwell over much on whatever Paul might have told Aaron, turning all of my focus toward Lyric instead. Whatever would come of their conversation was beyond my control, while the challenge of the cones course loomed before us with an almost sentient regard, as if waiting for me to show a weakness.

Judging by Lyric's sharp transitions, and the way she balanced herself for turns, any weaknesses would be mine. Never before had she come into day three with so much power still in my hands. I could have grown drunk on her playfulness if time allowed, but before I could sink too far the first bell rang out, signaling a driver to start the course. Most of us brought our horses around to face the arena, halting them outside the flow of traffic so we could watch our fellow competitors take on the beast set before us.

And the course was a beast in truth, meant to expose every flaw in one's training. If you neglected your fitness, your horse would not be fast enough. Should your dressage skills be lacking, you would not be able to balance and rate your horse, also losing to the clock. And heaven forbid you did not have your horse listening, because the slightest inaccuracy in steering would result in knock down penalties. This calibre of a course matched what one might find in Europe, as close to a championship level challenge as any I ever faced before. That impression was reinforced as Penny Winters steered her veteran saddlebred through the winding maze. Lyric made small fidgets in her eagerness to go, shifting weight from foot to foot and bobbing her head discreetly to ask for the contact that meant we were going to move. The customary movements were little more than white noise after our long partnership, no distraction at all as my eyes followed the route of my fellow competitor.

An overcorrection at the start of a slalom caused three balls to tumble to the wet turf, one of them splashing up a rainbow arc of spray as a hint of sun showed its face. Too much speed through a turn sent her horse down onto one knee in order to remain upright, and while he immediately stood back up, Penny lifted her whip high to signal her retirement. The bright chestnut gelding dropped his head and walked out of the arena, nostrils wrinkled with worry, but I recognized the soft love in Penny's eyes as they went by. When she looked up, I saluted her with my own whip, so thankful to see genuine horsemanship even at the pinnacle of our sport. She smiled, if weakly, which quickly disappeared as she passed by Maarten and Paul. Obviously, I was not the only person to bear the brunt of their derision, which intensified my burning urge to beat them. Not for myself, but for all of us who valued our relationship with our horses over anything else.

Lyric took a step forward in response, the supple leather reins telegraphing my every thought directly to her.

"Still now, lovely," I murmured, smiling faintly when her obedience came with a swished tail of opinion. There was no fault to be found in her eagerness, after all. To know she wanted to go to work after the exertion of yesterday held its own reward.

"Oh, my giddy aunt, someone really needs to give Malone a brain transplant," Cardi grumbled just behind my shoulder, which redirected my eyes to the ring.

Inside, Grady Malone engaged in a tug of war with his new Dutch Harness Horse, who had clearly reached his limit of being hauled around by the mouth. The poor animal threw his head from side to side, attempting to escape the heavy pressure of the bit, and when that failed, he reared.

There was a collective gasp from everyone watching as he wobbled on his long legs, but a flick of the whip brought him back to earth. Unfortunately, it also drove the wild-eyed creature to bolt forward, just as Grady's groom jumped from her perch to help. The girl lost her footing, stumbling hard as she struggled to right herself, and the horse lurched sideways away from the commotion.

For several tense seconds, every driver in the area readied for the horrific possibility of a wreck, including me. While I trusted Lyric to hold her ground in the face of a host of ridiculousness, the sheer chaos of another horse crashing through the crowd could not be accounted for. Once panic took hold, horses were like dominos, falling easily to the pressure of their peers. One could never forget their base nature, and the motto underlying even the calmest equine was to run away from danger.

As the announcer calmly asked the audience to remain quiet the ring crew leapt into action before things could escalate. Aaron confidently stepped in front of the frantic animal with his hands held out wide, several other people fanning out to either side. My heart flew to my throat for a breathless second, fearing the horse might run him over, despite the way his driver sawed at the reins. I need not have worried, as the animal dove for the perceived safety of the calm, steady human before him, desperate for some kind of relief.

However much I perceived myself in danger of falling in love, the moment Aaron took hold of the horse's bridle I knew myself for lost. My horsewoman's heart melted into a puddle as his free hand stroked the shivering neck, and his mouth moved with words I did not need to hear to know they were ones of comfort.

He relinquished his charge as soon as the groom reached him, waving away her thanks. Grady said not a word, his jaw clenched with anger and the purple flush of shame running over his cheeks. I might have pitied him, but this was the third horse in as many years that he had driven to act out publicly. While Paul and Maarten were both heavier handed than I preferred, they were emotionally cool. Grady tended to boil over when under pressure, which his sensitive horses simply could not stand.

Sides heaving and nostrils fluttering, the leggy horse jigged out of the arena as his groom walked beside him. Grady kept his hands quiet on the way past the whispering officials, lips clamped so tightly together they had gone white. I heaved a relieved breath as one of the ground jury followed in their wake, shadowing them back to the barn so that nothing untoward could occur behind the scenes. History did not need to repeat itself, for the horse's sake, even if one more infraction would likely see Grady blacklisted.

The competition quickly regained momentum, a beautifully turned out pinto mare putting in a workmanlike round for her driver. A slow, tickling drizzle picked back up as they went through the finish timer, renewing the deep black of Lyric's muscular body as the next driver took the course. One by one, our numbers dwindled, though we were joined by a few pairs and the first of several four-in-hands. I smiled every time I caught sight of Aaron striding around to set cones for the next carriage, nodded an encouragement to Sue as she trotted toward the ring, then turned Lyric away to get ready for my own round.

Tuning out everything but my mare, I barely noticed Paul as we shared the warmup arena. He became a shadow, of little consequence aside from the space he took up. Lyric quickly came into my hands, a musical vibration moving between us as though I held harp strings instead of reins. The carriage itself hummed along in her wake, rain droplets shivering and skidding along the patent leather dash, the lash of my whip swaying heavily with moisture.

We arced between a few sets of warmup cones, then I took her out to the open field where I could ask for a strong canter to get her blood up. Nor did it take much as she exploded into action with a squeal of excitement. Laughter bubbled up in my chest, overflowed out of my mouth, Cardi echoing our joy.

Just as I trilled my tongue to signal a downshift to the trot, Cardi tapped me on the shoulder. I turned my head to see the ring steward waving at us, and my body followed suit, Lyric responding to the change with a flowing turn. She balanced beautifully on the way down the hill, rocking her weight back to slow the carriage without conspicuous effort.

I had plenty of reason to smile as we were waved straight into the arena, and my lips remained fixed with happiness as we halted to salute the officials, waiting for the whistle that would give us

permission to begin. My lovely mare, who figured out the games
we played very early in our competitive journey, stood stock still
but for a faint shiver moving over her skin. When the whistle
sounded I felt her energy shift forward, eager to go, but she waited
when my hands remained relaxed. I had spent numerous shows at
the lower levels teaching her patience, for the one downfall to a
clever horse is they often anticipate your direction. But on the
other side of the coin, I did not seek to muffle her spirit. Which is
why I smoothly took up a trifle more contact and gave a spirited
cluck that launched her straight into a trot, rewarding her
obedience with a confirmation. *Yes*, every cell in my body told her,
you are correct, and clever, and oh so very right. In response, she
leaned into the collar of her harness, gleefully ready to affirm my
confidence in her.

Circling only once, I let her come straight at the perfect
moment, her neck arching in delight as we aimed for the start gate.
Her sturdy legs ate up the distance, lifting her muscled frame up
off the ground as if she were one of the more lightly built horses
that we shared this sport with. To be sure, there were horses of all
sizes and shapes in carriage driving, all welcome to play, but few
ever made it to Advanced.

But I put that thought out of my head as we entered the course,
condensing all my energy into the drive. The first several gates
were fairly straightforward, all on large, sweeping turns that were
merely a warm-up. In the slalom, I shaved portions of a second
away from our time by working the inside edge of the gates,
decreasing the needed bend. A high-pitched kiss of my lips sent
her into a canter as we came out of the turn toward the other end of
the ring, her hoofbeats muffled by the wet earth, my eyes already
locked on our next goal.

Owing to the damp conditions, and the earlier stumble by
Penny's gelding, I slowed her for the next turn. She shook her head
in response, but answered my hands, silently telling me she
thought we could do it. My reply was delayed by the three quarters
of a cloverleaf in our next obstacle, which demanded absolute
clarity of thought. The still breathlessness of the audience felt
palpable, though I could hear nothing beyond our breathing as we
threaded the needle back on itself with barely more than a
hairsbreadth to spare. Once clear, I answered her faith, giving her

leave to gallop toward the bridge. My heart thundered to match her feet, old memories of her refusing a bridge during competition causing my pulse to spike. Then memory after memory of her bravely facing this, and worse, since that day, smoothed my emotions into a mirror slick surface that reflected nothing back but our love for each other. That love, in and of itself, told me that together we could face anything.

Her wide, bare hooves landed on the bridge with a booming reverberation. She gathered her body and launched herself from the initial point of contact as if she were a jumper, the world eerily quiet after the first crack of noise. I took no time for concern at that point, only an infinitesimal gathering of the reins to support her, and the sharp inhale of Cardi to mark the time. Then Lyric landed on the other end of the bridge, the wheels of the carriage adding a softer tympani to the deep bass of her feet. The music lasted but a breath before she found the turf again, my lungs heaving gratefully as I remembered to breathe on the way to the next gate.

There were twenty-two efforts total before we reached the end, all coming together in a chorus of speed and agility. High-headed and bright-eyed, Lyric carried every note I asked of her. At the final gate, I gave her the reins, commands unnecessary to send her back into a gallop. She stretched out flat, coaxing speed out of every muscle, turf flying up from each tearing stride.

Then we were through, and I sat up to slow her, as grateful for the way she softened as I had been for her sharpness.

Applause filled my ears as we achieved a walk on a long rein and turned toward the exit. The familiar sound had an extraordinary edge to it, and I grinned all the harder to realize the addition came from Aaron. In the brief moments our eyes met I saw so much pride and warmth that I could have wept. He clapped his thick knuckled hands together in something more than the usual polite acknowledgement, each slap of his palms reverberating through me. Suddenly, I knew the blows for what they were: the final bites of an axe before a tree yields to gravity. I was falling and little could stop me now.

Would that the moment had remained unsullied, but I felt Lyric's hesitation in the reins and looked up to Paul's blaze-faced bay warmblood headed straight for us. I barely had time to say whoa before Paul steered around our now fixed position with a sadly familiar sneer. His disdainful voice flew by at a strong trot, invasive enough for every word to be heard.

"Watch where you're going with that plow horse."

I struggled to uproot the anger he stirred as I carefully manoeuvered back out to the waiting congratulations of my fellow competitors. After all, we had but one time penalty added to our score, and one of only three clear rounds thus far. My mare was content with herself, so happy in her own skin that I could not bring myself to care about the ribbons to come. But even as Paul knocked down one cone and scores were tallied for placings, the greasy film on my happiness remained. For I once fancied myself in love with Paul, much as I was falling for Aaron. If my judgement was so poor to offer that selfish toad my heart, could I really trust myself not to make the same mistake again?

Aaron

I'm not always the fastest on the draw, but my saving grace has always been accuracy. When I played baseball, I could put the ball over the plate with a precision few batters could combat. In rodeo, I'd caught damn near every steer I ever threw a rope at. By the time I took up jousting, I'd perfected my hand-eye coordination to an uncanny level. So as I watched Jaque navigate the cones with not even an inch to spare in some cases, I was understandably impressed.

The other thing I admired was how lit up she got, her smile so electric as she flew across the finish line that you could have powered a small city. And when our eyes met, I felt like I'd just gone zero to sixty in three point five seconds, every inch of my skin tingling with pressure. Yet, her visible joy also made it much more obvious that Paul Scott had said something that hurt her. My fists tightened immediately and my weight rocked onto my toes, everything in me screaming for his head. Why wasn't anyone calling him on his bullshit?

"Not worth going to jail over," Harv murmured from just behind my shoulder. He didn't even flinch when I turned a flinty stare his way, his own gaze completely stony despite the regret that bracketed his mouth. "I mean it, Aaron. He might deserve a good, old fashioned ass whoopin', but he's also a high-dollar criminal prosecutor. He'd nail you to the wall in court, then gloat over

Jaque's heartbreak. You think of her, even if you aren't worried about yourself."

Grinding my teeth in frustration, I settled for glaring at the prick on his way by. "A lawyer. Guess that explains why his head is so far up his ass."

Harv's chuckle helped lighten the air, and his broad hand clapped me on the back. "Probably so. God knows if I'd have ever recovered from the condition without my Joyce. Lawyering does tend to encourage a rather overblown ego."

Grimacing at my *faux pas*, I turned toward him. "Sorry sir, I have a knack for sticking my foot in my mouth, often up to the knee if you give me a minute. Not that I've got room to talk anyway. Being a jouster is about as ego driven as it gets."

Humor and sympathy filled Harv's eyes. "Ego drives us all, young man. But it's important that you don't let it do the steering. Keep that in mind."

Then he strode off to chat with the course designer about something, leaving me to stew in a mixture of unexpected emotion. I'd known him little more than two days, and he'd been more supportive than my own father had been in my entire life. Forming Gallant Company with Bart gave me a family the likes I'd never known growing up, and I hid in the refuge it afforded. But clearly, the world away from the Company held just as much good, if I were willing to risk myself a little. Hell, Jaque alone stood as proof of that. Asking her out had been a terrifying leap outside my comfort zone, but look at how it paid off.

Though Paul Scott maintained his lead by a tiny margin, I grinned unapologetically when he knocked over a ball in the cloverleaf. Sure, he might have a prancy, finely bred horse to brag on, but Jaque held the high ground to my mind. She worked hard, and her horse gave everything she had, not just out of obedience, but true affection. She was showing me a better way, both with her and with the horses. I doubted Paul Scott would ever understand what he was missing, on either front.

Just as with the rest of the levels, the awards were held until all the drivers completed the course, even the multiples. We worked through several pairs and an impressive array of four-in-hands, constantly resetting the gates for the different sized carriages. At the top level, I'd been shocked to see how little room for error they had. But when the last combination cleared the finish timers, I turned to hunt up Harv, itching to go see Jaque before they were called back to the ring. He waved me off with a grin.

Jogging around the warmup arena, I quickly reached my objective, coming up on the carriage from behind. Jaque had turned slightly in her seat so she could chat with Cardi, and thankfully, her smile was back. It warmed appreciably as she noticed my approach, and then Cardi turned around as well, laughing outright when she caught sight of me.

"Shoulda known it was you, Prince Charming. She sure doesn't smile like that for anyone else."

"Well, at least you're finally smiling at me too, Cardi," I teased, even as I approached Jaque's seat.

Cardi's loud laugh pulled some eyes, but most of them just smiled at her good humor. These carriage people were pretty great, by and large, always supportive and happy for each other.

"But honestly, I don't smile like this for anyone else either," I continued, taking the hand Jaque held out. Our eyes met and I let the smile I'd been reining in have its head. Not that it was particularly toothy or wide, but a particular slant to my lips that only happened when I thought of Jaque. Of how her lips felt against mine, and the way everything in me calmed when we spoke. Judging by the way her own lips softened, she felt it too.

Our fingers tightened on each other, and I pulled her down just enough to press a kiss to the warm sliver of skin between her glove and the cuff of her jacket. I wished the rest of the world could melt away for a few stolen minutes, so I could warm myself in the flowery scent of her skin, still prevalent beneath the wet leather of her gloves and the richness of the rain-soaked earth. But even that foolish dream got washed away as the announcer invited all the competitors back to the ring.

Not wanting to keep her from her well-deserved accolades, I moved to step backward, but her grip tightened on mine even as the other carriages began to move. "Aaron, I would very much like it if you would ride into the ring for the awards. You have worked as diligently as any of us this weekend, and should be there for the results."

I opened my mouth to say no. After all, she'd worked hard for this recognition, but she shut me up with lethal accuracy. "Please. I want you with me."

So I released her hand and circled the carriage to climb into the seat beside her. Her pleased smile created a well of peace deep in my chest, the restlessness that had always lived there inexorably changed. Not gone, not even chased out, but actually modified by the knowledge that this brave, glorious woman wanted me with her, valued my company. As Lyric stepped forward at Jaque's softly spoken command, I let myself relax into the cushions and settled an arm across the back of the seat. Owing to the raised, slanted driver's seat, this left me touching her low on the hips, but something about it felt just right. Like maybe I could fit into her life.

The question that plagued me as the carriage rolled forward was whether or not Jaque would want to fit into my life. My former fiancée had used those words in her tearful apology as she pressed the engagement ring into my numb hands. That our lives would never fit together, no matter how much she wished they would. And I'd let her go, because even though I'd thought our edges fit just fine, I for damn sure didn't want to be in a relationship with someone if they didn't want to be there with me.

I shook those heavy thoughts away as Jaque pulled into the lineup, sandwiched between the blonde lady I'd seen her speaking to on several occasions and a gal driving a splashy looking paint horse. A little worry threatened my calm, as I couldn't remember either of their names from when Jaque introduced them at the competitor's party. Not unusual for me, to be honest. Hell, it took me nearly a week to remember all the trainee's names last summer. But aside from some nods of acknowledgment, the drivers remained quiet, focusing on their horses.

We didn't have long to wait for the judges to make their announcements. Much like the other two events, they gave out ribbons for the best score for the day's efforts, walking from carriage to carriage to hand out ribbons. Everyone began to shed their raingear as the sun came out, giving the arena a little more color in the process. I got a little antsy as they moved up the placings, wondering when they'd get to Jaque. The impatience died on the vine though, when they called out Paul Scott in fifth and he looked like he'd just kissed the south end of a north bound donkey. Jaque landed a respectable third, but the blonde lady, Sue, and her bay mare, Rhapsody, came away with the blue ribbon. Once the judges finished up with the pairs and four-in-hands, the air thickened appreciably as they moved on to the overall placings.

For this, each driver was called forward in order of placing. Grady Malone, the dick head who'd abused his horse's mouth so badly, had never returned from the barn, so that was one less competitor to field. Another guy had retired on marathon the day before, and the lady who'd bowed out after her horse slipped was also out of the running. Not to mention, the class size at the Advanced level was much smaller than the others, which meant we didn't have long to wait before they were calling Jaque's name over the loudspeaker.

Her patient mare, who seemed almost sleepy during the lineup, stepped immediately into a trot as Jaque steered her toward the judges. While I'd seen them work all weekend, feeling the mare's power press me back into the seat made me a bit giddy. Horsepower in any format had my absolute admiration.

They halted beside the judges with a clean-edged sharpness that surprised me for its smoothness, not a single lurch transmitting to the carriage, further cementing my earlier comparison of the vehicle to a European sports car. The engineering that had gone into its construction was absolute art. The fact that the "engine" that powered it had a mind of her own made it all that much more fascinating.

They handed Jaque a large red ribbon twice the size of the yellow one on the dash, though this one she hung just above the handle of her whip. The flowing tails fluttered slightly as she thanked the judges, and then we endured photographs from the official photographer. Not that I had a hard time smiling, what with Jaque's happiness spilling over onto me. She dimmed not a bit as we gave up the spot to her dickhead ex, urging Lyric into a strong trot as we swooped along the rail. Applause in plenty rang out for her, from the audience and the center of the ring as well. Once parked back in the line-up, I risked a liberty, lifting the arm behind her back to squeeze her waist. She graced me with a flutter of eyelashes that I took for pleasure before angling her body around to chat with Cardi. I listened as they discussed what needed doing before Cardi left for the airport, and made note of any place I could help, but otherwise remained silent. The long, wet day had caught up with me, and the longer I sat still, the stiffer and colder my body grew.

Before long the announcer dismissed everyone, which couldn't have come at a better time. I shivered inside my rain jacket as we made our way back to the trailer, but felt grateful that I didn't have to walk. Or worse, ride back out with Harv. One would hope he'd drive a bit more sedately now that things weren't so pressing, but I'd watched him tear around all day, and his speed hadn't abated in the least.

While the rain finally stopped, the cloud cover barely thinned, which made the afternoon feel more like early evening. When we reached the trailer, I vaulted down from the carriage box, muffling a grunt as my weary body complained. All I wanted was a hot meal, a hotter shower, and the warmth of Jaque curled up with me in bed. But we had much to accomplish before any of those things would be within my reach.

I stood at Lyric's head and offered her the last of the tiny cookies in my jacket pocket. They were damp and crumbly after a day's worth of abuse, but the mare snuffled them up as if they were manna from heaven. The ladies climbed down off the carriage a bit more gracefully than my abrupt exit, shedding their soggy wool aprons as they moved toward our charge. They took less than a blink to have the black mare unhitched and secured to the trailer, and barely more than that to shed her harness. Jaque threw a fleece cooler over her to help ward off a chill, but I'll be honest, out of all of us, the mare looked to be enjoying the weather the most.

While Cardi worked on storing the harness Jaque went to change, and I did my damnedest to get the carriage clean. I was bent over, peering beneath the fifth wheel to get the last bits of mud when I felt a hand land on my ass.

"Jaque," I growled teasingly as I straightened, expecting to turn around and scoop her into my arms. Imagine my shock when I found Joyce grinning at me in pink cheeked amusement as she tucked her hand back into her jacket pocket.

"You'll forgive me, I hope?" she asked as my lips quirked in confusion. As a knight at the renaissance faire, I'd had my hind end manhandled on many occasions, but only very rarely by someone older than my mother. "I couldn't seem to help myself. It's been a long time since Harv had such a tight derriere, and yours is exceptional."

I never managed to make a diplomatic reply as another voice joined the conversation, one that sounded less than pleased. "He might, but I am not quite sure how to feel about it."

We both turned to face Jaque, myself with a bit of worry over the swirl of coolness that marked her clipped tone, and Joyce with a renewed blush. Lyric stood at her mistress's side, her ears swiveling back and forth to find the source of tension, nostrils flared as if she could scent out the trouble.

"Ah, Jaqueline, dear! My apologies to you both. I came to offer you my congratulations, and to thank Aaron for helping today. We really would have been in a bind without him."

"I appreciate the sentiment, Joyce, truly. I have always loved coming to your show, and never mind when you pet my dog…" Jaque's usually soft eyes narrowed, and a challenging edge sharpened her smile. "But I would thank you very kindly to keep your hands off my boyfriend."

Whatever chill I'd been feeling disappeared as lightning ran down every nerve ending I owned. Being claimed so openly by her did things to me I can't rightly give words to. I could have leveled cities for her, conquered civilizations to hear her say it again.

Before I could own up to the feeling, she unclipped Lyric from the trailer and marched off toward the barn. I looked around stupidly for a place to toss the rag I held, ready to walk away from my self-imposed task. Everything could wait until I cleared the air with Jaque. But Cardi stepped into the fray, halting both Joyce and I before we could take a step. Her eyes held nothing but sympathy as she addressed me.

"Charming, you might want to give her a few minutes to cool off." Then Cardi's fists hit her hips as she turned toward the other member of our party, ice in her thin smile. "And Joyce, while I'm sure Harv will be forgiving of your indiscretion, I hope you'll be the one to tell him about it. You know how the rumor mill can be, and I'd hate for him to hear about this second hand."

"Yes, yes, of course," Joyce answered, eyes as steely as her husband's had been earlier. "Harvey and I don't keep secrets, and it is beneath you to think otherwise, Cardinal Collins."

Joyce turned to me next, bright spots of pink high on her cheeks highlighting the matronly smile she wore. "I honestly don't know what came over me, Aaron. I'm not the sort of woman to randomly grope anyone."

"I never would have thought so either, Joyce." I tried for a smile, but it fell flat under the weight of my worry over Jaque. "Yet, here we are. I sincerely hope Harv doesn't take this the wrong way. He's a good man, and I really thought I'd like to see you both in Aiken." Then my eyes darted toward the barn, and I knew my patience was at an end, regardless of how impolite it might be. "And on that note, I'm going to see a lady about a horse."

"Go on, Aaron," Cardi responded for them both, her hand closing on Joyce's elbow when she took a step toward me. "I think I can get Joyce to help me with the rest before I have to leave. I'll call Jaque later, and I expect to hear you with her."

So I took off for the barn, jogging around a few rigs that were pulling out under the light of the setting sun. I needed to find Jaque, to know if what she'd said had been more than just the heat of the moment. Nothing in the world felt more important in that instant.

Which of course made it the perfect time for my mother to call. I forced myself to listen to her complain about my youngest sister Darlene, faking a patience I didn't feel as I gently explained that Darlene's divorce was completely understandable. But she dragged the conversation on forever, swearing up and down that she raised us all better than this. Why was she being punished, she asked, as if she were the one wronged. Every second she kept me from chasing Jaque felt like an eternity, but as I said goodbye one thing became abundantly clear. My mother's love, however much I craved it, stood up against the storm of feeling I had for Jaque like a flickering candle in a gale force hurricane.

Jaque

Anger was not an emotion I enjoyed nor wore well, no matter the motivation. I knew how ruddy my face grew and the way my lips disappeared as I frowned. I hated the way my stomach rolled and pitched, like a bucking horse bent on ridding itself of an annoyance. Worse, my hands grew stiff, balling up and trembling as I exercised restraint over my conflicting feelings.

What had Joyce been thinking, touching Aaron so inappropriately? Worse still, what had I been thinking, behaving so jealously? And heaven only knew what Aaron thought of the whole debacle. I felt like I might be torn apart by the maelstrom in my heart, jagged edges of dark cutting through the happiness I enjoyed during the awards ceremony. How could I have fallen from those heights so quickly?

However, my mare had earned my love and respect countless times over, regardless of the state of my emotions. She had given me everything she was capable of, all weekend and did not deserve the spillover from my frothing emotions. So I eased my marching steps, breathing through my nose to slow my heart rate, and made my way down the lane toward the stabling tent. As I calmed, my hand curled over the crest of her neck, the tight braids that lined the top of the muscular length threading between my fingers like we were two puzzle pieces. Thankfully, she gave me an anchor as we went straight past the three-headed hydra that plagued my steps all weekend long. Maarten's thick accent was unmistakable, as was the disdain that filled his words. "Ah, look, gentlemen, it seems as if even the most dogged of competitors will have a lucky day. We should applaud their futile efforts, for it is unlikely to happen again."

Their clapping rang out slow and muffled around the pounding that started in my head. The acid I swallowed over the course of the weekend finally spilled from between my lips, and I halted abruptly to level them all with a glare. Only Paul showed the faintest flinch, as he knew the bite of my temper. Rare it may be, but when riled, I made sure to leave an impression.

"Ah, yes, congratulations to you gentlemen as well," I replied sweetly enough, earning a gloating grin from Maarten that stoked my anger ever higher. "For proving once more that money may buy you lovely horses but will never give you redeeming personalities or compassionate horsemanship. Well done, truly. You must be so proud, Mr. van den Berg. A credit to your training program."

All three of them went wide eyed, Maarten and Paul rocking back as if slapped. But they did not concern me half as much as the curl of Grady's lip, like a dog threatening to bite. Menace blackened his expression, and I instinctively shivered, wanting to run away but unwilling to give ground. Still, I broke the eye contact, much as I would with a reactive dog.

"Jaqueline, that's not very lady like." Paul admonished, as if he had any right at all to be disappointed in me.

"I am sorry," I shot back, the easy apology making him smile. Yes, he had heard those words many a time from me, as he pushed me into believing everything wrong in our relationship was my fault. But that was well in the past, and I had removed my blinders long ago. "I am a lady, but only to those who have earned that side of me. You lost that privilege all on your own."

Then I left, unwilling to waste another second of my dwindling energy on those who would remorselessly suck the last of it from me. As I entered my own aisle, I wove carefully through the remaining tack trunks and harness racks that lined the path. Some people were in the middle of packing up, and I mustered smiles for those I knew. Aside from the flush still burning my cheeks, there would be little sign that I was crumbling under the strain of the day.

Getting Lyric settled took mere moments, as I had prepared everything earlier in the day before heading to the trailer. She tucked into her hay and dove for her feed the instant I retrieved it from the tack stall. Taking a stitch ripper to the yarn holding her braids in place provided a chance to channel some of my anger, viciously tearing the tiny knots from their mooring. But I remained careful all the same, Lyric too precious to risk to haste. Once done I latched the stall door shut behind me, making every motion incredibly deliberate to cover my impatience. I could come back for night check once I found my own dinner. Perhaps some food would help me sort through everything I felt? I always grew a little untethered by the end of a show weekend, and at the moment, all I could think about was a massive basket of french fries.

Back outside, I took the long route to avoid any more unpleasantness from my detractors. This left me passing by a sweeping panorama of the show grounds, all softened by the pastels of the setting sun. My feet stopped of their own accord, and I drew a deep breath of the rapidly cooling air, moisture lending a richness to every scent. Closing my eyes, I could almost imagine myself at my grandfather's farm, though I knew I would never stand there again. That melancholy thought added weight to my already roiling emotions, and I finally caved in on myself. No other outlet remained but tears, letting frustration bleed off as the salty heat made rivulets on my cheeks. Sobs came soon after, quiet ones, so as not to draw the attention of the people caring for their horses not more than thirty feet away. No one needed to see this, no one needed to know that I had been bled so cheaply. After all, we came in third in what had been our most challenging competition yet. Happiness came with the ribbon, did it not?

"Jaque?"

I sucked in a ragged, startled breath, not ready to face Aaron. Holding a hand out toward the voice behind me, I tried to allay him. "Just a moment, I shall be just a moment." Empty words, and they did not stay him any more than they calmed my righteous tears as I turned away to hide them.

His hands landed on my shoulders in a way that felt familiar. As if he had done it a thousand times before, and my skin had known just where his thumbs would press into the base of my neck. Fingers swept through the hollow over my clavicle, even through my jacket and I relaxed into that small embrace with relief. There. This, I needed.

"What's wrong? Is Lyric alright?

Oh, and that voice. I loved the way it caressed my heart, my body willing to release anger in favour of more pleasurable passions. That is, provided I had not ruined things with him as well.

"She is quite well, I assure you. And I will be well, soon enough." Turning my head, I pressed my cheek against the warmth of his hand, needing the reassurance of more contact. I could think of nothing that might distract me better than the simplicity of physical pursuits. Yet, he went still at the touch, and my stomach plummeted in disappointment. I had overplayed my position and would have to pay the price. An apology pushed behind my teeth, but frustration followed fast, riding the memory of countless apologies to Paul. "What, I cannot even touch you?"

His hands tightened on my shoulders and he spun me around. Sunset sparked off the anger in his eyes, highlighting the tightness of his jaw. Some part of me was drawn to the potential for violence in his athletic body, then softened in the next breath when he took my hand and lifted it to his cheek. The muscle there jumped then relaxed.

"Jacqueline, you may touch me wherever and however you like. But when I felt tears on your cheek, I felt the urge to rip someone limb from limb. That required an adjustment on my part."

"Adjustment?" I queried ridiculously, my brain moving slowly through the fog of embarrassment over being caught in helpless tears. I did not betray weakness to people. Years of being teased as a child had ingrained that particular coping mechanism.

"Yes." He shrugged his shoulders as if uncomfortable. "I grew up with three sisters. Tears are a trigger for me, and I feel quite strongly about yours."

Oh. That was the first moment I had heard a word about his family, which felt very important. Like a rare jewel. On the other hand... "While I am grateful for your concern, my noble champion, I pray your feelings toward me are not of a brotherly fashion."

That earned a dark laugh, his hands slipping from my shoulders to my back, and he pulled me against his chest. Burrowing my nose into the base of his neck, I drew in his scent, warming myself in the physical connection. He had respectfully kept his distance, allowing me to focus on Lyric all day long, which endeared him to my heart. Apparently, my body considered more than twelve hours far too long. My brain whispered for caution, but the rest of me did not listen, my arms wrapping around his back to pull us completely flush. Breath hitched in my throat as I felt the first stirrings of his passion pressing against my belly.

"No, my lady, I have no desire to be a brother to you."

"My gratitude knows no bounds." I slid my cheek back and forth against his sweater, the wool warm from his body. A lovely change from the damp jacket of earlier. "Nor does my desire for you."

"You aren't going to make this easy, are you?" I felt the words rumbling in his chest as much as I heard them.

"And why should I?" I followed the question with a kiss to his Adams apple, smiling when he swallowed hard. "Would it not be better to relieve the distraction? To forget for a little while."

He hummed deep in his throat, his hands back on my shoulders, setting me away from the fabulous temptation of his body. The power in his hands and potential for danger were an unexpected thrill.

"Jaqueline, I promise you, when we come together, there will be no forgetting." He stared into my eyes for so long I felt sure he could see my soul, a frightening vulnerability to allow. The deeper he looked, the more I feared he would turn away from what he found. "I don't want to be a distraction. I want your complete and undivided attention."

A pulse of desire moved through my body like one giant heartbeat as he cupped the side of my jaw, a calloused thumb brushing my cheek. I had never heard a man speak so straightforwardly of his intent, more familiar with stumbling permission and wordless consent. The stark honestly made me dizzy with want, and I swayed toward him, needing more contact.

"I can think of little else, Aaron. I am yours for the taking." His resolve held right up to the point my hand tangled in his hair, the thick locks slipping between my fingers. Then he capitulated, swallowing my moan of anticipation and feeding it back to me as he possessed my mouth. Hungry for his kisses, I cared little for breathing. His full lips felt as though they had been made to match mine.

When he pulled away, I was left panting, my hands fisting in objection so he could not escape. But he did not let go, simply stared as if unsure, like a colt assessing something new. "You..." He paused, swallowed, and tried again. "Jaque, please don't think this is a line, but I swear, I've never felt like this before. And it's..." Another pause, his eyes flickering away, and I released my grip on his shoulder so I could push his wild hair away from his forehead.

"Amazing, wonderful, glorious?" I offered, smiling tentatively as he relaxed into our embrace a little more. "Please, say yes, because I am terrified."

He hitched me up onto my toes, closer to his relieved smile, and tipped his forehead against mine. "All of the above."

Need morphed to something gentler, but no less fierce. Something that made me want to hold him for no other reason than to be close. Something that wanted to give him peace, though he was clearly no stranger to a fight. But before I could say anything, he let me go, slowly, so I could balance myself. What I remained unsure of was whether or not my emotional equilibrium would recover. While he had not shied away from my earlier impulsive declaration, I would not rest until I knew his thoughts on the matter. As if he knew the serious direction of my thoughts, his brow wrinkled.

"Come on, I saw Lyric was taken care of. How about we grab Soleil and go get some dinner? I think we'll both feel a hell of a lot more like talking with some food in our bellies."

I nodded and allowed him to steer us toward the trailer, hoping to get in a quick farewell to Cardi before she left. Much as she and I had to discuss, we were out of time, and I felt my focus shifting. Regardless of my fears, Aaron Drew had more than earned a good deal of my completely undivided attention, and I wanted nothing more than to give it to him.

Aaron

As I drove us into town, I thought a wet cat would have been more relaxed to pass company with than Jaque. The distance between us felt huge, even in the close confines of the truck. Nor did I understand why, considering her placing in the competition, but I had a pretty strong suspicion Paul Scott might have something to do with it. He'd pointedly sneered at me earlier, while I was hunting for Jaque. After talking to my Mom, I'd been short-tempered enough to flip him off. The glare I got in return had warmed the caveman portion of me that still wanted to pound his face in.

Finding Lyric alone had set off warning bells in my head, but I figured maybe I'd just missed her. On the way back out of the barn I'd paused to admire the sunset—it always had been one of my favorite times of the day, and lately became a prelude to my evening conversations with Jaque, giving it even more importance. As my eyes adjusted to the last bit of brightness after the cloudy day, I caught her form haloed in the light. My skin shivered with delight, recalling the fire in her eyes as she laid claim to me, and I hurried to catch up with her, wanting to share the quiet moment.

But that wasn't to be. Her tears refreshed my animal rage and also woke something markedly less familiar in my lifetime. Tenderness. I wanted to scoop her up, hold her tightly until the tears were less than a memory, to chase them away with kisses.

The anger she responded with only stung for a moment, and then she'd turned to passion, which distracted me entirely.

God, she felt so different, even in her upset. I'd be getting a week's worth of guilt inducing texts from my mother, after hurrying her off the phone. But Jaque didn't want her anger to touch others, always pulled back the instant she came close to hurting anyone. Even those who deserved it, were I to guess.

Her voice was carefully modulated as she directed me to a burger joint, and she maintained a careful mask as the waitress seated us in a booth. I missed the natural animation of her face as she stared fixedly at the menu, and the longer we sat there without speaking, the worse everything felt. No, I didn't think she meant to give me the silent treatment, but my youth had been rife with being ignored when I'd done something to upset my mother. It beat out being yelled at for every damn thing, but in that moment, I'd have preferred Jaque come uncorked.

While we waited for our drinks I slid my feet across the floor and carefully wrapped my legs around Jaque's, hoping to get some kind of response. She lowered her menu just enough that I could see her eyes, the usual warm brown unnaturally cool. Immediately, I pulled back, not wanting to add to her agitation. Her menu dropped to the tabletop in response and her mouth opened as if to speak... just in time for the waitress to return to take our orders. I waved for Jaque to go first, my stomach so tight with nerves I wondered if I could even eat.

"Pardon me, I would very much enjoy a large order of french fries with cheese. And a mocha shake with extra whipped cream, no cherry."

My brows rose over the amount of food she requested, considering her slight appetite over the course of the weekend. But I turned to the waitress and made my own requests, feeling the need to match the amount. If we were going to be sitting for a while I might as well refuel after the long day.

As soon as the woman turned for the kitchen the welcome warmth of Jaque's calves wrapped around one of mine. The hidden embrace eased the friction on my worry, and when I met her eyes, they were much more lively than mere moments before.

"I should apologize," she began softly, and I slid an open hand toward her. As soon as she took it, her shoulders straightened a bit more, seeming to gain as much strength from the touch as I did. "My mood is never at its best when I am hungry."

"Mine either," I confessed, squeezing her fingers lightly. "And I'd bet you haven't eaten since breakfast. In my case, Harv and Joyce provided lunch."

She stiffened, her lips twisting, and I realized my mistake. Hurriedly, I pushed onward before she could retreat. "You know, I don't think she meant to actually touch me. I was bent over and took a step back, probably right into her hand."

"That is kind of you to say, Aaron. You are ever a gentleman." Ow, that didn't exactly sound complimentary, but once more, she softened. Retreated, even, her shoulders rounding as if to protect herself. "Regardless of her intent, I must apologize again. I have no right to behave so jealously. You are not mine to claim."

The forlorn smallness that shrank that small sentence also squeezed my heart, and I responded instinctively. "Yes, I am."

Her smile wasn't the one I was hoping for, disappointment lacing her upcurved lips. "No need to say such things, Aaron. You have already won me over. I have no illusions about our lives, and I am well aware that you will have another willing partner by next weekend."

Before I could overthink, I slid out of my seat and moved over to her bench. She scooted over to make room, but I pushed right up against her side anyway so I could see everything that she felt for myself. Confusion clouded the earthy brown, but I preferred it to the defeat that had been there.

"What happened to the woman who climbed me like a tree in the restaurant parking lot? Who steered her horse around the hazards yesterday like she was a charioteer in a Roman coliseum? To the Jaque that wolf whistled at me, and publicly declared I was her boyfriend? Did all that courage disappear once the competition was over?"

"I beg your pardon?"

Though I thought she meant it as a statement of affront, all I heard was hurt. Maybe I was going about this all the wrong way.

"No, I beg yours, Jacqueline." I tugged her hand up to my lips, cupping it with both my palms as I pressed kisses to every knuckle. "I thought I'd been straight forward enough this weekend that you wouldn't doubt me. Seems my usually stellar aim has fallen short."

"Oh, no, I, um…" Jaque blinked rapidly, staring at my lips on her skin as if she were powerless to look away. "I did not mean…"

"Didn't mean it when you called me your boyfriend?" I asked softly, breathing it against the back of her hand. Her eyes flew up to meet mine, wide and finally, truly warm. "Or didn't mean it when you said I'd move on to another woman next weekend?"

"Aaron, I can't imagine…" But her eyes flicked up behind me, and she stiffened, alerting me to the approaching waitress. I released her hand and shifted slightly to give the impression of distance. My intent wasn't to embarrass Jaqueline and I'd been serious earlier. A meal would do both of us a world of good. Talking could wait.

We attacked our food with a will, Jaque systematically dismantling her fries with ruthless efficiency. I forgot to chew my burger when she used a finger to scoop whipped cream off her shake, then licked the dollop off with obvious relish. When she noticed my reaction, her pleased grin threw a wrench in the inner workings of my brain, and thinking threatened to cease entirely. Took a real effort to swallow the chunk of burger in my throat, and then I chugged half of my soda to aid the passage. Clearly, whatever she thought of a relationship with me, she remained determined to push for a closer physical connection.

As our stomachs began to fill we slowed down, and I felt the need to iron some things out before she took us right off the rails. Yeah, we had a little over a week of phone calls to look forward to, but some things I didn't want to talk about without being together. When I turned slightly to face her, she slowly bit into the french fry she held as if it required all her concentration.

"Jaque, I'm serious about being your boyfriend. Unless that was the jealousy talking. I haven't so much as flirted with anyone since New Year's Day, and I'm not interested in finding someone else."

Quiet reigned as she finished chewing, then took a long pull on her shake, her cheeks sucking inward with the effort. My libido tried to take it dark places, but I wouldn't be distracted. This felt too damned important. After she dabbed her lips, she finally gave me her attention, hand landing on my thigh.

"I had no right to be so bold, Aaron, not without discussing it with you first." Earnest disappointment pursed her lips as she paused. I turned toward her more fully, putting my arm along the back of the booth so I could caress her shoulder. The muscles there carried a humming tension, as if she were restraining herself. "I did not mean to treat you as if I owned the rights to you, to take your choice away. Moving too quickly is a habit of mine, one I am trying to improve."

"It's only a problem if the other party involved has a problem. Which I don't, Jaque. I want this with you, and only you." My heart twisted painfully as I realized the hole in my argument. "But it'll only work if you trust what I'm saying."

"I want to," she answered mournfully, the hand on my leg curling in on itself. "Sadly, it is myself I do not trust. I always push for more, then find my judgement misguided, and I am hurt once again. I cannot blame anyone for that but myself."

Even as my dislike of Paul swelled into something more like hate, the pain in her voice cut my insides into ribbons. Much as I wanted to pursue a connection with her, I knew myself too well to promise I would never hurt her. But I needed to give her some hope or risk losing her faith all together. Turning her hand upward where it lay on my thigh, I placed my palm against hers and offered her the truth.

"Jaque, I'm not very practiced at being in a good relationship, so I'm pretty certain I'm going to screw up here and there. But I can swear that I'll never intend to cause you pain, and I'm hoping you'll give me time to prove it."

"How much time?" The guarded way she clipped off the question made me worry I'd said the wrong thing. Yet, her eyes were bright with hope, which sparked an answering light in me.

"However long it takes, Jaqueline. You are worth every second I've spent here, and I hate that I wasted years not seeing how amazing you are."

Her lower lip wobbled, then firmed, clearly unwilling to show any weakness in such a public place. That sentiment, I could totally understand. I'd learned early in life to mask my feelings so they couldn't be exploited to anyone's advantage, and hated that she'd done the same.

"However much I wanted this between us, Aaron, I do not know that I could have been enough for you before. My driving has consumed the better part of these years, and I cannot promise it will not come between us now." Despite the determination in her voice, she pulled my hand up and kissed each of my knuckles just as I had done to her. Those soft lips on the knotted joints did more to ease my heart than anything else she might have done. The pain I'd endured when those fingers had first been broken still haunted me, but her loving touch easeed the ghostly memories. "Still, if you are willing to try, I should very much like to be your girlfriend."

Despite the narrow confines of the booth, I pulled her close and kissed her cheek. "Oh, I'm going to try harder than I ever have before, Jaque. Because I really, really want to be your boyfriend."

Then my girlfriend melted me faster than the remains of her milkshake, pressing her lips right to mine, in full view of everyone in the restaurant. Hell if it didn't feel a lot like falling off Byzantine at a high rate of speed. Bart would have laughed shamelessly if he'd been there to see it.

Jaque

When we left the restaurant Aaron thoughtfully shared a small piece of his hamburger with Soleil, which endeared him to me even more. She unbent enough to lick his fingers in gratitude, but still would not allow him to pet her. Someday, perhaps, she would release her prejudice of men and be at peace with his touch.

For myself, Aaron's touch gained esteem at every moment. When I placed my hand on the console in offer of a connection, he did not enfold it as I hoped. Instead, he rested his fingers in my palm, flashing a small smile as we passed beneath a rare streetlamp.

"I need to keep my hands free for the wheel, if you don't mind."

"No, not at all." I angled myself in the seat, the better to watch him in the light from the instrument panel. Truly, my silly heart thought nothing more handsome than Aaron driving. He seemed most himself, completely in the moment and unweighted by worries.

Our ride back to the show grounds had a misty quality, as if we moved in a fog that kept us apart from the rest of the world. By the time we reached the stabling tents only a few other vehicles remained, most trailers having pulled out with the setting sun. Quiet reigned, and I turned Soleil loose to sniff along the aisle as we went inside to look in on Lyric. Aaron shadowed me in the dim light, close enough for comfort but not so much as to be in my way.

I found Lyric dozing on her feet, eyes mostly closed and her lower lip hanging down enough to show off the pink of her gums. She roused slowly as we let ourselves into the neighbouring stall to replenish her hay, and I dropped several flakes into the corner without placing them in the net. No need to keep the stall tidy as I would be stripping it in the morning, and she deserved every last stem of the rich green fibre. No, actually, she had earned far more, but to her, food held a greater value than any bauble I could buy.

Aaron took one of her water buckets to refill it, leaving me to press myself against Lyric's sturdy side. She and I were a match, beautiful in our strength, our bodies capable and solid. Even our hair shared the same glossy wave, reflecting the faint overhead light. I ran my hands under the wool cooler to check her temperature, the skin beneath lively and supple. Thanks to the cooler weather, I knew she would rest well tonight.

Once Aaron returned, snapping the now full bucket into place, I gave her a sweet kiss on her browbone. Her eyes closed and she sighed, nuzzling into my arms for a moment. Then I left her to rest, closing her in for the night. As I slid the catch home, my eyes caught on the shiny ribbons that hung from her stall door, and I lifted them off, still marveling over our accomplishments.

But I flinched as I brought them up into the light. What in heavens name? Mud splattered over the long tails of the satiny ribbons, darkly obscuring the lettering declaring our placement. While the day had been wet and mud lay everywhere, they had been clean when I hung them up. The aisleway itself was dry, which made the mud ever so much more of a mystery.

"What's wrong?" Aaron asked as he turned away from securing my equipment stall.

"I am not sure." As I peered up and down the aisle in search of answers, I found no one else around who might be able to provide insight. Still wet enough to have been a recent addition, the mud on the stall door lay in thick and clumpy swaths, unlike anything in the immediate area. All the facts together made my nerves draw tight with the suspicion that someone purposely defaced Lyric's well-deserved accolades!

Pushing blindly past Aaron, I headed for the outside water spigot, wanting to wash them off before they dried. But as I bent to rinse them clean, Soleil shot around me in a streak of colour, barking wildly. Something in her tone gave me pause, put a quaver in my voice as I called her back. "Soleil, come here! Right now!"

She ignored me, disappearing into the darkness with a low snarl. I heard running footsteps which sent Aaron into action. Lethal grace carried him in Soleil's wake, long legs lending speed. He too vanished, and I trailed after both, ribbons hanging forgotten in my fingertips.

"Soleil?" I called again as my eyes adjusted to the moonlight, hoping for some kind of response. Aaron appeared first, dragging a hand through his hair even as he looked back over his shoulder.

"Sorry, Jaque, I lost her. Any ideas where we should look?"

"There are so few people left, I am sure she will stay close." I lifted my hand as if to shade my eyes from the nearly full moon but the cool mud brushed my face. Flinching away from the touch, I grimaced. "Ugh, I must clean these." As I turned to find a place to hang them, a low flash of white caught in the corner of my vision, which promptly resolved into the bib along Soleil's chest. "Mon petit chou! Do not scare me so!"

She trotted up to me with her tail aloft and her jaw gapping in pride, certainly convinced she had done me a service. But when I bent to pick her up, she shied away and growled, clearly bothered by the ribbons. I dropped them without hesitation, my concern for her superseding my upset over their ruin. "Come, *sucre*, I am sorry to be so upset. You frightened me, running away."

As she came close I reached beneath her, relaxing as she pushed up on her hind legs to help me lift. When I buried my nose in her thick fur she gave my cheek a rare lick of reassurance. Though I turned for the truck, ready to leave before another mishap could occur, Aaron did not follow. He bent to finish my work, carefully brushing the dirt away as water rinsed off the evidence of someone's purposeful defacing.

The care he took with me, with all the things that mattered to me, made my throat thick. I wanted to smile as he slid the hooks on the backs of the ribbons into his pockets after he shook them free of excess water. But anger swam in deeper waters, frustration causing eddies in my happiness. I looked up at the night sky, swaths of stars and the moon both shining all the brighter after the recent storm.

The gibbous shape swam as tears threatened, but I refused to cry them. Paul and his ilk would not bleed me ever again. As my resolve firmed Aaron moved in behind me, a bulwark of support as his arms came in under mine. Soleil did not grumble at his nearness for once. He tucked his chin against my temple and held me against his broad chest, silent and accepting.

We stood there for quite some time, as several more trucks left the showgrounds. But eventually the long weekend demanded I pay, and I muffled a yawn in Soleil's ruff. Aaron turned me toward him, a gentle smile wrinkling around his eyes.

"Alright, ladies, let's go get some rest. You've got a long drive tomorrow."

All my fight disappeared at that moment, gratefully set aside as he steered me for the truck. Not a single word was exchanged on the drive to the hotel, or even as we changed for bed. He kissed me on the forehead as I snuggled into his embrace but asked for nothing else. The passion that tempted me all weekend had curled up to sleep hours ago, and I followed it, too exhausted to object.

We overslept, both of us having forgotten to set our alarms in our exhaustion. If not for the text reminder for his flight, we might have missed it entirely. As it was, we rushed through packing our suitcases before scurrying to the barn to feed. I threw hay at Lyric with uncharacteristic alacrity, earning a slanted ear my direction when some of it hung up on her head.

"Oh, my apologies, Lyric." I picked the hay from her forelock even as she bent to her breakfast, forcing myself to slow down. However much I wished for more time nothing would make that happen, and my mare deserved better than haste. But as soon as Aaron returned with her water buckets we left again.

Monday morning traffic slowed our journey to the airport, and I fidgeted needlessly with the radio tuner as Aaron drove, needing something to do with my hands. Every commercial grated on my nerves, the morning show hosts far to chipper when all I could think about was letting Aaron go. I hated how deeply the ache in my chest went and marveled in the same breath to feel so much for him. When had anyone ever planted themselves so firmly in my heart?

"Jaqueline, here," Aaron said as he pulled onto the exit for the airport, hand held out for mine. When he threaded our fingers together, regardless of his need to play it safe while driving, my emotions steadied slightly. He too sought to maintain our connection as long as possible.

As late as we were, I expected him to pull up to the curb and head inside, but he steered the truck into the parking garage instead. "Aaron, what are you doing?"

He did not answer as he pulled his hand away to navigate the tight confines between rows of cars. Not until he pulled into a mostly unoccupied corner did he turn the engine off and look toward me. "You, stay right here. I'm going to drop my bag off and I'll be back." Then he shot out of the truck before I could protest, duffel in hand as he ran toward the terminal.

"Whatever has come over him?" I asked Soleil as she stood up and stretched to look out the back window. She appeared as confused as I was over his behaviour.

I barely had enough time to truly begin to worry as I caught sight of him on his way back, still at a run. Swinging the door open, I turned to slide off the seat, but he moved in before I could lower myself to the ground. My heartbeat sped to catch up with his as his lips found mine, and our bodies came together perfectly as he leaned his weight into me. The kiss progressed furiously fast, a rough tangle of teeth and tongues that stole my instinctive need to breathe. No, I could forget my own name if only he would keep kissing me that way.

"Jaqueline," he rasped as he moved from my lips to my neck, hot breath making me shiver. "A little over a week from now, you and I have a date."

I nodded feverishly, clinging to him with both hands as he sucked on my pulse. Though the edge of the seat pressed into my lower back, and the smells of the airport threatened to intrude on the moment, I shoved reality away. I would take every moment he offered and then try to steal more.

"I wish you could stay," I declared, though I knew the sentiment to be foolish. He pulled back from my neck, blue eyes dilated with passion, and my stomach lurched with regret. Why did I not wake up early to give him the sendoff he deserved?

"Me too." Reaching down, he grabbed my knee, hiking it up over his hip. Denim be damned, I took the hint and hooked the other one around his waist as well. We were as close as two people could get and still be dressed. "I'm sorry we don't have more time."

"I am sorry I did not reward you adequately for all your hard work."

He slanted a chastising look my way, and playfully slapped my butt. I am not ashamed to say I felt a zing of excitement at the contact. "Told you before, you're worth the wait. Besides, I wasn't kidding when I said I'd take the time to prove I'm invested in you. Knowing you'll be just as impatient as I am is going to keep me warm at night. Now, how about you show me how much you'll miss me?"

I tried, urgently tangling our mouths together as he hitched me further up his body. I could feel how much he wanted me, not only in the obvious evidence, but in his hands as they roved over my back. The touch felt both passionate and loving, and having the two things so deeply intertwined worked on me like champagne. I felt warm, and light, giddy from the bubbles in my head as he sucked on my tongue.

Alas, time was not on our side, his phone intruding on our fare thee well. He ignored the incessant buzzing for several long breaths, slowing our kisses, caressing my cheek with his thick knuckles as I slid to the ground.

"I've got to go, Jaqueline."

"I know." I raised my chin, keeping our eyes locked, determined to see him off with a smile. "You will call me when you land, I hope? No texts once I am on the road, but I will have my Bluetooth in so we can talk."

"I will, bossy woman." His teasing tone said he meant it in jest, my heart easing at the playfulness. "You be safe, okay?"

"Always." Not a difficult promise to make, after all. Lyric was too important for me to do otherwise. "You do the same."

"Never," he said lightly, pressing one last feathery kiss to my cheek as he stepped away. "I'm a jouster. Danger is part of the job description."

Then he grabbed his messenger bag from behind the seat, surprised when Soleil stood up and wagged her tail at him. Though she did not come close enough to be pet her opinion of him had shifted. "Goodbye to you too, little one. Take care of your mama."

To make sure I gave as good as I received, I smacked his magnificently tight behind as he turned back toward me. He pressed a grin to my mouth, and I wrapped my arms around him again, making sure our last moments together were as glorious as I could make them.

"You're not going to make this easy, are you?"

"Never," I breathed against his lips, then let him go with a sense of finality as I stepped toward the truck to close the passenger door. We both had schedules to keep and I wanted to get back to Florida before midnight. If I kept moving perhaps I could distract myself from the bereft feeling settling into my chest.

When I turned around again, he was already on the move, long legs eating up the distance toward the terminal. The dull ache intensified as he disappeared around a long line of cars, and my feet dragged heavily as I climbed behind the steering wheel. Whatever I hoped for, I certainly did not expect him to leave me without a backward glance.

Soleil climbed into my lap, tiny nose pushing under my numb fingers until I began to stroke her face. Concentrating on her silky ears, I pushed my disappointment away. My weekend had been all the better for Aaron's visit, and I could not regret a moment, even the letting go.

"Thank you, little one," I told Soleil, finding some delight in the slight tilt of her head at the new form of address. "You know how to set me to rights. Now, shall we go pick up Lyric? It is going to be a long drive."

She moved to her bed with little encouragement, yipping in excitement as I turned the key to start the big diesel. While the truck did not run half so smoothly as a newer one, it had served me well through the years. With luck, it would serve a few more.

Just as I shifted into reverse, looking over my shoulder to be sure the way was clear, my phone chimed. Thinking it might be my hosts in Florida, I picked it up, my heart thudding painfully to find a message from Aaron. With hope and trepidation, I swiped the screen to open the text.

'My lady, I'm sorry I took off. You deserve a braver man, but if I didn't walk away right then, I feared I might never. I hope this is only the first goodbye of many, and that I'll get better with practice. Until then, forgive me. Your boyfriend, Aaron'

The tears I had managed to hold back spilled over without contest as happiness burst to life, pushing my worries out of the way. My fingers fairly flew over the screen as I replied.

'You worried me. I shall exact penance from you when next we meet. But such a weakness I can well understand, as I miss you even now. With love, your girlfriend, Jaqueline.'

I stared at the screen for several moments, wisely not pressing send. Oh, I knew even then how much I could love him, but no matter how prettily he spoke, I worried to push him too far. In the end, I deleted the *love*, putting *affection* in its place. Taking the larger risk would be better done face to face, where I could read the truth in his eyes.

When the phone buzzed again my whole body warmed at the heat of his reply.

'I'm going to imagine a long list of ways you'll let me pay my dues. The possibilities are countless. Now put your phone down and drive before I jump out of the security line and do something reckless.'

I laughed at the last bit, thankful to find joy even in a goodbye I hated. Replying with a simple farewell, I tucked the phone into my cupholder and pulled out of the garage with a lighter heart. Ten days were all that stood between Aaron and I, and we were both resilient enough to endure the wait. We made it this far, after all, which gave me hope that we could find the strength to carry us toward something far greater than I ever dared to hope for.

❧ 6 ❧

Aaron

Despite an uneventful flight home, I struggled to be pleasant around Jo and Bart when they picked me up at the airport. Though I was glad to see them, their togetherness wore on a freshly sensitive set of nerves. From the backseat of the truck I had a clear view of their intertwined hands as he drove, which made my deprivation all the harder to bear.

Not that they did anything wrong, mind you. We all hung out at the dining room table after eating, catching up on everything. They had a schedule drawn up to get all the spare horses ready for jousting this summer, each of them in varying stages of training. Jo showed off several preliminary concepts for the new website, and Bart filled me in on all that needed doing around the farm. But they begged off before too long and headed for bed, leaving me alone again. I couldn't tell you which I hated more—being the third wheel or being alone. Either way, I felt the odd man out.

A series of disorganized dreams ruined my sleep, broken up by periods of wakefulness that ate away hours as I stared into the dark and tried to empty my mind. It shouldn't have been such a struggle. After all, I'd spent a couple hours chatting with Jaque while she drove, mostly talking about her problems with the douchebag contingent. Listening without getting angry hadn't been easy. The whole conversation, I'd been unable to sit still, pacing the floor in my room and rearranging the contents of my medicine cabinet twice. Kind of pathetic, since I didn't keep much in there anyway. But I couldn't do anything about her situation, and I needed to do something before I headed for the fridge for a drink. Jaque made me want to be aware and present, to never miss anything if I could help it.

Once she reached Ocala, I let her go, both of us ready for sleep. Turning down the blankets and fluffing the pillows felt comforting, the familiar first step toward oblivion. I followed every step of my usual routine, laying out the next day's work out clothes, and taking a long shower to help me relax. By the time I slid between the sheets and put on my headphones, my whole body felt heavy and slow. Soft piano accompanied by the sounds of the ocean lulled me straight to sleep.

But I didn't stay there. No, I woke at midnight, wired and edgy, my pulse far too speedy. Some breathing exercises helped me quiet, but even then, it took an hour to sleep again. This repeated several times, all with an increase in heart rate and vivid flashes of bad dreams I hadn't dealt with since the last time I stayed at my mother's house. Shitty memories I had no desire to revisit. My back felt like someone had gone over every inch of it with a wrench, tightening down each vertebra. On a car, that much tension would have made me worry about something sheering under strain.

I swung out of bed carefully, planting my bare feet on the hardwood, spreading my toes to really ground myself. While I hadn't gotten into serious yoga, one of the knights at the dinner theatre I'd started out at had shown me how to keep my body happy. A few good stretches relieved the worst of the aches, but once the blood was flowing I saw little point in returning to my bed. A damn shame, since I usually reveled in the peaceful comfort of that sanctuary. Instead, I went to the living room with my tablet and logged on to my social media account. Might as well catch up on my friend's lives, since I'd basically neglected everyone but Jaque over the weekend.

Call me weird, but I didn't do social media on my phone. I needed the disconnect, the ability to step away from the busy speed of the internet. Everyone wanted in on every aspect of my life in the real world, and while I enjoyed sharing energy with the crowds, I hated the compulsive feeling that drove people to post everything in their lives. Who the hell cared what I ate for dinner or what color socks I wore?

As I scrolled through pictures of my nieces and nephews, the posts were broken up by multiple notifications from my mother. She'd recently started selling makeup for one of those work from home companies, and while I felt happy for her, the sheer number of articles and beauty tips she shared threatened to overwhelm my newsfeed. Noticeably, all of the things she shared were what I considered over done faces, with very traditional beauty pageant standards. Not that all of the women on the circuit were quite as, ah, rabid about appearances as my Mom. Most were much more down to earth when they weren't competing. But chances were pretty strong that Mom would pop loose an eyelash extension if she ever saw Jaque's purple dyed highlights. The mental image had me grinning as I continued advancing the page, liking and commenting on my nephew's sports accomplishments and my little niece's first riding lessons, when I skidded to a halt on a post from Jo.

Accompanying a small photo collage of Bart and Jo together were bold faced words that came as no surprise.

Josephine Bowen got engaged to Bartholomew Clark

She had refused to post anything until they got back home, wanting to tell her family personally before she sprang it on social media. Over a hundred people had already left comments of congratulations, and I typed my own message of encouragement without much serious thought, because they weren't my hang-up anymore. Much as they occasionally freaked me out with their coupledom, I knew they belonged together.

Instead, my stupid brain latched on to my growing relationship with Jaque. Did she want to link us together on SocialTree? Hell, even thinking about it created a ball of warmth beneath my breastbone. Being connected to her so publicly would give things a kind of solidity, as if it couldn't be erased. But hot on the heels of that happy thought came a splash of bitter cold. If I made us public my mother would pounce on Jaque with the kind of fervor reserved for a weasel and an unsuspecting mouse.

I couldn't risk it. Not yet anyway. Maybe when things felt a little more permanent. I mean, I'd been months away from getting married when my mom ran my fiancée off. Jaque certainly had a good deal more spine than my former fiancée, but she deserved to know what she was in for before I dumped my dysfunctional family on her.

As if she knew I was thinking of her, the private message icon for Jaque popped up on the corner of my screen.

'*Good morning. This is early for you. Is everything okay?*'

'*Couldn't sleep anymore. What about you? Don't you get a day off?*'

She sent a laughing emoji. *'No such animal. While I do not have to work for anyone else today, Lyric still needs me to feed her. And she gets a massage this afternoon.'*

'You deserve a massage too.' I shot back, wishing I could help. No one deserved a day off more than her.

'Are you volunteering?'

My thoughts had noble intentions when I answered to the affirmative, but they quickly morphed into something selfish as I imagined running my hands over her bare skin. Which made me think of how I'd left her in South Carolina, with her kiss-swollen lips and so much emotion in her eyes. She could have asked me to conquer gravity and time in that moment before I walked away, and for her, I would have killed myself trying.

'I should warn you now, I am not one of those women who will only want a massage. My expectations are still quite high, particularly after our goodbye kiss.'

Electricity pinged me right between the eyes, eliciting a shiver to burn off the excess energy. How had I missed this woman? This gloriously delicious woman who met my every thought with her own and raised the bar in the next breath. *'I intend to meet every last one of them as soon as you get home.'*

She sent an emoji of a fast beating heart, a sentiment I echoed in real life. *'Continue with that line of conversation, Aaron, and I shall load my mare for the trip North before you can blink. Which I do not say lightly, considering our clinic this weekend.'*

Shifting uncomfortably against the worn leather of my recliner, I wondered over what I could say that might tempt her home sooner. Not that I would, regardless. I wanted her to succeed even more than I wanted to consummate the passion between us.

'Damned if I do, damned if I don't. Because my friend deserves every success for her hard work. And my lover, I want her more with every breath. Anticipation will make our reunion that much more intense, and the reward will be worth it.'

Her reply took a few minutes, the flashing icon letting me know she was typing, and I expected a novel in return at that point. Instead, I received a short statement that left me aching for her. *'I wrote out a detailed description of your reward but deleted it for fear I might take things too far. Suffice it to say, I shall reward you handsomely.'*

Too far? Was there such a thing? Is there anything I wouldn't give her, if she but asked? For her I would even risk my mother, the fiercest foe I could imagine.

'For you, there is no such thing as too far. I mean for us to go the distance, no matter how much distance is between us. Now I'm gonna go take an ice-cold shower before my roommates wake up. Because while I love the way you make me feel, I really don't want to spend the next week getting teased for the inevitable reaction.'

For good measure, I sent a little animation of a cartoon dog with his heart pounding out of his chest, hoping the typed words would come across the right way. Another reason to hate the distance between us. After the intense weekend I'd learned to read her better. Online, I didn't have all the little signals to point me the right way.

'Your secret is safe, Aaron, though I relish knowing I can affect you so. I will be thinking of you and look forward to your call tonight.' Tagged on to the end, she added a pair of kissy lips. Foolish or not, I pressed my finger against that tiny symbol and then on to my own. From this far away, I'd take whatever I could get.

Then I headed straight for the shower, needing the chill water to put me back in my own skin. I had so much to do now that we were home, and no time like the present to get started. Jo gave me a narrow-eyed inspection when she found me already up and dressed, but Bart kept us moving. We put in a good work out, sweat soaking through our shirts as we did circuits through various body weight exercises. While the tourney was over our work never ended, and none of us wanted to backslide. The more we sweat in training, the less we would bleed on the field. Or, that was the theory anyway.

But once the sweat began to dry, we went opposite directions. For my part, I had a tractor to get running, Jo needed to do some computer work for her clients and Bart had phone calls to make so we could get our workshop rebuilt. The burn scar had long since been cleared, and we had our hay in a fabric shelter down by the pasture, but we still needed to put up a new building. I would join him at contractor meetings, but until then, we needed to divide and conquer.

My old Ford tractor sat alone in the small garage attached to the house, looking almost forlorn with one small headlight peeking out from under the tarp I'd covered her with before we left for Cali. Her bright blue paint was faded in places, and as I dragged the canvas off her, I remembered I owed her a good going over. Rust grew along the fenders and around the control pedals, something I hated to see on my favorite girl. She deserved better from me now that Bart was back in action.

Patting her bonnet with genuine affection, I moved toward the seat. Many fond memories swirled around with the dust I kicked up. This old lady had been my first foray into the inner workings of an engine. She originally belonged to my dad, and I'd listened to him cuss and swear his way around her for most of my childhood. But the one truly good memory I had with my father had been when he showed me how to coax her into starting. You needed to hold the clutch exactly so, and set the choke just right, otherwise, she'd sputter and die. I'd been twelve, just able to reach all the pedals, and barely strong enough to turn the steering wheel to nurse her around the arena. But he actually smiled at me the first time I managed to drag the whole roping arena without help. I desperately clung to that memory for years, hoping I could make him do it again.

I shook the dusty memory loose as I set down my toolbox and climbed into the driver's seat, pleased to feel the choke slide smoothly in my hand. When I took the tractor as part of my inheritance, I'd gone over her from front to back, slowly replacing or rebuilding every bit of her. Sure, I could have bought a new one, but I couldn't bear the thought of my mother selling it off for parts or yard art. But when I turned the key, she didn't even sputter, just clicked weakly. The clicking gave me a bit of relief, since that meant the starter still worked. Hopefully, all I needed was a fresh charge on the battery.

But then I remembered the battery charger had gone up with the rest of the tools in the workshop. As I stomped up to get my truck so I could give the tractor a jump, I let the anger swell, frustrated at all we lost. Yes, we'd brought back the spare lyst equipment from California, but that barely touched the surface of our losses. Our tents were gone, as well as every bit of repair equipment, not just for the tractors, but the entire farm. Thank God Bart was in charge of all that shit, or I'd lose my mind trying to get it all replaced.

My big Dodge rumbled to life with the barest twist of a wrist, and within minutes we were parked in front of the garage, the low growl of the engine a warm comfort as I hooked up the jumper cables. Nor did I have to wait long for the tractor, which leapt to life with an abrupt grumble, like an old woman startled from her sleep. As I got her closed up and moved the truck out of the way, I managed to find a smile for the raw familiarity in the chores that waited for me.

The morning disappeared in a haze of light sweat and dust as I spread accumulated manure out on the neighbor's fallow field. I'd done the same thing this time every year, after all the potential fertilizer that occurred every winter from the frequent nights the horses spent in stalls. We'd repeatedly talked about putting a shed in the pasture, just to save our farm sitter the trouble, but time and energy always ended up spent on something else. Nor was it the only project I pushed back over the years, from building a few more paddocks near the barn to fencing off a new pasture on the north side of the arena. Only so much I could accomplish on my own.

Speaking of the arena, it needed a good drag, which took up most of my afternoon. Not a tough job, once I got the chain harrow hooked to the three-point hitch. You couldn't beat the calm and steady clinking of the harrow, or the resulting surface with the tiny furrows so very symmetrical and relaxing. Always made me think of the Zen gardens my sister Courtney liked, precise and easy on the eyes.

As I stopped in the middle of the arena to inspect my work, my mind went to the next item on my agenda. Byzantine. Judging by the lowering sun, I should put him off until tomorrow, but a small voice that sounded suspiciously like Jaque said I should go visit with him before calling it a day. Seeing how her mare responded to being made a priority had pointed out one of the major flaws in my relationship with him. I treated him as less than a partner, and more of a tool, only spending time with him if we were working. And I didn't even know if he would welcome my company, but I needed to start somewhere.

After I put the tractor up and took a stroll down the hill to the pasture, I found Byzantine and J.T. at the water trough. Both loved to play in the tank and were our resident troublemakers, often resulting in repairs and late-night round ups. Thankfully, they usually behaved themselves while we were on the road, but Bart said he thought it was because they were too tired from the day's work to cook anything up. The older I got, the more I sympathized with that sentiment, no longer feeling the need to go out or stay up drinking with the cast at the faire. Better to sleep and recharge for the next day.

The gate swung open smoothly, still in perfect shape after Jo suggested we put up a strand of electrical fence across it the last time we replaced it. I loved that woman, mainly for how good she was for Bart. But her ability to see ahead and save us future trouble certainly had planted the seed of affection. She fit into our team like she'd been custom made, even when she used her smart mouth to cut through bullshit or brought things to light I would have been more comfortable leaving in the dark. Yeah, I would have been happier if Cranston had never happened, or if Van Dougherty had never found his old horse with us. I know that reflected poorly on me, but I couldn't fix the problem if I wasn't honest with myself. But when unpleasantness arose I would stand shoulder to shoulder with her every time. I'd failed her once but resolved it would never happen again.

"Hey bud," I said softly as I walked up to Byz's shoulder, my hand lifting up without thought. But I pulled back before I could touch him, remembering the day he pulled away. My ego had been bled by that simple thing, particularly when Jo had to bring it to my attention. How had I misread him for so long? Maybe I misread him from the very beginning, and he'd just put up with me for years?

He turned his blunt Roman nose toward me, eyes more relaxed than I'd seen since I pushed him into the lyst to fill his brother's hoof prints. I rummaged in my pocket, having to dig past my keys to find the tiny treats I dropped in there for just this kind of occasion. When I offered it to him on a flattened palm I fully expected him to snatch it up like a land shark, hopefully without leaving teeth marks. He'd turned into a pushy bastard over the years, absolutely rabid about his food.

But instead, his nostrils fluttered widely, taking in the scent of my palm. With more delicacy than I ever would have imagined, he lifted the small cube from my hand, long winter whiskers feathering over my skin as he slowly chewed. Eyelashes lowered, he huffed out a deep breath as the treat crunched in his molars.

It's not like everything in our relationship suddenly became a Disney movie from that one quiet moment in the setting sun. As soon as he walked away, I left, still having not touched him. But looking back, it was a turning point for me. My resolve would be tested— he wasn't some complacent cow and I had amends to make. But we all have to start somewhere.

Jaque

To say I felt tired would be like calling the ocean a lake—more than a small understatement. Sleep had been fitful, though I managed a few decent hours once Soleil curled up against my back. After messaging with Aaron I muddled up enough energy to do Lyric's chores, then took her for a nice hand walk before the heat of the day sapped me entirely. Not that the native Floridians found it warm. No, the staff out feeding the horses that belonged to the farm were all bundled up as if they might freeze. The girl working in the barn wore a puffy jacket and sheepskin boots, and still, she shivered as she went about her business, changing out blankets on any of the horses who were body clipped.

Once Lyric settled back into her stall, content with a ceramic infused sheet to keep her muscles loose after the weekend's efforts, I retreated to my little studio apartment. There in my haven away from the bustle of the barn, I left the shades drawn down as I curled up on the loveseat. Soleil created a nest on the bed I still had not made, scratching the blanket into just the right shape.

Staring across the room, my eyes latched onto the blinking light from the microwave, unfocusing until it became a green blur. In that space slightly outside of awareness, I let my mind have free rein to explore. I would have loved to turn straight to my delicious memories of Aaron, but there were more pressing matters at hand. A few weeks stood between now and our next competition, and while I intended some longer drives to maintain fitness, and a few lessons to sharpen our dressage, Lyric needed little of my time. She was at her peak, and all I needed to do was not let her backslide. No, my real concern came from attending the competition itself.

Not that I worried over how we would place. No, we would rise to the occasion and the scores would sort things out. My hesitancy came from Maarten, Paul, and Grady. I did not look forward to the unpleasant exchanges they would provide. They stained my happiness like coffee spilled on linen, spreading in veins along the fibres of my joy.

Having someone in my camp always helped, mind you. Cardi stood in my corner, ready to rip into them at the slightest provocation. My trusted friends were so few, though I knew many good people on the circuit. Perhaps Aaron would be there to guard my back, but I did not know if our schedules would permit it. Nor would I have him fight my battles for me. This friction was mine alone to smooth out.

I might have dwelled on it a bit longer if not for the ringing of my phone. Soleil barked at the familiar music, Ride of the Valkyries reverberating off the walls of the little room as I scrambled to answer.

"Papa?" I queried pointlessly, knowing exactly who called.

"Ah, Junior! *Comment va tu ma chère fille?*" How is my daughter, he asked, a smile evident in his gruff voice.

"*Ca va bien, et toi?*" I am well, and you, I responded, not wanting to disclose my troubles to him. He often thought to come down and sort things for me, something I simply could not allow as an adult. Forever, he had wrapped me in cotton batting, stifling my growth with his overwhelming love. Though I understood why he behaved so, I would not permit us to fall into those old roles ever again.

"*Merveilleux! Mon vol de s'matin était parfait!*" Stellar! My flight was perfect this morning, he exclaimed before launching into a complete retelling of the adventure. I loved listening to the familiar cadence of his voice, the rise and falls in the same places no matter how the tone changed. Our language caressed my ears with the texture of childhood, memories freshened with the infusion of home. But even without that, I could have listened to him speak of flying forever. I could well remember hours of my youth spent in the rear seat of his little plane, the world falling away and nothing but the sky all around. In my work with Lyric the adrenaline rush I grew to love remained close even now.

Much of the technical details, like wind speed and elevation, remained a mystery to me. But I begrudged not a moment of his retelling, his love for every aspect making me love it too. My lips twitched as I thought of Aaron, and his own fascination with cars. No, I could not understand it, but I could love it for the joy it gave them.

"*M'écoute tu*," Listen to me, my father chided, and I dragged my mind back to the present.

"*Je suis désoler* Papa," I apologized, sighing heavily as I pulled my feet up under me, exhaustion bringing a chill with it. "*Je suis épuisée, l'événement équestre m'a demander tout mon énergie. Mais j'en regrette pas une seconde.*" I am exhausted, the equestrian event asked all my energy. But I regret not a moment. Lyric did so well, and we came in second!

He responded to the news with a glad cry, "*Félicitations, ma fille! Félicitations! Tu dois être vraiment fière!*" Congratulations, my girl! You must be very proud!

"Also, I have perhaps met someone," I ventured, switching to English as I thought of Aaron. I wanted to share all of my happiness, even if it were likely to create friction. "I think even you might like him, Papa. He is a horseman, but also works on cars."

"Is this the man who fixed your truck, Junior? I thought he was merely a business acquaintance." No one could have missed the coolness of his query and I winced, knowing for this reason too I had left home. "You cannot risk your success in your work against a relationship. What will happen when he learns you cannot have children? No man wants a barren woman."

Ah, there. No matter how much I loved my father, I could almost hate him for this weary old argument. In my current state I could not muster proper anger, only a resigned stating of the facts as I rubbed the back of my neck. What I would not have given for Aaron's strong hands just then.

"Papa, please, you know very well that barrenness is not our curse. Were that so, Mama would never have had me. And to this point in my life, I have not been able to keep a relationship long enough to consider children, let alone the risks involved. Your worries are pointless. Let me at least enjoy this little while of hopeful joy before you doom me to spinsterhood."

Papa's voice came back clipped, a sure sign of his displeasure. "I do not understand why you would risk yourself. You know the hurt will come; it always does."

Softly, I replied, "Papa, I risk for the same reason you do. I do it for love. That is the only thing truly worth risking everything for, in my relationships, and in my work."

"Love was not enough to save your mother," he answered bitterly, but for once, I could not find pity for his pain.

"If it were, she would have lived forever," I snapped, bending under the combined exhaustion of my body and heart. A single tear gathered in the corner of my eye, burning to be released, but I would not yield. "But we do not get the luxury of forever, any of us. We only have now, and I intend to enjoy it for as long as I am blessed. Yes, he could leave me, but so many others have without a word being spoken about a future."

Quiet reigned for several moments, only his tense breathing telling me we remained connected. My jaw ached as I fought to keep still, to hold back so many more angry words. They would serve little purpose but to agitate him further. Eventually, he yielded, "I am sorry, *ma fille*. Forgive an old man his prejudices. I wish you only good things, my Junior."

"I know, Papa. But I wish you could be happy for me; however momentary this might be. Let the past rest."

"I cannot let go of the past, it is all of your Mama I have left." His gusty sigh stole whatever upset I might have harboured. My own guilt for living when she did not never failed to overwhelm my personal affront. "But I can let you make your own future. Still, I pray you will be wise. To lose you would be to lose the only piece of her still living."

My heart fractured along the fault lines carved since I was old enough to understand my mother's death. I hugged my legs all the closer to my chest, hoping I could keep the broken pieces contained. "For all I know, Papa, Aaron may not want children. But we will cross that bridge when we come to it, and not a moment before. Now, before we bleed ourselves too much from old wounds, perhaps you will tell me when I can expect you for your spring visit?"

Good cheer returned quickly once he had a brighter subject to embrace. Every year, he flew his little plane down to Kentucky to see me compete. He hated flying commercial and enjoyed the freedom of planning his own flight. Details were exchanged, and I programmed my phone calendar, so I would not forget to pick him up in the midst of getting ready for the show. Shortly thereafter, we said farewell, and I dragged myself off the loveseat to find something to eat. After all, I would be of little use to my mare or anyone else if I did not take care of myself.

Later in the afternoon, I brushed Lyric off in readiness for her massage. Jill Arlington had a manner about her that set people and animals at ease, as if she traveled around in a cloud of calm that others could draw on at need. We would miss her when we left Florida, for that alone. Mind you, the body worker we used in Kentucky did fine work, keeping Lyric's body in shape for the rigors of competition. But I always felt that Jill's work lasted longer because it went much deeper than mere muscle or tendon.

The chuffing sound of Jill's little smart car alerted me to her arrival just as I finished checking Lyric's legs. As I patted the mare's muscular shoulder, the steady *tick tick* of her Corgi's toenails filled the aisle, which made Soleil shoot up from her spot in the corner with a bark of excitement. A quick flick of the wrist threw the catch on the door, and she launched toward her particular friend, inciting a flurry of noise as they spun around each other in a glad dance.

Jill's laughter could barely be heard over the chaos, but Lyric still nickered lowly, stepping up to my shoulder so she could look down the aisle. That reaction alone made Jill worth every penny, knowing my mare looked forward to seeing the woman so much. Dodging the bundle of flying hair made by the dogs, she met me with an outstretched hand, palm cool against mine. "You know, I'm going to miss how tired Tinker is after seeing Soleil, almost as much as Tinker is going to miss Soleil."

"Yes, tonight Soleil will sleep as if a rock." I agreed, wishing for what felt like the hundredth time that Jill could come north. But there were tradeoffs. I did prefer my farrier in Kentucky to the one in Florida. "As will Lyric. She rests so deeply after your visits."

"That's how it's supposed to work, my friend," Jill answered, though as she ran her hand along Lyric's crest I could not be certain if she spoke to the mare or me. "I'll loosen up all that lactic acid, and get the blood moving clean again, so you'll be all ready for your clinic this weekend."

As Jill moved in beside her, Lyric adopted a patiently aware posture, ears following the woman's touch along her body. Knowing fingers stroked along the bladder meridian, running in a flowing line from head to hocks, checking for any sluggishness. When she paused just below the curve of Lyric's haunches, rubbing a gentle circle, I knew she had found something. Still, Lyric leaned into the touch, rather than away, showing Jill that she appreciated the attention. That the motion was repeated on the other side allowed me to breathe easier, aware that Jill had likely found some residual soreness. No surprise, considering how great Lyric's efforts had been.

I watched intently as Jill touched on a few pressure points that might disclose internal issues, like ulcers or worms. Both showed clear, letting me relax even further. When Jill began rubbing Lyric's gums to aid in softness I went to fetch my stool, secure in the knowledge that all would be well. While I trusted my hands to know Lyric, having a second opinion unbiased by daily familiarity set my mind at ease.

Lyric and I both adopted a half aware manner, her with a cocked hip and low hanging head, myself propped up against the door jamb with soft eyes. I let my mind wander as my body mirrored the mare's state of tranquility, unsurprised when it turned toward thoughts of home. Once, home had been my grandparent's farm, but that had been lost in a legal battle with my uncles. Quebec's understated allure no longer beckoned me North, though there were days I missed the muffled quiet that followed a snowstorm. Lyric would have loved a romp in the deep drifts, frost glistening on the tips of her dense, unclipped coat.

No, now I thought of Kentucky, the rolling green hills and the soft twang of her people. They embraced me with a surety I had not expected, as warm and comforting as the earthy scent beneath Lyric's thick mane. I would return to Canada, eventually, once my visa expired, but by then I hoped we would have proved our readiness to compete for our country at the World Championships.

My coach in Canada had retired after an automobile accident left her in too much pain to drive anymore. At her recommendation, I took the leap to the States, where training and the competitions were much more plentiful. Lexington, Kentucky seemed a natural choice, being the horse capitol of the United States, but cost of living was prohibitive.

When I found a job listing with a commercial carriage company in Louisville, I leapt at the opportunity. With my extensive driving experience, the owners of French Silver Carriage Company, Frenchy and Lily Boudreaux, had been all too pleased to sponsor me for a visa, which included a place on their farm for Lyric and I.

After I proved myself trustworthy, working safer, smarter and harder than many of my co-workers, they promoted me to manager. I expanded their string by leasing Aaron's horses for the busy holiday season, increasing profits by a fair margin despite the extra mouths to feed. The following year, they stepped back and handed me the reins to the company, becoming silent partners so they could retire to Florida. If they ever decided to sell the farm and close the carriage company, I would lose my visa the instant I no longer had a job. That, in and of itself, would be a threat to my stay in Kentucky, which caused my chest to constrict enough that I quietly hissed at the pain.

"Are you alright?" Jill asked, a pinch of concern between her brows, though her voice stayed so even you could almost forget the physical markers. Lyric did not move, head hanging nearly level with her knees as Jill's hands worked deeply into the heavy muscles of her haunches.

I smiled, albeit thinly, and nodded. "Yes, only thinking of everything I need to work on at home. Silly, I know, when I cannot do a thing about any of it for now."

Jill tipped her chin in acknowledgement. "Ah yes, we humans have such a hard time living moment to moment. You have my sympathy. I've at least got practice at it." Her eyes softened as Lyric sighed into the pressure of her hands, and we both smiled. "No sense in keeping you still if your brain wants to be busy. How about you go make sure our furry dervishes haven't torn the barn aisle apart? I'll let you know when I'm done."

Though I followed her suggestion there was little for me to do on my one day off. I would be busy the remainder of the week, getting packed and fulfilling my obligations to my gracious hosts. Tomorrow, the two colts I worked with would be gelded, getting them ready for a year out in the field where they could grow in the plentiful sunshine and thick grass. And my favourite, the filly, would join them in a few weeks. Hopefully, I would return next year to help with the next stage of their development.

For today, nothing stood between me and thinking about the reason for the pang in my chest. Though I had no guarantees about Aaron and I's relationship, I did not want it to end over something so logical as nationality. Having him as part of my life made the world a richer place, and the more I fell for him, the more Kentucky truly became the place I thought of as home. But for now, all I could do is to get through the next week. Only then would I be free to explore the steady bloom of new dreams as they entwined themselves around the old.

Aaron

Though I spent far too long on the phone with Jaqueline that night, the few hours of sleep I did manage were restful. I rolled out of bed even before my phone began to chime an alarm and headed straight for the floor to knock out some pushups, ready to get moving.

After a steaming hot shower and a kale and blueberry smoothie, I settled at my desk. My biggest task for the day would be to find lodging for our upcoming gig. Our new pavilion was ordered but wouldn't be complete before we needed to get back on the road, and we still had a ton of shopping to do before our camping equipment was back up to snuff. So, I spent a couple hours on the phone hunting up a hotel room for Trace and me. After the debacle at our rodeo gig in November that had left the entire team sharing one room, I wanted to be sure there were no misunderstandings.

Thankfully, Bart and Jo had their little trailer to stay in where they could keep an eye on the horses. The thought of leaving our crew of troublemakers by themselves brought to mind the night Cappy and Argo got loose and raided the trash bins at a small venue in Georgia. We'd only gone to dinner and returned to the site to find the security staff trying to wrangle them back into their pens. It had taken hours to clean up the resulting mess.

Still, as I waited on hold to speak to a manager, I smiled at the memory. It had been a long time since I thought of my old horse with anything but sadness or frustration. I lost Argo during Bart's deployment, and once my brother had been injured, I'd pushed along on my own for what seemed like forever. Jousting stopped being fun, training Byzantine more of a dreaded chore than anything else.

Not that I had much choice in the matter. Horses needed fed, the mortgage had to be paid. But now, I had a chance to change things. With Bart and Jo shouldering much of the day to day weight of the Company, I could focus on all the little things I let slip by. Already, I felt lighter, new hopes springing up in the shade of old dreams coming back to life.

Once I had a room guaranteed, I turned my attention to the organizers of the faire. We were going to need a place to park the trailer close by the horses, preferably with power so they wouldn't have to use the generator. Took some time to track down the property manager, and I had to engage in a lively conversation to get my point across. Us not having the big tent meant some rearrangement of the layout, and the gentleman in question acted less than thrilled with the last-minute changes.

When I finally wrapped up business, my skin practically itched with the need to do something physical. As I laced on my boots with abrupt tugs, energy swirled up and down my spine, looking for an outlet. In retrospect, I should admit that probably wasn't the best mood to be in when I went out to the pasture to get Byzantine. I'd considered it a good sign that the horses were all near the gate getting a drink when I made it to the bottom of the hill. Even better, Byz appeared interested in me after our brief visit last night. He stood quietly as I secured his halter, accepting the cookie I fished out of the pocket of my jeans without a single bit of pushy behavior. I scrubbed the crest of his neck with both hands just to watch his lips wiggle with pleasure, and foolishly figured he'd be happy to leave the herd after all that.

He disabused me of that notion halfway up the hill, planting his massive hooves like he'd grown roots, and because I wasn't paying attention, I hit the end of the lead rope with more momentum than he thought acceptable. Instantly, he threw his sizeable head in objection, yanking me around like a puppet. Dust and irritation swirled around us, framing our standoff like gun fighters waiting for the other to make a move.

"Dammit, horse, does everything have to be a fight with you?" I grumbled, my jaw already tightening with annoyance as I yanked authoritatively on the cotton rope attached to his halter. A sensible man might have noticed the way his jaw tightened to match mine. "If you'd just listen, we'd get along much better."

A strangely harmonious pair of rude snorts undercut the brewing tension, followed by the sound of booted feet tramping down the hill. Turning to face the source of all the noise, I watched Bart and Jo approach, affection and exasperation welling in equal measure. Yes, I loved them both, yes, they were good for each other. But their togetherness stung me deeply.

"What are you laughing at, lovebirds?" I bit off, not even bothering to check my mood.

Jo said nothing, only smiled over at Bart, which should have scared me. Silent Jo was *far* more terrifying than mouthy Jo.

"I'm laughing at you, brother," Bart answered as they stopped in front of me, adopting nearly the same hipshot pose as if they'd practiced it in a mirror. Did they have to be so damn together all the time? "I'm pretty sure Byz is wondering why everything has to be a fight too. Listening to him would probably solve half your problems."

That deflated a fair portion of my ire, thinking back to something his Gramps said while we were in California. I'd called him a horse whisperer and he'd turned me down flat, claiming he was really a horse listener. Seemed absurd in the moment, but after seeing Jaque notice every little thing about her mare, and what it did for their relationship, I gave it more credence. But even as my hands loosened on the lead, I flung the last of my irritation at my brother, wanting a target.

"Well, great horse guru, you tell me what he's saying then."

Jo leveled gimlet eyes on me and stepped closer to Bart's shoulder, clearly ready to defend him if I kept attacking, but Bart shrugged it off with practiced aplomb.

"Brother, he and I have never warred with each other, so he's not mine to make peace with. You're the one who has to wave the white flag of surrender."

"Surrender?" I bit off a bit more harshly than I intended, unable to stop the flow of words even when I heard my father in them. "Bart, he's a horse. I can't let him win."

"Then be prepared to keep losing," Bart shot back, his hand cutting through the air as if to surgically divide us. "Until you stop seeing him as an opponent, the war will continue."

"Fine," I growled out like a hound with a sore paw, hating that he could see so much more than me. Hating that I needed him to point it out. "Then can you at least tell me how to get him to the barn without a tug of war?"

"Oh, that's easy," Jo filled in, surprisingly chipper sounding considering her defensive stance. "Let us go catch our boys and we'll all go up together. It's not like Byz has had to go anywhere by himself in a long time."

Then she set off down the hill, letting the slope speed her strides, leaving Bart and I alone. My brother lifted a brow in inquiry, clearly waiting for me to say whatever was eating at me. Though it chafed, I dug up my thoughts, careful to keep friction out of the words.

"Isn't he supposed to do what I tell him, Bart? I mean, if I tell him to leave his friends, he should do it. That's how it's supposed to work."

His chin cut sharply to one side in a wordless denial. "Now brother, you answer this while I go get my horse. Byz's not a machine. When was the last time you gave your partner any reason to prefer your company to that of the herd?"

With that unpleasant bit of gristle to chew on, I stared at his back as he followed his lady down to the gate. I couldn't really be angry at him for giving me the truth. He knew horses on a level I could barely comprehend, let alone hope to achieve. And he was right. Byz and I had been all business for a long time. As burnt out as I'd felt before last summer, it only made sense that my horse had borne the brunt of my mixed emotions about our work. I'd only just begun to rediscover the fun, and to be fair, I needed to find a way for Byz to enjoy things too.

Luckily, Bart and Jo already had fun planned. As we hiked back toward the barn, they filled me in. Jo had contacted one of the local Thoroughbred barns and arranged for some time to use their training track. Immediately, the skin that ran along my shoulders tightened with anticipation, recalling the hellbent gallops Byz and I once shared. Yes, this was exactly what the doctor ordered, for both of us.

Byz picked up on the anticipatory energy as we knocked the dust off our horses and loaded our tack into the trailer. He danced sideways as we walked outside, head lifted to scent the air, though Eros and Rowan's calm influence kept him at a low simmer. Clearly, he had some energy to burn, which was great to see after the tournament and the long trip home. My own restlessness could hardly wait to get us both pointed in the same direction, with the vain hope we might be able to outrun our mutual frustrations.

With only the three of us, we were able to take the small rig, renewing my gratitude that Bart was back in the swing of things. He'd been a missing puzzle piece for a long time, and when Jo joined us, we landed the invisible piece we hadn't even know we needed. This time, I had no qualms sitting in the back seat, appreciating the way everything worked out. Not just for Bart and Jo, mind you, but for myself.

When I originally left home to escape the demands of my parents, I'd ended up in Vegas, intent on drinking myself stupid and getting laid repeatedly. The allure of both burned up even faster than my small savings, and I decided to spend the last of my fun money on a ticket to the medieval dinner theatre, needing a distraction from my youthful problems. A chance conversation with one of the knights after the show turned into an invitation to join a bunch of their crew at a nearby bar. The socializing then morphed into a half joking job offer from one of the senior knights after I revealed some of my rodeo accomplishments. I later blamed my acceptance on the beer when my mother blew a gasket, but between you and I, I'd been stone cold sober. Those guys were living the way I wanted to live, confident and admired, obligated to no one. Add in the easy camaraderie they offered, and I bought into the mystique, hook, line, and sinker.

The knight life sucked me in fast, though I wouldn't call it a picnic. No, I worked as hard as I ever had, got yelled at as often as by my father. But the fact that the other guys in the show were sweating just as much, eating dirt just as often, kept me going. I pushed my body and mind harder than I ever had for rodeo, or baseball, because I didn't want to let my buddies down. Thanks to all my time in rodeo I felt zero fear of taking a fall, though it took a couple weeks to perfect a convincing unhorsing. The competitive streak my father had instilled railed against the idea of "losing" on purpose. I memorized the routines and adapted to the more controlled style of riding pretty quickly, leaving only one hurdle to overcome. The sword work.

Time and time again, in the heat of the moment, I choked up on the sword like I meant to swing for the fences, leaving the sword master cursing loudly enough to make the banners hanging from the rafters' shiver with the reverberation. Nor did my thickened knuckles help, stiff and inflexible as I changed grip on the sword, resulting in fumbles that caused my new-found brothers to swear profusely. I dropped my sword so much they joked that it ate even more dirt than I did, which was saying something with my new guy status. But eventually, with relentless practice, I grew proficient enough to start some weekday matinee shows.

The first few shows disappeared into a blur of fatigue. Being the new guy, that meant I got to lose, every single time. My dues were paid in bruises to both body and ego, taking falls from my horse and dying under the hero's blade. Yet even as a loser, the crowds cheered my character's name, and the maidens flocked to win my favor, every single night. Accomplishment and acceptance were a heady combo, leaving me even more lightheaded than the drinks often bought to gain my attention.

My parents hated everything about my work, which only made my success taste that much sweeter. I'd spent far too long caring about what they wanted and never gained anything for my efforts. When my dad came into Vegas for a rodeo, I'd invited him to stay with me, even left tickets at the will call desk like a dutiful son. Relief was all I felt when he refused both, not wanting his heavy-handed touch on the good thing I'd created for myself.

But even as I worked my way up the ladder of seniority, gaining a foothold with the weekend crew and mentoring new trainees, a restlessness stewed in the deepest confines of my heart. Vegas was fun in the short term but I had grown up rural, so the constant crowds and noise worked on me like fine-grit sandpaper, wearing away my peace of mind. Maybe it's callous to say, but when my mom called to let me know my father died, I'd found solace in knowing I wouldn't have to face his censure again. At the funeral, even as Mom hung on my arm sobbing inconsolably, I'd carried an indefinable flicker of hope into the dark with me. As if some deep part of my soul knew that my whole life was about to change.

A sudden downshift in speed brought me back to the present as Bart braked to make the turn down a long drive that wound between hills. Trees lined the asphalt, but the hard surface eventually gave way to dirt just as the tanbark oval of the track revealed itself in the valley below. We parked beside a large tractor barn and set to getting our horses ready, but even as I tacked up Byz my mind returned to the past. To the moment I'd first met Bart at my father's funeral, the brother I hadn't even known existed.

Before maturity and the Marines filled out Bart's frame, the resemblance between the two of us had been pretty marked. We stood practically the same height and weight, even with five years between us. While my mom venomously denied the possibility of Bart's parentage, I'd known better. In fact, knowing Bart existed made so much of my parent's divorce make perfect sense. Nor did it surprise me that my parents hadn't talked about him, owing to the favored tactic of ignoring problems until they went away. Sure, they yelled a lot when my Dad got drunk, which was a lot of the time. And, after my chance at a baseball career had been flushed down the drain by my broken hands, my dad hardly found two words to spare for me that weren't hollered. But this sort of secret struck me as something my mom would have wanted to sweep under the rug, because while my dad slept around from one coast to another, my mom enjoyed the singular dubious privilege of giving him children. That, as much as anything, had kept my mom going. To have actual, walking, talking evidence to the contrary, well, I'm pretty damn sure that was the real reason she cried all weekend.

She lost what remained of her mind when the lawyer announced Bart's portion of our inheritance, revealing a depth to her pettiness I never suspected when she publicly called Bart's mom a whore. I mean, it's not like we got millions or anything. But Dad had laid by a pretty good life insurance policy, not wanting his family left in the lurch if rodeoing took his life. No one would have guessed a heart attack would get him before a bull or bronc could. He'd been the kind of man you expected to die with his boots on.

When the truck came to a smooth stop, I had to shake my head to clear it from all the memories. But once the horses were saddled, I felt a decided sense of connection to my father's penchant for risk. As I swung up on Byz, I had the sudden mental image of strapping my incredibly mortal shell to the back of a bomb. So much power coiled between my legs I could feel a low-level vibration in my seat. He stood steadily, despite the excess of energy, grinding his teeth on the bit as we waited for Bart and Jo to join us. I needed to stay in the present, focusing on calm thoughts in hopes he would keep me in the saddle once we headed for the track. I imagined warm, sunny days where the thick pasture grass waved in the breeze, the way my truck gleamed after a good wash, or chocolate chip cookies from the sandwich shop in my hometown. Damn, I missed that deli. So many times, I'd snuck out after my mom made dinner and gotten a bowl of chili or a meatball sub. Without fail, Mrs. Campbell would put a couple cookies on my tray with a fond smile and a shake of her head. Because whatever my mom thought of her standing in the small community, nothing was a secret there. Repeated travesties at the booster bake sales and church potlucks sealed her fate as the worst cook in our county.

As I turned Byz in a circle to redirect some of his growing agitation, he fired off a halfhearted kick that jolted me firmly back into focus. My companions mounted their horses as I came straight again, and I sent him toward the track with a deep exhale of relief. Our combined restlessness carried explosive potential, enough to make a crater on landing if he launched me into orbit.

When we hit the well-churned dirt he started to jig, dancing sideways, trying to escape the light touch of my legs, pushing against the pressure of the bit as I kept him from going faster. Out the corner of my eye, I watched Jo hike her leg up over the pommel of her saddle so she could shorten her stirrups. Once adjusted, she stood in the irons, balancing her weight over her horse's withers. She threw a toothy grin at Bart, and he smiled back with the same level of fierceness, but a cool shiver ran up my arms as I had the overwhelming sensation I'd swum out past a comfortable depth.

Byz kept me from getting too sidetracked, pinning his ears flat against his neck as their horses picked up a trot, quickly moving up beside us. I let him match their speed, but he leaned on my hands with a will, nostrils pinching with frustration when I said no to the tightly wound power he wanted to turn loose. Before long the knuckles in my left hand began to complain at the weight, but I knew if I gave him an inch he would shoot off like a rocket. When he flipped his nose, trying to get the reins to loosen, I growled an objection. He promptly kicked out behind, voicing his own complaints.

"Mind if I make a suggestion?" Jo asked, sidling Rowan close enough to be heard over the chuffing rhythm of the horses' hooves. Caution marked the pinch around her eyes and the tight smile she attempted.

My ego stung like a hundred papercuts as I nodded my acceptance. "By all means, Jojo. I feel like I'm arguing with a steam engine."

In true little sister fashion, she stuck her tongue out at me, but I recognized the playfulness of the gesture. "Instead of trying to hold him in give him something else to do. Weave him back and forth so he has to think about where he's going instead of how much he wants to run. Holding them in just makes them pull harder, in my experience."

Recognizing the wisdom in her words, I turned Byz toward the rail, pleased to feel some of the building tension bleed off. His ears started moving, flipping back and forth with surprise as I switched directions again. With each consecutive turn he answered more readily, the hard marble of his granite gray neck slowly softening. We were only a quarter of the way around the track when I straightened him, and he lasted nearly a furlong before the pressure began to gather again. Twice more I repeated the exercise, but by the time we reached the track entrance again he'd settled into a steadier gait, content to pace his friends.

We let them walk a short while, since they weren't used to maintaining such a sustained effort, but I noticed all three recovered fairly quickly. No, drafts would never win in a speed race at any distance, but we kept our horses in work, which meant they were fit. It showed in the way their breathing quickly slowed and the easy strides they took.

As we came around the second time, I noticed a small crowd gathering, several bodies leaning on the outside rail with an expectant air. No doubt this was a rare opportunity for folks who spent their days with horses built for blistering speed. I just hoped I didn't embarrass myself when we finally revved the engines. It'd been a long time since I'd blown the cobwebs loose and even longer since the days I raced my rodeo buddies around the old fairgrounds track.

Bart moved in on my left, squeezing in between Ro and Byz with a casual air. Byz hardly reacted, quite familiar with the well-muscled stud, but as all three horses came abreast I felt an electric charge fill the air.

"Alright, once we reach the halfway point we're gonna turn counterclockwise on the track. I want to wait until we're almost around the bend before we let these beasts run. They've probably got about a quarter mile in them before they start flagging." Bart's deep voice held a level of calm I doubted I could have managed at that moment, not with so much adrenaline already dumping into my system. "I recommend we stick toward the outside rail so the horses don't have to deal with the deeper footing. We'll finish near the gate where our audience is. Everybody ready?"

"Yeah, Aaron, you ready to eat my dust?" Jo taunted, the familiar challenge in her eyes comforting in its sting.

"Hey, I'm sitting on one ton of gunpowder, Jojo. You're the one on the poodle puff," I shot back, raking my eyes pointedly over her fluffy footed Shire. "You aren't just racing Short Round this time."

Bart snorted at the old insult to Eros as he legged the thickly built stallion back into a trot. "Dynamite comes in smaller packages, big brother. More power per pound than you could possibly handle."

A thread of envy wormed its way into my brain as I watched man and beast move together like one animal, but I shook the emotion away. Their partnership wasn't something I aspired to. I just wanted my horse not to hate me anymore.

Conversation ceased for a few hundred yards, until the horses all settled into a fairly well-matched trot considering their vastly differing builds. But then Bart lifted an arm to make a circle in the air, a gesture familiar from our work as jousters.

"Come about!" he barked, every bit of Marine bite in the command and we wheeled our horses together as if we regularly practiced the maneuver. Jo gathered her reins and rose in her stirrups as I leaned forward, waiting for the word that would set us free.

Byz wound up more every second, pressing against the bit, digging further under his body with every stride. I put the reins in one hand long enough to clap my hand flat against his damp neck, the wet concussion meant to encourage. "Steady on, bubba. We've got this."

When his sooty colored ears flicked in my direction, I could almost feel his regard, as if he didn't quite know what to make of me. But I set my eyes around the turn, thinking about the finish line I couldn't quite see, and he lifted his head, clearly eager for whatever goal line I aimed him at.

"Charge!"

We were a half stride behind Jo and Bart, caught with my pants down, but Byz didn't need any direction from me at that moment. All I had to do is stay out of his way, floating the reins toward him as he surged forward, keeping my eyes on the horses ahead of us.

My companions gave a masterclass as I watched them. Bart's long legs wrapped around the stallion's barrel while Jo stood in her stirrups, hovering over her horse's withers. Two very different styles, and yet, both moved in perfect harmony with their partners. The best I could come up with was to stay out of Byzantine's mouth, the reins slack as he stretched his neck out in an effort to reach his herd mates. But he got no closer, despite the constant pressure of my heels against his ribs.

A quick look back from my brother had him hollering at me as we emerged onto the straight away. "He likes to pull, Aaron! If you want more speed, take a hold!"

But that was all he had time for as Jo threw out some kind of war cry and Rowan kicked into another gear, dirt coming up from his fast-moving feet. Much as I'd never understood her affection for the tentative creature, I had to admit they made a fierce team. Not one to be left behind, Bart leaned forward and grabbed a fist full of Eros's mane, his rough voiced words of encouragement lost to the wind whistling by my ears. The stud flattened out, pulling away, and I hurriedly gathered my reins, determined not be left too far behind. I was the captain, dammit, and I had a reputation to maintain.

Not that my vaunted accuracy factored into the situation, but I sure as hell meant to be in the mix. A sentiment Byz seemed to grasp with the same determination that I took hold of his mouth with. He picked up steam, plowing into the pressure of the bit with all the subtlety of a demolition derby car. While I'd been trying to not create conflict, in this case I could harness his fighting spirit.

"Let's get um, bubba!" I hollered as I leaned toward his neck, words made hoarse with the effort of tossing them into the wind. The ache in my knuckles from holding him completely disappeared as he spread out into a full-length gallop. My competitive spirit roared its approval as we began to close the gap, but for the first time in a long time, the sound of my ego came out muted. Joy bubbled in my chest, a geyser of addictive warmth that held no selfishness.

For two hundred yards, I let everything go but that feeling. Absolute freedom poured down the reins until even Byz lightened up, though his mouth remained wrapped firmly around the bit as if he were trying to suck the marrow out of the moment. Cheers and screaming barely registered as we neared the finish, three tons of horse flesh pounding out their own music against the earth.

We drew level with Bart's stirrup as Jo roared across the finish line ahead of us both, her laughter brash enough to be heard over the pulse of my own heart and Byz's roaring breaths. Despite the mildly labored sound he refused to answer my hands as I sat up to slow us, and we zoomed past Eros as Bart dropped him to a trot. I didn't feel like Byz meant to run away as a rebellion, more like he channeled my competitiveness and didn't want to stop until we were in the lead.

Then we were past Jo, her eyes wide with concern as she shouted something at me. My brain took a couple strides to translate the garbled sounds, but once the words reassembled themselves into something intelligible, I went straight into action.

"Take him in the deep stuff," she'd shouted. Bracing my outside hand on the base of his rock-hard neck, I pulled determinedly on the opposite rein, his stride stuttering as we moved into the deeper footing on the inside rail.

"Whoa, dammit!" I hollered as his body bowed, resisting all forms of guidance even as he began to slow. We were close enough to the thick white rail that I began to worry for my leg, so I changed tacks before he could rub me off. At the change of direction, he slowed, which brought back to Jo's earlier advice. So as soon as he rebalanced, I switched reins again, losing momentum by increments. Softer and softer, he slowed, neck dropping down, no longer pulling against me. Before long, we were at a trot, then a walk, his ribs heaving beneath my legs at a rate that had me a bit worried for his well-being. But as I turned him back toward his herd mates who were waiting back at the finish, the rhythm began to slow, and his spine loosened up beneath my seat. Relieved that he was none the worse for wear, I let him have the full length of the reins and took a deep breath of my own.

That relaxation proved to be my downfall as twenty feet from our companions he shook like a wet dog fresh from a bath. I came loose in a heartbeat, sliding off his side before I could even think to grab hold of something. At the last second, I remembered to let go of the reins so I wouldn't catch his mouth. But then all I could do is tuck my shoulder into the fall as the well-turned earth welcomed my body. I finished flat on my back, limbs spread to stop the roll, the blue sky pleasant to look at while I sorted out my feelings.

Irritation came first, but I shunned that deeply rutted road into the darkness, looking for another way out. I'd almost come to grips with resignation when something large and warm blotted out the bright sky. Drops of moisture landed on my forehead as I struggled to focus, but clarity came as Byz blew out through his nostrils, showering me in snot. Then he touched my cheek with his whiskered nose, the eye he tipped my way wearing a concerned wrinkle even as I caught a glimmer of amusement in the slant of his brow. After all, he'd never managed to lose me unless someone with a stick knocked me out of the middle first.

Before I could stop them the giggles hit me like an incurable disease, overtaking every cell in my body with wheezing laughter. I sat up in an effort to stop the convulsions but every time I looked back up at my horse they started again. Tears blurred my vision as I leaned over my knees, my diaphragm aching more from the need to breathe than from the fall.

The space around me fell into shadow as Jo and Bart pulled up around us, serious concern on their faces as they vaulted off their mounts. But I waved them off with a limp hand, using the other to pat Byz's neck as he continued to hang over me.

"You alright, Captain?" Jo asked, the use of my title giving away her worry.

"Fine, fine," I answered easily, wiping away residual tears and horse snot as I pushed to my feet.

Bart grinned, burly arms crossed over his chest as he looked at me. "You sure about that, big brother? It's not like you to come off your horse without assistance. Maybe you hit your head?"

I resisted the urge to roll my eyes and scratched the sweat curled hairs on Byz's withers, smiling when his big, sledgehammer shaped head turned my way with a far softer eye than I'd seen from him in a long time. "Yeah, little brother, I think everything is gonna be just fine."

The feeling intensified as we all headed back to the gate, leading our horses as we greeted our hosts. They were a rowdy bunch, laughing over my fall, admiring our big horses with loud voices and hands that did half their talking for them. Byz stood at my side through it all, relaxed in my company, even touching me on occasion as if testing the new connection we were forging.

Back home, I spent hours working the dried sweat out of his coat, reveling in the quiet camaraderie of his company. He still needed some reminding about good manners when we gave them their evening grain, but even then, I stood with him, greedy for more peace. We'd made a huge step in the right direction, and I almost missed him when I headed upstairs to have my own dinner. Maybe there really was something to be found in the close relationship Bart and Jo fostered with their horses. And maybe Byz and I could find something like it for ourselves.

7

Jaque

The laughter in Aaron's voice brought me a good deal of pleasure, but despite the humourous way he told the tale of his fall, the subject matter made bands of fear constrict around my heart. I had not ridden a horse in many years, after a particularly harrowing spill. The mere thought, even now, put knots in my throat that I struggled to swallow down. Still, I would not sully his happiness with my old scars.

"I am happy you and Byzantine are finding your way together," I encouraged, keeping my tone full of sunshine and warmth. "There is little I love more than connecting with a horse, and the tough ones can be so very rewarding."

"Yeah, though I've got a feeling Lyric and you have never had bad moments." While I appreciated the admiration in his voice, I flinched as he struck so close to the nerve his story had exposed. "You are like Bart and Jo, so connected and in tune with your horse it's uncanny."

Except that once, though I shoved the thought away with impatient mental hands. "We are deeply bonded, since her birth in fact. I can still recall how it felt to hold her wet little body against mine while her mother licked her clean. Outside, we had a blizzard blowing in and the barn doors rattled with the wind, but once she had her first drink, she lay down and took a nap with her head in my lap. I loved her from that day on."

"Wow," The whispered awe in that small word shivered along my skin. "I've never even met a foal, let alone a newborn. That had to be pretty powerful."

I smiled, warming with the sweet memory of Lyric's tiny head laying on my thigh. "Incredibly so. You are missing out on a very special experience, Aaron. If you would like, I can take you out to meet some little ones when I am back in Kentucky. Foaling season has already begun, and I am friends with several breeders. One of my jobs during the fall is to work with weanlings, just as I have here in Florida."

"Is that what you want to do in the future? Raise horses? Because it sounds like you really enjoy it," he surmised, the sincerity of the query taking me by surprise. Not even my father guessed that to be my goal, and I shared nearly everything with him.

"Yes, it is. Lyric is meant to be my foundation mare. The Canadian Horse is incredibly rare and I cannot bear the thought of them dying out. She is fourteen this year and will not compete much longer. With a horse so incredible as she, I want her line to live on." Indeed, I could imagine the future that saw her round with a foal, or the night I might help bring her offspring into the world. But I flinched as that brought to mind carrying my own children, a foolish dream I might never realize. Aaron had that effect on me, setting loose hopes long kept in the shadows. "But enough of me. What is your hope for the future? Is there a plan beyond jousting?"

He sighed heavily, and I wished I were there to kiss away the worry I heard. "To be honest, I just want to see the Company succeed, even expand if possible. With Bart back in the lyst and Jo trotting us out to the public, I think we're pointed in the right direction. And I want everyone else in the Company to be happy. Ridiculous, but there it is. They're all family to me, closer than my actual family, and I want the best for every last one of them."

I bit my lip at the heartfelt affection in his voice, deciding I would never have a better opportunity to learn more about the one thing he never spoke of. "That is a worthy goal, Aaron, truly. Though I hope someday you will tell me more about the family that raised you. I am greedy to know you better."

The silence on the line made me fear I pushed too far, but then he sighed. "I can't imagine you'll find anything in my history that won't make you think less of me. If I lost a future with you over something in my past, it would hurt like hell."

My fist knotted in the pillow at the vulnerability of his confession. I could not leave him unanswered. "Your past made you into the man I care for, and for that alone, I must love it. But I would not cause you pain for my curiosity."

"No, I suppose it's only fair to share my past if I want any kind of future with you."

My heart flared painfully bright to hear he considered a future between us. I had kept my hopes to the simplicity of a physical relationship, with no plans beyond that. Yet, the smile in his voice let me dream a bit further. Perhaps, if I were careful not to run him off, he could come to love me even half as much as I already loved him. Yes, that would be more than enough for my needy heart.

"Would you at least tell me about your family, then? I know you have sisters, and your brother, but little else. What of your parents?"

"I have three younger sisters, actually. All of them married with kids, though my baby sister is going through a divorce. They all live in Iowa, near my Mom." A sheen of ice worked its way into his voice as he spoke, dampening his usual earnestness. To hear it applied to his family made me wish I could be there to lend him some of my own warmth. "Life for them is very different than mine, so we don't always see eye to eye."

"And your father?" I ventured cautiously, smoothing the pillow I so recently wrinkled as if I could so easily soothe the tension from his voice.

"He's dead."

The utter flatness of his reply smothered any desire I might have to know more. My throat constricted, making my reply far too soft. "My sympathies. I could not imagine losing my papa, though I was never blessed to know my mama. She died while I was very small." So small, I had barely known the touch of her hand before death stole her away. But my pain was easier to handle, familiar in its ache. The pain I felt from Aaron made for new wounds, wishing I could steal his troubles so he would not have to bear them.

"Aw, Jaque, I'm sorry. I didn't mean to bring you down. My dad and I had a complicated relationship. I guess it makes me an asshole that I don't miss him more."

Ah, but I managed a slight smile, confident I could steer us toward a lighter subject. "We must stop apologizing so much to each other. I do not regret asking. I only wish it did not weigh so heavily on you to speak of these things. I find my only sorrow when it comes to you is that we are apart. But all the same, I am glad we are able to talk. Here in the quiet of the night, you seem so close."

Heat pooled in my gut at the faint friction that chased each word of his reply, as if he spoke through sand. "Not nearly close enough, Jaque. I hope you've got some down time available when you get back home, because we're due some time alone."

Though I knew I risked pushing us too fast, too far, my mouth had a mind of its own. "We are alone now, Aaron. I am yours to enjoy."

Silence again, only this time, I felt like I stood on the edge of a cliff with a thunderstorm at my back. Energy crackled as my skin grew taut, anticipation and fear consuming me from the inside. But as with every other time I gambled his reaction, he stepped up with the confidence I always dreamed of in a partner.

"Then tell me what you're wearing, Jaque, so I can imagine you here in my bed. Tell me where you want this to go, and I'll take you there."

To my everlasting gratitude, he made good on every word.

Aaron

Sharing intimacy with Jaque, even from a distance, hit me low in the gut with all the accuracy and power of a major leaguer swinging for the fences. Shaking in the aftermath, I stared up at the dark ceiling, simultaneously grateful for this experience with her and hating that we couldn't be together yet.

Silence felt right at first, words too flawed to express my emotions. But as it continued to linger, it gained weight, pressing down on me like a bad dream.

"Jaqueline, you really are glorious." Awe filled every word, and still didn't feel adequate. "I've never felt this much. It's like all of me was numb until you."

"Oh, Aaron." The barest edge of a sob marked my name, which had me rolling toward the phone as if she lay on the bed beside me. Before I could overthink, I pressed the video chat button, needing to see her. As it rang, I heard her shifting, then her strained voice. "What are you doing, Aaron?"

"Come on, Jaque, we've gone this far. Be brave, let me see your flushed cheeks and beautiful eyes."

She gave no answer, but the icon on the screen spun as it connected. Then, in all her glory, she appeared. With only the screen for illumination she was refined to her essence, eyes glowing with pleasure, full lips showing bite marks. Her hair tumbled forward over her shoulder, the thin strap on her chemise playing peekaboo through the thick strands. Propped up on her elbows, her breasts created a deep valley I wanted to get lost in.

"How is it you look even more amazing than the last time I saw you?"

Her eyelashes fluttered as she tipped her chin down, clearly uncomfortable with the compliment. "No need to play the flatterer, Aaron. You have won me already."

"Oh Jaque," I admonished, smiling to soften my tone. "This isn't about winning you. It's about deserving you. Everything you give, I can never come close to earning. But I intend to try."

She offered a cautious grin before twirling her hair around a finger. "Then I must commend you for the effort, because despite your lack of faith I would say you were incredibly smooth."

Huffing a half syllable of laughter, I shifted onto my belly to match her posture. "I've never gotten into the whole phone sex thing before. But you make it easy to get lost in the moment, Jaque, even the unexpected ones."

Her whole upper lip disappeared into her mouth, and she looked away again, my arms tightening with the need to hold her. "I am sorry if I was too bold."

"Never," I swore, giving it all the vehemence I might a curse word as my hands vibrated with impotency. No matter how much I wanted to pull her to my chest and keep her there until her doubts disappeared, I was going to have to resort to words. "I'm serious, Jaque. You are hands down the most fiercely alluring woman I've ever known, and I never want you to hold back. While I kept things slow for my visit, once you get home we can go whatever speed you want. Fast, slow, I don't care, as long as we go together."

Nostrils flared, Jaque sucked in a deep breath then buried her face in the sheets. All I could hear were muffled exclamations as her fist thumped the mattress hard enough for the phone to bounce. Seriously concerned I'd just caused a blowout on the one purely good thing I had in my life, my tongue glued itself to the roof of my mouth, unable to think of a damn thing I could say to keep myself from wrecking.

A solid knot of lead weight gathered in my stomach, and the sweat of passion that had gathered between my shoulders went cold with dread. Both sensations left me well behind the curve when Jaque righted her phone, revealing an unexpectedly serene expression.

"I pray you will forgive the unladylike display, Aaron. I am not usually prone to such fits."

"Excuse me?" I answered dimly, brain losing traction at the sudden change of direction. "I'm confused. What just happened?"

A complete blush darkened her cheeks, and she licked her lips nervously. "I have a tendency to rush a relationship. To discover we were on the same page made me a little ridiculous. I am ashamed to say I cursed profusely, and at a rather high pitch. Neither you nor Soleil needed to hear that."

My heart slewed around the corner of relief and amusement, then squealed to a halt with a genuine laugh that made the weight in my belly vanish. That she giggled in response made my head swim with overwhelming happiness. "Honestly, Jaque, I thought I'd upset you."

"Oh, not at all." Eyes round with wonder, she stared at me as if afraid I might disappear if she blinked. "I never thought to feel so happy, particularly when we are so far apart. At this rate, I fear I shall have to fall in love with you."

My heart stuttered like a misfiring cylinder, then roared forward with an overabundance of fuel, but I managed to keep my equilibrium this time. "That's the plan, Jaque. And when it happens, I hope we can fall together."

She smiled so softly I could practically feel the feather brush of her lips on mine. I would have pledged my heart to her on the next breath if she gave me the slightest encouragement. But happy or no, she behaved more wisely than me, turning us away from the beckoning edge of love.

"I hope so too, Aaron. But for now, we should say our good nights. Our work has no mercy for tired eyes or weary bodies."

"True enough, my lady. Though I hope to see you in my dreams, I'll look forward to talking with you tomorrow night."

"*Je te verrai dans mes rêves*, Aaron." Her throaty voice covered the miles between us with feeling and emotion, providing another ounce of hope to weigh against the darkness of doubt. Then she pursed her lips in a playful kiss just before the call disconnected.

Grumbling under my breath, I rose from the bed, needing to clean up before I could rest. Afterward, I flopped back into my pillows, expecting sleep to be elusive. But no, it sucked me down into a whirlpool of oblivion, giving me my first full night of sleep since I'd left Jaque behind. No dreams broke up the quiet night, but I'll be honest... dreams had nothing on my waking hours now that Jaque was in my life. Now, if I could get her back into my arms as easily as she made her way into my heart.

Jaque

While Aaron and I kept our late-night conversations much more tame the remainder of the week, breaking down such an intimate barrier brought us closer. He told me a little about his beauty queen mother, and how Bart had been born to another woman, which allowed me to guess at his father's faithless nature. I hated to think of how he must have treated his children if he could not even be true to his wife. While I never would begrudge my father if he found a new love, I felt blessed knowing my Papa loved my Mama so faithfully. Evidence in its purest form of what a true marriage of hearts could be.

Friday night our call was brief by necessity, so I could rise early the next morning. This clinic carried the potential to set me up for a chance at the North American Single Horse Championship. If we could place well, the World Championship might be next. Not that I knew how I could afford to fly Lyric overseas, but I would not worry over something that had not made itself a problem yet. One step at a time.

Lyric nearly pulled me onto the trailer in her eagerness to go, parking in her accustomed spot with little guidance on my part. She picked at her hay as I clipped her lead into place, staring out the window with clear expectation as I closed the ramp and Dutch doors.

A twenty-minute drive deposited us at one of the better-known farms in Ocala, tree lined lanes and white vinyl fences in every direction. I had barely put the truck in park when my phone vibrated on the dash. A short message from Aaron filled the screen as I unlocked the display.

'*You ladies show them what you're made of. I know they'll see what I see, an incredible team that can handle anything.*'

I sent him an emoji of kissing lips, grateful for his faith. Having someone in our corner made me feel that much stronger as I unloaded horse and carriage. We were early, giving plenty of room in the schedule to fuss over my partner and see her quietly hitched.

You could not have ordered more perfect weather, the cool, foggy morning giving Lyric an extra swing to her steps. Her traditional leather harness accented the curve and play of her muscular form, elegant and powerful. I exchanged easy smiles with two other drivers as I passed them on the way to the main arena. Their horses also moved out happily, though by the sweat marks beneath the harness, they already had their lessons. The relaxation and contentment boded well, showing none of the tension horses had carried at the van den Berg clinic.

After a slow, lengthy warm-up, I parked myself out of the way to watch the team before me. They were a familiar pairing, Sue's bay mare flashy in a way that had nothing to do with her colour and everything to do with her movement. Every limb sliced through the air as if to cut it, whether collected or extended. She carried her head high, neck arched and ears pricked with full awareness of her own magnificence. Even when she threw in a snorting spook at a sandy spot in the middle of the grass, she moved with all the ease of a bird in flight.

The clinician, a woman I knew only by her judging at our most recent show, rode on the back step of the carriage so she could look over Sue's shoulder. I could hear nothing but a low murmur over the steady hum of the wheels and the rhythmic swing of the single tree moving to the cadence of the mare's strides. Thick, dew wet grass carpeting the huge arena absorbed every hoofbeat, lending to the overall feeling of quiet. The marked difference between this and our last clinic felt so massive, I could hardly put them in the same category. Here, out from under the oppressive weight of domination and ego, Lyric and I could learn.

Oh, did we learn! Lillian Beard put us through our paces with a thoroughness that would have impressed my old instructor. She did not hold back because Lyric was not a high dollar warmblood or well-heeled show horse. No, she pushed, challenging me to get more from my mare with every exercise. Never had I been more grateful to work with someone who knew us from a competition, because she had seen us at our best and pointed directly at the places we could improve.

"Ask for more give in the shoulder there, right there," she admonished, prompting me to touch Lyric's shoulder with a flick of the whip, a whispered reminder to pay better attention to that portion of her body. A grunt of effort accompanied the next stride of canter as she adjusted her balance, her top line flexing with the effort.

As we rounded the corner Lillian directed us into a downward transition. She required us to maintain the same level of push as we found at the canter, to let the forward power fuel an extended trot. The result made my eyes sting with awe as Lyric boomed across the diagonal of the arena as if her feet had grown wings.

Lyric answered the softening of my hand, stretching to reach the bit as we shifted to a more collected trot before we curved along the rail again. I half expected Lillian to ask us to repeat the exercise again, but she gave us leave to walk. Though I did not give the reins away with the same totality I might have on my own, just a few inches were enough for Lyric to uncoil her now damp muscles, mouth chewing thoughtfully at the bit.

"You've built an amazing connection with your horse, Miss Sauveterre." Her smooth voice carried clearly from her station on the back step, and I turned my head to assess Lillian's sincerity. The smile that greeted me looked genuine to its core. "While I could see some of it from the judge's box it's a pleasure to get an even clearer picture."

"Thank you, Miss Beard. She is my heart, and I doubt I would have reached this far without her." Though I spared Lillian a quick smile, my attention shifted back to Lyric, clucking sharply to encourage her to keep up a longer stride. No sense in puttering during a lesson. "This is our first season at Advanced, and I never thought we would do so well, so soon."

"May I be honest, Miss Sauveterre?" Lillian asked, a hint of reluctance marking her question. At my terse nod, she continued. "You did a lovely test, gaining points for accuracy and obedience that your fellow competitors were having more difficulty with that weekend. But those things alone would not be enough to have placed you so high if the more experienced drivers had laid down their best test."

Oh how that soft, yet implacable truth slithered into my ears, dropping to my gut to pool, leaden and chill. Lyric reacted to the change in my energy with alacrity, steps slowing as her head rose, the twist to her neck telling me she wanted to stop, to look back at me. But I could not let us be so affected by such honesty, anymore than I would ever let insults bleed us.

"Walk up, *sucré*," My voice carried a firmness of resolve, a call to action for the both of us. As she strove into the harness again I pushed aside my emotions and squared my shoulders, ready to move on. "Then, Miss Beard, I would be grateful if you could help us find our best test."

One could almost feel Lillian's smile, like sunshine at my back, warm with what I hoped was approval. "Miss Sauveterre, I would love to. Let's take the power you are storing in your core right now and do some more canter transitions. I think we can lighten up your mare's front end, which will help in all three phases."

To which I complied, beginning another half hour of intense exercise, mentally and physically. By the time I dropped Lillian off beside her next student, I felt so contentedly exhausted that I did not even flinch to find Grady waiting. His sneer hardly reached me as Lillian and I exchanged handshakes.

Headed back to the trailer I observed Lyric moving in the same relaxed way the other horses had traveled, and I wondered if she felt the same blissful contentment I did. Physically, she could have gone longer thanks to hours of fit work. Mentally, we were cooked to perfection, and whether in spite of or because of it, I found myself excited to repeat the experience tomorrow.

Aaron

The excitement in Jaque's voice as she shared her experience at the clinic lit me up from the inside. There'd only been one other person in my life I believed so strongly in, and what I felt for Jaque made my faith in Bart seem dim in comparison.

Which is probably one of the reasons why I noticed the difference in her the following night. All that joy felt smothered from the first moment she answered the phone, though I could tell she wanted to remain positive. Yet, the false cheer jangled through the phone regardless.

"We worked on some very complex bending lines and played with sharpening transitions to make up time between gates. Lyric grew so fired up over the exercises she squealed at one point. Grunting I have heard, but not a squeal. She has never been so wild with excitement."

Carefully, as if I were handling my mother's prized tiara, I attempted to dig a bit deeper without breaking anything. "And yet?"

Fragile silence stretched thin again, though this time I didn't feel like the haggard nature of her quiet was directed my way. She couldn't get home soon enough for me. At least then, I could hold her. "I hope I'm not screwing this up, Jaque, but I feel like you're hurting. I want to help, if I can."

"I am not hurt," she answered hastily. "Though I am thinking about some of what I learned today. Lillian is very honest, which I appreciate. But I am afraid I have been wearing blinders, and the truth seems overwhelming at the moment."

I paced off the length of the room, too edgy to be still. But when I heard Bart and Jo tromp up the stairs, back from their dinner out, I dropped onto the edge of the bed to quiet the echo of my angry footsteps on the wood floors. "What can I do, Jaque? If you want, I'll jump in the truck right now."

Her low chuckle carried a bit more warmth. "Much as I would love to be selfish, I know you have your own obligations. Those must come first if our relationship is to last."

I won't lie, I hated that itty-bitty word, if. But I appreciated that she thought of how our lives could fit together.

"Still, I'm willing. You're important to me, and I know Bart and Jo can hold down the fort. You deserve to have someone to lean on."

"Thank you, sincerely. You are very important to me, as well, which is why I cannot ask you to come. This, I can endure. It is simply unpleasant."

Is it possible to be thrilled and hurt at the same time? The combo felt eerily similar to when Bart and I pulled a double unhorsing in California. My body had ached from the impact, but I'd been giddy to have my brother back. In this case, she'd both denied me and drawn me closer in the same sentence. The positive sensations were enough to help me push through.

"So what happened? You don't sound like you did yesterday. Is Lyric okay?"

"Yes, thank you, she is in fine form." Some brightness returned to her voice, enough that I could tell she'd found her smile. "In fact, she is currently staring over my shoulder, wondering where your voice is coming from."

"Seriously?" Though she couldn't see it, I shook my head in disbelief. "I swear, your horse is almost dog-like the way she behaves."

"It is a breed trait, this intelligence," she responded, warming to her subject. "I am afraid she has spoiled me for any other breed. No other horse could possibly compare to this level of work ethic, connection and temperament."

Her voice shifted, words coming out more briskly as her mood changed. "Which is a portion of my problem, as I have been informed if I ever wish to reach the true pinnacle of our sport, I will require a more suitable breed." Anger simmered, pressure building under the lid she had covered it with. I found my body responding involuntarily, teeth grinding in an echo of her tension. "And while I enjoy all horses, I find myself unwilling to imagine a competitive future with anything less than I now enjoy."

"Nor should you have to, Jaque," I bit off, angry at a faceless enemy for their callousness. Even in my ignorance I thought Lyric's connection with her mistress as glaringly obvious as a neon sign. For that matter, blind people could probably see the strength of Jaque's relationship with her mare. "They must see you as some kind of threat, to undercut you like that."

"No." Resignation stole her fight in one word. "I would have thought that, coming from van den Berg, or many others. But Lillian was very kind, and only offered her advice as she feels I have a significant chance at becoming an upper echelon competitor."

Confusion wrinkled my brows together. "I'm confused. Aren't you already an Advanced level driver? You've proven your abilities. What more is there?"

"She was speaking of the World Championships, as I shared my goals with her. And while I am currently a top three driver from Canada, I have little hope of achieving a decent placing at the championship level." The anger roiled up again, in her voice and in my gut. "Lyric is simply not a stunning enough mover compared to the others, which will not garner the dressage scores needed to win."

A discordant ping echoed in my mind, as if something important were buckling under strain. This didn't sound like the woman I knew, the one that told me the ribbons meant nothing compared to her relationship with her horse. In fact, it sounded far too much like something my father said when my old roping horse could no longer make the fast breaks needed for high placings. I didn't know what to say, afraid no matter what I did I'd piss her off. But it turns out I didn't have to say a thing.

"Well, it does not matter anyway." She sighed, that outward breath pushing away all the conflict in her voice, making room for peace. "Lyric and I do not need to beat anyone. She has nothing to prove. In fact, we could never compete again, and I would be content."

Though I still wished I could stand between her and her disappointment, I felt so proud of her for sticking to her truth. Yeah, I might have gotten a bit lost along the way, but it had taken quite a struggle to stand up to my parents when I decided to break out on my own.

"Whatever you choose, Jaque, I'm in your corner, though I do love watching you do your thing. Lyric and you, to my eye, have something much more enviable than the other teams."

"You flatterer," she teased, and I breathed a little more deeply at her easy acceptance of the compliment. Little by little, we were growing to trust each other. Maybe what we built would be strong enough to endure when tested. "I am grateful to have your faith, Aaron. I have felt lonely since you left, an unfamiliar sensation, and certainly not enjoyable."

"But you'll be here soon, Jaque, and I promise we'll steal some time away. When do you hit the road?"

"In the morning, once traffic thins. We will rest at a farm belonging to a friend, once we are through Atlanta. Lyric can stretch her legs and have a good roll while I take a nap. Sadly, this will put our arrival near to midnight, but I hope you can find some time for us the following evening?"

Damn, so close, yet so far away.

"Do you need anything done at your place? After all the practice I got at the show, I could go make Lyric's stall up." Maybe if I were lucky, her mistress might invite me in to share her bed as well. Not just sexually, either. Every part of me wanted to be close to her, to drown in her scent and feel her ribs rising and falling with each breath. I craved her company with even more intensity than I desired her body and would gladly forgo intimacy if it meant we could rest together.

"You do not need to do a thing, Aaron, though I would be grateful for the gesture. Both Lyric and I will be looking for our own beds at that late hour."

"Then consider it done. Byz and I are going for a ride in the morning, but I'm otherwise at your disposal." Would it be creepy to sit there and wait for her to arrive? Desperate? Mind you, desperate wasn't far from the truth. "Feel free to call if you need company while you drive. I'll make sure I have my Bluetooth on."

"Thank you. We are both ready to be home, I think. Florida holds little allure aside from the competitions, and after today, even those have lost some of their pleasant glow. In the morning, all I have to do is load Lyric and Soleil and pray for clear roads." She paused as if measuring out her next words. "I am even more ready to see you. Would you have time for a date on Wednesday night? We could have dinner, perhaps see a movie?"

My heart pumped double time at the hope in her voice, such an echo of my own emotions. Any reservations I had disappeared, and I committed entirely to saying what I felt, urgency roughening my reply. "Honestly, Jaque, I don't care what we do, as long as I get to spend time with you. This week has been rough. We could go out, we could stay in, or we could do a little of both. Details don't matter past being able to touch you, to see you. Video chat is great, but not nearly enough."

"Oh, Aaron!" I caught a muffled sniffle before she continued. "You once told me you were full of lines to get a woman out of her pants, and I find myself praying you are not using them now. I want to believe you, so dearly."

Stifling a curse, I pushed onward, ready to bare all my secrets if it would help gain her trust. Hopefully, I wouldn't shatter it in the process. "Jaqueline, I'm never, ever going to lie to you. So believe me when I say I've never felt this strongly about anyone. Not even my former fiancée."

She sucked in a breath of surprise, and I held mine, terrified over how she might respond. Would she withdraw? Would she lash out? Would she hold my reticence in reserve against some future argument?

"Why did you not marry?" she asked, so little inflection in the question I hardly knew what to think. But I knew I needed to answer, so I ripped the old scab off as fast as I could manage.

"Melissa gave me back the ring. Said our lives wouldn't fit together. Even when I offered to cut back on traveling, she still left." The wound to my heart didn't even bleed, now just a faded part of the cratered landscape of my past, so I kept going. "But if I'm giving you the whole truth, I don't think that's why. I think she bolted because of my family."

"What?" Indignation turned the rhetorical question into more of a squawk than anything. "That is completely ridiculous! Clearly, whoever this woman is, she was not worthy of you. Who does such a thing?"

My concerns evaporated in the face of her reply. How could I hold out against a woman who thought me so worthy? But I did need to temper her response. "In her defense, we were young. I could hardly stand up to my mother then, and still struggle with it. Can't expect her to manage what I couldn't. She did what she needed to do for herself, and I think, in the long run, I have to thank her for it."

"Thank her for abandoning you? What kind of love is that?" Though the question came out gentler than before, she still punched out the words.

"Yes, thank her, Jaque." Smiling, I imagined her lips flat with displeasure, maybe her dark brows pulled together in consternation. God, I appreciated that fight in her. "I had some growing up to do. She forced me to realize I needed to make my own life, regardless of my family, to figure out who I was. All of it led me to you, eventually, and for that alone, she's got my thanks."

"Well, I, um..." Flustered now, she pulled in a deep breath, then forced it back out. "While I am grateful for these late-night conversations, Aaron, I cannot help hating the distance between us.

I would prefer to kiss you after such a statement, rather than say thank you."

"You're welcome. And I can wait, Jaque." Didn't want to, mind you, any more than she did. "Kisses keep. But I wanted to get the hard stuff out of the way now, so when you get back here I can focus on us."

"*Sacrament*," she muttered, the tone one of frustration. I heard the whump of blankets being thrown back, a long zipper being pulled, both sounds hasty. Then the distinct clicking of her dog dancing on the tile of the apartment. "Tell me you have plans, tomorrow evening? Stop me now, before I am foolish."

Though the tightness of her demand worried me, instinctively, I felt a pull that spoke to my own need for her. "No, no plans except to go get Lyric's stall ready. Why?"

"Rest will be futile after this conversation. So, I will leave now, while I can use all this excitement I feel." Every hair on my scalp tightened as if eager for the grip of her fingers as I heard the jingle of keys, then the opening of a door. "And you, I expect you will be at my home no later than sunset. While I cannot guarantee my energy level will allow for lovemaking, I hope a few of the kisses I have been deprived of will refresh us both."

"Jaque, I'll be there waiting for your truck to pull in," I swore, impatience and excitement driving me to my feet, though I kept still, letting the euphoria build. "Keep me updated so I know when you get close."

The door clunked shut and I heard her suitcase rolling as her breathing quickened, my own lungs working to keep up though I hadn't moved an inch. "I keep a spare key to the house beneath the purple and silver planter beside the porch. Make yourself at home. I will be there as quickly as I can."

"Be safe, Jaque," I implored, her truck dinging repetitively as she opened the door and slid the key into the ignition. A slightly different tone alerted just before she turned the key, the older model diesel engine turning over with a mild delay. "No matter how much I want to hold you, Jaque, don't rush on my account."

She made a noise of disbelief, even as the rumble of the engine faded, then I heard the low nicker of horses, which made me suspect she had returned to the barn. "Aaron, however much I feel for you, Lyric's safety is my responsibility. I can assure you that nothing, not even your delicious kisses, will sway that."

My ego took the blow like a champ, because something greater shored it up. I was in love with this woman, every single bit of her, including the parts that loved her horse like a family member. "I would be disappointed in anything less. You ladies travel safely and well. I'll see you at home, kisses at the ready."

"We shall," she answered, a bit more softly as I heard the stall door slide open and then the soft *whoosh* of Lyric breathing her in. "I lo.." A pause intervened, though she covered it quickly. "I look forward to seeing you, Aaron. A week is forever to be away from you."

Had she been about to say what every cell in my body hoped she'd say? My chest felt tight, like I'd just taken a lance blow from Bart. I sat back down on the bed, my legs trembling. I fought to breathe around the sensation without making her worry. "I look forward to seeing you too, my lady. Now, focus on your girls. You can call me back later, once you're on the road."

"Thank you, I will," she shot back, almost panicky sounding. "Goodbye."

Then the line went dead, and I sat there for damn near thirty minutes, staring blindly into space. Half of me wanted to shoot out the door at that very moment, to go to her place, turn on the lights, fix up the stall, to do *something* before anticipation tore me apart. The much more rational portion of me remembered the time. At eleven o'clock at night, I couldn't accomplish much, and that would still leave me with more than a dozen hours to sit and wait.

But then I heard Jo's voice in the living room, and I leveraged myself back up onto wobbly legs, steadying as I headed for the door. Much as I would never, ever ask my actual sisters for their advice about a woman, I knew I could trust Jo. Practically family already, she had an eye for what needed doing, and Jaque called her friend as well. If anyone in the world could help me get through the night sane, it would be the family I'd found, not the one I'd been born into.

When I waded into the kitchen, I faltered slightly. Bart and Jo sat at the island, angled to face each other as he held up an Oreo for her to nibble. A tender moment I didn't want to interrupt, since I'd been the one to keep them apart for so long. I owed them the time alone. But they both waved me to join them, so I headed for the fridge to pour a glass of milk. Jo handed me a pile of her precious cookies as I slid on to the remaining stool, keen eyes missing nothing. I even managed to swallow one down despite the tightness that wracked my entire body, all that excess energy desperate for an outlet.

"So, Jaque's on her way home," I began, pausing to check in with my audience. Jo wore a surprisingly soft smile, though I caught a hint of smugness around her eyes. "And I want to make sure she has a warm welcome. Any ideas?"

Bart shared a grin with Jo and shook his head, then reached past her to clap me on the shoulder. "I know I said I would laugh my ass off when you took the fall, Aaron, but I'm too damn happy for you to manage it. Whatever you need, I'm in."

Jo laughed as she leaned back against Bart's chest, but I felt no malice in it, only the usual banter we traded. "Oh, you men. Jaque will just be happy to see you. No grand gestures needed. But if you really want to go all out I'm pretty sure we can come up with something appropriate. When is she getting in?"

Thus began a steady hour of conversation as Jo lined out a simple, perfect strategy that my over excited brain never would have come up with alone. Most of my tension dissipated by the time Jaque rang me back, wanting some company as she drove, and I said a quick goodnight to my roommates before heading back to the bedroom. Though I still didn't sleep much I found my rest in the knowledge that the woman I loved would be back in my arms soon, and that no matter how dysfunctional my family might be, Gallant Company more than made up for it.

🍃 8 🍃

Jaque

Knowing Aaron waited made my coffee stops obsolete, though I drank down the chocolate laced caffeine out of habit, hoping to remain alert. Were I lucky, I would have enough energy to enjoy his attentions before exhaustion overtook me.

During our layover in Georgia, I managed a few solid hours of sleep on the couch in my friend's tack room. But when a barking dog outside set Soleil off, I woke completely alert, unable to be still a second longer. I might have tried harder to rest, but when I looked outside Lyric stood at the gate as if expecting me. So we resumed our travels, three ladies usually so happy on the road all eager to be home.

Oh, how I longed for my own bed, the flannel sheets and cashmere blanket wrapped around me, the faint lilac scent that rose from the candles I kept in every room. The tiny two-bedroom home had become a haven, at first because I did not have to share it with my father. Yet now I found myself unaccountably excited to have Aaron there. He had never said a disparaging word about the hints of purple I surrounded myself with, from the paisley carpet in the living room to the chair cushions at the dining table. The splashes of colour reminded me of my grandmother who originally fostered my obsession by gifting me a bed set on my fourteenth birthday. I had been desperately looking for a way to claim my femininity after a childhood spent at the heels of my father and grandfather, always embroiled in their pursuits, which left little room for being girly. But as my body changed to reflect my sex, and I began to notice boys, I struggled to find a middle ground. Pink had been too garish, like I tried too hard. Purple felt powerful, something fit for a warrior queen rather than a helpless princess in need of saving. Much better for a tomboy finding her way in the world.

As soon as I embraced the colour, it began to show up in unexpected places. From my first truck, which had been a bone of contention with my father who complained over the glittery plum paint, to the day I bought Lyric her first halter in the prettiest shade of lavender. Conversing with the owners of the carriage company in Kentucky, I had been tickled to find their logo was a silver fleur de lis with purple lettering, as if calling out specifically for me. When Aaron answered my online ad looking for draft horses to lease, I took it as a fine omen when he wore a dark purple shirt at our first meeting.

When I finally pulled into the gate at my little farm and found Aaron in another dark purple shirt, the setting sun making the colour more vivid, I could have wept. He stood in the open doors of the barn, smiling enough to make up for the fading light of day, and I nearly sobbed over my inability to contain the love I felt. How could I deserve all this happiness? Surely, this feeling would not last. Each time I had loved, allowed myself to believe in the possibility of forever, reality would come crashing down. This between Aaron and I, being so much more intense than anything I had ever experienced, would wreck me completely if it fell apart.

But I could not dwell on such things, not with Lyric relying upon me. She made a fine buffer as I climbed from the truck and accepted a brief embrace from Aaron while Soleil ran circles around us, barking her excitement. I pulled away, knowing my mare deserved my full attention. Sadly, I loved him all the more for how he let me go, hands sliding away with slow intent. My skin ached where he had touched across my hip and shoulder blade as he followed me to the trailer. We worked together quickly, silently, no words needed as the ramp came down and I stepped inside to retrieve Lyric. She politely walked to the barn, but I felt a hurried tension in the lead, as if I could not move quickly enough. When I stopped outside her stall to strip the cotton sheet from her body, she shook violently as if to shed the feel of the fabric. Now that we were home, she could be as dirty as she pleased, and we did not have to worry about what anyone else would think of how we looked. Which is why I pulled off her halter and pointed to her open stall door, as was our habit.

"Stall, *mon tresor*."

She did not wait for me to change my mind and went straight in the door without a backward glance. I watched with a fond smile as she spun around once, then dropped into the thick bed Aaron had made, grunting happily as her legs waved in the air. In the oversized stalls meant for full size drafts, she found plentiful room to wiggle around to reach every itch. I could understand her feeling as the road often left me itchy as well, forced to be still for so long. But my hand stilled as I scratched my arm, Aaron stepping in behind me to lift my hair. When his lips touched the skin he bared, I shivered with delight, forgetting the aches of my body in less than a moment.

"She looks happy to be home," he murmured, settling my hair over my opposite shoulder as he tucked his chin against the edge of my jaw. The warmth of his body beckoned, even though he made no move to hold me, and I leaned into him with a sigh of contentment. "Does she need anything else before I take you away?"

I blinked to clear the haze of lust clouding my vision and took in the stall. Lyric had spread herself out, taking up as much space as possible as she exhaled deeply into the pine shavings, so she needed nothing from me at the moment. Much as at the show, Aaron had found the hay nets and filled one to bursting, hanging it perfectly in the corner. Her water buckets were clean and full to the brim, and he had even opened the top half of the outside door, allowing the still twilight air inside. No, he had done everything perfectly, and that left me free to focus on my own needs.

Without a word I slid the stall door shut, making sure the spring-loaded latch caught securely before I turned to face him. The eyes I had dreamed of looked back with so much more tenderness than I expected after our separation. Passion still lingered in the upturn of his lips, but gentleness filled the touch of his fingers on my cheek. "Everything else can wait until morning, though I will come check on her later. Until then, I am yours."

His hungry smile grew, though his touch remained sweet as he cupped my jaw and leaned in, rough voice filling the air between us. "Mine. That's what I like to hear, my lady."

Then he claimed my lips with a desperation I echoed, my hands flying up into his hair as we dove into each other's mouths. I stood on my tip toes, increasing the pressure so perfectly I thought I might faint with delight. Nor did he leave me alone to it, leaning down to meet the contact, one gloriously strong arm banding across my back to pull me closer. Hot, wet kisses were more delicious than anything I had ever tasted, our tongues exploring with a determination that reflected the passion we denied ourselves in South Carolina.

When he softened his grip and began to pull away I could not help a whine of complaint, earning a throaty chuckle. "Don't worry, Jaque, this is only a pause. But I've got dinner in the oven, and I've had enough of burning things for this lifetime. Let's get you fed, then we can get back to satisfying our other hungers."

Dinner? He made dinner? My brain could not handle the idea that he would go to such trouble. As his mouth made another feathery landing, I caught him, pouring my gratitude into the little nibble I gave his lower lip before I let him go. "Thank you."

He blinked repeatedly, which gave me a thrill to see my effect on him. In one week I had almost convinced myself I imagined the intensity to be mutual, but the proof shone in his heavy-lidded eyes. "Anything for you, my lady."

Those words would have felt empty from anyone else. But as he turned us toward the house, I believed them. After all, he continued to prove them with his actions, over and over again.

We walked as we had from our first date, moving together without awkwardness or hesitation. Soleil trotted ahead, leading the way up the walk. He opened the door, gesturing us in ahead of him, and I stepped into the comforting embrace of my home with actual tears in my eyes. The table had been set for two, one of my candles flickering in the centre beside a bowl of lavender roses. Rich scents came from the kitchen, prompting my stomach to protest the abuse it endured while we traveled. Even the healthiest fare to be found at a truck stop could not compare to the promise of a home cooked meal.

"I did not know you were a cook," I said dazedly as I turned to face him.

He pushed the door closed with a sheepish grin, so boyish in that moment I could almost see the child he must have been. "I can cook enough to keep myself fed, but I called in an expert for this. One of our knights, John, his wife is a chef, and she jumped in to help."

I smiled knowing his friends were involved. Such efforts implied a blessing, which counted much more heavily now that I knew the Company. Each had introduced themselves at the holiday party, making sure of my welcome, and embracing me warmly. Even the icy cool Alex had clapped me on the shoulder as he shook my hand, his smile much warmer than the false one he cast at his date when she cattily stepped in between us. As for John's wife, Caroline, she literally embraced me, folding me into her arms as if we were long lost sisters. That her loving care went into our meal made it all the more enjoyable.

"I shall have to thank her." I meant to step closer to him, to thank him as well. But the itch I ignored earlier returned with a vengeance, reminding me how badly I needed a shower. However much I wanted his attentions, I would feel much more comfortable if I were clean. "Can our meal wait a little? I want to wash the road off my body before we eat."

The itch went quiet as he stepped into my space, one hand on my hip as he leaned in to kiss my cheek. "Go hit the showers, champ. It'll keep just fine." Then he turned me toward the hall, swatting my butt to send me on my way. "But hurry. I'm hungry."

Though the contact on my rear held little sting, I still felt a zing which gave my reply a dark promise. "So am I."

Judging by the way his fists tightened, as if he held himself in place, he clearly understood the hunger I referenced had little to do with food. And with that delicious image to tide over my appetite, I took myself off to the bedroom to hunt for clean clothes, Soleil prancing daintily at my heels.

Much as I wanted to be back in Aaron's embrace, I lingered in the shower, grateful for the familiar surroundings. In Florida, I only had a cramped box to clean up in, but at home I enjoyed the bench to sit on while I shaved my legs. A full array of soaps and lotions were at my disposal, and I luxuriated in the chance to spoil myself a little. Once clean, and my hair toweled dry, I went into the bedroom to dress. Thanks to Aaron's thoughtfulness, the furnace was set on high, leaving the room uncomfortably warm if I meant to sleep later. But still damp from the shower, the heat felt divine as I slid back into clothes.

Wearing pyjamas occurred to me, either my fleecy bottoms or the satin chemise I sometimes wore, but much as I wanted to enjoy those things with Aaron, I chose to redress entirely. I did gamble enough to put on one of my nicest sets of underthings, hoping he would be peeling off all the layers I wore, and a soft cotton camisole that soothed my over-sensitized skin. The jeans I pulled on were my oldest pair, thin in places from constant wear. Then I reached for my favourite cardigan, the one I wore on our first date, wanting the comfort. While I felt reasonably sure our night would end back in this bedroom, the layers would give me some armor if he decided we were moving too fast again.

That thought made me wince, even as I pressed a hand to my chest, holding in the heart I wanted to give him. I both loved and hated his carefulness, feeling so cherished, yet so guilty. Was I moving too quickly again? Did my constant want predestine us toward an inevitable burn out? Fear welled up, pushing at my happiness, making my hands hasty as I dragged a brush through damp hair in an effort to calm myself. The reflexive motion helped steady my nerves, as did the memory of his expression when I left him in the kitchen. By the time the tangles were removed a sense of calm overcame me. I would let him set our pace, no matter the speed. Maybe then, we would have a chance at something lasting.

As I walked back out to the living area, he turned away from the stove with a warm smile that practically begged to be devoured. When he pulled out my chair so I could sit, I thought I might melt from the way his hands smoothed over my shoulders as he bent to place a kiss on the top of my head. "This is going to sound cheesy, but I missed the smell of your shampoo."

At that, I did melt, my heart puddling in my chest, the warmth trickling lower to join all that want I struggled with. As he moved back into the kitchen to dish our food, I bit my lip, want increasing at the rear view of his muscular body. Though his brother wore a broader frame, carrying more bulk, Aaron's athletic shape appealed to me far more.

"Please, be as cheesy as you like," I offered as he worked over the stove, then turned back to deliver my dinner. Though I reached out intending to pull him down for a quick kiss, thought derailed at the familiar sight and scent of the food, my hand landing on his stomach in order to keep grounded. My voice came out as a choked whisper when I finally managed speech. "Oh, oh this is lovely."

"Jaque?" Clearly concerned, he crouched beside me, gathering my hand in his. "Did I screw this up?"

Oh, we were a matched pair with all our doubts and fears. That realization allowed me to find an unsteady smile as his calluses stroked back and forth over my knuckles. "No, my champion, you could have done no better if I planned this myself. Beef bourguignon is one of my favourite meals, so much a reminder of my childhood with Grandmere and Grandpere. Even the bread is toasted like she used to make it, and the memory grew achingly clear."

"I'm sorry," he offered, which strengthened my smile and tightened my grip on his hand.

"Is that not my line? And you would tell me there is nothing to apologize for." When the furrows in his brow lightened, I stroked his shaggy hair away and placed a kiss on the ones that remained. "Now, we should enjoy our meal before it grows cold. Caroline's work should not be wasted on my nostalgia."

Nor did the meal disappoint once Aaron ladled his own portion and returned to the table. The savoury herbs in a rich wine and beef broth satisfied both stomach and heart. I sopped up every last drop with an extra slice of toasted bread, then leaned back into my chair to watch Aaron finish his last few bites, not at all self-conscious to have finished before him. Such trivial things bothered me little, not after being raised into adulthood by men. Besides, then I could appreciate the play of emotions across his features, moments so dear to me after our time apart. When he pushed his bowl away with a satisfied groan, my lips tipped up in amusement.

"You know, I worried when she brought that big cast iron pot over." He wiped his mouth with a napkin before continuing, revealing a tight edge to the corner of his smile when he met my eyes. "My mom uses something like it to make pot roast, and I swear, it's like eating a salt lick made of cardboard. Thank God Caroline is much more gifted in the kitchen."

A twist of sadness made my contentment taste slightly bitter, knowing he had so many unpleasant memories with his family. While I would have loved to take them away, to salve the hurts, all I could offer were new happinesses to balance them. "I am grateful as well. I have such beautiful memories attached to this recipe, and to share this with you adds another."

Pushing to my feet, I stretched from toes to fingertips, trying to shake off the stiffness left over from the drive. Sluggishness persisted as I settled onto my heels again, but I forgot it when I looked down into Aaron's eagle sharp eyes. The want that I ignored during our meal roared back to life, like an incoming thunderstorm that blackened the horizon with its power. I did not weigh the risks, or worry over the future, only responded to the swell of emotion between us. "Perhaps you would care to make some other memories?"

He sat forward in his seat, bracketing my waist with his hands as he looked up, and I gulped down a breath at the potential in the air. "Oh, we've got plenty of memories to make tonight, Jaque, but I'm still not hurrying. If I'm not mistaken, I volunteered to give you a massage."

Choking back a laugh, I raked both hands through his hair, letting my nails run over his scalp. His eyes closed, and his nostrils flared as his grip moved up my ribcage. More of me ached to be touched, but I kept to tenderness, cherishing every moment. "If that is your attempt at seduction tonight, I am afraid I might fall asleep before you get very far."

His eyes flew open, studying me intently before letting go of my waist. I had no time to grumble an objection as he immediately reached for my cardigan, slowly sliding it off my shoulders. "Liar. You're as buzzed on me as I am on you. But I still want to help you relax for a bit, before we hit the bedroom."

Shivering with a surfeit of feeling, I could hardly deny him, letting go of his hair so he could tug the sweater down my arms. Gooseflesh rose as he tossed the garment on my recently vacated chair, then reversed the caress of the cashmere, his calluses tracing up the line of muscle in my forearms. Which left me wholly at his mercy when his thumbs made firm circles in the tender skin at the bend of my arm, soothing the ache of loading my trailer and several days' worth of driving both Lyric and the truck.

"Aaron," I breathed his name out so softly, even I could barely hear it. My eyelashes fluttered wildly as he continued his ministrations, working his way along the muscles until every bit of tension dissipated. When he took one of my hands in both of his and began to massage my palm, my knees buckled, making me sway enough that I had to put my free hand on his shoulder to remain upright. He could not know how lovely that felt, when my hands worked so hard every day. They needed to be soft enough to have whispered conversations with Lyric's mouth, then strong enough to shift carriages, which I carried a good deal of pride over. But no one had ever given my hands such undivided attention, and when he lifted my palm up to place a kiss in the middle of it, I could barely remain upright.

"I need to sit, Aaron. My head is spinning." A half-truth, I admit, since my heart had joined hands with my head for a merry game of ring around the rosy. Both were giddy with joy when he guided me backward a step so he could stand, his hands anchored on my hips.

Soleil looked up from her bed beside the TV, but promptly forgot us once she realized we did not carry food. Aaron guided me onto the sofa, then knelt, the hands on my waist sliding down to massage the outside of my thighs. His grip felt divine, so powerful, so controlled, and his very avoidance of the inside of my thighs made me squeeze them together, needing some kind of pressure.

"Hey now, that kind of defeats the purpose," he teased carefully as he eased my knees apart again and moved between them so he could reach me for a kiss. When I tried to scoot closer, to deepen the kiss, he pulled back, and I whined my displeasure. He quieted my objection with a sympathetic softness around his mouth, and another long caress of my thighs, thumbs pressing deeply into the softer flesh toward the inside. Not quite where I wanted him, but my muscles were too occupied with turning into putty for me to raise any objection. "Just wait, Jaque. I promise I won't leave you wanting, but I really want to do this for you. Let me take care of you."

Not that I could muster an ounce of power to deny him as he worked over my other hand, my body melting into the deep cushions as if I meant to become a part of the furniture. A peaceful lassitude filled me up, though I never once felt sleepy as I watched through half-closed eyes while he worked on my calves. No, I reached a zen-like state of waiting, his touch sensitizing me one portion at a time. He reduced me to groans of delight, rough calluses giving added friction as he pressed into the arch of my foot.

Once both legs were tended, he leaned forward and pulled my upper body out of the cushions, guiding my forehead to lay at the crook of his neck. He smelled wonderful, like a deep forest, yet not piney. Something less astringent, and a little ancient that I drew deep breaths of as his hands slid beneath the edge of my camisole to trace the line of my spine.

"Is this okay, Jaque? Or would you rather I stayed over the shirt?"

Oh so careful, my Aaron, though I looked forward to breaking down those barriers between us with a good deal of relish. I turned my head just enough to be sure he could hear me, adoring the soft feel of often washed cambric against my cheek. "You are welcome to remove it entirely, if it would be more convenient."

"We'll get there soon, my lady, but for the moment, this is enough."

His fingertips dug into my flesh with intent, as if he could excavate the tightness that came from sitting in the truck for so long. Concentrating on every breath, the endorphins did their work as I relished the flex and release of his thighs beneath my hands. Keeping them still took an effort of will, though the warm denim felt lovely against my palms. Were I not turned on more completely than I had ever been, I might have even dozed off as threatened.

Instead, I felt the electric sting of his lips when he pressed them to my shoulder. I reveled in the power in his body as he gathered me against his chest and stood up. And I sighed like a truly love-struck fool when he whispered the kind of sweetness that guaranteed him my heart.

"Do you want to go check on your girlfriend before I monopolize your attention?"

Shaking my head emphatically, I kissed the edge of his jaw, wiggling my arms out from between us so I could embrace him properly. "No, I am all yours for the moment. I usually go out right before midnight, if that is okay?"

"You mean I have to let you out of your bed later? That's going to be difficult, you know," he teased before nipping at my lips with his own. "But I'll do my best."

"I surely hope so," I answered, stepping back enough that I could watch his response for the truth. "As your best has already knocked the rest of my dating life completely out of the park, you have created high expectations." Then I moved out of his arms, snagging his hand as I moved the few steps toward Soleil's little kennel built into the end table. She dragged her feet with enough dramatics that I smiled, ruffling her full mane as she stepped inside. Once I had her secure, I looked back at Aaron with a saucy grin. "Now, where were we?"

"I believe you were about to take me to bed," he replied, play and passion both giving his answer depth.

My fingers tightened around his when I took my first step toward the hall, as if I feared he might let go. But he held on just as tightly, and never looked away as we moved toward the next stage in our relationship.

Aaron

As Jaque led me down the short hallway to her room, I drew in a deep breath trying to calm the roar in my chest. Restraint wasn't something I exercised very often, and every cell in my body wanted to race ahead. But that inhale filled my senses with Jaque, her particular blend of flowery dusk calming me enough to regain control.

When she paused at the threshold, I stepped in close, my hand hooking around her hip to press us together. "You smell divine."

Her feminine chuckle whispered in the darkness, and I heard a slight click, followed by soft light from the bedside lamp. "The way you hold me feels divine."

I took our linked hands and wrapped them around her waist, tucking my chin into the feather softness of her hair. We walked forward, together, each step taking us deeper into a surprisingly feminine sanctuary. The king bed frame was constructed of silver metal scrollwork that reminded me of vines. The mattress was covered in a Heather purple blanket that looked incredibly soft, with more kinds of pillows than I knew existed piled at the head. The lamp cast a lavender hue over everything, from the chest of drawers covered in a variety of hat boxes, to an old-fashioned vanity that reminded me briefly of my mother.

But I shoved that memory away, too enthralled by the warmth in my arms to let it intrude. "Who knew my woman was so girly behind closed doors?" I teased carefully, releasing her hip to pull the hair away from her neck. She tipped her head back immediately, a mysterious smile enchanting me just before I put my lips on the soft skin just below her ear.

God, I loved the way she trembled as I traced the curve of her neck down to her shoulder, nuzzling over the thin strap of her camisole. Even better, her hand came up to anchor in my hair, encouraging me each step of the way.

"Aaron." She said my name like a sigh, the sound fluttering over my heart like the most delicate of butterflies. "I do adore your mouth. Such lovely words come out of it and it gives the sweetest of kisses."

Oh, how I looked forward to putting said mouth all over her tonight. No more waiting, no more longing, just satisfaction for both of us. But I wanted to drag it out until sweetness wasn't enough, until we were both frantic with need.

"I've barely begun, my darling." I teased again, before gently biting the tendon that ran between her neck and shoulder. She arched against me, the pleasure so acute as to border on painful, but I rode it out sucking on her honey sweet skin.

"Jaqueline, I've never been so enchanted," I whispered against the ruddy blush I left to mark my place. And it was totally true. She felt like magic in my arms, something I sorely lacked in my life.

The hand sandwiched between mine and her belly came loose from its restraint. But it didn't go far, landing over mine to encourage further exploration, my palm gliding beneath her silky top to explore the soft skin of her belly. "Ah, greedy woman."

"Only for you," she responded huskily, not knowing how that simple statement knocked me off balance. "I have never wanted anyone as much as you, my champion."

God, what value she placed on me. Not long ago, so much expectation would have felt claustrophobic, stifling. Now, I wanted to live up to it.

"I promise you, Jaqueline, tonight is ours. Nothing will stop me from fulfilling the potential we've both been fighting." I traced her lowest rib with my thumb, emboldened by the way her back flattened against my stomach.

"God, woman, you're going to drive me crazy." I groaned as my arms tightened to bring her impossibly closer, but I froze when she went still. "Jaque, are you still with me?"

"Yes," she said, but it came out thin and strained. "I'm s..."

The apology cut off, but I couldn't even smile at the effort she made to silence it. I turned her around so I could see her face, the usually full cheeks gaunt with worry, then sat down on the edge of the bed so I could pull her between my knees. Looking up into her eyes, I hunted for a hint that might guide me through. "What did I do wrong, Jaque? Tell me, so I can fix it."

She flinched, but bravely kept eye contact. "You cannot fix everything for me, Aaron, no matter how much your noble heart wants to." Finger combing my hair, as if the motion soothed her as much as me, she continued. "Only I can fix it. And the best way is to make new memories with you."

For a second, I lost perspective in the kiss she bent down to deliver. But my heart refused to leave her hurting, so I pulled away with a gut-wrenching groan, tugging her hands from my scalp to press them to my chest. "No, darling woman, not this time. Tell me, please?"

In the diffused light, I almost missed her blush, which intrigued me a great deal. What could such a graceful, gracious woman have possibly done to be embarrassed over? "Come, Jaqueline, the sooner you give over, the sooner I can return my attention to your gorgeous body." I taunted playfully, lifting her hands so I could kiss along the knuckles.

Her eyes went soft, her lips parting in such a way that I longed to kiss them, but I stayed still. I'd waited this long, a few minutes more wouldn't hurt too much. Baser parts of me emphatically disagreed with that assessment, not with a warm willing woman standing in front of us.

"I am embarrassed to admit to a tendency to drive men crazy," she blurted out, shame making her pull against my grip on her hands, but I kept her close. While the thought of anyone else touching her tasted like ash, I wanted to know what I was in for. "When you said as much, I know you did not how you meant it negatively, but I grew scared I might do the same to you."

I frowned, confusion muddling my response time. Nothing about her had ever struck me as crazy making. Unless you counted wanting her so badly my brain was slowly caving in on itself. "I don't understand, Jaque. You're one of the nicest people I've ever known, with a huge heart. Nothing about you could ever make me crazy."

"No, no." She sighed heavily and tried once more to step away, but quit at the slightest tightening of my grasp. "English is not my best for this explanation. I am sure there must be a word for this, but I do not know it." Her lips twisted as she hunted for words. "I am, as best I can say, a fan of sex."

Okay, that startled a chuckle out of me. "So am I. How is this a problem?"

Frowning deeply, she finally stepped in close, but it put my chin right into her glorious cleavage. Temptation assaulted me with a club, and though my muscles strained, I kept still.

"I am not proud of this, and I understand if you don't want to stay, but I must confess it all." Guilt and fear narrowed her face. "When he said I was driving him crazy, he meant because I wanted more sex. And he did not. I wanted more than he did."

The seriousness of her speech that made me think past the grand prize-winning party going on below my belt. Now, I wanted to pummel her ex-lover for more than just outright jealousy. Clearly, he was a moron. Sure, maybe having such a willing, responsive, enthusiastic lover would have over faced him. But for him to make her feel bad for it made my knuckles burn with the need to hit something.

"I will restrain myself, I promise," she offered, a hint of panic in the words pulling me from my thoughts.

"No, Jaqueline, that won't do at all," I said, releasing her hands so mine would be free. "I can't let you feel guilty over something that should be cherished." Right back to the edge of her shirt I went, determined to chase away the shadows dimming her desire. "There was no fault on your part. He simply wasn't a good match for you."

"But, I wanted too much, Aaron. I always want too much," she said plaintively, though the last word shot up an octave when I pressed both thumbs gently into her belly button and massaged outward.

"No, my darling," I soothed as I lifted the hem to expose a sliver of her belly. Kissing along the trembling skin I exposed, I looked up into her liquid gaze and spoke with every ounce of conviction I owned. "You weren't too much. He simply wasn't enough."

At that, she wrapped her arms around my head, and I buried my nose in the warmth and scent of her skin. When I laid her down a few minutes later, I made it my mission to be enough for her.

Jaque

Soleil's whine worked its way into my subconscious, bringing with it a slow blooming awareness. Warmth came first, both of my body and the air I breathed. My nose tickled as I inhaled, and I drew in the heady scent of my own desire and a hint of musk that made me want to bury my nose deeper. My limbs felt sluggish, but not in a drained way. More of a satiated heaviness. And then I remembered, in a quick flash of input that had me blinking my eyes at the powerful influx of feeling. Aaron.

Aaron blew my old doubts away with kisses and caresses. But after the long drive and his devoted attentions, I am afraid I yielded to exhaustion before we reached a mutual conclusion. Noble soul that he is, he soothed me to sleep, cuddled in his arms.

Soleil whined again, this time more urgently, and I silently begged her for just a few more minutes. I wanted to revel in his embrace, to enjoy the feel of his bare leg tucked between mine. Then I forgot to breathe. Last thing I recalled, he still wore jeans. Then I flushed all over, embarrassed to have left him hanging. Or had I? I could not recall, which left me panicky.

Despite that, I still did not want to move. I wanted to linger in his strong arms, listen to his heartbeat. I gloried in the memories I did have, of the way he chased my pleasure down until it was too sated to run. Surely, I knew passion before, but never with the sort of thoroughness that made my body heavy even now. And three orgasms! Three! Who even did such things?

Of course, my core throbbed, reminding me of the single hunger that had gone unsatisfied. I shifted my hand so it could run down his chest, determined to remedy the lack. But Soleil whined again, this time more plaintively, and I groaned. She could wait no longer.

As I gently extracted myself from his embrace, Aaron grumbled and rolled to his back, throwing an arm over his eyes. Though I wanted to take a moment to study the physique it exposed, the needs of my tiny companion superseded my own at the moment.

Tying the belt on my robe, I shuffled down the hall until the light left on in the living room could guide the way. Soleil danced from side to side on her front feet, then spun a circle as her whining increased in volume.

"Shush, my little cabbage, we have company. You must not wake him."

She quieted, lifting her nose in the air, likely catching the scent of Aaron and the effect he had on my body. But the instant I opened the door of her crate, she shot for the dog door without a backward glance, and I sighed under the weight of guilt. Judging by her speed, she had been trying to wake me for some time.

Taking advantage of her potty break, I slipped my bare feet into an old pair of wellingtons for a short trip to the barn, Yes, I know decency should have dictated I at least wear pants, but there lay the glory of having my own place. No one would see me running around in my bathrobe except the horses, and they did not care what I wore, as long as I fed them on time.

With only Lyric currently in residence, I had even less to worry about as I let myself outside, the cold tightening my bare skin. My mare was not the only one to prefer winters to summers, and I relished the sensation of pulling the brisk air deep into my lungs to cool myself off as I crossed the gravel drive to the barn. I had left the aisleway lights on, which aided me now as I peeked around the edge of Lyric's stall door. She stood hip shot, posture entirely relaxed from head to tail. Only her tidy ears and soft eyes moved as she took me in. I stepped fully into the opening so she could see me better, and my heart filled with love as she moved forward to greet me with a soft brush of her muzzle.

"I do not mean to disturb, *mon tresor*," I murmured, cupping the strong bones of her jaw so she could lean into the touch. "But I am glad to find you content."

She drew deeply of my scent, taking in the familiar and the changes with easy aplomb. No, my girls knew me, neither of them surprised to find me well loved. But I wondered if they could feel the difference between before and now, how deeply this affected me, how fundamentally terrified I felt. But then, I laughed softly at my own foolishness. Of course they knew. Lyric in particular made me own my fears in order to be her partner, to be honest with myself because she knew the truth. Only one fear remained, one that I pushed to the background over and over. Thankfully, she allowed it to stay in the shadows, tolerant of my flaws.

As if to reinforce that acceptance, she stepped close, hooking her head over my shoulder to pull me into an embrace. Rubbing my cheek against her neck, I ran my hands through her thick mane, the short strands wild from her earlier roll. More than likely, my own hair looked the same after such stimulating evening activities. "Thank you, *ma fille*. Now, you rest. I shall see you in the morning."

She watched me leave, the deep well of her calm still lingering in my chest as I crunched along the gravel. As always, she brought me completely into the present, no worries for the future, no cares about the past. What would come, would come, and we would face it down as we had everything else in our lives.

As I let myself back inside and kicked off my rubber boots, Soleil skittered through the kitchen, almost losing traction on the tile. I laughed softly at her antics as she snatched up a stuffed mouse from beside the sofa and ran a fast lap around the coffee table.

"No, no, *sucre*, we have hours until dawn." I bent down to hold open the door of her crate. "Come, back to bed."

Horrified, I watched her shoot down the hall, realizing my mistake. Bed meant my bed, and I did not know how the current occupant would take to such an intrusion. As I scurried after her the silence frightened me as much as a sudden bout of curses would have. But when I cautiously peeked in the dimly lit door, my heart warmed.

Aaron sat up against the headboard, Soleil crouched on his legs as he offered to throw her mouse. Her tail never stopped wagging, even as they both looked over at my entrance. "Well, at least she isn't growling at me anymore." He smiled sheepishly and shrugged his shoulders, tossing the mouse to the foot of the bed. Soleil pounced on it, shaking it ferociously and gnashing her teeth. "She's quite fierce."

"Very. And while I'm pleased to see the two of you getting along, I must admit to a bit of jealousy." I smiled gently to take the sting from the words, and tugged teasingly at the belt of my robe. "I really had other plans for this morning."

His eyes went from heavy with sleep to wide and dark, and he threw back the blanket to invite me closer. "Me too, Jaqueline."

I visually feasted on him, taking my time to study every inch of exposed skin. The fact that he still wore his boxers eased my heart, knowing he had not gotten too far ahead of me. Now that Soleil had been taken care of, and I knew Lyric was well, I could be selfish. I did not even look at my dog, simply snapped my fingers. "Soleil, down."

She reluctantly took her toy and dropped off the other side of the bed, and I heard her scratching around in her nest of blankets on the floor. And I climbed back into Aaron's arms, my fallen heart as eager to be held as my needy body.

Aaron

A few hours later, I woke to an unexpected weight on my hip. The woman in my arms shifted, her warm skin lulling me to stay still, but the weight moved and I peeked over the edge of the blanket. Soleil looked back at me, dark eyes reflecting even the low light in the room, the uncanny stare completely unnerving.

"Hello, little one," I murmured roughly, effort and exhaustion thickening my throat. When she did not move, I cautiously snuck a hand from beneath the covers, encouraged to see her tail wag as I reached out. She sniffed my hand with all the deliberation of a queen inspecting her army, and when her tongue darted out to rasp over my knuckle, I felt like I'd just received an accolade.

Her thick coat felt downy soft as I pet her for the first time, but the moment didn't last long, as Jaque moved against me. Soleil dropped back off the bed with a barely discernable huff, and I focused on my lady as she wiggled around to face me, her body brushing against mine in the most alluring way.

"Aaron, are you awake?" Heavy lidded eyes told me she was barely awake herself, and I reveled in the softness of the moment.

"If we're still sleeping, I'm currently in the middle of one of the best dreams I have ever had," I murmured, pulling her hand up off my chest so I could kiss her wrist. She smiled from her eyes outward, and slowly leaned in. I met her kiss with hopeful tenderness, wanting the feelings in my chest to be real. I tasted more than passion on her lips as I rolled to my back and pulled her over me with a hand in her hair, but also companionship and a strength I wished were mine.

"Ah, perhaps we are still dreaming," she offered. If we were, I wanted to dwell there, to drown in her sweetness and never breathe the bitter scent of loneliness again. Doubt tried to remind me I'd loved before and failed, but Jaque stole it with another exquisite kiss.

"You are a vixen, my darling," I groaned, as we drew back to breathe, my arms linking across her back to keep her in the moment with me.

"You drive me to it, *mon amant*," she responded, leaning down to steal another kiss. "We are matched, meant to be together this way."

I pressed my agreement into the kiss, losing my worries, my fears in the velvet stroke of her tongue. Even first thing in the morning, she tasted familiar. Like something from my youth that I couldn't remember, but had always been searching for.

"Ah, *mon amant*." Her whisper brushed softly over my lips, a glorious sensation, but it could not distract me from a sense of deprivation. In the aftermath of our lovemaking, she had called me her love, and I wanted that back. We could have laid there forever, sharing the same air, our hearts beating in time. But I took a risk and broke the quiet.

"You called me *mon amour* before, Jaqueline."

I saw her face pale before she turned her head away and hid against my shoulder, shrinking in a way I instinctively hated. When she moved as if to get away, I tightened my arms in panic, though I did not want to keep her against her will. Again, I'd done the wrong thing, and I struggled for a way beyond my mistake.

"I'm sorry, I shouldn't have said anything."

At the apology, she cautiously turned to meet my eyes, the tears in them crashing against me like a tidal wave. "You are not upset?"

I frowned, smoothing a hand up her back. "Why would I be? I consider it a great honor to have such a glorious woman call me her love, though I cannot imagine what I did to deserve such a reward."

Her gasp of surprise was eclipsed only by the delight that came on its heels. Dashing her tears away, she smiled more brightly than the sun beginning to peek through the curtains. "You do not think me too fast? Or forward?"

Winding a finger in the midnight dark of her hair, a few strands of the twilight purple in the mix, I slowly pulled her down so she could read the truth in my eyes. "No, *mon amour*. I am lost in you."

"Oh, Aaron," she choked out, before capturing my next breath. I found peace, even as she stormed over me, half sobbing and half laughing as we kissed. "You truly say the most beautiful things."

"You make me feel the most beautiful things, Jaqueline," I answered, peppering her cheeks and chin with playful kisses. Her smile was radiant as she pushed herself higher, offering her neck up for the same treatment. As we tangled in the sheets once more, I put a prayer into every touch we shared that this time love would prove stronger than blood.

Jaque

We spent an entire day together, Aaron lending a hand with the chores I usually would have accomplished alone. They all went more quickly for the help, despite the fact that we often paused to share a kiss, or even a brief embrace. Never once did he pull away from the work, or from my touch, both blessings of unimaginable proportions.

Once my fancy trailer had been unloaded, I parked it behind the carriage house and switched over to the steel stock trailer. No longer fashionable or particularly pretty, the old girl was nonetheless quite safe. Built extra tall for the draft horses, partitions inside allowed me to haul the larger carriages for my commercial work. Aaron already knew its foibles after hauling me back and forth several nights during my last busy season, and we had it hitched in mere minutes.

As we drove over to the farm where my remaining carriage horses had been staying, he spoke of how he would like to go over my truck again, to be sure it would not fail me in my travels. I offered to come look over Byzantine, to see if I could find any physical reasons for the changes in his mood. Yes, things were getting better for them, but he said the gelding still ground his teeth while being girthed up and hunched his back after being mounted. Such signs pointed to discomfort and would be a significant roadblock to their continued improvement.

Aaron balked a little, defending his brother's care of the horses in a way I could only consider admirable for his loyalty. "I don't want Bart to think I don't trust him. He's the best horseman I've even known, except for his grandfather."

"Nor am I discounting his knowledge, I assure you." I touched his elbow as I drove, still wanting contact, though the painful edge of need had been blunted. "But we all have such vastly different experiences, and if mine can save you a bill from the vet, then all to the better."

His hand covered mine, though I never looked away from the road with all the morning traffic. "I appreciate it, don't get me wrong. But I want to ask his opinion before I say yes, if that's alright."

"Of course." Pulling my hand away so I could make the next right, I threw him a smile as my head turned his way. "I do not want to cause trouble."

"Oh, I don't think it's any trouble, Jaque." His tone smoothed out and warmth skated up my back as if he were caressing me, though we were not touching. "He'll probably be thrilled, and Jo will skip down the aisle to welcome you in. She's been much too smug about us getting together." Amusement coloured that last statement, and I found my lips widening in agreement. Jo had caught on well before Aaron had, I felt sure of it.

"But I need to ask. Being partners with my brother makes every decision a little more complicated, and he's just now getting back to himself after some trouble. I want us to stay strong, not undermine him, even if I think I know what he'll say."

I could say nothing against that. His level of commitment to his family only made me love him more, giving me hope that he could be so committed to me. In most of my relationships, I had been an afterthought. Someone to spend time with at night, or on a weekend, but rarely brought into the circle of a lover's regular life.

Once I pulled around a barn and parked beside a field, I reached for his hand. The sun-wrought wrinkles beside his eyes smoothed out as I gently kissed his rough knuckles, the thick joints a dichotomy against the rest of his handsomeness. Words came easily, without the slightest struggle, though I knew the risk in them. "It would seem you are not just my champion, Aaron, but a champion to all. For that, I love you more."

Our eyes never blinked as he pulled his hand back, bringing mine with it. With a reverence I could hardly warrant, much less comprehend, he kissed my knuckles in return. "And for that, I love you more."

You would think we might spend hours gazing into each other's eyes after finally saying such tender words, but a multicoloured tangle of dogs came spilling around the corner of the barn, preceding their owner. I looked away to gauge how much time we had before he reached us, and when I looked back, Aaron grinned, his eyes sharp enough to shave my nerves in the most delicious way. "Let's get this done. I'm having very private thoughts right now, and I can't make good on any of them until we're back at your place."

The instant he let go of my hand, I moved for the door. "You have no idea what you are in for, Aaron Drew."

"Maybe not," he replied calmly as he slid out the passenger side, our eyes meeting across the width of the cab. "But I'm looking forward to finding out."

Then we were swarmed by dogs, several trying to climb in the cab to see Soleil. She growled and snapped at a particularly forward border collie that shoved his head behind the driver's seat, settling once I pushed the dog back with my hip.

Aaron intercepted a giant white livestock guardian that shoved his paws in the door.

"Whoa there, now, big guy!" He collared the animal with an arm, ruffling its ears with the other hand as the dog attempted to lick his face.

A sharp whistle from their master got all of the creatures bounding to his side, giving us enough breathing room to close the doors. He sent the dogs back toward the house with a low command, most trotting off happily, except for the border collie, who slunk around the corner of the barn with mournful eyes. Aaron joined me, casually wiping off some of the white hairs that clung to his clothing as we approached our host.

Though a bit shorter than me, my farrier Dan was larger than life, eyes twinkling with enough mischief for a man a quarter of his age. The hand that clasped mine was even more work roughened than Aaron's but that did not surprise. He had at least twenty years on my boyfriend, and a lifetime of working under a horse to account for, not to mention a youth spent on the rodeo circuit.

"Jaquie, my girl! How's our mare doing?" He dragged me in for a hug that I returned in earnest, having missed his forthright company and horse-centric philosophy. Though I opened my mouth to reply as I stepped back from the embrace, he turned to greet Aaron with another outstretched hand. "Young man, nice to meet you. I'm Dan Craig, the farrier, the myth, the legend."

Aaron laughed easily, which earned him a deeply creased smile from Dan. "Sir, nice to meet you as well. I'm Aaron, Jaque's boyfriend."

Dan's gaze shifted to me as his smile grew. "Is that so? Well, it's about time you got yourself a proper chore boy, Miss Jaquie." Then lightning fast, he turned back to Aaron. "Glad to see there's a man out there smart enough to step up to the plate. If'n I were a younger man, I'd have courted her myself. There aren't many like our girl Jaquie."

My cheeks pinkened at the praise, though I'd heard it countless times before. Something in me shifted last night, my emotions living closer to the surface in the face of Aaron's love. "Ignore him, Aaron. He is a shameless flirt."

Aaron looked over at me, hand coming to rest on my hip as he drew me against his side. "Actually, sir, there's no one else like her. If I weren't so blind, I would have noticed that years ago."

That blatant declaration, his firm but gentle touch all combined, left my heart whispering 'For that, I love you more'. Which had my body stridently reminding me we should get home, where I could say such things. Though I returned Aaron's embrace, I looked back to Dan, his knowing eyes saying he could see right through me. The older man grinned with unrestrained glee when my cheeks went pink again.

"Dan, my apologies, I do not mean to rush you, but we have much to get done now that I am home. Where can we find the herd?"

"Aw, I saw them down by the creek crossing earlier. Give me a minute, we'll see if we can't rustle them up for you. No sense walking all that way." Then he turned toward the empty field and whistled a sharp, five note tune that echoed back from the far tree line.

On the next breeze, you could hear the rumbling of many hooves off to the south. We all turned to face the growing sound in time to see a mini mule crest the hill ears first, a mass of horses at her heels. They traveled along a twenty-foot-wide lane that ran all around the field, the track encouraging them to move about much as horses in the wild might.

"Bring 'em in, Baby Agnes!" Dan hollered at the little mule, encouraging them all to greater speed. Just behind Agnes came

Clint, my solitary pony, his half black, half white face lifted high to catch the wind. Two tall black geldings were in the middle of the bunch, shoulder to shoulder as they often were. No surprise that the half-blood Percheron brothers worked so well as a team. Then behind the entire lot, jogging slowly so as not to overtax herself, came the white-grey mare, Constance. She lived up to her name in so many ways, as reliable as the rising and setting sun.

Once she entered the main corral beside the barn, Dan swung the gate closed, and we gave the herd a chance to settle at the hay feeders scattered haphazardly around the area. Constance selected the nearest one, the other horses calmly accepting her presence as she never brought drama with her. Nor would she tolerate it, which meant the brothers avoided her like the plague. That did not stop them from harassing everyone else as they waded from feeder to feeder, pushing other horses out of their way by dint of size alone. When they moved toward Agnes, intending to bully the tiny grey faced matriarch of Dan's herd, I stepped into action. Climbing up on the bottom rail of the board fence so I could hang my arms over the top, I barked at them. "*Garçons, soyez poli!*"

Four black ears swiveled my way immediately, the command far too familiar for them to ignore. Many times, I had used it on the streets, in the barn, and beside the trailer, to discourage them from pawing or messing about with each other's harness. Cobalt, the sweeter of the two, waded through the herd just ahead of his brother, Corbin, so he could reach me first. Do not think his motivation entirely affectionate. Cobalt knew how to play the cute game and hoped he might get a sugar cube from me before his brother pushed him off.

But I fed neither one, content to pat their necks and look them over. "They were not too much trouble, Dan? You have kept them up very nicely."

"Naw, I kept them apart from the herd for a couple days, let them all get to know each other over the fence. Everybody stayed pretty reasonable, except for Clint."

I heard the faint annoyance in his voice, something that tended to happen with anyone who knew the pony well. The little monster lifted his head up at the sound of his name, and I groaned to see him standing right in the middle of one of the big square feeders. Aaron started to laugh, but choked it off when I crossed my arms and glared at the brat. Clint earned his name for the size of his personality, and when you squared off with him, he always regarded you with a lifted brow that asked you if you felt lucky.

You might ask why I kept the animal, but I can honestly tell you there were few animals on the planet that would take better care of a new driver. He knew his job, had faced down aggressive dogs half his size, stood stock still in front of a train crossing, and managed himself perfectly in traffic. Better still, as your skill increased, so would his antics. This made for capable, confident and solid drivers, making him priceless to me as a lesson horse.

"Yes, he is a trial. I apologize." Then I looked around at the rest of the herd, finding a familiar shape missing. My heart panged with worry as I looked to Dan again. "Where is Oscar?"

The rough boned standardbred came to me for some retraining after Dan rescued him. The gelding had been an absolute delight to work with. Gentlemanly in all things, and content to drive down the trail for hours once he understood he no longer needed to hurry. I hated to think the winter had taken him.

"Don't you fret, Jaque, that fella is living in high cotton now." Dan grinned, his earlier displeasure over Clint forgotten in the face of Oscar's success story. "He's living with one of my clients out near Elizabethtown, in a big pasture with a couple minis. She wanted something that could pull the whole family, and he walked off the trailer like he owned the place, making sweet with the grandkids. Probably one of the best placings I've ever had, thanks to you."

I blew out the breath I held, and headed for the barn to fetch halters, both men falling in behind me. "Good. He deserves spoiling after all the races he finished. Time to slow down and smell the flowers."

Dan kept all of the horse's halters just inside the main door, each with their own hook and nameplate. Fully half of the barn served as hay storage, while the remainder had been reimagined into one large communal space that the horses shared in inclement weather. He did not believe in stalling horses separately, unless absolutely needed, so they lived as a herd, as nature intended.

We were derailed from our objective as an unusually fluffy and vocal cat jumped up onto the counter beside the tack room door. He stared at Aaron with an uncanny regard, as if they knew each other, though Aaron moved to step wide around him. The dark grey animal meowed insistently, reaching out to catch at Aaron's jacket with an impressive set of claws.

"That's Boris. Sorry about that," Dan said as he unhooked the cat and shooed it away. "Hope he didn't do any damage. He got dumped out here last month, and is a fine mouser, but the cats I already have in the house won't let him come in."

"No, that's alright. It's just a barn coat." Aaron answered as he took the halter I handed him, but I noticed he looked toward the hay stacks where the cat stood vigil, staring down with an unblinking regard. "I didn't know cats were like that. We only ever had ferals where I grew up."

As we turned back to the corral Dan chuckled and clapped Aaron on the shoulder, having to reach up a bit to manage it. "Young man, cats are like women. Just when you think you've got 'em figured out, another one will come along and blow everything you thought you knew completely to hell."

I fought a grin to listen in on the discourse of men, well familiar with it after being raised on the farm and the airfields. Though my grandmother had guided me toward my femininity, men had helped me find my strength, pushed me to succeed. No matter how much I adored being a woman, I would always find comfort in the company of the rougher sex.

The horses loaded easily, all except Clint, who sat back on the lead like a world class jackass. If we gave him to a child, he would have climbed on as sweetly as pie, but he loved to test anyone who had a reasonable chance of outsmarting him. In this case, he well knew that I hated to argue, and I believe he only did it to be sure I had a candy in my pocket. The very instant I crinkled the treat, he stepped onto the trailer as if it were all his idea.

On the ride home Soleil whined and paced several times, looking through the back window of the truck. I saw nothing in the rearview mirror to concern her and discounted the behaviour to her sensitivity. Sometimes, the smallest things could upset her. If I so much as relocated a piece of furniture in the house, she would circle and growl suspiciously, daring it to move again.

Lyric whinnied as we drove alongside the pasture, though not to greet the familiar horses. No, she whinnied for me, far more interested in my company than theirs. I had left in the trailer without her, an offense that could hardly be borne. Cobalt called out to her, the trailer rocking as he began to paw, and I tapped the brakes to put him back on all fours. The poor gelding had a hopeless crush on her, though she ignored him with righteous disdain.

There were squeals and small dust ups as we turned the animals out together, sorting through the social niceties with alacrity. But they knew each other so well all it took was some posturing and a few wide kicks to remind everyone of their place in the hierarchy. Constance and Lyric ambled off toward a copse of naked trees once I begged my mare's forgiveness with a maple candy, and the boys took off for the far end of the field, Clint pinning his ears as he struggled to keep up with the longer legged brothers.

That left me free until we met Bart and Jo for dinner, so I turned toward Aaron with every expectation of returning to our earlier flirtations. He waited, hands tucked in the pockets of his jacket, looking for all the world like a rugged male model in an outdoor wear catalog. With a lovely shadow of beard on his jaw, his hair slightly windblown and the quiet confidence he had in his body, I felt a little outclassed for a moment. But then he smiled and reached out, pulling me against his chest, and I forgot my doubts. This man wanted me. He did not have to say a word to prove it; his actions spoke loudly enough for anyone to hear. And I would accept that gift for as long as he offered it, be it for now, or eternity.

Our kiss came together perfectly, and he kept things slow, as if we had all the time in the world. A fiction, as work would pull us apart the very next day, and soon he would be back on the road. But I pretended, let myself get absorbed in the way he cradled the back of my neck in his hand, in the way his hair twinned around my fingers as he cherished my mouth.

But I was shocked from the fantasy as he pulled back, my eyes flying open to watch him wince in pain. "Son of a bitch!"

I might have asked after his trouble if not for a loud meow, which made me look down to where the cat from Dan's wrapped his paws around Aaron's denim clad thigh. Irritation at the cat warred with my amusement over the predicament, but when the animal began to climb, I hurried to help before damage could be done.

"Here, *mon coquin*, none of that," I spoke soothingly as I unhooked the cat's nails one at a time, petting his ears to distract as I worked. Aaron stood stalk still, though his thigh trembled when the cat tightened his grip, but I saw anger in the jut of his chin. Hopefully, this Boris had not ruined my plans for the afternoon.

Once loose, I scooped the young animal up and headed for the trailer, looking to contain him until Dan could retrieve him. As I walked away, the creature set up a piteous yowling, struggling against my hold. Though larger in length and breadth than Soleil, he had the lanky frame of youth. Most of his bulk consisted of a plush coat that should have given me plenty to hang on to. No such luck, as the soft strands slid through my fingers as he twisted in my arms.

"Now, now, be still," I pled, walking faster before I lost my grip. My jacket would keep him from causing me harm, but it also allowed better traction, and for such a young creature, determination lent him strength. Soleil did not help, appearing from inside the barn to run circles around me, barking the alarm every time the cat cried. "Soleil, *maison!*"

Thank goodness she listened, heading for the house at a fast clip so I could focus on my burden. I had barely closed him into the tack room of the trailer, where he could do little harm to the contents during his imprisonment, when Aaron headed my way. He no longer looked angry, though a pained pinch appeared as he shook his leg out while he walked. Our stowaway pawed at the door, his meow shifting toward desperate when Aaron spoke.

"Is he okay?"

"Are you?" I asked, looking pointedly at his thigh. To my amusement, he pulled himself to his full height and put his hands on his hips.

"Jaque, he just startled me. If I were scared off by a few scratches, I wouldn't be trying to get you back in bed anytime soon."

Remembering our night of passion, my pulse throbbed insistently, but I ignored it for the moment. The score marks on his lower back both pleased and disconcerted me. "I am sorry, I am not usually moved to scratching."

He grinned then, something full of male pride and innuendo that left me ready to jump him right there in the middle of my driveway. "Oh good, I must be doing something right."

My body tensed, preparing to launch into his arms, but the cat interjected another complaint. This cry could have melted a heart of ice, piteously young and sad. Aaron looked to the door and frowned.

"Maybe we should take him inside with us? At least until we can get ahold of Dan? He sounds miserable."

Unable to resist Aaron's softness, or the cat's desperation, I opened the door and reached for the animal. He leapt into my arms, but did not linger, launching from my shoulder to reach Aaron. Upon landing his higher perch, the feline wound his tail around Aaron's neck and immediately began purring loud enough for three cats combined.

"Well, clearly, he wants you," I teased as I shut the trailer back up, unuttered laughter making the words dance.

"Clearly, so do you," Aaron shot back as we turned toward where Soleil waited for us on the porch.

"Took you long enough to notice," I returned breezily, as if my entire body did not hum with his provocation. As we walked inside, I threw a parting shot, warming it with a grin. "Now, if you will put your kitten down, I will make sure you never forget me."

He yanked me around by one arm, and I hit his hard chest with an oof of surprise. The cat jumped down onto the sofa with a hiss as Soleil leapt up to make his acquaintance, but I had no thought to look away from my lover. Eyes sharper than a thousand diamonds bored their way into my heart, so he could deposit his reply where I could never unearth it, even should I want to. "Jaqueline, a head injury could take my memory, a fall could take my life. But even in those two situations, my heart will never, ever forget yours."

From that point, I cannot recall the exact path that led us to the bedroom, but I can assure you it was littered with clothing and kisses so fierce my lips were tender when we sat down to dinner with Jo and Bart. Nor did I regret the lamp we broke in the hall, or the scratches I added to Aaron's collection. To have a partner who challenged me, supported me, and loved me as he did, I would have given anything. Well, except for Lyric and Soleil. A woman's girlfriends were sacred, after all.

Aaron

So, I guess this was how you got a cat. Dan said he couldn't come get the animal until the next day, but it only took one night to realize I'd miss his big block motor purr and the weight of him on my shoulder. Boris had followed me diligently over the past several days as I'd replaced the fuel filter on Jaque's truck. He watched from a bench in the aisleway as Jaque checked Byzantine for ulcers. Byzantine reacted violently when she palpated the pressure points, kicking out a warning that sent Boris scurrying away. When I moved to correct the gelding's rudeness, Jaque soothed us all with quiet words as she explained a course of treatment that would help. The next morning, Boris played in the grass as Jaque joined the Company in starting a fence line for a new pasture to the north of the arena. That same afternoon I left him in the house with Soleil while I played ballast when Jaque took Lyric out for a long trot at her neighbor's place. He just fit himself into my life with little drama.

Kind of like Jaque. No matter what she and I did, things went more smoothly when we were together. I didn't want to lose that, even for the coming weekend. We fit together like the gears of a high-end transmission, easily shifting from friends to lovers, then back again when needed. Even when I fired up my truck on Thursday night, needing to get back to the farm so I could pack for the weekend, she made it easier on me. No pouting, no guilt that I had to go, only kisses to remind me of what would be waiting when I got home again. When I finally made myself climb in the truck, she maintained a serenity I envied, picking up Boris so I could make my escape. We shared a rueful smile as the feline meowed noisily, and I put the big Ram in reverse before I could second guess my leaving them behind.

Muffled swearing made me stomp on the brakes before I'd gone more than a few feet. Jaque chased the cat as he ran away from her, concern puckering her brows together. Boris jumped up on the hood to stare at me and started caterwauling his complaints loud enough to be heard in the next county. I used it as an excuse to get out of the truck. But when I scooped him up, he latched on for dear life, which made Jaque smile again. Which meant I needed to kiss her one more time. Which led to a make out session that dislodged the cat and gave him time to jump in the cab. In the end, I drove off with a purring cat on the back of my seat, while I muttered under my breath about how he'd better not scratch the leather. And I had to stop for necessities on the way home.

Not that the farm felt like home anymore. I mean, I still liked my king-sized bed, but it felt too big without Jaque. I'd missed my ratty old recliner, even with its trick footrest and worn upholstery. I loved my blender the next morning as I made my first smoothie in several days. But the hardwood floors and granite counters that Bart and I put together with our own hands lost some of their shine. I missed the softness of Jaque's little house, from the plush carpet to the featherbed, even the dog hair that stuck to my socks.

Bart opened his mouth to say something about the cat when I walked up the stairs with the furry appendage wrapped around my neck, but I guess something in my expression made him reconsider. In an effort to keep the peace, I installed the little brat in my bedroom, making sure to show him the litter box I set up in the bathroom and the water dish by the dresser. He settled in pretty nicely, curling up at the foot of the bed while I packed my bags for the trip. But the instant I left the room and closed the door, the meowing started again. So, I let him follow me, never more than twenty feet away at all times as I hooked up our big trailer and loaded Byzantine's tack.

Jo quickly made friends with my shadow when we went back upstairs, pouring out a tiny bit of milk on a saucer I didn't even know we owned. But as soon as I dropped into my recliner, Boris joined me, curling up on the deep cushion behind my head to take a nap.

Apparently, cat purring is synonymous with general anesthetic, as the noise knocked me out harder than the time I had surgery on my knee. I woke to a darkened living room, my phone buzzing in my pocket, and my mouth fuzzier than the bottom of my socks.

"Hey there, Jaque," I mumbled as I answered the phone, sure it must be her at such a late hour.

"Who's Jack?"

My youngest sister's voice registered in a nanosecond, and I struggled upright in the recliner with a grunt. "Sorry, Darlene, what's up? Is William okay?"

"Will is fine, thank goodness, though he may shortly be a ward of the state." Her fierce tone made my eyebrows rise to the worthy heights Bart usually achieved as I leaned forward to prop my elbows on my knees. It took a lot to rile Darlene up, which meant this conversation was going to last a while. "I might have to kill Mom, and that'll put me in jail for a long time."

"Darlin', don't tell me another word," I cut in, using the nickname Dad gave her when she was little. It'd annoyed the hell out of her during her teenage years, which is why I'd resurrected it, but all these years later, it remained a special thing between the two of us. "I need plausible deniability."

At least she laughed, bleeding off some of her likely justifiable anger. "Okay, I'll zip my lip, but only if you'll let me vent. Otherwise, I can't be held responsible for my actions."

Then I laughed, because as the baby in the family, she'd rarely, if ever, been held responsible for anything. "Sure, you spill. I'm not going anywhere until the sun is up."

"Oh, good, that gives me at least five hours," she shot back, lightening the mood even further. "Should be just enough to get the job done."

In reality, she only used a half hour to blow off steam, understandably upset over our mother's continued attempts to get her to patch things up with her ex-husband. Mother had invited him for second Sunday supper, the once a month dinner our family was obligated to attend if they were in striking distance. When Dar complained, furious over the intervention, Mom had the audacity to claim Will needed to see his daddy. Ridiculous, considering the man hadn't made a single attempt to see his baby since the night he was born. I'd been there, witnessed his detached manner as I pointed out his son through the glass window of the nursery. Worse still, I'd listened to him answer his phone as he turned to leave, not even saying goodbye as he told his new girlfriend he was on his way home from the golf course. Even now, I couldn't wrap my brain or heart around such a reaction. His own child, born of what he professed to my sister to be love, his oath made into ashes when he turned to the arms of another woman. Yes, I claimed my share of weekend affairs, but how could a person feel even a tenth of the love I felt for Jaque, and violate the trust that came with that sort of intimacy?

My own anger simmered as she continued to pour out her grievances. Mom had also spread rumors that Darlene was seeing other men in an attempt to make her ex jealous. This backfired completely, rumors floating around town that Darlene was an easy lay, women whispering behind their hands while men leered at her as she walked down the street. Darlene laughed without humor at the very idea she might be entertaining men.

"Do any of them have the slightest idea what my life is like right now? I'm a full-time stay at home mom and I'm juggling online classes to finish my bachelor's degree so I'll be ready for a decent job by the time Will is old enough for preschool. My apartment looks like a storage unit and a toy store collided in a back alley, and those catty bitches are lucky I bother to shower before I go to the grocery store once a week. And Will hardly sleeps well enough for me to get a decent nap, so I hardly think I'm going to be getting any nookie anytime soon."

"Ugh, Dar, really? I'm your brother. The last thing I ever want to hear is you and nookie in the same sentence."

She scoffed at my discomfort and soldiered onward. "Will didn't come from a cabbage patch, big brother. And speaking of babies, don't you think it's about time you took the attention away from my failed marriage and found yourself a lady? Then she could start harping you about a grandchild to carry on the Drew name. Maybe the ulcer I'm developing would go away."

A goofy smile hit my lips as my brain ran away with the idea marrying Jaque and making babies, but Darlene cleared her throat after I forgot to answer her. "Hello, earth to big brother? Have you been hitting the beer again?"

My lips wrinkled in distaste as I thought back on that particular weakness. Pridefully restraining from anything stronger than beer, refusing to overindulge like my father, I'd dulled my emotions just the same. Hell, alcohol was probably all that kept me from running out of Christmas dinner with my family. But I had no call for it anymore and looking back at how blessed I'd been even then, any excuses for my behavior evaporated. If I wanted a future I couldn't let it be muddied by my past. "Nope. Maybe one a week since Christmas. Been too busy making a life for myself. As for the lady, that'll happen in its own time, so don't you worry over me."

"Well, thank sweet baby Jesus." Darlene threw a heap of Midwest on the colloquialism, and I laughed. Her talent on the pageant circuit had been impressions, and I still thought she could have been a damn good comedienne if she hadn't married so young. "But seriously, Aaron, what am I going to do? If Mom keeps this up, I'm either going to go on a murder spree or become a recluse. William doesn't need his mom to be the town cautionary tale."

Weight landed on my shoulders, no less heavy for being emotional and not physical. But I'd carried it for so much of my life that the ache felt familiar, and for my sister, I'd never shirk the load. Bethany and Courtney toed the line, bowing to my mom's rigid standards without complaint. As for me, I could piss on the county courthouse steps in broad daylight and Mom would make up a story about me having to put out a fire that would have burned down half the town. In her eyes, I was the culmination of her marriage to my Dad. She provided him with a son, the ultimate duty of any wife, and bragged on me with exaggerated pride all my life. The only real sins I ever committed in her eyes were the day I moved away, and every time I turned down a date with the beauty pageant contestants she threw my way.

"I'll talk to her, Darlin'. Probably not until Monday, since we've got a contract this weekend, but I'll talk to her. In the meantime, try out the recluse avenue. Who knows, you might like it?"

Another scoff hit my ears, a mumbled curse on its heels. "As if. You and I are way too social to hide away from the world. At least you found the good sense to escape this backwater when the chance presented itself."

Ah, that came off bitter. I wondered for a moment if she'd had a chance and not taken it. "Darlin', you just say the word, and I'll come get you myself. You don't have to stay if you don't want to.

Guilt shadowed her reply. "No. I can't leave, which you know better than anyone. I do want to be here, where it's familiar and safe, with family just down the road. I want Will to grow up going to the same schools we did, to ride the sun faded merry go round at the park and take his bicycle to school with the rest of the kids. But thank you for offering, Aaron. Just knowing it's an option lets me breathe a little easier."

We nattered on for a few more minutes, but then I heard the crackle of Will crying over the baby monitor and she begged off. After I disconnected the call, I checked my messages, finding three from Jaque, sent hours ago.

'Hope Boris settled in, Soleil misses him. Almost as much as I miss you.'

This was followed by a photo of the dog and Jaque curled up on the sofa, both wide eyed with sadness. I might have believed Jaque's were real if not for the slight curl on the corner of her mouth that told me she meant it to be a tease. What she followed it with nearly had me jumping back in the truck, despite the late hour.

'Would have loved to talk before you crashed, but with the workout schedule I have had you on for the last several nights, I understand if your stamina flagged. Will have to work on your fitness level when you get back, so you do not require such a serious recovery period.'

Yes, we'd set a wicked pace for ourselves since she arrived home, but no matter how many times we made love, I craved her even more. It wasn't ego that made me want to rush down the road and wake her up with urgent kisses and seeking hands. I had nothing to prove, even with her taunts. No, I wanted to make love to her until she understood exactly how perfectly matched we were, and that all her passion had found a home right beside mine.

But instead, I stood, picking up Boris when he meowed a sleepy objection as my sudden motion made the recliner rock. I crawled into my own bed, no longer comforted by its embrace, and stared at the ceiling until Boris curled up beside my head and began to purr. As I fell asleep, my tired brain confirmed that this was indeed how one ended up with a cat. And while I knew how foolish it sounded out loud, in the silence of my own head I was free to wonder how exactly one went about getting a wife? I mean, sure, I'd risked asking once before, but this time, I really wanted the commitment to stick.

Aaron

Whatever doubts I harbored about Byz were pretty much erased over the course of the weekend. He came to me in the pasture when we went to catch horses in the pre-dawn light. We led everyone up the hill, his square head right beside me the whole trip up to the barn, then he stood relaxed and calm while I groomed him. A big change from the tension that marked our relationship for the last few years, one I needed to thank Jaque for. She'd given me the last missing piece of the puzzle when she found his discomfort, and we were already seeing results with a few changes to his feed regime.

Not that he suddenly turned into a plug. No, he still half launched up the ramp onto the trailer, and I had to slap his butt so he wouldn't lean on the partition as I tried to latch it. When we got to Alabama he came off the trailer like a wind-up car pulled back to its limits, just shy of dragging me toward the familiar pasture. Our horses enjoyed a sizeable slice of acreage at this festival, with plenty of bushes and trees to bulldoze through in search of grass. Considering the way he took off when I removed his halter, J.T. at his heels, I thought there was no way he'd be willing to be caught the next morning.

There, he surprised me again, coming straight to me with a confident stride and bright eyes. Maybe it was the cookies I'd started carrying, or that he knew we were headed in to feed breakfast. But the way he watched me changed. I no longer felt like we were dudes eyeballing each other and talking shit at the start line of a drag race, searching for a weakness to exploit. Now, we were more along the lines of partners, checking to make sure our buddy had their head on straight before we waded into a brawl together.

Bart and I decided months ago, when he first started getting back into the lyst, that we would take turns playing emcee. A coin toss that morning meant Byz and I went into the ring to play up to the crowd before we presented the knights for the first joust of the day. Unfortunately, Byz hadn't read the memo, which left me riding a lightning spitting leviathan as I made introductions.

"My gentle lords and good ladies, I am Sir Aaron Drew, Captain to the Gallant Company of Knights." That I didn't choke on any of the words kind of surprised me, considering the way Byz hopped around, hind legs carrying most of his weight as his front hooves barely touched the earth. "We are jousters on an eternal quest for victory, winning over crowds from one end of the faire kingdoms to the other. But the truest conquest we face is not to defeat one another. No, it is to better ourselves, to unite in the bonds of brotherhood found only on the lyst field."

A cheer rose up from the sparse early morning crowd, garnering the attention of other patrons still wandering along the lane. I channeled Byz's energy into a rollback, which came easily with how much he'd already shifted his weight to the rear. We earned a smattering of applause at the flashy move, and Byz's neck bowed up in pride to be so recognized. For all his hard headedness, his soft spot was vanity, and he tended to preen if given half the chance. A fact I'd all but forgotten in my single-minded goal to just get our job done. Yet another reason to be thankful for Bart's return to jousting.

"Are you ready to greet your knights, people of the shire?" The audience's collective voice gained strength as people filtered in, and Byz gave me another glorious rollback, even more balanced than the last. "Are you ready to watch lances shatter and bodies fall?" There, I noticed a bit more bass from the male contingent, the prospect of violence always a potent lure.

"Then first, let us greet our patrons, Their Royal Majesties Edward and Katherine!"

A roll of percussion from the kettle drums filled the air, the vibration thrumming along my skin, and Byz responded to the sensation with a bold leap forward. Not a runaway, since we moved toward the source of energy, but a declaration of his power that humbled me. That also I had forgotten. The athlete and warrior I partnered myself to.

As the King and Queen processed onto the dais, I recalled Byzantine's early exposure to the sights and sounds of the festival.

While Jo had taken Rowan straight to the lyst, our usual progression was much slower. Once the horses were working well at home and began to learn the rhythm of the joust, we would often take them on rides around our home festival grounds before the season began. We accustomed them to the crowds in stages, first by tying them in the standing stalls at our encampment so they could watch everything from the safety of the herd. Then we rode around the arena between jousts, allowing the patrons to pet them so the horses could learn that the wild costumes and raucous behavior were nothing to fear.

Next came a much larger step, as we asked the new horses to carry the emcee. To quietly wait while the royal entourage processed, to take in the drums and the loudspeakers, to ignore the constant background hum that came from every direction. Most drafts were content to stand, but from the first, Byzantine had been out to prove his courage. He paced toward the drums with a snort of challenge, carried his neck all the higher as the trumpeters filled the air with brass. Nothing got past him, eyes and ears picking out and evaluating every new thing with a determination that impressed me. You see, to my understanding, Eros and Rowan did things for their riders because they didn't want to let them down. But Byzantine did things because he had something to prove.

That attitude had also been in his brother, Argo, but tempered by the wisdom that comes with age. He too had been watchful, nothing ever surprising him as his training progressed, which made him easier to work with in the lyst. When I lost Argo to colic in the middle of the jousting season, Byz had been forced to step into his brothers hoof prints. In my frustrated grief, I expected him to be exactly like his more experienced sibling, and when he did not conform, I took it personally. A mistake I would always regret, though now, we were bridging the rift I made.

I patted his neck as he settled beneath me, rewarding his calmness with an easing of the reins. He blew out through his nose as the King droned on about the beauty of the day and the loveliness of his queen, and I fought down a laugh. Clearly, my horse and I were of the same mind about pompous windbags.

Not that the guy portraying the king was actually a wind bag. I'd met him last night for the walk through and found him pleasant. But every cast at every festival played their roles a little differently. Region and ownership often influenced the tone, as did how well the cast themselves got along. At every one, the King or Queen set the tone for the festival, their example leading the way. Sometimes, you got the jovial Englander who loved his ale even more than his queen, sometimes you got an aloof and pious Spaniard that looked one step away from starting an inquisition. In this case, we had a Frenchman who loved the sound of his own voice, and probably checked the fit of his crown in every available mirror.

When the pontificating ended with the King's blessing on our tournament, I began the introductions, calling Trace to the lyst with a wordy exposition on his handsome face and loyal heart. The women in the crowd gave a collective sigh as he rode in, long blonde hair flowing with every stride Cappy took. He'd matured during the trip to California, filling out and growing comfortable in his own skin. Now that he had started training with our armorer, I began to see a man whenever he looked me in the eye. Having a purpose tended to do that to a guy, as I well knew. A big change for the defensive, desperate kid that jumped at a chance to join us when we met him at a small-time fair in rural Pennsylvania.

Once the applause began to die off, I moved on to my brother, Bart. Usually, I could play up his Scottish heritage to win the crowd for him, but in this case, he faced another Scotsman. So, I ran with the spiel about his returning from war and judging by the hollering I heard as Eros blasted through the gates to claim the field, I struck the right cord. Always nice to have military in the crowd, and in most cases, folks were pretty vocal in their support of veterans.

We went through the warmups, the guys lancing some rings, then throwing a spear at a hay bale target we'd freshly painted that morning. I had to give it to Trace, while he hadn't placed highly at the California tournament, he'd come out the other side of the experience with a much stronger arm. He buried the spearhead up to the wood shaft, showing a resolve I could hardly believe. Even his riding had improved, but a good deal of his focus remained on keeping his horse going rather than aim.

Bart and Eros put on a masterful performance, one I could practically copy with Byz, though they owned an effortlessness I couldn't manage to achieve yet. Hell, even on my best days, I wouldn't have made each stride so incredibly orchestrated. On occasion, the itch of jealousy would crop up, but every time I dug it up like the weed it was, I always found shallow roots. I didn't really need what Bart had, and I'd seen all the work that went into his relationship with the stallion. All the heartbreak beating them both down until the pair leaned on each other for strength. No, I was glad Byz had been spared Eros's wretched beginnings, and that I never faced the trials my brother endured during his enlistment. For us, I would be perfectly happy to make it through a weekend without sniping at each other. Some fondness would be icing on the cake.

Byz danced sideways a step or two as his herd mates ran around, but otherwise kept his cool. Not that I thought for one second he'd become a My Little Pony. Nope, the instant the guys adjourned to their separate ends, I laid the rein to his neck and he spun away as handily as my old rodeo mount. As I made a quick pass along the rail to ramp the crowd up, my self-consciousness winced to think of the disservice I'd likely done to every horse I'd ever ridden.

As the leader of Gallant Company, I prided myself on recognizing the efforts of my teammates. I'd even talked a good talk when it came to acknowledging our horses, since jousting would be much less impressive without them. But I barely scratched the surface of rewarding my own partners, complacently falling back to my father's way with horses. Treating them as tools, easily discarded or replaced, ever since my dad sold off my very first horse when he'd no longer been competitive. Hell, he'd even made me watch the rangy chestnut be auctioned off, and while he'd gone for a decent price to a younger kid who wanted to learn to rodeo, my dad wouldn't have flinched if he'd gone to the kill buyer. Countless other old, used up horses were sold for pennies on the pound that day, a memory that still stung my eyes. I'd manned up about it, because my father wouldn't have forgiven me for sentimentality, and because numbness seemed a better alternative than sadness. But when the time came to purchase horses for our troupe, the auction yards had been the first place I'd gone. If I could save even one horse from the fate those poor souls had suffered, I would do it time and again.

Argo and Byzantine came from one such auction, though they were never in dire straits. They were well muscled, slick with good health, both steely gray with some white fading around their faces. We picked them up the year after Bart found Eros, when the stallion finally began to come around. They came into the ring to be sold as a matched pair, not afraid of the chaos of the auction house, and I bid on them on impulse. Bart liked to say it was because they had alphabetical names like we did, two brothers who looked similar, but not identical. And while that never factored into the decision on the surface, I could admit those similarities appealed.

Speaking of brothers, my smile came easier as I watched the guys pick out ladies to hand off roses to. Jo had given Bart hell about giving her roses while they were working, and he'd argued right back just as fiercely, not wanting to be unfaithful in any way. I admired his resolve, particularly now that I had Jaque to think of, but as Captain, I breathed a sigh of relief when she verbally bludgeoned him into giving flowers away to the crowd.

Bart eventually agreed, but judging by his choice, he planned to keep the romance aspect to a minimum. He gave the rose to an older woman who looked fit to date his Gramps, pointedly ignoring the hopeful mass of women who were trying to get his attention. Trace didn't fail the crowd though, flashing his model perfect smile as he looked over the clamoring women. Several bodices were tested for structural integrity as some of them bounced up and down, displaying all their charms in hopes he might pick them. Not that I really looked at the cleavage anymore. Too many years doing this gig made it normal, like the white noise of tires humming along the highway. At this rate, I barely noticed.

Oh, but if it were Jaque. I cleared my throat and shifted in the saddle to break away from the very vivid image of Jaque in full on wench kit. I adored the sight of her in a cotehardie, but in a bodice? I would be lucky if I could remember my name, let alone how to ride.

Trace decided on a slim elvish looking girl, her hair a vivid pink over the prosthetic ears she wore, sticking to a trend I'd slowly noticed over the years. He always went for the cosplayers, the ones wearing fantasy costumes rather than the historical. Probably from all the time he spent playing D&D and shit. I'm not sure he ever played anything non-fantasy, excepting the rare times we dragged him into a first-person shooter or racing game with the rest of us.

Then we were back to business, the guys headed to the armoring blocks to get the rest of their kit on. I almost hated to watch Jo help Bart, truth be told, their ease together making me ache with missing Jaque. They never got mushy. She didn't kiss his cheek, he never took her hand. But their love was so thick in every touch, even as she bolted on his buffe and grand guard with practiced ease. Something in the way her fingers lingered a few extra seconds, and his eyes followed every move she made. And they stared at each other for a whole breath just before he pulled his visor shut, that simple intimacy more telling than a thousand shouted words.

But then, his helm closed, her fingers secured the hasp, and she sent him on his way with a slap across his backplate that made my fingers sting in sympathy. Even with the silent conversation they held, Bart rode out ahead of Trace, waiting for his opponent with a negligent air.

Jo wasted no time, heading over to check on the squire's progress with Trace. That work ethic, that drive to make things happen, had been the deciding factor in my endorsement of her knighthood. Sure, Bart talked up her horsemanship and her willingness to engage the crowd, but for me, I'd been more concerned over finding someone who could pull their own weight. In Jo's case, she could pull her weight and several other peoples', all without flinching. Add in an absolutely fearless demeanor in the lyst, and I swear, I would have moved heaven and earth to have her on the team.

Once she showed the squires how to properly secure Trace's helm and sent the knight on his way, she got all of the kids appropriately situated with new tasks. We'd practiced the routine with them last night, all on foot, but now faced with the crowds and the potential violence swirling through the air, they needed some direction. I paid very little attention as they scurried about, except for one girl that darted in front of me as I made a few passes on the rail to chat up the crowd. In her case, I had to sit down hard and haul on the reins to keep Byz from running her over, all while maintaining a steady patter for the patrons in the stands. He stopped just short of the frozen girl, close enough that I could see the blood drain from her cheeks and her eyes glaze over with fear. As we turned away he ground his teeth around the bit, and I felt his back hump up as we headed for a back corner of the ring where we would not impede the view. Clearly, I needed to get my head in the game and quit thinking about the past.

Through the clash that followed I kept up a decent flow of words, getting the crowd to cheer in all the right places, and building their anticipation as lances shattered as sharply as any lightning crack. I admired Trace's new-found resolve as he doled out some incredibly solid hits. In the third pass, he actually loosened Bart's seat, a big step up in his game. But in the last, Bart answered him with an emphatic blow that got the audience screaming as lance pieces arced high in the air, Trace flailing his arms to remain upright. The kid nearly saved it too, but in the end, gravity tugged him down with an inevitable power.

People surged to their feet before Trace hit the dirt, a wall of jagged noise going up that made Byz's ear twist. He liked applause, and even cheering, but the screams never sat well, putting wrinkles in his neck as he pulled back in distaste. I scratched at those wrinkles, hoping to appease him even as I channeled the energy of the crowd.

"Huzzah and ten points to Sir Clark, for providing the first of many unhorsings you are like to see on this festival day. And a hearty cheer for Sir Trace as he rises from the dirt, who received three points for a touch." Bart was already on the move, steering around the end of the lyst toward where Trace lurched to his feet with a hand from Jo. "Final score is twenty-seven to eighteen, the win going to Sir Clark!"

Applause and huzzahs from the court blended together in a more pleasing tone for Byz, who danced sideways beneath me as if the win were ours. My throat tightened up at the display, even as my body absorbed the movement and stilled his feet. He'd been so angry for so long, and to see him proud again made the moment sweeter than any victory I ever enjoyed. My hand shook slightly as I stroked his neck, but my voice remained steady as I spoke to the crowd beginning to leave.

"That, lords and ladies, is a mere taste of the competition to come! And for those of you who would like to meet your champions, our knights will meet you at the fence with their brave steeds for the next fifteen minutes. We will return at the hours of one and five, with new and exciting combinations of jousters for your enjoyment. Until then, fare thee well!"

With that, I flicked off the belt pack for my microphone and vaulted from the saddle, quickly loosening Byzantine's girth to cover for the overflow of emotion still trembling over my skin. But Byzantine laid me low even further, turning his head to touch his muzzle to my elbow, his eyes glowing with pride and slowly blinking with contentment. I never, ever expected to see so much softness directed at me again, and certainly not so soon. Clearly, I underestimated the equine capacity for forgiveness in a big way.

"Good job, bubba," I intoned lowly, unwilling to share the moment with anyone. My free hand fished in my belt pouch for one of the little cookies, which had his lips quivering with delight before I even held it out. He took it more gently than he ever before, as if we owned all the time in the world to enjoy this communion.

The moment shattered with the call of an eager young man at the rail, waving wildly to get my attention. Even as I plastered on a smile and turned to greet him, I held the memory of Byzantine's forgiveness close to my heart as one of the most priceless experiences of my life. And damned if I couldn't wait to tell Jaque all about it.

The remainder of Saturday, I played a conservative game in the lyst, protective of the newly rediscovered connection with Byzantine. Not that I reined him in, or held back, but I took a page from Jaque's playbook, and sought to value my horse over a win. To have fun, in a low-key kind of way. He hardly knew what to make of me, I think, pausing briefly before taking action. We were in new territory for both of us and needed to muddle through a bit.

That decision resulted in a loss to Jo, though she didn't unhorse me. She simply broke more lances than I did and judging by the odd look she slanted my way as we shook hands at the end of the passes, she hardly knew what to make of me either. Several times that afternoon, I caught her staring, and once, she stopped beside me as if to ask a question. Even if she figured out what she wanted to ask, I doubt I would have managed an answer. I didn't lose the will to win by any stretch of the human imagination, but learning to balance that drive with the shift in my perception would take a little time.

Nighttime provided a reprieve, as I sat on the tailgate of my truck with Boris pressed up against my leg and watched the horses move around in the moonlight. Eros was barely visible, the flickering edge of a shadow at rest, Cappy even less so, as his winter coat tended to absorb light rather than reflect. You could see Rowan clearly, with his blinding white feathers and tail shifting with every movement. Somehow though, my eyes were drawn to Byz, camouflaged in the darkness due to his darkly mottled gray color. I tracked him by the way he moved, always forward and purposeful even in his down time, marching from one pile of hay to the next with a sort of authority. Rowan cleared out well before Byz reached him, Cappy would move off with an affable slowness, with only Eros standing his ground. When Byz approached Eros, he did so with a slower step, making sure the stud could see him coming. Not that he bowed to Eros, as the stud had morphed into a pretty laid-back guy over the years, but Eros wouldn't take any flack either. Pushy behavior would be met with a very deliberate bite, which Byzantine was more than familiar with. In fact, you could see the old pattern of them in Byzantine's coat, small white parentheses that blended in with the gradually appearing flecks of lighter hair as he paled through the years. Someday, you wouldn't be able to see them at all, since he would inevitably lose his color with age. I threw out a quick prayer that he would outlive his brother, who never grew old enough to become fully washed out.

The tableau made a lovely backdrop as I shared a late call with Jaque, her voice a steady anchor for my ever-expanding heart. I thought being away from her would ache more, as intense as my feelings were, but two things dulled the pain. One, I had Boris, who had a knack for knowing when I needed him. Anytime I grew antsy, he appeared. Though youth made him lean in appearance, the fluffy creature was fully large enough to stand up on his hind legs, wrap his paws around my thigh with just enough claw to get my attention, then shove his head into my hand in a firm demand to be pet. As soon as I complied, he began purring loud enough to compete with the two-stroke engine in a weed eater, the noise and vibration shaking loose whatever bothered me.

Number two felt a bit more complicated to explain. I'm not very accustomed to the sort of emotions running around in my chest, so I kept struggling to pin down what they were. Ever since Jaque shared her love with me, my heart felt lighter, like a balloon on a string. I'd experienced the feeling a few times in my life, but before, the sensation came with a bit of panic, as most balloons are only tethered by a tiny ribbon, capable of snapping at the slightest provocation. I'd been cut adrift so often it felt practically inevitable.

But the link that ran between Jaque and I, even stretched over the miles, held strong. Not a ribbon, more of a thin chain that gave us the freedom to chase our dreams, but would always guide us back to each other.

Thanks to those two things, I slept pretty well, Boris taking the pillow beside me where I could hear his motor running. I didn't even need to put on my headphones and listen to music with his low rumble soothing me to sleep. Trace didn't appreciate the cat's company at first, though he'd been clear that his main qualm was allergies, so we solved that with a stop at the drugstore. And I needed to sneak the animal into the hotel, since I hadn't expected to bring a pet. He stowed away again, hiding in the tack room of the trailer, and I couldn't bear to leave him alone overnight. Sure, I grumbled about it in front of everyone, but I'd been pretty impressed with his tenacity. I had a cat now, but he made it pretty obvious to all that I was his human.

What he didn't like was being shoved in the trailer during our jousts on Saturday, so I took a wild swing and picked up a harness at the big box store the next morning. He gave me a withering look when I put it on him, and the leash too got a disdainful sniff. But once I lifted him up onto my shoulder, he settled with a happy chirp, ignoring the ignominy of his get up.

The most amusing portion of the morning came as I went through a fast food drive thru. When I pulled forward to pay, Boris eeled around so his head sat right beside mine. As the kid at the window took my card, Boris loudly announced his presence and reached out as if to swat, his huge paw spread wide to display a formidable set of scythes. The kid startled and jerked away, eyes wide with shock.

"Holy shit! What the hell is that?" I contained a snort of laughter as the kid clapped a hand over his mouth once he realized he'd sworn out loud. "I mean, I'm sorry sir, I didn't mean to cuss."

"No, he's a bit of a surprise to everybody," I offered as the guy ran my card and tentatively offered it back to me, well clear of Boris's significant reach. "Besides, he's cranky before he's had breakfast." As if he understood every word, the fluffy bastard employed the comedic timing of a genius, growling lowly.

The pimply faced teenager blanched white and took a slow step back. "Well, I'll just go check on your order then."

As soon as the window closed, I reached up and scratched the cat's sizeable ears, rewarded by a revving of his motor as he rubbed his cheek into my hair. "You are something else, cat."

An impression that intensified as we went through the morning routine, Boris perching on the stall partition as I groomed Byz, then clambering up onto a box to watch as I helped Bart get armored. His displeasure came at high volume when I tied him to my armor trunk, but Jo suggested I give him my old arming jacket to lay on, which he deemed a passable stand in with a few discerning sniffs. I left him sitting there in a full-on display of haughty indifference, stretched out to his considerable length and refusing to even look my direction as I climbed into the saddle to do my job.

We went through the usual to-do with introductions of the knights and acknowledgement of the royal court. Jo threw bold grins and low lashed looks at Bart as they worked the nearly full crowd and warmed up their horses with a few games. Bart's brows were drawn down so far you could hardly see his eyes, but judging by the twitch at the corner of his mouth, he was scowling to fight off smiling. I doubt anyone else would read anything into the flirtation, since they never played up their romance in public, but it still put my teeth on edge. I'm not ashamed to admit that jealousy fed my irritation. I'd have given up my favorite set of socket wrenches to have Jaque with me, even for an hour.

Got to admit, all their flirting made for an exciting joust. They went at each other like mortal enemies, clearly determined to gain the upper hand. Lances blew apart as if we had pre-scored them, a technique used in theatrical jousting to make sure the audience got a good show. The crowd responded accordingly. Despite the early hour, the stands were almost full, and each hit raised a growing wave of cheers that made the very air vibrate. Byz stood rigid with awareness, his ears flicking toward the lyst then back to me, limbs locked into place. That stillness held about as much potential for violence as the power struggle we watched, and I hoped he could contain it a little longer. Or that when he finally let it go, I'd come away unscathed.

Pass one and two saw a little wobble from both knights, but not enough to see daylight under their seats, and I took a moment to egg the crowd on as they reset at the ends. "The score is tied, eight to eight! Come, let your knights hear you! Call out for their victory!"

The third charge, Jo whipped around her end like a house on fire. How she managed to keep her lance upright against the momentum, I'll never know, as even I would have hard time compensating. Bart wasn't far off the same mark, and the audience screamed as they closed in. Three strides out, lances were coming down, at two, they were level, and at one, everyone watching forgot to breathe, even me.

Crack went the lances as they made contact, then the split lightning strike of one of them shattering in a wild spiral of shards. But not Jo's. Jo's held, bowing so hard I felt sure we were going to see her ejected from the saddle much as before. Every muscle in my core tightened down in sympathy as I willed her to hold on, and Byz's back humped up as if we were the ones receiving the blow.

She held, bearing down long enough to jostle both of them before the lance sprung out from under her arm, twisting across her body and Bart's like a perverse sort of teeter totter. As it spun around, catching Eros along the base of his neck, the stud flung his head up in a chain reaction that tipped Bart past the point of no return.

Not that Jo remained seated, but that didn't stop my arm from flying into the air, and my voice from roaring approval. "How about that, folks! A double unhorsing, and the first time Dame Bowen has dislodged Sir Clark! Give them your cheers!"

Blood thirsty screams were underscored by worried gasps as the horses left their riders in the well churned dirt. Jo rolled up on her knees pretty quickly, as did Bart, but her posture worried me, a

certain hunch in her body making my stomach clench with
memories. The first time I'd been truly laid out by Bobby Arnot,
the mountain of a man that mentored Bart and I in full contact
jousting, I'd almost thrown up in my helm, my body objecting to
the trauma. Bile burned the back of my throat at the very thought,
but I kept up the steady stream of words for the sake of the crowd.
Hopefully, they'd take the extra rasp in my voice for excitement.

"That was a hard hit for both our knights, and it's going to take
them a second to get their breath back. They have plenty of time as
the squires have to reset the lyst ropes and get the horses back to
the mounting blocks." Indeed, said squires were in the thick of
things, scurrying around to good effect. The horses were in hand,
and the end stanchion for the closest barrier was being muscled
back into place. Trace crouched by Jo's head, pulling her helm
open so she could breathe easier, and her hand clutched his leg as
she struggled to push herself up. Bart had one foot on the ground,
balancing the rest of his weight on the other knee, throwing his
arms in the air to encourage the crowd. As Jo got her legs under
her all the way, bracing against Trace's arm for balance, I did a
pass on the rail to pull everyone's eyes to hide her wobbly steps as
she headed toward the mounting block. Bart started moving too
once he heard me speak, relying upon my narration to keep him in
the know.

"Ah, here we go, lords and ladies, give another cheer as they get
to their feet. We've got one more pass to go, with a tied score, and
one more chance for our knights to take the lead! Dame Bowen is
tougher than a rocky Welsh mountainside, and Sir Clark is a canny
competitor. It's still anyone's game!"

My emotions were a mixed bag, both thrilled for the show they
were putting on at the same time I worried over Jo. Not that I'd
ever tell her, mind you. She got touchy about being the lone girl,
thought we might coddle her for it, which was my first instinct.
Bart stared at Jo so hard I could almost see a line connecting the
pair of them, and I wondered for the hundredth time how he could
do this with the woman he loved. No way could I have done the
same with Jaque. Hurting her would wreck me. But my
apprehension vanished in an amused puff of breath as the squires
got Jo's helm off, giving her a view of Bart standing on the steps
across from her. Her fist pumped up into the air so hard, she spun

herself around, nearly toppling off the block as she cackled with glee. "Yes, yes, yes!"

Thankfully, Trace grabbed her by the elbow and kept her upright. Bart broke into an uncharacteristically large grin that only Jo could ever pull from him, and he gave her a stiff bow as the crowd caught on to her enthusiastic celebration. She blew him a kiss that held all the passion of a grapefruit, and twice the playfulness of a Labrador puppy, mouth wide with laughter as he caught it.

People shouted "You go, girl!" and "Woohoo!" at a volume that made it hard to distinguish one voice from another. She sobered quickly as she caught my eye, though nothing stifled her grin as she sketched a nod with her chin to acknowledge my regard. Much as I wished I could end on this note, we were contracted for at least four passes at each scheduled time, unless a knight was rendered unfit to continue. As I had let her further into the business side of the Company, she'd read those documents for herself. However much she enjoyed the moment, her sense of duty to the Company would not allow her to indulge too long.

In moments, both knights were back on their mounts and headed for the lyst. Trace got his side of the crowd chanting "Bowen, Bowen, Bowen!", so I reciprocated, trotting Byz over to the rail to get the other half on Bart's side. "Come on, raise your voices! Sir Clark, Sir Clark, Sir Clark!"

One of the squires caught on to my intent, jumping up on the fence rail to clap his hands to the rhythm, and I tossed him a grin as I turned away to give my attention to the joust. Helms now secure, Jo and Bart both waited calmly, lances in hand, for me to turn them loose.

"Knights at the ready!" I called out, the mic picking up my booming words so that they raced through the air, tension mounting as the sound ran circles around the arena. The squires at the lyst ends raised their arms to wave the riders about, and as if the movements were choreographed, Bart and Jo paced their horses around the lyst ends. Just as they came straight, I threw out the command everyone waited so breathlessly for. "Charge on!"

Jo's sensitive horse hesitated briefly as she laid her heel into his ribs but flattened into a canter as she urged him forward. Neck held out straight, his eyes squinted on approach, clearly anticipating another rocking blow. Eros harbored no such qualms, and ran forward as if he led an army, neck arched with power. But Jo still didn't flinch, the eye slit of her helm focused entirely on her target, completely ignoring the impending violence to her body. The hits were textbook, twisting both of them toward each other as their lances landed. Yet, the one Jo held popped out from under her arm within a millisecond, her arm no doubt exhausted from the earlier effort. Bart's broke nicely, cracking into several pieces right along the wood grain. Plenty violent enough to satisfy our audience, but not so intense as to see either of them unhorsed, it also broke our tie.

Bart and Jo exchanged an odd embrace once their helms were pulled, clasped fists lifted up between their bodies as they leaned toward each other. Eros and Rowan didn't move a muscle for the brief moment of communion, apparently familiar with their rider's habits. As they released each other, I announced my brother as the winner, but it occurred to me that winning meant something different to everyone. Clearly, Jo felt proud of her efforts, of having left everything on the arena floor. And Bart wanted no accolades for himself, waving toward Jo to acknowledge her success. Every direction I turned anymore, another arrow of realization struck me, widening the hole Jaque had opened during a game of miniature golf. Hopefully, this lesson would override those of my father, and I could get on with the business of living without the high cost of thoughtless victory.

I vaulted off Byz to greet the crowds once the knights dismounted, trying to focus on the many faces that swam in front of me. But the energy crackling through the air between Jo and Bart should have left singe marks on everyone in a ten-yard radius. As for myself, the burn didn't show on the surface. No, it struck me in a far deeper and more profound way.

Every glance they exchanged as they signed lances, every stride they matched as they walked back to the encampment, drove home exactly how much I missed Jaque. Not like a limb, or even an internal organ, as important as those things were. Because at that moment, I'd have traded either for the chance to hold her, for the sense of wholeness I felt when she wrapped her arms around my waist.

Once we returned to the encampment Boris tried his best to distract, running over to join me as soon as Jo untied his leash. He walked the edge of the stall like an acrobat and chirped to get my attention, but I barely mustered the brain cells to get Byz untacked. In fact, I earned a dirty look from the gelding when I whacked him on the elbow with the stirrup iron as I dragged his saddle off.

"Sorry, bud. My bad." He shifted onto his offside leg as I reached to soothe the spot, and I nearly pulled back, not wanting to alienate him further. But before I could give him space, he settled his weight back on to all fours, accepting the contact with a gusty sigh. Instinctively, I exhaled my relief as well, grateful for every second chance he gave me as I cupped my hand over the joint I'd struck. The thick bones and heavy muscle felt solid yet supple, his athleticism a gift I cherished. Argo had been the heavier type of Percheron, built like a semi-truck, but Byzantine reminded me far more of my pickup. He could haul a load or haul ass, whichever the occasion called for.

Once I'd made amends and stowed my saddle on the stall wall, I turned to take stock of the little encampment. The horse's simple standing stalls were set back behind the arena, beyond the reach of patrons, affording a chance for all of us to decompress between jousts. Without exception, they all munched contentedly from their hay nets, hipshot and relaxed. One squire sat under a shade tree up by the gate to answer questions, but beyond that, the rest of us were free to roam the faire or lounge. Trace took advantage of the latter option, sprawled negligently in a camp chair underneath our armoring pavilion now that Jo and Bart were divested of their gear. Unsurprisingly, I glimpsed Jo pushing through the curtain in the canvas wall that marked the back of our space, with Bart a few strides behind her. My gut soured, and my fists knotted up with the knowledge they were headed off to enjoy some alone time. Not that I begrudged them a single moment, but their happiness drove the sharpness of my own deprivation that much deeper. Why couldn't I find the same sense of peace I'd known just the night before? I would see her soon enough, after all.

Unwilling to wallow in the pain, I scooped up my cat, his cheek rubbing against mine with a low rumble of affection. I wish it had been enough to satisfy the growing hunger in my heart, but his love didn't have the flavor I craved. After depositing him back on my trunk with a good chin rub and admonishing Trace to keep an eye on him, I strode out into the faire looking for some food. No, a roasted ear of corn wouldn't silence the growling beast in my chest, but maybe I could at least quiet the one in my stomach.

Jaque

Thanks to Dan volunteering to check on my herd, I was able to sneak away on Sunday to surprise Aaron. Jo knew my plan, as I needed directions and insight into the trip, but I said not a word to anyone else. Usually, my Sundays were spent schooling Lyric, but I took the day off and promised her we would make it up tomorrow.

The four-hour drive to the southern border of Tennessee went quickly, anticipation filling my veins with energy. Though I watched countless videos of Aaron jousting, I never experienced it in person. With luck and a little help from my friends, I would now be able support Aaron much as he supported me at my show. With willing hands and enough familiarity with his herd to be of some help, I could also cheer with the best of them.

I texted Jo as I pulled into the big field full of vehicles that stood between the road and the main gate. Before climbing out of the truck, I checked the braids in my hair one last time, far more nervous than I anticipated. What if I had overestimated our relationship? What if Aaron was not happy to see me? Thankfully, Jo's quick reply provided plenty of distraction. Action was the surest cure for my nerves.

'Go to the ticket booth all the way to the left of the gate, ask for Betty. She'll give you directions to where I'm waiting. Bart's covering for me, so hurry!'

The secretive nature of my visit made the blood hum in my veins as I threaded my way through the parking lot. I jogged the last stretch up to the ticket booth, too excited to be patient. Betty wasted no time once she knew who I was, guiding me through a small side gate in the painted plywood castle façade. She pointed toward a carved wood statue of a unicorn, the weathered surface greyed with age.

"You turn left just after that unicorn, sweetheart, and follow the lane down the hill until you see a big stuffed pig hanging over a food cart. Two shops down on the right, you'll see Esmeralda's. Jo's waiting for you in the back."

By the time I scurried down the lane and found the shop she spoke of, I had to gulp the humid air down like water. The weather for the day was shaping up to be warm, and I originally dressed for the cooler temperatures in Louisville. But I had little time to recover, as Jo's arm emerged from between clothing racks and beckoned me to follow.

"Okay, we don't have long, but Essie is going to help us out," she barked, excitement giving her voice a girlishness that reminded me how young she was. I never would have guessed her age when we first met, not as maturely as she behaved. In this case, her high energy proved contagious, and I relished the rare bit of girl time. As she originally predicted, we had fallen together as friends, and I wanted to deepen the relationship. "Do you want to go with your usual purple, or are we dolling you up in Aaron's colours?"

My eyes squinted as I considered the question. "The dark blue would be attractive, but I am afraid the yellow does terrible things to my complexion. We would need to find a different shade than his usual." Then I turned the inquiry back on Jo, her grin fading at the edges under my regard. "What would you do, Josephine? Be your own woman, or wear Bart's colours?"

"Good question. I haven't really thought about it, because I'm always in my own kit." She motioned toward her fitted tunic, the pewter grey fabric clinging to her slim curves to show off her athleticism. "And I really am my own woman, which Bart seems to appreciate. I think Aaron likes that about you too, but now that you've got me thinking…"

One arm crossed her body and her fingers drummed against her ribs as she studied my face. "For now, I'd play up who you are. But if you two stick things out, I'm thinking we'll surprise the brothers gallant sometime. Do things up properly to show the world they have our full support." A completely predatory grin overtook her then, and her eyes narrowed as she met mine. "It'll be fun to let them beat their chests and claim us. Bart will hardly be able to contain himself."

How my skin tightened as my body caught up with her line of thinking! Aaron truly would be overwhelmed, an imagining that appealed to me a great deal. Thus far, he had been a vigourous, but careful lover, and I relished the idea of driving him wild. But my purpose today was to surprise, not distract, and I did not want to put him off his game. So, I bowed to her wisdom, and decided to be wholly myself. "Purple it is then."

Everything happened in a whirlwind then, clothing and questions flying everywhere as Jo strategically shoved me into a little alcove with a curtain and ordered me to disrobe.

"Excuse me?"

"You heard me, Jaque. All but the underpants and your boots. Trust me, you do not want to have to put your shoes back on once we get you laced in."

I barely had my jeans off when two blousy shirts were shoved through the curtain. "Which one?"

The purple cotton was lurid grape, and I reflexively pulled away from it to reach for the white instead. "Oh, nothing quite that bright a purple, thank you."

"Got it." The purple disappeared, more questions falling fast and hot. "How much cleavage are you comfortable with? And what size bra do you wear?"

Thinking back to all the times Aaron's eyes lingered on my breasts, my skin flushed as I replied. "36C, and cleavage is acceptable as long as everything is secure. No wardrobe malfunctions."

A giggle I didn't know came from behind the curtain, immediately followed by a tan arm holding out a pair of bloomers that looked to match the top. I assumed it was the barely introduced Essie. "Oh, I like her. And remember, the bra has to come off too! You do not want that rubbing under your bodice!"

The curtain pulled back just as I tugged the bottoms up past my hips, and Jo waved me out to stand in front of a mirror. They layered me like a cake, sliding several skirts over my head. Deep plum made the base that draped to my ankles, then a gauzy violet came to my knees with a variegated hemline. Lastly, a dusky grey overskirt joined the rest, Essie fussing it into bunches that accentuated my hips.

But the crowning glory came in a rich plum brocade, Essie lacing the corseted bodice in such a way that my waist looked impossibly smaller. Mind you, that came from how much more my breasts drew the eye, and I grinned shamelessly. While my original

intent had been a more sedate surprise, I did not mind being a bit of
a distraction to the right eyes.

"Essie, you are a goddess, and I owe you a heck of a lot more
than money for this!" Jo pronounced, handing over a credit card
with a dramatic flourish. Before I could find my voice to object,
she held up her other hand in the universal gesture for stop.
"Shush. A girlfriend helped me with my first bodice, and I
promised to pay it forward someday. Besides, it's going to be
worth every single penny to watch our captain swallow his
tongue."

I found little will to fight her when she looked so completely
puckish over the prospect. Seeing Aaron at a loss for words would
be delightful. "And what did your fiancé say the first time he saw
you in such attire?"

She blushed prettily, all the fair skin between her freckles
dawning pink. "He said I looked good. But his eyes were a lot
more than complimentary. When we got tired of dancing around
our feelings for each other, he said he felt lightheaded and
lecherous. He really wasn't supposed to be thinking of me as a
woman, and I completely undermined his efforts."

Girlfriend to girlfriend, I lowered my voice to a whisper and
leaned in close. "You know, I think I did the same to Aaron. I wore
a dress for our first date, and he could hardly look away. Thank
goodness too, since I have been half in love with him for years."

Jo snorted and rolled her eyes, though the lift to her cheeks said
she held on to a smile. "Men! So blind sometimes!"

"It's the boobs," Essie interjected as she reappeared with Jo's
card and the receipt. "Every man's kryptonite!"

Though we all shared a laugh at that incredible truth, Jo's phone
chimed an alarm. We made a quick exit after thanking our new
friend, and Jo led me to a back door that took us behind the scenes.
There, the shops were much more cobbled together, some clearly
in need of improvements and nothing like the embellished fronts
that faced the streets. Costumed people lounged in the odd patch of
shade, but otherwise, our route was unimpeded as she strode along
ahead of me.

Even if there had been a crowd, I knew my friend would have
carved a path. While she carried a hint of her natural authority
when we first met, it had strengthened since then. And much as I

could not wait to see Aaron in his armour again, I imagined seeing Jo in hers would prove to be equally as impressive.

She led me into the back of another shop, this one looking out over a roped off arena where pennants danced in the breeze. At the threshold, she turned to face me, all her earlier mischief tempered with genuine affection. "Alright, Jaque, here's where I leave you. Once the crowd starts to build, you find yourself a spot close to the rail, preferably toward the left. Aaron favours that for his starting position."

"Are you sure I will not distract him?" I asked, anxiety making my stomach clench against the bodice. Perhaps this was a bad idea. I had not asked him if I could come, and I hated to think that he might not welcome me.

As if she could read my emotions, Jo reached out and squeezed my shoulder. Sympathy softened the shape of her eyes, but her jaw firmed with conviction. "Jaque, I'm absolutely counting on you to be a distraction. He needs a little something to shake him up. So when I hand him a rose to offer to a lady in the audience, I want you to step up to the rail with the brightest smile you own. Give your knight something to fight for."

Then she strode out into the sunshine, head held high as she greeted a little girl who called out her name. I watched her go with no small amount of admiration, for whatever her age, clearly Josephine Bowen owned a gift for seeing things few would ever notice. And heaven help anyone who stood in her way as she sought to put things to rights.

๖ **II** ๛

Aaron

When I walked back into our roped off encampment, Bart was already there, fussing over the strap barding Eros wore during his forays as the emcee. We had a set made by a very talented leatherworker at our home faire, in the company blue and gold, adjustable to fit a wide range of horses. But as that set needed some repairs after the California trip, today, he used his own green and silver. The colors were striking against Eros's ebony black coat, and the decorative dagging seemed to point out every rippling muscle the horse possessed.

At thirty minutes to the hour, we had plenty of time still to prepare. I took a page from my brother's book and started grooming my horse. With the help of a metal curry, I made short work of the dried sweat in Byzantine's coat, then ran a firm bristle brush over every inch of him until his variegated gray coat looked smooth. He still appeared a little dull to my eye, the color muddy this close to shedding time. That spring ritual couldn't come soon enough for me, even though I hated the several weeks of flying hair that got into everything. Between the travel to warmer climates and the longer daylight hours, it came every year shortly after this faire. Then, Byzantine would look his best, my dark blue and gold caparison bringing out the high carbon steel color of his coat.

At twenty to showtime, I headed for the armoring pavilion, leaving one of the squires to finish tacking up. Boris hardly groused when I tied him up, now familiar with the routine. As Bart joined me, I asked after Jo's whereabouts, and he shrugged his shoulders with all the urgency of a sloth as a smile flavored his reply. "She said something about paying forward a favor. But you know her. She's as reliable as the sunrise."

Not a sentiment I could argue after nearly a year of proof. But I worried over her uncharacteristic absence just to distract myself as

Bart helped me into my kit. What could keep Jo away from the Company so long when there was work to be done? Trace didn't seem too put out as he strapped on his leg harness and secured his gorget, working on all the pieces he could handle himself. But Bart had finished with me and buckled Trace's cuirass into place by the time she ran in the gate, face damp from the effort and the warmth of the day.

"Sorry guys, I got waylaid by a couple kids and lost track of the time! Promise it won't happen again!"

I scowled as she jogged past me, though my heart really wasn't in it. Hell, my heart wasn't really into jousting at the moment either, but we all had jobs to do. "Come on, Jojo. I'm not going to cut you slack just because you're marrying my brother."

Though I meant the words to come out teasingly, they rasped with the shadowy unhappiness I wrestled with. Her spine went rigid even as she lifted Trace's arm harness so he could slide his hand through the articulated steel. I felt the weight of her unseeing regard like a man in front of a firing squad, knowing my slaughter to be imminent. My lungs stopped working, probably to keep me from saying anything else stupid, and I winced in anticipation of the coming retribution. Any second, she would pull the trigger, and I'd accept the shot, because I'd earned it.

But strangely, she remained silent, still giving me her back. The only punishment I received were withering looks from both Bart and Trace as she continued to work. I hid a sigh of relief by turning around to pet Boris before we had to go, hoping the constant sounds of shifting armor would mask the gusty exhale. No one said a damned word to me except the squires as we mounted our horses and headed for the ring, driving home the point that I'd been an ass. After growing up in a houseful of women I knew the silence for the rebuke it was, all the more potent coming from someone who had no qualms speaking her mind. An apology definitely lay in my future.

Bart's rumbling voice filled the air as he stirred up the thicker afternoon crowd, a melting pot of humanity in the growing temperature. All the faces on the rail melted into a blur when I finally made my charge onto the field, Byz taking advantage of my divided attention to show some real speed through the turns. The heat that bothered him so greatly in California no longer seemed to be an issue, a positive thought I clung to as I tactfully bent him around into a stop. We still earned a smattering of applause, as the maneuver showed off the thick muscles in his neck and made the caparison flutter impressively around his legs.

My fingers were tight on the spear as we played our games, as if that grip would rein in my scattering emotions, but I maintained a light hand with Byzantine. No matter how I felt, he deserved better from me. I'd shortchanged him for too many years, along with many of the others I shared my life with. Never again.

Which made my next course of action much easier to follow through on, as I rode up to Jo to take a rose from her. The ladies had Trace to distract them as I wrapped my hand firmly around hers and met her guarded expression. "I'm sorry, Jo. That was uncalled for. How can I make it up to you?"

For a moment, her eyes narrowed and her lips trembled, and I panicked at the thought that she might cry. But before worry could settle its hooks in me, her whole face bloomed into a delighted smile that almost knocked me off my horse as she replaced her hand with a large lavender rose. My fingers fumbled closed around it, heart clenching at the memory of Jaque's pleasure over the bouquet I'd given her. I couldn't bear to give this one to some random patron, job or no. But then Jo gave me something else to cling to. "That's easy, Captain. You can take this purple rose and ride off to your left to find the woman it belongs to."

I swear on my mother's cherished tiara that my limbs lost function for a second as my brain caught up with what my body already understood. My head swiveled fast, desperate to confirm what I hoped to find waiting for me. Byz followed my eyes, turning us to face the far end of the arena as I cued him to pace forward. He moved with a mature gravity that reminded me of his brother, clearly understanding his part in the weighty moment.

She stood up as I approached, drawing my eyes to a flash of purple that gave me something to aim for. As I drew closer her serene smile calmed my clamoring heart, and I could see her raven hair had been braided into a crown that beat out anything I'd ever seen on a beauty queen. The crowd ceased to exist as I reached the rope rail and swung Byzantine sideways so I could get closer to the woman I loved. My ears became deaf to their noise as I waited for her to speak.

"A pleasure to see you, Sir Drew." The breathy words carried far more heft than they should have, and her smile grew impish as her next inhale drew my eyes away from her face.

You probably could have struck me in the head with a lance and it would have done less damage to my brain cells than the sight of Jaqueline's glorious cleavage framed in a well fit bodice. How the hell was I supposed to mimic any kind of honorable behavior with so much temptation laid out before me?

An earthy, knowing chuckle snaked inside my armor, pummeling me with a desire I had neither the time, nor the leisure to indulge in.

With more willpower than I gave myself credit for, I managed to steer back on track, wrenching my eyes back up to her heated regard. The sooner I could finish this joust, the sooner I could hold this magnificent woman in my arms. "My lady, I ask you to accept this rose as a token of my favor. Would you do me the honor of allowing me to champion you in this joust?"

Her deft fingers reached for the stem, barely breaking eye contact long enough to be sure of her destination. And while I loved the lightning flash that jumped from her skin to mine, warning of the storm building between us, her eyes were calmer than a still pond, giving me an anchor.

"My champion, I am the one so honored. Thank you."

Then she pressed her lips to the rose with a sweet smile before pulling it away, the gesture enchanting me completely. As she stepped back the volume of the crowd returned, murmurs of curiosity pushing me back toward my responsibilities. But as I turned to the block where Jo waited with my helm, a teasing grin on her freckled face, I still felt Jaque's gaze like a physical touch. Knowing she had come, that she would be waiting for me when I finished, made my heart feel so light it is wonder the damn thing didn't fly right out of my chest.

Trace waited too as I moved in beside Jo, a strained grin putting wrinkles in his smooth features. I looked to him with a measure of concern, even as eager delight bubbled in my chest like the low idle of a turbocharged engine.

"Everything alright, Davies?"

He nodded, dark amusement now more obvious in his baby blues. "It will be, provided you don't scatter my body parts all over the field. I know I'd be showing off if I had a lady, so I'm pretty sure I'm in for it. Just remember, you break me, you pay."

Then he held up a bright white bite guard to be sure I saw it before he shoved it in his mouth. Not a usual piece of equipment for him, which piqued my curiosity. Maybe he picked it up in California?

When he tossed me a cartoonish grin before slamming his visor down and riding away, I found myself both touched and amused. His support and good humor cut loose another mooring line holding my heart down.

Jo bit down on her amusement, saying not a word as she tightened the wing nuts that secured buff and grand guard to my chest.

"Don't think I won't repay you for this someday, JoJo. That was incredibly sneaky."

Her lips stretched wide with unabashed pride as she lifted my helm above my head. "No scorecard on this one, big brother. We all get love. That's prize enough for anyone." Then she jammed the clamshell of metal down a bit rougher than usual, a challenge in her eyes that worked like a spark on dry kindling. "Now, go out there and fight for your lady. You manage it properly, and we'll send you off to spend some time alone at the hotel with her instead of making you wait out the day with the rest of us."

Before I could muster an answer she dropped my visor closed, effectively trapping me in my own head while base desire drove arrows up my spine. I fumbled the manifer as she pushed it over my numb fingers, and barely managed rational commands to my limbs as Byzantine paced toward the lyst.

Mechanically, I backed him into place, his grinding teeth a signal I should have responded to. Yet I couldn't remember why. Or even how. Stiff armed, I reached out for the lance I knew would be there, robotic fingers clamping down without checking my grip.

With all that inattention, Byz took over, following the circling arm that gestured us around. I didn't stop his headlong charge, hazy eyes searching for more purple rather than the grand guard. On autopilot, the lance lowered, but with no guidance, something happened that defied my years of expertise. The moment slowed down, my pulse thudding thick, and... I missed completely.

That missing jar to my hand shook me like a pup held by the scruff of its neck by an irritated mother. The impacts that followed rang in the deepest parts of my soul. Firstly, Trace struck true, driving into my shoulder like an industrial rivet gun with a vendetta. That alone, I might have endured. But Byzantine answered my complacency with a wakeup call I felt to my bones, responding to my unbalanced seat with a full-on ejection. Not enough air existed in my helm to prepare me for the brief flight I took, nor did I regain my wits adequately to control the landing.

Ever driven a t-post into the ground? That jarring velocity of your body as you throw your whole will into parting the stubborn earth with implacable steel? Well, now I knew what the t-post felt like. My shoulder dug the first divot, the rest of my body weight driving it home with a thunk I felt from scalp to toes. Time ceased to exist for me, as I lay there mentally checking to make sure all my parts still worked. I wish the impact had been enough to shake the stupid loose from my brain, but my agitated brain cells were too stunned to counteract what followed.

Anger moved through me like a volatile wave of lava, devouring reason, obliterating responsibility. My aching body didn't even register, the ringing in my ears totally ignored as squires levered me to my feet. So help me, I meant to get back on my horse and show him who was really boss, by whatever means necessary. I would not allow him to ever embarrass me again.

I know. Not my best moment. Ever. I had some doozies before, believe me. But never that strong, never so completely encompassing. Every muscle I owned trembled with unspent rage, wanted nothing more than to fight! Looking back, I know Byz wasn't who I was really angry with. I was angry with myself. I've always been angry with myself, as if my father's disappointment didn't die with him. No, I inherited it. Nothing I did would ever be good enough. That same rage that caused me to break my own hands drove that ten second internal temper tantrum like a flame belching funny car drag racer dumping fuel.

But thankfully, I had an ally. As the visor of my helm went up, cooler air rushing over my sweaty face, I ran my rage right into a wall. A brick edifice of implacable concern that spilled out of Jo's worried eyes, caring about me with a fierceness that left no room for my own self-loathing. No, it wasn't Jaque's loving gaze, but I don't know that I could have faced such purity in that moment. I wouldn't have been worthy of such unconditional affection. I needed a fellow warrior who took no bullshit and understood my flaws already.

Eyes narrowing and lips thinning, Jo reinforced that impression by grabbing my grand guard and shaking me. "You have your head on straight now?"

I grimaced, then winced as we turned, feeling what would be a lovely bruise on my shoulder and upper arm. But everything moved just fine as I tested the joints, so I ignored the ache. "Jury's still out. Though this is your fault. Maybe you and Bart can joust while thinking dirty thoughts about each other, but I'm not that gifted."

For all her toughness, Jo still had enough innocence that the comment made her blush violently. But as she guided me under the lyst ropes, she didn't back down either. "Well, lesson learned. Next time, I won't exceed the limits of your miniscule attention span."

I might have rebutted but said short attention span flicked over to the mounting block, drawn by Byzantine's braced neck. He looked two seconds from nipping the squire holding him in place, mouth working the bit violently.

"Fuck," I cursed under my breath, well aware I'd screwed up. Again. And I didn't have the luxury of taking my time with an apology. If only I had a cookie to give him, it might be enough of a band aid to get through the joust.

As if reading my mind, Jo's hand appeared in front of me, an unwrapped mint in the valley of her upturned palm. When I looked over at her to say thanks, she shook her head and flicked her eyes meaningfully at the waiting audience. Ah, right. Time to get the show back on track.

Byz turned to stone under my hand the instant I touched him, holding his breath so hard it's a wonder he didn't faint. I sighed heavily, sure I'd totally ruined things between us again. Before the breath fully left me, he softened, echoing the sigh, neck curling so he could see me better. What I saw in his face almost knocked me to the ground again.

Worry wrinkled his brow, eye tight with concern even as his nostrils quivered hopefully at the scent of the mint. I saw not one ounce of the anger or resentment I expected. Hell, it would have been justified, given my own response to him ditching me.

Reflection kept me silent as I fed him the mint and stroked his damp shoulder before remounting. Maybe he hadn't done it on purpose? I thought, as Jo secured my visor and sent me back to work. After all, if I'd missed my target, chances were pretty strong my riding hadn't been top drawer either. Wouldn't have taken much to rattle me out of the saddle. Dammit, why did all of this have to be so complicated?

Then I was out of time for the past, patting Byzantine's neck before I accepted a lance. This time, I stayed firmly in the present, able to smile in the privacy afforded by the armor that the last flash I saw as I made my turn was the deep purple of Jaque's bodice. I didn't hope for kisses later, I didn't imagine the heaven of her arms. Only reveled in the knowledge that she loved me enough to come all this way to see me.

As my lance came down this time, my vision remained crystal clear. I dropped the reins two strides out, inhaling deeply of the close, humid air. My outside leg automatically tightened in response to a slight balk from Byz, which I guessed was him making sure I had my head in the game. The tip of the lance thocked into place as if drawn in by a giant magnet, my torso contracting against the ripple of violent energy that pushed back at us.

Hitting Trace always felt like that. Even from the beginning, when he'd been easier to tip over than a Jeep trying to corner at high speed. He carried a natural density beat out only by Bart, and our old friend Bobby. Sure, he'd originally missed more than he hit, and his horsemanship skills were merely passable, but between the density and absolute devotion to the team, he'd become one of our most reliable players.

Something between Trace and I gave way, and I wrung my body free of the torque as I threw the lance away. Wouldn't do to get through the blow, only to get tangled up in a lance that wouldn't be reusable after that impact. As I shoved against the outside stirrup to re-center my weight, my left hand reached out for the reins, hoping to prevent another unseating. But I'd barely made contact with the braided rope when I felt Byz downshift smoother than a high-end luxury car, balancing us both as he gently came to a stop.

As I finally found the reins, my eyes swam at the gift he'd just given me. Again. Gut clenching and lungs heaving, I held my eyes wide to prevent some very uncharacteristic tears. How could he do that? Unseat me with extreme prejudice, then carry me perfectly moments later? Squeezing my eyes shut hard enough it made my head ache, I heard Bart's Gramps clear as day, talking in my head.

"Boy, the biggest handicap you have in talking to this horse is all your worry. He doesn't give a rat's hairy butt cheek for what comes later, only what comes now. If you could pull your head out of your ass long enough to live in the moment with him, the two of you might just learn to get along with each other."

I'd spent weeks trying to figure out what he meant. So much of my life, I'd been thinking ahead, and the habit wasn't easily broken. After all, I had other people relying on me, expecting things of me. I couldn't let them down. The goals and objectives ahead were everything. But now, I sat stunned by the absolute proof of his words.

A hefty slap against the thigh of my leg armor brought me out of the shock though, and I sucked in a huge breath, as if I could pull the truth so deep inside of me that it would soak into my very cells. One hand reached out for the lance as the other adjusted the reins slightly, giving Byz another inch of slack. Clearly, I could trust him with it as long as I did my part of the job.

Little existed for the next several seconds except the roll of his mouth around the bit making those reins shift slightly in my hand. Every breath he took pressed against my calves, and I felt the minute shift of his weight as the signal to come about rose in the air. A sense of right vibrated through me, and if we'd had one more moment to wait, I swear, I expected to hear him speak. Never, in my whole life with horses had I ever felt so intensely connected, more in sync.

We made our turn, pivoting around my inside leg and for the briefest second, I thought I might know what it was Bart and Jo felt with their own horses. That knowledge made a lie of my earlier statement that I didn't want what they had. As we raced toward whatever may come, my heart beating in time with the thunder of

Byzantine's hooves, I suddenly wanted it more than anything else in the world.

Well, except for one thing. I still wanted to be part of Jaque's life, to love her with every ounce of my being. Which is why I brought my lance to level with unmatched conviction, determined to be worthy of the love she offered me. I might not have the faintest clue what I was doing with lady, or horse, but I was going to give both everything I had.

Jaque

Sacrament! If my heart beat any faster, I worried it might give out from the strain. Seeing Aaron fall twisted me into knots of concern, and my nails buried themselves into my palms to keep from leaping into the ring. The intensity of my fear had no comparable measure, stealing space in my chest, limiting my ability to breathe. Trembling against the urge to fling myself through the ropes, the old break to my clavicle throbbed with sympathy, certain he would be making a trip to the hospital. How could he possibly recover from something so violent?

While Jo wasted no time getting to Aaron's side, her facial expression remained incredibly relaxed as she offered him a hand up. I tried to take my cue from her, breathing sharply through my nose as I uncurled my fingers, but that is as far as my body would unbend. Perhaps if I focused elsewhere?

No, that did me little good as I watched his horse. Poor Byzantine looked rigid with distress, each step he took slamming into the dirt with the sort of tension that boded ill for both his ulcers and the ones I suspected Aaron also harboured. So often in times of stress, I watched Aaron's stomach clench in on itself, a mannerism I recognized from my father. That both man and beast struggled did not surprise, owing to all the times Lyric's physical problems echoed my own. The tightness in her shoulder that influenced her lengthenings absolutely mimicked my old injury. Wringing my skirts with both hands, I struggled against a whimper, wanting so much to help them both.

"Mi'lady?" an unfamiliar voice interjected, drawing my eyes to the side. A woman much my age leaned around her gentleman companion with a sympathetic wrinkle marking the outside of her eyes. "No need to worry. These guys are pros, and I'm sure Sir

Drew will be fine. Zach and I have been watching them for years, and we've never seen any of them seriously injured."

The man nodded in agreement, the kindness in his gaze almost more than I could bear in my overwrought state. "Yup. Besides, judging by the way he looked at you, I doubt there's much that would keep that guy from your side."

My lips pursed around the questions I wanted to ask, stupid as they were. I felt sure that over the years, Aaron had carried the favour of many a lady at this very faire. How could he not have? Seeing him in his element, I could understand why women might throw themselves into his arms given even half a chance. Something extraordinary overcame him, donned in his armour, a kind of surety, a justifiable pride that lit him up from within.

"Zach's right, you know," The woman interrupted my musings again, her tone full of wonder and her eyes speculative even as her hand folded around her companion's bicep. "Can't say I've ever seen him so interested in a lady, though he's usually full of pretty words for everyone. You're a lucky woman to have caught his attention."

I smiled softly at the memory of his reaction to my appearance, but then movement caught my attention. "Lucky, indeed," I murmured offhandedly as Jo escorted Aaron to the mounting block. Years of watching Lyric for the slightest stiffness had me studying every stride he took. My heart rate calmed at the relative ease he showed, even in the full suit of armour. At the competitor's party, he wore only the parts that covered his arms and legs. Now, entirely encased in steel, I wondered at how comfortably he wore the ensemble, as one might wear a bespoke wool suit. No wonder our cultures fostered the mythos of the knight in shining armour, if this is what it did to a man, to wear such a thing. And while I held no interest in wearing one for myself, I found curiosity nibbling at the back of my thoughts, wondering what it would do for a woman like Jo. Perhaps luck would allow me to discover the answer at the later joust.

After a moment to placate his horse, Aaron swung back into the saddle with an ease I envied. But I shoved my own baggage aside as I scooted to the very edge of the bench, watching him manoeuvre his Percheron gelding back into the rope lanes they used as barriers. Such insubstantial guidance against the will of a massive animal some might say. I knew better though, after watching the first run. Aaron had dropped his reins well before the impact, and his horse could have easily shied away. Only hours of training, familiarity and trust kept the horses inside those ropes, just as my driving horses could kick themselves free of a carriage if they were of a mind to.

When they came around the turn to charge, my heart leapt against my ribs as if we could ride with them. Unlike the last run, Aaron moved smoothly, his own lance lightly brought to bear as if he wielded a blade of grass rather than a length of wood. I sucked in all the air I could muster as the younger knight did the same, holding my breath as they closed in on each other.

My muscles seized tight as the lances struck, bits of them shattering into the air as if to celebrate the inherent violence. How these riders could find this fun, I would never understand, but as the crowd roared, I could appreciate the energy in the air. Even as the men halted their horses, a hum looped between every person present, warm and alive like the sun. You could power the nearby city off that expectant air. Would that you could channel them at full cry—the national energy crisis could be solved in an afternoon!

Shivering with the current of humanity, I let myself get swept up. My gaze sharpened, focusing on Aaron, finding pride in calling him mine. This daring, vital man, so full of energy, worry, tenderness, and fractured heart; he belonged to me as I belonged to him. For him, I could forget my own worries over the impact, my old memories of falling, and simply celebrate his mastery of this rare skill.

I saw a subtle shift in Byzantine. Nothing overtly obvious, since dark blue fabric covered most of him, and certainly nothing from Aaron, encased in steel. But Byzantine's body grew lighter, yet all the more intense, so very focused on his rider that nothing else mattered. Perhaps most horse people would not have recognized it from behind like this, but as a driver, I knew the look of coiled energy very well indeed. Understanding how it felt to find those moments with my own horses, I shimmied on the bench, excited to see what Aaron would make of it.

Byzantine bent around Aaron's leg like water around a boulder, but when he straightened, he leapt forward like the same water breaking through a dam. My breath came in short pants at the visual impact the pair of them made, sunshine catching on Aaron's armour, the speed of their approach causing Byzantine's colourful blanket to snap around his legs. They were all things powerful and right about the world, and as Aaron and Trace traded hits, I could feel an echo of it in my chest. The pain of the blow moved through me, welcome and powerful, bringing up a collage of adrenaline from my own memories. Yes, this I understood! To pit yourself against risk, to come out the other side perhaps more whole, even with the fear of failure threatening to clip your wings. I knew the strain of body and heart leaping toward the goal, the exaltation that came from reaching it.

Looking back, I wondered if that is part of what doomed all my other relationships. Perhaps I needed a man who understood that part of me, who did not feel threatened by it. I had always been the one putting my heart to the hazard, throwing myself after my goals, and harnessing myself to men who were not like-minded dragged me down.

True, Paul and I had enjoyed a similar goal and drive to reach it, but he never accepted my need for balance. Every step forward, we argued about which direction to go until we could no longer stand being together. Add in his hesitancy over my need for physical affection, and I chose to leave before the mere sight of him drove me to hate. He had been the one to throw in with van den Berg afterward, driving a firm wedge into the split between us. I did not know if anything could bridge the gap now, even as friends.

But Aaron... Ah, this man, he not only supported me, he threw his weight into the harness beside me. He did not always understand me, but he never stopped trying. When I had a need he could fill, he did, but he never took anything away from me, recognizing my mastery in its own right. And he never failed to answer when I reached for him. Never had being a woman felt more powerful than by his side. No wonder I fell so easily into love with him.

By the time he unseated Trace in the fourth run, I wanted nothing more than to fling myself over the paltry fence to reach Aaron's side. As an adult capable of controlling my impulses, I limited myself to jumping up with the rest of the crowd to scream with excitement. Bart declared Trace the victor, but I did not care, recognizing something far more important than winning had taken place for Aaron. My emotions ran so close to the surface I could have wept for the display of brotherhood as Aaron vaulted from his horse and walked over to meet Trace as the squires lifted him out of the dirt. Backslapping hugs ensued, despite the armour, and they were both smiling widely when their helmets came off.

I could not sit back down after all of that, shifting restlessly on my feet as I waited for the crowd to move out. Perhaps once things settled, I could make my way to Aaron. Before I could work myself into too much of a state, Jo waved me over to a small gate and let me in the arena. Aaron turned away from Trace to give his horse a pat as the squire led the gelding off, but then his eyes were for me alone. They sparkled with genuine happiness, and he held out a hand in welcome. Too much armour stood between us for a true embrace, but I stepped in as close as I could.

"Glad you came, my lady."

I smiled up at him, wishing I could kiss his dazzling smile. "I am too, my champion."

Bart hollered his name, and Aaron looked past me for a moment, his mouth quirking sideways. "Let me go appease the masses, then I'm all yours, okay?"

How I wanted to say something alluring at that moment, something to hurry him along, but if I wanted a future with him, this was a part of his life I needed to accept. Still, I ran my fingers through his sweat damp hair to tidy it, allowing my nails to firmly brush his scalp. Judging by the thready puff of air that escaped him, he felt both the affection and temptation in my touch. "Do your duty, Sir Drew. I shall be waiting."

Then I playfully pushed him away, content to help Jo. We moved around the field, picking up bits of armor and placing them in a wagon as the squires worked at carrying broken lances back to the camp.

The horses stood at the rail near their knights, accompanied by a squire so people could pet the big animals. Eros, and the big gelding Trace rode were fairly tolerant of all the touching, standing expectantly as hand after hand reached for their faces. But Byzantine endured the unwanted adoration with a flat expression, ears tipped out to the sides and a wrinkle over his eye that concerned me. When I mentioned it to Jo, she sighed.

"I know, he's not a big fan of group interactions like this, but not all the squires pick up on his body language. Give me a second."

I admired the way she walked across the arena with both authority and softness. In less than a shake, she sent the young man holding Byzantine on another errand, and he went with a smile on his face. Then she waved me over.

"Here, Jaque, could you take him? I'm basically sending all the kids to get their lunch break in. Kind of unorthodox, but I think with your help we'll do just fine."

Before I could nod my agreement, she pressed Byzantine's reins into my hand and turned for Bart to make a similar arrangement. Shaking off my shock, I put on my best smile and headed to the rail. Eager hands reached out as we approached, but I stopped shy of three squealing girls pushing against the ropes. "Ah, ladies, I see you would like to meet a warhorse! Have any of you pet a horse before?"

"No," cried the middle girl, her face twisting with impatience. "But I LOVE horses. Someday, I'm going to get one and ride it everywhere."

The other two shook their heads, but those greedy hands remained aloft, demanding their due.

To one side, I spotted another girl, this one much calmer. She studied Byzantine with a hopeful tilt to her head, as if memorizing everything about him. Certainly, a better prospect for the wisdom I wanted to share, though I made sure my eyes touched each of them as I spoke.

"Let me tell you a secret about horses, fair ladies. Not all horses enjoy being pet the same way. In fact, most horses consider it rude for you to pet their face unless they know you. It is like a total stranger walking up to hug you, without any introduction."

Mouths twisting with confusion, and in the case of the middle girl, a bit of pique, their hands slowly lowered to the fence. The quiet girl fixed her gaze on me, rapt with attention, soaking up knowledge like a sponge.

"If you would like to make friends with Byzantine, I can show you how he likes to be pet the best. Then he might consider you a friend."

Middle girl sneered outright. "This is stupid, come on, let's go see the other horses." She turned in a huff, her friends following a bit more reluctantly as she stomped toward where Jo now stood with Capstan. Jo's eyes narrowed as the girl pushed in front of a little boy, and I knew she had their measure, which allowed me to smile gently as I turned back to the remaining girl. Her parents sat behind her, focusing on their phones rather than their child, so I took my time. "How about you, brave lady? Would you like to make friends with Byzantine?"

Her eyes widened with anticipation, but she remained calm. "Yes, please. I mean, I rode horses at summer camp, but not as much as I want to. My parents can't afford lessons." Her cheeks flushed as she darted a look at said parents, embarrassed to have admitted such a thing.

"Never you worry, young lady. If horses are in your heart the way they are in mine, I am sure you will find a way to the knowledge you seek. But for the moment, perhaps you would hold out the back of your hand for Byzantine to smell?"

I have known many people to thrust their hand out in nervousness, but this child had no fear in her gaze as she held out her arm. I coaxed Byzantine forward, wondering if she might flinch at his sheer size, but I saw nothing in her gaze except hope. Byzantine's nostrils widened as he took in her scent, and when I asked for another step, he answered more willingly. A promising level of discernment, considering his earlier distaste for the fans.

"Ah, very good! It would appear he likes your smell. Did you recently eat something sweet? He does love sweets."

"A caramel apple," she breathed the words out slowly as his whiskers grazed her knuckles. "I wish I saved some for him." Then her eyes shot to mine. "Can I touch him now?"

He likely would have welcomed her quiet hands on his angular face, but I had a lesson to finish. "Certainly, though let me show you how he enjoys it best. Do you see here, on his jaw?" Her eyes followed my pointed finger, and she nodded, watching as I cupped my hand around the bones and began to rub at the sweat I found. Immediately, he tucked his nose to press against the friction, wanting more. "He is sweaty from carrying his knight, and that makes him itchy. If you scratch right here, he would enjoy it very much."

Bless her, she did not flinch as I moved away and her fingers curled into the same damp groove. He did not push on her as much as he did me, in part because she had neither the strength or the practiced touch, but his eyes half closed with happiness all the same. We spent several minutes more as I turned Byz sideways to the rail and showed her all the best spots on his neck, and she giggled with delight when his lips began wiggling. Better still, when some other children, and even adults approached, the girl found the confidence to share her newfound knowledge with each of them.

Byz stood completely at ease, even with multiple people touching him, when a voice broke into our little scene. "I see Lady Jaqueline is teaching you all how to properly spoil my war horse! Well done, ladies and lords!"

I turned my chin to take in Aaron, his most affable smile on full display as he swaggered over. His audience giggled appropriately, and he amped up the charm as several kids thrust out broken pieces of lance for his signature. One lady even had him sign her t-shirt, though I thanked Christ that she only offered him her shoulder. Objectively, I appreciated his act. Less rationally though, as I continued to supervise those petting his horse, I hated the pretense. I wanted to pull him away from the crowds, to have him all to myself.

Then he moved from one side of Byz to the other, his hand scooping around my waist, squeezing lightly on the way by. My heart lightened to know the man I loved still lived under the practiced facade. That knowledge made it much easier to endure the remaining minutes in the ring, and I watched him work the crowd with a bit of pride. He gave every fan personal attention, making each feel special before he moved on to the next.

Still, relief swelled up when the crowd truly began to dissipate, and Jo turned her charge for the large gate at the corner of the arena. I followed suit, with Bart shortly on our heels, the horses our priority now. As Rowan whinnied a welcome for his herd mates, Jo pointed me to the furthest stall, and I settled to my work. Byzantine headed straight for his water bucket once I removed his bridle, and I took advantage of his stillness to watch the others work. Following their example, I managed to shuck off his tack and other trappings without much fumbling. Beneath his saddle, sweat

soaked through his thick coat, and I set to work with the towel
hanging on a hook beside his stall door, scrubbing with a will.

Other women might have worried for their finery in the face of
so much flying hair and sweaty work, but I reveled in it. To be able
to support Aaron as he supported me brought a sense of
satisfaction that I felt in my bones. I worked every inch of the
towel until the whole thing grew heavy with moisture, Byzantine
leaning into the circular strokes with barely audible grunts of
appreciation. He deserved no less after his efforts, both physical
and mental.

"Hey, Jaque."

I turned my chin to find Jo standing in front of the stall, a
contented expression on her features. "I'm sure Byz would be
perfectly happy for you to keep doing that for another month, but I
thought you might like to go help Aaron out of his armour." She
pointed behind her with a thumb, and my eyes landed on the man
with unfailing accuracy.

I grinned widely and tossed her the towel before giving
Byzantine a last stroke over his rump and leaving him to his hay.
"How useful I might be is questionable, but I will enjoy the
experience all the same."

She laughed as I moved past her, then clipped the rope barrier
closed behind me so the horse would remain contained. "Oh, he
can walk you through it. You'll catch on fast, I promise. It's like the
world's noisiest strip tease."

I returned her humor in kind. "I shall remember that later, if I
catch you helping Bart."

Her grin held no repentance. "See that you do."

Then she left me to cross the grassy lot alone, eyes fixed on my
target as he stepped beneath a shade pavilion. The other two
knights were already at work at another trunk, metal clattering
noisily as it piled up. I slowed, stifling a laugh when I noticed his
cat straining on the end of a leash, meowing insistently. The
sizable feline reared up and hooked his claws in Aaron's chain mail
apron, shoving his head into Aaron's open hand with particular
relish.

"Am I intruding on a private moment?" I teased as I came close
enough to be heard. A bark of laughter came from Bart as he

worked on removing the last of Trace's armor, and Aaron turned toward me with a grin. "I could come back later."

"Ah, no," Aaron replied, before stepping in close so his companions wouldn't overhear. All the energy of earlier snapped against the inside of my skin, searching for an outlet. "I'd much rather pet you, given the option."

"A possibility," I purred, flashing him a saucy grin. "But you are assuredly wearing inappropriate attire for such activities. Perhaps I should help you shed your shell, my champion?"

A hacking noise came from behind him, and we both turned to face Trace. He made a disgusted face, the wrinkled lip and stuck out tongue out of place on his pretty features. Thankfully, I found it more teasing than genuine. "Okay, I'm gonna go before all you couples start ripping each other's clothes off. Bart and Jo are over at the horses making googly eyes, and I can only take so much."

Stifling a giggle, I watched him stalk toward the gate until Aaron's fingers wrapped around mine.

"Come on, my lady," he beckoned, a thousand indecent promises in his low voice. For the blood that rushed to my belly, I could have appreciated him, but the affectionate plea in his eyes brought me to love him more. "The sooner we get this pretty tin can off of me, the sooner I can reward you for your help."

"I am well rewarded, simply being with you, Aaron," I responded as Boris rubbed against my skirts to say hello. He settled back on to a pile of fabric beside the trunk after I rubbed a hand down his spine, remarkably relaxed about the whole affair. Not something I would have expected from a cat, but Boris defied the usual in every respect.

"Then let's get this done for my sake, *ma fleur*," Aaron said, smiling tenderly enough that I could hardly deny him anything. "Because I find myself in desperate need of your kiss, and this," His hand gestured the length of his body before rapping his knuckles against the breastplate. "Severely limits my ability to show you how happy I am to see you."

Thinking of the desire in his eyes as he rode up to me, I smiled back, though the upturn of my lips struggled against my guilt at distracting him. Still, I kept my eyes on his, determined to see the truth in them, however unpleasant. "I might venture a guess you were very happy earlier, *mon amour*. Though I wondered if that warmth would last after the spill you took. My heart ached to see you laid low, and I admit to feeling some blame for it."

The sun wrinkles around his eyes deepened considerably as he cupped my chin in his hand, never looking away. "Jaqueline, that fall was nothing compared to how hard I've fallen for you, and I'd repeat it a hundred times to prove how much I love you." Then he heaved a deep sigh and shook his head ruefully. "And much as I hate to put a pause on this conversation, I really need to get out of this armour. I'm cooking in here."

"Oh!" I flinched up onto my toes as if stung by a bee. "Please, show me how to help."

His relieved smile soothed my guilt as he pointed at the piece of segmented armour covering his shoulder. "Start here. There's a buckle under my arm, then another up by my neck."

To say I fumbled the whole process would be a very kind understatement, but Aaron remained patient throughout. I dropped several things as we went, the stainless steel weighing more than I anticipated, making a great deal of noise. The din covered the occasional curse word I let slip, and I frowned at my inept fingers. By the time we removed the armour from the waist up, my brows were in danger of remaining permanently knit together.

As I straighten from placing his neck protection on the pile of steel, determined to see things through, Aaron's hand reached for mine and he tugged me into his arms. I crashed against his chest, my breasts heaving against the edge of the bodice that shaped them as I sucked in a surprised breath. His eyes, however, remained firmly fixed on my face, pupils dilating so widely that the blue became a decorative rim. "Good enough for the moment. I need a kiss."

Our lips met with more haste than tact, but I could not spare a thought for the impact around the greed that welled up in my belly. Kissing him filled up the loneliness I carried around in his absence, obliterated any embarrassment over my ineptitude. Hands clutching the thick quilting of his jacket, I might have whimpered as our tongues danced against each other if I could have spared the air in my lungs. He tasted my desperation, answered it with a groan as his arms tightened across my back. Our bodies pushed into each other, instinctively impatient with all the layers that still separated us. I might have climbed his like the solid bulwark he had become to me, if not for a very loudly and pointedly cleared throat, which made both of us step back on a gasp of surprise.

Bart stood a good ten paces away, eyes politely averted, though I caught the edge of a grin on his wide mouth. "Brother," he said conversationally, as if he hadn't just walked in on a passionate exchange. Aaron's visage looked in conflict, stuck between amusement and frustration. "Methinks you might want to shuck the rest of that armour. Then you could go check the trailer for that vambrace you were talking about earlier." He turned to face us, green eyes full of sympathy and mischief before he redirected his gaze to where Jo spoke to some people at the fence. Though I rarely blushed, my cheeks flamed explosively over my unseemly conduct. What must Aaron think of my wanton behaviour in public? "I expect it could take you awhile. Jo and I will keep an eye on the camp."

Aaron nodded tersely, the mask sliding back into place, and I wilted a little. How could I have forgotten myself so completely? He must be disappointed. "Thanks, brother, good plan."

With the growl in those clipped words, I turned away, determined to put some distance between us. But I did not make half a stride before the callused rasp of Aaron's fingers slid around my wrist, shackling my steps in the process. "Jaque, do you mind helping me with the chainmail?"

"Of course," I said, voice pitched as low as my spirits as I moved to comply. He turned to give me his back, lifting my hand up toward a large, double tongued buckle. As my fingers closed on the wide leather belt that rode over his hips, he let go. The loss of his touch ached, but I found some steel for my spine and managed the thick leather as he held the weight of the linked chain cloth. Once that lay folded upon his trunk, I knelt to undo the tiny buckles that held on his leg armor, unable to bend over comfortably in the bodice. Not only would it have cut into my breathing, I did not trust the neckline should I upend myself.

My scalp began to prickle with heat as I set down the first leg. When Aaron did not move to help me access the second, I heaved a sigh and looked up, unprepared for the naked hunger in his eyes. All earlier concern that I had disappointed him vanished like steam as he stared down at me. Swallowing the moisture pooling in my mouth, I put a hand on his thigh to steady myself.

"Aaron, whatever delicious thoughts you are having, perhaps they would be easier to fulfill if you allowed me to remove this last piece?"

He smirked so illicitly that I felt the heat melting me from the inside out, and I clutched the leg of his pants with desperation. The rumbled mix of passion and humour in his voice shook my brain enough that I could see around the desire for a moment. "Then you might want to let go of my pants, Jaque."

For any of my former lovers, I might have released them. But Aaron and I traveled new territory, and I took another risk, nearly certain of my reward. As my hand tightened further in the fabric, he grunted as my blunt nails raked the meat of his leg, eyes losing focus as I pulled him around to face the other direction. When he stood correctly, I took my time, stroking the side of his thigh as I undid the buckle there. His half chaps prevented much I might have explored, but I loved the tic in his jaw as I rubbed circles in the back of his knee with my thumb. By the time I added the last bit of armour to the pile, he panted, barely audible over the clatter of steel. World's noisiest strip tease, indeed.

For all that I had driven him to the limits of his control, he cleared his throat and bowed at the hips to offer me a hand up with all evidence of pleasantness. "My lady, I am grateful for your assistance. Could you spare a few minutes to help me track down an errant piece of equipment?"

"A few minutes, my champion?" I teased, loving the firm, possessive clasp of his fingers as he hauled me upright as if I were a feather. "I should think we can manage better."

He tucked my hand into his elbow as he turned us toward the back gate. "Well, should we locate the armor in a timely manner, I have several other ideas to pass the time pleasantly."

Thick passion and soft love made a lovely harmony in my answering laughter. "Should you fall short of ideas, I am sure I could provide you with multiple possibilities."

No sooner had we pushed through the fabric drape of the gate, he dropped all pretense of manners and dragged me around to face him. Giddy with the wild promises in his gaze, I threw my arms around his neck, ready for whatever I had stirred up.

"Jaque, I'm sure a lifetime wouldn't be enough to fulfill all the fantasies I have about you."

Hearing him mention a lifetime, without an ounce of guile or prompting, stole my breath. Whatever remained in my lungs, I lost in the kisses that followed. Neither of us paid much attention to whether we were alone as he hauled me up his body and my legs wound around his waist. Later, when sense returned, I felt gratitude that we managed to make it to the horse trailer without interruption. But in the moment, I barely waited for him to step up into the tack room before I began clawing at the padded shirt he wore.

In the aftermath of perhaps the hastiest lovemaking I have ever known, we were a panting tangle of limbs and clothing. Yet despite the roughness of the scene, happy tears leaked from my eyes. This man fulfilled every part of me, and somehow, I did the same for him. Such a miracle felt like more than my heart could contain, but perhaps, if I were very lucky, his heart would hold on to the rest.

❧ **12** ❧

Aaron

I swear, I didn't mean to go all caveman on Jaque, but she spurred me on every stumbling step of the way. Nor did she allow me to feel sorry about using her so roughly, thanking me for the experience as she pressed kisses to my scalp in the aftermath.

My legs wobbled with effort and bliss as we got ourselves cleaned up. After straightening out her skirts and readjusting her bodice, we took turns at the horse trough to wash the worst of the sweat away. As she scrubbed a towel across my back, much as she had with Byzantine earlier, her touch lingered on the still faint bruises I gained during the jousting. The contact held no censure or hesitancy, only an acceptance I couldn't get enough of. Her gentle laughter as she put my hair back to rights put butterflies in my stomach. Not a sensation I'd ever experienced, far more familiar with the burning roil of stress. Lastly, I donned a dry shirt and clean tunic for the afternoon, prepared to do my duty on the field one more time before I invited Jaque back to the hotel.

As we ducked back through the curtain into the encampment, hand in hand, everything felt idyllic. The humid, low hum of warmth gave the scene a sleepy air. Horses quietly chewed their hay as Jo and Bart lounged beside the stalls. Trace had returned to his spot in the shade, and a haze of peace lay thickly enough that you could practically see it. Though I offered to take up the master of ceremonies duties for the late afternoon joust, the Company had made plans without me.

"I think you deserve a break, brother," Bart said, Jo standing at his elbow nodding her agreement. "You've held the line long enough."

Blinking hard against an upwell of emotion, I struggled to find a reply. "Thanks. I mean, seriously. Not that I regret an instant I spend in the lyst with you lot. Every day is a privilege."

Jo crossed her arms and threw a mock glare at me, the vehemence ruined by a half grin. "Well, maybe you should take the afternoon and show Jaque around. Might remind you why you fell in love with this life to begin with."

As Jaque rocked forward on her toes, excited at the prospect, I rubbed the back of my neck to relieve the strange prickles of shame. Jo hit the nail dead on, once again seeing a need and giving it a voice.

"Yeah, that's probably well overdue." As I looked to Jaque, the unabashed smile she offered answered the questions I asked before I gave them voice. "What do you say, my lady? Shall I show you around the Shire of Auburnwood?"

"My champion, I would be delighted to see your world through your eyes."

Which is how I ended up escorting Jaque up and down the lanes of the small faire, sampling candied nuts, smelling soaps, and stopping here and there to watch cast members create magic for the patrons. She delighted in the magic show put on by a mime, laughed outright at the bawdy singing nuns, and stared in fascinated horror at a sword swallower. We shared a lunch of chicken kabobs while sitting on a bench in a shady grove listening to a trio of ladies play their harps. As she lingered over a pouch at the leather workers booth, the front flap wrought into a deeply etched fleur-de-lis, I wrapped my arm around her waist and leaned in to be heard over the other people in the shop.

"That suits you, Jaqueline. Will you let me buy it for you?"

She startled and quickly set the pouch back on the shelf, her mouth turning into a slash. "Oh, no, Aaron, I do not require gifts."

I plucked the pouch up with my free hand and steered her now stiff body toward a wall of belts. My hand massaged her hip, urging her to relax even as my own tension spun tighter. The risk I needed to take in that moment held a greater edge of danger than any joust I had ever faced.

"Need and want are not mutually exclusive. In this case, I want to give you this. Seeing you dressed to fit into my world is a treasure, and as you know, well-made leather goods will last a long time. I'm investing in the hope that you'll be joining me at events for years to come."

Wide eyes flew up to mine as if we stood alone on an island, rather than in a cramped little shop. Her answer held a firmness of resolve that belied the trembling of her breath. "I will be by your side whenever our schedules allow, Aaron. For however long you will have me."

To that, I smiled, now surer of my advance. "Then be prepared for more shopping in the future, Jaque, because I mean to have you for as long as you will have me. Which will require a lot of outfit changes over time."

"I will make room in my closet when I get home then, Sir Drew," she murmured, her body melting against my side from hip to shoulder as she smiled up at me. "Though I warn you now, I am known to collect hats. This could prove to be an expensive endeavor."

"Worth every penny," I assured her, before dropping a light kiss on her cheek. Though we had washed up, I still caught a faint hint of my own sweat on her, and my body tightened in response. To cover for the sudden shift in mood, I gestured toward the belts hanging on the wall. "Now, let's pick you out one of these before we head back to camp. You said you wanted to watch Jo joust, and it's nearly time to start armoring up."

She didn't let me rush past the moment though, her free hand coming up to rest over my heart. "What you feel, I feel too, Aaron. Never stop wanting me. I need that, as surely as breath."

"Couldn't stop if I wanted to," I shot back, covering her hand with mine. "But I don't want you thinking that's all I'm feeling, Jaque."

"I know." She tipped her chin up and kissed the edge of my jaw, that simple brush of lips reaching the steadily filling emptiness in my heart. Seems that spot had been waiting just for her. "And for that, I love you more."

I might have responded in kind but a little kid barreled into the back of her legs, and words morphed into a barely discernible growl as I swept her around my body. Not that I aimed any anger at the kid, but every protective instinct I owned flared to life as if I were standing between her and a speeding car.

A young man shot after the tyke, worry lacing his shout. "Billy! Get back here!"

Jaque looked after the danger with laughing eyes. We both watched as the young man snagged the little boy around the waist, hoisting him into the air to the accompaniment of a shrill lilt of delight. She buried a giggle against my shoulder, keeping her words low as the pair reentered the shop. "Aaron, he is barely knee high to me. I believe I could fend off an attack to my ankles."

I cleared my throat with a grumble of embarrassment at the overreaction but managed a self-deprecating grin. "Sorry. I'm sure you'd have no problem charming him into submission, much like you do with my horse. And me."

"Ah, I am well acquainted with what works for the two of you," she offered, though her eyes slid sideways toward the little boy now being strapped back into his stroller. "Admittedly, I am far less familiar with the proclivities of very young children. As an only child, my exposure to them has been decidedly limited."

"Ah, not so in my case." I relaxed my hold on her and turned back toward the belts, fingering the long lengths of tooled leather as a nervous outlet. Talking about family always put me on edge. "With three younger sisters, all of whom have kids, I'm well acquainted with playing uncle. I'll even admit to knowing how to change a diaper."

"I am sure you are a wonderful uncle. And that you will be a boon to Jo and Bart when they have children." Jaque turned to the belts as well, studying them with single minded focus, completely unwitting of the wrench she tossed into my brain. "Speaking of, we should hurry. I do not want to miss out on a moment of the joust, now that I have you to explain it all to me."

I functioned on cruise control, hovering at her elbow as the shop owner fit a belt to her hips and we paid for the purchases. Jaque's casual mention of Jo and Bart having babies sent me skidding, hunting for traction. What the hell would we do when that time came? Would they move out of the apartment? Maybe off the farm entirely? Yeah, Jo said she wanted to take kids on the road, but her being pregnant would leave the Company short at least one jouster for a time. Sure, my brothers-in-law were chauvinistic dicks, and hadn't been much help to my sisters, but I knew in my bones that Bart would want to be there to help Jo. Was this something I needed to think about sooner rather than later? The way the two of them were with each other, my gut feeling said they wouldn't hold out long.

We made it back to camp in time to help with armoring, Jaque fascinated with how everything fit together. But even there, I had a hard time focusing, because thinking about my brother and Jo led me straight into another treacherous stretch of road. Did Jaque even want kids? We'd talked about many different things over time, but never once come close to the subject. I knew I did, at least in the abstract. Much as my mother's constant nagging wore deep grooves into my psyche, a family still remained one of my long-term goals.

However much I wanted to know if Jaque and I were on the same page, two things made me bite my tongue as we got the jousters mounted and followed them into the arena. On one hand, we'd barely begun our relationship, however strong my feelings were. And on the other, my stomach rolled itself up in a tightly aching ball at the possibility of having to give up either Jaque, or the misty dream of a family. Either would hurt, in ways I didn't want to contemplate. So, I shoved the question down deep, hoping to lose it in the mess that filled the back of my mind, and turned my attention to sharing the largest facet of my life with the woman I loved. If I were lucky, the worry would be for nothing, and our dreams would run parallel, at least where it counted.

Jaque

The question in Aaron's eyes looked as obvious to me as a marquee sign, but I shied away from giving an answer. Partly because I did not truly know my answer, some because I feared for his response, but all because we did not have the time to discuss things properly. No sense opening a door we could not enter, though I knew we would have to walk through it soon.

Needing a distraction, I allowed the whole of my attention to shift to Jo. She sat her gelding as if they were a whole piece of cloth, he the warp that lent them strength, her the weft that held them together. But the dense weave of their hearts made it difficult to discern where one ended and the other began, like the fine wool of my favourite driving jacket. All you could do is admire the smooth fabric of their partnership, the way they rippled and shifted together in the smallest movements.

In this particular moment, they stood just before the open gate to the arena, attention firmly fixed on Bart and Eros as they pranced along the far rail. Bart had a magnificent speaking voice, filling the air with a commanding, yet approachable tone, calling on the audience to stand for the entry of the royal court. My eyes followed as man and stallion turned toward the far end of the arena, where trumpeters heralded the entry of a finely attired group. They processed two by two toward the raised and shaded platform they occupied at the last joust. At the base of the stairs, the pairs parted, forming an aisle as the King and Queen moved up the middle. None of them took their seats until the monarchs sat down, then the various members of the court arrayed themselves elegantly across the stage as the King gave Bart leave to begin the joust.

Aaron's hands folded over my shoulders as he stepped in close enough to be heard over Bart, the weight of his palms delightful. "Do you want to sit down?"

I turned my head to look up at him, tempted to kiss his jaw, but unsure of how much affection I should display while in the public eye. "If I will not be in the way, may I stay in the arena with everyone?"

Approval lit his eyes and stretched his lips upward. "My lady, it would be a pleasure to show you the ropes. Just stick close to me once we are in the ring." Then he dropped a brief press of lips to my cheek, his thumbs sweeping deliciously up the back of my neck. "There, one last kiss to see us through until later."

I might have lingered there in the lee of his body if not for the thudding rhythm that vibrated up my legs and drew my attention away. Trace charged forward to the cheers of the crowd, his Percheron shaking the earth as they cantered ponderously around the far end of the arena. Though I missed the weight of Aaron's hands as he stepped to my side, I studied the younger knight with a bit of wonder. He relied upon his horse's good nature rather than any real skill as a rider, but I could admire that he stayed out of Capstan's way, not tugging uselessly at the reins or kicking extravagantly. The blonde cut a pretty picture, long hair floating in his wake, a smooth jaw and noble brow causing a flutter among the ladies present.

As they slowly lumbered to a stop, Bart's voice lifted again. I had hardly appreciated the timbre of it earlier, all of my focus fixed on Aaron. Now, I heard an extra bit of richness infuse his tone as he introduced Jo as a rose of uncommon strength, known for the sharpness of her thorns.

Though I did not see her cue him, Rowan rolled into a canter within the first stride, Jo smoothly following his motion. They moved much more quickly, arrow fast, yet feather soft. She dropped the reins and let him run, lifting her arms to encourage the audience to greater volume. Cheers joined Rowan's hoofbeats, a harmonization that made my pulse leap to join in the chorus of excitement.

Jo herself more than fulfilled my earlier imagining. The armour she wore, so wholly different from that of the men with its graceful lines and subtle etching, made her every movement all the more impressive. While her fellow jousters looked comfortable in their gear, she gave the impression that the weight of her armour was carried in her heart. As if she understood the strength she could inspire in women everywhere. I imagined the first hero she had inspired with her big dreams had been herself. A feeling I understood so deeply that my eyes welled with tears as I watched her take her place at the opposite end of the arena.

I startled at pressure against my lower back, so caught up in everything that I had lost track of my surroundings. Aaron pulled away at my wide-eyed regard, then waved me forward through the gate so he could close it behind us. Stationing ourselves beside one of two large mounting blocks, we watched as the King and Queen gave their blessing to the jousters. Once the formalities were concluded, the squires ran up to give each knight a rose, and I frowned as Jo rode right past Bart to hunt for someone in the crowd.

Touching Aaron's elbow to gain his attention, I spoke barely loud enough to be heard over the hum of the throng. "Why does she not give the rose to Bart, as you gave yours to me?"

Aaron's stubbled jaw thrust forward as if to point at Bart. "Oh, Bart has given Jo roses before, but Jo determined they needed to favour the crowd instead. To be honest, that one rose may be the only one I can ever offer you so publicly. We play to the audience we are paid to entertain, and this is part of the game." His mouth drew down in a subtle frown. "I hope you won't feel slighted for it."

When Jo beckoned a young girl to the rail to accept the big yellow bloom she held, I shook my head. "No, Aaron. Roses are a passing trifle compared to the knowledge of your love. I understand."

Tension seeped away from around Aaron's eyes and his smile returned as Trace settled on an older woman in wizard's robe. "For that, I love you more," he said softly, bumping his shoulder against mine.

I could not reply though, as the squires ran over to snatch up some rings from beside the block and then scurried about the arena. Their actions were unfamiliar from the joust before, and I watched them all with sharp fascination. Nor did I have long to wonder, as several squires lined up along the jousting lane and held a ring aloft, while another offered a spear to Trace. Bart's commentary assisted my understanding.

"First, our knights will test their aim at rings, ensuring they are prepared for the more dangerous joust. Cheer for Sir Davies, good people, give him cause to rise to the challenge."

Trace kicked Capstan into a canter, dropping the reins as they ran between the ropes of the lyst. To my eye, he did a passable job, certainly far better than I might have managed back when I still rode horses. My hand-eye coordination had never been particularly fabulous, even during my fearless Pony Club years. Though always last picked for teams at the gymkhana, I had excelled in dressage and turnout, which served me well even now.

Ah, but Jo's pass caused a twinge of very hungry jealousy. I missed the feel of a spine undulating beneath my seat, the flow of energy between horse and rider. Much as I loved Jo, in that moment, I almost hated the ease of her movements, unhampered by fearful memories. Nor could I understand how she could put herself to the hazard, over and over, risking injury to herself or her mount.

Men, I understood. They thrived on risk, ego and pride a driving force. Even Aaron, who balanced his competitiveness a bit better than other men I knew, had the same edge of challenge in everything he did. I adored them for it, to be honest. The simplicity of going after what you wanted without as much overthinking had to be an easier way to live.

Before long, the riders approached the mounting blocks, Bart's voice no more than background noise as I followed Aaron's direction and stepped up to Rowan's head. I did not touch him until Jo let go of her reins, and even then, I only offered him the back of my hand for a sniff. Though his hooves remained firmly planted as Aaron worked on the remaining bits of armour, he stretched his neck out to touch my skin with the pink between his nostrils. He had the softest eyes, even with the thoughtful wrinkle that popped up whenever Jo shifted in the saddle. Ringed with long white lashes, they regarded me with the sort of calm that lured you in. Even with the activity around us, I stood in a bubble of quiet I usually only enjoyed with Lyric.

My jealousy washed away on an easy puff of air as he blew out against my fingers. While I could envy Jo's skill, I could harbour no ill feeling in earnest. Her horse showed me the truth of things, that they were each other's safe place even in the violence of the joust. For that, I had only earnest admiration and a deepening sense of sisterhood.

Which made watching the match ever so much easier. Trace's style could best be described as utilitarian, much like some of the commercial carriage drivers I worked with. Safe, and he would always get the job done, even if you could not call it beautiful. Aaron had an extra edge when he rode that made the violence into art, like a broken glass catching light, or the jagged edge of torn silk caught in the wind. And he matched his horse, move for move, as long as he kept his mind in the moment. Still, each served to bring Jo's work into stark relief.

Jo and Rowan were purposeful in every movement, no motion wasted, each stride measured. Even their hits were precisely timed, my body flinching sympathetically with every impact. They were clockwork steady, but with the sort of exactness that became beautiful in its execution. The care they took with each other was palpable, as he carefully slowed so she remained centred after the hit and she stroked his neck after each pass. They were the soft flow of watercolour paints blended together with fine watchmaking, bringing a lump to my throat as I thought back to old rides with my own glorious partner.

I nearly choked on the lump when Jo and Trace tipped sharply back in their saddles on the final pass, startled into a hoarse yell along with the rest of the crowd. Thank God for Aaron's restraining hand on my shoulder, or I might have leapt into action, not even knowing if I could help.

"Wait," he said calmly, steadying my nerves as the horses slowed and their riders struggled to right themselves. Which allowed my thoughts to slow enough to see clearly. Capstan remained on a steady path, unwavering in his aim, while Trace tried to heave himself upright without the use of his hands. Why did he not grab onto something?

But Rowan sidestepped, lifting his head in alarm, intentionally trying to remain under his rider. For her part, I could not imagine her struggle with gravity, arms tightening in toward her centre after being blasted backwards. Somehow, despite her thinner form, she curled her body in on itself and shoved her weight upward, using her outside stirrup for leverage. By the time they came to a halt, she sat hunched forward over the saddle pommel, looking completely spent by the effort.

"Is she well?" I asked Aaron, leaning in to be heard over the applauding crowd.

"She'll need to catch her breath, but everything's fine." He squeezed my shoulder in reassurance before letting go. "Trace is in the same shape, I'd bet, and she'll probably recover faster. I don't know that I've ever known a tougher jouster than Jo."

"Truly? But she is so much smaller! And a woman!"

My exclamation made Aaron grin, even as he watched the jousters shake hands. "Size and sex has little to do with mental toughness, a lesson I learned from my sisters well before I knew Jo." Then he slanted a knowing gaze my way, warmth bubbling up in my chest as he finished the explanation. "A lesson you've only reinforced, Jaque. You aren't a jouster, but you've got just as much guts and determination as Jo. Don't sell yourself short."

Then we were busy divesting Jo of her extra armour, leaving me to stew in my own thoughts for a few minutes. My eyes studied her face for signs of pain, stroking Rowan's neck to feel for tension that might signal something was wrong. I found nothing but the peace that comes from embracing your challenges and the glow of a job well done.

When Jo climbed from the saddle, Bart rode up to meet her, their hands tangling together in a quick squeeze of affection before moving on. But when she turned back to her horse, I saw the secret hidden in her palm.

Rowan's ears swiveled to complete attention, nostrils aquiver with anticipation as she opened her fingers to offer him a mint. A simple gesture, but so telling of the connections that abounded in Gallant Company, forming bonds stronger than the steel the knights wore. Aaron elbowed her on the way by, teasing like one might imagine a brother would. "Hurry up, Jojo, the public awaits. You can spoil your pony later."

She stuck her tongue out at him, then turned to me with a twinkle of humour in her eyes. "Jaque, would you be so kind as to keep Rowan company while I play my part? Aside from Bart, there's no one else I'd trust more."

I nodded mutely, struck by the compliment. Thankfully, my hands knew their work, and I loosened his girth automatically. We walked the rail, allowing many to stroke his long salt and pepper forelock, sharing the magic of the day with the masses. Later, as I followed Jo back to camp and joined in the rhythm of caring for the herd, it occurred to me that I had gained far more than a boyfriend in Aaron. As each of the horses and humans accepted me into their ranks, even Byzantine unbending enough to allow me to kiss his broad brow, I realized I had found a family. One I wanted to belong to almost as much as I belonged to Aaron. But as I drove home alone later that night, I thought I might have one more massive challenge to face if I wanted to join their worthy company. For how could I call myself one of their number if I allowed fear to stop me from even riding my own horse?

Aaron

Jaque didn't stay much past getting the horses fed for the evening, and while I felt her absence as we settled around a small campfire that night, I didn't begrudge her leaving. She had given me a huge gift in coming, offering up her own time to become a part of my life. No one had ever made such a big effort, and the way she fit into the Company made it feel like she'd always been there.

By the next afternoon, we were back together as she came out to the farm to join us for dinner. Just sandwiches, since we were all beat from packing and unpacking, but no one complained. We stretched out on the worn leather furniture in the main house, discussing plans for the new workshop as Boris lounged on the cushion behind my head.

"I'm thinking we should keep the hay out in the new shelter, Aaron," Bart offered as he leaned forward to drop his used paper plate on the table next to everyone else's discards. We'd left nothing behind but a few crumbs and grease stains, but Soleil still sniffed hopefully at the table edge. "It'll reduce the fire danger and it would give us more room for an actual workshop if we store more equipment in the loft."

My eyes narrowed in contemplation as I considered the idea, though the feel of Jaque's fingers stroking up and down my arm melted away the stress that usually came from a change of plans. Life felt pretty amazing at the moment, and it would take an awful lot to ruin the glow of contentment I sat in.

"Yeah, and with Trace heading up to work with Ambrose, maybe we could make up a little area for him to practice," Jo added, using air quotes as she said practice. "I'm pretty sure we've got some dents for him to work on already."

Trace shifted in his seat like someone had put a burr under his butt. "I dunno about that, Jo. I'd probably make things worse right now."

"Right now, I can handle the fixes," Bart reassured him, leaning back to put his hand on Jo's leg. "But I think it's a good idea, for the future. Ambrose thinks you've got a knack for this stuff and having the proper tools down here will mean you don't lose too much practice when you're home."

Trace scrubbed his knuckles against his jaw before settling back into the lone recliner. "Yeah, I mean, that'd be great. But don't go to the trouble on my account."

I turned a narrowed gaze on him with a smile to soften any sting he might get from my rebuke. You could never be sure what he might take seriously. "Trace, though we may go to a great deal of trouble for you, you've always been worth it. You're family, and no matter what, we take care of family."

Jaque's hand tightened on my bicep and she leaned in to press her cheek to my shoulder, the silent support buoying.

"Well, shit, what do I even say to that?" Trace asked, back to squirming again.

Jo's socked foot lashed out and caught him in the shin, just hard enough to make him go still. "Geez, now who can't take a compliment? How about thank you?"

He mock glared at her and mimed a swat at her leg as he stood up. "Yeah, we must be family. Only a sister could be such a pain in the butt." When she stuck her tongue out at him, he rolled his eyes before stepping around the coffee table to approach me with an outstretched hand. "Thanks, Aaron. You guys saved me, and I hope you know how much I appreciate it."

Though I hated to move away from Jaque, I stood to meet him and dragged him into a back-slapping hug. "You're welcome, Trace."

On the way back to the apartment, I stopped by Byzantine's stall, our evolving relationship requiring more time and attention. Jaque tugged her fingers out of mine as I leaned over the Dutch door, then migrated down the aisle to greet the spare horses she leased over the holidays, leaving me to face my partner alone. He ignored my appearance at first, something I might have taken exception to in the past. Given the choice between his food and me, I could sympathize with his decision, particularly considering his possessive response to most anything edible. So I upped the ante, digging in my jacket for the last remaining cookie of the handful I'd shoved in there at the beginning of the day. Being an opportunistic land shark, he moved toward me the instant I held my hand out, one ear pointed my way. The other remained fixed on his hay, as if someone might steal it while he stepped away.

"Bubba, nobody wants your food, they all have their own," I said. Humor made my chest feel airy as Byz chewed on his reward. Just to make a liar out of me, J.T. appeared at the door of the stall beside us, tossing his head to get my attention. Byz pinned his ears and gave a high-pitched squeal as he twisted toward the other horse, and I might have chastised him for the behavior if not for the way he softened when he turned back to me. Busy lips rubbed over my jacket sleeve, but he carefully kept his teeth to himself, clearly showing me he understood our social contract. I'd be good to him, he'd be good to me, and all would be right with the world.

Such clear evidence of the positive changes between us had my hand lifting up to his neck, automatically curling my fingers to scratch beneath his mane. Seconds later, we were engaged in a full-blown itch fest, him leaning against the door frame with all his weight, lips stretched into the air as I increased the pressure. He grunted like a pig, enjoying every second until my arms and shoulders complained about the workout, and I dropped my hands.

After a yawn of contentment that rolled his eyes back in his head, he looked to me with by far the cutest expression I'd ever seen out of him. Broad ears pricked forward hopefully, and his lips flapped together as if to ask why I'd stopped. I patted his shoulder and laughed as I used the other hand to brush off some of the hair he'd shed all over me. "Sorry, big'un, I'm all worn out now. But I'll get you again in the morning."

Jaque reappeared at that moment, her knowing smile telling me she'd seen it all, and helped me dislodge the liberally scattered hairs. "I believe the two of you might become friends after all."

"Yeah, we just might," I agreed as Byz disappeared back into his stall with a shake of his boxy head. Then I lifted an arm and turned my body to invite Jaque close again, for once, excited by all the possibilities in my future. Surely, if Byzantine and I could right our relationship, hope remained for the one remaining source of personal conflict in my life.

As if the mere thought invited trouble, my phone rang, this time with the opening strains of the Miss America pageant theme.

"Mother," I answered quickly, concerned over the late hour of the call. "Everything okay?"

If not for Jaque's arm around my waist, I might have staggered when my sister Bethany delivered news I always feared would come.

"Aaron, Mom's in the hospital."

❧ 13 ❧

Jaque

Aaron went uncharacteristically pale, and his weight sagged against me as all the breath left his lungs. While I had no idea what he had just heard, I understood that something must be wrong for him to respond so physically. When he listed to one side, I steered us toward the wide bench beside the wall. However strong I might be, I thought perhaps my energy might be best conserved for the moment. Who knew where this bad news would take us tonight?

"Is she okay? What's wrong?" he wheezed as he blindly reached for the seat, then slowly lowered himself down, every motion stilted. All his attention rested on whoever spoke on the other end of the call. I did the only thing I could in such a situation and sat beside him, my hand stroking up and down his spine. "Okay, I'll jump in the truck. There's no way I'll get a decent flight this late, but if I drive I'll be there by morning. Rest if you can. I'm on my way."

He lowered the phone from his ear and stared off into the distance, not seeing the warm light of the barn aisle or even the darkness outside the doors. His opposite hand ran through his hair, then tightened into a fist as he pulled at his own scalp, eliciting a groan that stemmed from something much more painful than that simple tug accounted for. Then he shoved to his feet, ignoring my presence completely as he shot toward the door that led upstairs. I caught up with him as he slammed open the door to his bedroom, the abrupt sound resulting in a shout of alarm from Bart and Jo's room.

Aaron paid no attention to Boris's meows, upending his duffel into an empty laundry basket before throwing it back on the bed. Like an automaton, he grabbed folded clothes from the chest of drawers and shoved them into the bag, pushing away Boris's entreaties for attention. That uncharacteristic action, more than any of the rest, pushed me to approach.

"Aaron?" He made no indication he even heard me, and I might have tried again if not for Bart's appearance in the doorway.

"What the hell's going on in here?" Bart barked, surveying the scene with a frown.

"Mom's in the hospital. Gotta go," Aaron responded, the words wooden and disconnected coming from a man I knew to be so deeply feeling. "I don't know what's wrong yet, really. Just shortness of breath and dizziness. They're still evaluating, but I gotta be there."

Bart softened immediately, as did I, my heart panging with sympathy. No wonder he was upset! I would be a mess were my father in a similar situation.

"Okay, we've got things handled here. I'll call the guys, see if they can play any coverage for next weekend, just in case." Aaron did not even look up, though I caught a relaxing of his shoulders that said some of it must have registered. "And Aaron?"

At that, Aaron froze, his head slowly swiveling up to regard his brother. The despair in his eyes tore me to shreds. "Yeah, Bart?"

"You need anything, you call." The conviction in Bart's words filled up the room clear to the high ceiling, and I half feared Aaron might buckle under the weight. Relief overtook his entire body, even his knotted fists loosening. "I don't care what time it is. I don't care what I'm doing. I'll be there for you, brother. We all will." At that, his eyes flicked to me, and I felt Aaron's regard shift my way as well. "I'll leave you two to talk. Drive safe."

Then Bart quietly pulled the door closed behind him, and I took a tentative step toward Aaron as he lowered himself to the edge of the bed. One of his hands stroked over Boris's dense fur as the other lifted toward me in supplication.

I took it without hesitation, wanting to be whatever he needed me to be. "What can I do, *mon amour*?"

Suddenly, for the second time in as many days, I found Aaron's head buried in my sternum. He pulled me close then wrapped his arms around me like steel bands. My hands found purpose, one threading into his hair as the other softly stroked his back. He did not cry, or even shake, only held on as if he might never let go. But I knew he needed to leave, much as every selfish cell of my body objected to the idea.

He turned his head to the side, nuzzling against my ribs before he spoke. "I wanted tonight here, with you, Jaque. I'm sorry."

Throat thick with emotion, I bent to press a kiss into his wild hair. "No apologies, my champion. Life will part us from time to time, but I will be here, waiting for you."

At that reassurance, he looked up. Though the pinch of worry on his forehead remained, his cheeks did not look quite so drawn. "You make this too easy on me, Jaque. I wish I could shrink you down and tuck you in my pocket, so we didn't have to be apart."

My brain and mouth were, for once, in perfect accord, requiring no real thought. "Would you like me to come with you?"

His eyes, up to this point quite dry, dampened. "No, I couldn't ask that of you, though I appreciate the offer. Means a lot."

A small smile tugged at my lips. "You are not asking. I am offering because I love you, and if my being with you will make things easier, then I want to be there."

His lips thinned, and a tremor moved through his arms. A denial was in the offing. So I leaned in and whispered, "Let me be your navigator, Aaron. Surely, someday in our long future together, you will return the favour." Then I kissed him, sealing my words against his lips, stopping his objection until it softened and fell away.

His acceptance came on a shared breath. "Okay."

In less than an hour, we were on the highway, Soleil and Boris curled up in the back seat on top of our bags. We spoke little for a change, the mile markers flashing by to the hum of the big diesel engine. A flurry of texts took care of my own obligations, Dan happy to cover the farm in my absence. Cardi promised to exercise Lyric for me, so her fitness would not suffer, and Laura, one of my drivers, would take over the wedding that the carriage company was obligated to do. Then I turned my undivided attention to Aaron. While he looked at home behind the wheel, this time, I read impatience in every flick of his eyes.

"Do you want to tell me what waits for you?" I asked gently.

He shook his head, though not in denial. "Don't really know, yet. Which is what scares me. Mom and Dad were both smokers, and while Mom keeps telling me she's quit, we all know she hasn't. So it could be anything related to that. Or something else entirely. I'm going in blind."

"My father was a drinker for many years," I commiserated, turning a little more in the seat so I could see him better. The warm leather embraced me, and in any other circumstance, I might have been tempted to nap. But not when Aaron needed me. "Addiction can be difficult to overcome."

"Yeah." I caught many untold stories in the weight of that agreement. "I think she does it because it reminds her of Dad. But I don't know. She's not much into talking about him unless she's bringing up the past. We don't talk about the divorce, or even his death. Just how good things were when we were a family, which is a load of crap."

The bitterness of his statement fouled the air in the cab, and I sought to lighten it. "Grief is a strange beast. It makes us remember only what we wanted, and none of the bad. My father has my mother on a pedestal, as if she were a heavenly creature beyond reproach. I am sure she must have been as human as the rest of us, but I will never know."

One knotted hand left the steering wheel and spanned the distance between us. I took it, bending over to kiss his knuckles, grateful for the sweetness that allowed him to see past his own troubles to my old hurts. "I'm sorry you lost your momma, Jaque. But I'm grateful she brought you into this world."

"I am too, Aaron," I replied, content to hold his hand as the sweet sentiment cleared the air. "And I look forward to meeting the woman who gave you life as well. I have much to thank her for."

He stiffened before exhaling forcefully, as if pushing out whatever troubled him. "And I hope she doesn't give you cause to regret coming with me. She can be a little distant with strangers."

My free hand ran up from his wrist, firmly massaging the muscles of his forearm until he began to relax again. "Aaron, I assure you, whatever happens, I will never regret a single moment as long as we are together."

Concern, and an unaccountable fear shaded his gaze as he looked away from the road for a moment. I did not blink, wanting him to understand the depths of my resolve. To have him let me so deeply into his life was a mark of trust, and I would not betray it. In less than a second, he turned his attention back to driving, but the shadows faded from his cheeks as his hand squeezed mine.

"And for that I love you more," he rasped out softly.

A simple enough statement to make, but it perfumed the space between us with much needed hope in such a bleak situation. Would that it could have lasted beyond those mindless hours we shared on the highway, but when the sun rose the next day, I discovered Iowa held far more troubles than I could have imagined.

Aaron

We parked on the lowest level of the multi-tiered garage, leaving the windows cracked for Soleil and Boris. With the cool weather, they would be fine until we got a better idea of what we faced.

The hospital itself loomed like a giant silhouetted by the rising sun, hunched and easily capable of tearing my world apart. Terror and concern warred with each other in the tight confines of my chest as we crossed the rain-soaked parking lot toward the main entrance. Barely constrained by the chain of love that linked Jaque and I as surely as our joined hands, panic beat an implacable bruise on the inside of my sternum as we entered the foyer. Selfishness had fueled my acceptance of Jaque's offer to come with me, but now, selfishness wanted to keep her away from my mother.

Bethany had texted with an update, saying her oxygen levels were stable and her breathing had eased. Already, Mom had begun to annoy the nurses with her demands, insisting they change the temperature in the room, fussing over the drab colors of her hospital gown. Too much ice or not enough in her water cup. Couldn't they make the beeping of the machines quieter? At least Beth had been able to appease her for a while, offering to help her with hair and makeup so she would look presentable when the doctor came around.

I love my mother. Probably more than I should, but there you have it. That didn't mean I was ignorant of her temperament. High maintenance hardly did justice to her and she could give master classes in guilt trips. Screw that, the woman could argue a PhD dissertation on the topic. And while my ex-fiancée never confirmed my suspicions, I had a strong feeling my mother had been the catalyst that shattered that relationship so spectacularly. The odds were in favor that she'd pull something similar with Jaque, and I needed to warn her before we faced the inquisition of my sisters.

Once inside the elevator, I pulled her around to face me, sucking in a deep breath for courage. "Jaque, I..."

She shut me up despite my good intentions, kissing me with a sweetness I greedily consumed. Blood pumped through my veins with renewed fervor after the long night of driving, shoring me up as easily as a cup of coffee. Worry and stress faded under the assault of her tongue and the clutch of her fingers in my hair.

"Ahem," A dry voice intruded on the passionate moment, and we broke apart to find an amused nun holding the door open. "I am assuming you were looking for the C level. If not, I would be happy to let the door close and wait for the next available elevator car. I hate to break up such a devoted scene." She punctuated the offer by looking us up and down like we were two naughty children, a hint of humor glinting in her peaceful eyes as the wrinkles around them deepened into a map of fond memories. "God is love, after all, and I am glad to see it alive in such a heart-weary place."

"Ah, yes, thank you, sister," I managed, waving Jaque out the door with an approximation of a courtly bow, then I turned to regard the nun for a moment. "We appreciate your understanding."

"Bless you, children," she answered kindly as the doors slid closed, and for several moments, we stood there in silence. Until Jaque broke the silence with a very girly giggle.

I turned toward her, surprised to see a hard-red flush on her cheeks as she fanned at her face and stared at the ceiling tiles. "Oh, *sacre*! I do not think the nuns of my youth would have been so gentle had they found me in such a compromising position. I would have been writing lines on the chalkboard for days!"

However inappropriate it might be, my animal brain latched on to the thought of Jaque as a Catholic school girl. Hardly a fantasy that had ever crossed my mind, but I found fertile soil for many a midnight imagining in the rich chocolate of her eyes and the warmth of her embrace. "What, no confession required? Or hail Marys' to make?"

Her chin tipped back down so we could regard each other, and she smiled with a bit of hesitancy. "I would imagine those as well, though I never got into enough trouble with boys to earn such punishments. Nor was I friends with any of the girls who did, so the exact penalties remain a mystery."

I scoffed playfully, stepping closer so I could take her hand. "If we'd been at school together, I'm sure you'd have been in plenty of trouble."

The flush rushed back, and a twist of pain hunched her shoulders as she looked away. "I doubt that, Aaron. You were likely quite popular, and I would have admired you from afar, but never spoken to you. I was a chubby girl, given more to studying than socializing. You never would have seen me."

Much as I feared she was probably right, I tried to think better of teenage me than that. I might have been a screwed up, washed out athlete, but I hadn't been a jerk to anyone. And while it had taken me awhile to notice her as an adult, I wanted to hope that daily exposure to her kind heart would have brought me around. So, I reached for her chin, cupping it gently as I brought her eyes back to mine, and exposed a bit more of my damaged soul.

"Jaque, your sweetness would have called to me. I craved it then, as much or more than I do now." Her eyelashes shuttered shyly, and she smiled, prompting me to continue. "I wouldn't have been much of a knight in shining armor. But I think you would've saved me anyway."

Shy disappeared, conviction blazing in the grip of her fingers as she met my eyes. "We will save each other. Now, and in the future. Whatever waits for us, I will be by your side as long as you will have me."

Trying to keep things light so I wouldn't choke on my ever-thickening emotions, I faked a laugh. "You keep saying stuff like that, and I'm going to take you seriously."

"You should," she replied quietly as the doors to the ward opened, divulging a couple of nurses in brightly colored scrubs who barely spared us a glance on their way to the elevators. Then she pointed toward the same doors with our joined hands as a brightening sense of hope grew in my chest. "For now, let us see to your mama. Then, I shall see to you—we could both use a good meal and a chance to sleep."

At the mere mention of sleep, my jaw reflexively stretched in a yawn, eyes watering with the force. Jaque immediately followed suit, covering her mouth with a hand as I managed a genuine chuckle. "God, that sounds amazing. I know just where to go, too.

Let's see what the doctor has to say then. I'm ready for a full belly and a flat spot to curl up with you in my arms."

So I turned her toward the doors and picked up the phone by the door so we could be buzzed in.

Bethany stood up from the chair beside the nurse's station as we approached Mom's room, her face pale with exhaustion and worry. Though her eyes quickly flicked over Jaque, she managed a tight smile when she looked up at me. "Thank goodness. I'm about done in. Do you think you can cover for an hour before Courtney can get here? She has to drop the kids off at school."

"Sure, sure," I promised her, giving her a brief squeeze before she shrugged me off. Bethany had always been a bit chilly in terms of physical affection, so I wasn't surprised. Each of us were incredibly different, to be honest. Courtney could be the most clingy when she was stressed, needing reassurance, and Darlene was more of a comfort giver, rather than receiver. Personally, I liked touching and being touched in equal measure. Dad had done his best to discourage such unmanly behavior, but time had muffled his disapproval, and Gallant Company had done the rest. Thankfully, both set me up to be ready for Jaque, whose touch meant more to me than a thousand accolades.

"Thanks. I've probably got a disaster zone waiting for me at home. Frank can manage to get the kids to school, but not much more." A heavy sigh made her shoulders slump, and she looked longingly toward the door. "Just play nice for a bit, please? See if you can't charm her into being more patient. The nurses are already fed up."

A squeeze from Jaque's fingers around my bicep reminded me of my manners before Beth could scoot off. "I'll do my best. But if you can spare a second, I'd like to introduce you to my girlfriend, Jaqueline. Jaqueline, this is my nearest sister, Bethany."

Bethany gave her a longer look, lips thinning before she formed a semblance of a smile. "Nice to meet you, Jaqueline. Good of you to come up with Aaron on short notice."

Jaqueline offered her a hand, and while Bethany took it, I couldn't say the greeting was warm. My eyes narrowed, but I kept my mouth shut. We already had enough upheaval going on. "Of course. While I wish the circumstances were not so urgent, I am glad to meet you as well. I hope we will have time to get to know each other better?"

Bethany shrugged and looked away, a clear sign she wasn't comfortable answering. "Maybe. Depends on how long Aaron can stay, and what the doctors have to say. They kick us out of the ward at shift changes, so perhaps we can all meet for supper at some point."

Jaque's smile widened with genuine delight. "I would be thrilled. He has told me about Nessie, and I should very much like to meet her. As well as hear stories of his misspent youth."

Eyes rounding with surprise, Bethany looked back to me with a much warmer smile. "Oh, there are plenty of them. I'll talk to Courtney and Dar, see if we can make anything happen." Then she slanted her eyes sideways at Jaque, skepticism muddying her voice. "We'll see how long you last."

And while Jaque assured her that she would be happy to listen to everything they had to say, I knew Beth was referring more to Mother. My gut roiled with an acidic burn, all the more unpleasant for the knowledge that it would probably get worse before the day was out.

Bethany made her exit shortly after making sure the nurses knew who I was. That left me alone with Jaque, and I turned toward her with a regretful frown.

"I hate to ask it, but do you mind waiting out here? Mom is going to be flustered enough, and I don't want to surprise her."

She smiled like the sun coming out from behind a cloud, soothing the pit in my stomach. "Aaron, you once told me that maybe someone should take care of me for a change. Please," Her hand released mine, but quickly came up to touch my cheek. "Allow me the chance to return the favor. I will check on the animals, then see about some coffee from the cafeteria. You let me know when I should come back."

A kiss hit my cheek, barely a whisper of contact before she turned away. I smiled as I watched her walk off, not just because I appreciated the shape of her, but because I loved the whole of her. Then she turned back around with a mischievous grin, jogging the few steps to fetch up against my chest. I grabbed her shoulders to steady her, then froze when I felt her hand sliding into the front pocket of my jeans. A quick dart of my eyes confirmed no one would be watching, then I focused entirely on her touch.

"My apologies, I forgot the truck keys."

I swallowed my tongue as she purposefully took her time fishing them out, her puckish smile growing in potency as she lifted them up in between us.

"You really are going to drive me crazy in the best way possible," I rasped as I let her go again.

She backed away, a toss of her chin giving her ponytail a saucy sway and not an ounce of regret dulling her spirit. "Consider it a mutual effect. I will be waiting for you and thinking of a million delicious ways to distract you from your troubles." As her hand touched the door, all the heat mellowed dramatically. "I love you, Aaron Drew."

Then she disappeared, the double doors hiding her from view. I stood there for a moment more, savoring that last glimpse like the finest of liquors. Because while I appreciated the distractions she offered, the love in her eyes gave me the strength to face down my greatest fears.

Which is why I was still smiling, ever so faintly, as I poked my head in the open door of Mother's room. The beeping of the monitors and the hiss of oxygen sobered me completely, and I braced myself on the door frame before I could speak. "Mom? May I come in?"

"Of course, my dear boy!" she exclaimed, though she began coughing the instant the words stopped, and I shot inside to see if I could help. Though my feet didn't slow, I flinched inside to see her look so very small in the hospital bed. Her typical makeup job did little to hide the deep hollows of her cheeks or the sagging under her eyes. In fact, as I poured a glass of water from the pitcher beside the bed and held it out, I would swear the caked-on foundation and contouring made her look like a mannequin against the white sheets. Add in the plastic cannula bisecting her upper lip, and I barely recognized her.

A few breaths later, she accepted the cup, hands trembling as she brought it to her painted lips. A sheen of sweat broke out on her upper lip as her chest rose and fell with an effort, and my heart broke a little more. This is what I'd always feared, with all her years of smoking, and I hated being right.

"Do you want me to get a nurse?" I asked gently, compassion surging forward like Byzantine charging off the line. Whatever had come before no longer mattered, only the present would make a difference.

Her lips twisted sourly, and she waved her perfectly manicured hand in denial. "No." A sharp bark, then a pause for breath as she calmed herself enough to speak in a much quieter voice. That didn't make her statement any less cutting. "Those clueless, heartless harridans won't do anything for me until the doctor comes again. They say I'll need more tests before they can treat me with anything more."

"Mom, I'm sure they know what they're doing," I placated, despite the urge to tell her off for being so rude. Much as I hated every hospital stay I'd ever had, I maintained a great deal of respect for the nurses who cared for me. I'd get them some flowers or something, later, a thank you they would likely never hear from my mother.

"Doubtful. They've done nothing but bruise me with their needles and keep me up at all hours to check my vitals. I would be fine if they had just let me sleep." She set her now empty cup down with the same ladylike deliberation that she always maintained, which gave me a bit of hope. But in the next, she fretfully plucked at the blanket across her lap, a whine taking over her voice. "I'm so tired, Aaron."

Pity joined the party of upset in my stomach, and I tightened the muscles there against the oncoming burn. "Mom, if you want to close your eyes for a few, Beth said the doctor won't be in until about nine. I can go sit in the cafeteria with Jaqueline, so you aren't disturbed."

Her eyes sharpened so fast, I recoiled against the sting as they cut me. "Jacqueline? Do I know her? Jacqueline Forbes from Des Moines?"

I cleared my throat but didn't look away as I answered. "No, Jaqueline Sauveterre, actually. She's the gal we lease horses to over the holidays. And my girlfriend."

Though her breathing trembled, the set of her jaw went from weak with exhaustion to rigid as steel. "I cannot believe you are just now telling me. How long has this woman been involved with you?"

Holding my chin high, I told her the abbreviated truth. "Since New Years, Mom. But she's been in Florida for a couple months, and we've just started getting serious."

The chill of disappointment filled every word, and her eyes looked even colder. "And you brought her here to see me at my weakest. I'm in no shape to entertain visitors, Aaron Allen Drew. Why would you embarrass me like this?"

Huffing a breath in annoyance, I nonetheless reached for the clawed hand she had wrapped around the bed rail. I cupped it in both of mine when her frigid skin met my palm, still worried despite this little conflict. "Mom, you don't have to see her if you don't want to. I'd never do that to you, and Jaque is far too kind to impose. She simply came along for moral support and to help keep me awake while I drove. I haven't slept since Sunday night, and I worried about falling asleep at the wheel."

Like the flip of a coin, her face changed, the deep lines of anger giving way to hollows of worry. "Oh, my boy! You should have rested. Your sisters shouldn't have made you worry so much. I'll be just fine."

"I know you will, Mom. You're one of the stubbornest people I know." I kissed the back of her hand in hopes I could keep her temper soothed, noticing a faint bluish tinge to her nails that spoke to her breathing difficulties.

"Your Daddy often said the same thing." Her eyes watered with memories, as if their story were some kind of fairy tale, but I remembered something much less sweet. A plate shattering against the door as he walked out, calling her a stubborn bitch over his shoulder. But I pushed the darkness back, unwilling to bring it into the light of day. "Either way, the hospital doctor should set things right once he talks to Doctor Mullins, and I can get out of these wretched robes."

She mustered a weak smile as I squeezed her hand in encouragement. "That's right, Mom. We'll get you out of here. Bart has things covered at home, so I can stay for a few days."

Her lips pinched in, the artificially pink color disappearing into her mouth as her nose lifted in the air. "Home? You are home, my boy! And don't you ever forget it!"

I shook my head over the old argument but said nothing to refute her. Wouldn't do any good to get her wound up. "Mom, please, just rest? We'll talk more later, after the doctor comes by, and once we hear what the plan is, I need to go get a little shut eye. Otherwise, I won't be any good to anybody."

She patted my hands, then looked down at the thick joints with a sigh. "A shame you lost your chance at a baseball scholarship, dear boy. You could have done great things, then come back here to be the hometown hero. I could have you close, like all the rest of your siblings."

Gently, I extracted my hands from hers, forcing a smile. "We all have our own roads to travel, Mom. And I'll always come when you need me. But for now, please, rest?"

Eyelids suddenly heavy, she blinked a few times as her shoulders slumped back into the pillows. "You'll be close though, my boy?" The rasp in her voice seemed as much from melancholy as her difficulty breathing. "You won't leave me alone like your daddy, will you?"

The plaintive note in the question tore at my heart, so I gave her the best truth I could. "I'll be here when you wake up, Mom. And if I'm not, you just call me. I'll be right downstairs."

As she pulled the blankets up around her shoulders and turned her head toward the wall, I stepped away. A nurse met me at the door, a finger over her lips as she gestured me to follow her. Neither of us relaxed until the door closed without a voice calling us back. "Thank you for getting her settled. She's been agitated since she regained consciousness. No surprise, if she's in nicotine withdrawals."

I didn't bother to deny Mom's habit, even though I thought she would if anyone asked. Instead, I shrugged and ran a hand through my hair, which made me miss Jaque. I needed her with me to keep my hands busy. Or to tangle her own hands in my hair. Both, preferably. "I get it. She's not an easy person to get along with in the best of circumstances, and this is bound to bring out the worst. What time will the doctor do their rounds?"

Sympathetic eyes took in my sagging posture, reading me with unerring accuracy. "It'll be after shift change, which is in ten minutes, and we'll be closed to visitors for about two hours. That should give you a chance to get some food and caffeine before you get back. Give me your number, and I'll call if she gets agitated again, okay?"

With a smile of gratitude over having found an ally, I scribbled down the number and said thank you again before heading for the double doors with weary determination in my steps. Two hours might be just enough time to get checked in to the local motel and grab some food. And if I were very lucky, maybe I'd get a few minutes to close my eyes, with Jaque's soothing hands stroking through my hair.

Jaque

I hated to wake him, whatever the clock said. After heading straight for the hotel, we had dozed off together, face to face, his weary eyes falling closed as our heads hit the pillows. No sooner had Boris curled up behind his head and began to purr before he fell asleep in earnest. Soleil took up the pillow behind me, as well, sandwiching us together in a comforting well of love and peace.

Judging by the wrinkles of worry still creasing his sleeping brow, Aaron needed this peace. Physical exhaustion played its part, but the emotional weight he carried strained his stamina far more. Whatever had gone on with his mother did him no favours, and while I would not press for details, I hoped he would share some of the heavy load with me soon.

But time slowed for no one, so I gently brushed the hair back from his ear, slowly, repetitively and firmly stroking his scalp the way he seemed to enjoy most. His eyes twitched and his jaw worked for several seconds before he blinked awake and produced a drowsy smile. "It's time, then?"

"Yes," I affirmed, pressing a soft kiss to his chin. "If we are to pick up something to eat, the time is now. Much as I would love to shelter here, I would not keep you from your family."

"Yeah, and I'd rather beat the doctor there than be late." He blew out an incredibly gusty breath as he rolled away and upright on the edge of the bed. But it seemed the effort did him in, as he slumped over his knees and folded in around his middle. An inescapable ache welled up in me as I slid across the mattress on my knees and wrapped myself around his back.

"Aaron, how can I help? Whatever you need, please ask."

"I can't…" The words ground to a halt, overtaken by a sob for air, his body rattling beneath me. "Jesus, Jaque, she can't breathe and I can't help her. This could kill her!"

"Oh, *mon amour*." My throat closed around a thousand useless platitudes. I missed my mother on a cellular level and I had never known her. All I could do is hold him while he dissolved into grief, a few burning tears dropping onto my arms as he pulled them tighter around him. The grip of his hands felt just shy of bruising, but no pain registered around the ache in my heart. *Sacre*, how I wished I could take the burden from him, even for a moments release. "I am sorry for your hurt, my heart," I whispered against his shoulder, letting my hands fist in the belly of his t-shirt.

He laughed wetly, a surprisingly warm sound in the midst of his troubles, and his hold on my arms gentled. "What did we discuss about apologies?"

Loosening my grip, I mustered an encouraging smile as I eeled around beside him. "In this, you cannot stop me. While I cannot apologize for something I did not do, I am certainly full of remorse for your pain, as if I caused it myself."

"I'm no stranger to pain," he said, looking down at his once broken hands with a twisted frown that made me suspect he did not mean only physical suffering. A warm trickle of sympathy spilled from inside me like I had cut my own heart.

"None of us are, Aaron." I covered his thick knuckles with my smaller hands, pressing some warmth into him however I could.

"You gotta understand, Jaque, before I pull you any further into my life..." Pausing, he turned toward me enough to deliver a kiss to my forehead. He lingered as if it might be the last time his lips might touch me.

I refused to accept such a fatality and tipped my face up to align our mouths. When he made no move to deepen the kiss, I pushed his endurance, licking his lower lip. He groaned and capitulated, the very flavour of him changed by his sorrow. As if I could draw it from him, I strove to deepen the kiss, twisting into his lap to bring us together more fiercely. Strong hands grasped my waist, pulling me closer as our embrace turned fierce, clutching.

"Jaqueline," he moaned, rolling us onto the bed in truth until his body covered mine. Then he pushed up on his forearms, anguish maring his beautiful eyes as he looked down at me. "God, I want to lose myself in you!"

"You can," I assured him, though I understood the conflict that made his arms grow rigid. "Though I do not think now is the time. But I do want you to remember that you can. I am yours."

Gently, he lowered his body over me, one hand cupping my cheek. So much emotion filled his damp gaze, I felt sure the tears would return. "I hope you never change your mind. Because I am yours too."

For that confession, I gave him a soft smile and stroked over the rough stubble on his chin. "Unless you tell me you kick puppies and ride your horses into the ground, I am confident that nothing you tell me will change how I love you, Aaron."

His jaw flexed under my hand, deep shame and shallow hope making his reply turbulent. "No puppy kicking, but my horsemanship was once non-existent. If you can forgive that, then I will happily love you for the rest of my days."

Guilt coloured my joy over that sweet declaration, though I leaned up and kissed him for it all the same. Selfishly, I wanted to linger, hiding from the troubles that waited for us just down the road. To swim a while in the languorous bliss of his touch, his unflinching affection. But that would not be very loving to him, in the end. His family needed him.

When I let myself slip back down onto the mattress, he sighed again. Thankfully, while I heard the pain and regret in it, I also felt the affection in his hands as he pulled me up off the bed after him. We quickly washed our faces, changed shirts and made sure the animals needs were provided for. Then we stepped out the door, his hand firmly wrapped around mine, prepared to face whatever came.

Thankfully, we still beat the doctor to the ward, and I settled into a chair in the waiting area as he headed off to his mother's room. One of the nurses made sure I knew where to find the vending machines and restrooms, but otherwise, I was left alone. This gave me time to text Jo, updating her with the little I knew. Shortly after I sent the text, my phone vibrated, showing a call coming through in reply to my message. Scurrying back out the doors, I accepted the call with a whispered greeting.

"Hello?"

"Jaque! Sorry, I hate to bug you, but I wanted to see how you are holding up."

I frowned as I dropped into a chair near a window alcove, not wanting to disturb the quiet. "I am well enough, though worried for Aaron. I want to be with him, but his mother is not comfortable seeing me yet."

Jo snorted, which I came to understand could convey many emotions, from humour to disgust. In this case, the snort wore a sharp, edgy quality that made me sit up straight. "Well, don't expect you'll be comfortable meeting her either."

"What do you mean by that?" I asked brusquely, instinctively defending Aaron's mother as I would my own father. "To have raised such a wonderful man, I am sure she is delightful."

"Look, it's not in me to gossip. I hope she'll be perfectly charming, in fact. But as you are my friend, I don't want you walking in blind either. The woman can be difficult at the best of times, and an outright cow at the worst." She sighed heavily, followed by the familiar noise of a horse pushing hay around, both sounds stealing some of my tension. I knew Jo to have a beautiful soul and had never heard her say an unkind word about anyone until now. But from Aaron's stories, I also understood she was not one to allow her friends to be hurt. "Just be careful, okay? Stay strong. Strong enough for both of you."

"Oh, I will not fail him," I affirmed, letting a bit of steel fill the words. Though I would not share the bleeding of his heart, I could admit to the injury to mine. "I did not know that loving someone so much could make my heart ache so deeply for them." And because I knew her to be as fierce a horsewoman as me, I lowered my voice and made a confession that perhaps only she would understand. "There is a better chance of my giving up Lyric than giving up on Aaron. And as you well know, I would sooner lose a limb than forgo my mare."

Jo chuckled and her reply came in a much lower tone as she shared a similar secret. "Though I'll categorically deny it if you say a thing, I can understand completely. While it would be one of the hardest things I ever did, if I needed to give up horses in order to marry Bart, I might just do it." Then her voice took on a tone of absolute confidence as she added, "Not that he would ever ask for such a thing."

"No, Josephine, I do believe the both of us are equally blessed to have men who love us just as we are." A bloom of contentment filled my belly as I gave the words to the air, as if that made the truth even more solid. "They would move the heavens to be sure we never gave up our horses, in fact."

"So true."

The love that laced those simple words had a strength in them that reverberated between us, gaining power. Jo had always felt like more than a casual friend, from the very first, and now, I could see our relationship for what it truly was—a sisterhood.

"Jo, before I go, I want you to know how much I care for you. I know we have not known each other long, but you are precious to me."

After a pause long enough to make me worry I had overstepped, she replied in a language unlike anything I had ever heard, musical to my heart. "*Adar o'r un lliw ehedant i'r un lle.*"

"Your pardon?" I asked, desperate to know what those beautiful words meant.

"Oh, forgive me." I could tell she smiled, even without seeing her. I felt its echo on my lips. "It's Welsh, the language of my roots. It means that birds of the same colour fly to the same place. And in this case, Jaqueline, I think it's safe to say the two of us were meant to love these men, to be part of their lives, and each other's."

"*Il n'y a que les montagnes qui ne se rencontrent jamais,*" I answered back, pleased to share my own language with someone. "There are only mountains that never meet, which would mean that no one is so fixed that fate cannot bring them to where they are meant to be. For my part, I am blessed many times over to have come to this place in my life."

"Then, dear friend, I will leave you to travel the road ahead of you and Aaron. And I'll trust that no matter the ruts and bumps, you'll find your way back home. You'll find family waiting for your return."

Connection confirmed, we said our goodbyes, and just in time, as my phone buzzed with a message from Aaron, wondering where I was. I rose from the tiny alcove as I typed my reply, and headed back to meet him, on much stronger footing than when I sat down. For as much as I believed in the love between Aaron and I, knowing someone else in the world had faith in us lent me a measure of surety I would be drawing on to get through the days ahead.

Aaron

We were back in the truck shortly after meeting with the doctor. Courtney stayed with Mom for the day. Mom had asked me to go by the house for her dressing gown and her knitting, which I would bring back to the hospital later when I took over the watch. The doctor had outlined a catalog of tests to be done, refusing to even guess at a diagnosis until he saw the results, but he'd been pretty firm about Mom needing to rest in between. She acted entirely too compliant, simpering and sweet over every request the doctor made, which confused me. The man was younger than me, so I couldn't call it flirtation. Still, my shoulders itched with the surety that some sort of intent lay behind her actions.

I parked beside Mom's older model Cadillac and turned toward Jaque, who had remained silent for the short trip. Conversation felt redundant when I met her eyes, that gaze a soft caress against my over wrought heart. Instead, I held out a single finger in the universal gesture that asked for a minute, and quickly slid out of my seat. She watched as I walked around to her door and waited patiently as I opened it and held out a hand to help her down. I know she didn't need my help, and I wasn't doing it to impress anymore. But I needed her touch, craved it like breath. With her hand in mine, I could face the wretched memories that permeated the walls of my mother's house without getting overwhelmed.

She said nothing still, letting me lead her up the concrete steps to the front door. The old deadbolt made a creepy grinding sound as I unlocked the door, an omen of the stale nightmares waiting within. Normally, I could compartmentalize like a champion, keeping them at bay with a false cheer. But with my heart in shreds over Mom's health, I felt stripped bare, all of my armor useless against the remembered shrill shatter of china plates hitting the door frame as my father fled the house.

Jaque's hand tightened, reminding me I no longer stood alone. The warmth of her touch and the happy memories we were making gave me a fixed point of joy to work from. I exhaled slowly as my eyes adjusted to the dim interior, but I didn't bother with the lights as we walked up the short flight of stairs. Even with Jaque's presence, I didn't want to face the faded, yet somehow still garish colors of the living room. My nostrils were teased by the faintly acrid scent of cigarettes, which made my stomach lurch. Usually, Mom smoked outside, or by the kitchen window, but something had changed. Knowing that unrelenting train of thought would lead me to a wreck, I held my breath and turned down the hallway.

While Mom's bedroom sat to the right, I detoured quickly to the left, ducking into my old room. As if we were being chased, I pulled Jaque around me and quickly latched the door before falling backward against it to suck in a deep breath. Sure, the air still tasted heavy with memories, but some of them were sweet enough to balance the bitter.

"Aaron?" Jaque's voice soothed me like honey to a sore throat, easing the rasp as I swallowed down the last of the phantoms. Her brown eyes were as gentle as her hands as she stroked over my face with both. "What is wrong? How can I help?"

I couldn't even smile for her, though I leaned into her touch. "You're here. That's enough. And I'll be okay. Just a lot of memories in this house, few of them good."

Her lips pursed into a moue of concern. "I am sorry for your hurts. Should you care to talk about it, I am willing to listen."

"No." The denial came out a bit sharper than I intended, though she didn't flinch away, her hands firming on my cheeks as if to hold me in place. Many of the other women in my life would have taken offense, answering the carelessness with even sharper words. But Jaque just waited, eyes still soft, patient as a saint. I continued, practically whispering as if to make up for the mistake. "I can't face them right now. I'm too tired, too worn down. But thank you."

Tipping her head slightly to the side, her lips relaxed. "Then perhaps you would share some of the good memories with me? I would love to know the younger you, even a little bit." She looked around the still dim room with a hint of tease in her voice. "How many girls have you snuck into this room over the years, Aaron Drew?"

For that, I actually managed a hint of a smile as I flipped on the lights so she could explore. "If you don't count my little sisters sneaking in when they couldn't sleep, that would be exactly one. You."

Hand halfway up to a photo of my favorite horse, Cal, she shot me a doubtful look, though her eyes were warm. "Truly? I would have thought you quite the catch in high school and full of mischief as well."

Shaking my head, I walked the scant few steps to my old twin bed and dropped onto the mattress so I'd be out of her way as she poked through the best parts of my past. "No, I didn't bring people over. I didn't want anyone to know about my real life. Any trouble I got up to was usually down at the river or at the rodeos I went to with my dad. Though even that stopped after my parents finally split up."

God bless her, Jaque didn't fish for more details, just let the statement fade as she perused the shelf full of model cars I'd built on the nights I couldn't sleep.

"Which one?" she asked, pointing to the dusty models.

My brain couldn't grasp her meaning, exhaustion dragging every thought through a layer of mud, so I hunted clarification. "Which one what?"

"Which car is your favorite? The one you want to drive across the country. I still want to navigate for you."

My throat clogged with emotion as I remembered the night she offered, and then closed entirely as I imagined our future together. Tears threatened for the second time in one day, though I gulped them back with a will so I could breathe again. "It's the dark blue one on the end, with the black stripes on the hood."

She carefully picked up the car and turned it around in her hands. "A Charger? Really?"

The pointed inquiry left me a little behind the curve, and my jaw dropped. She knew what it was? "Um, yeah. I've always been a Dodge guy."

Her lips tipped up with mischief and faux innocence laced her words with rare sarcasm. "Truly? I never would have known. Not like you are at all devoted to your truck."

"Well, yeah." A real grin erupted, even though I felt a bit guilty for it with all the trouble my Mom faced. "Dodge vehicles don't have the same rate of breakdown as your beloved Ford."

After setting the little car back on its shelf, she swung toward me and planted her hands on her hips, playful challenge in her gaze. "I would argue that point, as said Ford has seen me through many thousands of miles with little trouble. However, as the last breakdown served to bring you further into my life, I cannot even be upset. The truck did me a favor."

I hauled her into my arms so I could kiss that sassy grin, as in love with the challenge as the softness. Not a passionate embrace either, but something infinitely sweeter that lingered on my tongue even as I drew back to meet her gentled gaze. "Yeah, me too. Don't think I've ever been more grateful for a blown radiator hose in my whole life."

I was even more thankful for the way she eased me into talking about my childhood, asking questions about my old baseball jerseys that hung on one wall, and the rodeo buckles arranged on another display over the head of the bed. But before long, we were both yawning, and I left her behind for a moment to gather the things Mom wanted. Thankfully, her robe hung undisturbed beside her vanity, and her yarn bag was in its usual spot beside the rocking recliner. Within minutes, we were back on the road.

We were both so tired that after getting back to the hotel room, we barely managed to take the critters out and get ourselves into pajamas before yielding to the siren song of the king-sized bed. For the first time since our relationship began, neither of us wanted anything sexual. We sought comfort, pure and simple, shared breaths and tangled limbs quickly lulling us toward oblivion. Much as I appreciated our moments of mutual release, this felt like another critical ingredient in our love story. To know we could find peace as well as pleasure together made the possibility of forever seem so much more real, whatever troubles we faced in the next several days.

Jaque

Before returning to the hospital we enjoyed dinner at a small restaurant near the centre of town. Aaron looked a little more himself, the haggard slant of his mouth now softer, and the shadows under his eyes fading. He had taken care with his clothing, making use of the iron in the hotel room to press his shirt and jeans. The soft cotton button-down he wore matched the blue of his eyes, and he had donned a pair of polished black cowboy boots and matching belt with a silver wrought buckle. While I had never seen him in western wear, I enjoyed the visual very much. His shoulders seemed broader, and the dark jeans perfectly framed the art of his muscular legs.

For my part, I did my best to dress appropriately, on the off chance that his mother would like to meet me. While I had not packed a dress, I did have several nice blouses that would suit. I wore a pair of wedge heels that never failed to make me feel more confident. Something about the extra height boosted my ego. Aaron took advantage of those extra couple inches and kissed me repeatedly on the short walk to the restaurant.

So many people walked up to our table to offer their well wishes for Aaron's mother, manly handshakes and kindly hugs passed around with a genuine warmth that let me see ever so much deeper into all that made Aaron into the man I knew. While he implied many less than gentle memories at home, the people of his hometown had made a big impact in his life, and still cared for him, even after he moved away.

There were a few women who cast doubtful glances at me, most with perfectly done up hair and makeup, including one of the waitresses. But I did my best to smile and be supportive of Aaron, because that was all that truly mattered. I needed no one else's acceptance but his.

Our waitress, an older woman who treated Aaron with a motherly sweetness and concern, made sure we got plenty to eat and even boxed up some slices of pie for later. She gave me a lingering hug before we left and smiled approvingly when Aaron and I walked out hand in hand. That small endorsement reinforced my decision to be there for him and put a bounce in my step as we made our way across the parking lot.

Better still, after we reached the hospital, Aaron cleared his throat and turned toward me with a tender hope softening the sun wrinkles around his eyes. "Jaque, before I have to leave you in the waiting area again, would you indulge me in a few kisses? Something to tide me over until later?"

Oh, yes, that I could definitely do, and not for him alone. I said not a word in reply but pushed up the centre console on the bench seat and slid as close as I could get without being in his lap. He took my hand and pulled it up to his neck, though I needed no encouragement to tangle my fingers in his hair as our lips met. Much like our earlier cuddle before we slept, this felt different. I still felt passion in the slow slide of tongues and the way his arms tightened across my back, so I did not worry over fading interest. But despite the fact that we were sneaking kisses in a parking garage, I no longer felt like he needed me as a distraction from his worries. Our kisses were an affirmation, a promise so sweet I tasted it on the back of my tongue, savouring it long after we let each other go.

I spent several hours on the barely padded couch in the waiting room, mostly texting with Cardi. After driving Lyric yesterday, her excitement for our next show bubbled over.

'OMG woman! Your mare is game right now! I had a time getting her to stay on the rail and not anticipate turns. She wants to do the cones something fierce.'

'LOL' I replied, fingers flying over the keyboard, though I paused briefly when a short video popped up. Sure enough, Lyric's ears swiveled to lock on to every little orange cone, her head tipping slightly to ask Cardi for permission. Her steps were elastic, bounding and I loved the bunch and flex of her muscular haunches. Even her tail reflected eagerness, the black waterfall of thick silk held away from her body, yet softly swaying in time to her strides.

'*She looks wonderful, Cardi, and I owe you a case of chocolate bars for keeping her going. Aaron's mother is stable, though we have no diagnosis yet. Hopefully, we will be back soon. He has his own work to get back to as well.*'

'*You do whatever you need to, girlfriend. I'm happy to play with your girl, now that Vinter is retired.*'

After a successful season at Intermediate, Cardi had retired her old Welsh pony from any competitive efforts. He now enjoyed the softer life of teaching her husband's grandchildren about the joys of horses. Desperate for some sort of humour in the morass of emotions Aaron swam in, I shot back with something one might consider both offer and threat to anyone who knew my pony. '*Clint is currently unoccupied, should you feel the need to get back in the driver's seat.*'

She sent a string of emoji to convey her feelings on the matter, from a horrified scream to a skull and crossbones. '*I thought we were friends Jaque! Are you trying to kill me?*'

Muffling laughter behind a hand, my eyes darted around the waiting area to make sure I did not offend anyone with the sound. The whole ward felt swathed in wet wool, nurses quiet as they went from room to room and the other visitors sombre or exhausted.

Not long after Cardi wished me good night and good luck, Aaron reappeared from the hallway. A tight smile made his cheeks sharp, and I stood immediately to reach for him, wanting to soothe. I could not fix his problems, but I would do my best to always be there for him as he faced them.

"How is your mother?"

He did not answer until his hands were wrapped around one of mine, his grip gentle, yet vibrating with urgency. "She's better tonight. Looks like I'm not the only one who got some rest today, and she's asking to meet you."

While my heart thrilled at the request, something in his voice smacked of hesitancy, which made my reply guarded. "If you think I should?"

Fingers tightening on mine, his gaze bore a weight I could hardly fathom. "I think the two women I love most should meet. But I'll warn you now; she can be as cutting as she is charming, and her moods are extra shifty right now. I'll understand if you'd rather not."

Touching my free hand to his heart, I hoped I could answer in a way that would reassure him. "Aaron, I am here for you, no one else. What would help you best?"

While the knot of worry between his brows remained tight, he let his lips relax and a bit of boyish innocence snuck into his eyes. "Well, I don't think you can fix her health, so that's right out."

"No," I murmured, a pang of longing squeezing my heart as I wished it were within my grasp to relieve the worry that drove him.

"Then how about we pop in for a few and visit before she gets ready for bed?" The statement came as a question, still giving me a choice. "We'll be heading back to the hotel after, since she's feeling well enough to be alone tonight, then I'll be coming back in the morning. We're all going to sit in on the conversation with her doctor, see what we're dealing with and where we're going from here."

"I cannot think of anything better than a full night of rest, for all of us. Little could be more healing," I said, already wishing to hurry the introduction along. Longing ached in my bones with a steady throb, so different from the usual lightning flashes along my nerves. I wanted to make love to him, to deepen our connection, affirm the strength of our feelings.

His eyes, already the deepest blue of twilight, filled with a rich echo of my hunger. "After our earlier nap I've got more than rest in mind, *fleur de nuit.*"

A flush burned my skin, though it barely reached my cheeks, most of its heat concentrating on my thighs and belly. My voice came out hushed and throaty as my hand tightened on his shirt. "*Mon amant*, I shall enjoy applying that particular salve to both our hearts."

He nodded a terse acknowledgement to cover for the emotions rioting between us, then turned to lead me down the hall. Towed in his wake as much by our heart connection as the grip of his hand, I took several deep breaths for composure. His mother deserved my respect and complete attention. I wanted her to meet the woman that loved him with all of her heart, not the impatient hoyden that wanted to drag her son into a mop closet and get lost in his kisses.

The underlying hospital scents of antibacterial hand gel and bleach halted at the door, held at bay by thickly applied perfume. Though the perfume itself held a pleasant hint of flowers and musk, the overwhelming use of it made the back of my throat burn as I pushed my way through the odiferous barrier. I blinked around the sting as Aaron let go of my hand, momentum carrying me the rest of the way to his side.

There, I clutched his elbow for support until my eyes cleared enough to meet the bland gaze of his mother. Reserve cooled her expression, something I could not fault her for considering the last several days of stress. Her shoulders, thin even with the quilted satin dressing gown to disguise them, were held back with ingrained hauteur. Not even the oxygen tube beneath her nose or the IV in her manicured hand could take away from the air of superiority that wreathed her as heavily as the perfume.

I saw Aaron in the colour and shape of her eyes, but there the resemblance ended. Where his mouth had wrinkles from sun and smiles, hers looked carved by chronic unhappiness. Most people in the hospital wore their humanity plainly, but this woman defied her circumstances with finely penciled brows, a far too even complexion and enough mascara to turn her eyes into the focus of her face. Her gaze bore down on my hand where it rested on Aaron's arm, and she smiled so thinly I wondered if her heart looked as gaunt as her painted red lips.

Aaron cleared his throat, and before I could remove my hand from him, he covered it with his own. While her eyes narrowed at the touch, they warmed considerably as her attention shifted to Aaron. Whatever my first impression might have been, I could not fault the way she looked at him as if he hung the stars in the sky. In fact, my heart panged, having never seen that look from my own mother.

"Mother, I'd like you to meet Miss Jaqueline Sauveterre, my girlfriend. Jaqueline, this is my mother, Mrs. Francine Ellen Drew."

"Jaqueline?" The woman asked, as if she did not believe him, then turned that questioning regard to me. A thread of trepidation ran up every vertebra in my spine, as if a spider plucked at my nerve endings to see if something had caught in her trap. "French, if I am not mistaken."

"Yes, Mrs. Drew," I answered, lifting my chin with pride as my accent thickened slightly. Prick me, and I would bleed Quebecois. "French Canadien, to be specific."

"Oh, Canadian, how quaint!" She smoothed the blanket across her lap, a calculating slyness in the batting of her lashes. The low hiss from the oxygen gave her words a breathy vulnerability, but also a hint of menace that I fought to ignore. "And how did you meet my lovely boy? I don't recall him traveling north of the border."

"Aaron and I have been friends for several years, thanks to his horses," I offered, hoping to reassure her that my feelings for him were long standing and strong. "We have only recently come together as a couple, though it feels as if we have been together far longer."

"Ah, yes, he did mention you using his horses for the holidays," she replied, the coy lilt of her voice targeted to point out Aaron's generosity. "And now, here you are, making yourself comfortable in the rest of his life. How beneficial for both of you!"

I stiffened at the implication that I might be taking advantage of his kindness, but bit back any kind of reply. Instincts well-honed by years of competing with people who would stop at nothing to shake your confidence told me that she hunted for a weak spot. While pride clawed at my throat, I swallowed it down and forced a serene smile.

"Indeed, I believe Aaron and I do an admirable job taking good care of each other. He has supported me in my endeavors, and I shall continue to support him." Though my smile never faltered, I let my eyes harden so she could not mistake my intent as I finished the declaration. "Unwaveringly."

Her nose lifted up with a superciliousness that said she smelled something fishy in my reply, but I spoke only truth. Not that she could have smelled a dead tuna around the perfume she had bathed in.

"Mother," Aaron sighed with the sort of tiredness that sucked all the anger out of me, righteous or no. "Speaking of support, can I get you anything else before we go? I'd like to get a solid night of sleep so I can be here for you in the morning."

Immediately, she softened, though her maternal warmth came off as suffocating as her perfume. I wanted to drag Aaron from the room, not caring for the blood she tried to draw from him with fangs of guilt. "Oh, my darling boy, I understand. No one would willingly spend a night alone in this sterile room when you can have the warmth of someone who cares for you and a softer bed than this chair." She waved disdainfully at the duck yellow recliner in the corner, then brought a hand up to her forehead as her body slumped back into the mattress. "You go, and I'll do my best to sleep. Morning will come soon enough, and then maybe the doctor will tell us how much longer I'll be stuck in this purgatory."

Aaron stepped away from me, the warmth of his touch cooling fast as he leaned down to embrace his mother. She threw a look of triumph at me over his shoulder. I had to physically shake my head to dislodge an image of a spider gloating over its prey, his spirit visibly dimmed by her manipulation. "Mom, if you really want me to stay, I will."

My stomach churned with objection, but I held back the bile-laced denial that struggled behind my teeth as if my life depended on it. I was not there for me, or for this woman. I stood in Aaron's corner, no matter how much it rankled his mother and ate at my nerves.

As she mocked sniffling against his shirt, he handed her a tissue from the bedside table, and she pressed it under her eyes as if to catch tears before her makeup could be mussed. He crumpled even further as she cried, and I understood why my own tears affected him so much. She used them to manipulate, making him sensitive to the slightest hint of hurt.

"No, no, my dear, you go. Leave your old mother to rest and I'll see you here, bright and early tomorrow. No sense depriving both of us of comfort when yours is close at hand." She cast a quick look my way as Aaron sat back, judgement in her stare as if she knew what sort of comfort I offered. But I looked away, allowing my gaze to soften as I took in both the hope and fear in Aaron's eyes when he searched her face.

"You'll always be beautiful and young to me, Miss Iowa," he said, appealing to her obvious vanity as he cupped her hands in his. "And I'll bring you a cinnamon roll from Harper's, if you feel up to eating."

There, her attention shifted beyond the little room, calculation in the quick shifts of her eyes before she smiled like the sun. He perked up like a flower long deprived. "You make sure you bring enough for your sisters too, Aaron Allen. And the doctor. That boy needs to be sweetened up so I can go home."

He shook his head even as he smiled indulgently. "Oh, I think if you put your mind to it, you could charm him easily."

"It's not *me* that needs to charm him," she said coyly, waving Aaron away when his eyes narrowed. "Don't you ruin my fun, Aaron Allen. I've got so few pleasures in my life and you've still years to enjoy your own. Go, take your pretty little girlfriend and find some happiness for as long as it lasts."

The wistful sadness that marked her last words did a number on me, pity cropping up to drown my earlier pride. Could I begrudge her the connection with her son when she had already lost her husband? Surely the old memories that haunted Aaron, whatever they were, hurt her as well. But her words also strengthened my resolve as Aaron did as she bid, and we let ourselves out of the room. He and I would last a lifetime if my aching heart had anything to say about it.

Aaron

A tempest of emotions buffeted me from the inside as I drove back to the motel. None of them could be indulged for the moment, knowing I was responsible for Jaque's safety and that our animals waited for us. So, I firmed up the walls of my heart against all the sadness, anger, pain and even love that formed the clouds in my mind, and gave the road my full attention.

Thankfully, my hometown was small and the drive short, but the instant Soleil heard the key in the lock, she began to whine. As Jaque pushed the door open and bent to shush her little dog, I moved across the room to open the bathroom door before Boris could start caterwauling. We took them both outside, carrying them out to the grass for some well-deserved recreation in a fenced enclosure behind the pool house. Soleil rushed to relieve herself as Boris explored beneath the base of a hedge, and I blew out a breath, relieved for my own part to be back among those I loved.

No, wait. I still loved my mother, but Jaque and these animals were different. Perhaps it's better to say that I felt more peaceful surrounded by love that held no conditions. I didn't have to dance to please them, and that freedom made me feel lighter. The inner storm faded as I watched Soleil pounce on Boris's tail, and he mocked a swipe at her pointy nose to discourage her.

"Be gentle, *petite chou*," Jaque chided, even as her arms wrapped around my waist. Warmth and peace moved over me like a blanket, stilling the last of the ugly vibrations remaining in my chest.

I returned the embrace, tipping my chin down so I could bury my nose in the dusky flower scent of her hair. Though the night air held a chill we stayed for quite some time, watching the fluffy dog race figure eights around the almost as fluffy cat. Low growls of play punctuated the air with energy each time Boris swatted at Soleil's blurred shape. The dam I'd built after leaving Mom melted away, and softer versions of the storm clouds settled in my belly. Laughter snuck out around the edges when Soleil took a turn with too much speed and lost her footing. She slid sideways several feet, like a runner stealing home, then popped up with a startled expression that was almost cartoonish.

Jaque laughed too, then stepped around to face me, her hands spreading across my back to hold me close. "Sometimes I envy animals their ability to live so much in the moment."

"We're lucky to have them around to remind us," I said, one of my hands reaching up to pull the heavy comb holding Jaque's hair up off her neck. Much as I'd been stressed out, I'd still noticed and appreciated her efforts to look her best for my mom. Still, I would always prefer her hair down, the raven locks heavy against the back of my knuckles and the purple strands catching the light. "And in that vein, I'd be happy to take you upstairs and live in the moment with you."

Immediately, her thickened lashes swooped down, the natural palette she used to accent her eyes making the chocolate brown look even deeper. She wore no lipstick, the true rose of her mouth rich enough on its own, and my lips were greedy to taste hers. But despite that allure, I caught a glimpse of hurt that dimmed her passion. "I am always willing, Aaron, though I do not think your mother would approve."

My gut stewed, fear that I would lose her making a bitter broth while chunks of regret and anger swam to the surface. "I'm sorry, Jaque. In any other circumstance, I'd have stepped in and said something to derail her. But I wanted to leave her somewhat peaceful so we could all rest. Picking a fight, however warranted, would be counter to her recovery. I can't thank you enough for enduring her temperament."

A flash of fierceness lightened her gaze as she looked directly at me. "I am tougher than I look, my champion. A few veiled prods are easy to bear as long as I know that we are still strong. You need not defend me, and I will not engage her, not while my faith in us remains."

I hitched her closer, wanting to kiss her even more for such kindness, relief cooling the contents of my stomach. But she held me off, leaning back and pressing a hand against my chest. "Aaron, my pardon if this seems too blunt, but before we lose ourselves to more physical distractions, tell me why you let her pull your strings? Though I would give almost anything to have a mama I cannot imagine why yours twists you so."

Immediately, the storm clouds returned, fierce winds pulling my heart in too many directions at once. My face drew down, and when I ground my teeth in frustration I felt it all the way to my boots. But rather than shying away from the maelstrom, Jaque grabbed on all the tighter.

"This is not a judgement, Aaron. Your relationship with your family is completely outside my relationship with you. But I want to understand, to know you better, good or bad, dark or light. Do not shut me out, I beg you. Let this make us stronger."

My muscles ached with the effort to keep still, to not tear out of her arms. I didn't want this negativity to touch her, to touch us. Couldn't something in my life be free from the stain of my past?

Eight fan shaped pinpricks set my upper thigh on fire and I looked down into Boris's huge green eyes. The grip on my jeans softened once he gained my attention, and he meowed with a demand even an idiot could understand, including me. I reached down and scratched his head, immediately rewarded with a rumbling purr that ran up my arm, carrying with it a physical wave of affection.

Not quite enough to hold back the storm, but the feeling slowed things down enough that Jaque could set her hooks in me too. Literally and figuratively. Both hands, one at my back and the other now at my neck, curled inward. Her blunt nails found purchase in my skin and my clothing. My heart too, felt her strength, and as I looked into her eyes once more, I saw the fairy creature that captivated me on our first date. I recognized her power from the beginning, but now, I understood the absolute truth. This woman would never quail away from the storm, she would unfurl her wings and draw strength from the wind, dance with the clouds and refuse to let the rain ground her. Lightning would call her sister and thunder would name her friend, and I, poor, lucky bastard, had no hope of resisting her.

I gusted out a breath, the hurricane losing potency as I yielded to her implacable grip. Boris released me to her care, his claws gone, though the sting remained to keep the memory fresh. Needing Jaque's strength, I covered the hand on my neck, pressing her nails into my skin even more. A slow blink and the hint of a pleased smile softened her features. I bent to press a kiss to her cheek, savoring that warmth against my chilled heart. She settled back onto her heels and sighed before asking, "Better now?"

"Better, but still conflicted. I'll explain as best I can, but let's go inside, okay?"

After hugging me with a fierceness I loved as much as her softness, she let me go and wordlessly turned to gather up Soleil. Boris still sat beside me, thick tail wrapped around his feet and a wisdom in his eyes that I defied any Zen master to duplicate. When I scooped him up, he immediately leveraged himself onto my shoulder like an ancient gargoyle, still and silent except for the mighty purr that vibrated both of us.

Jaque and Soleil led the way back to our room. While I appreciated the shape of her body, in that moment it wasn't the full curve of her ass or the soft sway of her hair that held me captive. No, I fixated on the confidence in her steps, the set of her shoulders, both telling me I could follow her through any storm and come through the other side. Perhaps not unscathed, but neither would I be alone in the aftermath.

Our motel room held little in the way of extra comforts, the furnishings dated and the walls thin. But the old heater under the window kept it comfortably warm, despite being a bit noisy when it started up, and the owners, members of my mother's church group, kept the place scrupulously clean. We also didn't have neighbors, owing to this being a small town in the middle of the week. Sure, we could have stayed at Mom's place, but the privacy alone made a motel worth the extra expense. My sisters couldn't barge in unannounced and I wouldn't have to endure a guilt trip from my mother when she discovered we'd brought animals with us. Growing up, we'd never been allowed to have indoor pets, and I certainly would never ask Jaqueline to be without Soleil. Not to mention how much I now relied on Boris to lull me to sleep when I struggled.

Jaque deposited Soleil on the faded but soft comforter draped over the bed, watching as I secured the door for the night. Once the security latch had been thrown, I turned toward her, but she forestalled me with a raised hand.

"We should get ready for bed, Aaron. Once we settle in together, I do not want to get back up."

"Me either," I agreed, swallowing down the urge to ask her to forgo pajamas. Much as I feared this confession would wring me out, I still hoped to make love to her. I ached to explore the new softness of our connection. Passion still permeated every touch, every glance, but we were entering unexplored emotional territory.

Judging by the way Jaque watched me undress, we were on the same page. Her eyes followed every motion of my hands as I unbuttoned my shirt, unzipped my jeans. I returned the regard, appreciative of the creamy flesh she exposed, but just as enamored with the hunger in her gaze. Couldn't find it in me to be disappointed when she donned a slinky chemise that hugged her curves, the purple fabric deepening the color of her eyes.

After tugging on a pair of sleep pants, I joined her and the animals on the bed. Boris eyed me with no small measure of censure when I slid him over one pillow so I could fit in next to Jaque. "Don't look at me like that, you giant dust mop. This is my spot."

He chirped with indignation but settled fast when I stroked his ears. Jaque laughed even as she curled against my side.

"This is all your fault," I teased as I pulled her closer. "When we started out, I hoped to be sharing a bed with you. I didn't know we would have so much company."

Soleil jumped up to put her paws on Jaque's hip and barked at me, her curled tail waving madly when I reached over to stroke her ears too. Jaque's hand joined mine, fingers lost in the silky coat. A playful twinkle made her eyes bright. "Had I known you would be willing to share with my dog, I might have invited you into my bed much sooner."

"Jaque, if you're in a bed with me, I don't much care who we have to share with. As long as I know you're mine and I'm yours, I am content." Then I released the dog, planting both hands on Jaque's ribs instead. Between the silky fabric and her warmth, I let my troubles slip further away. Surely, they could wait a bit longer?

But she kept me on track, planting a firm hand on my sternum. My ego might have suffered but for the regret that twisted her lips. "Much as I appreciate the sentiment, my champion, I would feel much more at ease if we could put the matter of your mother to bed first."

While my gut clenched in anticipation of pain, Jaque's closeness kept the worst of my frustrations at bay. "Yeah, sorry. Just not something I like talking about."

A parenthesis of sarcastic disbelief bracketed the left side of her mouth. "Truly? I never would have guessed."

I kissed that saucy curl of her lip before settling against the headboard in preparation for the discomfort that lay ahead. "Yes, my lady. I, Aaron Drew, am not accustomed to talking about my feelings. Not really a skill set in much demand when you beat up your friends for a living. But for you, I will put myself to the hazard."

"I promise I shall do my best to salve your wounds when it is over, brave knight."

Easy to believe words, as she sprawled over my stomach and gently kissed my chest. I brought her hand to my lips to seal that promise, then placed it over my heart before covering it with both of mine. "I'm relying on it, Jaqueline. Because I'm afraid this isn't going to put me in the best light..."

She said nothing, setting her chin on our joined hands and waiting. So I took a deep breath, as ready as I would ever be to take a dive off the deep end.

"My parents weren't what you'd consider sweethearts, at least not behind closed doors. Not to each other and not to their children. Both of them could play the part very well in public, but at home, nothing was ever good enough. Grades were allowed to slide sometimes, but performance could never suffer. My sisters weren't lady like enough at their pageants, I needed to toughen up, be more manly."

Jaque made a huff of disagreement that I cherished. "I have never once found your masculinity in question."

I squeezed her hand in thanks, but kept going, maintaining momentum. "Yeah, well, when your dad is relying on you to bring back his own glory days, I don't think it makes him very objective. And for a long time, I did my damnedest to make him proud. Was all set to be an asshole, just like him. Win at all costs. Sometimes, when I get stressed, I fall back into that rut."

Sympathy filled Jaque's expressive eyes, rather than the disgust I expected. Jaque kept her priorities straight, her heart always in the right place. My former fiancée once found that winner-take-all ambition attractive, but even at a reduced strength I found it exhausting to maintain. With Bart around, it was so much easier to let my idea of success soften a little. But between losing my fiancée and Bart getting deployed, the need to be the best returned with a vengeance.

"Winning is not a bad goal, Aaron," The back of Jaque's fingers danced along my jaw, soothing my ragged edges. "And I will admit, your prowess in the saddle is incredibly attractive. But it has nothing to do with my loving you. You could lose every match for the rest of your life, and I would still love you, so long as your heart stays the same."

A cocky grin split my lips. "Well, I hope you aren't expecting me to go soft, either. I thrive on competition, particularly with Bart. It's part of who I am."

"And I love that part too." A saucy wink caught me in the solar plexus, my gut getting squirrely with passion rather than nerves as she slid her body further up mine. "All the soft parts, and all the hard parts."

Gritting my teeth to maintain control of the desire she stirred, I leveled a stern look at her. "And you're making this conversation harder."

"That is not the only thing…" she shot back, her voice singsong, and those enchanting eyes entirely unrepentant. Her belly felt divine against mine, putting pressure where my body wanted it most. "But such is not my intent. Only to ease you with a bit of distraction, to remind you of what delights wait at the end."

Immediately, I pulled back on the reins of desire. Couldn't change my physical response, nor did I want to, but tonight I wanted things to be different. To give her everything I'd held back so far, with the patience she so often graced me with. Nothing could change the pain in my memories, but it was time to face it with the same sort of fevered exaltation that kept me going back to the lyst. After my fiancée, I thought I'd never find a partner worth the risk again, but loving Jaque was worth every drop of blood in my veins. For her, I would chance far more than these old shadows.

"Aw, Jaque, I don't need any reward for this. I want to tell you all my secrets." Softening my touch, I cupped her cheek, hoping like hell that she could feel how much I loved her. "And not just because you asked."

A warning flash passed through her eyes, like heat lightning in a summer storm. "It is not meant to be incentive. I am not the sort to promise my body for favors, Aaron."

My jaw tightened, hating her defensiveness, hating whoever caused it to begin with. But my touch stayed soft. "And if you point them out, I will happily kick the ass of any man who ever thought you might. Truly, Jaqueline, I want to give you all of me. Tonight, and every moment of our future."

She blinked several times, butterfly fast, and the defensiveness disappeared. "Whatever you give, I will gladly accept. Now, and in the future."

Felt damnably like a vow, reaching deep into my soul and wrenching free the last of my reservations. If she could deal with everything I meant to unload, then nothing would stop me from loving her for the rest of my life. "And for that, I love you more," I swore, leaning up to kiss her chin. She went one better and gave me her lips, our promises making the kiss rich and sweeter than chocolate.

I lingered until my neck began to feel the strain, the muscles there still a bit abused after my fall over the weekend. As my head fell back to the pillow Jaque made herself more comfortable, resuming her spot at my side. Her hand remained on my heart and her leg still hooked over mine, like a living blanket of affection. Boris chose that moment to shift closer, his body pressed up against the soreness where my shoulder and neck met, his determined purr giving both physical and mental comfort. Most surprising though, was when Soleil jumped over Jaque's hip and curled herself into a ball on my stomach.

She was still touching Jaque, her back pressed against her mistress, but she looked right at me. The narrow-eyed suspicion was gone, black eyes meeting mine without reservation. Even as Jaque moved her hand off of my heart to pet Soleil's little ears, the regard remained, a weight behind it far greater than her tiny size could account for. Throat tight, I stroked her pointy muzzle with a careful hand, swallowing hard when she pushed into the pressure. Never in my life had I ever felt so completely accepted, so entirely surrounded in love.

"I hope you can understand how amazing this is, Aaron." Jaque's eyes were wet, her smile so soft as to be blurry around the edges. Or maybe that was just because my own vision swam with emotion. "She does not even cuddle with my father. You are the only man she has ever trusted well enough for this."

Clearing my throat, I looked back at the little dog. She pulled her head away and delivered the tiniest lick to my knuckles before tucking her nose under her tail. "I feel very honored," was all I could manage, the tether on my emotions slipping further out of my grip.

But Jaque's hand landed back on my chest, the caress anchoring me into my own skin. Silence reigned for several minutes, broken only by the rattle of the heater under the window and Boris's purr. I took that reprieve to gather my scattered thoughts and when I finally spoke, my voice came out relatively normal.

"As I was saying…" She nodded for me to continue, so I pressed on, determined now. "My dad was probably the standard for what you might call toxic masculinity. He had to be the best at everything, and by his standard, so did I. He got me on a horse at a very young age, toughening me up with mutton busting competitions and drilling me on roping like other kids learning their ABCs. I played tee ball, then little league when I showed some promise as a pitcher. I never really got to just be a kid when dad was around. His expectations were high, and I idolized him enough that I tried to reach them."

Even with years to soften the memories, an ache still built under my heart and my stomach rolled, realizing how close I'd been to growing up into a carbon copy. But rather than rub at the ache, I kept my hands on Jaque, finding her touch infinitely more soothing.

"I understand, Aaron." Her lips formed a smile, but something bittersweet tugged the corner of her mouth. "I grew up without a mother, shadowing my Papa at the airfield and my Grandpere in the barn. Most of my life, I wore ballcaps with grease on them and jeans with holes in the knees. If not for Grandmere, I might never have become much of a woman. They called me Junior, even."

God in heaven, I knew in that quiet moment that I wanted to marry Jaque. A picture formed in my mind and heart of a chubby cheeked girl with pigtails lying next to me under a car, giggling when I rubbed grease off her nose. Jaque's voice rang out in the background, calling us in to the house for the night, so real in my mind I could have wept at the beauty. I longed for that future with an intensity that defied explanation, the ache countering all my old pains.

"If that's the case, I'd have fallen in love with you at a very young age, Jaqueline." Her doubtful grimace firmed my grip on her arms. "I mean it. Sure, I dated popular girls, the ones well known on the pageant circuit, but only because I thought I was supposed to. For a damned long time, I tried to fit the mold my parents laid out. But it never felt right. Those girls weren't for me. You were for me, all along."

Jaque trembled as if shaken by my declaration, but she held my eyes with the courage of a warrior. "You say such beautiful things, Aaron. My heart hoards each word like gold. But I am hungry for the truth of you as well, beautiful or no. Tell me all the things the younger you would have shared with me."

So, I pushed on, unable to deny her anything. "Well, I tried to fit the mold, even as I outgrew it, until I was about sixteen. My parents filed for divorce and spent too damn much time trying to turn us against the other. Dad bought me an old truck to fix up for my first car, a reward for getting on the leaderboard for high school rodeo, but also to tick Mom off. To make her happy, I started dating a girl from the pageant circuit. So, when you ask why I let my Mom act like she does, then the answer is guilt. Always guilt. How could I pick my Dad over her, when he divorced her and left us, and everything else? Then, after Dad died, I felt bad for not being there for her."

Shuddering at the old memories, I started stroking Jaque's arm, needing the warmth to keep me in the present. Her frown echoed my feelings exactly, no doubt because she'd met my mother. Jaque's flowery scent filled me as I inhaled deeply, pushing away the shadows even further.

"Anyway, I made it onto the high school all-star baseball team. An absolute golden boy among my peer group. But then, I injured my shoulder part way through the national semi-finals. Dad yelled at me to push through, and I tried, determined to make him proud. But the coach pulled me to prevent further injury and to my dad's way of thinking, I lost the game."

I felt Jaque's anger building, like the wall of humidity that came with a summer thunderstorm. But I didn't flinch away, only pressed forward, determined to get this over with now. "In the aftermath, I couldn't do anything right. Every night, he'd find something to yell at me for, and Mom would yell right back. As soon as I could get away, I'd head for the garage to work on my truck."

When my hands tightened much as they had that fateful night, Jaque cuddled closer. Not an ounce of fear colored her gaze, only conviction. "I am glad you found a refuge, Aaron. Though I wish you had not needed one."

I shook my head, unworthy of her faith in me. "A refuge, perhaps. But I think being alone drove me to make some very stupid decisions." My knuckles twinged with phantom pain as I drew close to the moment of truth, my heart throbbing with a bit of panic as I stepped to the edge, viscerally afraid of the fall to come. "My parents fought, screaming blame at each other, my mom throwing things to chase him out of the house. Though I kept my sisters holed up in the basement, my gut rolled with fear and anger over the unfairness of it all. It shouldn't have been my job to take care of them. I didn't want to be responsible, to have to carry all this weight on my shoulders."

"So, this has been a part of you since childhood, this need to take care of everyone," Jaque murmured, smiling when I narrowed my eyes. "Do not look so doubtful. I see it in the way you treat everyone you care for, Aaron. Your brother, your team and your family. It has marked our relationship from the outset as well."

Sighing heavily, I nodded. "Yeah, I guess so. But at that point, it was way too much for me to handle. And that night was a breaking point in more ways than one. I was under the hood, fighting with a rusted bolt on the intake manifold when my hand slipped. Scrapped the skin off a few knuckles and I cussed a blue streak that would have made both my parents lose their cool. Thought to myself it'd serve my dad right if something messed up my chances to play again."

Jaque went preternaturally still. Like the thin zap of quiet that comes right before a lightning strike. Her eyes gave no clues, their depths a swirling morass of emotion that felt like a match for everything rolling around in my chest. Unwilling to draw the moment out, I took a deep breath and made the plunge.

"Which is what led me to slam the hood of the truck on my hands. On purpose. Broke three knuckles and did a shit ton of damage to the cartilage and connective tissue. Told Mom it was an accident, but I think Dad guessed the truth." Jaque remained silent and my lungs tightened until it felt like Byzantine sat on my chest instead of Soleil. "Effectively ended my career as a high school athlete. Mom home schooled me the rest of junior year, since I couldn't even hold a damn pencil. Wore nothing but sweatpants for almost six months because buttoning jeans was too difficult."

I might have rambled on more, desperate to fill the silence, but then the storm broke over me in the shape of the woman I loved. Jaque pushed Soleil off my belly and our lips crashed together even as she threw her leg over my hips. Tears sprinkled my skin, hands curled in my hair until the roots stung, and her mouth drew on mine as if she could pull all my old hurts out by will alone. I embraced her tender fury, so thankful she hadn't let me fall alone and kissed her with an abandon that I only ever felt with her.

The storm eased quickly though, softening into a gentle washing of my soul as our kisses turned sweeter. I'm no fool. Even in blessed relief, I knew I still had troubles to face, but knowing Jaque would love me through it made my eyes wet with gratitude. Jaque made no mention of the tears that ran down my temples when she drew back, though her eyes followed their path. She didn't question why I'd done anything so stupid, made no judgments, asked for no clarification. No, she reached for my hand on her hip instead, lifted it to her lips and kissed each of the thickened joints with a sweetness that surpassed any kindness I'd ever known. But as much as her touch healed me, it was her words that filled me with light like the sun breaking through the clouds, until all the old darkness fled in fear.

"Whole or broken, Aaron, I shall love you."

Bright with the need to share how she made me feel, I pulled her back down and kissed her. Hope flavored every soft touch that followed, every gentle caress we exchanged, because whole or broken, my heart would always belong to her.

Jaque

No one would ever question Aaron's physical courage, but after his confession, I knew it to come from his very soul. I'd felt his fear as if it were mine, a cold rush flooding through my veins as he hurried through his words. Anger nipped at its heels as my heart broke for the lonely boy he had been, but I shoved past it in the same breath I pushed Soleil away. By the time our lips met, I made a conscious choice to feel nothing but love.

Not only the romantic, passionate feelings I enjoyed, but the meaningful and unconditional emotions that could withstand the most extreme tests life might see fit to subject us to. Something we both needed as desperately as air.

Without saying a word, he matched the intensity exactly, every brush of lip steady, firm. The urgency that often marked our lovemaking morphed into something different. Less desperate, more inexorable, the conclusion forgone but still longed for. I tasted a new sweetness in the seductive sweep of his tongue against mine, meant to be savoured, lingered over.

He shivered deliciously when I gripped his hair again, holding him in place so I could kiss along his jaw. But he did not remain passive either, hands finding my bare knees, gliding over the silk of my chemise until he caressed my hips.

"*Épater*," I sighed as I tore my lips from his neck, distracted and enchanted in the same breath by his touch. "So divine."

Taking advantage of my malleability, his calloused fingertips traced my spine until he could press my shoulders. Grip achieved, he rolled us over, my thighs a perfect cradle for his weight. But even then, he remained unhurried, the friction in his fingertips dancing over my ribs as if he were painting on me with warmth and delight. When I growled in complaint, he stilled, drawing my eyes.

"Jaqueline, you'll not rush me tonight. Please, let me set the pace? I promise you it'll be worth it."

Sacre, much as my body wanted to demand, my heart saw into his. This, he needed, he wanted. For him, I could wait. "I am at your mercy."

A hint of the devil filled his smile as he leaned in to kiss me. "And you'll be well rewarded, I swear it."

"I always am, my champion," I reassured, my palm stroking his tight back. "You never fail to answer my passion. Never once have I felt like I want too much, a gift I often imagined but never received until you."

His expression shifted from devilish to elated, the ever-present worry lines fading from his forehead. "No, Jaqueline, never too much. Because with you, I always want more. Not just sex either. I want more time, more feelings, more experiences." Radiant hope filled my heart, making my belly tremble. But he gave me no time to reply, continuing to obliterate all my old fears even as he created another. "I want more commitment, when you're ready. I know it's too damn soon to say it, but I want a lifetime of this. I want to make love to you until we are old and grey. To make a family, if you want. To make enough memories together that your heart is full to overflowing and you forget anyone ever thought you were too much."

Rendered speechless for fear I might blurt out something stupid, I dragged his mouth down to mine. He obliged me with kisses, though he kept his tongue light on mine until my frantic pulse slowed its pace. Then he migrated downward, clever lips drugging me with sweet sensation as they danced over my neck. The wet heat left me oh so vulnerable when he pressed a question into the hollow of my throat.

"Too much?" The vulnerability in his voice came through clearly, even when husky with desire. I responded as much to that need as the other when I shook my head, knowing he referred to his confession rather than his touch.

"No. Never too much. Give me more."

A tremor wracked his body as if something physically gave way inside him. But those delightful lips never stopped their assault down the front of my night gown, blazing a slow trail along my sternum that melted my natural impatience. Even the slight friction of his recently shaved chin added to my enjoyment, all glorious in their own right.

I gloried in the languorous attention. Lovers past, an urgency marked every coupling, a desperation to grab hold of every moment while I could. But Aaron made me feel safe, as if we could take forever for this alone. Our passion had no bottom, feeding off each other in a whirlwind of light and energy, so I knew there would be desperately needy assignations in our future. But this time, and for many hoped for future moments, we had the leisure to linger.

By the time he reached my stomach, even through the silk my skin had become sensitive enough for his touch to tickle as he kissed around my belly button. When I vibrated with a muted giggle, his breath huffed out in mutual amusement, further tickling my sense of humour along with my skin. I looked down at him, grinning like a fool when he met me with a smile.

"What's so funny?"

"My best friend in high school once told me about an idiom for sex that I never fully appreciated until now."

"Do tell," he encouraged, even as he bent down to nip my belly, igniting electricity amongst the fluttery feelings in my middle. "That way I can be sure to revisit it in the future."

"*Faire des pirouettes sur le nombril*," I murmured as the heat of his tongue soothed the skin he stung. "To make pirouettes around the belly button. Which you do so very well."

Lips still touching me, his eyes darted up, humour and desire warming the deep blue colour. Purpose in his movements, those lips slowly traced a dancing spiral around the indent in the softness of my belly. I shivered from the arches of my feet to the backs of my elbows, my hands clutching his hair as his tongue darted into the small hollow.

"Never thought I would be so in love with the French language, *ma fleur de nuit*," he whispered against my hip as he migrated lower. "But I'm looking forward to years of lessons."

"Years and years. You shall grow weary of them," I promised, my spine arching upward as he followed the crease of my leg.

He moved past the hem of my chemise, chuckling darkly when he kissed the inside of my knee and I twisted in his gentle grip. "I don't know about that, Jaqueline. I've got a lot of incentive to be a good student, if it makes you squirm like this."

"Oh, mon amour, it is not your skill with languages that causes that, much as I appreciate the beautiful things you say. It is the anticipation of your rather gifted mouth being applied to other efforts."

"I have no idea what you're talking about," he huffed indignantly, startling a laugh out of me before he chased another shiver along my leg. For a countless while, his body spoke a language that needed no words, telling me a thousand times over how much his heart loved me.

Aaron

I didn't have the words to convey my feelings, so I put my emotions into touch. Not because we were perfect. Nothing so trite as all that. But because we answered each other's needs, time and again, willingly and without qualification. I'm no fool. I understood from watching Jo and Bart's families that conflict still existed in loving relationships. But I recognized the differences between my birth family and the one I had become a part of. Jaque would not manipulate me with tears, though she did not fear to cry. She was honest with her emotions, as giving of every part of her heart as her body. Nothing was kept in reserve. Which is what let me let go, let me get completely lost in Jaqueline's passion.

She held me to her with hands that were equal parts tender and demanding. Nothing mattered but us as we slowly climbed the peak of pleasure. We clung to each other like two lost souls caught in a hurricane, surrendering to the storm we created.

When the burning energy finally faded she seemed in no hurry for me to go. She was still but for her hands, which brushed ever so lightly through the sweaty curls at the base of my skull. And her gaze, always so soft, stroked over my face like the richest of velvets.

"I am…" she paused, swallowed, tried again. "I am undone, Aaron. I did not know love could be so sweet, yet so… strong."

I knew exactly what she meant, and leaned down, grateful when she offered me her well kissed lips for a brief caress. My trembling hands toyed with her tangled hair as I pulled away, absolutely enchanted by our connection. "That's our love, my lady. Sweet, yet strong. Fierce, yet gentle. And I think we've some other layers still to discover."

Her eyes flashed with excitement even as her mouth stretched into a patient smile. "I look forward to exploring them all. In fact, I would be pleased to explore more new territory with you tonight."

Took me a bit to recover and fulfill her hopes, though this time it was her that began a slow build of the next storm. No doubt in my mind that there would be a lot of storms in our future, both the ones we created and the ones we endured. But with Jaque, I would always be willing to risk the lightning in order to dance in the rain.

Jaque

Rain slashed across the windshield with punishing force as we drove to the hospital the next morning, but nothing could dim my blissful mood. Aaron satiated me so well the night before that I slept like the dead, oblivious to the storm that rolled in, or even the alarm as it blared beside the bed. He woke me with sweet kisses, even started the shower so I could step straight into the hot water, and I emerged to find he had taken Soleil out to do her business.

We took care with our appearance again, Aaron's well creased jeans and button-down shirt much the same as the night before. Only the pattern on the shirt had changed, now a blue and grey plaid that seemed fitting for the stormy skies outside. I twisted my hair up into a chignon to conceal the purple strands I felt sure would upset his conservative mother, even though Aaron encouraged me to leave it down. I could keep the peace for his sake.

He left the engine idling after parking beside a bakery, then hurried inside to procure the cinnamon buns he promised his mother. But to my absolute delight, he returned to the truck bearing much more than pastries. The scent of coffee and chocolate flooded the cab as he set a large rectangular box in the back, then hastily clambered in the driver's door, holding out a paper cup even as he settled into the seat.

"My lady, I come bearing gifts."

I wrapped my hands around the proffered cup with a whimper of anticipation, holding it under my nose so I could draw deeply of the rich mocha he thoughtfully purchased. "This further cements your position as my champion."

He chuckled as he put the truck into gear and cautiously pulled back out into the street. "I thought you might like that. Hospital coffee leaves a lot to be desired, and I don't know how long we'll be this morning."

"You are worth waiting around for, good sir," I answered playfully, rewarded with a widening grin that chased some of the worry from his brow.

At the hospital itself, we hurried up to the ward, finding his sisters already waiting. Of the three, I enjoyed Darlene the most. She balanced a no-nonsense attitude with an approachable kindness. Qualities I admired in anyone, but especially in a situation where my welcome was less than warm from the remaining family. While Bethany and Courtney were not as acidic as their mother, they surveyed me with a reserve that said they still withheld judgement.

The one redeeming factor remained that they all loved their brother, an impression they reinforced as we met the trio in the waiting area of the ward. They all hugged him tightly, even Darlene, despite the baby she held on her hip. No calculation in their actions, filling the small space with much needed light. But I had little time to observe their interaction, all of my attention stolen away as the most petite fingers wrapped around my wrist, my gaze dropping to meet startlingly large brown eyes.

"Hello," I ventured softly, unsure if I should look around for the child's mother. "Who are you?"

"Nessie," she answered, so quietly I could barely hear her over the chatter of the adults. But that was all the confirmation I needed before I crouched down to meet her at eye level. She smiled shyly, half hiding the expression behind a very tattered stuffed cow that was missing an eye and one horn, but her eyes remained fixed on me regardless.

"I am Jaqueline, your uncle Aaron's friend."

"Mama said you were bringin' sweet rolls," she stated, though the plaintive tone made it more of a question, as if she doubted the information. As if to back up the words, her tummy growled loudly, resulting in her bringing the cow up higher so she could stifle a giggle.

Grinning even wider, I risked poking her belly, eliciting another delightful laugh. "Yes, we did, though we will ask your mama before you have one. They are very big cinnamon rolls and I am not sure you can eat a whole one on your own."

The cow dropped down again, revealing a firm chin and thin lips as she delivered the most serious look possible for someone who resembled a sprite in a fairytale storybook. "Can too."

Turning my chin to one side as if in consideration, I looked her up and down. "I would be astonished if you did. It would be like magic."

Her little chest puffed out with pride, delight making her eyes shimmer. I leaned forward, eager to hear what clever thing she might say next, when she looked behind me and a wide grin overtook the entirety of her face. "Uncle Aaron!"

His hand landed on my shoulder as I turned to look up at him, and I caught the briefest glimmer of something in his eyes that made my middle go soft. I might have tumbled over without that steady grip to balance me. But then he looked to his niece, smiling as if she were a lost treasure found, and I wobbled right over the edge of falling more in love. Better still, he let me go and lifted her into a hug, her little arms wrapping around his neck. While I pushed against my knees to get upright, it was only to cover for the sudden yearning to raise a family with this man who loved his niece with so much sweetness.

She chattered about the toy cows he gave her for Christmas, and I turned away from the beautiful picture they made. Bittersweet hope overwhelmed me at the sight of his strong hand spanning her back, his other forearm supporting her across the thighs. Those same hands could cradle a baby to his chest, those arms could toss a toddler in the air much as my papa had done for me.

Instead, I watched his sisters descend upon the nurse's station with the pastry box, inviting the people on shift to help themselves. I doubted a few sweets could make up for Mrs. Drew's fractious temperament, but judging by the smiles passed around, the nurses appreciated the effort.

That done, the three women turned back to us, Bethany scooping up her child with a bit more impatience than the little girl deserved. In moments, she settled Nessie at the colouring table in the corner with a firm admonishment not to make a mess of the massive sweet roll she set down. Perfect timing, as one of the nurses called everyone's attention to the doctor headed into Francine's room, halfway down the hallway.

Hastily, Aaron scooped out a big roll and set in on a napkin before kissing me on the cheek. "Do you mind watching Ness? Hopefully, we'll be quick."

I smiled as I darted a look at the child who already had decimated half of her roll. "I believe we will get along without supervision. Take your time."

For the barest of seconds, he favoured me with a look that appeared to mirror the hope that pooled in my belly. But we had neither the time nor the privacy to discuss our future or my past, and his family needed him to be present.

When he walked away I settled on the floor beside Nessie to watch the little sprite make her breakfast disappear. Nor was that the only magic she could perform, as she drew me into her imagination with stories of cows in space, demonstrated ably by her tatty stuffed toy. I told her stories my grandmother had shared, of clever princesses and the strong knights that loved them. In fairytales, there were challenges to face and dragons to beard, reminding me of the challenges that stood between me and my own happily ever after. But Nessie's childlike faith reminded me that anything was possible if you believed.

Aaron

My mother had done herself up like it was pageant day, hair teased into a full mass. Eyelash extensions were glued in place as firmly as her practiced smile and genteel manners. You'd have thought she were pouring tea for Miss America rather than plying a young doctor with pastry. He took one, though judging by the way he set it aside after a couple bites it was more to appease his patient than out of genuine interest.

I stood at Mom's beside like a sentry, as if I could protect her from the bad news I read in his pinched expression. Not that Mom helped make his job any easier as her true goal in bribing the doctor became terribly obvious as she introduced us all to the man.

She patted my hand where it rested on the bed rail, gazing up with every semblance of pride. Bragging on the accomplishments in my youth, she glossed over my current work with a vague mention of the trials of running my own business. Bethany and Courtney too received a loving look and brief description of their successes. But then she looked to Darlene, and a calculating narrowing of her eyes ruined the appearance of warmth.

"And this is my youngest, Darlene. Hard to tell with a baby on her hip, but she was runner-up to my title of Miss Iowa a few years back. Recently single, she'd make a beautiful date if you've any social functions to attend, Dr. Alderwood."

Darlene went completely pale, body rigid as she bit down on the helpless anger I could see in her eyes. William shifted restlessly on her lap, agitated by his mother's tension I'd bet. But Darlin' drew on all the grace she learned from her years on the pageant circuit and filled the awkward silence before the obviously embarrassed doctor could manage a reply.

"Thank you for thinking of me, Mama, that's very kind. But I'm sure Dr. Alderwood has more important things to worry about this morning than my availability. His patients deserve all his attention, just as little Will deserves all of mine." She hitched the now fussing baby up to press a kiss to his cheek, finding a smile as she stared at my nephew. Then she turned it on all of us, a beatific gift even the doctor seemed to appreciate as the mood in the room relaxed.

Well, except for Mom. Her mood ratcheted up like a brake line under too much stress, and I needed to bleed it off before she lost her grip. So, I filled the silence, redirecting everyone's attention to the real reason for our gathering. "On that note, Doc, what news do you have for us?"

Relieved to have a modicum of control again, the young doctor launched into a wordy summary of the test results and the specialists he was referring her too. To break it down in simplest terms, he was concerned about her lung function, emphysema or COPD being most likely with her history of smoking.

Ever been in a car wreck you could see coming? Like, you know your tires are a little bald, conditions are slick and people around you are driving too fast. You keep your eyes open, your hands on the wheel, as prepared as you can be for things to go wrong. When they do, you don't even really panic, because hey, you felt it coming. But that still doesn't prepare you for the impact.

My heart slammed into my ribs like a fender into a guard rail, so hard I half expected it to knock me over. But I didn't flinch, watching the doctor's lips move as he detailed the drugs we needed to pick up at the pharmacy and the oxygen concentrators that she would need for the time being. He tried to give us some hope, saying that with treatment he'd seen plenty of patients regain their previous quality of life, but one of his admonitions stole my hope away with icy spikes of dread.

"But Mrs. Drew, in order for all this to work, you'll have to do your part. That means giving up your cigarettes."

All three of my sisters went still as the last word fell from his lips, horror making their pretty faces appear gaunt. They hadn't looked like that since my father's funeral, which told me my fear was valid. Nor did Mom do anything to ease it, waving one manicured hand in the air as if to chase off an irritating insect.

"Oh doctor, I'm sure I have no idea what you are talking about. I gave those up ages ago."

The stern set of his chin said Dr. Alderwood wasn't buying it, but he drove his point home with the one appeal she might listen to best—the one to her vanity. "I hope so, Mrs. Drew. Your health is in good hands at this hospital, but the most important hands in your treatment are your own. Cigarette smoking would undo any good from the inhalers, and you absolutely do not want to smoke around oxygen machines. They can ignite and cause serious burns, which scar significantly."

Mom's hands fluttered up toward her face as she sucked in a breath, and I had to hand it to the guy. He didn't pull punches, which I appreciated in my line of work. Nothing less than the blunt truth would ever pierce the strange bubble of denial my mother insulated herself in.

"Burns?" she whispered, her voice barely more than the scratch of a pile of dead leaves shifting in a breeze.

"I'm sure you'll have a care, Mrs. Drew," the doctor continued, affable and smooth as he shifted her patient file under his arm and took a step toward the door. "Nurse Hines will be in shortly to go over your home care and follow up appointments, and we should be able to get you out of here by this afternoon."

When none of us tried to stop him, he fled, leaving behind his half-eaten roll and a foreboding silence no one wanted to break. Mom stared blankly at her lap, stroking her hands together one after the other while my sisters and I tried not to fidget with impatience. We wanted to get her home before she made herself anymore of a nuisance to the staff, but what new challenges would we face? Who would stay with her? How would we make sure her needs were met?

Thankfully, we received answers in short order, as the nurse I met the first morning strode in. Briskly efficient, she gave us the rundown on where we needed to pick up drugs and immediate oxygen, the numbers to call for the more long-term machines, and who we needed to speak with regarding follow up appointments. Mom did little except mutter under her breath, complaining continuously about the cost, the fuss, though the way she stared fixedly at the nurse made me think she wanted a physical target for her upset.

Knowing that, I quickly thanked the woman, then excused myself as she left, wanting to apologize for Mom's misplaced wrath. "Nurse Hines?"

She swung around with a tired smile, though it felt genuine enough. Wouldn't have blamed her for shrugging me off, but like a saint in scrubs, she waited for me to speak.

"Do you know of any home care services in the area? Just to lighten the load for everyone?"

Her eyes narrowed as she considered the question. "For the sake of your family, that's a good idea. But to be very frank, Mr. Drew, your mother doesn't exactly make it easy to help her. Do you have a family friend who might be willing to stay with her for a week or two?"

I sighed, thinking of all the people she alienated over the years, then shook my head. "Thank you, but no. We'll figure something out. But if you think of anything that might work, I'd appreciate it."

She nodded sharply, though her eyes, as ever, remained kind. "Absolutely. Watching your family have health problems is never easy since we can't fix it for them. But we do the best we can."

"Yes ma'am, we surely do," I answered before leaving her to get on with her work, trying to ignore the way her words echoed in the hollow spot in my chest. Jaque and Nessie did a good job distracting me, as I found the pair on their bellies, leaned over a scattering of coloring books and markers. Nothing could fill in the hole, I knew, but seeing Jaque with my sweet little niece made my heart feel a size larger.

Though I didn't disturb them, Jaque noticed me, her warm smile shoring me up even as I lifted a finger to my lips to keep things secret. She nodded ever so slightly before returning her attention to the page in front of her, and I walked back into my mother's room with a little breathing room against the sense of doom hanging over my head.

Shortly after eleven, Bethany headed out with Nessie to make arrangements regarding the oxygen while Courtney and Darlene took turns keeping Mom distracted. We received permission to take Mom down to the cafeteria for lunch, though she fussed all the way there about people seeing her in her house-coat. But it got her out of the bed, and out of the hair of the nurses for a bit, well worth the bevy of compliments I paid to ease her anxiety.

Jaque joined us, engaging my sisters in polite conversation about their families and helpfully loading a plate for me so I could cater to my mother. Good thing too, as the woman fussed endlessly about the selection available, changing her mind several times before settling on making a plate at the salad bar.

We passed a relatively pleasant hour in the sunshine of the garden atrium before returning to the ward to begin paperwork for Mom's release. Before too long, we were loading her into Courtney's car for the short trip home, an oxygen pack humming in accompaniment to the return of Mom's unending muttered complaints.

At the house, I helped her up the stairs and we got her settled in her flower-patterned recliner with a blanket over her legs. She seemed momentarily content to check all her voicemails, reveling in the people who called to wish her well. Courtney took her leave rather fast, needing to get back to her own family. Jaque, on the other hand, appeared agitated, fussing with the ruffle on one of the gaudy pillows decorating the sofa while the rest of us moved around the house.

"Hey, Jaqueline, could you help me in the kitchen for a minute?" I asked casually, though Mom's eyes cut toward me with a hard edge. "Mom, we're going to see what groceries you need. Shouldn't be long."

Covering the receiver of the phone as if the person who left her a message might hear our conversation, she spoke up. "I'll be perfectly content with some canned soup and crackers, Aaron

Allen. But you might toss out the leftover casserole on the bottom shelf and check the milk. Don't go to any trouble, though."

I nodded to placate her as Jaque snuck past me without looking up. "I know what you like Mom. No worries there."

Her lips relaxed and she smiled, expression almost warm with the affection I craved. "I know you'll take care of me, dear boy. You always have."

The praise inherent should have lit me up like main street at Christmas time, but instead, it bounced vacantly around in the hole that my childhood left in my heart. To cover my swallow of disappointment, I nodded again and retreated as she turned her attention back to the phone.

God, I was tired of taking care of her. Not that I didn't want to. Hell, the responsibility had been part of me for so long I might fall apart if I even considered letting it go. But no matter how much I gave, she would always want more, would never be satisfied. Which didn't leave me much to give the other people I loved, including the woman currently hidden behind the refrigerator door, her denim clad curves poking out most alluringly as she inspected the interior.

"You don't have to do that, Jaque," I offered, even as I slid in beside her, my hand coming to rest on the hollow of her back.

She shook her head as she straightened, eyes wide with something like astonishment. "Not certain I could be of any help, Aaron. There are butter containers on every shelf! How much butter does one household need?"

Chuckling, I reached for the yellow tub in the doorway and held it up. "Just this one. The rest all have leftovers in them. Mom keeps the empty containers and reuses them. And even then, it's not butter. She likes non-fat margarine."

Abject horror pulled her head back on her neck as far as it would go. "Not butter? I am sorry, but my French roots object to such a travesty. Perhaps I could use less fat in my diet, but I would rather do without than to worry so much over my figure that I eat something so tasteless."

Considering I only ate the yellow colored spread when I visited Mom, I couldn't find it in me to object. "I love that you love butter. And french fries. And chocolate. All things delicious and worth savoring."

She melted into me like said butter, then, her arms wrapping around my waist as I tucked the tub back in place and let the fridge door close under its own weight. "Speaking of delicious and worth savoring, could I kiss you before you go back to your mother? I know she needs you, so I will not monopolize your time."

"Monopolize away," I bent to meet her lips with a contented sigh, happy to give because I knew she would return the affection equally. Her hands went into my hair, a touch I adored from the very first moment and would likely cherish until the last kiss we ever shared (may that be a long time in coming).

Those few stolen minutes saw us through the early evening, Darlene showing up just before six with Will on one hip and a cardboard box on the other. The unmistakably sharp scent of sesame and soy preceded her up the stairs from the front door, and I jumped up to relieve her of the burden, as much from hunger as chivalry. Chinese food had been a strange pleasure growing up, something we brought home after our parents fought so Mom wouldn't have to cook. While I hated those fights, it had been a relief to eat something with flavor for a change.

We all moved to the dining table, Mom unwilling to bend her rules about eating in the living room even to make things easier on herself. But she walked there under her own power, the long cord from the oxygen concentrator following her like a snake's thin tail. While she picked at her plate, Darlene, Jaque, and I attacked our food. Mannerly, mind you, in deference to Mom, but the sesame chicken and fried rice disappeared off our plates with a haste even my gluttonous horse could appreciate.

I took charge of Will after dinner as Darlene helped Mom get ready for bed, a task I didn't envy considering all the complaining we heard floating down the hall. Much like the baby, once tired, Mom tended to get whiny. Will was easier to appease, as I held him to my shoulder and paced slow laps around the living room while Jaque watched.

"This is a good look for you, Aaron," Jaque murmured as Will's fussing quieted, reduced to sighs and gurgles as he snuggled against my neck.

I turned to meet her eyes, stilling my steps so I could study the pinch of tension surrounding her usually soft mouth. It didn't match the hopeful tenderness I heard in her voice. "I watched you with Nessie earlier. You wear it well too. Hope it's a good look for us both, someday."

If I hadn't been watching for it, I might have missed the way her face paled and her hand clenched on the arm of the sofa. "I also hope so."

Again, her voice held longing, but she kept something back. Stroking Will to keep him soothed, I crossed the room and sat down beside her. Close enough to touch, though she kept her hands to herself, that action alone speaking louder than words. Jaque always reached for me if we were alone, and I missed the contact.

"What's wrong, lady mine?"

"Nothing that we must face right now, Aaron," The defensive sharpness in that simple statement was no reassurance. "Let us take care of your mother, then we will have the time to focus on us."

I might have objected, her happiness of greater importance to me in that moment than my own, but then Darlene emerged from the hall. Relinquishing Will to his mother made my arms feel empty, and the worried ache in my chest expanded, no longer distracted by the baby's weighty warmth. Worst still, Darlene told me Mom wanted to see me before she'd sleep. I left Jaque alone, the unanswered question cutting the space between us.

"Hey there, Mom, how're you feeling?" I asked as I stood in her doorway. Amongst the pink satin and ivory lace, she looked much more herself. Confident with her place in the universe, even with the bruising showing under her eyes now that her makeup was off. Few ever saw her without her face on, and she tended to be a bit sharper without the mask, as if you'd peeled away one of her defenses.

"It's good to be home, Aaron Allen, though it's bringing to light fresh worries. Here, pull up the chair and sit for a moment."

Though I cringed internally, knowing I probably wouldn't like this conversation if she needed me to sit, I gingerly lowered myself onto the tiny stool from her vanity. Though the damn thing had held me for years, the lace and scrollwork made it look too dainty to bear up under me. When it made no indication it might collapse under my weight, I leaned forward and took Mom's thin hand.

"How can I help you, Mom?"

She wasted no time and jumped directly onto her usual soap box. "You need to come home, Aaron. Stop it with this foolishness, come back to where the people love you and settle down, start a family."

"I've told you before, Mom, I have my own home." Her mouth opened as if to run over my denial, but I held up my free hand to hold her off. "I have a job, one I am good at, and makes me happy again. I even have a family, one that's growing every day. And you know I'm just a phone call away."

She pulled her hand out of mine, crossing her arms over the comforter pulled up to her chest as her lips disappeared again. "That's not what I meant, don't be so obtuse. By your age, your father and I already had four children, a house of our own, and a solid place in the community here."

Tired of having the same argument over and over, it took as much effort to hold back a retort as it did to keep myself in the saddle after Bart hit me with a lance. My jaw ached with the strain to bite back that they'd also had a dysfunctional marriage and were the source of much gossip around town. While I no longer felt the need to run far and fast from that past, I'd also built a present I was insanely proud of. And, looking to the future, things were promising for the first time in as long as I could remember.

"I told you when I left for Vegas, Mom, I've got my own road to walk. And I like where it's heading. With Jo and Bart around, now I've got more time to come see you and the girls. Jaque and I are building a strong foundation. The Company is expanding too."

She sniffed with derision, the gesture cutting even with the armor I'd developed against her displeasure. "Hmm, well, much like your father and his rodeoing, at some point your age and injuries will overwhelm you. And then you'll come crawling back home, begging for a place to belong. What then?"

Considering my injury list was much shorter than my father's at this age, I hoped I'd be at it much longer than him. But just as I was about to say so, she shoved further into the fray, trying to get a win in before I could rebut her.

"And don't tell me you are planning a future with that Canadian woman! She's not nearly woman enough to keep your attention with all the groupies throwing themselves at you during your travels. You'll stray before too long."

Anger flared like a meteor, though it burned icy cold, freezing me into complete stillness. Usually, Mom interpreted quiet as a sign of victory, but her instincts must have screamed a warning as her mouth slammed shut on anything else she might have said. Eyes locked on hers, I watched awareness dawn, then a hint of fear. For once, I didn't look away, needing this honest evaluation of her behavior, unclouded by old guilt. That fear gave over to her own anger, then slid into the wide-eyed innocent look that she employed to wheedle her way out of trouble. But I didn't give her a chance to speak this time.

"Mother," She shrank into herself, losing any of the strength she'd gathered being home, and I hated that I'd stolen it from her. But I had taken the blow, even knowing it was coming. Now, it was time to answer it. "I am not my father. My whole life has been about proving that, and that you would assume I'd ever behave like him tells me you don't know anything about me."

"Well, you live so far away, how would I know anything about you, Aaron?" Mom whined, the high tone helping along the headache I'd started with my clenched jaw. "It's not my fault. You never call unless it's to ask me for something, you never come visit unless I beg and you always leave as soon as you can. You're practically a stranger! I didn't even know you were dating anyone until just the other day."

Steeling myself against the guilt, I answered her with a calm I didn't feel. "And I didn't know you were having problems breathing until I came up here."

A flash of anger lit her eyes, the blue color that I'd gotten from her lost as her brows drew down. "It's just a short spell, Aaron, I'll be fine in no time. But at least it got you home for a bit so I could talk some sense into you."

Ignoring her attack against me, I leaned closer, gratified when she went silent again. "Speaking of talking some sense into someone, are you going to finally quit smoking? You heard the doctor. It'll kill you if you keep going."

"Would serve you right, boy," she shot back waspishly, face twisting into an ugly mask as pain stole her humanity. "You killed your father with your rebellion. Might as well drive me to the brink as well."

All my anger drowned under a flood of guilt I couldn't hold back anymore than a line in the sand could stop a tsunami. In fact, I bowed under the pummeling weight of it, hunching over my knees as I stared blindly at the carpet. Didn't matter that I knew his death wasn't my fault, logically. Didn't matter that I knew her smoking wasn't my fault. Nothing I did would have ever influenced either of my parents.

When I could breathe again, I shoved to my feet, looking down at my mother with a combination of pity and sadness. "Mom, I'm gonna go. Darlene is staying in my room across the hall tonight. I'll be back with breakfast. Love you."

She went pale, as if understanding she'd gone too far, and her hand lifted to reach for me, but I was already walking away. Everything hurt in that moment. Love, hate, guilt, forgiveness, storm or calm. Even as I fell into Jaque's embrace later, my heart bled, the wound of my own doubts so deep nothing could heal it.

Jaque

The previous morning's bliss made for a harsh comparison to the following one. Where it had been rainy, the next dawned clear and bright, not a cloud in the sky. And where I then felt completely happy, now, I knew only a defenseless ache.

Aaron said nothing about what transpired with his mother, but I felt his pain as if it were my own. The hurt spread out from my middle, radiating to every limb, much like the time I came off of Lyric and she had gotten injured. My guilt, my helplessness to fix things, to stop it from happening to begin with, ate at every bit of warmth Aaron and I had gained. When he reached for me I did my best to soothe his hurts, but no matter how much I loved him, it was not enough.

We stopped to pick up groceries before heading to his mother's house. But as we pulled up in front of the split-level home, I suppressed a shiver of foreboding. While I had originally been excited to see where he grew up, to meet his family, now, I wanted to encourage him to drive away. We could go anywhere but here, chase the road until it ended and choose our next turn on the flip of a coin. Anything would be better than the chill in my stomach that said we were headed for a wreck.

He didn't go in to wish his mother good morning, simply marched into the kitchen and began preparations for breakfast. Darlene emerged from the hall as I cracked eggs, the scent of cooking sausage and brewing coffee now an alluring aroma that warmed the cluttered kitchen. In yoga pants and a wrinkled, oversized t-shirt, she looked exhausted and every inch the youngest of Francine's brood. Will rested on one hip, the little guy grimacing as he waved a sippy cup.

"Please tell me you bought juice?" she entreated as she collapsed into a chair at the tiny breakfast table by the sliding glass door. There in the sunlight, I could see bags under her eyes, so I darted to the refrigerator to grab the apple juice Aaron insisted we buy.

"No added sugar, even," Aaron answered, a promising bit of lightness in his voice as he flipped the bacon. "Got you some hazelnut creamer, too. You know I've got your back, Darlin'."

"I know, big brother, and I thank the heavens for you daily," she replied, even as she poured juice for Will. I darted for the coffee maker as soon as it beeped its readiness and pulled the largest mug from the hooks under the cabinets. When I carried it over to her, along with the creamer, she sagged with gratitude. "Thank you to you too, Jaque. I'm running on fumes. Will was fussy and I spent most of the night walking him so he wouldn't wake Mom."

Crouching down so I would be level with the cherub cheeked little monkey in her lap, I held out my hands toward him. "William, would you like to come see me, so Mommy can have a break?" I did not baby talk, speaking to him as I would one of the young horses I worked with. Gently, evenly, and with warmth. He looked intently at my face for a moment, before gazing up at his mother for reassurance.

"It's okay, Will. Jaqueline is nice, I promise."

His answer to my question was to reach out toward me with a chubby fist. I slid him easily from her lap to mine, making sure I had a good grip on his surprising bulk before I stood. "Ah, *mon canard*, little wonder your mama is weary, to have carried you all night! Come, we shall go make toast for our breakfast. Surely you are hungry?"

Little noises I took for agreement passed through his lips, and his eyes followed my every motion as I put bread in the toaster. His giggles each time the toast popped up lightened the mood in the kitchen considerably. By the time breakfast was ready to serve, Aaron managed a genuine smile when Will offered up a bite of half-chewed bread to his uncle. I melted a little as he mimed taking a bite and made sounds of enjoyment. To move beyond his own upset in order to make his nephew smile proved beyond all reason that this man deserved all the love I could possibly give.

Bless her, Darlene pulled a lap tray out of the pantry and offered to take Francine her breakfast. The momentary respite was a treasure as Aaron and I settled at the table with Will between us. For those few minutes alone, I could envision having a family with this man, conquering all the obstacles that stood in our way.

When his sister returned, Aaron stood and moved over one seat so she could sit next to her baby. Once she spooned some eggs onto his plate, he proceeded to mash them thoroughly on the table and his face, giggling the entire time. Darlene sighed. "I am going to regret this. He always gets gassy after eating eggs, but if he gets a full tummy, maybe he'll take a nap so I can get my homework done."

Grateful to be useful in some way, I leapt into the silence following her statement. "I could watch him, Darlene. There is little to occupy me otherwise."

She leaned back in her chair, eyes wide at the offer. "Oh, no, I couldn't ask that. He's my responsibility, and just because he's being darling right now doesn't mean he will be later. Gas makes him fussy and the diaper changes are not for the faint of heart."

I looked to Aaron, grateful to find a pleased surprise softening the forehead that had been pinched all morning. "With Aaron's help, I am sure we can manage. You can get your homework done that much faster if you do not have to worry over your baby. Maybe even take a nap."

Groaning, she yielded to the offer. "A nap would be divine, but an uninterrupted hour to take a bath would be even better. But only if you're sure."

Aaron patted her arm. "Absolutely sure, Darlin'. Take advantage of the time, okay? I'm not here very often, but when I am, I'll always help."

"Myself, as well," I confirmed, grabbing Will's sippy cup as he knocked it off the table for the third time. "Consider the offer open any time I can manage to come visit with Aaron."

Her eyes darted back and forth between Aaron and I several times, but I had eyes only for the man I loved. His steady gaze held promises, and I accepted every single one with a grateful heart.

Then he confirmed them out loud. "Yeah, Darlin', Jaque is family. Or she's gonna be soon enough. And her heart is plenty big enough to love you all just like I do."

Well, maybe not just like. I would always love him more than them, would defend him ferociously against anyone, family or no. But I could love them, certainly, if they let me.

Darlene left us shortly after finishing her food, called away by Francine's thready but still imperious demand. As soon as she disappeared down the hall, Will twisted in his highchair, whining when he could not see his mother. Aaron wasted no time, scooping him up and heading for the sink to wash the baby's face and hands. It took both of us to get the drying egg out of his hair, the dark, fine curls reminding me of Aaron's unruly locks. Then, we marched downstairs to get him into a clean change of clothes, the miniature jeans a copy of the ones Aaron wore, his t-shirt emblazoned with a bright green tractor.

The diaper change was not nearly as dramatic as I feared, only wet, not dirty. I admired Aaron's efficiency and had a thought to be grateful. While I found myself willing to fantasize about babies, it was reassuring to know the one man I would risk such a danger for had some experience with the tiny people.

We were in the middle of playing with a box that you were to fit shapes in when Darlene returned, proclaiming herself done with the morning responsibilities. Aaron left us for a few minutes to get his mother settled in the living room now that she was dressed, leaving me alone with his sister and her baby. For several minutes, we focused completely on the little boy, but then her attention swung to me.

"Tell me you're in this for the long haul, Jaqueline." Despite the hushed delivery, her words held a weighty combination of dread and hope. "Because I don't know if he can take another rejection. Bethany doesn't think you'll last once Mom gets to steamrolling you, but I'm hoping you're made of sturdier stuff than the last woman he gave his heart to."

Perhaps I should have felt slighted for their doubts, but I understood the sentiment sprang from love. For that, I could find no fault. "Darlene, I have made my promises to your brother, words meant for him alone. But to you, I promise this—whatever may come, I chose to remain faithfully by his side. He deserves no less than the faithful devotion he so generously gives to others."

She nodded in agreement. "Can't say as I have the pretty words you do, but I agree. Aaron's got a big heart, always gives and gives." Darlene reached over to squeeze my shoulder, as much an embrace as she could manage with William sitting between us. "I'm glad he's found someone who will give back." Then she headed for the stairs with a laptop and a stuffed full messenger bag, leaving me to help William press a slobber covered rectangle into the appropriate cut out.

Aaron came and went throughout the day, introducing me to the intricacies of soothing the baby when he fussed. Much as the crying could induce a headache, I did not begrudge William his tears. He had no words to tell us what troubled him, any more than a horse might, and I equated his small tantrums to moments when a horse might buck or kick to express discomfort. And when we would finally hit on whatever he had been trying to communicate, little could be more charming than the way he softened into your arms with relief.

Shortly after lunch, I sat down in a rocking chair, gently soothing William to sleep as he curled against my chest. One tiny hand clutched at a length of hair that had escaped my ponytail, the purple strands fascinating the baby beyond all reason when he discovered them. Just as William's grip loosened with sleep, Aaron crouched in front of me, every stress wrinkle in his face relaxed. He said nothing, only watched, eyes caressing both the baby and me. In the face of that much naked adoration, my excuses for holding back fell away, swept under by what I prayed was unconditional love.

"Aaron, what if I cannot have children?" A sliver of fear made my throat prickle the instant the words left my lips, the burning intensifying when his eyes snapped up to meet mine with a sharpness I had not seen before. But I pressed on with a quiet calm, not wanting to disturb the sleeping child. "My mother died giving me life, and the condition which took her from my father is hereditary. However much I would love to give you the family you long for, I do not wish to leave you to raise that family alone."

His face paled a bit, and I stopped rocking when he wobbled forward. But he caught himself with one hand on my knee, turning the needful gesture into a caress the moment he found his balance. "Jaqueline…"

Whatever he meant to say halted immediately at the tinkling of a bell, his mother's method of summoning help since she could hardly draw enough breath to yell. Aaron tensed at the first chime, the stress wrinkles reappearing like a horrible magic trick. "Dammit."

Much as I hated the timing, I admired his devotion to the woman, even if I doubted she returned the sentiment in any meaningful way. Had I a mother, I am sure I would forgive her much as well, particularly in a moment of need. "Go, Aaron. Your nephew has me held captive for you. We shall be here waiting."

"Thank God," he murmured as he pushed up onto his feet, so much conflict in his eyes I wished I had kept my secret. With so much to deal with already, I had piled even more onto his plate, none of it easy to chew. "Be back in a few minutes."

Some might consider me foolish for worrying as he disappeared back up the stairs, his voice a soothing rumble as he asked after his mother's wants. After all, I hardly considered the possibility of children before Aaron. Why should I fuss over it now? But it was far more than the medical concerns, or the threat to my own mortality that tore at my heart. For the real tragedy that loomed over me now was this—I had finally found the one man who I was not too much for. If what tore us apart was my not being enough, then I feared not just the loss of his love, but the possibility that no man would ever love me just as I was. Could I survive? Surely. But now that I flew at such glorious heights with Aaron, I found the mere prospect chilled me to the core.

Aaron

It took twenty minutes to get Mom situated for an afternoon nap. I tried my damnedest to channel the patience I always managed for my nieces and nephews, but it was hard to stomach that much whining when nothing you do is ever going to help. Worse still when the majority of my mind and heart were caught up in the bomb Jaque dropped.

When she finally told me what weighed her down, I hadn't had a single thought beyond denial. Not denying what she said, but a deep-down, visceral rejection of the possibility of losing her. I would sooner give up Gallant Company than risk the chance of her dying, and that wasn't a statement I made lightly. The Company was so much a part of me that I'm not sure who I would be without it. But without Jaqueline, I'm not sure there would be enough of me left to scrape into a suit of armor, anyway.

As I brought Mom a fresh glass of water for her nightstand and tucked the blankets up to her shoulders, she shocked me out of my spiraling thoughts with a raspy statement I had never heard her utter. "I'm sorry, my boy."

Frozen in place, one hand still clutching the edge of her comforter, I finally met her eyes after spending all morning avoiding the contact. She looked so tired, and more than a little terrified, all the makeup in the world unable to mask her mortality. In the face of what I just learned about Jaque, that fear resonated well past any of my residual anger from the night before.

"Thank you," I acknowledged, patting her shoulder before straightening to my full height. I'm no dummy. I knew better than to tell her it was okay, because she'd take it as permission to run roughshod over me again. But I appreciated the apology more than a thousand words of praise, which made it easier to muster a tired smile. "Get some rest, Mom. I need to go check on Will. He's about due for another diaper."

She harrumphed as she turned her face deeper into the pillow. "If you ever start a family it would be better to saddle yourself with a woman who knows how to care for your children."

Ah, yeah, there was the salt rubbed into the wound, particularly as said future family now lay swathed in shadows of doubt. My stomach dropped, but I jacketed my reply in steel, so she couldn't mistake my seriousness. "Mom, anyone can learn to change a diaper, and Jaque is a quick study. But not everyone can love as unconditionally as that woman, and I expect her to be treated with respect. I love her, she loves me, and that's all that matters."

Silence was her only reply, weariness overcoming even my anger on Jaque's behalf. The emotional blows just kept coming, harder to endure than hits from a lance because they struck so deeply. How much more could I bear? So, I pulled the door closed behind me, leaving it open a crack in case she called. Maybe Darlene would be willing to listen for her while I sorted things out with Jaque?

But no, when I knocked softly on my old door and peeked into the room, I found my sister sprawled across the bed. She still had a towel wrapped around her hair, which told me she'd gotten that bath she wanted. Barely audible snores made my heart feel a little bit lighter. At least I hadn't failed as her brother. Felt good to know I could help, even though she could have muddled through just fine without.

Speaking of muddling through. As I quietly made my way back downstairs to check on Jaque and Will, I came to terms with a few things. Could I get by without Jaque? Yes. Could I give her up and find another woman who would be able to have children? I could. I wouldn't, mind you. My heart, my mind, and my body were so irrevocably in love with everything about her and I could never be satisfied with anything less. Was it possible I could devote my lifetime to her and lose Jaque to something other than childbirth? Absolutely. Lives ended every day, gone in a breath. But as I stepped into the family room and my eyes took in the sight of Jaque dozing in the rocking chair with William clutching a lock of her rich purple hair, the one truth that mattered pushed past all the rest in the demand to be heard.

I had a family. A beautiful one that grew all the damn time, related not just by blood, but heart. And whether we were ever blessed with children or not, I knew this woman was the one I wanted to be a part of that family. Love was a choice, an action, not just a word, and I wanted to make that choice with Jaqueline for the rest of my life.

❧ 16 ❧

Jaque

Williams's warm weight lulled me to doze, and another warmth woke me, splayed hands stroking gently up the outside of my thighs. I smiled as my eyes fluttered open, Aaron's touch always a gift, but the expression stalled out when I met his gaze, remembering where we had left things. Swallowing my apprehension, I made sure of my grip on the baby before leaning forward.

"How is your mother?"

"Tired. Seems to be a theme." One hand moved further up my leg as he settled onto his knees, fingers coming to rest on my hip. But the caress I truly enjoyed was his eyes, so kind and open as he studied my face. "You, the baby, even Darlene."

"I think this week has been difficult for everyone."

"Be more difficult without you, my lady." Then he smiled, and while weariness muffled its potency, I clung to the honesty in it. "And no matter what, I love you. Children or no, our love is more than enough for me."

I leaned back into the rocker again as my spine sagged with relief, tears pricking my eyes. Yet my arms tightened as self-doubt raised objections. "But,"

He held a finger to his lips, eyes flicking down toward Will when the baby began to shift restlessly. "Shhh, let me talk a minute. Relax, or you'll wake the baby."

I settled, forcing a sigh. "I am at your mercy, then."

His eyes twinkled with a mischief I cherished. "Perhaps later, I'll take advantage of that. But for the moment, I want you to know I'm at your mercy too. My heart has always been meant to love you, and I'm grateful every moment you allow me the privilege. To think of snuffing those moments out before their time, even for children, is physically painful." He pressed a hand to his heart as if rubbing at an ache. I wished I had a hand free to touch him. Something to renew our connection with.

"I am willing to try," I offered, then amended my statement when he looked ready to object. "No, I want to try. Not only for you, but for me. For who I am in loving you. I want to see you holding our baby, Aaron, with a desire so deep I have rarely felt it for much else. It may be that the doctors can treat the problem, or even that I am not at risk. But I wanted you to know, before our hopes ran away with us."

His smile crept up a notch. "I remember you saying something about the hazards of carriage driving. How a driver needed to be committed because when things went badly they had to stay in the carriage no matter what, for the safety of their horse and everyone around them. Well, this is me, taking up the reins, risking the runaway. Because no one around me will like the wreck I'll be if I let go of you, least of all me."

I sniffled gracelessly, trying to hold back tears. "You truly do say the most beautiful things."

"And I mean every word," he promised, as if everything he already said wasn't enough. Then his arms wrapped around my waist and he lowered his head to my lap, as close as we could get without disturbing the baby. Embracing me, even in a moment that would gain him little in terms of sexual satisfaction. Something I did not know I needed until he gave it to me.

Darlene came downstairs to retrieve Will shortly before dinner, just as I managed my first solo diaper change. She ribbed us about the domestic little scene and joked about making our own babies instead of trying to steal hers. That she included me in the tease took any sting out of my fears, particularly when Aaron squeezed my hand in reassurance.

We ordered out for dinner, another salad for Francine and pizza for the rest of us. Darlene and I set the table with paper plates before taking our seats, William happily burbling away in his highchair as we waited for Aaron and his mother. The rigid dining room appeared much more inviting now that I felt secure in my welcome there. Well, from all but Francine, who audibly gasped in dismay when Aaron helped her walk to her seat.

"What is that?" she hissed, pointing one of her perfectly manicured nails at me.

I swung my head from side to side to look at myself, worried I might find a spider on me considering the vehemence of her reaction. "What?"

"Is that purple in her hair?" she continued, as if I were little more than a fixture in the room, staring up at her son in entreaty. Nervously, I fingered the strands. While I had never worn it down around her before now, surely my choice of hair colour was my own business?

"Isn't it pretty?" Darlene asked, firmness in her chin as she glared at her mother in outrage.

"I think it's beautiful," Aaron stated as he steered Francine into her chair and scooted the seat closer to the table. "It's her personal colour, just like red lipstick is yours, Mom."

Then no one mentioned it again, though I felt Francine's disapproval like a specter hovering in the corner of the room. Darlene and Aaron maintained light background conversation, discussing her progress with her studies. Her goal was to become an accountant by the time William started school, a career she could rely on for steady work. Though Francine grumbled about her daughter's choices, including some pointed barbs about giving up on her marriage too soon, Aaron's pride in his younger sister made a fine counterpoint. Had his whole life been like this, I wondered, always stepping between his sisters and the unpleasantness of his parents? He had divulged more about his father since his confession a few nights ago, so I understood how little praise any of them received as children. Little wonder he always found a way to encourage others. Aaron intimately knew how it felt to be starved of such warmth.

As I dished a third slice of pizza the shadow of Francine's censure grew and found its voice again as she dabbed delicately at her lips. "A lady should never eat more than a gentleman."

Aaron pointedly grabbed two more slices from the cardboard box, but otherwise ignored her, leaving me free to indulge however I liked. The cheese lost a good deal of its allure with her snide comment seasoning things, but I ate every last bite in defiance. No sense wasting Aaron's noble gesture.

After dinner though, everything quieted. We settled in the living room for a bit while Francine knitted, and Darlene went to give William a bath. This turned my mind to the little creatures in our care who had been locked up most of the day. While Boris would use the litter box, Soleil had no such means of relief.

"Aaron," I touched his arm to draw his attention from his phone. Though it vibrated several times during dinner, he had waited to answer. While cleaning up our mess in the dining room, I learned they were from Bart, so he was now deep in conversation with his brother about the team leaving tomorrow. Judging from the pinch over his brows when he looked up, he worried about something. "If we are staying for much longer tonight, I should go to the motel and attend to our companions."

"Companions?" Francine inquired, for once, no hint of criticism in her voice. But confusion abounded as she directed the question at Aaron. "You've brought friends with you?"

Aaron's concerned expression bled over into humour. "No, Mom, she means her dog and my cat. We didn't have time to find someone to watch them, so they've been staying in the motel room."

I smiled at the fondness in his voice, loving how sweet he was with both animals, but the moment shattered as Francine hissed her disdain. "A cat? Why would you have such a dirty little beast, Aaron? You know very well that I cannot abide them in the house."

Aaron turned a flat stare on her. "Which is why he's at the motel, Mom. I'm not asking to bring him over."

"And dogs? Inside? Shedding on things and tracking in dirt. Animals belong outside!"

To that, I could no longer keep my silence. "We are all of us animals, Mrs. Drew, and I would no more ask my little Soleil to sleep outside than I would baby William. My dog is one of my chiefest joys in life and her place is beside me. As for Aaron's cat, he is a delightful creature. Boris would be broken hearted were Aaron to leave him behind."

Faster than the shifting wind in a tornado, she rounded on me with a similar chill. "A woman's duty is to make a safe home for her husband's children, so that confirms all my doubts as to your suitability to be part of this family. I won't have any of my grandchildren forced to share a home with animals!"

Before I could recover from the shock of such a categorical denial of acceptance, Aaron stood. The motion drew Francine's dagger sharp gaze away, giving me a chance to swallow down the maelstrom of emotions bombarding me. But the rest of the room seemed to dim as Aaron drew a deep breath, those emotions also swirling around him. His warmth and kindness were swiftly buried under heartache, pain and a righteous anger. I did not fear it, as it was not directed at me. Instead, I feared for him, terrified of what this might cost him.

"Mom, that's enough." The chill in his voice felt like it came from the heart of a blizzard. I shivered in reaction, wishing I could cuddle close to him, chase the cold away from both of us.

Not realizing how close she stood to the precipice of disaster, Francine railed against his warning. "Don't you presume to boss me, Aaron Allen Drew! I gave you life, young man, and that gives me a say!"

Desperate to stop the wreck I saw in the way his jaw tightened, I jumped to my feet. "Excuse me, I think I will go check on Darlene. Perhaps she could use my help with William?"

One step was all I managed before Aaron's hand closed gently around my elbow. "Wait, Jaque, just wait. I want you to hear this so it can't be twisted later." His grip would not have been enough to stop me, but the plea in his eyes rooted me to the ground. "Stand by me?"

"Of course." When his fingers loosened, I pulled my elbow away and reached for his now empty hand, though whether that anchor was for him or myself, I could not say.

Then he turned back to his mother, who despite having a few moments in which she could collect herself, still looked incensed. A sneer stole every ounce of her beauty, her exterior now a match for what I guessed must be a very withered soul. "Oh, no, by all means, run away. Don't let us keep you. Aren't the French all cowards?"

For many reasons, I would have happily turned the other cheek, but one thing could not be borne. Never insult what I love, my heritage included. Still, my general good nature and my love for Aaron prevented me from trading insults with his mother, however vilely she might behave. So, I turned to face her, shoulder to shoulder with her son, presenting a united front. Whatever vitriol she spouted, we would stand together against it.

Aaron

I'd spent so much of my life shuttering my emotions, hiding them away, that it hurt to let them loose. To finally be angry, upset, and yes, outright hurt by how my own parents had treated me. One sought to squash them under the heel of his boot in an effort to make me into his image, and the other took advantage of that squashing to mold me into whatever shape she liked. All my old guilt turned to dust in the face of my mother's unmasked disdain though. Careful peacekeeping went by the wayside the instant she insulted Jaqueline.

"I'm done listening to you, mother. You can say whatever you like now, because I won't be around to hear you. You've never once listened to me, never once offered a word of encouragement if it didn't suit your purpose. But you'll listen now, or they'll be the last words you ever hear from me."

A motion in the shadows drew my eye, Darlene standing at the edge of the hall, giving me pause. Mom took that hesitation for a weakness and plowed into the opening.

"Don't you threaten me, my boy. I'm all you've got left now that your Daddy is gone, and I won't tolerate your disrespect."

Darlene's eyes, already wide with fear, bloomed with something much more intense—after all our late-night conversations, I guessed it was quietly bottled anger. Fed by constant cutting criticism from our mother, Darlene had believed her husband's infidelity might be her fault. Our mother who should have been a safe place. That anger made her nod at me, backing my play, whatever happened. So, I pressed on, shored up as Jaqueline's hand tightened in mine, lending me her own strength.

"No, Mom, you aren't all I have left. I've got people at my back who understand what family really is. I've got a woman at my side who shows me every day what unconditional love really means."

Her lips disappeared and her eyes became nothing but black slashes in her face as she turned her ire on Jaque again. "This hoyden? Oh, I'm sure she keeps your bed warm, but that's not what makes a marriage last. You're a fool if you think otherwise."

God, I wanted to sag under the weight of her displeasure, but I couldn't. Not just for my sake, but for Jaque, for Darlene. Even for Bethany and Courtney, though they wouldn't thank me for stirring the pot like this. Knowing my mother like I did, the fall out would make itself felt by even the innocent. Nothing was ever her fault; she was always the wronged party.

"She doesn't just warm my bed, Mom," Okay, in retrospect, Jaque tended more to outright burning the bed down, but Mom didn't need to hear that. Nor would Jaque have thanked me for the praise in that moment. But she thanked me later for what came out of my mouth next. "She warms my heart. And I'll never live long enough to thank her for it, since it has been cold for so long."

Though I could see her anger beginning to take a physical toll, shoulders round with weariness, Mom fired one last desperate shot. "If you chose her over me, Aaron Allen, I will never forgive you."

Right then, Jaque chose to speak, her voice so full of the sadness I couldn't let myself feel yet that I nearly broke. But what she said gave me strength enough to withstand the end of the world as I knew it. "That you even ask him to choose, to divide his heart which is capable of so much love, I wonder how you shall ever forgive yourself."

Mom sat in stunned disbelief, as if Jaque physically slapped her, her mouth working but no sound emerging. While I worried for her breathing, I knew now was the time to walk away. Any further words would be pointless. Jaque and I moved toward where Darlene had ducked back into the hall, tears leaking down her cheeks in steady succession.

"Sorry, Darlin'," I murmured, pulling her into a rough hug that she returned with desperate strength, as if she were afraid to let go. "I made a mess of things."

She shoved away from me with a determined set to her shoulders. "Nonsense. They've always been a mess. It's about time we started shoveling the mess into the trash, where it belongs."

I gave a strained grin, thankful for her sass even if I felt like shit. "Just don't throw out the good memories with the bad, okay?"

The way she rolled her eyes reminded me of Jo. "Don't be ridiculous, big brother. You are so many of my happy memories, and I've few enough as it is. But what're you going to do now?"

Looking to Jaque in question, I saw nothing but faith. I knew she'd back me whatever I decided. Even if that meant staying to see my mother taken care of. But that's not what my heart wanted. "You know, Darlin', I think I'm going to head home. It's time. How about you? You need help before we go?"

She shook her head immediately. "No, Will's asleep, and I'm pretty sure once Mom gets done venting her spleen, she's going to need to sleep too. I'll stick around, see if I can't keep shoveling some of the mess."

"But you've already got so much on your plate, Darlin', you don't need this too," I objected, fighting the urge to tuck her under my arm and take her with us. "Will needs you, and your schoolwork is important."

A grin of mischief spread over her face, showing off all the beauty and character that our Mom would have, if not for her bitterness. "Sure, but you guys let me catch up on my sleep today. I feel like I could run a marathon. A few days of getting Mom settled will be a piece of cake." Then she turned to Jaque, arms open wide, and they embraced just as fiercely as we had moments ago. "And you, lady, make sure he still comes to see us. Momma may have lost her mind, but the rest of us still want him around."

"Of course! But please, you are welcome to come visit us as well. Bring William, too."

"I see, you just want me for my baby," Darlene responded, though her smile said it was all in fun.

A wheezing screech from behind us said Mom had regained her voice, though judging by the unintelligible angry sounds, not her wits. Warning enough. Time to go. I hugged Darlene one more time before stepping out of the hall and onto the stairs. Jaque's hand came to rest on my shoulder as I paused to get one last look at my Mom, some faint hope still living that she might come to her senses.

"Bye, Mom. Don't know when I'll be back, but when you're ready to apologize, you know the number."

She exploded then, hands clutching at the arms of her recliner as she attempted to rise. "Get out! Get out and never darken my door again, you ungrateful brat!" The words trailed off as her breath grew short, the shouting too much for her weakened lungs. Collapsing into her chair again, she rasped out a final epithet. "Get your whore out of my house."

Hope snuffed out even as my conviction grew that I'd done what I needed to. Jaque didn't deserve such disrespect, whether I loved her or not. I walked out the door under a full head of steam, not really angry as much as sure we were on the right track and felt not an ounce of regret as we pulled out of the drive and headed for the hotel to pick up our pets.

No, the regret came a hundred miles later, shortly after we crossed the Mississippi River. After fueling up I parked in a darkened corner of the truck stop to call Bart and let him know I was on my way home. He'd called in Fillmore for the weekend, since we were supposed to be working a faire in his home state, so they didn't need me. But I needed to get back in armor and hit something, before I shattered under the strain of what I'd done.

Call finished, I lifted the center console to invite Jaque close, needing a respite. She crawled into my lap without a word and offered me her lips, giving without my having to ask. But instead of stopping what I felt, she gave it an outlet, channeling the pain and even the hard-won pride into a storm we knew how to dance in. I cried like I hadn't cried since my childhood as I kissed her, years of suppressed feelings pouring out of my eyes. My hands clenched just a little too tight, my mouth rougher than she deserved. But Jaqueline answered with loving touches, welcoming the embrace and held me tighter still. Even little Soleil whined in concern, worried about my distress.

By the time the sobs stopped, I felt wrung out. With Jaque's weight pressed against me, one hand in my hair as I snuggled against her chest, I felt safe. But I also knew we couldn't stay there. When I lifted my head to stare up into Jaque's tear streaked face, I somehow knew she'd been crying for me too. "Thank you."

"I would say you are welcome, but I would give a great deal for this pain never to have been yours," she answered, pressing a comforting kiss to my brow as she stroked my hair out of the way.

I wished I could have found the beautiful words she deserved for her devotion. But failing that, I tried for a weak smile. "You ready to go home, my lady?"

She smiled back, her expression looking far less weary than mine. "I am, my champion, though I pray you will forgive me for asking, as I know how much you love your truck. Would you allow me to drive? Let me take the wheel for a time, and you can rest."

Which is how I came to doze off in the heated passenger seat of my own vehicle, the rumble of the diesel and Boris's purr a fine lullaby. But I did it with a tiny smile, closing my eyes on the vision of Jaque at the wheel. We spoke of playing navigator for each other, not so long ago. But that night, I discovered Jaque had become far more than a driver or a navigator. She was the compass I could rely on to steer me homeward.

❧ 17 ☙

Jaque

We arrived at Aaron's place in time to help with morning feeding, though the sun still hid behind the horizon. Soleil happily darted around the aisleway as we mixed breakfast for the impatient herd, which made me long for my own horses. Though I regretted not a moment of my time with Aaron, I yearned to kiss the tiny snip of white on Lyric's lip. To inhale her warm comfort, to reconnect with one of the purely good things in my life. Perhaps then I would feel less adrift.

Still, my heart healed more than a little to see his big gelding, once so determinedly defensive, whinny like a colt when he heard his rider's voice. He nuzzled Aaron's pockets for treats but did not shove or nip. They shared a moment's communion that made Jo stop in her tracks to witness it, as Aaron leaned over the stall door and fully embraced the stout neck, vigourously scratching beneath the mane in the process. Byzantine wiggled his lips against the light jacket Aaron wore in defense of the cool spring air, clearly enjoying the contact.

"I'll be damned," Bart rumbled as he stepped out of the feed room with a stack of rubber pans in his arms. "'Bout time you two made up."

Aaron delivered a few hearty pats to Byzantine's shoulder as he grinned at his brother. "Yeah, it is. Hopefully, he and I can make good on our potential this weekend. I know it's going to be weird now that you've called in a ringer, but maybe we can get in at least one joust."

Bart laughed and shook his head. "Brother, when I texted him last night Fillmore was relieved he wouldn't have to joust. He's coming anyway, since we're close, but only to help out."

At the news Aaron's face gained colour, the paleness from last night chased away as his blood ran hot with excitement. While I imagined he had much to heal after the upheaval with his mother, that change alone gave me hope he might come through the experience without lingering suffering.

Once the horses were fed, we all retreated to the loft apartment and settled at the small dining table with cups of hot caffeine, coffee for all but Jo. She cradled a tumbler of tea in both hands as we listened to the brothers discussing what little needed doing before the team could depart. Though Soleil sprawled at my feet, I felt like an unnecessary accessory to the conversation but did not want to rush Aaron either. He relaxed by the moment, now back in the familiar embrace of what I considered his true family.

My patience lasted as long as my coffee, which proved timely. Aaron made noises about heading to his room to repack his bag, then turned to me, a wealth of softness in his midnight eyes.

"My lady, would you accompany me? I need a few minutes before we say our farewell."

I struggled not to ruin his solemnity by smiling. Hard to do, when Jo hid a pleased grin in another sip of her tea. Instead, I held out a hand and replied in kind. "Of course, my champion."

He took my fingers with chivalrous delicacy, guiding me up out of the chair and down the hall to his room. Soleil took her place at my side as Boris trotted ahead, certain of our destination. Once inside, he urged me to sit on the edge of the bed before turning to rifle through a drawer in his bureau. A confused crease took up residence between my brows at his suddenly furtive movements, the quiet holding an expectant quality.

When he faced me once more, a small velvet bag lay in his palm and a tentative hope marked his every movement with sweet tension. "I meant to give this to you Monday, when we stayed here together for the first time, but... life." He shrugged, almost boyishly shy as he held out the offering for me. "The thing is, Jaque, it seems pretty insignificant now. You've given me so much the last few days, and I can never hope to equal that gift."

Plucking the little pouch from his palm, I was surprised to find it weighty for its size. But before I opened it, I addressed his comment. "Aaron, gifts are not given in hopes of repayment."

Then I tipped the contents out into my hand, gasping as the blue heart caught the light. Dark as his eyes, but still, possessing an inner glow. Though not very large, the pendant lay heavily against my skin, warming to my touch as the attached chain slithered between my fingers. "It is lovely. When did you have time to find such a thing?"

Pride and still a bit of worry punctuated his reply with a raspiness. "It was in one of the shops we went to at the faire." Then he cleared his throat, cupping my hand in his as he destroyed my reserve with sweet words. "When we're apart, I wanted you to know my heart is with you."

"Oh! Oh, Aaron!" I stammered, eyes filling with stinging happiness as I looked up at him, a flush moving over my shoulders like a thousand fiery kisses at once. "Oh, mine will be with you, as well. Near or far, I have given it to your keeping."

"That's all the repayment I'll ever ask for, Jaqueline. You keep mine for me, I'll keep yours for you." Then he stepped in close and gathered me to his chest, pressing his lips to the top of my head. I wanted to wrap my arms around him in return, to always give back whatever he gave, but his strength lured me to cuddle into the embrace. Surely I would have a chance to hold and be held many times in the future, to give without reciprocation, much as I had the night before. Nothing would please me more.

"I know you must go soon," I murmured into the thick cotton of his shirt, letting my lips brush over his muscular chest in the process. "Else I would give you something to remember me by so you would know what waits at home."

He chuckled, and while I knew he must still be hurt from the falling out, I heard heat in the rumble under my ear. "I promise you, Jaque, not a single cell of me will ever forget how it feels to be with you. Having to say farewell will only make our hello that much sweeter."

After that declaration, we kissed, trading between sweet sips of each other's lips and a ravenous hunger that made for a clash of teeth. A perfect balance, to my mind, before he pulled away and helped me put the necklace on.

Clasp secure, he cupped the back of my neck with both hands and stared into my eyes. I vow to you, it felt as though he exposed the depths of his soul with such an honest gaze. So much love spilled over the raw edges of his fractured heart that I knew beyond a doubt he would heal. Perhaps his mother would come around, perhaps not, but he truly accepted how much he was loved, and not by me alone. "For everything, I love you more, Jaqueline Sauveterre."

Grasping his wrists to increase the weight of our connection, I answered him solemnly, "May we always love each other more, Aaron Drew."

While I left him to his work not long after, I felt him close, even as I missed him. Partly in the weight of the pendant just below the hollow of my throat, but mostly in the weight of love that pulsed in my chest. His memory filled the passenger seat of my truck as I drove home, he lingered in the shadows as I parked Lyric in the aisle and curried her until she gleamed. That night, when I climbed into bed to wait for his usual evening call, I felt him in the way Soleil curled up behind my legs, avoiding the spot where Aaron had last slept. Even she knew his place in my life, and I would gladly wait for him to come home and fill it again.

Aaron

Our new tent came in while I was gone and the weather was decent, so Friday night felt like shades of the good old days once the horses settled in. With the recent rains to reduce fire danger and the approval of the management, Bart built us a little blaze to congregate around. Fillmore brought a few six packs of beer with him, so between the heat of the fire in front of me and the cool bottle in my hand, I felt pretty mellow. Everyone in camp seemed to be in a similar mood, with Trace and Fillmore trading stories in low tones while Jo and Bart stared into the flames with matching smiles of contentment.

I felt like the odd man out, watching them. Though not with the abrasive irritation that I felt before Jaque and I came together. It morphed to the dull throb of an old bruise, more a constant reminder that I missed her than a stabbing pain. And I wasn't entirely alone, with Boris draped across my shoulders like a weighty scarf, his purr relaxing the muscles in my neck where stress usually manifested.

But stack that on the recent break from my mother and I had some serious aches to nurse. I didn't regret having stood my ground, but my sisters bombarded me with texts, keeping the sting fresh in my memory. Bethany delivered a blistering series of messages, all of which I tolerated well until the last. Mom told her

Jaque was just after me for citizenship, using me to get into America.

I never knew you could laugh angrily before that, which was an odd sensation. Sort of an acid burn in my throat along with the bubbles of humor. First off, Jaque had made it very clear that her objective was to represent Canada in the World Championships. No dice if she were an American citizen. And I'd listened to her talk about her home country, the love in her voice palpable. That knowledge made my response to Bethany easy to formulate.

'Well, you can tell Mom it's much more likely I'll end up becoming a Canadian. I'm sure that'll blister her ears.'

As if she knew I could use some support, Jaque texted me shortly afterward. *'You are loved and missed.'* That alone pulled my shoulders out of my ears and let me relax enough to enjoy the evening again.

When it came time for night check on the horses, I got up and followed Jo and Bart. Their surprise over my joining them was quickly eclipsed by their shock when I haltingly spilled my guts over what had gone down with my mother. The words were easier to say in the dim light coming from the moon and the distant fire. The heat in Jo's eyes when I finally looked up from fiddling with a piece of hay string could have cracked a glacier. I half feared she would saddle up that instant and go give my mother a piece of her mind.

But she stayed silent as I told them where things stood, and the anger faded to the background, drowned out by a wave of acceptance as she hugged me tight. "Big brother, I know it was hard. But I'm proud of you for standing your ground. And for your sake, I hope she comes around."

Then, she disappeared into the darkness toward the trailers, likely off to bed. Which left me with the hulking edifice of my brother, who had borne my mother's sharp tongue through the years and all of my excuses for her without once condemning me.

"You saw this coming, didn't you?" I asked, voice cracking with the strain of holding back my feelings for so long.

"No," He sighed, a deep exhale I knew he often employed when trying to steady his own emotions. "I hate to say I hoped for it, since I knew it would hurt you. It's been hard to watch you take this kind of beating. You deserve better, brother."

My heart, so tired from the upheaval over the last week, finally broke wide open. Not because I needed to let out any more anger, but because I wanted to let in all the love I felt. From Jaque, Bart, Jo, and even Byzantine, who wandered over to stand with us while I let tears of gratitude run down my cheeks.

Once the waterworks dried up, I finally turned to Bart and hugged the hell out of him. He returned the embrace with all the manly backslapping I could ever need, proving emphatically that our brotherhood came from far more than the DNA we shared. It came from enduring trials together, cherishing the good and facing the bad. There would be more of both in our future, and I couldn't have asked for better people to share the journey with.

Weight lifted from my chest, I headed for my own bed after saying goodnight to Bart and Byzantine. The gentle crackle of the fire that Trace and Fillmore still enjoyed, the faint sounds of the horses chewing and Boris's rumbling all made another fine lullaby. I fell asleep easily, which made for a better than usual morning, waking when the horses nickered for breakfast. My face tingled after a bracing splash of cold water from the bottle I'd left beside my bed got the blood pumping. When I regarded the motionless lumps of the younger men still swaddled in their sleeping bags mischief I hadn't entertained in years came to the fore. Boris paid little attention to my antics, curled in a dense ball in my bedroll, not even mustering a meow when I left the tent to hunt up a couple of fresh bottles from the ice chest outside.

To be fair, I did give them warning, stomping back into the tent, noisily changing my clothes, but they remained resolutely unaware. Even the clearing of my throat garnered no effect, nor did the increasing sounds coming from outside that told me Bart and Jo were starting morning chores.

"Guys, time to rise and shine," I said firmly, though I held back amusement as I said it, hoping I'd get to follow through on my plan. They obliged, the only movement coming from Trace's cot as he pulled the sleeping bag tighter around his shoulders.

So, I stood just out of reach and shot each with an icy cold blast from the bottles, BAM, BAM, right on top of their scalps. This resulted in horrified squeals one might expect from a baby goat deprived of the bottle as both flailed around in their well-zipped cocoons. And I shot out the tent flap before they noticed, biting down hard on my knuckles to keep from giving myself away.

Bart shook his head and grinned as I joined him tossing out hay for the herd. "Good to have you back, brother," was all the acknowledgment he made. The now understandable cursing in the tent finally drove Boris outside, his plaintive meow quite disgusted as he trotted across the field.

Took until we finished setting out the feed pans Jo showed up with for Bart's statement to settle in my bones. I needed to finally accept the truth. I had been so caught up in everything I ought to do that I hadn't done much of anything I wanted to do in a long damn time. So as I stood with Byz to make sure he didn't run his herd mates off their own feed, with Boris winding around my ankles to beg for attention, I made a resolution. It was time to take a step back from quite as many responsibilities and begin stepping up to the things that mattered to me, personally. My eyes drifted over to Jo and Bart hanging out with their own horses, reminding me to start with the family I right in front of me.

At least I was afforded a little time to plan my words. We first needed to deal with Trace and Fillmore, who finally emerged from the tent with outrage plain in the set of their narrowed eyes. The young cowboy who came in as a trainee at the same time as Jo had filled out a bit over the last year, arms and shoulders stacked with muscle, but he still needed some time to get comfortable enough to speak his mind. We hadn't found the time to really play with him on equal footing since his knighthood. Trace, however, experienced no problems airing his grievance after so many years with us. Dragging his long blonde hair into a ponytail as he stalked to the edge of the electrical tape, he wisely stopped before touching it. You only bumped into it accidentally one time before you got understandably cautious of the sharp sting it could deliver.

"Who the hell dumped water on my head?" he growled, eyes going immediately to Jo as she was the most likely culprit for a practical joke in his experience. "That shit was cold!"

He even shivered to reinforce the image. But Jo, completely innocent for a change, just shrugged her shoulders as she sipped her tea before answering. Her words made a trail of frosty puffs in the cool morning air, though the temps were already warming with the sun. "Not me, fellas, much as I'd love to lay claim to the mischief. I was at the trailer making feed pans."

Fillmore looked incredulous, eyes wide with disbelief that either Bart or I would do such a thing. Trace, however, tried to stare us both down in turn, waiting for some sort of crack in our defenses. He found no such weakness, as Bart stepped up next to me and folded his arms across his considerable chest and stared right back. You know that saying about staring into the abyss and the abyss staring back? Well, Bart was the abyss, and he had a layer of dark in his stare that could curdle your blood when he saw fit to level you with it.

When Trace finally broke, all the tension bled right out of his body like you'd poked a straw in a juice box and sucked it dry. "Alright, fine, whatever. I'll just go get started on the manure shoveling then."

Bart broke into a broad grin. "Now there's some clearheaded thinking. Maybe next time the two of you won't stay up so late, then we won't have to resort to extreme measures to get you moving. I'm sure Mr. Lee remembers the rules about being up in time to feed."

Fillmore quickly turned away, heading straight for the wheelbarrow and forks sitting by the gate, aware of his *faux pas* now. While Jo held open the gate for the guys, Bart and I turned away to pick up the now empty feed pans. We always went for Tuck's pan last, as the rotund Belgian tended to drool like a mastiff. I bit the bullet since Bart had covered for me, and held the pan pinched between thumb and forefinger as gobbets of saliva dribbled from the rim.

"Disgusting," I muttered, even Boris eschewing my company in order to avoid the slime. "Bart, didn't you say something about getting Tuck's teeth checked to see if we can fix this?"

He snorted as I joined him by the hose to rinse the pans clean. "Vet said it's not his teeth, though she gave him a quick float to be sure. Might be an overactive salivary gland, but not much to be done for that. Just part of his charm."

"Yeah, charm," I grumbled as we made short work of the chore, then moved on to the next. We didn't have individual pens for the horses this time, as this was a small-time fairground in northern Georgia, tucked in between the suburbs and a more rural area.

However, Bart got the organizers to provide a large rental tent to use as shade, set right up against the metal railed fence surrounding the main arena. This way, we could tie the horses securely, keep them and our equipment in the shade, and still get plenty of visibility with the patrons. Last night, we had distributed and filled buckets, but still needed to hang them and the hay nets before we brought the horses in for the morning.

About the time we finished, our volunteers began arriving. Jo appeared out of seemingly thin air to take them under her wing. That left us to go bring in the herd, with the help of the guys, all of the familiar activity giving me time to think. Which meant right about the time I was out of stuff to do, I was ready to wrangle with my first real task.

"Hey, Bart, you got a minute before I go hunt up breakfast?" I asked nonchalantly, as I scooped up Boris and started walking toward my truck. Judging by the purposeful way he fell in beside me, I don't think he was fooled in the least.

"What's up, brother?"

As I plunked Boris down on the driver's seat, I straightened my shoulders, hoping my instincts were as good as they used to be when it came to reading him. From the first time I'd met him, still a little scrawny with youth, Bart had been an open book if you slowed down and took the time to read him.

"I'd like to propose a change in the Company," I began as I turned to face him, appreciating for the millionth time his tendency to listen, to wait before answering. Saved us a ton of arguments over the years. "Now that we're both getting into the swing of things, I'm wondering if you're ready to go back to the co-captaincy." Pointing toward where Jo introduced the volunteers to the horses, I gave a half grin to go with the tease I delivered. "After all, it looks like Jo is stealing your job. Might as well take the next step."

He grinned too as he watched her work, expression remaining light when he turned back to me. "I had a feeling she would, even in the beginning. But there's gotta be more to it than that, Aaron. What's your reasoning?"

"I've got a few answers to that." Ticking them off on my fingers for emphasis, I began. "One, you're back in the game, no holds barred. Two, I think you might be even more ready than you were when we last shared the title. Three, if I'm going to keep myself accountable to my own progress, I think I need to step back from the line a little. The stress has been…"

When I paused too long to search for an appropriate word, Bart tossed out a few accurate choices. "Acute? Chronic? Painful? Absolute shit?"

"All of the above," I agreed, though a rueful chuckle lightened the answer. "I know we never planned for your overseas deployment with the reserves, and you getting injured never crossed my mind, with your role in supply. Not that I regret holding the line for a singular instant when all that went down."

My heart clenched with remembered fear when I'd gotten a phone call from his Mom. She'd been a veritable rock, even with the worry in her voice, a far cry from my own mother's penchant for hysterics. When I found Bart hiding out in the dingy hotel almost a year later, his skin sallow, eyes practically lifeless, the pain had increased a thousand-fold. For a while there, I truly feared we'd already lost him. But I shook away the dark memory, facing the now whole man in front of me with pride overflowing in my heart. "That's what partners, what family, is supposed to do. Hell, you've been stepping up for me the last few months while my own crap came to a head. But I think we're both ready now."

He regarded me for several moments, that abyss in his eyes coming back. That look always made me feel like he was rifling through the contents of my soul, even at seventeen. Freaking uncanny then, and with a wealth of experience behind him, it was absolutely surreal. Thankfully, whatever he found seemed to satisfy him, and he held out a hand. "I'm in."

We shook on it, and I was all set to leave without any further fanfare, but then he hit me with a parting shot. "Besides, if Jo gets her way, we'll have to increase our numbers to cover simultaneous contracts. Better to have a captain to manage each crew."

Then he walked off to whatever task came next on his never-ending mental list. That left me staring after him while my truck whined a complaint because I left the key in the ignition and the door open. If not for a well-timed meow from Boris, I might have sat there much longer, wondering how in the hell we'd ever gotten so lucky in finding Jo. She had seen the needs we had, then answered them one by one. Now, she was taking us well beyond our wildest dreams, driven on by seemingly limitless faith in our humble company.

Jaque

The morning came with a familiar pounce from Soleil's tiny paws upon my shoulder, a more reliable alarm than any ever created by man. She had been remarkably forgiving with the odd schedule we kept while in Iowa, but we were home, and business must be attended to.

I shuffled into the kitchen, yawning and stretching even as I pulled loose the cover on the dog door so she could go out into the tiny yard. The pendant Aaron gave me bounced against my breastbone as I straightened, and I wrapped my hand around it as if to embrace him, even with the distance. Yes, a foolish imagining, but one that warmed me from the inside as I turned to start my morning coffee and oatmeal.

Once Soleil skittered back into the house, morning needs met, I left the little pot of oatmeal to simmer and pulled a zip up hoodie over my pyjamas. As I slipped thickly socked feet into tall rubber boots, I smiled, remembering the morning Aaron had first seen me traipse across the yard in my usual morning uniform. I had been caught between embarrassment at having the man I was attracted to seeing me at less than put together and wanting to know what he wore to bed. That morning, I had spent a good portion of my chores imagining how he would look with sleep tumbled hair and bedroom eyes. Now that I knew the truth of it, I am unashamed to say that it was my favourite look on him. He softened so much in the intimate confines of the bedroom, not only from our passions, but from the peacefulness we created in that space.

While I spent time with Lyric the day before, grounding myself in her steady company, she still nickered loudly the instant the front door opened. How my heart flooded with joy to watch her pick up a trot on the way to the barn, movements full of easy power, earthy grace. Though much of her remained covered in a bright purple blanket, owing to her short-clipped coat, I greedily drank in the jaunty lift of her tail and the way her thick limbs articulated. Even with a bit of dirt to mar her deep black colour, the healthy shine was unmistakable.

On her heels came the remainder of my herd. Clint pranced with high knees like a wooly carousel pony, while Cobalt and Corbin flanked his shadow like a pair of burly flunkies on the heels of a diminutive mob boss. Constance, as always, ambled to the gate last. While she loved her food with the same enthusiasm as any draft horse, she refused to waste an ounce of energy to get it.

I let them through the gate one at a time, reminding Corbin to whoa when he attempted to muscle through with his brother. He responded immediately, rooting his hooves to the muddy threshold even as he watched Cobalt head inside. Still, his ears flattened out in displeasure, lower lip dropping into his equivalent of a pout, certain he would be starved. We devoted a good deal of time to working through his impatience when I first began work for French Silver Carriage Company. After spending all his young life paired with his older brother, he had little confidence in being driven alone. But time and miles convinced him I could be trusted to keep him safe, to provide for his needs, resulting in a surprising amount of affection and an astounding level of obedience. Even when he did not like it.

Once they were each in their stalls, I closed the doors behind them. When I first came to the United States to work for the Boudreaux family, the boys had been rude and impatient at feeding time. But now, we had a system worked out that kept them from kicking their stall doors down. I provided treat dispensing balls with hay pellets in them, which added an interesting skirling sound as they butted the toys around on the floor. Only Clint occasionally tested me now, putting his treat ball in a corner where he would knock it incessantly against the wall until I arrived with his bucket of supplements.

I did not feed them on a regular schedule, typically. My life was too erratic to be consistent, and to be fair, they hardly needed anything beyond grazing or hay. In fact, soon I would have to start rotating them to the dry lot, so they would not plump up too much. But I enjoyed feeding them, seeing their eyes blink shut in bliss as they took their first mouthful of mush, hearing the soft, or not so soft, sounds of slurping as they cleaned their pans of every last drop of food.

Upon delivering the last bucket to Lyric, I lingered in her stall, slipping the blanket from her body to inspect her. Nose to tail tip, I took my time, fingers tracing all the familiar lines, hunting for the slightest deviation from normal. Aside from a few mussed patches of hair from rolling, she was in perfect shape, ready for whatever challenges awaited us.

This set my mind to a challenge I had not contemplated in quite some time. Aaron had mentioned the possibility of going on a trail ride together, and I longed to join him with the same enthusiasm we did everything else. Could I ride her again? The mere idea of risking her drew my hands down to the slight thickness over her knee, reminding me of the huge wound I spent six months crying over as I worked to heal it.

I taught Lyric her job as a driving horse from a very young age, ground driving her everywhere in a halter from her first birthday. For her third birthday, we hitched to a cart for the first time, a complete non-event in her mind. Nothing ever phased her faith in me as we slowly learned each other, including her inaugural ride as a four-year-old. By her fifth birthday, little pleased her more than long rides in the fields and woods surrounding my Grandpere's farm. Ears up, eyes bright, she looked to every stretch of new road with an open heart.

Until one beautiful autumn day when then soft ground slipped from beneath her nimble hooves as we trotted along. Images of her disappearing from under me as she fell off the trail flashed behind my closed eyes with breathless intensity. That fall had been the single most terrifying experience of my life, resulting in a separated shoulder as I tumbled down the incline. But worse still had been her coming down the hill in my wake, unable to see me below her. I had thrown my arms up to cover my head and cried out her name in a desperate prayer.

She answered, dropping her head so she could see me with one bright eye, then launched herself into the air as if she owned wings. Her devotion stole my breath more forcefully than the fall itself, sacrificing her own safety to keep from hitting me. When she crumpled to a stop on the trail below me, I slid down the hill unable to even cry out around the bands of fear constricting my chest.

Bless her, she lifted her head as I came to her side, a slight whine in the nicker she gave me that said something was hurt. Oh, my heart broke as she pushed to her feet and blood began to run down her leg, a river of red pushing loose the dark debris that covered the wound. I cried myself raw as I worked to stop the bleeding with the kit in my saddlebags. Unable to get a signal on my phone, we slowly limped homeward, mindful of the bandage and both of our stiffening bodies.

The vet cautioned me against hope, as close to the joint as the wound had been. Infection had been a constant threat. Nor did they hold much hope against scarring, as stitches were difficult to manage around an area with so much movement. But, thanks to Lyric's trust and our relationship, we persevered. Even with my own injury to slow my movements, she had been an admirable patient, enduring countless cleanings, bandage changes, and months of stall rest that would have driven a more hot-blooded creature to madness.

When I began to rehabilitate her with light exercise in the jog cart, she had quickly picked back up the knack of things, busy brain always working. I sought out a trainer then, to teach me more of the craft that my dear mare seemed to have an affinity for. And while she occasionally looked to her saddle hanging on the wall with a bit of a wistful sigh, I decidedly avoided the possibility. Anything that might risk her so much was not worth the price.

I am no fool. I knew in my heart that every day was a risk. Each trailer trip could be an accident. A slip in competition might cause a career ending soft tissue injury. A kick in the pasture could break bones. I risked far more with my commercial horses, working in traffic, on pavement, with the unknowns inherent in an urban environment.

But perhaps it was time? Perhaps taking a risk in loving Aaron gave me a measure of courage, having my bravery rewarded so fully.

"What do you say, dearest friend?" I asked Lyric, looking up from where I crouched beside her leg, reassured by the strength beneath my hands. "Would you like to be ridden again?"

She turned her mush covered nose toward me, lips flapping genially. The softness in her eyes gave me all the answer I could have hoped for. How much trust had we gained over the years? No earthly measure existed, and I would never cease being humbled by it. But I also had years of wisdom to draw from, telling me that much like our journey to this point had been guided by wiser, cooler heads, perhaps we should have help in this as well. My emotions could not be relied upon, and I needed the reassurance of someone to keep me on the right track. I would not risk her needlessly in order to prove something to myself.

I stood, shaking the feeling back into my legs before pulling a lighter weight sheet off the wall to cover Lyric against the cool spring morning. Smoothing it in place, I smiled, despite the anxiety that nibbled at this reemerging dream like a rabbit finding the tender new shoots of lettuce in a garden. I would need to act quickly, before it was consumed to the roots. There were calls to be made and a grey mare to bathe. Later, Laura would arrive to pick up the carriage for the wedding, and I would not be caught unprepared. Risks were inherent in all things, but I would meet them all with the same devotion my own mare gave me every single day.

Aaron

"Settle," I murmured as Byzantine shifted restlessly at the armoring block as we waited for Jo to secure my helm. Raring to go since I put his saddle on, he fidgeted endlessly in his own skin. When I stroked his neck, a flinch met my fingers, raising a bit of concern. This kind of energy could easily go explosive, and I didn't want to fight with him.

"Remember, side to side," Jo said, breaking into my thoughts as if she could hear them spinning in my head. She never stopped working on my armor, attention remaining on her hands as she continued to speak. "If you pull, he'll fight. Make his brain work instead."

"Right," I answered, so she knew I'd heard her. Carefully, I took up the right rein to ask him to bend his neck. The kid at his head wasn't really paying attention, more a roadblock than any active influence, so I was able to achieve a slight yield. An immediate release rewarded the effort, causing Byz's head to dip into the give, some of the tension under me bleeding away. "Thanks."

Jo smiled before tipping the visor closed, acknowledging both the word and the effort. Before stepping away, I asked for the left bend, which he resisted for the slightest breath before exhaling into the motion. Trying my best to match him, I exhaled too, though my nose wrinkled at the close-up smell of my own breath. The morning breakfast burrito had been a bit on the heavy side, leaving a greasy feel on the tongue and a sourness in my gut.

Still, my mood could hardly be beat. Over breakfast, Jo shared a couple inquiries she'd received about new contracts, and while it would be interesting to juggle, I could barely wait to get in touch with the interested parties. The Gallant Company eagle had been in a holding pattern for too long. It was time to spread our wings again.

Speaking of wings. Byz used his, dancing with barely contained excitement as I continued to bend him back and forth around my leg. We were up against Trace this round, which allowed me to focus on my horse more than my opponent. I could count on all of my teammates to provide a solid target, but Trace was the least complicated of them, steady and reliable. Jo was fast and sharp, demanding a bit more attention, and Bart would have required an utter devotion to the hit I didn't have the energy to deal with in the mornings.

We entered the lyst, then I swung him around to back into the lane, reassured by Jo's appearance in my field of vision. She was a rock to be relied on, in so many ways. Fillmore was shadowing her for the day, getting caught up in how we did things on the road. I felt sure he'd catch on fast, though he didn't have quite the same confidence level Jo came to us with.

When the call came to come about, Jo's arm drawing a circle in the air above her head, I struggled against the urge to pull on my horse. He blew off the line like a drag racer stuck in high gear, revving too high, too fast for me to follow that well. But I let go of the reins and got my lance down with a serious effort, leveling just in time for the sharp *crack* to reverberate through my body.

After I threw the lance away Byz juttered to a trot, his gait rough with tension, which made his cooperation all the more a miracle. I'd half expected him to run down Fillmore, flicking off any attempts to stop him with a toss of his head. But no, he halted just before the end, neck so upright I got a clear view of his sharp ears pointing back at me through the narrow slot in my visor.

"Good man," I praised, voice rough with gratitude as I found the reins.

The next turn, he leapt again, throwing me back against the cantle as if to nail me in place. But I let him go, refusing to fall back on the old fight that fueled our relationship for so long. Instead, I concentrated on my part of the job, delivering a smooth, accurate shot to Trace's beat-up grand guard. My reward came in a loud shout from the audience as I fought to stay in the middle of the saddle, the blowback enough to strain every muscle in my core. Judging by the noise and the thumbs up from Jo as Byz came to a stop, Trace had yielded to the pull of the ground.

I didn't worry overmuch for his condition. This particular arena was deeply tilled, making the going a little slow for anyone on foot, but perfect for falling in. Unless he got tangled up, or just took a bad angle, the impact shouldn't do much damage. Didn't take him long to get back in the tack either, his every move relayed to me by Bart's well-honed background narration. But it was enough time for Byz to take some deep breaths and settle into his skin.

For turn number three, my resolve to not fight finally yielded a prize. When my leg closed on his side, Byz moved, already anticipating the rein I would have laid against his neck. Yeah, he still launched himself down the lyst with a good bit of muscle, but it felt more purposeful, directable. I sighed into the stride, bringing my lance down with all the time in the world...

Moments later, I found cause to rethink my corresponding relaxation as Trace returned my blow with interest. Sure, I controlled the tumble once I figured out I couldn't save it, but I ended up choking on the cloud of dust I kicked up as I rolled onto my hands and knees. Hell, I needed to spit several times to clear my mouth of the red clay as Fillmore got me aimed toward the mounting block. But I had the clarity of mind to notice that Byz was back to fidgeting, shifting foot to foot and chewing the bit with worry.

"Hey, bubba, my bad." His ears tipped toward me as I acknowledged my fault in the equation, and the chewing slowed as if he were tasting my tone for sincerity. "We're gonna get this, I promise. No matter how long it takes, we'll make this good."

His feet stilled as I climbed the block, angling his neck to keep me in clear view as my hand closed on the reins, my foot found the stirrup. The only tension that remained was the anticipation of my weight. I swung back on, taking the time to get well settled since Bart could keep the crowd entertained with fancy maneuvers and suave words. "Hey, Lee, grab me a water?"

He scuttled quickly to retrieve a bottle from the shade beneath the block, and I swished a couple times to get the grit out of my teeth. On the upside, I couldn't taste my breakfast anymore around the minerally taste of clay. Then I grinned at the young guy as I tossed him the now empty bottle. "You sure you don't want to have a go this weekend, Fillmore? We can make it happen."

Shaking his head, he managed a sheepish grin I hadn't seen since he'd been in training. The expression made him instantly likeable, like a long-eared hound that wanted to be useful. "Naw, I'm not gonna steal anybody's fun unless I gotta."

"Then get me pinned in, man, because I've got some ass to kick." Then I tapped my visor closed and waited for him to secure it. Byz felt me coming, started moving before I even put my leg on.

The last pass wasn't much to write home about, in terms of drama, but I considered it remarkable none the less. Because when my big, rawboned, hammer headed war horse slung around the corner like a European sports car on a switchback, I found the sweet spot. The place where steady burning competitive edge met up with the giddy joy of doing what I was born to do. The moment where I finally, truly felt like we were on the right track. And the conviction to continue chasing that feeling, even when it meant learning to let go.

Jaque

In the midst of readying Constance's fancy harness for the late afternoon wedding, I received a text from my boss, Lily Boudreaux. While I had been left to run the business she, and her husband Frenchy, had built, we still touched base on occasion. Likely, she simply wanted an update on any upcoming contracts. I set down my rag and tugged off my gloves to open the message. The contents stole every ounce of warmth gained while working in the afternoon sunshine.

'Jaque, I know this won't be an easy pill to swallow, but Frenchy and I are ready to sell. We have a few months to hash things out, so no major rush. Just wanted you to have as much notice as possible.'

For several moments, I stood transfixed, staring at the phone with my mouth agape. Yes, I felt hints of this coming, but thought I had more time. At least through the holidays, when the company did its best business. To say I felt blindsided would be a drastic understatement. Some sense of betrayal tried to push to the forefront of my feelings, but I squashed it quickly. If not for Lily and Frenchy's kindness, I would never have come so far.

When I shook free of the selfish reaction, a frisson of fear ghosted through me with a wave of cold that belied my earlier cheer. I had no recourse for this. No savings to expend in an effort to buy the business or its assets. No means to purchase the land. My home, small though it might be, would pass to another. The horses I shared so many hours of my life with would be turned over to new families who did not know their foibles. Who knew them better than me? Who could love them better than me?

Additionally, my work visa would be in jeopardy. Without a job to keep me in the United States, I would have to return to Canada. How could I leave? I had a life, a small, but wonderful circle of friends, and at long last, I had found love. To leave Aaron would tear me to pieces.

Though a foolish part of my heart cried out that he would not let our relationship wither, I knew his own work demanded he stay in Kentucky. No amount of emotional upheaval could steal that knowledge away. In a very real way, I faced losing everything I held dear, except for my beloved Lyric and little Soleil.

I steadied myself with a hand on the tree I worked under, the bark of the oak a familiar friction. Tears threatened, pushing at my closed eyelids, thickening my throat. But I refused to cry yet, no matter how hopeless the situation seemed. It was not in my nature to give up because of a little adversity.

After blinking repeatedly to clear the sting in my eyes, I looked back down at my phone and carefully crafted a polite response.

'Thank you, Lily. You and Frenchy are very kind to think of me. As you originally offered right of first refusal to me when it came time, I would very much appreciate a chance to purchase the company's assets and the horses. While the property value is well beyond my scope, I may be able to carry on the French Silver legacy in your stead.'

When no reply was forthcoming, I went back to my work, humming under my breath in an effort to lighten the strain on my heart. The multitude of chrome spots decorating Constance's harness required a fine attention to detail that appealed to my senses. Even the thick black leather, so much heavier than Lyric's show harness in order to hold up against all the decorations, soothed my mood with its mellow shine. I infused every ounce of hope I could muster into my work, praying that this would not be passed on to other hands.

Soleil's barking broke into my reverie, followed shortly by the crunch of tires on gravel, both informing me of Laura's arrival. There were many things to appreciate about Laura, I thought as she parked beside my yard. At that moment, though, I focused on her reliability. She always arrived on time, and if she said she would do something, you knew beyond a shadow of doubt that it would be done. I also loved her beagle, Belle, who often rode in the carriage with her during the holiday season. Soleil loved when they came to visit, as evidenced by her whirling spin of excitement when Laura stepped out of her truck. Belle's tan and white body vibrated with repressed excitement, but she waited for Laura to give permission before launching herself from the seat. Our two dogs danced around each other in a blur of colour, tails held aloft and wagging madly as they said hello. Oh, whatever would I do if Soleil had to give up her friends as well?

But when Laura limped toward me at a more sedate pace, I also remembered that sometimes the woman accomplished things even at her own expense.

"Are you well?" I asked as she approached, my brows drawn together with concern that had nothing to do with my own worries. "I can take this job if you would rather not. I was not sure if I would be home in time."

She smiled, even with a pinch of discomfort maring her upper lip with wrinkles. A shame, as Laura had a smile that could lift the mood of a confirmed cynic when she was at her best. While she had little tolerance for fools, she was warmth personified to all others. "I'm okay, Jaque. Just the old injuries complaining about doing yard work all day yesterday. Nothing that'll stop me from driving Constance."

To that, I returned her smile with genuine affection. "She is easy to work with, I agree."

Her eyes inspected the swath of leather and chrome beside me, expression lightening a little more. "And, you've already done all the hard work. I'd put money on Constance being as spit polished as the harness."

I laughed without an ounce of self-depreciation. She knew me well. "Of course. There is nothing like a bride in her lily-white gown to make an old grey mare appear dingy. And we cannot have our Constance looking less than camera ready."

To which Laura nodded agreement, whistling sharply to call her dog before we headed down the aisle to fetch the mare in question.

It took little time to load the horse and harness, the blindingly clean vis a vis already secured in place at the front of the trailer. For weddings, we used a white carriage, this one tastefully appointed with chrome accents and subtle black pinstriping. I had already changed out the flowers decorating the dash and canopy to match the wedding colours of green and white, fitting for the springtime. To give up that little ritual of decorating the carriages before a job seemed an outright travesty.

While Laura fetched her formal attire from her vehicle, I cranked over my truck to let the diesel warm up. As I sat waiting, my phone chimed, which I answered with now ingrained eagerness. After all, Aaron often sent me random texts to maintain our connection, and I always hungered for more. But alas, it was Lily, responding to my request. She quoted me a figure well below what I originally estimated, followed by another text that eased my heart more than a little.

'We know how much you love the horses, and no one is more deserving of a shot at the company. It would be in worthy hands. Frenchy said he'll have a cost breakdown emailed to you by this evening, and we're willing to work with you on financing. We really just need to sell the property so we can retire in earnest and not have all the taxes and business finances adding to our worries.'

For their faith, I had nothing but unrelieved gratitude. This still left me with a hundred other worries, such as where to live and how to keep my work visa, but those concerns felt much less overwhelming with the knowledge that I would not lose my equine partners.

I took the time to send off a grateful reply before Laura's voice broke the wall of my distraction. "Jaque, are you okay?"

Considering the emotional rollercoaster I rode, it should surprise no one that I began to shake with the letdown. The phone slipped from numb fingers to hit the floorboards. "Not altogether well, but better than I feared, my friend."

Her light brown eyes softened with sympathy, but I caught a sisterly sharpness in their depths that shored me up enough to still my shaking hands. Yes, for the people that I shared this company with, I would do my level best to keep us together. A deep breath fortified me further.

"But it is nothing to concern yourself with. A minor annoyance in the greater scheme, and you best get on the road if you are to get the bride to the church on time."

Eyes narrow with disbelief, she let me have my deception as neither of us liked to be late. "Fair enough. But if you want someone to talk to when I get back, I'm free. The husband is out with his buddies for the weekend, and I'm at loose ends."

Faking a smile for her benefit, I slid from the seat so she could take my place. "My hope is this little problem will be less than a memory by the time you return. But if you would like to go out for supper later, I am sure the dogs will happily keep each other company while we gossip."

"It's a date, then." While she smiled, I detected a firm resolve in the set of her posture that said I would not be let off the hook so easily. But she said nothing more, only whistled several times to get the attention of her Beagle. The little thing was completely invested in scenting along the fence line of the pasture, ears dragging along in the wake of the furrow her nose made in the grass. But then she loped to her owner with a happy grin and a wagging tail before leaping into the cab of the truck at her mistress's command.

"She is still the best-behaved beagle I have ever known," I said, desperate to end our conversation on a happier note.

Predictably, Laura grinned even as she handed me my phone. "And still the worst behaved dog I've ever had." Then she climbed into the truck without another word.

While the phone vibrated several times, I did not look at it until Laura safely pulled out onto the road. Even then, I did not look at the messages that came in, hunting only for Cardi's speed dial icon. I refused to bother Aaron with these troubles. He had enough to deal with, not only in his work, but with his own recent emotional upheavals. No, this particular situation called for a girlfriend, and there were few I could count on more than Cardinal Collins.

❧ 18 ❧

Aaron

"I guess I'm just a bit lost right now," Fillmore mumbled down at his Coke as we waited for our supper, as if embarrassed to admit such a thing. Remembering how lost I'd been at his age, I felt a good deal of sympathy for his situation. But I had enough wisdom to know he was a damn sight braver than me. I never would have admitted to such a thing.

"I got nothing against farm life, and I admire my brothers, Hank and Rory for keeping the farm going for Dad after Mom left us. If Dad had to sell the farm, I dunno what would have happened to the rest of us. I'm even proud of how we all grew up helping out. There's no shame in hard work."

He raised his chin stubbornly, eyes suddenly hard, an expression I'd never seen on the affable country boy. As if he expected any of us to disagree, but his audience, one and all, understood the value of sweat equity. I might have said something to that effect, but Bart beat me to the punch.

"We get it, Fill. There's no one present who hasn't busted their ass to get shit done." His deep voice pulled the attention of everyone at our table, each of them nodding as Fillmore looked around to test the truth of Bart's words. "And your willingness to do what needs to be done is one of the main reasons I kept you in the training program. Even when you weren't quite sure, you soldiered on, and that's a skill a thousand times more valuable to us than any fancy degree or loads of money."

While Fillmore leaned back in his chair, relaxing under the reassurance, I noticed he still glanced furtively over at Trace. If you went on appearance alone, Trace looked like he hadn't seen a proper day's hard work in his life. Even as the last year broadened his jaw and his mind, one could be forgiven for assuming that our golden-haired, model-perfect poster child only ever played video games. That his whole life had been one of privilege, completely swaddled in upper middle-class advantages. Not far off the mark, for most of his life, until his perfect existence imploded with all the violence of a bomb.

Trace showed a pretty impressive level of discernment when he turned into Fillmore's stare with a self-depreciating grimace. "Yeah, even me, hay seed. I spent over a year working for a traveling carnival, doing everything from cleaning fryers to selling souvenirs. Took me awhile to work my way up to running games, but even then, I still put in the dirty work during set up and tear down. Believe me when I say working for Gallant Company is a freaking cake walk compared to that. Just the smell of funnel cake still turns my stomach."

Jo lit up like a slot machine that just hit a jackpot, leaning forward like she might jump out of her chair. "Oh my God, no wonder you were so out of sorts at the fair in Oklahoma!"

Trace's fair cheeks flushed, and he looked up toward the ceiling as if hiding something. I wondered to myself what might be causing his discomfort, since we all knew he'd been dealing with some painful family memories. But Jo's gaze sharpened as if she smelled blood. Might have worried for the kid, but Bart redirected everyone pretty handily.

"See, so you're preaching to the choir here, Fill. And it's fine if you want to come work with Gallant Company for a bit until you figure out what you want to do with yourself. No pressure. If you decide it's not your thing, we'll send you on with our blessing."

Fillmore's forthright, solid brown regard swiveled to me for confirmation. "Is that true, Captain? I don't want to disappoint anybody."

I nodded. "Absolutely, Fillmore. You don't stay in jousting for the money. You stay because it's part of you, because you love it. No sense keeping anyone around if their heart isn't in the game. The only beating you'll ever get in this company is in the lyst or during a workout. The rest of the time, we're all on your side."

Some of the stress making his eyes look too small bled off, and Fillmore mustered the first real smile I'd seen since we sat down. He must have been pretty worried about what we might say. "Thanks. I mean, Trace said you guys would understand, but it helps hearing it from the source."

As if she'd just been waiting for a break in conversation, our waitress arrived with a heavily laden tray of food. We were reduced to grunts and groans of enjoyment for a while, all of us starving after a long day of pounding on each other and caring for our horses. Once I'd swabbed the last bit of gravy from my plate, I leaned back in my chair and let conversation continue without my participation. Rolling a half empty pint glass between my hands, I let the cool condensation on the glass absorb into my calluses, the chill soothing to my sore palms. I'd jousted Bart in the afternoon, both giving and receiving several massive blows. One of the passes, the wood under my hand gave way, leaving the center burning with the impact that I could still feel. Almost like a tiny sun lived under my skin, rays of heat radiating from the middle of my palm out toward my fingers. Nothing broken, per Bart's examination, but I'd be feeling it for a few days at least.

We gave Trace a chance to play emcee for the very first time, something we wanted everyone to take a crack at. Jo would get her chance tomorrow. While the young guy fumbled with the wording, I knew he would get better with practice, just like Bart and I had in the infancy of Gallant Company. What he'd been a total natural at was crowd interaction. Clearly, his time as a carnie served him well, as he drew the people in with a natural charm. Genial and good looking, he made perfect strangers feel comfortable, engaging them like they were old friends. It was nothing like Bart's authoritative boom, or even my practiced patter, but people responded warmly. For my part, knowing we had another arrow in the quiver should we need it was an absolute gift. If we were going to be splitting the team up to cover simultaneous jobs in the future, it would make things easier if we could switch out jobs as needed.

By the time we left the restaurant, I itched with the need to call Jaque, to fill her in on all the changes the day brought. Almost as if it wasn't real, wouldn't be true if I didn't share it with her. Sure, we couldn't be with each other all the time, but I still wanted her to be part of things. And I wanted to hear all about her day, the ups, downs and in between. Those months she'd been in Florida proved a hundred times over how intimate those shared details could be.

Took a bit before I could indulge my desires though, having to make sure the horses were cared for and the camp readied for the next day. The young guys headed off toward the campground where I could hear a few musicians doing a passable rendition of Whiskey in the Jar. I left them to their fun, having attended many a campfire in my younger years. Bart and Jo made themselves scarce, leaving me standing alone in the dark with my cat winding around my ankles.

I didn't waste any time pulling out my phone, scooping Boris up with one hand while I dialed Jaque with the other. When the effort garnered nothing but her voicemail, worry put a kink in my shoulders. It wasn't like her not to answer in the evening. Still, I left a quick message, sure she would return my call before long. But even after I grabbed a shower at the gym building we'd been given access to, and made my way back to the camp, she still hadn't called me back. Just in case she hadn't seen the message, I sent a text to say good night before plugging my phone in at the truck. I mean, I wasn't the kind of guy to be needy, and I knew she had a life aside from me. She wasn't obligated to be available, and I never wanted her to feel pressured. But sliding into my cot without hearing her voice still didn't sit right.

Took a while to fall asleep. Managed a couple hours, thanks to Boris's determined and weighty purring. But then the guys came in, whispering in that too loud way that only the drunk could manage as they stumbled toward their cots. Once Trace crashed, the snoring began. I tried my damnedest to find some form of restful oblivion, staring at the seams on the tent roof. You could see the triple folded and stitched lines like rafters overhead, thanks to the low lights still on near the arena so people could navigate the darkness. No amount of quiet reflection soothed my frayed nerves, and while I dozed fitfully until dawn, I got up as soon as the sun did. No sense laying around wallowing in my own misery when so much needed to be done.

Didn't know whether to be grateful or disappointed that the guys got up as soon as I woke them. Might have been therapeutic to douse them again, but I couldn't be sure my temper would survive another encounter with their youth. That didn't stop me from talking a little too loud when they winced at my wake-up call. Served them right for overindulging.

But worse than their drunken consequences, I found not a single message from Jaque when I headed for the truck to go fetch breakfast for the team. No voicemail, no text, not even an acknowledgment that showed the message had been read.

My worry intensified then. While I wanted to believe that the lack of contact didn't mean anything, old hurts welled up in the pit of my stomach. They painted my gut feelings with acid sting, past experience certain that she'd come to her senses and left me behind in order to save herself. But pride wouldn't let me crawl for her attention, either. So, I soldiered on, much the same as I had to get through the years without my brother to cover for me. I was a grown man, after all, and twenty-four hours was a minor obstacle to get over before I could see Jaque again. Hopefully, I'd find her waiting with open arms. Otherwise, Bart would have to drag me out of a black hole of despair.

Jaque

"Jaque," a voice croaked somewhere to my right, and I forced my swollen eyes open a crack. A swath of daylight bathed the woven rag carpet in the middle of my living room, the bright colours making me squint as a throb of discomfort lanced from one temple to the other. A thick film coated my tongue and acid burned the back of my throat, bringing all the memories of the night before into sharp relief as my eyes slammed shut with disgust.

"Please tell me we did not polish off all of the wine last night?" I groaned, sure that the voice I heard belonged to Cardi. Laura had returned from the wedding job and joined us for dinner at an Italian restaurant. Cardi and I polished off an entire bottle of Cabernet on our own, since Laura did not drink. Then we adjourned to my little cottage after a stop at the liquor store for two more bottles, and both women kindly listened to me wallow in my cups while the dogs played at our feet. While I vaguely remembered Laura saying goodnight, everything beyond that remained a drunken blur.

Cardi grunted as the couch sagged with her movement. The heavy thunk of glass against wood made it easy to picture a dark green bottle landing on my coffee table. "Yup. There's less than a swallow left in either bottle. But hey, the alcoholic lubrication was warranted."

While I grumbled something like agreement, I turned my face into the arm of the sofa to block out the light still pressing on my closed eyelids. I had not overindulged to such a significant degree in years. However, the damp fabric beneath my cheek made me flinch upright so I could peer suspiciously at the wet spot. "*Esti de marde*, I drooled!"

Cardi sniggered unsympathetically. "And snored. Profusely."

I finally found the motor control to sit upright, which allowed me to favour my best girlfriend with a halfhearted glare. She looked in slightly better shape than I felt, though tangles riddled her dirty blonde hair and the bags under her eyes looked heavy. Hers were merely carry-on sized, while mine felt like steamer trunks. "Well, you farted. I told you not to get extra cheese on your pasta."

"Bite me, baby cakes," she shot back. Harsh words, but her tone held no rancour. We had broken down numerous barriers last night, between venting our problems and consuming an inadvisable amount of carbohydrates and wine. While we solved nothing, I felt a thousand times stronger for the experience. Hangover or no. "Lactose intolerance is a risk I'm willing to take when everything is so up in the air for you. And me, by extension. A little more parmesan felt warranted."

"Completely fair," I responded, nodding slightly to reinforce my agreement. Not enough to jostle my throbbing head, mind you.

While I held no regrets for the impulsive decisions of the night before, at least in the abstract, I experienced massive regrets in a physical sense as Soleil skidded through her dog door like a furry missile and barked sharply to get our attention. The sound lanced through my brain like a knife through a melon, cutting the little bit of rational thought I gained into shreds. Light danced behind my closed eyelids and I breathed heavily to stave off a wave of nausea.

"Shhh," Cardi growled lowly, obviously no happier with the level of noise. Soleil's ears flattened at the admonishment, but she sat down to contemplate us both in silence. "Seriously, munchkin, you've got a sonic level bark at the best of times, and I can't handle it."

I giggled at the apt description before choking on the amusement when the vibration made my head pound all the harder. Even with both hands pressing inward to contain my brain, I worried it might run between my fingers regardless. "Oh, new rule! No laughing while hungover!"

"We need several rules, in case this ever happens again." She grunted, added sounds of friction causing me to open my eyes enough to see what she was up to. When she reached into the sleeve of her t-shirt, I almost asked her what the hell she was doing, but the moment her bra began to slither out, I understood.

My skin began to itch, now that the grievous error had been brought to my attention. Few women alive would voluntarily sleep in their bra, particularly not one with an underwire. Mine felt permanently welded into the flesh along my ribs and sweat lined the base of the cups with unpleasant moisture. Thus, I began my own shimmy, trying not to jostle my head over much as I worked the hooks at my back.

Though I fumbled getting the undergarment out from inside my shirt, little could compare to the relief when the bra pulled away from my skin. I collapsed back into the deep couch with a groan, letting the satin and lace dangle from my fingertips with little regard for how graceless it must look. "We should never do this again."

Cardi harrumphed peevishly, but I refused to look at her, fixating on the texture of the ceiling. While I always hated the popcorn plaster, now, fond feelings for all the memories made beneath its shelter made it less awful. Sad to think those days were coming to an end. "Speak for yourself. I think we should do it again. Regularly. It's therapeutic."

"Therapeutic is not the word I would use to describe my hangover." No, torturous was more apt. Or perhaps, inhumane. I rarely drank myself into such a state. Considering how long it had been since the last time I overindulged, I felt woefully out of practise.

"Well, no. My mouth tastes like the inside of a shoe and probably smells about the same." I looked over to see her breath heavily into her cupped palm, then her face collapsed in on itself in clear disgust. "Nope, worse. But despite that, I'm damn glad we hung out." Her eyes were damp along the bottom lashes as she looked over at me. "I needed the girl time. The way things are with you right now, I don't know how much longer we'll have to hang out."

When the tears hanging off her lashes finally overflowed, cutting glistening trails down her flushed cheeks, I leaned over and put my head on her shoulder. "No tears, silly woman. Even if I have to go back to Canada, I can still come visit!"

Her head dropped on top of mine, setting off the throbbing around my brain again, but I refused to react. My head would recover, given time. "Yeah, but it wouldn't be the same!"

I patted her knee in agreement, but otherwise kept silent, leaving an opening in case she wanted to champion me further. Listening to her rail against my leaving had made it very clear how much I was loved. When she too kept the silence, I let my eyes close, grateful for the peaceful moments. I did not let myself think about my personal worries, simply wallowed in the warm bubble of companionship.

But then, she drew a deep breath and straightened purposefully. "So, there's got to be something we can do to keep you here. I'm gonna tell Kristoff when I get home. He's a great problem solver. And on that same thread, since guys like to fix things for us, have you told Aaron yet?"

I sat up fast, as though yanked upright by an invisible puppet master. My vision swam with both a renewed headache and tears. "No! Oh, Cardi! Whatever can I do? I cannot lose him over this! What if there is no way I can stay? I cannot abandon him after the falling out with his mother. It would be absolute…"

"Shit," she provided when my words stalled, her usual forthrightness returning. My heart throbbed with happiness over that normalcy, allowing me to hope all would come out right. I focused on her eyes, now amazingly dry and sharper than a blade. The edge I saw might have made me flinch if not for the humour wrinkling her nose so adorably. "But here's the thing you gotta remember, Jaque. We all have shit to handle. Some piles are bigger than others, or stink to high heaven. You and I, we're horsewomen, which leaves us extra qualified for managing whatever flaming manure gets in our way. We'll grab shovels and get to work."

I laughed, which I would bet was exactly what she intended. Heart a bit lighter and warmer with her honest conviction, I took a step closer to my personal pile of *marde*. "So true. But that gets me no nearer a solution regarding Aaron. I do not want to lose him, to give up the love we have found."

Her mouth slanted in a half grin. "Well, Jaqueline, judging by the weekend I spent working with Prince Charming, he's a pretty experienced manure mover. If you want to make a future with him, I'd say you need to let the guy know what you're facing. You'll know he's a keeper if he pulls on the rubber boots and picks up a shovel to help you dig."

Several minutes passed as I digested that bit of wisdom, my brain beginning to work around the fuzz from my hangover. It threw me bits of random information, such as the time shown on the clock over the television. At ten AM, I knew Aaron would already be working, meaning I would have to wait until the evening to call him. But to call him, I would need my phone, which was not in the pocket of my jeans.

Before attempted to hunt for it, I turned to look directly at Cardi. At this close distance, we had room for nothing but honesty between us. Her bloodshot eyes made mine water with sympathy, but the muddy blue depths were warm with genuine affection. Yes, I found love with Aaron, and did not wish to lose it to distance. But I also had the truest of sister-friends in Cardi, and Jo held the potential for something similar. Laura was a dear, ever so much dearer for the time we spent together the night before. Even my farrier, Dan, held pride of place amongst my friends. To give up any of them was more than I cared to contemplate.

"Thank you, Cardinal Collins. What would I do without you on my backstep?"

She blinked slowly, her smile widening to full effect. By her expression alone, I could tell she knew I meant the question to cover so much more than our time together on the carriage. "Either go to slow or tip over in the turns. But, much as I wish we had all day to wax maudlin, I think it is time we focused on the fellas we're paired up with. Kristoff is probably fretting himself silly, since I haven't texted him all night."

To which I groaned in reply, remembering my own lack of communication with Aaron. "Oh, *sacre*, I did not reply to any of Aaron's texts during dinner either!" What must he have thought?

Cardi did not allow me to wallow in self-pity over the uncharacteristic forgetfulness, only shoved herself up off the sofa before offering me a hand. When we were both mostly upright, she steered us for the kitchen. "I think the men will wait a bit longer. First, we need coffee."

When she turned on the lights, I winced, the white cupboards harshly reflecting the overhead fixtures. My skull resumed a steady throb, though not quite as violently as before. "And anti-inflammatories. Many anti-inflammatories."

She grunted an agreement and we fell to work, companionable in the relative silence as the coffee pot percolated. Soleil whined, drawing my attention as I shook pills into my hand. She sat pointedly beside her purple food dish, button eyes bright with hope, which made me wonder if I forgot to feed her the night before. Happily, she was easier to appease than my aching body, requiring only a scoop of kibble before settling down.

I needed another half hour, sitting at my little table beside my best friend, caffeine and ibuprofen absorbing while we stared into space. We cleaned up our mess in the living room, brushed our teeth and combed out our hair. I lent Cardi a clean shirt for her drive home, even if it sat a bit tight on her broader shoulders. By the time I walked Cardi out to her car, we both felt a little more human.

As I went about my barn chores, I also felt more confident in the future. With every pile of manure I tossed in the wheelbarrow, my smile grew, reminding me that I had experience aplenty. And so did all the people I loved.

Aaron

Turns out Josephine Bowen could claim a weakness beyond her inability to play video games and an absolute hate for being wrong. After several awkward silences during the action and tripping over her words for the entire afternoon joust, we now knew she was a horrible emcee. Listening to her fumble the scores had made me bite my tongue with shock. Considering how wordy she usually was, capable of dancing verbal circles around anyone, I never expected her to fail so dramatically. And repeatedly.

But Jo's truest redeeming feature was that she didn't know how to quit. She soldiered on, throwing herself onto her own blade with self-deprecating humor that got the audience laughing. Each mistake was owned up to, and jokes were made about lance blows being detrimental to brain cells. By the time I dismounted to greet the fans at the rail, my estimation of Jo's courage expanded to a level nearly on par with Bart's. Considering everything he'd faced and overcome, I never thought anyone would come close.

She graciously took some teasing from the people who wanted to meet her, even taking pictures despite the painful looking blush that covered her cheeks. Her façade of confidence remained completely believable, except for one important factor. Bart kept casting worried looks her way. Their love might be coloring his vision when it came to Jo, but however much they were wrapped up in each other, they never let it affect their work. Which made me think he saw something in Jo that I didn't know her well enough to grasp. Past experience with Jo said that if she did get upset, she might steamroll anyone that got in her way.

Gotta give the woman credit though. She maintained her cool, smiled, laughed, and made sure everyone felt welcome. People still gravitated toward her, particularly children. Bending down to greet them at eye level, and even kneeling so a toddler could reach through the rails to hug her, Jo never showed an ounce of upset.

Even when we went back to the little shaded area to untack the horses, she maintained her aplomb. It wasn't until most of the people meandered back toward the main vendor area, leaving us in a pocket of semi-privacy, that she finally allowed herself to crack.

Long legs churning with unspent energy, she crossed the tent to the equipment area where I lounged with Boris. He sat on my armor trunk, purring happily, though the sound cut off abruptly when I stopped stroking his head. Something told me Jo would need my complete attention.

When she stuttered to a halt in front of me, her generally pleasant features were lost in a welter of wrinkles. Even her recently red cheeks were stark white, every freckle in high relief. Her eyes were unflinching on mine, but the roiling worry in them made my stomach clench with sympathy. "I'm sorry, Aaron. I can't believe I screwed that up so epically! You've got every right to be upset. If I'm not up to par I understand if we need to renegotiate my contract."

Shock set me back for a second, as I rethought everything I'd been about to say. I hadn't expected her to beat herself up so entirely. But I didn't take too long, not with Bart heading our way with a concerned glower that made him look like a shadowed cliff face, dark and implacable.

"Do I look upset?" Her mouth opened as if she already had an answering salvo pre-loaded. But then she swallowed it, surprised by the question. "Seriously, Jo, I'm impressed! I mean, sure, you dropped the ball so many times that three runners could have made it safely around a baseball diamond. But damn it all, you kept picking it back up and trying again."

"But I totally wrecked! I mean, honestly, I couldn't even say Percheron correctly," she bleated in objection, throwing her hands up in the air in disgust. "Honestly, Pear-Cher-Roan? My Welsh ancestors rolled in their graves faster than a greased wagon axle to have me slaughter a word like that."

I choked on a laugh since I hadn't heard that particular misstep. Might have felt bad about it, but even Bart slapped a hand over his mouth to muffle his amusement as he came in behind her. She didn't notice him in her distress, prompting me to keep her talking. "Hell, even experienced emcees have bad days, and we've had professional hires buckle under the strain of a testy crowd. And even if you did screw things up, it's not in your contract to work as an announcer. This was a total experiment."

Her shoulders scrunched up toward her ears as she crossed her arms. The narrow-eyed stare she gave me brought to mind Byz leaning back against his halter in a clear refusal to follow. All she was missing were the pinned ears. "But it's my fault we might need to split the team up. I need to be able to help fill the gap!"

"Your fault?" Bart interjected, his eyes narrowing to match hers when she swung toward him. "Yeah, I guess it is your fault. Your fault we're better than we've been in years, that we're gaining new clients and have a growing reputation as the best full contact jousting troupe East of the Mississippi. I mean, if we're throwing blame around, you might as well get all of it."

"That's not what I mean, and you know it, Sir!" Her nostrils flared in warning, and for the briefest second, I kinda worried for my brother's safety. She never called either of us sir anymore unless she wanted to make a point. He was seconds from getting flattened if he misjudged how much she loved him. Were I a braver man, I might have stepped in, but she wouldn't even flinch when she ran me over like an indecisive squirrel. I'd be roadkill without mercy. "I failed! I can't help!"

J.D. Harrison

He snorted like his stallion might, a heavy sound that made the air vibrate. "No, you didn't. Failing would have been giving up, and we know you better than that. You don't know how to quit. No matter how many times you get hit, you keep getting back up."

"I made the Company look bad!" she shot back, arms unfolding and her fists tight, as if she wanted to lash out with more than words. "I care too much about this Company to mess things up!"

Bart didn't retaliate, didn't even refute her. In fact, he softened, going from jagged granite to affable bulldog in record time. "Jo, we've talked about this. You've gotta give yourself as much slack as you do everyone else."

Her jaw tightened with an audible grind of teeth, but I had a sneaking suspicion it was to hold back the moisture making her eyes glisten. "Bart, you aren't fighting fair!"

Squirming with discomfort over the sudden turn in the conversation, my eyes flicked away from the scene to watch Fillmore and Trace discreetly slip out the gate, herding our squires off toward the main body of the faire. Smart guys. I'd join them, if I thought I could get away without being noticed. This fight felt too personal, too intimate.

Worse still, as I stoppered my ears to keep from hearing what he said when he stepped in close to her, my heart throbbed. Even when they fought there was so much damn love between them, which intensified my own longing. I wanted this with Jaque. The struggles as much as the sweetness. We could overcome anything, as long as we kept loving each other.

"What do you think, brother?"

I shook my head to clear away the wispy dreams building in my mind and looked up at Bart. Couldn't even find it in me to be ashamed, since Jo and Bart were standing there holding hands. "What? Sorry, I didn't hear the question clearly."

A lazy smile broke his lips apart from the serious expression he'd worn. "I suggested we give Jo another shot, after some coaching. She was trying not to use the same lines I do and started stumbling over the words. I figure we could help her come up with her own script, if you're willing."

I smiled, leaning back in my little camp chair with smug delight. "Don't know what you're asking me for, co-captain.

403

You've got the same decision-making power I do. If you think she can do it, then I'll follow your lead."

Jo's head swiveled so fast I expected to hear vertebrae pop, and she stared at Bart. "When did this happen?"

Bart's neck flushed darkly under his scruff, but he met her gaze anyway. "Just yesterday. We haven't really worked out the details yet. But this isn't about me, right now."

She might have refuted him, but I shoved into the gap in conversation before things went too far off the rails. "No, this is about you, Jo. And I think Bart is right. With a bit of training you'll be able to tackle this again. If you'd quit, if you'd tossed the mic to Trace, I might be inclined to give it up. But you didn't." Then I stared hard at her, tossing down a challenge in the one way I knew she could never refuse. "Unless you want to quit on us now? If you think it's too much? We don't want to push you into something you aren't ready for, Jojo."

If the rest of the goad hadn't already done the work, the purse dog nickname drove my point home with unfailing aim. She grew several inches taller from my seated point of view and looked down her nose with mixed irritation and amusement. "Don't think I don't see what you're doing, Sir. You know very well I'm going to make you eat your words."

Grinning back with a complete lack of shame, I shoved to my feet so I could meet her at eye level. "I'm counting on it, Josephine. Hell, I'll even bring a little steak sauce the next time you emcee, so I can actually enjoy the experience. I trust you both to do your best for Gallant Company, now and in the future." Then I thrust out my hand, pleased when she pulled away from Bart and slapped her palm against my forearm. I gripped her arm in return, then yanked her into a rough hug. While she hugged me back, we didn't embrace long, she in a hurry to get back to my brother. Seeing him slip his arm around her shoulders in welcome intensified my desire to reconnect with Jaque.

"On that note, I'm gonna leave you two to watch the camp while I go call my girlfriend." Then I stalked off toward my truck, secure in the knowledge that they had everything under control. Being able to chase my own personal dreams without worrying about the Company was so liberating I felt drunk on the sensation.

Jaque

Much as I wanted to spill all of my concerns at Aaron's feet, to get them off my chest, I held my peace. My reasoning was two-fold. For the first part, Aaron sent several texts and voicemails while I had been unavailable, the worry in his voice thick enough to stitch into a blanket. The final message, left while I showered after finishing morning chores, had sounded much more relaxed. Though little more than a profession of his love, an underlying thrum of eagerness said he couldn't wait for the day to end so we could talk.

For the second part, perhaps it was wisdom, perhaps selfishness. When I unloaded my troubles I wanted to be able to wrap myself in his arms. To be grounded in his physical strength, surrounded by the warmth of his touch that I needed as much as breath.

My convictions were easy to hold to when he called me that evening. Though I apologized for being unavailable the night before, he quickly set me at ease.

"Jaque, Cardi has been your friend for much longer than I have. Even if that weren't the case, I don't expect to be your be all, end all. I've got all of Gallant Company to share my time with and won't ever begrudge you time for yourself. Mind you, I'd still rather be spending time with you than anyone else. You feel like home."

That simple statement left me awash in a flood of acceptance that warmed me as if I just slid into a hot spring that stole every ounce of my tension. Suddenly, losing my little house did not seem so catastrophic. As long as I had Aaron, as long as I had people and animals to love, it did not matter where I lived.

Mind you, then he worriedly babbled on, pulling me back into the present. "I mean, how home is supposed to feel, not like my Mom's home."

"Aaron," I said softly, pleased when he fell silent. Happiness made my voice raspy as I pushed the words through a surplus of emotion. "You feel like home to me too. Even speaking to you from so far away, I am at peace. No matter how our passion swells, nor how our troubles threaten, loving you gives me faith that we will come through the other side of every storm."

He cleared his throat and I heard a restless shifting before he managed a reply. "You know, I'm really looking forward to being back in your arms, Jaque. I hate being away from you, even if I love my work. Every time we're apart, I get impatient for the day we can make our own home, our own safe harbour."

With that, the last of my tethers to the cottage I enjoyed for so many years was severed. Not an ounce of pain marked the cut, nor did I bleed. His confession healed me instantaneously, left me looking forward to the day he and I embarked on the next step of our journey, together. Were I lucky, that day might come sooner than later, though I would keep that hope close to my chest until I could speak to him in person.

"No matter how far apart we are you make the distance feel so close, so intimate," I whispered, as if he were beside me rather than sitting in his truck, hundreds of miles away. Another truth, one that drove deep into my heart with the knowledge that even if I returned to Canada for a time, Aaron and I would come through the experience stronger. Too many times in my life, distance killed the relationships I tried to keep alive. But even from the beginning, Aaron reached out, spanned the space between us. We were closer than I had ever been with anyone, even when we were not together.

I instigated a deepening of that intimacy, laying in the dark of my room and whispering the miles away with words of passion. He answered me with an intensity that stole my breath and killed my worries at their very root. By the time we said goodnight, my muscles were lax with satisfaction, and my heart overflowed with Aaron's never-ending echo of my need.

The experience kept my nerves from fraying too badly the next day, as I went through the motions to kill time. Only my commitment to Lyric's fitness kept me from blowing off the day in favour of waiting on Aaron's doorstep for his return. Soleil and I took the mare for a short trot down the road to a farm where we used the dirt lanes around the corn fields for conditioning. Though I added weights to the backstep to mimic having a navigator, it was not the same as live company. But aside from a few moments when it would have been nice to have the shifting weight of a human to steady us over some ruts, I remained content. The quiet allowed plentiful time to think as we worked through a series of trot sets meant to maintain Lyric's condition. She required little management as I let her take as much rein as she liked, raising and lowering her neck for balance as I adjusted the contact accordingly.

I did not check out, by any means. Her safety and mine required I be mindful of our surroundings in case something arose that concerned my brave mare. A rare event, anymore, but I had failed her once with my inattention. I would never do so again, no matter how much weighed on my mind.

On our way back to the farm, I took my time, waving at passing traffic and even stopping in a driveway to chat with one of the neighbours. Lyric enjoyed the social interactions, her ears pricked as she followed the conversation, tuned in to people's body language and tone. She never rushed home, felt little need to be with the herd as most horses did. Aside from our first few solo rides when very young, she was content to go on adventures with only my company.

By the time we returned to the barn, she was completely cooled out. I needed only to curry the sweat from her short coat and put her blanket on in preparation for the evening chill. She went in her stall to enjoy a bucket of mush in reward for her hard work, then I put her out in the pasture. It took longer to wipe down her harness and put the carriage away, but even then, I had the whole afternoon before Aaron would be home.

Those hours taunted me, moving slowly despite the ways I kept busy. Still, I felt a huge sense of satisfaction as I worked in the kitchen, preparing a meal to welcome him home. Not just Aaron, either, but the entirety of Gallant Company. They were his family, and I flattered myself to think they were coming to be part of mine as well. The tourtiere came together quickly, as I had made the filling and shortcrust that morning, and the sugar pie was simple to complete with the help of my mixer. Before long, the hot oven scented the entire house with all things sweet and savoury, a perfume I could not wait to transfer to Aaron's apartment.

But first, I took the time to shower, readying my body to welcome him. Once clean, I applied lilac lotion to my still damp skin. He would not care if I smelled fresh from the barn, but I did it all the same. So many memories of him tucking his nose against me and inhaling deeply made me well aware of how my signature scent appealed to his senses. My worries would wait one more night; for tonight, I needed only to love my man. To build one more layer of the foundation for the home we found in each other.

Aaron

Jo groaned as she pushed her plate back, a sentiment I agreed with entirely as I chewed on the last bite of sugar pie. Arriving home to Jaque standing in the well-lit barn aisle had been glorious enough, warming my heart and lifting my spirits to see her waiting as I once waited for her. But having dinner ready once we finished getting the horses turned out in the field had been an unimaginable bonus.

We needed to bring in Bart's computer chair in order to fit all of us at the table in the apartment, since Jaque specifically invited Trace to join in. But sitting there beside Jaque, surrounded by my brothers and sister, made me feel full in a way that completely eclipsed the obscene amount of food I ate.

Putting her hand over Jaque's arm, Jo leaned forward, then caught my eye. "Can we keep her, Captain?"

Chuckling into my napkin as I wiped my mouth, I looked over at Jaque to gauge her reaction. She and Jo were friends, I knew, but it took time to get used to Jo's brand of honesty. Jaque's eyes widened with surprise, the chocolate brown catching light from the living room. But more telling was the slow parting of her lips, the soft flush of pleasure moving up her neck before she turned her regard from Jo to me.

"I'm hoping so, Jojo," I answered, though I never looked away from the woman I loved. Even more amazing to my mind was that she loved me back. "Every day, I find another way I don't want to live without her."

Trace coughed uncomfortably into the silence that followed, Jaque startling at the noise enough to disrupt our connection. But I couldn't be upset at him, because while Jaque looked away to say something to Jo, her hand dropped to my thigh. We sat at the table for a bit longer, chatting over Jo and Bart's plans to get the spare horses used to armor. She leaned forward with fascination as Trace talked about his work with our armorer and participated completely when we hashed over the notes from our contractor on rebuilding the workshop. Every moment integrated her further into my family, confirming my desire to have her be a permanent fixture in it.

Once the dishes were rinsed and in the washer, and the leftovers put away, everyone adjourned to their own pursuits. Trace begged off to do laundry, since he would leave for Ambrose's in the morning. Jo and Bart made noises about making sure the horses were all settled, which told me they would be gone for a bit. My brother further confirmed the privacy I hoped for, winking none too subtly as he followed Jo down the stairs.

For several minutes, I remained content to sit there, Jaque leaning against my side. We didn't say a thing, only shared space. God, I'd missed that more than anything else. But my lady wanted something more, turning her head to press her lips to my shoulder. Her hand slid further up my thigh, just enough to make me shift gears.

"Would it be asking for too much if I wanted you to take me to bed now?"

"Never too much," I responded, the rasp in my voice intensifying as her fingers drew a circle on the inside of my thigh. "Though I hope you know I'll be keeping you there as long as you'll let me."

Her husky laugh told me she wasn't bothered by the prospect, even as she stood. My groin, already throbbing in anticipation, went even tighter as her touch slid away. I hardly needed the crooked finger she gestured with to get me up out of the chair, but that hooked little digit scooped me up with a casual strength that barely hinted at the power she held over me.

As I followed, I left that power in her hands, allowing her to steer me toward the open door to my bathroom. "Go, take a shower, wash off the road, my champion. Then we will have our way with each other."

Then she slipped into my bedroom, her dog and my cat on her heels. Like any reasonably intelligent individual, I did as I was told. Nor did I rush, taking advantage of the hot water to loosen muscles tight from the weekend's work and the long drive. I even shaved, not wanting to mark her skin with friction burns. Took willpower not to hurry, knowing she waited, but our entire relationship proved out the old adage of the best things in life being worth the wait.

Wasn't until I finished toweling my hair mostly dry that I realized I'd forgotten to grab my pajama pants. For the first time since Jo moved in with Bart, I would have to dart across the hall with only a towel wrapped around my waist. While Bart's bathroom was directly attached to his room, mine was the one we allowed visitors in. This made me consider the logistics if I were to ask Jaque to move in with me. Would we all be able to survive living so closely together? Or maybe I could move into Jaque's little house, its cozy, comfortable environs a perfect retreat.

All rational thought disappeared as I let myself into the bedroom. Jaque had laid herself out on my bed like a confection, displayed to excellent effect by a deep blue negligée. Her cleavage nestled the heart pendant I had given her, and shadows cast by the bedside lamp barely hid the line of a thong on her hip. A bow just below her breasts looked to be the only thing keeping the mostly sheer fabric on her body. Even more alluring was her knowing smile as she rolled up on her knees to move toward me, the midnight fall of her hair swaying heavily against her shoulders.

I might have made a comment on her beauty, might have said something about how much I loved her, but she pressed a finger to my lips as her other hand tugged loose the bow on her nightie.

"However lovely your words, Aaron, I want no more of them tonight. Show me how you feel."

So, I kissed that finger, and all the rest of them. Then we kissed so much my lips forgot what it felt like not to touch hers. And when we finally came together, my once neglected heart forgot what it felt like to be without love.

❧ **19** ❧

Jaque

"I want this, always," I murmured against Aaron's shoulder. He smelled of salt and plain soap, a potent drug to inhale even as my limbs objected to the mere idea of movement. Boneless in the aftermath of ecstasy, I still wanted more of him.

His arm tightened around me and he grunted with effort as he leaned up enough to kiss my forehead before collapsing back into the pillows again. Knowing he too was spent by our lovemaking made the constant pool of desire in my belly swirl with delight. "Me too. I'd invite you to move in, but I won't ask you to give up your privacy. You've worked hard for what you have."

To hear that, my heart ached with happiness and dread both, as I still had not shared my news. Nor did I want to disrupt the post-coital bliss we swam in. But the unresolved thoughts stole into me anyway, tendrils of worry thieving my peace. Though I tried to keep it from transferring to him, he grew restless as my stress level increased. When the pressure grew uncomfortable, I pushed up on my elbow, hoping I could kiss away the concerns for a little while longer.

The tension cutting furrows in his brow made me think it might be too late. When he finally spoke, his concerns proved easier to address than mine.

"Jaque, I didn't mean to put pressure on you. I'm willing to wait until you are ready for the next step."

My eyes ached with pressure from tears I could not indulge in. "Oh, no, Aaron, never think I do not want more. Never!" Pressing kisses to his face, I endeavored to soothe the misunderstanding away. "I would happily vault straight to marrying you, my faith in my feelings is so strong."

He went completely rigid at my confession, and I worried that I had pushed him too far. Everyone had limits, after all, and I was known to push boundaries well past the comfort level of my lovers.

If not for his eyes, I might have panicked entirely, certain I had ruined everything. Those midnight depths, however, were tender enough to calm my racing heart.

"Me too," he whispered back, as if he too were afraid. I knew love had betrayed him many times over, which left me in awe of his courage. "But I didn't want to say anything. I know you want to compete for Canada, and I didn't know if marrying an American might jeopardize that. I never, ever want to get in the way of your dreams, Jaque, no matter how much I want to be with you."

Oh, every cell in my body wanted to throw myself on him. To celebrate the sheer joy I felt over the knowledge that he also wanted that elusive more. But my brain maintained a practised grip on the reins, keeping me still. I could not take such a step with him until he knew everything. Until he understood how tenuous my life was, how little I brought to the table. It was possible that he would want no part of my troubles, and I wanted no promises made when so much remained unsaid.

"There is more to this, though." I sat up and turned away from him, pulling the blankets up to guard against a chill. As the cold feeling came from inside me, it did little good. "So much has changed since you left."

His arm snaked around my waist, pulling me into the shelter of his body. Wordlessly, he moved us up the bed until he could lean into the headboard, then he shifted the blanket until it covered us both. Only then did he tuck his chin down and whisper in my ear.

"As long as it isn't goodbye, nothing you have to say is going to make me feel any differently. The boy I was loves you. The man I am loves you. And the creaky old cowboy I'm going to be loves you."

Sacre! He undid me with his tender words, held me together with his strong arms, and I followed his leap of faith with one of my own.

"Even if I lose my home?" I asked, turning my head so I could gauge his reaction. My voice cracked with strain as I continued. "My employers are selling their property, and I shall soon be homeless."

"I'm so sorry, *mon amour*." He snuggled me even closer, the touch entirely non-sexual despite all the skin to skin contact. Kisses pressed to my cheek, hands rubbed soothingly over my arms. "I don't know if I can say anything that will make you feel better. You've worked so hard to grow the business."

I let myself cry then, allowing grief to bleed off while wrapped in the safety of his acceptance, his understanding. He did not say a word as I tipped my head back on his shoulder, the tears running freely down my temples into my hair. Even that was another layer of comfort, as I knew tears could make him uncomfortable, but he did not try to stop them this time.

No, I stopped them, determined not to drown the joy I felt only minutes before. Knuckling the last of the salty moisture from my eyes, I endeavored to relax into the soothing warmth of his embrace.

"There is a silver lining, if I can make it work." Exhaling slowly to gather my thoughts, I decided to tell him everything. He knew the difficulties of running a company, the ins and outs, far better than I. Yes, I managed things for Lily and Frenchy, but always had them as a buffer. This leap of faith would leave me with no fall back. "The owners and I are in discussion for me to purchase the company on a payment plan. Thus far, the terms seem incredibly reasonable, though we have things to hash out before a contract is written."

His chest rose and fell with what I took for relief, and he squeezed me tighter before relaxing again. "Then I'm happy for you. You've earned this chance with a lot of hard work. I know we only talked a little bit over the years, but it doesn't take a genius to put the pieces together. You started out needing two extra horses, and now need all four. You've got a team of drivers every holiday season, and still manage to juggle it with your competition schedule."

Were it possible, I would say I fell even more in love with Aaron in that moment. He had said many beautiful things to me since the start of our relationship, but few were more meaningful than his recognition of my work. "Thank you, it truly has been a labour of love."

"I get it." A chuckle vibrated against my back. "Bart and I don't get rich doing what we do. Sure, we're doing well enough now, but one rough joust could put an end to our careers. Life with horses is always a gamble. But we wouldn't trade it for a million dollars."

Yes, he understood exactly. I sat up, hating moving away from his warmth, but I now approached the more difficult part of this complicated equation. Seeing his face, looking in his eyes, would lend more strength than hiding in his arms. It took some creative repositioning of the blankets to cover both myself and him. Perhaps another woman would be able to keep her eyes from wandering, but Aaron's body provided a wonderland of delights that I could not resist. And, though he chuckled at my contortions, he helped get us settled. I flatter myself to think he would have a hard time resisting me too, if we remained exposed to each other. Such a blessing to know we were so well matched that way.

Leaning forward over my crossed legs, I picked up where I left off. "There are still many unknowns. Without a United States employer, my work visa is in jeopardy. While I hate thinking about it, that could take me away from here. I have a buffer of several months before the ownership of the carriage business transfers to me, but it is still a concern."

His brow furrowed deeply, a sure sign he was thinking, but the twist at the corner of his mouth that usually indicated stress remained absent. A good thing, as my stomach twisted more than enough for both of us. When he reached for my hands and looked directly in my eyes, I thought my heart might stop at the seriousness that filled his gaze.

"I'll handle this better if you give me a chance at it later, but I want to put all my cards on the table so you know I'm serious. Would you be able to stay if we got married?"

My body jerked, the muscles along my sternum clenching with shock, and I pulled my hands from his. Soleil responded to the sudden shift in mood by jumping up on the bed and growling lowly as she paced around me, as if she could defend against the pain in my heart. "Aaron, I do not want you to marry me for citizenship!"

He flinched just as hard as I, grooves of guilt twisting his features into a caricature. But he did not look away for a singular second, allowing me to see the fear that dimmed his eyes. I might have softened to it, if not for the hard edge that sharpened his words. "Jaque, I feel like I failed somewhere along the line if that's what you think. I want to marry you because I want to commit my life to loving you. Hell, I'd wait years, if we had years. But you want to stay here, and I want you to stay too."

Looking away from the hurt painted all over his face, I petted Soleil to quiet her, using the action as an excuse for not replying immediately. She settled against my leg, the small weight a comfort as I sorted my own feelings. Difficult to do with all the ups and downs of the last hour. Not looking up from my fingers tangled in the dog's thick sable coat, I ventured a reply. "My apologies for the overreaction. Pride goeth before the fall, it seems. I know you are trying to help."

"No," he denied, and I looked up as he leaned forward. An earnest hope lit him up, dulling the defensive clench of his jaw. "I'm not saying any of this because think I have to, or because of your concerns about staying in the country for your carriage company. Dammit, Jaque, I want to marry you for me. For us. I want to see where our relationship takes us, together. Hard to do that if you have to go to back to Quebec. It's one thing if we have to be apart for short stretches while you're competing or I'm working. But a full-time, long-distance relationship would be a strain."

He said everything I needed to hear, but still, I could not muster a proper reply. Then, he sealed the deal with an accuracy that no other man in my life, even my dear papa, had ever managed. With a sigh that sounded like it came from the depths of his enormous heart, he won me entirely. "Tell me what you want to do Jaque, and I'll hitch myself into the harness next to you to get us there. Give me a little time, I can even follow you to Canada. It'd be a hell of a commute for jousting gigs, but I'm by your side one hundred percent."

I grabbed hold of his hands with an unbecoming desperation to reaffirm our connection, pressing kisses to his once broken knuckles. The unique patchwork of old scars and hard-earned calluses felt delightful against my lips. "Oh, Aaron! I would no more ask you to give up being here with Gallant Company than I would ask Lyric to walk on two legs! They are your family!"

"And so are you." The tenderness in that sweet answer reverberated in my soul, and every bit of defensive tension bled away. "You don't have to decide anything tonight, *mon amour*, but whatever happens, I want to share a life with you."

I quickly went up on my knees, smiling both for Soleil's disgusted huff as I dislodged her, and the surprise in his eyes as I leaned in for a kiss. Not caring an ounce that the blankets slid from my body or that my thighs trembled from holding myself in place, I lingered. Only when we were both breathless and my lips were puffy did I pull back enough to catch his gaze. Waiting for his eyes to focus was worth it, as I wanted his absolute attention for my acceptance.

"Aaron Allen Drew, I will happily marry you."

His pupils widened with delight right before he scooped me into his lap and pressed his lips back to mine. A new flavour filled our kiss, one that made worries fade from my mind. Not just the passion I craved, nor the kindness we always gave each other, but the honey sweet taste of unadulterated joy. He fed it to me with every slick of his tongue, each breath from his lungs, and I passed it back until my head swam with happiness.

When we finally came back up for air, it was potently obvious both of us were ready for another round of lovemaking. But he did not immediately press me to the bed, only held me close as he whispered promises into the sliver of space between our faces.

"I swear, Jaque, I'll give you the proposal you deserve. You'll never have a reason to regret this. You can move in tomorrow if you want. And it doesn't have to be all of us in the apartment forever. I'll figure something out. We just built those pastures, so you can bring your horses here, and I'll get with the architect on changing plans so you've got someplace we can put your carriages. This'll work. It has to work."

Needing to stop the frantic flow of words, I tangled a hand in his hair, tightening my grip so I could watch his eyes pin with desire. Chuckling at the surety of his reaction, I answered all those promises with one small caveat. "No, my champion, we will figure things out. Together."

He smiled, hunger roughening his voice, but love lending tenderness as he echoed my promise. "Together."

Then we slid down into the now tangled blankets to seal our vows in a very physical way. As we chased our bliss, sweat slicked and hearts galloping with the same stride, I knew it would not matter whether he proposed again. These moments, however tumultuous, were precious because they were ours alone. I needed no one to witness them to make the words any more binding.

Aaron

The next morning, I let Jaque sleep in while I took another shower. She still hadn't moved by the time I finished, so I headed for the kitchen to make a smoothie. Every move I made felt brand new, as if I'd been reborn in Jaque's arms the night before. It still felt a bit surreal, to be honest. I'd proposed to a woman once before, all wine, roses and down on one knee. But it never felt even a quarter as intense as my promises to Jaque. As her promises to me. To my mind, together was the most beautiful damn word in the English language.

Bart and Jo clomped up the stairs from the barn just as I flicked on the blender to do its thing. They were sleepy eyed but grinning as they dropped onto the stools at the counter. Neither said a word as I turned the blender back off and grabbed a glass from the cupboard. No, Jo struck at my greatest moment of weakness, just as I tipped my wrist and began to pour.

"We're keeping her, aren't we?"

I didn't flinch like I had before Jaque and I got together. Instead, I turned to look at Jo in slow motion, my hand nervelessly following my body. The splash of liquid hitting the granite counter hardly registered around the stupid grin of happiness that overtook my face. Wasn't until Bart began laughing that I realized I missed the glass entirely.

"Shit!" I cursed reflexively, though there wasn't any venom in the word. Though the grin morphed into something rueful, I couldn't stop smiling enough to really get upset. Setting the glass carafe back in its base, I regarded my brother and someday sister-in-law. Jo grinned like a house cat with a mouthful of canary, and Bart held a hand over his mouth to muffle the laughter he couldn't seem to stop. They still wore the clothes they were wearing at dinner, which confused the hell out of me. Not hard to do when my head still floated in the clouds. "Did you guys need to do laundry or something? Why're you wearing dirty clothes?"

Valid question, I thought. Neither one flinched away from being dirty, but they were fastidious given the option.

"We stayed out in the trailer to give you two some privacy for your first night," Jo answered lightly, rubbing Bart's back as he leaned over his knees, still smothering snickers. "But we forgot to grab PJs. Now, answer the question, Captain. Are we keeping her?"

Before I could formulate a simple yes, Jaque's voice cut through the room, still husky with sleep. "I hope so. Though I thought it best to discuss arrangements with you before we assumed anything."

She stood beside the sofa, swaddled neck to toes in my old fleece robe. The faded dark blue gave her rumpled black hair extra highlights, and immediately brought to mind the lingerie she wore the night before. Cad though it might make me, I was grateful to have the counter to hide behind. No one needed the obvious proof of my desire to make an appearance in the conversation.

Jo jumped up to hug Jaque, squeaking with excitement. A full head shorter than Jo, standing barefoot on the hardwood, Jaque embraced her like they were sisters. When they began chatting animatedly, I turned my attention to Bart, attempting to mimic his constantly raised eyebrow. When he looked up, he immediately started laughing again.

"You gonna live, brother?" I asked dryly. While I waited for him to catch his breath, I managed to pour what remained of my smoothie into the glass. I'd started mopping up the puddle of sticky goo on the counter by the time he answered.

"Maybe," he wheezed, then pushed to his feet to grab the trash can so I could drop sopping wet handfuls of paper towel into it. "I couldn't help myself. Told you I was going to laugh my ass off when you took the fall. This was long overdue."

I chuckled as I corrected him. "But I've been in love with her for months now."

He slapped me on the back once I finished cleaning up. "I know. But the expression on your face was too much to resist. The last time I saw you look like that, Bobby Arnot knocked you for a loop. You had a concussion and asked the ER nurse if she had any plans later that night."

Jo and Jaque both giggled as they joined us, and Jaque's arm wrapped around my waist like it belonged there. Oh, wait, it did. "Why is that funny?" she asked, favoring me with a sweet smile. "You are a handsome man; she would have been foolish to turn you down."

Bart choked on another laugh as I answered her. "Because she was old enough to be my grandmother. Which is precisely what she said as she wheeled me in to get my head x-rayed."

This time, when Bart couldn't control his amusement anymore, we all joined in. Happiness overtook me again, intensely blessed to be surrounded by so much love. Maybe I hadn't been born into this family, but I wouldn't trade my shaded past for the brightness of my future. Even when Bart and Jo headed to their room and Jaque left me to get dressed, the feeling lingered. I wished fervently for a lifetime of similar mornings, my soul washed clean in the purity of joy.

Jaque

While we went our separate ways to get showered and dressed, before long we all reconvened in the barn aisleway. Aaron and his brother seemed intent on walking through their plans for the new workshop building, carrying a roll of blueprints out toward a large, flat patch of ground across from the barn. Riding the rising wave of happiness pushing me through the morning, I asked Jo if I could join her when she mentioned heading down to the pasture to look in on the herd. I needed a co-conspirator for my plans to get back in the saddle and could think of no one better than her.

Though as we strode down the hill, I began to have my doubts. Jo seemed fearless. While I wanted to be fearless in the same way, what were the chances she would understand my problem? She fell off her horse regularly and simply laughed it off. My worries over riding Lyric would seem silly in the face of the risks she took every day.

I nearly talked myself out of saying anything, but true to form, Josephine owned a knack for sussing out what truly mattered. "Much as I appreciate this nostalgia trip, I've got this sneaking suspicion you wanted to talk to me alone. If it's about you moving in, then let me put your mind at ease. I couldn't be happier! You're as much a part of the Gallant Company family as any of the knights."

My feet stopped moving of their own accord, as if the ground swallowed my boots. A whirlwind of gratitude and fear tore through the joy that filled my sails, for she soothed one fear, but woke others. She turned toward me, a concerned pinch around her mouth. "Jaque, what's wrong?"

Throat tight, I swallowed repeatedly before I could give an answer. "Oh, Jo, I am a fraud if you think I belong among your number. There is much you do not know."

She scoffed and rolled her eyes, the dismissive actions goading my unease into a gallop. But her words were another matter entirely. "Jaque, you've got heart aplenty to have stood up to Aaron's mom. And you've been part of the crew here far longer than I have. You've influenced the horses for the better. Not to mention how much happier Aaron is with you around. You make us stronger."

The bands of fear around my chest loosened enough to let me laugh sardonically. "I am a sham compared to all of you."

Jo stuck her tongue out and crossed her eyes, the silly expression startling an actual giggle out of me. "Jaque, if you think getting armoured up and hitting each other with sticks makes us brave, I would argue that most sane people would call us stupid for taking the risk. Heck, they'd probably think driving your horse around like she's a racecar is pretty nuts too. So really, you're in grand company." Then she snatched my hand and yanked me back into motion, my boots scuffing up dust as I fought to keep my balance. "Come on, whatever's on your mind will be easier to talk about with the horses around. They make everything better."

She let go of my hand once I found my footing again but kept us at a brisk pace that got my blood pumping. It also stole so much of my breath I could not have said a word even if I were of a mind to. I am certain she did it on purpose. The woman never did anything without thought, which is what set her apart.

Once we were in the field, with the herd slowly making their way toward us from the farthest corner, she stopped and tipped her face up into the sun. I searched for the best words to explain myself, but before I could begin, she filled the peaceful air with her own worries.

"You know what's stupid? Like, epically ridiculous? I'm engaged to my best friend, I'm happier than I've ever been in my whole life, and I'm letting one stupid hang-up get in my way. Something I'm sure most women in the world would think the best, coolest, most fun thing ever. But it gives me anxiety like you wouldn't believe."

Her silence after that statement gave my mind ample room to wonder what she could possibly have to worry over. She was one of the most courageous women of my acquaintance, and as I knew many brave women, that held some weight. "Surely not?" I said, more a question than statement when the silence stretched too long. "What could you possibly have to worry over? You are so capable and organized."

Shoulders rounding up toward her ears, she shrugged the compliment away. "I'm serious. You'll probably laugh, but since I'm hoping you'll be my maid of honour, I'm gonna tell you anyway. You deserve to know what you're in for."

"Excuse me?" I asked foolishly, far more surprised by the awkward offer than I had been about Aaron's proposal of marriage. "Your maid of honour? Surely you have a best friend to ask. We have not known each other that long."

She swung toward me, skin paling beneath the multitude of freckles. "Oh! You don't have to do it if you don't want to! There's no pressure. See, I already suck so bad at this wedding stuff. Ugh!"

This time, I grabbed her hand, yanking a bit roughly to halt her panicked babble. Oh, what a pair we were! Perhaps she would understand my silly fears better than I thought. "Josephine, I would be delighted. I simply wanted to be sure. I have so few close girlfriends, only finding them in recent years. No one has ever asked me to stand up with them before."

Her free hand smacked over her face, fingers widespread as if it might hide her sufficiently. "Oh, thank goodness! I need someone to hold my hand through this." She squeezed my hand as if to make sure we were still connected, then peered between her own outspread digits. "You really are going to laugh though."

"Test me," I challenged, grinning with a sudden upswing of courage. "If you share your worries, I will share mine. Then we will be on level footing."

"Fair." She dropped her hands down and shook out her arms, then squared her feet with her shoulders as if prepared for a fight. No surprise from such a warrior woman. Then her words took off at a dead gallop, like a runaway horse with the bit in its teeth.

"Okay, dumb as it may be, every time I try to sit down and make plans for a wedding, I break out in a cold sweat. Bart is trying to help me, but there's only so much he can do. He already suggested we elope, but my Mom would be devastated, and my Gran would probably swat me for even thinking about it. I swear, that woman has a sixth sense for when I'm straying from the path. I mean, I could let those two plan something, but if I do that, then it'll be the whole dog and pony show, only minus dogs or ponies. I'll be trussed up in a bunch of lace and satin, trotted up the aisle of a big church, made to pose for a million pictures while wearing shoes that make my feet ache. A torture that I'd endure to marry Bart, because he's worth it, but I don't think that's the way to start a life together. Fancy and expensive doesn't mean a thing to me, unless it comes from the tack shop. And I loathe the idea of being dolled up like a confection. It makes me itch."

As if to punctuate the tirade, she scratched at her elbow, then clutched it tightly. Her eyes flew to mine, wide with actual fear. "I'm so screwed, Jaque. I've never wanted and not wanted something so badly in my whole life."

Oh, that feeling I understood quite well. It summed up my situation with riding Lyric to perfection. But first, I needed to reassure my friend before she imploded with worry. "Oh, Jo, you are not, as you say, screwed. At least not when it comes to your wedding. While I have no experience in these matters, I have several friends who can help us figure things out. We will come up with something perfectly suited to your love story, a beautiful chapter in what I am sure will be a long happily ever after."

The breath whooshed out of my chest as she flung herself at me, wrapping me up in a most unexpected hug that threatened to crack a rib. No mean feat, since I was built more thickly than her, but her strength overcame any differences. As I returned the embrace, Jo felt like she was built all of muscle and resolve. A potent reminder that I could not have picked a better woman to be in my corner for the challenge before me. Her strength and her vulnerabilities both made it ever so much easier to spill my guts when she finally stepped back.

Nor did she flinch in the slightest when my weakness lay bare before her, the spring sunshine chasing shadows away. No, she asked pointed questions that were easier to answer as the horses finally reached us, their calm acceptance as much a balm as hers. We did not linger terribly long, her cell phone beeping with a message from Bart asking if we would be back soon, but by the time we rejoined our men we had developed a plan of attack for both of our problems. Likely, we would reevaluate our strategies multiple times before all was said and done, but having allies made the coming fights so much easier to face. Courage might shiver in the face of fear, but in Gallant Company it would not fail.

Aaron

As Jaque had a competition coming up, and a thousand things to do to get ready, we were at her farm for the rest of the week. I helped where I could, riding the backstep for a few drives and going over her truck to be sure it was ready. Though the drive to Lexington wouldn't be long, I felt better knowing we didn't have to worry. Besides, her dad was flying in to visit, and the last thing I wanted was for him to think I wouldn't take good care of his daughter.

Cardi sometimes joined us in the afternoon as we cleaned carriages and harnesses. We all enjoyed dinner together one night when Gallant Company helped us get the trailer loaded. Jo surprised both women with t-shirts, a new design Bart had come up with to celebrate Jo's influence in our troupe. The women exclaimed over the feminine design, a jousting helm surrounded in thorny rose vines, with Jo's signature 'Fight Like A Girl' in bold print. Fitting, considering how hard Jaque fought to chase her own dreams. I gave Jo extra credit for doing this batch of shirts in purple. While my sister in arms often favored less overtly feminine colors, she knew my lady very well indeed.

Once the hum of appreciation died down, they discussed the carriage company buy out, and I rested easier listening to the relaxed way she answered everyone's questions. With our chosen family around us, anything seemed possible.

We spent nights at her place, falling into bed exhausted, but content. I would miss the little cottage when she gave it up. Though I entertained the possibility of trying to buy the place, I gave it up when I heard the preliminary figures. Property values in this neighborhood were beyond my means, much closer to the city and its amenities than the Gallant Company farm. Someone with much deeper pockets than mine would be scooping up the place as soon as it went on the market.

Barely past dawn on Thursday morning, I returned to the farm in question to pack a bag. We would be leaving for the show as soon as I got back to Jaque, and she had asked me to bring a jacket and tie. Cardi would not be able to play ballast for her on Friday, as Jaque's dressage test was scheduled during office hours. This was an international level competition, which meant she needed to have a groom on board at all times, so I'd been drafted. Being involved excited me, and I was determined not to let Jaque or Lyric down.

When we arrived at the barn Boris trotted down the aisle ahead of me, meowing loudly. To my surprise, Byz's coltish nicker answered, and his hammerhead poked out seconds later. When he caught sight of me, his ears went up with interest. Like a trained monkey, my hand went straight to my pocket, fishing past my truck keys and some change for a cookie. He accepted it greedily, and I smiled. Until he blew his nose all over my jacket.

"Thanks, bub," I said sarcastically, though I petted his neck so he knew I wasn't actually upset. Then I watched with a bit of wonder as Boris put his paws up on the door and meowed at my horse, his tone one of demand. Byz dropped his nose down to snuffle the cat, lips moving through the thick fur with a delicacy I'd never seen from him. "Well, I'll be damned!"

The moment ended on the next breath, Boris chirping as he dropped down and trotted toward the door to the apartment. Still a little stunned, I gave into his demand and opened the door before stumbling up the stairs on cruise control. Jo sat on the sofa, laptop balanced on her knees. Without looking up, she pointed a thumb toward the back corner of the dining room where Bart had his computer station. "He's deep in the code but should be done soon if you need him."

"Nope, I'm good," I said, heading straight for my room. Boris paused at the couch to beg pets from Jo, so I left the door open for him and went to the closet. It wasn't very big, which never seemed to matter with just me in the room. But I did wonder where we would put Jaque's things when she moved in.

Didn't take much time to get my things sorted, though I took extra care putting my dress clothes in a garment bag. Jaque took so much pride in her appearance at the shows, I felt called to do the same. Thankfully, Alex had turned me on to his tailor a couple years ago, so I owned a gray wool suit that would make a passable match to what I'd seen her wear in South Carolina. None of my ties came close to her preference for purple accents, but I grabbed a few different options, figuring I'd let the lady chose what would work best.

As I rolled up the rest of my clothing to stuff in a suitcase, my thoughts drifted, causing my hands to slow. There would be more difficulties than just where to put Jaque's clothes. My room could easily accommodate more furniture. But how long would four adults be able to share this apartment? We never planned for more than just Bart and me.

Not only that, but our barn was at capacity. Sure, there were plans in the works to put run-in sheds in the pastures and thank goodness we'd already fenced the two extra fields. We could make it work in the short term. Jaque's carriages needed to be inside though, and we required storage space for all her harness too.

A pair of jeans fell from numb fingers as my brain shifted back to the human portion of this equation. What about kids? While the possibility remained in question for Jaque and I, Bart and Jo definitely wanted children. Probably sooner rather than later, no matter how much Jo liked to remind me they weren't in any rush. I'd seen all three of my sisters through having babies, and I saw that same hungry glimmer getting brighter in Jo's eyes. Not that Jo ever did anything by the same playbook as most of the women I knew, but I needed to plan for the eventuality.

Rationally, I worried. Jo was an anchor player in the lyst, devoted and reliable. Sure, she wanted to come back after pregnancy, but it would still take her out of the brackets for at least a year. But we had Bart back now. Fillmore would be joining us this summer, to refresh and refine his skills. There would be another group of trainees, and if I got desperate, I could always call Bobby to recruit a temp.

The business concerns resolved, I sat down on the bed, staring into the empty room without seeing. Emotionally, I nursed other concerns. Would Jaque be okay sharing an apartment with a growing little family? Would it bother her to have babies around when we might not be able to have our own? And there were other babies to concern myself with. Jaque's dream of raising Canadian Horses needed its own room to blossom and grow.

Boris broke into my swirling thoughts with a butt of his head against my elbow. I shoved back to my feet with a grunt, pausing to pet him. None of my worries needed answering today. All my focus needed to be on Jaque and getting her through the weekend ahead. Anything else could wait.

But as I walked back into the living room and caught sight of Jo cuddled against Bart's side, my footsteps faltered. I needed to touch base with them, now, without Jaque around. To know they truly were okay with all the changes upending our little world. They looked up as I set my bags on the dining table, then I dropped into my recliner with a sigh. Being wrapped in its familiar comfort eased my heart another notch.

"All set?" Bart asked, voice as placid as a still pond in summer. Jo didn't move an inch, lounging against her fiancé with a negligence I no longer envied, but her eyes tracked me with an intensity that belied her posture.

"Yup. Just wanted to chat with you two before I headed back out. Things are going to get hectic, and we won't have a lot of time later." Bart's regard shifted minutely. If you didn't know him, you might not have noticed how still his eyebrows became or the flexed edge of his bicep that said he would spring into action if needed. "Are you two okay with Jaque moving in? Honestly? Because I don't want to put undo strain on our relationships with each other."

Jo sat straight up, her hand bracing against Bart's knee. "It would be pretty selfish of me not to welcome her, Aaron. You welcomed me, after all. And I love her like a sister. It'll be good to have some feminine energy around the place."

"Ha!" I barked, pointing a finger at her so she couldn't mistake the aim of my tease. "One of you troublesome wenches is enough."

"Then maybe you aren't the man I thought you were," she shot back, grinning unrepentantly at the comfortable banter. "Because your girlfriend and I may not be peas from the same pod, but we do grow on the same vine. I'd hate for you to bite off more than you can chew."

Unuttered laughter made my reply sound bubbly. "Well, Jaque is a damn sight sweeter than you are!" Bart scowled, and I felt a rebuttal coming on, so I headed him off. "At least she is to me." He settled at the qualification, allowing me to shift my original question to him. "What about you, brother? It's about to get cozy up in here, you know. I don't want you to feel crowded out."

He pulled out this beatific smile that would have looked more at home on a marble sculpture of Jesus than his granite mug. "I'd be an asshole and an idiot to deny you. She's a good person, all on her own. We help our friends if we can, and she's more than worthy of our help. But more than that, she's good for you, Aaron. You deserve each other, to love as deeply and freely as Jo and I do." He looked to Jo with a sweetness that seemed sickening before I understood it, and Jo softened as she met his gaze. Their love lapped at my toes like a massive wave that eventually dissipates on the beach, so powerful and then soft. "Now that we know how strong love can make us, how could we possibly stand in the way of anyone who has a chance at the same?"

Jo's hand gentled, cupping his knee with a caress that mocked my earlier tease about her sweetness. I didn't begrudge their connection, but it did provoke my own need to be with Jaque. Might have made my subsequent farewell a bit brusque, but they only smiled as I thanked them and scooped up my belongings. Three stairs down it dawned on me that I could solve one problem today. One that might go a long way toward thanking them for being so accepting.

Felt a little like intruding as I turned to face them, Jo now snuggled against Bart's chest. They looked up expectantly, but with an edge of impatience that told me I'd better get the lead out.

"Hey, it's not like it's up to me anyway, but I know you've been worried too." I shifted uncomfortably as they stared, feeling like a selfish moron for ever getting in their way. "Being with Jaque gave me some perspective, so I want you to know I'm totally cool with you two having kids. Whenever. Now, later, don't worry about the Company. We're family, and we'll make it work. More love is always a good thing."

Then I turned away, running from my own guilt as I dropped noisily down the stairs. Waiting for a second at the bottom for Boris to catch up, I paused a moment more to give Byz another cookie. Just long enough for Bart to catch up, barreling out the door like a juggernaut, a little breathless as he skidded to a stop.

"Aaron, wait!"

Now nervous over his unusual behavior, I turned away, wanting to keep moving. "Here, walk me out to the truck. I've got to get back."

He fell in beside me, hands shoved into his pockets as if he couldn't keep them still otherwise. "Thank you for what you said up there. Means a lot to us both."

I waved off his gratitude, my own hand moving a bit erratically. "Never should have been my business in the first place. I had no right to keep you apart. Jo is part of this company whether she's jousting or not, and I hate that I couldn't see past my own worries. You both deserve better of me." Then I shrugged off the last of my guilt and mustered a smile. "Besides, her being off the roster is going to be the least of our problems if you two start building a family. That apartment won't hold much more than the four of us, and kids need space!"

Bart didn't say anything until I'd stowed my bags in the truck, Boris perching on the center console like a fuzzy gargoyle. But when I turned toward my brother, the goodbye on my lips stalled out. He wore an expression I had come to love, a glimmer of an idea lighting him up from within. The first time I saw it had precipitated the formation of Gallant Company, and every time since then, it had heralded terrifyingly magnificent changes.

"You know," he began, feeding out the words so slowly I wanted to yank them from his mouth fully formed. "Mr. Teller just put out a for sale sign. He's transferring out west with his job, wants to be closer to his kids."

Jim Teller was our neighbor to the east. The one mare in our herd lived with his small flock of sheep, which worked perfectly for many years. If Bart had given me this news a few months ago, I might have worried over where to put the pale-yellow mare. She hated Bart's stallion, and we didn't need the drama. But now we had the new pastures, which left me confused as to why he brought it up right at this moment. "So? Does he want us to move Buttermilk?"

Bart shook his square head, one infuriating eyebrow mocking me. "No, not at all. Hell, what I'm thinking isn't even strictly necessary. I can always do a remodel on the house if we need to have separate spaces, because I'm pretty sure you and Jaque are going to be making your own family…"

The urge to throttle him increased significantly, and I fished out my keys, jangling them with impatience. "Will you get to the point, man? I'm out of time and brain cells for this guessing game!"

His second eyebrow lifted, and as it clicked into place beside its twin, so did the puzzle pieces in my head. Hope dropped into my gut like I'd swallowed swirling clouds, and my brain latched on to the idea with every claw it owned. "Do you think we can manage it? I know the property needs a little clean-up, but he's got plenty of outbuildings for all Jaque's stuff. How much is he asking?"

Bart shrugged monolithically slow, a pleased smile cracking his face in multiple places. "Don't know. But I can find out. It's a by-owner deal, so it could work for or against us. It's only about twenty acres to our eighty, but with some management it could work for Jaque's needs...and yours. There's a detached three car garage for puttering in."

Okay, yeah, I was excited before he said that, thrilled by the prospect of something just for Jaque and I. Nothing to do with the Company. But when he mentioned the garage, my breath hitched with long denied interest. Judging by the deepening laugh lines on his face, Bart knew he'd struck his mark.

"Don't gloat, asshole. If this happens, that'll leave you over here with all the horses and the rest of the Company. You sure you want that?"

His amusement overflowed in a quick chuckle, but in no way muted the soberness in his eyes. "Absolutely. It's what Jo and I both want. Living above the barn is perfect for us, and you'll still be close enough to be involved, work your own horse. We can still be a family." Weighted with possibility, his hand landed on my shoulder and he stared me right in the eye. "You want me to make the call? You ready to take this risk?"

I lifted my hand to his opposite shoulder and grinned, much as I had any other time he and I took a leap. But this time, it was for a much worthier reason than anything that came before.

"When does Gallant Company ever shy away from a risk?" I scoffed, but my heart throbbed, pushing a wave of emotion up into my throat. Made my words hoarse, but Bart understood me anyway. "I didn't see this fall coming, but I'm committed to it now, with every fiber of my being. I'll make the calls, see where it gets us."

He hauled me into a rough embrace, and I slapped his back, unable to muster a reply when he choked out, "Come home covered in glory, brother."

Then he left me to climb in the truck, a little stunned by the abundance of possibilities spread out before me. I got myself up the drive on autopilot, pausing at the edge of the road to shove my Bluetooth in my ear. Filled with fear and anticipation, I punched in the number on the for-sale sign hanging on the gate next to ours, fully committing to the path ahead as the phone began to ring.

ᔑ20ᔐ

Jaque

The whole drive to the horse park Aaron remained uncharacteristically distracted, fiddling constantly with his phone. When I inquired if everything was okay, he dissembled, though the pleased smile that accompanied his non-answer kept me from worrying over much. Jo even called at one point, and they engaged in a stilted conversation that I could make no sense of!

However, once we arrived, his phone went away. He fell to preparing Lyric's stall as soon as I checked in, and I settled into a quick braid job for the afternoon jog. Unlike the competition in South Carolina, this was under international level rules. We would have to present our horses to a panel of judges to prove their soundness before the competition began.

That done, I put her away, covered nose to tail in a lycra hood, a sheet, leg wraps and a tail bag. We dropped off the trailer nearby and deposited both Boris and Soleil in the tack room before hurriedly making the short drive to a nearby airpark. Papa messaged from his last fuel stop, and we would just make it in time to pick him up.

Aaron remained relaxed as we parked and headed for the small terminal, though his eyes constantly scanned the area. Whether a nervous habit or genuine interest, I could not say. The first I could well understand, as I had been a mess before meeting his family. The second would bode well for his relationship with my father, giving them something to bond over aside from me. I had enough to worry about this weekend without babysitting the two of them.

We were directed toward a waiting area where a computer screen showed all the incoming aircraft. There were not many at this time of day, so I spotted it readily when Papa's flight information flashed up to join the rest. Before long, I watched his little plane taxi past the bank of windows. Aaron squeezed my hand when I bounced on my toes, responding to my excitement with a huge grin.

"I told you before, I am a daddy's girl." His grin faltered, likely thinking of his own father, and their strained relationship. I squeezed his hand in return, then bounced on my toes again, this time pressing my lips to his cheek. "I am sorry, Aaron. I wish…"

He shushed me with a quick kiss, lip to lip, and I felt his smile return before he pulled away. "No apologies, remember. Besides, I'm looking forward to discovering more about the girl you were growing up. The boy I was is intensely curious."

Warmth flooded my limbs as I settled to wait beside him, and I prayed one last time that the two men would hit it off. They must. I could not bear to have both of our parents against us. My stomach went hot and cold intermittently, and I checked my phone obsessively as we waited. Papa would not leave his plane until he knew it was properly secured. One did not take undue risks with one's passion, a feeling I well understood from my care with Lyric.

Then my phone vibrated, and I choked back a whine of excitement more fitting from Soleil as I read the terse message. '*On my way in.*' Several more minutes passed, a hodgepodge of people coming through the doors from the tarmac. My heart leapt when I caught sight of his faded blue ball cap, and I pointed at him for Aaron's benefit. "There! There he is!"

Aaron scanned the area, a confused wrinkle popping up beside his mouth. "Where? I don't see anyone." But then he froze, staring at the ball cap moving along barely above the bottom of the windows, and I realized my error. Now, it was too late, and I hoped he would adapt quickly.

Releasing his arm as the doors swung open, I called out, "Papa! Over here!"

Then Jack Sauveterre rolled through the door, a wide smile splitting his weathered features. Strong arms, hands as callused and capable as Aaron's, propelled him toward us. His duffel bag was slung across the back of the wheelchair he used to travel, the sport model nimble and stable in all types of footing. In the carpeted area that lead to the waiting area, he zipped along as if the wheels had wings, and I bent to hug him even as he came to a stop.

"Junior," His voice was husky with emotion, something I always cherished whenever we had been apart for so long, telling me without a word that he missed me as much as I missed him. "*Vous êtes belle, ma fille.*"

"English, Papa! You do not want Aaron to think you are telling secrets," I chided as I straightened back up. Though he said I had my mother's eyes, when I looked in the mirror, I always saw his shrewd gaze staring back. Now, those eyes turned to Aaron, and I was pleased to see the man I loved had shaken off his shock to offer his hand to my father.

"Aaron Drew, sir. It is a pleasure to meet you." I covered a smile to hear his most precise diction coming to the fore, something I found charming from our first conversation. "You have raised an amazing daughter."

Papa scoffed. "No, my Junior, she is her own woman. I gave her love, her *grand 'mere* gave her guidance, my own papa gave her horses. Otherwise, she grew as she pleased." But he took Aaron's hand all the same, gripping more firmly than necessary. Such had been the case whenever meeting one of my boyfriends. He wanted them to know that the man in the wheelchair would still protect me. Even when I did not want him too. "You may call me Jack."

Aaron's eyes widened in surprise, as my nickname was pronounced exactly the same despite the difference in spelling. Then he nodded respectfully as Papa released him, not even flexing his fingers to show that the treatment affected him. "I would be delighted. Thank you."

I would have liked to linger, but the clock was not my friend and I had much to do before we were ready for the jog. "Gentlemen, while I look forward to long conversations tonight, could we perhaps move things along? Lyric awaits."

They turned to face me and nodded sharply, almost as if a matched pair. In fact, the similarities took me aback. Though Papa's hair was as black as mine, compared to Aaron's many shades of brown, they both had tan, weathered skin. They both smiled from their eyes first and carried themselves with a calm confidence that held just enough cockiness to intrigue you. But the biggest similarity could not be seen, for their hearts were even more handsome than their faces.

I swiveled away to hide my smile, leading the men out to the truck. Aaron hurried ahead to open the passenger door for my father, the epitome of politeness, but Papa harrumphed as he passed me. I could help him, but anyone who offered aside from close friends and family chafed his pride horribly. Later, I would explain that to Aaron. In the interim, I patted Papa's shoulder in reassurance. "*Son coeur est bon.*"

This earned another grumble, but he tempered his mood as he rolled up to where Aaron waited. "*Merci*, Aaron."

"*Je vous en prie*," Aaron answered back, though he slaughtered the enunciation so badly I stifled a laugh behind my hand. He tried so hard to pick up bits and pieces of French from me, but his accent remained atrocious.

"I would stick to English, were I you," Papa said blandly, looking up at my boyfriend with a mock glare. Then, thank *Cris*, he smiled. "At least until Jaqueline has time to help you refine your tongue."

Aaron froze, clearly unsure how to respond, while Papa made sure to leave an impression. Reaching behind his chair, he took the duffel bag and tossed it easily into the bed of the truck. Before anyone could offer to help, he navigated right up to the door of the truck. He pushed up on his wheelchair with one hand, grabbed the handle over the door with the other and smoothly deposited himself in the passenger seat without disturbing so much as the crease on his jeans. From there, he used an arm to scoop his motionless legs the rest of the way into the vehicle before favouring Aaron with a wry expression. "Something to keep in mind; my arms work perfectly well. The motorcycle wreck took my legs, but I am not helpless." Then he pulled the door closed, leaving Aaron and I standing there with his things.

"I apologize," I began, but he broke into a blazing grin, pressing a finger to his lips once his back turned to the truck.

"Shh, Jaque, it's fine. I deserved that." Then he pointed at the wheelchair, thinking wrinkles appearing on his forehead. "Now, would you mind showing me how to fold this up so I don't embarrass myself any further?"

We stowed the chair in mere moments, then he walked around and opened the driver's door for me. Papa nodded his approval at the gesture once Aaron closed the door. "He is good to you, Junior."

Not many words, but they were telling. I smiled tenderly but said nothing, firing up the engine as Aaron climbed into the back seat. This beginning looked to be much more promising than I feared.

Back at the show, I found barely enough time to prepare, even with Aaron's help. We took Lyric to the trailer and pulled off her garments, brushing her until not a single hair lay mussed. Her tail became a sable waterfall as I released it from its braid, belling at the bottom with a few passes from a wide toothed comb. Papa made himself of use as well, taking a damp rag to Lyric's presentation bridle while I hopped in the dressing room to change. Boris darted through the open door, meowing in admonishment as he found his person. Aaron spoke soothingly to him even as he brushed oil onto Lyric's hooves.

I closed the door on the happy scene, making sure to pay my dues with Soleil before I dressed. She was contented with a rub of her ears, allowing me to hurry into my outfit. Makeup was minimal, a bit of powder to take the shine off my face, some mascara and a quick brush of dusky lavender eyeshadow. I knew better than to use lipstick anymore, as I had a nervous habit of chewing it off. No one found lipstick on teeth an attractive look. Best to do without.

Looking at my phone to check the time, I hurriedly twisted my hair up onto my head and covered it with one of my favourite hats. The short-brimmed fedora gave full range of vision, and always looked jaunty. Then I let myself out of the trailer, certain I was going to be late!

My nerves subsided in an instant, and I paused to appreciate the vision before me. Boris lay curled up on Papa's lap, pressing into the hand rubbing his head. Aaron sat on the running board of the trailer, one hand on Lyric's reins, though I doubted it was necessary. She stood listening to the two men converse in low tones, ears flicking from one to the other with relaxed interest. Only when I dropped to the ground did her attention shift, head lifting up to find me, which made the two men turn as well.

"*Ma fille*, you look exceptional!" Though the words came from my father, Aaron paid me a silent compliment, eyes lingering appreciatively on the curves set off by the fitted waistcoat. I had forgone a jacket for the jog-up, owing to the warming spring, and their praise helped bolster my decision.

I did a once over on Lyric, not that I thought Aaron neglected her. But having help remained a novelty, and would not always be available, so best to keep the habit of doing for myself.

Then we took a short walk to the main arena where a small crowd gathered along a straight track of hard-packed footing just outside the fence. Horses, and their human attendants, were grouped nearby, most of them waiting patiently. A few of the hotter horses walked, their handlers watching out for the shenanigans that sometimes ensued with fit animals who were ready to compete. One never knew when you might find yourself flying a kite with a mind of its own.

I marched off to join them after waving Aaron and Papa toward the spectators. A few resolute breaths centred my emotions so that Lyric and I could move into the thick bubble of energy created by so much anticipation. Sue and her Rhapsody were one of the pairs walking on the periphery. As were the horses belonging to van den Berg's followers, though their drivers were conspicuously absent, leaving the grooms to do the work. No, the men were clustered off to the side, chatting about who knew what. Holding back a sneer of disgust took an effort of will. Did they not understand how important the little things were to their relationship with their horses?

I did not fault the drivers fielding multiples for not walking their own horses. With two to five horses under your care, it was all hands on deck. In fact, I waved at one of the pony pair drivers, Sharyl, as she walked along with her husband and son, each with a bright chestnut pony in tow. However, singles drivers had no excuses but their own arrogance, which to my mind was no excuse at all. Our horses gave us everything at these competitions. The least the men could do was offer fair exchange.

The jog-up moved quickly, once the officials called us to order. Singles went first, as we took the least time, though I still waited for all the smaller equines to take their turns. The ponies came in all shapes and sizes, from a diminutive Shetland, the elegant Welsh, all the way up to a sturdy Haflinger. All were adorable, though Clint taught me well that small size had little to do with the size of their heart. They were as fit and fierce as their larger brethren, and twice as determined to prove they could compete with the best of them.

Several of the more refined horses in my group gave admirable displays of their athleticism as they trotted down the strip of compressed dirt, more creatures of air than earth as they leapt and kicked. When Paul's big Dutch gelding reared up at the end of the lane as they made the turn back toward the ground jury, his face turned pale with fear, then red with embarrassment. He yanked unduly hard on the reins, as if he could force the big horse to behave, which resulted in a few uneven trot steps as they began the return run. They were sent to the holding area to re-jog once the rest of us were done, and he shoved the reins at his groom as if the whole thing were her fault. I sighed, wondering how I missed the signs of his selfishness before.

I am not blind. I knew Aaron still struggled with his Byzantine, but he was trying to be a better person for his horse. Setting aside a lifetime of poor habits was never easy. That he pressed on, and admitted his fault in the problems, lifted him well above the level of Paul's punitive attempts at dominating his horse.

Lyric's jog proved a non-event. Though my heart picked up speed as we approached the judges, swelling with excitement, and the tiniest hint of anxiety, Lyric found the experience entertaining. People stood all around, watching her, a circumstance she took advantage of. She modeled perfectly, standing square, her posture in a state of readiness. Her body language said "*Look at me, am I not lovely?*"

Then we trotted away, matching strides as if harnessed together. Her bare hooves beat an undertone of music against the hardpack. Unlike the shod horses, who always kept a hollow beneath their feet, hers spread out, and made full contact. She moved with all the earthy power she owned, showing off without acting up; ready, willing, but always lady like. When I patted her neck as we slowed to a walk for the turn at the end, she arched into it, accepting her due.

We were given clearance to compete as soon as we stopped beside the judges. I thanked them, smiling widely as we cleared the way for the next team. My smile withered on the vine as Grady Malone approached, his horse already rolling its eyes with discomfort. He ignored us as if we were beneath his notice, which suited me perfectly well. Avoidance beat out antagonism any day.

But seeing his poor horse already stressed when the competition had not even started made my heart ache.

The salve for my worries clapped softly as we joined them, Aaron and my Papa looking so handsome and proud. They proclaimed us to be lovely, then Papa escorted us back to the trailer while Aaron went to the office to pick up the keys for my golf cart. Swathed in their faith, I put my focus back where it belonged. I could not change the way Paul or Grady treated their horses, but Lyric and I could set an example. One that would mark us as winners, no matter how we placed in the competition.

Our prize lay in bettering ourselves, creating closer communication, and greater love in everything we did. A championship ribbon paled in comparison to that golden goal.

Aaron

Over dinner, I spent so much time listening raptly to Jack's stories that I hardly tasted my food. The man held little back, sharing not just his glories in the Royal Canadian Air Force, flying transport aircraft into some of the most rugged terrain Canada offered, but also his challenges raising Jaque after his accident. Hearing about his dip into alcoholism brought to mind Bart's fall into his own pit of despair. But it also made me admire Jack all the more, knowing he'd fought so hard to be the father his daughter deserved. I could see where she learned to love so unreservedly and said a silent prayer of thanks that she decided to share that love with me.

Through it all, he mentioned losing his wife only once. "I have no regrets in raising Junior. Being a father kept me alive, brought out the best in me." He patted her hand to cement the words but turned his attention to me. Brown eyes went from warm with love to cold with a warning that caused my blood to frost over like an icy pond. "But losing her mother crippled me even worse than being paralyzed. I cannot feel my legs, but the empty space where my Angeline is not will never stop aching."

Though propelled into a change of subject by a very uncomfortable Jaque, I let conversation go on without me. Let her father's truth sink in, felt it wind around my heart like barbed wire. Because for the first time in my life, I loved someone so much that I could not imagine my life without them. I didn't miss my dad. I felt guilty for not being around more, for not trying harder to have a relationship with him, even though I knew I couldn't have changed things without hurting myself. And I would feel even worse about my mother when she went, sooner or later. When Bart got hurt, and I didn't know if he would survive, I felt like someone kicked me in the chest.

But to lose Jaqueline? My God, falling in love had been like taking a fall from Byzantine. Exhilarating, full of risk, and at the end, a breath stealing impact. I fell more every day, as if I had stepped off the edge of a canyon and had yet to find the bottom. I plummeted, yet flew, experiencing a freedom I never could have imagined. Losing Jaque would be like hitting the bottom of that canyon, and since my fall gained speed with every minute, I knew the impact would destroy me even now.

I carried that knowledge with me as we dropped Jack at the hotel so he could get some rest while we checked on Lyric one more time. The mare needed a little more hay, then Jaque spent several minutes communing with her after we tended to the physical needs. Witnessing their bond was a thing of beauty, two females of very different species acting more like sisters than partners. They did nothing but breathe together, but in those few moments, I knew they communicated on a level that none would understand but them.

Once back to the hotel, I gave thanks for whatever luck assigned us to the third floor. Jack had a room close to the lobby, which meant Jaque and I could share a room without worrying about her father on the other side of the wall.

After a hot shower, I felt no closer to any kind of equilibrium. My insides were twisted around; upside down. They didn't relax until Jaque took her own turn in the bathroom and then joined me in bed. Only when her skin and mine were pressed together could I muffle the worries eating away at my happiness.

"My champion?" she murmured against my chest, even as her fingers strummed my ribs. My skin sang with warmth, and I returned the caress in kind, massaging her neck until she moaned.

"Yes, my lady?" I encouraged after a few minutes of silence, neither of us escalating our seduction yet. Contentment grew apace with desire, and I didn't know which might win out on a night like this one. Of course I wanted to make love to her; I always wanted to make love to her. But I needed this comfort too, feeling her safe and well beside me.

She sighed, breath washing over my pectorals, then hooked a leg over mine to snuggle even closer. Predictably, my body expressed interest in pursuing further intimacy, but I ignored it. My heart had too much on the line, no matter how willing my fabulous girlfriend proved to be. As if she recognized the vulnerability of that particular organ, Jaque struck, her hopeful inquiry so soft, yet intensely powerful.

"Do you think, if we are blessed to be parents, we could name a little girl after my mother?"

My emotions buckled like a car in a head on collision, folding in on itself until no one would recognize its original shape in the wreckage. The sweet pain was so acute I couldn't breathe for several heartbeats. When I finally dragged in a much-needed lungful, it burned all the way down, as if I were inhaling all the tears I wouldn't let myself cry. Strength was what Jaque needed, and I would not fail her, even as we addressed my deepest fears.

"If there's even the slightest chance that having babies will hurt you, then I don't want to try. But if you decide to be a mom, and we get lucky enough to have a girl, then I can't think of a better name." Grasping for some sort of lightness before I suffocated, I relaxed my hold, then looked down at her with forced amusement. When she tilted her face up, eyes shining with happiness, I couldn't help the true smile that overtook me. "As long as you don't decide to alphabetize the rest of their names, you can call our babies whatever you want."

She laughed, her joy dazzling. "No? I thought perhaps we would keep the tradition alive. Angeline Aurora has a certain ring to it!"

I dramatically smacked my palm against my forehead, groaning as if in pain. "No, God no. I refuse! I will cut you off, so help me, woman. No baby making will happen if you persist in this madness."

This time, when she laughed, it resonated in my center as if she had plucked a cord. The now husky tone held a direct line to my desire, which she encouraged with a hand that moved down my belly with intent. "Well, no, no baby making now. Though perhaps we should practice?"

I caved; my willpower made of tissue paper where she was concerned. We fell into each other with laughter on our lips, Jaqueline taunting me with a slew of possible names for our hoped-for children. Ridiculous combinations like Brandon Boyd and Camilla Collett. Before long, I was tossing names back, starting on the other end of the alphabet as I worshiped her creamy skin with my lips. "Zachary Zane, then!"

Though we continued in that vein for a bit longer, soon, we were too consumed with the pursuit of pleasure to manage much beyond animal noises of enjoyment. The edge came upon me fast, and I clung to my sanity barely long enough for her to catch up. Then we flung ourselves out into the abyss, falling without fear. At least for the moment.

Jaque

Dressage day dawned bright and cloudless, people shedding jackets as the temperature rose into the promise of spring. In the t-shirt Jo gave me, and a pair of worn jeans, I enjoyed the hum of my fellow competitors as people and horses came and went around us. The sun warmed my back as I stood on a stool beside Lyric, putting her braids in again. She dozed as I worked, tail flicking lazily, ears moving to follow Aaron's movements. He had pulled our presentation carriage out, not an ounce of hesitation in his actions as he attached the curved shafts and the groom's seat. The lamps followed, and I noticed he wore the white cotton gloves that would protect the chrome and glass from smudges. Having been to his mother's house, seeing her in action, I now understood his aversion to the innocuous gloves on a much deeper level. Having him use them now, without prompting, meant a great deal to me.

It was a superb day, perfectly temperate. The trees were beginning to bud, a faint green haze outlining the naked branches, and already, the rich bluegrass Lexington was renowned for thickened into a carpet. The barns were abuzz with activity, many Novice level drivers already headed for the arena to take their turn on the evenly tan footing. The horse park was considered by many to be the epitome of show grounds, everything manicured and so much history traced along its tree-lined lanes. I did appreciate it for those reasons, but a part of me preferred the personable, intimate feel of less showy events. Still, if we were looking to make our presence felt in the small world of combined driving, this was the level where we needed to play.

Just as I shifted my little stool around so I could braid Lyric's forelock, a familiar and welcome voice gave me pause. "Jaqueline, your mare looks well!"

Turning to face Lillian Beard, I smiled broadly to see her in the driver's seat of a pony pair. The two buckskin pintos were walking toward me, eyes bright with interest, and Lillian's hands light on the reins. She trilled softly, focusing on her ponies until they came to a stop.

"Thank you, Lillian, we are as prepared as we can be. How was your drive?"

"My little troopers were wonderful. This is their first show as a pair, but they are behaving like old campaigners. Only Intermediate level, but if they keep this up, I'll be unsurprised if we end up at the Pony Championships the next go round."

"Well then, I will be sure to keep an eye out for you at future shows," I assured her, knowing the ponies could not have a better driver to help them reach their potential. Lillian had made an impression on Lyric and I after just one clinic. "Though I did not expect you here. Are you not from the west coast?"

She shrugged, her tailored sunflower and black jacket ruching up around her shoulders for a moment. "Life takes us in unexpected directions sometimes, don't you think?"

My gaze darted over to Aaron for the barest moment, and my heart blazed with happiness. When I looked back to Lillian, she wore a knowing smile that brought heat to my cheeks. But I lifted my chin with pride. "Yes, I believe it does. Hopefully, yours takes you where you wanted to go. If you will be here through the season, would it be possible to arrange coaching? I very much enjoyed working with you in Florida."

Delight brightened her expression. "I would be happy to come to an arrangement. I'm still figuring out a few details, but we'll exchange contact information." One of the ponies shifted restlessly, turning his head as if to rub it on his teammate. Lillian immediately asked the pair to walk on, keeping them out of trouble, but waved her whip at me on the way by. "We'll see you at the barbeque tonight!"

When I turned back to my work, I carried the warmth of the exchange with me. Between that and the sun, I felt relaxed, ready to face any challenge that lay ahead. Though my life might be in a state of transition, everything so far led me to believe that the risks I took would pay off, just as when I left Quebec to come here.

The impression continued as I changed into my show clothes that afternoon. After putting my hair up, I secured the hat firmly in place with several pins. A quick shake of my head confirmed it would not go anywhere, short of a sudden gale blowing in. Patent leather flats peeked out from beneath the hem of flared pant legs, and the deep plum jacket with its profusion of buttons angling across my torso looked sharp. I thought it a fitting match to my mare, with her glossy coat and elegant harness.

Then I headed out into the sunshine, where said mare and my handsome groom awaited. It was not lost on me that someday I would play bride to his groom. Soon, I hoped.

Lyric radiated good health, breathing calm, but ears pricked with eagerness as she turned toward the sound of my footsteps on the concrete. Aaron wore a charcoal suit almost a match for the colour of my pants, an unexpected surprise. Highly polished brogues caught the bright sun, and the bowler hat I gave him to wear in the arena was tucked under one arm as he held Lyric's reins with the opposite hand. I would have given up every last french fry in the world to have a picture of them just then, two of the great loves of my life looking to me with so much happiness in their eyes.

Hitching Lyric to her carriage took mere moments, though I did not rush. Our safety was too important for me to risk missing anything in order to beat the clock. Aaron waited until I took up the reins and climbed into the driver's seat, watching my every move as if he meant to memorize them. Only when I had my apron on and properly tucked in around my body did I nod to him.

"We are ready, Aaron. Are you?" He nodded back and released the reins, taking a step toward the carriage, but stopped when I shook my head. "No, not quite."

Then I offered up my own surprise, the first of several planned for the weekend. With a quizzical tilt to his head, he took the small box I pointed to on the groom's seat behind me. He cracked it open to reveal a deep purple tie with thin stripes of silver, and a matching pocket square. Judging by his grin when he looked back up, he had no issues with me branding him mine, ever so subtly.

"You realize I'm imagining you all decked out in my colours now?" A faint growl edged his lighthearted words as he replaced his blue tie. Anticipation zinged through my body at the prospect, but I smiled serenely. We would have plenty of time to pursue the idea of laying visible claim to each other later. For now, I needed to keep my composure. Lyric deserved all of my attention. That did not mean I could not poke holes in his composure, however, which I took advantage of once he climbed into the seat behind me.

"Hmm, I thought I was wearing your colours the other night in your bed, my champion?" Judging by his stifled groan as I asked Lyric to walk on, I struck my mark well. A promising beginning to a test that called for accuracy. Now, to see if I could continue the trend when we reached the arena.

Aaron played his part to perfection at the warmup arena. He had driven my father and Soleil over to the arena in the golf cart earlier in the day, leaving a small bucket of grooming tools with them. Once Lyric's muscles were sufficiently loosened by a short warmup, and her mind tuned into the game ahead, we stopped on a bit of tarmac near the golf cart for touch ups. Aaron jumped down with an easy athleticism that few present could have matched, then immediately set to touching up our turnout.

Sacre, he cut a fine figure, even when crouched to brush dust from Lyric's legs. This time his hands were confident as he took a damp rag to her eyes and muzzle. And I, foolish woman, stared, remembering those same hands caressing my own skin. When he caught me watching, his lips went from thin with concentration to upturned with pleasure. As if I beckoned him, he moved to stand beside the driver's box, eyes glimmering with mischief as he handed me an open bottle of water.

I gulped it noisily, needing the icy liquid to cool my blood from the inside. But it did little good as he used the cover of my apron to trace his knowledgeable fingertips over the bones of my ankle. The seductive caress would seem innocent to anyone watching, as if he were dusting my shoes or tucking my apron closer, but the effect on my senses felt absolutely sinful.

Then he pulled back, reaching for the bottle in my nerveless hand as if he had not just upended me. His eyes still held passion, but they were tempered by a sober knowledge that cleared the haze from my mind. "I'm sorry, I know you've got bigger things to think about right now."

Perhaps he meant the words to calm the storm building in my belly, but in a way, he only strengthened it. To have him see me so clearly, to not just accept, but support my goals, was another turn on. However, thanks to an impatient flick of Lyric's tail and the sudden awareness of all the carriages milling nearby, I was able to contain the craving he stirred.

"Thank you. But you should know that this is not bigger, not more important," I answered softly, even as I took the reins back up. "Never doubt that you mean more to me than this."

He nodded, appreciation in his smile. Then the softness bled away, morphing into the guise of a knight who sought out challenges for a living. Sharp eyes called on all the fierceness that lay dormant in my belly until I let it come out to play. The sleeping beast stirred like a leviathan in the darkness, purring with pleasure as it recognized an echo of itself in Aaron's gaze. When I smiled back, it was nothing like the usual sweetness we gave each other. No, this was toothy, an acknowledgement from one carnivore to another that we were hungry. Not for blood, not even for glory, but we craved these tests of will. Something in us would starve if we did not take these risks.

When the ring steward called out my number as being in the hole, my head snapped up, breaking contact with Aaron. The first set of eyes that met mine were Paul's as he trotted along the edge of the warmup arena, but he flinched away from the greed in my gaze, much as he had in our relationship. My blood thrummed as I realized the truth in Aaron's proclamation the first night we came together. I had never been too much. But Paul had certainly never been enough, and that gave me a power that I intended to harness.

I looked down, making sure Aaron could see everything I could not say in that moment. He nodded with satisfaction, saying plenty for the both of us as he stepped up into his seat again. "I'm ready. Are you?"

I answered by sending Lyric back into the fray, unflinching in the chaos, prepared for whatever came. With Aaron at my back, my glorious mare before me, and my Papa to cheer us on, I had never been more ready in my life.

Aaron

Riding on the carriage wasn't a big challenge. I'd watched the grooms in South Carolina, and Jaque had explained the rules. The gist of it was I had to be a mannequin. No noise, no undo movement, nothing that could be construed as helping unless she requested assistance if things went wrong. Otherwise, they could be disqualified.

Didn't make it any less thrilling. Jaque spoke so softly I could barely hear her over the whirring of the carriage wheels, soothing or encouraging by turns. Transitions were easy to anticipate if I listened to the sounds she used to cue the mare. Words precipitated a change in gait, either up or down. "Step up," usually meant an increase in speed within a gait, and "Easy," slowed us down. She never touched the brake, letting the mare propel or slow the vehicle with her own power.

I loved the canter. Yeah, the big trot across the diagonal was powerful, dynamic. But the canter hinted at the potential for speed that I craved. The mare's energy swept back through Jaque until even I could feel it, bounding and condensed. What would it be like to really let her run? The mere idea made me eager to learn more about helping Jaque, so I could be useful to her on marathon day as well.

Only the halts caused me mild trouble, but by the time we trotted crisply up the centerline toward the main judge's box for the third time, I was prepared. One foot tucked slightly back beneath me, the other slightly ahead, both bracing so I wouldn't slide forward on the seat when Jaque asked her mare to whoa. Otherwise, I never moved but to turn my head to follow the track of the carriage, hands clasped in my lap as if I were sitting at Sunday supper.

That is until she made her final salute and let her mare walk out of the arena on a loose rein, her voice warm and light with praise. Then I waited until she sat back again before putting my hand on her elbow, hardly enough pressure to draw a smidgen of her attention. She kept her eyes ahead, though I felt her regard in the breath she held, waiting for me to speak.

"Felt great from here, my lady."

She sighed out an audible gust. "Thank you, felt great from here too."

Once outside the arena, she quickly navigated back to the golf cart. I jumped down, fishing out a maple candy to reward Lyric as I walked toward her head. She breathed deeply, nostrils flared as she came down from her exertions, but the rhythm evened out in mere seconds as she crunched on her candy. I waited, keeping company with the contented mare until Jack showed up and began shifting himself into the golf cart. Despite the physical effort required, he still managed to grin widely at his daughter and offer his congratulations.

"Well done, *mes filles*!" Which I now knew meant my girls, and I loved how the praise made Jaque light up again. She had been fucking radiant before her test, so achingly fierce I wanted to crow my elation to the heavens. Though the raw elemental power had mellowed to something more palatable to the mere mortals that surrounded her, the glow was still plentiful enough to tan yourself in.

But we couldn't linger, even for the tender father-daughter moment. So I jumped behind the wheel of the golf cart and followed Jaque back to our encampment. Within moments, Soleil stood with her front paws on my lap, nose lifted into the air with every evidence of delight over the myriad of scents in the humid air. The little dog and I had come a long way since South Carolina, when she wouldn't so much as take food from my hand. Now, she was as integrated into my life, my family, as Jaque herself.

"You treat her well, Aaron." Jack stated quietly, so Jaque wouldn't overhear. I turned my chin in his direction so he would know he had my attention, though my gaze remained on the carriage. No matter how much I wanted to bond with her father, it would not be worth the possibility of a wreck.

"I do my best, sir. She deserves no less."

He gave a dry chuckle, though I heard no amusement in it. Apprehension moved over my skin, lifting the hairs on my arms even as sweat made my shirt stick to me. "No, she will always deserve more, my Junior. She is a treasure of a woman, and so much like her Mama. Were I to lose my Jaqueline, the last part of my Angeline, I would be lost as well."

Though my heart clenched with fear, I answered his unspoken admonition with complete honesty. "Loving Jaqueline as I do, sir, I don't know how you survived the heartache to begin with. But I'm glad you did, because I needed her so badly. I need to love her like I need to breathe."

Jack's voice rasped with a pain that sounded acute, even with time to buffer the rawness of loss. "Until you need to love more than you need to breathe, then you do not love her nearly enough."

My lungs burned with an objection. I wanted to tell him I was already there, but I held it in. The unuttered words were not his to hear. No, I would save such a confession for the woman herself. Add to that the heartache of realizing her father may not think I loved his daughter enough to be worthy of her, and I felt like Byz had a hoof on my chest. Yeah, breathing seemed pointless under the weight of that worry.

Once back at camp, Jack remained on the golf cart as we unharnessed Lyric. Jaque changed as I wiped down the carriage, then she rinsed the sweat from Lyric's coat as I took time to shed my own suit. Felt intimate, hanging my jacket next to hers, two complementary shades of storm gray that brought to mind the dark granite of Byz's coat when I first met him.

Jaque walked Lyric back to her stall, her father and I close behind in the golf cart. We were going to have a full house for this tour of the marathon course. Cardi would go around with Jaque in the early morning, before the first novice driver started. For now, Jaque showed her father around. I sat on the rear facing back seat with Boris beside me, listening intently to everything she said in hopes I might glean a little knowledge that would help me understand her passion.

As the late afternoon shadows lengthened into early evening, we cruised the course in the company of what seemed like hundreds of other golf carts and a veritable herd of ATV's, scooters and off-road side by sides. Jack charmed everyone he met with the same ease as his daughter, some people remembering him from his last visit. I settled happily into my role as sounding board when Jaque evaluated obstacles, though I hardly said much, just listened to her talk herself around. Soleil capered with other dogs, though never went far from Jaque, and Boris rode on my shoulders, keeping away from the chaos underfoot.

She introduced me to more people than I could possibly remember. I met so many spouses who were supporting each other. Some looked a bit weary, or even resigned, but even more gave me the impression that they loved this sport almost as much as their partners did. Those couples reminded me of Joyce and Harv, though I winced a little, hoping Joyce's mistake hadn't taken any of the shine off their relationship. Gallant Company was due near Aiken in a couple weeks, and I still wanted to meet up with them. Question was whether or not Jaque would be okay with it. We hadn't talked about the incident since it happened, and I hated to be the reason such a warm friendship hit the rocks.

By the time we left the showgrounds after the barbeque dinner, it was full dark. Crickets chirped, frogs called, and we rode with the windows down in the truck, enjoying the oncoming spring. Jaque asked me to drive. I leapt gratefully at the chance, hoping the soothing familiarity would help clear my mind. As father and daughter chatted in the background, I finally made sense of what Jack said. Not the way he meant it, probably, but it was no less true. He thought I needed to love Jaque more than I needed to breathe, but the truth for me was much simpler than that. Without Jaque in my life, I probably would have suffocated myself under the weight of my responsibilities. Without her storm to blow in and wash my troubles clean, breathing would have stopped all on its own.

❧21❧

Jaque

Helpers were everywhere on Saturday morning. With Jo grooming Lyric, Bart cleaning the stall and Aaron tending to the hay net while Papa scrubbed out buckets, I had the freedom to take Cardi out for a course walk in the dawn hours. We made record time through section A, and I began to feel a little invincible, as if nothing could stand in our way.

But on the actual marathon track, something, or more accurately, someone did stand in our very physical way. Several of them. Paul, Grady and Mr. van den Berg occupied the middle of obstacle one as Cardi and I parked outside the flagged area. Likely, the two sycophants were hanging on Maarten's every word as if he dripped gold from his lips.

To be fair, van den Berg had avoided speaking to me since the first day in South Carolina. I am not naïve, however. The unspoken disdain in his gaze felt palpable as I stood in the middle of the timer gate and ignored him in favour of the work ahead. This obstacle was not horribly complicated, meant more to warm the horses up for the greater efforts ahead, but I knew better than to underestimate a single stride. I needed to focus on the course, our true opponent, rather than the condescending attitudes of men who meant nothing to me anymore.

Cardi, however, bristled as if she were my guard dog rather than my navigator. Her glare dripped with venom as we walked to the first gate, though she softened the instant I pulled her attention to the map in my hands. We evaluated the two routes I plotted the night before, and she agreed completely when I opted for the line that would allow us to maintain speed, rather than risking losing momentum for tighter turns. As we walked through, passing close by the clump of men, they had the gall to laugh. Not genuine laughter, but an over rich sound of superiority that made my hands fist on the map I held. Cardi made one huge stride that took her right up against the rail Grady leaned on, loathing twisting her lips into a snarl. Grady almost fell to his knees as he scrambled away from her reach, which made me hide a laugh. Better still, Paul and Maarten flinched as she fetched right up against the thick beam, her hands curling into the wood to hold her in place.

"You got something you wanna say, gentlemen?" she said sweetly, smiling as if she were asking for the time. "Because I am sure us delicate flowers would be beside ourselves to learn at the feet of such esteemed men."

Had I been drinking something, I might have shot it out my nose. Thankfully, my amusement only escaped in another muffled chuckle as I slipped past the little scene to reach gate C.

"I didn't think so." While I did not see her sneer, I could hear it accenting every word. Then she turned and caught up with me as I rounded the left-hand turn from C to D. We maintained our sober façade all the way through to gate F, but found our exit line took us right through the alley occupied by the three men.

Narrowing my eyes to see through them to the exit, I addressed Cardi. "What do you think? Should we go around or through?"

Cardi sprouted a fiendish smile that I hoped to never see turned on me. Cartoon villains could take lessons from the evil delight shining in her eyes. "Oh, through, always through. Follow my lead."

So, I fell in a half stride behind and slightly to one side, not wanting to miss a second of whatever chaos she meant to unload. Three feet from their huddle, she dropped her bomb. They never knew what hit them.

"Gosh, Jaque, we need to find a portapotty! I think I'm bleeding through my tampon. And my uterus feels like someone is taking a chain saw to it. Do you have anything for cramps?"

Their eyes widened with panic, conversation grinding to a halt as she stepped in between them. Each man backed up as far as he could, horror in the tight line of their shoulders as they froze. Perfectly positioned for me to drive home the nail she had started.

"Oh, of course! I have tampons, and pads too. My first day is always like Niagara Falls meets a slasher movie. One can never have enough supplies for one's menstrual cycle."

Grady actually shuddered, and Paul made a sound like a distressed chipmunk. Victory flooded my veins with a potency stronger than hard liquor as I stalked down the hill away from them. Cardi, who believed in total annihilation of the enemy, added in a dramatic groan of pain as we reached the golf cart. "Oh God, it feels like it's coming out chunky!"

I rolled my eyes as I climbed behind the wheel but kept up the fiction. "Hang on, do not bleed on the seat!" Then I stomped on the gas pedal, managing to spit a bit of grass from under the tires as I steered down the lane toward the second obstacle. We managed to keep our composure until I turned a corner and saw a portapotty off to one side of the path. The mere sight started us giggling, which did not subside until we reached our next stop.

Thankfully, the rest of our walk remained trouble free. We toured the water complex with Sue, which I found refreshing. Always good to get someone else's perspective on the questions set up by the gates. How to rate according to footing, change of elevation, and even your horse's particular strengths and weaknesses.

Sue's mare, being of slighter build than Lyric, was quick through the turns, up headed and had a massive trot stride. This gave her the speed advantage, as she rarely lost time when her mare needed to drop out of the canter.

Lyric, on the other hand, was powerful and compact. I could collect her as long as we had enough space on approach, maintaining a canter even in tight spaces. Where she lost momentum was on the straight away, unless we were trotting down the road. Then, she was capable of a respectable speed. Oh, and Lyric loved uphill stretches! Give her a load to pull and she threw every ounce of muscle fibre and heart into the harness, which in her case, added up to a lot of pounds.

When we finally approached camp, I found the helpers had multiplied! Caroline Barry stood beneath one of the shades set up beside the trailer, busily arranging as if expecting highbrow clientele for a meal. A purple cloth covered a folding table, rolls of silverware wrapped in napkins sat in a basket and she had a bouquet of dried flowers sitting in an antiqued silver vase. Her husband John unloaded coolers and boxes from the back of a small SUV, and as he caught sight of me, his perpetually cheerful expression brightened even more. "Jaqueline! Glad to see you!"

While part of me reveled in the warm welcome, another part chafed. I needed quiet as part of my preparations for the coming challenge, not this well-intentioned chaos. But I could not send them away. I wanted them to like me, to accept me as one of their own. So, I hugged him, and introduced Cardi, then asked after the rest of the crew.

"They should be here anytime," Caroline replied as she hooked her arm through John's. "I've brought breakfast for everyone, so you can fuel up for the long day."

Wincing at the pain of denying her, I shook my head. "Caroline, much as I would adore another taste of your renowned skills in the kitchen, I will have to bow out. I cannot eat much before competing. Between being comfortable for the effort ahead, and sheer nerves, my stomach will not tolerate much."

She touched my crossed arms with delicate fingers. Warmth spilled into me from the slight contact. "Never you fear, Aaron told me. He also mentioned your predilection for hazelnut spread, so there is a Nutella croissant reserved just for you."

Cardi made a pained noise, staggering a half step as if she had been struck. Considering her weakness for sweets, her distress was keenly felt. "Please, oh goddess of the kitchen, tell me there's more than one!"

Caroline's full cheeks coloured prettily at the compliment, but she accepted it with grace. "What sort of kitchen goddess would I be to neglect the most important member of Jaque's team?"

Cardi laughed heartily. "To be fair, the most important member of Jaque's team would be Lyric. But she can't have even a little chocolate while she's competing. It'll mess with the results when she gets drug tested, which is almost certain at an international level event like this."

"Oh, I didn't know horses could eat chocolate?" Caroline looked up at John with a moue of inquiry. She resembled nothing so much as a porcelain doll, with her heavily lashed eyes, fine complexion, and rosy cheeks. "John, does Tuck like chocolate?"

"You know, poppet, I haven't tried it. He eats most anything that isn't tied down though, so I wouldn't be surprised. We'll have to check with Bart before we try though. I don't want to make him sick."

"Check with Bart about what?" Bart's unmistakably deep voice made me spin around in hopes his brother was with him. Jo strode along at his side, though Aaron remained conspicuously absent. She did not deserve the frown that overtook my features, but she did not shy away from it either, stepping up to hug me.

"You look like you could use a break from the throng," she murmured as she embraced me. I gave the tiniest nod before she let go, my throat thickening with appreciation for having such a lovely friend. To know we would someday be sisters made my heart clench with an overabundance of emotion, but I held it in as I met her eyes.

"I am not used to so much assistance," I offered, shrugging my shoulders with discomfort. However much I appreciated everyone's support, I needed some time to be quiet with Lyric.

"Gallant Company can be a lot at the best of times," she sympathized, squeezing my elbow before stepping back. "Let me grab your breakfast, then you can run off. If you don't eat something Caroline will be devastated, and Aaron will worry."

I stood on the outskirts of my own camp, listening to Bart explain that horses should not really have much chocolate, but Tuck could have a taste without doing any harm. Jo returned with two flakey croissants, each swaddled in a napkin. After pressing one into my hands, she pointedly looked toward the barns, the tiniest ghost of a smile in her eyes. "Go. I'll hold them off for a bit."

Then she turned toward Cardi, catching her attention with the offer of the other croissant she held. And I, unwilling to waste a moment of respite, fled. Lyric nickered when she caught sight of me, my heart aching with a sudden need to touch her. But someone else waited for me too, Aaron rising from the chair beside her door. Yes, I loved him, so dearly it should have terrified me, so I stepped into his open arms with a sigh of relief. He asked for nothing, only let me rest against his chest and breathe the clean scent of him deep into my lungs.

"Where is Papa?" I asked, letting my lips remain half pressed into the dark plum polo shirt stretched over his muscular frame. I had given him one of my too large spares, Bonterre Farms embroidered onto the left breast over a silver fleur de lis. He had not minded in the least, either to wear my shirt, nor to match, as I wore exactly the same thing.

"He took himself off to the restroom. I offered to go with him, but he said no rather…emphatically."

I turned my face fully against his pectorals to muffle a snicker. "I will presume he said something about not needing help handling his equipment? There were likely a few swear words added for colour?"

Aaron chuckled. "You've got it, my lady."

In any other circumstance, I would have spent hours in the refuge of his arms. But after a few moments of quiet, I shifted restlessly. As if he could sense my distress, he let me go, hands cupping my shoulders. Narrowed eyes met mine, and I struggled not to flinch from his knowing gaze. If he truly loved me, then he would accept even this about me.

"What's going on, Jaque?"

Lifting my chin to feign courage I did not feel, I took a leap, hoping he would understand. "I love you, my champion, but I need you to do me a favour."

"Anything," he answered emphatically, hands tightening as if he could lend me some of his strength. Instead, I borrowed strength from the surety of his reply, though my body habitually went rigid. I could not afford to be weak right then.

"While I adore your company, could I have some time alone with Lyric? It is nothing personal, I promise you. I am sorry to ask it."

Whatever I expected, the predatory glint of bared teeth surprised me. He had offered a similar expression the day before, and just as then, I felt the hum of blood picking up speed in my veins. Then his hands slid from my shoulders, one dropping to take the hand not cradling my croissant.

"Jaque, don't be sorry. I love this part of you. Seeing the joy your mare gives you, the courage you display when you drive her, is as satisfying to me as my own competitions." Then he kissed my hand and stepped back, though I felt our connection as if we were still skin to skin. "You will never be too much."

As he turned away to fetch Boris and Soleil from the tack stall, I blinked several times to clear my vision. When he strode away, cat over one shoulder and my little dog trotting at his heels, no hesitation marked his movements. Silly me, I stood stock still until he disappeared around the end of the barn, too full of feeling to move. When he was lost to sight, I turned toward Lyric on wobbly knees and sighed. Her ears flicked back and forth, likely as curious about what I held in the napkin as much as my roiling emotions.

Rather than share my treat, I dished her a small amount of pellets as a distraction, then dropped into the chair Aaron so recently occupied. The fabric still carried a bit of his warmth, and I sank in with a sigh of relief. The croissant tasted even better than it smelled, melting on my tongue as I closed my eyes to fully savour the buttery, nutty, chocolatey layers. By the time the last bite passed my tongue and I licked my fingers clean, every ounce of my tension had disappeared.

Lyric joined me, her muzzle coming to rest on the softness of my belly. Deep breaths, in and out, pushed warmth into my middle. I set one hand on the thick muscles of her neck, offering my own energy to her until we felt like one continuous circuit of power. She and I would never be the lightning strike of the quicker teams. We would not be the mutable water of the more athletic, or the wind of the faster. But we could be the thunder, passing on the power that reverberated in our connection with every beat of our hearts.

Aaron

Soleil still skirted a wide path around Bart, though he made an effort to crouch down when we walked into camp. But once I opened the tack room door, she hopped in and curled up on her bed, well familiar with the show day routine. Boris joined her, dropping off my shoulder with a chirp in order to knead his blanket into a suitable pile. I needed to get him a bed of his own, so he could be comfortable no matter where we went.

With Bart's help, I pulled the marathon carriage out, then we all took advantage of Caroline's generosity. She had prepared breakfast sandwiches on hearty whole grain bread, with fried eggs and cheese, kept warm in foil and a cooler. Not for the first time, I wished it were possible to take her with us on trips, along with John. But both had their own careers, lucrative ones that also made them happy. I'd never ask anyone to give up such a combination to come on the road with the Company.

Bart seemed to be thinking on the same lines though. After wiping the last bit of butter from his mouth, he voiced my thoughts. "Caroline, it's a shame we can't pack you up to play camp mom for us when we travel. Drive thru food gets old fast."

Caroline looked up from packing the trash away and shared a grin with Jo, who was helping Cardi get the remaining marathon equipment loaded in the golf cart. Then she favored Bart with her attention. "Actually, Jo and I have been discussing just that. With enough notice, I can prepare meals as I would for a catering client. Some would require a little assembly or reheating, but nothing too time consuming."

Bart rubbed his belly as if to confirm his full stomach, the wheels turning in his head. "I'm thinking we can come to some sort of arrangement, Caroline. Would you be available for a meeting this coming Wednesday?"

I left them to discuss the details without me. While I remained the initial contact for clients, Bart's specialty continued to be the running of the Company itself. Between his excellent view of the bigger picture, and Jo's penchant for details, I knew they had things well handled on the back end. This development alone would save me the trouble of hunting up breakfast at every stop. All to the good when I wasn't at my best first thing in the morning. Better to save my energy for the jousting, and we'd never have to worry about ending up with breakfast gut-bombs that we regretted for the rest of the day.

Jack rolled in a few minutes later, his rugged little chair handling the ruts in the field without hesitation. His corded forearms propelled him into camp with ease, and I waved him over to Caroline before he could ask after Jaque. She deserved all the quiet she could steal before we jumped into action again. Jack quickly charmed Caroline with his gentlemanly ways and the faint accent that came from speaking French most of the time. I loved it on Jaque, like a caress came with every word, but on her father, it carried a bit of mystery.

When the alarm on Cardi's phone went off, I shot into action, determined to keep my girls on track. Jack volunteered to stay with John and Caroline, as he could show them the best places to watch from. That left me free to focus on Jaque's needs, so I grabbed the shafts on the carriage and turned it toward the barns, grateful for something to do. For the briefest of seconds, I had to throw a bit of weight into the job, every muscle from my forearms to my feet tightening down like a ratchet strap. In the next breath, the carriage rolled with ease as my brother stepped in to push from behind. Cardi and Jo passed us in the golf cart before we even hit the asphalt, but it worked out well. By the time we reached the aisle way, they already had the equipment bins unloaded.

I stood to the side and began pulling together the things we would need at the vet box. Jaque gave me a list the night before when I asked what I could do, and it felt pretty damn good to be trusted with something. Sure, Cardi and Jaque didn't need all this help, but they made me feel like part of the team anyway.

Between my own busy work, I watched the ladies get armored up. They dressed Lyric first, not only the harness, but an extra pad along her ribs to keep the short shafts from rubbing in the tight turns. Her usually lush tail had been braided up, and she wore a crocheted dark purple bonnet over her ears with the silver fleur de lis embroidered in the middle of the brim that hung over her broad brow. Protective boots were velcroed over the vulnerable tendons in her lower legs, straps taped down to keep them from coming loose.

Jaque put on hoof boots as well, to prevent her hooves from getting worn down over the long distances they would be traveling. She had explained her preference to keep her horses barefoot, how beneficial it was to allow the hoof to expand and contract for proper blood flow. Not a choice many at her level made, when shoes were the standard, but with her farrier Dan's help they had found boots to fit the mare's large feet.

Well, not large compared to the Gallant Company herd, but certainly when you compared them to the lighter bred horses. Our horses never needed shoes, since they weren't asked to work for sustained amounts of time. With an occasional trim to keep them balanced, they managed just fine.

The two women had just secured the last strap on the mare when a commotion came from down the aisle. Hurrying footsteps bounced up off the concrete in a frantic rhythm, pulling everyone's eyes to Sue, the woman with the Morgan mare. Her eyes were wide with worry, and she mumbled a hasty sorry to the people next door as she dodged around where they were rinsing off their sweaty ponies.

"Jaque! Good, you're still here! Shit!" Nostrils flared wide, she sucked in a deep breath, trying to relax as Jaque stepped forward to meet her. "My gator just fell off the trailer fender and broke her wrist! I don't know who to ask for help, and I've got to be on course before you!"

Big hearted as she was, I saw the conflict in my lady's expression as she scanned over all of us. She would give up Cardi if it came to it, unwilling to win at the expense of another. But before she could make the offer, a throat cleared behind Sue.

"Excuse me?"

Everyone turned to face a petite blonde, a pale blue helmet and vest still in place, sunglasses covering her eyes. But her smile made me want to like her, genuine and warm, a slice of reassurance in the midst of the sudden upset. "I couldn't help overhearing. I'm Sharyl, from Spitting Llama Ranch, and we just finished our marathon. While my husband Paul navigates for me, my son is a pretty excellent stand in."

She hiked a thumb back toward where two men stood, each leading a shiny chestnut pony with vivid white markings. The younger man on the right waved genially even as they turned to put the ponies in their stalls, his tall stature making the ponies look diminutive.

"He stood in for Cardi last fall when she got the stomach flu, so Jaque can vouch for him. He can calculate times on the fly, and if you go over your routes with him while you do section A, he won't forget a thing."

Jaque nodded emphatically, grabbing Sue's elbow to turn her toward Sharyl. "Yes, Sue, Kent is wonderful to work with! He is a good weight to backstep for Rhapsody, and you will not regret the bargain. Go! None of us can afford to be late!"

The blonde waved Sue forward, and I barely heard her introducing the woman to her son, the anticipatory energy in our own camp creating a humming in my veins. Once they saw Sue heading off with Kent in tow, Jaque and Cardi moved in tandem, donning their own protective gear. Everything matched, from polo shirts like the one I wore, to black impact vests trimmed in silver. The helmets were black as well, with a broad strip of silver in the middle. Cardi pulled a tabard over her head before securing her helmet, blazoned with 143 to match the number attached to the mare's bridle.

Then Jaque led Lyric over, beckoning me to hold her while they attached the carriage. The mare stood obediently enough, but I recognized the sharp light in her eyes, the tensing of her muscles. Our warhorses did much the same as we readied them for the lyst, so I stroked her thick neck exactly how Jaque had shown me she liked, keeping my voice calm as the women moved around her.

"Steady on, war mare. It'll be time soon enough."

She blinked as if just realizing I stood in front of her, then exhaled with a flutter of nostrils. Her nose bumped my sternum, an impatient but tactful cue that she wanted to go. Just in time, too, as Jaque did a last walk around to double check her equipment, then took up the reins before stepping up into the driver's box.

This carriage was built like a rally car, more a cage on a high-grade suspension. You sat at an angle that allowed you to brace your feet for the turns, the sides of the seat also deep so you stayed in the middle even when the road got rough. There was a wide step behind the driver, low to the ground so the navigator could help keep the carriage stable in fast turns. Cardi stepped up into her place, checking the multiple stopwatches attached behind the driver's seat, making sure all her notes were in order. Once everything was properly secured, she quietly patted Jaque on the back to signal her readiness.

My hands went light on the bridle in preparation for them to leave, but Jaque did not ask me to release her just yet. Instead, reins and whip in one hand, she pressed a kiss to the fingertips of the glove on her other hand. Then, she blew it to me, a sweet action that meant all the more with the thrill of competition beckoning. My cheek warmed as if the ephemeral kiss had landed, and I returned the gesture. Her cheeks colored just as they had the first time, and I offered them the same encouragement I had then. "You've got this, ladies."

"Damn right we do!" Cardi responded, leaning around Jaque to make sure I could see the mischief in her smile. "See you at the ten-minute hold, Prince Charming!"

While Jaque groaned at Cardi's silliness, she also nodded at me to let Lyric go. I stepped back, making plenty of space for them, and she spared me one last smile before asking the mare to walk on. They were at the end of the aisle, just turning the corner, when Cardi dramatically leaned back and blew me a kiss too. I laughed at the display, grinning all the harder at Jaque's indignant squawk of objection as they disappeared from view.

When I slid into the driver's side of the golf cart, I found my brother in the passenger seat and Jo on the back, holding on to the equipment for the vet box. My heart swelled hard, seeing all the people I loved coming together. But as I executed a U-turn to head for the golf cart path, Bart made his own dig, voice drier than stale bread. "Prince Charming?"

Then Jo leaned over the seat, determined to get in on the action. "Do they even know you?"

I pushed her back with a palm to her forehead, groaning under the combined weight of their amusement. But truth be told, the ribbing told me as much as anything else that they were happy for me. Trading blows was what Gallant Company did, after all, and we were damn good at it. But what made us family is the way we helped each other up after every single fall.

Jaque

I would happily write you a detailed account of Section A, but there are really only so many ways to describe the glorious sight of Lyric's muscular haunches powering down the road. With the tight braid in her tail, I enjoyed an unobstructed view of her impressive engine. From the point of her croup to the bottom of her hooves, she became an undulating and continuous circuit of energy that pushed off the earth with the intent to fly.

Much as I loved the tight turns and adrenaline pumping risk of the marathon, Section A held its own appeal. It was freedom of movement, Lyric and I whispering to each other through the reins. Her supple body did not need guidance, she knew herself far better than I, adjusting stride and balance to suit herself. I needed only to suggest a turn, and she bent like a willow bough in the wind. A very thick, sturdy willow bough, but still, supple and lithe.

We took a few walks in the flat spots, those hard to come by in such hilly country. However prepared we were for the work, she was still a heavily muscled, solid black animal working in full sun. Judging by the white lather gathering between her haunches, and the flecks of sweat on her neck, I wanted to be careful. It would not do to make time only to run out of gas in the marathon.

Thanks to Cardi's meticulous timekeeping, we rolled into the ten-minute hold barely under the time I allowed for in my planning. Lyric stood politely for the vet to check her temperature and heart rate, well familiar with the routine. But what surprised me was how as soon as I asked her to walk on, she homed in on Aaron's voice when he called out to get our attention. My direction was entirely unnecessary as she went right to him, stopping just shy of where he waited with the buckets.

He must have coached his teammates, because they launched into motion without an ounce of hesitation. Sponges threw arcs of glistening water as they left the buckets, sunshine creating rainbows in the mist. With Aaron at her head, Lyric stood perfectly still for the treatment, thick muscles now shimmering like volcanic glass under the onslaught of water. Cardi joined the fray, scraping the water off with practised efficiency. Lyric was allowed a brief drink from the smaller bucket Aaron held before I asked her to walk, not wanting her to stiffen up.

Three times, we repeated the process. Lyric behaved like an absolute lady throughout, even when the veterinarian reappeared for the invasive use of the thermometer. I could tell even before he gave me the nod that she was in good shape, as much from his smile as from the excitement rebuilding in her body. The zing of energy moved along the reins, even slack, and she held her head up, looking for the exit that would lead to the course. She wanted to play!

When our countdown came, Lyric's ears pricked so high I though the tips might touch. Every fibre of her being was prepped, waiting only for me to let her loose. I held no room in my thoughts for Aaron, or my friends, only my indomitable, incredibly generous mare.

"Five, four, three, have a good drive!" the starter called, my cluck of permission coming as the last syllable fell. Lyric launched directly into a trot, pushing my hips back into the seat even as I softened the reins in encouragement. Then the carriage caught up with her powerful stride, scooping me forward into a sensation much like an airplane leaving the ground. A breeze brushed my cheeks, cooler than it had felt earlier, which gave me some peace of mind. Combined with the damp still on her skin, it would give her a little extra energy for the work to come.

Cheers split the air, a chorus of whoops and hollers from my friends as I swung around the side of the vet holding box. The swell of encouragement rose under us like a wave, and I barely had the wherewithal to lift my whip in thanks as Lyric found another gear, carrying us away. Just shy of breaking into a canter, she bowed her neck and curled into the breastplate with a grunt of sheer enthusiasm. Laughter pushed up from my belly and exploded from my mouth, Cardi joining in on the excitement with a whoop of her own. However we placed by the end of the day mattered not one iota, as long as we carried this feeling with us.

Somewhere between the start and the first obstacle, that truth settled into the marrow of my soul. Much as I told Aaron that the ribbons did not matter, some time over the last several years, I had strayed from that path. Not far enough that I could not find my way back, more as though I were just off the track, making every move more difficult because we were not in our groove. The instant I steered myself back, I felt the slightest release as serenity washed over me like chocolate melting on my tongue. Stress disappeared, for I no longer cared whether we competed at a World Championship. Sure, I would aim us in that direction, but now we would take the easier road. The one smoothed out by our connection, colored vividly with joy. It was much easier to navigate when the path was lit so magnificently with love.

Cardi said nothing in those few moments, but I felt her at my back like a ray of sunshine. Many navigators came and went over the years that I chased this dream, but she quickly became much more than a member of the team. She was my friend, the kind that would never hesitate to fight for me, or with me, if that is what I needed. I would not hesitate to step into the struggles she faced either. We were sisters, as much as Lyric and I, and as I was becoming with Jo. Warriors, all of us. Aaron called us fierce, and it was time for me to own that aspect of myself.

"Remind me of option B," I threw back at her, knowing she would catch my meaning without explaining my decision. She answered immediately, the crinkle of paper letting me know she already held the requisite notes.

"From A, we make the third right, first right toward the red butterfly at B, second left hard turn to C, left right serpentine to D, by the purple snail." A quick pause for breath interrupted her excited recitation, but she launched back into it with the same enthusiasm Lyric had come off the start line. "Right turn to head outside, circle right to the second left to get you to E, then another sling to the left for F, by the ladybug. Out is straight over Mount Menstruation!"

I snickered over that particular memory, the horror in Paul and Grady's eyes still vivid in my mind, though not one bit of my attention wavered from the road ahead. Our marker leading toward the first obstacle winked into existence just beside the porta-potties, which brought another feather light brush of humour. I would never look at a porta-potty without remembering, ever again.

"Are you ready?" I asked Cardi, feeling the slight bounce in the shocks that told me she tested her footing.

Lyric felt it too, her focus tightening down, shoulders lifting as I asked for the slight side to side give in her neck. She answered immediately, flexing even as Cardi replied. "Let's give it all we've got!"

And we did, Lyric blasting into a canter as soon as I kissed my lips, Cardi hollering out our number as we shot past the gate into the obstacle. Whatever happened, anyone watching would know that we were competing with our whole hearts.

Aaron

Nerves ate at me as we waited for Jaque to appear at obstacle two. Standing next to her father, I tried not to let it show, but after I bounced on my toes one too many times, he clucked his tongue in what seemed to be a chastisement. Looking down, I found no censure in his expression. Instead, I saw sympathy and no small amount of humor.

"Settle yourself, Aaron. Our Jaque knows what she is about, and her Lyric will not fail her."

"I don't doubt either of them, Jack," I assured him, meaning every word. "Those two are magic together."

His eyes narrowed, studying me so carefully that I went still under the regard. "I am pleased you can see that."

"Even if I went blind, I'd still see their connection." I smiled broadly but looked away when I heard hoofbeats coming in from behind us. A quick glance spotted an up headed bay horse, one I recognized as belonging to Sue Grayson even without a clear view of the driver. While I wished her well for all the kindness she'd shown Jaque even in the brief time I knew her, I tuned them out as they entered the obstacle. I needed Jack's blessing if I had any hope of gaining Jaqueline's acceptance of my upcoming proposal. "Honestly, Jack, your daughter is magic in every way. I've never known a more fiercely giving woman and people respond to her just as readily as the horses do. She's added balance to our Company over the years, becoming an integral part of our team."

Jack waved his hand at me, his lips twisting wryly. "No need to flatter, Aaron. I know what a treasure she is, and I have no doubt she means to make a life with you. She is the only one you needed to convince." Then his gaze went glass sharp, threatening to cut by proximity alone. "Though, should you hurt her, I assure you this little chair will prove no impediment to my beating the hell out of you. Your own mother would be unable to recognize you."

I choked out my reply around a mouthful of gallows amusement, as my mother hadn't recognized me in a long time. A few bruises would do little to change that. "Jack, if I hurt her, it'll never be because I mean to. I'd sooner open my own veins than harm her in any way."

He nodded his acceptance of my answer, though followed through with a lower timber in his voice that had me leaning in close. "I will assume she told you how we lost her mother."

"Yes." I didn't bother to hide the emotion rasping my voice. But I played my words out carefully, not wanting to share too much without Jaque herself being present. "And I don't want to chance anything like that happening, if the doctors find Jaque is at risk."

"That is all I can ask for." Jack sagged in his chair, though he waved me off with a grumpy frown when I touched his shoulder in concern. "Junior, I am sure, has her own mind on this much as she has in all other things."

"You know your daughter well," I confirmed with a grin, then made a quick change of subject as Sue and her horse shot through the final turn in the obstacle, Kent hanging out over the fender to counterweight the speed. We needed something light to pass the time until Jaque appeared. "I heard she spent a lot of time working on airplanes with you when she was little."

A hazy smile of remembrance overtook him, eyes going distant. "Oh, she has no true desire to work on them. But she did everything in her power to insure I took her with me whenever possible. While I could direct her to loosen or tighten a nut as needed, she preferred to hand me tools and talk my ear off as I tinkered. She was a chatterbox in her youth, though it faded some in her teenage years."

And so I listened to him talk, drawing a picture of the Jaque I would have fallen in love with even as a teen. Hell, chances were good I'd have been a goner as soon as I got over the girls have cooties stage. He even showed me a few photos on his phone, from a round faced toddler, to a full cheeked young woman. Each one only confirmed that I loved her more. I would love her when our shoulders were rounded by time and our hair grayed with a thousand worries from a life well lived.

When conversation lulled, my friends, my family, moved closer so that we stood in an expectant knot of humanity. Just in time, too, as deeply thudding hoofbeats came up over the hill. I turned to see Lyric appear through a gap in the massive hedgerow behind us, bright eyes already fixed on the upcoming challenge. Salt foam flecked her chest, but she showed no signs of strain, only an eagerness matched by the people in her carriage. Cardi bounced on her toes, crowing out their number to the people tasked with judging the obstacle. Jaque wore a giddy grin, broken only when she pursed her lips to kiss the mare into a canter.

They blazed through the start markers in an audible gust of wind as they shot past. I leaned forward as if I meant to join them, my stomach growling with the excitement it usually reserved for a good joust or a fast car. By now, I'd watched enough carriages go through that I had memorized the route, so I leaned into the first turn, muscles tightening with a sympathetic thrill. Cardi hung out past the edge of the carriage to keep the wheels on the ground as they dropped down a small incline into the bowl the obstacle had been built into. The whole thing was a mad maze of triangles, set at mind-boggling angles that made the horses work against not just momentum, but gravity as well. Several of the turns held dislodge-able elements, tennis balls balanced precariously on corners. They would fall, causing penalties if the drivers were not careful.

Lyric dropped to a trot the instant they fell into the warren of questions, her ears flicked back toward her driver with unshakable focus. Jaque moved back and then forward in her seat depending on the angles, giving and taking rein length with an enviable ease. All three ladies were a concert of motion, making their extreme sport into art. My heart thudded painfully in my chest when they slung around a turn on the outskirts, dirt flying out in an arc from under the rear wheels as Lyric launched them back down the incline into the middle.

As Jaque shouted at Lyric to gallop for the exit, my vision went blurry around the edges. When they shot through the timer markers in an explosion of violent grace, my knees went weak with relief. It wasn't until Bart pounded me on the back that I remembered to take a breath, which I sucked in with manic desperation.

"Damn, brother, I thought you were past that!" he teased, still slapping my shoulder a few times as I bent over my knees and got my lungs back into a normal rhythm. Then he turned toward Jo when she made noises of concern, revealing my old failing. "He used to hold his breath when he was jousting, sometimes."

"Oh, that's a bad plan! You okay?" Her voice held not an ounce of the amusement she usually enjoyed when she found a weak spot to exploit. "Totally understandable, though. I used to do the same when I was riding in jumper classes. Took a lot of work to fix it."

John chimed in as I straightened. "I about passed out the first time I watched Caroline in a fencing competition, I was so scared for her. Can't imagine how you stayed upright for that demonstration of speed."

Then he *oof*ed as Caroline's elbow met his stomach, her serene smile unwavering as he rubbed his belly in reaction. She always reminded me of old renaissance paintings, a certain gentle acceptance in her manner that invited you to be at peace. "Do not exaggerate, husband. You were fine for the bout. What made you green were the bruises afterward. It amazes me that you became a jouster at all, with your aversion to wounds."

He smiled ruefully as he gathered her against his side in a protective embrace. "Wife, I've never been averse to bruises on me, only you."

To which I nodded agreement. Now that I loved Jaque, I had a better grasp of how difficult it must have been for John to watch Caroline go through her own troubles. You would not know it to look at the beatific woman, but she hid a spine of steel that had endured a greater battle than any jouster might face. Bruises and broken bones from a fall were a small inconvenience compared to fighting against your own body.

Still, I shook off the memories of their struggles and turned to point everyone to the next destination. We had a bit of time to cover the small distance, since Jaque's route demanded a long loop compared to our straight line. Thanks to some skillful planning by the course designers, the last two challenges lay close to each other, and I meant to be there for Jaque for both. In fact, I meant to be there for every obstacle life threw at her, as long as she would let me. Some trials, I'd be able to help her with, but thanks to the examples set by the two couples accompanying Jack and I, I also knew there would be plenty of times I'd have to stand back and cheer Jaqueline on. Luckily, my fierce-hearted fairy made it easy. I would always be her biggest fan whatever challenges she undertook.

❦22❧

Jaque

Perhaps you would like me to tell you we won the marathon, but this is no made for television movie where everything wraps up tidily in beautiful bows. We did move up a placing over-all, and held the best time in obstacle number one, when Lyric was at her most fresh. With two more third best times, one coming from the last obstacle, I could not have been prouder of my mare. She had given me her very best with every beat of her glorious heart.

But my true prizes came later that night, well after all the ribbons were awarded at the competitor's party. Gallant Company departed after they helped with evening chores, Jo being able assistance when it came time to wrap Lyric's legs and Bart helping Aaron get my carriage cleaned and stowed away. John and Caroline's gift came in a basket of snacks to see us through the next day. Cardi had gone home for the night, preferring to sleep in her own bed for a change.

Kent came by our table to say thank you for my endorsement earlier in the day, then lingered for a bit when Aaron engaged him with specific questions about calculating times for marathon. The young man lit up with an energy I envied as he scribbled numbers on a napkin, clearly in his element. Even when I was freshly rested and at my best, I needed to use a calculator for the math involved. But he made his excuses when Malone's pretty groom, Trina, rose from the table behind us. I sensed a romance in the offing there.

That left Papa and Aaron flanking me like sentries. Friendly sentries, mind, and I was grateful for it, with van den Berg's clique sitting so close. It kept the sniping to a minimum, though I felt their comments grow sharper the more wine they consumed. For myself, I sipped slowly at a pleasantly mild white wine, making the glass last as I leaned companionably into Aaron's warmth. The efforts of the day were catching up with me, and now that I had stopped moving, I wanted little more than to curl up with my lover for a long sleep.

"It's a wonder her fat mare made it around the course without having a heart attack." I heard behind me, the words making Aaron tense in readiness for a fight. But I sighed heavily, leaning into his comfort all the more. No sense rising to their bait. They did not mention names, and I did not have the energy for their petty games tonight. Nor would I have wasted it if I did. I was too happy, even in the midst of exhaustion.

Papa excused himself to go sample another bottle of wine, our party tonight sponsored by a local vineyard. Only when he left did my nemeses grow truly bold, Grady leaning back in his chair until he bumped into us. When we turned toward him with matching expressions of disgust, the scent of liquor on his breath overwhelmed me.

"Oh, sorry, didn't notice you there." He addressed Aaron as if I did not exist, smarmy superiority thick in his fake smile. Then he pointed my way with his glass, the amber contents sloshing dangerously close to the rim. Obviously, he was enjoying the work of our title sponsor, a whisky distillery of some renown in the region. "Too bad about her being on the rag. Go to all the effort to help her out, get no reward."

Aaron looked shocked for all of a millisecond. He knew everything that had happened with Cardi and I, and laughed uproariously at our retaliation, so was not surprised there. No, I think the blatant rudeness startled him more than anything else. But my brave knight pushed into the glancing blow and struck back with alacrity, speaking so low that Grady needed to tip his chair back even further to hear.

"Nice thing about being a jouster is that I'm not afraid of a little blood." Grady paled while Paul actually choked on the swallow of wine he'd been in the middle of. "Too bad you pansy asses probably faint at the sight of a paper cut." Then he looked directly over at Maarten, tossing a devil may care smile at the now wan looking man. "Maybe if you grew a pair of balls, you'd be man enough to think for yourself instead of pandering to your coach. But that's probably asking for too much."

As Aaron turned back toward our table, I stifled a laugh against his bicep as Grady actually fell out of his chair. Not so muffled cursing sprang up from the ground, unoriginal invectives about my parentage and Aaron's manhood, but I ignored them as other people around us caught wind of his tirade. He was hushed in short order, and I heard Paul suggesting Grady head to the hotel for the night, a sentiment seconded by multiple parties.

After he was hustled off, I relaxed even further. Much as Paul could be a single-minded jerk, sure that his way was the only right way, he did not have the rabid bite of Grady. As for Maarten, he remained quiet, letting his groupie take the fall without him. I could not imagine the depth of insecurity that led someone so successful in his own country to such petty behaviour in ours.

Yes, ours. If I did not earn a slot for Canada this year, I would regroup, make my life with Aaron, pursue my other dream of breeding horses. If another horse came along that I could chase the World Championships with, I would try again as a citizen of the United States. Perhaps by then Grady would no longer be a thorn in my side, and Paul would let the past lay quiet. But, if not, I would be content having given this particular dream my very best effort. A good legacy to carry forward into the future, whatever it might be.

I nearly dozed off against Aaron's side as I contemplated my dreams, relaxing further as Papa rejoined us. Perhaps my body thought we could indulge in the fantasies all the better if we were asleep. But I was not allowed such a pleasant escape as Aaron straightened in his chair. I followed suit, determined not to be found weak, frowning as my eyes focused on Paul.

He did not address Aaron but spoke directly to me, sky blue eyes I once fancied myself enamored with now flinching as I stared him down. How did I ever think he might be enough for me? "Jaqueline, may I join you for a moment? I don't want to trouble you, but I owe you an apology."

I waved him toward the singular open chair, not at all sorry as both Aaron and Papa regarded him with suspicion. He deserved to squirm. While I wished him no ill will, I would not save him the trouble he heaped on himself. They knew he had done me wrong, and neither were likely to forgive him as quickly as I would. "I am pleased to see that Baltic came through for you today. You must be very proud."

"Kind of you to say so, Jaqueline. Your mare proved her breeding as well," he answered diplomatically, though I refused to allow any wiggle room, immediately calling him out.

"You mean, for a dull work horse?"

He shook his head with a vehemence I could hardly credit. "No, for any horse, Jaque. I've never thought your horse of lesser quality and am sorry for ever making such a petty comment. She may not be fast, or even flashy, but your Lyric is no less an athlete than any other horse competing today. You've both earned your place at Advanced."

"Kind of you to notice," I shot back dryly, letting go of Aaron so I could lean forward onto the table. "Not that we ever needed your approval, even when you and I were an item."

He flinched harder this time, the hand holding his wine goblet visibly shaking before he regained his composure. One did not become an assistant district attorney by falling apart easily. "Fair enough, and lesson learned on my part. Sorry I didn't figure that out sooner." His eyes flicked sideways to Aaron, but quickly came back to me, a tentative smile pushing at his lips. "Though it looks like that's all worked out for the best for you. It's good to see you happy."

"Very happy, thank you," I assured him, dropping my free hand beneath the cover of the table to rest on Aaron's thigh. Though the man beside me looked relaxed, his muscles told me he stood ready to leap to my defense should I ask it. That he remained still in the face of the perceived threat made my heart swell with happiness. He believed I could handle this myself, did not flinch away from my power. Suddenly, I wanted to end this conversation, not to escape from Paul, but to run away with Aaron. To affirm all the love in my life now. "Paul, I hope you find such happiness in your own life. It is absolutely liberating. But while I appreciate your candour, I hope you will be keeping this conversation brief. I do not have the endurance for more upheaval tonight."

He nodded again, this time, as if to himself. "Also fair, and I thank you for your patience thus far. Let me leave you with this," Setting down his wine glass, he spread both hands out on the table as if to show all his proverbial cards. "I'm sorry for being a chicken shit, and for not valuing you. You deserved better, and I'm glad you've found it."

"Thank you. I hope we can be civil with each other going forward, though I will not offer the same to your *friends*." He could not miss the doubtful chill I gave that word, as my idea of friends and his were vastly different.

This time he shook his head, a disappointed cant to his lips. "Yes, well, my association with van den Berg and Malone is at an end. I'm on the hunt for a new coach, it would seem. The cost of their *friendship*," he mimicked my tone almost exactly, "was far too high in many ways, none of them to do with money."

I allowed a small smile then, as we had once argued over how little value money actually held. Lawyers did so love to argue, and at his level, Paul tended to go for the throat. When he told me I only held such noble ideals because I was poor, I had ended our off and on relationship. Life was too short to be with someone so poor spirited, and now I was rich in all the ways that mattered to me.

"For your sake, I am glad." I meant to hurry him along then, but a pair of people approached the table with intent, the woman waving to catch my eye.

As I recognized her, every muscle in my body thrummed to life as if I were back at the start line with Lyric. Adrenaline swept through my veins like lightning racing through the clouds, not quite ready to touch the ground. If not for Aaron's hand smoothing up and down my lower back, I might have flown from my seat in fear and anticipation.

"Jaqueline Sauveterre, I'm Fleur Valentine," the woman said, offering me her hand as she drew up behind my father. Papa turned his wheelchair toward her, causing her to step back. Her face fell into polite lines as she looked down at him. "My apologies, sir, I did not mean to crowd you."

He delivered his most charmingly boyish smile, waving her to step into the space he vacated. "No apology needed, *mademoiselle*, I am simply making room for you to speak with my daughter. Please, go about your business."

While she gave him a doubtful look, the steel nerves that made her a legend in our sport rose to the fore. "Thank you, I appreciate the kindness. Miss Sauveterre, I do not mean to bother you long, but I wanted to be the first to extend congratulations. As the team coach for the Canadian National single drivers, it is my honour to say you have been selected for this year's team."

My eyes darted past her to the man I vaguely recognized as one of the committee members for Equestrian Canada, the governing body for horse sport in my home country. He nodded, the image swimming as I fought back tears of happiness. My knees wobbled as I stood to shake her hand and then his, only Aaron's touch on my back keeping me from collapsing into my chair. "Thank you, I am immensely honoured. Lyric and I will do our best!"

"Judging by your performance over the last several years, that much is stunningly obvious," the woman assured me, a broad smile softening her hawkish regard. "Now, you get back to your handsome companions, and I'm going to go indulge in one last glass of wine before they close the bar. Have a lovely drive tomorrow, and I will be contacting you soon to discuss a training schedule."

Then she melded back into the crowd, moving between tables with ease until I lost sight of her. Still, I stared after her for several seconds, not quite sure I had not imagined the whole thing in some sort of dream. Maybe I had dozed off on Aaron's shoulder, and I would awaken at any moment?

Only Papa rolling back into place so he could clap me into a hug convinced me of the encounter. Half numb, I hugged him back, eyes burning as they stretched wide with shock. We had done it. Lyric and I would represent our country of birth on the world stage. I accepted what seemed to be genuine congratulations from Paul before he made his excuses. Likely, he would spread word of my acceptance, gossip tending to flow even faster than the alcohol at these parties.

Aaron said nothing, which might have concerned me if I could have spared him an ounce of attention. But my brain buzzed too loudly, overwhelmed by a throng of people surrounding my table. They offered advice on all the best ways to travel, what to pack, where I should go to train in the month leading up to the Championships. Much of the information, I let slip through my grasp, knowing the bulk of my itinerary would be set by my coach. I lost track of all the hands I shook, cognizant of only one hand in particular as it rested on the small of my back. Without that touch, I felt I might dissolve away under the well-meaning flood from my peers.

When I finally broke away, Papa pleading his exhaustion, it took a load of will power not to run from the pavilion as if the hounds of hell chased my heels. A strange sensation to struggle with for a woman who had everything she ever dreamed of. I clung to Aaron's hand as we moved down the wide concrete lane toward the barns, sticking to whatever pace Papa set. He maintained a good clip for a man who claimed to be tired, but I could not blame him for being eager to get back to the hotel. I felt wrung out like a dirty, wet towel, and wanted little more than to collapse into a dark corner for a time.

We stopped to check on Lyric, and I moved woodenly into her stall, not even bothering to turn on the lights. The aisleway was lit well enough to show me her relaxation, and my hands told me the rest of the story, her body evenly warm and supple to the touch. Only when I turned to leave again did Aaron finally speak, catching my upper arms in his hands before I ran into him.

"Jaque, your dad and I are going to go get the truck. Do you want to spend a few minutes alone with Lyric?" I stared up at him with a slack jaw, not quite comprehending his meaning. The aisle lights behind him cast his face in shadow, so I could not read his features for clarification. But his thumbs caressed my arms as I began to tremble, and when he leaned in to press his lips to my forehead for a lingering kiss, I felt nothing but his love. "Stay. Talk to your girl. I'll be back shortly." Then he let go of me, turning toward Lyric for a gentle stroke of her neck. "Congratulations, war mare."

He left without another word, cutting me adrift, but I was not alone. No, I had another anchor inches away, her damp breath skating over the back of my elbow as she approached. I turned, managed a calm touch to her chin. She immediately lifted her nose, presenting the tiny white mark on her lip to me. Tears of gratitude filled my eyes, a wash of salt and emotion quickly dripping down my cheeks as I kissed that delicate spot.

"*Mon coeur*," I meant it to be a verbal caress, but it came out as a hoarse sob that I tried to choke off. She deserved so much better than my fractured emotions.

Proving my point in the extreme, Lyric slid her chin over my shoulder and curled her neck, pulling me into her. My hands clutched into her mane with an unflattering desperation, but she

leaned in, going against the nature of all horses to escape the
grasping of a predator. She had held me through worse, in all our
years together. The only difference was that this time, these were
not tears of heartbreak. No, they were sweet tears of happiness too
long contained, joy finally breaking the dam I constructed when
faced with so many people. Here, I could safely let it pour out,
wetting the shoulder of her wool sheet with evidence of my
overwhelming bliss.

I had mopped up most of the mess when Aaron returned,
toweling Lyric's shoulder dry before putting on her light blanket
for the night. He did not rush me, patiently waiting as I said one
more goodnight to my partner, my oldest friend. When I finally
latched the stall door and turned toward him, he cupped my cheeks
in both hands and stared into my eyes with a reassuring intimacy.
"Happy tears, yes?"

"Yes," I promised, giving him the genuine smile I could not
find before. Covering his hands with mine, I loved how his thick
knuckles pressed into the cup of my palm. "Thank you for seeing
what I needed."

He smiled with a tenderness I cherished, my lips tingling with
the urge to kiss him. "I may have taken a long time to truly see
you, Jaqueline, but now, even if I went blind, I would still know
your heart. Now, how about we let your lady friend get some well-
deserved rest. I'll take you back to the hotel where I can love you
to sleep."

An offer that answered my need again, one I replied to with a
kiss, content in the knowledge he would hear me without a word
being said.

"Hurry up, Prince Charming!" Cardi called out as we walked
slowly down the aisleway of the stabling area. I needed to make a
brief trip to the vendor area, Lyric's hoof oil having leaked all over
the bottom of my grooming tote. While I could salvage the brushes
with a good washing, I did not have the time nor leisure to fix them
before the afternoon. I would have to buy some new things to make
do, not a cost I looked forward to when I had a down payment to
make on the carriage company buy out at the end of the month.

Soleil barked and spun a circle on the end of her leash, excited by the sound of running feet. I looked back, grinning to see Aaron carrying his big grey cat like a giant fur collar, both hands supporting the creature so he did not bounce over much. They caught up with us before we made the corner, my champion not even out of breath from the short sprint. He marched along beside me with the barest hint of a smile on his face, as if some secret teased at his thoughts.

"All is well at home?" I asked, knowing he had just wound up a phone call to Bart. As co-owners of their jousting troupe, they were in constant communication regarding business decisions. Being brothers, they tended to share much outside their professional obligations as well. Soon, I would be in the thick of that close-knit relationship, sharing their home, and their farm. While Aaron assured me that everyone wanted me to join them, I could not help feeling concern. How long would it take for us all to drive each other crazy in such tight proximity?

"All is perfect," he answered, touching the small of my back as if he could feel my worry and meant to soothe it. "Though we might need to swing by the farm after we drop off Lyric, if you don't mind? I've got a quick bit of paperwork to get signed before the day gets ahead of us, then I am yours until Wednesday's joust practice.

Though I could not understand why he might need me to go with him, I agreed readily. He gave so much of his time to me, the least I could do is return the favour. Besides, I looked forward to having him to myself for a while. A more than fair trade.

We arrived at vendor's row in short order, cargo trailers of all sizes parked between massive oak trees as people wandered along in the spring sunshine. Papa had made himself at home, sitting beneath an awning attached to a massive semi-trailer, chatting with one of the shopkeepers. He waved as we passed by, but did not look inclined to come with us, so I continued on. Much as I appreciated petting over finely tanned leather and admiring the clean lines of a new carriage, I needed none of those things. Today, my needs were much smaller and more specific.

I lost Cardi at one of the hat shops, my heart twinging with the urge to join her. Hats were my one fashion vice, but I would not buy another until we knew how much room Aaron had for my already extensive collection.

Several vendors later, I came to a smaller trailer adorned with fancy scrollwork, the rear gate lowered to allow entry. A petite woman in a giant sun hat waved us inside from the little counter built into the nose of the trailer. "Come on in, folks! What can I help you find this morning?"

I stepped inside, inhaling deeply of the perfume known only in tack shops. Leather, metal polish, coat conditioner and the sweet sharp scent of new things combined to intoxicate the horse lover, more effective than even alcohol in loosening one's reservations. That smell beckoned you to open your wallet, to use that charge card. Surely our horses deserved the very best, after all.

But, with a goal in mind I was determined to maintain some sort of budget. My grip on Soleil's leash tightened, mimicking a firm hold on my resolve. "I am in need of new grooming tools, thanks to a mishap with the hoof oil. If you could point me the right way?"

Oh, she went me one better, sweeping around the counter to give me the complete tour of her available selection. There was so much to tempt me, from a new on the market massage tool, to the raw silk rub rag imported from Europe. I admired a set of brushes with all-natural fibres and leather backs, even though they were too big for my hands. She even showed off a collection of hand-crafted wooden grooming totes that were more finely made than most furniture. I nearly yielded to the one painted in my colours, running longing fingertips over the handle as if I meant to pick it up. But, in the end, I resisted, stepping up to the counter with only three brushes and a new container of hoof oil to pay for.

She smiled when I produced my wallet, pointing toward the back of the trailer. "My apologies, miss, I am under orders to refuse your payment. That gentleman there already gave me his card."

I swiveled around, objection already on my lips. Much as I appreciated his generosity, I refused to allow Aaron to cover for me. However, the man at my back was not Aaron, but my Papa.

"Happy late birthday, Junior," he said, stealing away my pride in an instant as he rolled down the narrow aisle to join us. I should have known. Every year, he surprised me with something to support my carriage driving habit. Last time, it had been a hat I coveted. In fact, it was the hat I meant to wear that very afternoon.

"Papa! Thank you, but there is no need. I am capable of paying for Lyric's things."

"I have no doubt, *ma fille*, but you will let me have my way in this. I am allowed to spoil my girls, am I not?"

Considering that he served as one of my three sponsors, I flinched away from accepting more help from him. He made good money flying tourists around and ferrying people to and from the backcountry. But he deserved to keep a little back for himself.

"And I am grateful you love us so, Papa," I conceded, knowing he would only grow more stubborn if I argued the point. "Thank you."

"Only the best for my girls!" He patted my arm, then patted Soleil when she reared up to ask for her share of the attention. "Yes, all my girls! Now, what else do you need? Surely, there is more than this!"

The shop keeper, being a savvy saleswoman, swooped around me to show him all the things I admired. By the time they finished, the tote I wanted was full to overflowing and a bag besides, Papa scooping up everything purple or silver that he could find. We owned a new array of shampoos and conditioners, sprays to detangle and shine, and even a liniment for after exercise. I did object to the brushes that were too big for me, or anything I truly would not use, but in the end, Aaron needed to help me carry everything back to the stables.

I endeavored to use as many of the new things as possible when it came time to ready Lyric for her afternoon showing. She gleamed in the sunshine, her coat picking up colors from everything around her. The braids along her neck sparkled faintly, silver rubber bands looped at the base for extra decoration. An onyx work of art from nose to hooves, offset only by the brightly polished chrome hardware on her harness. Her wavy-haired tail hung heavy, swinging lazily like a church bell not quite ready to ring. Papa rolled around her, inspecting the results of his purchases, running his hands over every inch he could reach.

"She looks fit and ready, Junior. Every inch a champion, like her driver."

"Thank you, Papa." I leaned down and kissed his cheek, reinforcing my gratitude. It was not often I could touch him, and I meant to take advantage of every second. Tomorrow, he would fly north again. "Now, would you keep her company? Cardi will be back soon, but I must change quickly if we are to be on time."

He waved me away. "Go, Junior. Your mare has known me almost as long as she has known you. I am sure we can pass the time together amiably enough."

Driving home the point, Lyric stretched her neck out and lipped my father's hair with easy familiarity. So, I hurried off, determined not to shorten my warmup time. I could sacrifice some of my own grooming in favour of Lyric, if need be.

Before my alarm rang at the hour mark, I was not only dressed, but Lyric was hitched, every member of my wonderful team coming together in concert. I had plenty of time to let my mare walk, loosening every muscle as the blood warmed. She looked her fill at the circus of the warmup arena, drew deep breaths that lifted her ribs, and slowly limbered every joint along her lengthy spine. We even took advantage of a relative lull in activity to have our bit checked for legality and the rear axle of the carriage measured so the cones would be set correctly.

For myself, I tried not to look too closely at what went on in the middle of that circus. While they had a massive area to work in, Grady Malone worked his horse in tight circles around his coach. The poor animal reached so far behind the bit that his nose nearly touched his sweaty chest. Lather raised on his neck, scraped and muddied by the reins. Likely, his mouth would have gaped away from the ruthless pressure of the bit, but his jaw was held shut with a noseband so tight it would leave creases in his skin.

Physically shaking myself to take my mind off the travesty, I knew I was powerless to change things. Nothing they did flouted the rules, though the ring steward kept an eye on them, a small reassurance. Should Grady stray too far, the powers that be were ready to intervene. All I could do is focus on my own horse.

When I took a turn at the practice gates set up to one end of the arena, my nerves got the best of me for a moment. I second guessed my angle, over adjusting the bend, then promptly ran over the cone on the inside of the turn. The distinct thump of the rubber cone against the inside of the rear wheel made Lyric hunch in distaste. She hated the way my body changed whenever we hit a cone, echoing the way my tummy clenched tight. Noises, vibrations, actual physical bumping from the carriage, those she could ignore as if they were insignificant dust specks. But when I felt off, she mirrored me completely.

This worked to my advantage as well, which she promptly demonstrated when I blew out a breath from my cheeks and let my belly go soft. I let her move on around the perimeter of the cones, lifting my whip hand to thank the kind person resetting the cone for me. Lyric settled back into a free-flowing trot, stretching her neck down as I fed her the reins, then coming back up as I shortened them.

"Lighten those feet!" I heard as we made an approach toward another set of gates, my eyes flicking sideways to see Lillian Beard just outside the arena. As if our lesson were yesterday, my body responded, shoulders rolling back, lengthening the distance between my lap and the underside of my ribs.

Lyric coiled up like a snake, her back shortening, shoulders lifting. From there, I could turn her with the slightest breath along the reins. This time, we came through the tightly grouped cones with clearance to spare! I kept her at a strong trot, swooping back around so I could offer Lillian a salute in thanks before I asked Lyric to walk again.

"That the gal you're gonna train with?" Cardi asked as we stopped for a short break under one of the shade trees near the main arena.

"As often as I can," I assured her, though my eyes drifted to the cones course as we spoke, tracing the pattern from beginning to end. Only one spot truly concerned me, the cones facing toward the arena wall with barely enough space to make a proper U-turn toward the next gate. The team on course slowed down in order to safely clear the gates without knocking down a ball, proving my concern. I thought Lyric and I could safely handle it with a little more momentum, but not much. "She has recently relocated to Kentucky, conveniently. Between her and the team coach for Canada, I have no doubt we will make improvements."

Two more teams completed the course as I studied their lines, but then the ring steward called for me to make ready. Lyric felt my attention sharpen well before I even began to gather the lines in readiness to move. She stepped out smartly, following my guidance toward the in gate while several people offered us well wishes for a good drive. I smiled at them all, but never met a single person's eyes, keeping my focus on Lyric.

That is, until I heard Aaron's usually crisp voice stumbling through the language of my childhood. "*Bonne chance, mesdames!*"

Oh, he said the sweetest things, even when he did not say them perfectly. I gave him better than a smile, blowing him a silent kiss as he stood beside my Papa. He caught it, pressed it to his heart, a knight in every deed, even when out of his armour.

For good measure, I blew another kiss to Papa, who flushed with the unexpected affection. Though I wished I could have stopped, to have lingered with them both, my number rang out with a note of command that could not be denied. So, I exhaled, sat up tall, and went to face the waiting challenge.

As I drove into the arena, the boundaries marked with a low white fence and a thicket of orange cones growing prolifically in the middle, my attention went first to the judges occupying a station along the rail. Halting Lyric nearby, I lifted my whip in respectful salute. One of them rang a bell signaling we could begin, and a vibration of energy ran up the lines into my hands as Lyric's ears perked. She knew our time had come.

Still, I kept things light, clucking softly to set us in motion. We curved to the right, tracing half of a perfect circle in the turf to aim ourselves for the start timers. The silence in the arena felt thick, as though we carved our way through an invisible fog. No breeze moved the flags over the bleachers, only Lyric's muffled hoofbeats and the soft whir of the carriage wheels breaking the quiet. Almost as though we were completely alone.

Except we were not. Lyric's ears tuned in on the first gate and I felt Cardi's excitement behind me like a shadow made of light. As we navigated a serpentine, I saw Papa's faith in us reflecting in the shiny glow of Lyric's coat. When we shot over the bridge at full charge, I felt Aaron with us, throwing himself completely into our world, seeing us as fierce warriors in our own right. And when I made that U-turn, barely escaping the second gate without incurring a penalty, I felt all the other drivers present. Each of us faced these same challenges, and for the most part, we felt each

other's successes and failures with a keenness I had never
experienced in any other sport. When we broke into a flat gallop to
chase the time to the finish line, I grinned, knowing in my soul that
I was exactly where I belonged.

My elation lasted all of a minute, though, as I emerged from the
arena to the sight of Grady Malone's poor horse balking. The lanky
gelding backed away from the gate, eyes rolling, hind legs
spraddled as he pushed into the breeching. Grady cracked his whip
overhead, desperately trying to send his horse into the main arena.
All this accomplished was causing nearly every horse present to
lurch forward, even Lyric tensing in preparation to go. I joined the
rest of the drivers on the far end of the arena, our low voices
soothing even as Grady began to curse.

"This is bullshit! Trina, get your ass down, give him a lead in!"

His petite groom jumped down from her seat on the back of the
carriage, scurrying for the horse's head. Her hands went to the
bridle and the horse shuddered in relief, bowing down to meet her.
Sadly, Grady chose that very moment to smack the horse with the
lash again. The gelding flung his head in objection, catching the
tiny woman right in the temple with the side of his bony cheek.
She dropped like a stone, falling right at the feet of the now frantic
horse where he could not see her!

"God damn it, horse!" Grady shouted, sawing the reins in an
attempt to regain control. This made things worse as the animal
reared up in the shafts, seeking some kind of relief. He twisted to
the side, hooves coming down less than a foot away from the
woman on the ground.

My heart raced even as I calmly steered Lyric away from the
madness, fearing that any moment would see a tragic wreck.
"Cardi?"

"On it," she answered, carriage shifting with the loss of her
weight. In seconds, she stood at Lyric's head, though she did not
touch her. If things got worse, the best thing would be for me to
leave entirely.

Like leaves being chased along on a brisk wind, people moved
into the arena with feigned calm and needful urgency. The breath
left my lungs to see Aaron in their midst, striding to put himself
between the fallen woman and the horse without an ounce of
hesitation. Some of the others moved to surround Grady, and while

we were too far away to hear them, you could not miss the growl of demand in the very way they stood. The reins slackened as Grady deflated like a stuck balloon. Aaron stepped up to the animal's head then, hands going straight to either side of the bridle just as I had shown him.

A pair of EMTs converged on Trina as members of the ground jury herded Grady further away with Aaron's help. Urgent motion rose and fell like waves as capable hands tended to needy souls. In short order, Grady's horse was unhitched from the carriage, determined volunteers pulling the carriage toward the exit as Aaron followed them out with the still shivering horse. They paraded from the ring, Grady bringing up the rear like a dilapidated caboose as he shuffled past his groom with a look of true worry on his pale face. That sign of humanity was the only flash of hope, though, as the medical team strapped Trina to a backboard and the ring steward asked us to clear the area so the ambulance could come in.

I let everyone else go first, as Lyric had done her time in urban settings. Little would surprise her, if I let her watch, but many of the more high-strung animals might take exception. Only when the last of the four-in-hands cleared out did I head for the exit, Cardi jumping into her seat on the move.

Thankfully, this horse park had plentiful room for the various turnouts. Some of the drivers headed down the asphalt path, making a pleasant Sunday drive out of an otherwise tense situation. Others parked in the shade, either because they had plenty of time before their drive or they were finished. But beneath all the feigned calm remained a buzz of worry and no small bit of gossip.

Sue pulled up next to me, her sensitive mare tense from all the energy, fidgeting with the bit and flicking her tail. "Well, I think that's the last we'll be seeing of Malone."

"It better be," Kent grumbled from his seat behind Sue, the young man glowering toward the flashing lights of the ambulance. "Trina's a nice girl, she didn't deserve that. Malone's an ass."

I nodded but kept my peace otherwise. No sense adding to the drama. "I hope she will be okay. And the horse. Poor fellow did not mean to hurt her."

"I think they'll be fine," a welcome voice interjected. Aaron appeared between us; jaw still tight even though he smiled. "I overheard the EMTs working on the woman, and they thought she was just going to have a heck of a goose egg. She was talking when we walked out, worried about Bruno."

A heavy breath escaped me, taking much of my worry with it. "Ah, that is promising. Any good horse person would be thinking the same."

"What about the horse?" Sue asked, leaning forward a bit as her mare began to relax in Lyric's steady company.

Aaron patted my knee as he walked past, the brief touch as reassuring as the way he made sure Lyric could see him around the blinders before he touched her. After a soft stroke along her neck, some of the tension left his shoulders too. My dear mare had that effect on so many.

"I'd say Bruno is gonna be alright too. His owner, one of Grady's sponsors, was making arrangements to take the horse home as I left."

What worry remained blew away on the soft breeze that chased his words, as if the world held its breath as we waited for the news.

It took a bit of time to get the show back on track. Lyric enjoyed a lovely nap in the shade as our class completed their rounds, and Papa joined us as well. As we all chatted, I caught Aaron throwing speculative looks at my father, as if he were trying to finish a particularly challenging puzzle. Before I could ask what was on his mind, word spread that they were gathering the Advanced single horses for the awards ceremony.

"Aaron, would you ride with me again?" I asked as I gently gathered the reins, allowing Lyric to wake up without rush.

He cleared his throat and ran a hand through his hair, a gesture I had not seen from him in some time. "Actually, Jaque, maybe your dad would like to go?"

My cheeks flushed as I looked to Papa, hating that Aaron put him on the spot. While I had taken my father for rides in a cart, getting him up high enough for the carriage had always been beyond our means. But Papa looked to Aaron, staring him in the eye for several long seconds that made my heart stutter. Had my boyfriend alienated my father in one fell swoop?

A quick jerk of Papa's chin put Aaron into motion, Papa following suit. They moved right up to the side of the carriage,

Papa locking the wheels of his chair as Aaron crouched down to his level.

"Cardi!" I yelped, now more worried than I had been over the near wreck with Grady's horse. While I trusted Lyric more than any other horse alive, if she were to move at the wrong time, it could end in disaster!

My steadfast navigator appeared in a blink, heading Lyric with low murmured words and familiar hands. Papa looped an arm around Aaron's neck, the other reaching up for the metal arm of the passenger seat.

"One, two, three," Aaron counted, standing up on three, his muscular arms flexing with the effort of cradling a grown man. I could hardly breathe as Papa transferred his grip to the back of the seat, hauling himself sideways as Aaron kept him in the air. With a thunk, Papa's weight hit the cushion, then he deftly scooped his thin legs into line with his body. The heavy combat boots he favoured weighted his feet into place, and he swiveled toward me with a boyish grin of accomplishment that Aaron echoed.

"Jaque?" Cardi nudged verbally as the ring steward called my name, leaving me out of time to thank Aaron for this gift. Lyric picked up a trot the instant I clucked, Cardi swinging up on the back as we moved. Emotions buffeted me with hurricane strength as I accepted our yellow third place ribbon, its tails fluttering gently as we rejoined our peers in the lineup. But I let those grand emotions scour my heart, so much goodness creating a beautiful ache in my chest. Papa smiled as though he were king of the world, a completely happy expression I only ever saw when he flew.

When we fell in for the victory pass behind Sue and Paul, my joy finally bubbled over in another set of happy tears as we made a lap around the arena. Lyric responded to that energy with an offer to canter, but I channeled it instead into an extended trot that she carried all the way through the exit gate. Like a giddy boy, Papa egged us on. "*Voler sur, mes filles!*"

To be courteous to my fellow drivers, I brought Lyric to a walk as we emerged from the arena. She felt fresh enough for a good gallop, but that would only stir up the other horses. We made the quiet walk back to the barn, Lyric's hips swinging with contentment as Aaron followed in the golf cart. But I vowed to myself that next time Papa came to visit we would show him our wings. After all, he was the one who first believed Lyric and I could fly.

Aaron

While Jaque called me a hero for helping Malone's horse and groom, I played it off. Because what I'd done paled in comparison to the chest swelling pride I felt when she watched me lift her father up into her carriage. Not an easy feat, either, as the man was packed with muscle from the waist up. But it was totally worth every burning second of effort to see them take a turn around the arena with matching expressions of delight as Lyric flew along.

After the whirlwind of activity and emotions of the weekend, we were all subdued at dinner. A contented quiet linked us all as we chewed through the burgers and fries that were Jaque's end of competition treat. She only ordered a small french fry, so I wasn't much surprised to find her picking at mine once hers were gone. When I pushed my plate toward her in open invitation, she demurred with an embarrassed frown. But not ten seconds later, her fingers strayed with unconscious hunger. I leaned back and put my arm around the back of her chair, happy to give them over. She deserved every reward, and I intended to spend my lifetime making sure she received as many as possible.

On an even lighter note, I caught sight of Trina, Malone's former groom, at a table with Kent and his parents. The guy couldn't have been more solicitous of her, making sure of her comfort before his own, his attention fixed on every word she said. No surprise considering his earlier vehement response to Malone's treatment of her. I grinned to myself. Being in love with the right woman brought out the best in me, and I had only admiration for anyone else willing to risk their heart for another.

The next morning, we made sure of Lyric's comfort before returning Jack to the little airstrip where he proudly showed off his plane. We spoke of another visit in the summer, if he could get away from his work. He hoped we might have time to take a flight with him, which I immediately agreed to. I already got a hell of a rush flying commercial and could hardly wait to go up in his much smaller DeHavilland Beaver.

We stayed long enough to watch him take off from the lounge area, the heavy bodied white plane quickly lost to sight in the vast expanse of blue sky and fluffy clouds. Jaque didn't cry as she stared after him, but her arms tightened around my waist as if she were afraid to let go. I said nothing, only returned the embrace with equal fervor. There would be many times in our life together when one or the other of us would have to leave. But I hoped she knew I would always return to her, as soon as I was able.

That hope drove me the rest of the morning as we hooked up the trailer and loaded Lyric for the trip home. Traffic conspired against my plans, two accidents making a snarl of the highway. While I was grateful neither one looked very serious, I hated the delays. Thankfully, with Jaque in the driver's seat, I could keep Bart and Jo informed of the change in plans. We texted with rapid fire speed as the miles crawled by, my knee starting to jiggle with impatience.

"I am sorry to make you late." Jaque's needless apology made me aware of how much my mood affected her. Her mouth thinned into a line of distress, likely worrying that the delays were impacting the paperwork I told her about. "Is Bart upset? Will this cause problems with your contracts?"

"Takes an awful lot to make Bart upset, *ma fleur*," I assured her, blowing out my cheeks in an effort to calm down. Boris got in on the action, leaving the bed he shared with Soleil in the back seat to curl up in my lap like a living pillow. My hands began petting without conscious thought, his instant purr allowing me to relax even further. "And the paperwork will keep. Bart just rearranged some things, which he's very good at. More than anything, I'm looking forward to an afternoon in your company. No work, no schedule, no obligations."

A smile softened her cheeks as she put her attention back on the traffic around us. "I cannot tell you how much I am looking forward to it. We shall only have the cottage for a few more months, and I intend to take advantage of the privacy."

I agreed, for her sake, not wanting her to worry a second longer when she was already so concerned about her horse as cars dove into the space in front of her truck. She handled it like a pro, keeping the rig at a slow crawl, eyes constantly searching her mirrors and the road ahead for hazards. Much as I preferred to be the one in the driver's seat, I'd finally found someone I didn't mind playing passenger for.

Well, navigator, really. When she needed a place to pull off and use the restroom, I got on my phone and found the nearest gas station with enough room for a large rig. I took Soleil out to stretch her legs, Boris draped over me like a protective cape. My neck was sweaty by the time we got back in the truck, and I wondered how we'd make things work once summer arrived. He was too much cat to wear in the hotter months.

As I climbed back in the truck, Jaque emerged from the gas station convenience shop with a paper coffee cup cradled reverently in her hands. She walked with purpose, likely as ready as I was to be home, which drove me back to my phone for a possible detour. By the time her seat belt clicked into place, I found an alternative route to suggest.

Taking the backroads, we arrived at her place just before lunch. The horses in the field broke into a run as we pulled in the driveway, strident neighing welcoming Lyric and Jaque home. Soleil barked with equal excitement, making circles in her bed as Jaque parked in front of the barn. Having been to the Teller's place on multiple occasions, I felt a thrill knowing Jaque would still receive a similar greeting. There would be a great place to park, and plenty of room to turn around her big trailers. Which made me all the more eager to get Lyric settled in for the day, so I could watch those same realizations dawn on Jaque's face.

We didn't take terribly long, with Jaque so concerned about keeping me from my work. Lyric went out in the field with her friends, stripped naked of any blanket now that the day had warmed. There was a bit of squealing as the horses crowded around her, but she cleared them off with the threat of teeth and hoof. Once social concerns were met, she promptly trotted over to a patch of dust and dropped down to roll, wiggling with enthusiasm as she worked the dirt into her shiny coat.

"I don't envy you that grooming job," I said as Jaque watched Lyric regain her feet, launching herself into the air for a spectacular buck that testified to her wellbeing. After working hard for the entire weekend, I would have expected a lengthy nap, not the victory lap she led around the pasture. Tail in the air, head held high, she galloped a circuit of the field with the rest of the herd strung out behind her.

Jaque smiled broadly as the group slowed, then stopped near the water trough, Lyric taking a dainty drink. The rest waited their turn, keeping a respectful distance until she finished. "Worth every ounce of sweat to let her be a horse, I think. Your own horses appreciate being kept outside, as you well know."

"Yeah, true enough." I'd argue they were field kept mostly because I didn't want to have to shovel that much manure on a daily basis, but they certainly seemed happier outside. Byz in particular got extra squirrely when kept in, so I considered it a good trade for the extra grooming required. "Anything else need to be done before we head out? I can get things unloaded while you tend the horses."

She shook her head, hair rippling like a living thing as it caressed her cheek. "No, everything else can wait. I have kept you long enough."

A quick whistle called up Soleil, though Boris remained absent until I started my truck. He came trotting around the side of the carriage barn, chirping indignantly as he came close enough to be heard over the engine. The sound chastised me more ably than any guilt trip from my mother, though it morphed into purring the instant I scooped him into my arms. I'd never be able to sneak away from him, that was for sure.

Not that I wanted to. I didn't want to miss a minute with those I loved, not one second. There would be time enough where I would be away from them, which made the moments we did have so much more precious. Like when Jaque took up her spot on the passenger side and immediately reached forward to adjust the radio to the station she liked. I grabbed hold of her fingers before she could fiddle with the knobs, smiling when she froze.

"My lady, for your traveling enjoyment, I've programmed your favorite to button number three."

She relaxed into my grip then, until one small finger poked between mine. I followed her motion as she gently tapped the correct button, her ready smile blossoming as the mellow sounds of a contemporary jazz vocalist filled the cab. Then she drew my hand toward her, pressing a kiss to one of my thick knuckles. "Thank you for making room for me in your life."

"The room was always there," I assured her after gulping my heart down out of my throat. Her eyes, so rich with warmth, looked suspiciously damp. To be fair, mine stung with emotion too. "Thank you for finding the door."

Then I pulled my hand away before I could jump the gun, and shifted the truck into gear, suddenly in a much greater hurry to get where we were going.

Quiet reigned as we motored along, Jaque's eyes half-closed as she stroked Soleil's ears. The small dog looked to be in the same almost doze, both of them worn out from the long weekend. Made it much easier for me, as I didn't have to worry as much about the way my leg kept bouncing. My palms prickled with dampness, causing me to constantly adjust my grip on the steering wheel. I resisted the urge to scrub a hand through my hair, knowing it was my worst tell. Besides, I didn't want to look completely deranged when we got to the Teller's place.

Jaque didn't notice we weren't headed for the Company farm until I pulled into the gravel lot between the house and the barn, eyes flying open with surprise as I set the parking brake and turned off the engine.

"Aaron, where are we?"

"Just the neighbor's place," I assured her, surreptitiously scrubbing my prickling palm along my thigh as I exited the truck. "Bart and I come over to check on things whenever they go out of town. He asked me to stop by and make sure Buttermilk had enough hay."

"Oh! I would like to see her, if you think they will not mind my being here." She climbed out of the truck before I could get around to open the door for her, much to my chagrin. So much for playing up the romance. Still, I appreciated how invested she was in the wellbeing of a horse she only spent a month out of the year with. "She is a lovely girl."

"And you are a lovely woman." I pulled her in next to me, guiding her toward the big, open barn where Buttermilk kept company with a small flock of sheep in inclement weather. Only half of it was fenced off for them to use, the rest serving as a storage area. As we stepped into the dark interior from the bright sunshine, my eyes needed a moment to adjust. But memory steered my free hand to the light switch, revealing piles of wood, some tarp covered cars and a stack of hay that nearly reached the rafters. Teller kindly lent us hay when our supply was obliterated in the fire, and I returned the favor, restocking him in full once the insurance money came in. But in that moment, what I saw in my mind's eye were Jaque's carriages filling up the space. It would be just big enough.

A quick check of the hay manger maintained the fiction I created, though Buttermilk delayed progress, trotting inside to see if she could scam a treat off of us. She had trained Jim's wife to bring her carrots, not hard to do when you looked like a storybook unicorn even when filthy. Those same doe eyes sucked Jaque right in, resulting in a lengthy bout of petting as the two reacquainted themselves.

That left me to poke around in the barn, the tarp covered vehicles tugging at my curiosity with a strength I didn't even try to resist. I knew Jim liked to restore cars—I'd seen him head out for weekend drives in a motley collection of antiques, from an immaculate Packard to a rickety looking Model A. Judging by the boxy shape hiding under the first dust-laden canvas, he had an old delivery truck. Under another, that I lifted the corner of for confirmation, I found a roadster up on blocks.

But the one closest to the main door looked to have a much leaner profile, completely unlike the rest of his collection. Experience told me there was a muscle car under the fabric, and I paused before touching the tarp. My stomach, already a tangle of fast paced butterflies racing qualifying laps, gave a gurgle of hunger that had absolutely nothing to do with how long it had been since breakfast.

Tentatively, I cupped my palm around the corner of the car, then shivered as I found the steel in the exact shape of the car of my dreams. Before I could chicken out, I grasped the canvas, noting it looked cleaner than the rest of the them. Holding my breath against the dust, and in sheer anticipation, I stepped back, pulling the canvas slowly after me. Regardless of my excitement, I didn't want to scare Buttermilk with any sudden noises.

Though the blue paint appeared faded with age, I recognized the slight angle of the rear end immediately. I'd stared at far too many photos of the late 1960's Dodge Charger not to know its lines with ridiculous intimacy. On the rare occasion I'd been able to get to a car show, they drew me in every single time. By the time I exposed the car, I was almost hyperventilating with excitement. Every sleek line whispered promises of speed on a dark highway, the chrome glimmering even in the meager light provided by the lone bulb.

When Jaque touched my arm, I jumped, so lost in my fantasies I forgot my purpose in being there in the first place. "Oh, sorry, I didn't know Mr. Teller had this. Let me put the cover back on, and we can go make sure his cat has food."

Judging by her sympathetic smile, she wasn't fooled in the least. Still, she grabbed a corner of the tarp and helped me guide it back into place. "Hmm, it would seem to me you need to have a talk with your neighbor. It would be a shame for such a beauty to remain hidden away when it could be very cherished."

My heart panged with delicious pain as she confirmed one more time how right she was for me. Made it much easier to turn away from the car of my dreams when the woman of my dreams waited.

I led her to the house, walking slow so I could study the property with a critical eye. Bart was right, there was work that needed to be done to get it ready for more horses. But the bones were excellent, and we were more than capable of the work. Sweat equity would polish this jewel into something Jaque could be proud of.

The house itself looked most promising. A small yard would suit Soleil perfectly, and there were plenty of sunny windows for Boris to bask in. Though not as big as the crew house at the farm, the mere fact that it looked nothing like my childhood home made it easier to imagine growing a family with Jaque. We still had no idea if it were possible, but I wanted to plan for every future. We could even adopt, if she were willing. This place was big enough for a family, but not too much for just the two of us either.

We went in through the kitchen, since that's where the cat bowl was kept. I didn't expect to see the actual cat, as Jim said it didn't care for strangers, so I quickly tipped a little extra kibble into the dish by the counter. They would be back before dinner, contrary to what I told Jaque. This was all a ruse, an excuse to show her the property.

"They've got a pretty nice place, I think," I ventured, as Jaque stood awkwardly in the middle of the attached dining room, holding her elbows. A hard posture to read. Could be she just felt weird being in someone's home without knowing them. Or maybe she was getting a bad vibe off the place? "Wouldn't mind having a house like this, to share with you. Reminds me a little of your cottage."

She thawed a bit at that, eyes filling with speculation as she began to look around. "Oh, yes, that would be lovely. Though the yellow paint is a bit bright for my tastes, I think it very homey." Peeking through the open door that led to the front room, she softened completely. "There is a fireplace. Would be a cozy place to curl up at the end of the day."

Blowing out a quick breath to steel my nerves, I reached for the little box Jo left on the counter for me, hidden behind the cat food canister. The soft leather texture gave me something to fiddle with as I walked over to Jaque and put my arm around her.

"On that thought, how would you feel about moving in here when your time is up at French Silver?" She went so still against my side, I feared I'd screwed up, which made my mouth start running in a desperate attempt to salvage the situation. "I mean, I know there's plenty to do before its ready for Lyric. And we can change the paint easily enough. Bart and I can fix practically anything you want. There's another barn on the other side of the house, for the horses to have stalls, and there's plenty of room for your carriages and trailers. But I figured you'd be happier if we had our own space, so you could do your own thing without all of the Company coming and going." I sucked in a quick breath to fuel my babbling, then continued. "If you don't like it…"

At that, she stepped around to face me. The tears on her cheeks wrecked me more thoroughly than if I'd taken a sledgehammer to the car in the barn. Walking out on my mother, the hurt from my former fiancée leaving me, combined with the guilt over my Dad, and the sadness from losing Argo all made a tiny ant pile compared to the mountain of hurt avalanching into my chest. Shit, shit, shit!

"You hate it. I'm sorry…"

There, she finally cut me off, a deft finger pressed to my lips. A wrinkle of humor curled her mouth. "No needless apologies, my champion. I love it. I love you for thinking of us. This is far more than I ever dreamed of, just as you have been far more than I ever imagined."

My knees went weak with relief, which left me clutching her arms for support. But then I remembered the little box in my hands, and let my weakness drive me to one knee. Her eyes went so wide I could not miss the shock in them. Sure, we discussed this, but never gave it a timeline. But I knew, with a certainty that I felt to the very depths of my soul, that I wanted to commit myself now. No wasted days wondering. I was so committed to taking this fall that I held no part of myself back, heart wide open.

"Jaqueline Sauveterre, there's no part of me that doesn't love you. Past, present, all of me is yours. Would you be willing to let future me love you for the rest of our lives?"

She crumpled into my arms, nodding even as her hands threaded into my hair and dragged me in for a kiss. I felt her yes thrum through me as if I had been dropped inside the engine of a race car at the start line, roaring, vibrating, absolutely singing with power. It blew out the tiny flicker of joy I felt the first time I risked my heart, obliterated the pain of eventual loss. In its place, she ignited a surge of emotion so overpowering, I knew I would never be the same.

I embraced her there for a long time, greedy mouths too busy for further words. Respect for her and my kind neighbors kept me from escalating things, though I felt pretty certain we were going to consummate our new commitment to each other as soon as we found some privacy. But when we finally broke apart, she barely let her lips leave mine before whispering "Yes," into my open mouth.

Stealing her for another kiss, I let that breathy word linger in our joined mouths. Savored it slowly, wanting this memory to last a lifetime. Only the ring box still clutched in one fist kept me from dawdling further. Letting her go just enough to pull it around between us, I used my thumb to flick open the lid.

"I know it's not much, but I figured it would work until I could afford better. Putting earnest money down on the house kinda killed my budget."

"Shhh, it is perfect." She looked down at what I offered her, and I felt tears hit the web of my hand. As if it might break, she carefully plucked the tiny ring from the box. Jo had helped me hunt for something suitable, owing to needing to be at the show for Jaque, but I thought we'd done damn well for the last minute. Though the band was plain gold, two tiny silver fleur de lis bracketed a central blue sapphire cut into a heart. My heart, facetted to catch the sunlight we knelt in like two supplicants at the gates of heaven. "I will never want more."

Then her eyes met mine, the happiness in them warming me from the inside out. "Would you put it on?"

Took a lot of concentration to grasp the ring without dropping it, as my hands began to shake from a combination of joy and relief. But take it I did, holding it grasped with my thumb and first two fingers as she held out a steady hand. She watched as I threaded it over her fingertip, then pressed forward, hastening the moment. It slid on as if it belonged there, making me heave a sigh of relief. Guessing at a size had been a real risk.

I kind of expected her to look at it some more, maybe take a photo to share with her friends. Instead, she looked up at me, promise in her eyes. The promise that waited there even when I was too blind to see it. "I will never take it off," she swore before burying her hand in my hair again. I didn't even flinch when a few strands caught on the setting, thrilling at her touch. "Now, unless we are taking possession of this darling house immediately, I do believe you should take me somewhere more private. For I want to know what it feels like to wear your ring, and nothing more."

On that note, I shot to my feet, taking her with me. Her legs wrapped around my waist as I scooted her higher on my body, and I managed to get us out the door without crashing into anything. When I deposited her in the passenger seat with a perfunctory kiss, she giggled, egging me on with a well-placed stroke over the zipper on my jeans. Though I growled with excitement, I fished out my phone and tossed it in her lap without yielding to the temptation in her laughing eyes.

"I'm going to take you back to your place and make love to you until I can't move anymore. But you get to text Jo and let her know we're going to be delayed. She's making dinner for us."

While she went still, likely weighing the options in her mind, I closed the door. Moving around the truck to take my seat, I scrubbed my hands through my hair with a violence bordering on masochism. The sensation did nothing to help me calm down, but I faked a calm smile as I turned over the engine. Only Jaque's hand on my arm helped at all, this touch meant to comfort rather than thrill.

"Aaron, I think perhaps we should go see your family." Gentle fingers stroked from inner elbow to wrist, drawing my eyes along the path she created on my skin. When she stopped, I looked up, willing to follow her lead anywhere. "I am committing to them as well as you, and I would like to thank them for their help."

Nodding carefully, I focused on steering us up one drive, then down the other. We could have walked, which might have helped calm my libido. But as I parked the truck in my accustomed spot near the trailers, I discovered that it wouldn't have done me a damn bit of good. Jaque shoved up the center console, slid across the empty expanse of seat, and plastered her body into the space between the steering wheel and me. Nails curled into the back of my neck as she nipped at my lips. One of my hands clutched her closer, the other fumbling for the seat controls to give her enough room to move. In seconds, she straddled my lap, need pressed to need, mouths a hairsbreadth from each other.

"We will fulfill our obligations to our family, Aaron." God, I loved that she called them our family. My hands tightened on her hips, pulling her close enough that she could feel all of me. "But make no mistake, I intend to get you out of your pants as soon as possible."

Soleil growled in the back seat, clearly responding to the mood in the truck, but neither of us moved to hush her. No, we stared at each other, frozen but for panting breaths until Jaque broke the silence. "Too much?"

I grinned so hard my cheeks hurt, loving that the question she once would have asked in earnest was now said so playfully. "Give me more," I answered, hauling her in for a kiss that said all the things man had yet to make strong enough words for. And she did, answering me with a passion that I would strive to match for the rest of my life.

℘Epilogue℘

Jaque

Lyric stood stock still as I tightened the girth on her saddle one more notch, her posture one of anticipation. We stood in the sunshine just inside the barn doors at the Gallant Company farm, activity swirling around us as jousters arrived for their weekend practice. I would not be participating, thank all the saints in heaven. No, Lyric and I were heading to the arena for a private lesson with Josephine, before the chaos truly began.

Not that my heart understood that. No, it thudded with sludgy fear, so unlike the bright joys of the last month. I tried to channel the happy memories as I led Lyric outside and began the slow walk up the hill to the arena.

We were days away from moving into the farm next door, a bittersweet ending and even sweeter beginning beckoning. Though I hated packing the little cottage, it would be easier to sell Frenchy and Lily's property if I were not there. Not that I stayed there much, as Aaron and I spent our time working on the new bungalow, and all the surrounding outbuildings. My commercial carriages were all that remained to move, once we finished cleaning out Buttercup's old abode. When I signed the contract to buy the carriage company, my horses were moved to the new pastures at the Company farm, Lyric given a stall in the barn until we could find time to do repairs at our own place. Much easier to manage my life with everything in one place, and I could spend more time wrapped up in Aaron's arms at the end of the day.

Then there was the weekend in Aiken that I joined the Company for, reuniting with Harv and Joyce over dinner. We stayed an extra day, going for a drive in the Hitchcock Wood with their four-in-hand of Dutch Harness horses. Though the weather was chilly and damp, that time together healed the small rift left when Joyce had groped Aaron inappropriately. Joyce even let me take the reins for a time, prompting Aaron to inquire if I would be needing more horses so I could have my own hitch. I demurred immediately.

While I could drive the four-in-hand along the wide trails without much coaching, I harboured no interest in trying anything at speed. One horse, one magnificent mare, to be specific, was more than enough.

Speaking of that magnificent mare, Lyric and I also enjoyed another lesson with Lillian, elevating our communication to hitherto unknown heights. Challenging ourselves always brought us closer, a thought I tried to cling to as I crested the hill and walked into the arena where Jo waited. She sat on the edge of the huge mounting block that the knights used to climb aboard their draft horses, calm as a mirror still pond. We had grown closer over the last month, united in a hundred mutual efforts. From caring for all the horses, to working on the new place and developing marketing ideas for my own company, each moment gave me reassurance. Jo would let no one fail if she could help it. It was not in her nature to leave anyone behind, unless she were being challenged. Then, it was best to step back and watch her own the situation.

All of that knowledge eased the knot between my shoulder blades. As did the camaraderie that developed as we spent hours perusing the internet for wedding ideas. While we were still no closer to making serious plans, she was beginning to relax, no longer nervous over the various aspects involved. Bart had laid down a challenge which worked to motivate her as well. They now had a date picked out, the weekend after the home faire ended, and the deadline galvanized Jo like nothing else.

But that prompted her to challenge me, now that we had a weekend with everyone home. Past time for me to get back on the horse, quite literally. Still, I was sweating as much with anxiety as from the hill climb as I came to a stop in front of my friend.

"You ladies ready?" she asked, voice gentle yet implacable as she stood.

I met her eyes and swallowed hard, trying to force a smile as I twisted the reins in my hands. "Lyric, I am sure, is beyond ready. I confess, I am not as confident as she."

Jo did not answer my smile, quite serious as she walked around us, inspecting our equipment with her usual thoroughness. Though I had not used our riding equipment in more than a decade, I had kept it clean, conditioned, and ready for the day my nerve would return. She would find no fault there, or in Lyric, the mare still fit for chasing dreams.

I remained the weak link, even though I dressed the part. My helmet alone felt familiar, but it had been so long since I wore the rest of the kit that I felt like a fraud. Though my old chaps still fit, they rubbed in places, my skin unused to the pressure.

"Well, you both look good," Jo encouraged, finally smiling. "We should definitely take some pictures as we go. You two seriously are masters of matching. Rowan and I need to step up our game!"

The teasing compliment startled me into a laugh. She was not wrong. We were purple on black in every direction, from Lyric's polo wraps, saddle pad and woven ribbon browband, to my helmet cover and gloves. One could easily mistake us for a tack shop advert. "I confess, between my weakness for pretty things for Lyric, and Papa's determination to spoil me, we have more purple in our wardrobe than not. Though, I have seen you in your jousting finery, Jo, and you are no slouch either."

She grinned with justifiable pride, drawing her shoulders back. "Yes, well, we all have our weaknesses. Some women like shoes, or jewelry. You and I shop for our horses instead." Then she threw me a sly look, poking me gently in the arm. "Now that you don't look like you're facing a firing squad, how about we get you on your pretty mare?"

To that, I laughed again, though a bit weakly. Disheartening to know my nerves were so very transparent. But reassuring to know that my friend saw through the façade and thought no less of me. I put a hand on Lyric's neck as I led her toward the mounting block and said a prayer that my noble mare would feel the same.

After fussing with girth and stirrups, I climbed the sturdy steps, grateful the heavy block did not shake beneath my quivering legs. My palms were damp as I pulled on my gloves, and my shirt clung uncomfortably as sweat sprung up along my shoulders. Swallowing down a knot of apprehension that I hated myself for, I stepped to the edge and took up the reins with a handful of Lyric's thick mane. For the briefest second, I grasped more than her mane, but a chunk of our history, a reminder of a hundred happy memories in the saddle. This moment should have been full of nostalgia, of power and promise. Before I could lift a foot to the stirrup, Jo cleared her throat. Desperate for any sort of reassurance, I froze and stared at my friend, standing on the other side of Lyric to counterweight the stirrup.

"You've got to breathe. I know it's not easy, but you won't do Lyric much good if you pass out."

Looking up at the sky, I drew in a breath, the air shuddering down my throat on its way to my burning lungs. After a few more, the bands around my chest loosened. The knot of my fingers relaxed around Lyric's mane, and she took a big breath in response. I might have taken a moment to berate myself for pouring my tension into her, if not for Jo's timely intervention.

"You don't have to do this, you know." She spoke in a whisper, keeping the secret of my weakness even when we were alone. While I had told Aaron about my lessons with Jo, I kept my fear close to my breast. "You're a good partnership without riding, Jaque. So why do you want this? What makes it so important that you're willing to risk this kind of fear?"

My chin trembled and tears sprang up, fury I had not known I harboured finally spilling over. "I miss it, Jo. I miss being close, and it was stolen from us with that accident. She could have died, we both could have died, and it is not fair! And I never even tried to take it back! Never once. I wasted all these years with her!"

Jo quirked the oddest little smile. "Well, wasted might be a little harsh. The pair of you have kicked a lot of ass."

Managing a damp laugh, I pushed the tears from my cheeks, the suede of my gloves harsh against the faint sunburn on my cheeks. Hours fixing fence at the new place quickly chased away the winter pale of my skin, even with sunblock. "Yes, I suppose we have. But still, I have been a chicken. I thought I was doing this so I could ride with Aaron, but no. This is for her and I alone. I want to be close to her again."

Through all of my emotional upheaval, Lyric stood unmoving. But in the silence that followed my impassioned outburst, when the truth finally found the open air, she responded. Her hooves remained planted as her neck curved around. Nostrils fluttering with a calm exhale, she hooked me behind the knee with her chin and pulled hard. Grabbing the saddle for balance, I shuffled right up against her ribs, almost toppling under her strength. Then she blew a hearty sneeze, putting an exclamation point on her demand.

Jo laughed. "Well, on that note, I think we have our marching orders. The mare has spoken!"

"Indeed," I giggled, amusement now free from my frustration. Fear still lurked in the shadows, but it was an unwelcome guest I felt one step closer to evicting. "And we betide us all if we do not listen!"

So, I regained the reins, took firm hold of my courage, and swung aboard my oldest, dearest friend. The motion came easily, as if we had ridden yesterday, not more than a decade ago. I settled into the depths of the dressage saddle, my body quivering as much in anticipation as anxiety. Jo slid my foot into the right stirrup for me, something I watched her do many times for the knights, which gave the action a peculiar sort of honour.

As I exhaled my way deeper into the saddle, the breath gusted over the nervous sweat along my forearms. The reins fell into place between my fingers, that connection unchanging in its intimacy even from the closer vantage. Lyric answered me with the gentlest curving of her neck, stretching into the touch, and sighed. Tears threatened at her acceptance, even as I worked to settle my leg along her barrel. But I did not want to miss a moment of this homecoming, even if my tears were from happiness.

A snapping sound drew my attention, and I found Jo waiting patiently at Lyric's head. She fiddled with the clip on a long line, slowly uncoiling the supple rope until it lay ribboned back and forth in her hand. I watched as if transfixed, clinging to the sure, soothing movements. Anything to keep from overthinking the moments still to come. When she looked up, eyes squinted against the sun even beneath her ball cap, I saw a gentle determination there that quieted my nerves. My friend would not let us fail, if she could help it. And to be fair, I do not believe even the universe would deny Josephine Bowen when she set her heart to a task.

"Okay, ladies, here's the plan." She looked us both over, including my mare in her explanation. "I'm going to put you on the long line. Not because I think she needs the management, or that you can't control her. Lyric clearly wants you up there, and no one could ever fault your communication with each other. But this first lesson isn't about the technicalities. This lesson is about connection. About reminding yourself that you belong up there.

So, I'm going to help you two be able to focus on each other. Does that sound good?"

I nodded, not sure I could speak around the lump in my throat. Quickly, but with infinitely courteous hands, Jo threaded the line through one ring of the bit, over Lyric's head, then clipped it on the opposite ring. She did it so smoothly, I barely felt the movements in the reins. But in the next instant, she tugged those reins with the intent to take them away. For a moment, my fingers turned to claws, clinging to the supple leather as if to the edge of a cliff.

"Trust me, Jaque," she murmured, maintaining her own tug, all without disturbing Lyric in the slightest. "And if you can't trust me, trust her."

When she tipped her chin toward the mare, I realized the foolishness of my panic. Lyric's ears swiveled to and fro, following the energy moving between Jo and I, but they always returned to me. My beautiful girl always looked to me for her cue, and my actions all but screamed at her that something was wrong. Not a burden she needed to bear.

Dropping the reins as if they burned my fingers, I put my hands to better use petting the strong crest of Lyric's neck. Jo quickly twisted the reins, then secured them through the throatlatch of the bridle, ensuring they would not come undone. The Pony Club kid in me nodded approval, adding another measure of reassurance to our endeavor. She knew how to keep us safe in even the smallest ways.

At long last, she stepped back to the end of the line. I made sure of my posture, heels under hips, back straight, eyes looking ahead. But Jo's faintly amused tone reminded me that I had forgotten an important step before moving. "And exhale…"

Chagrined, but undeterred, I did as she instructed. My shoulders came down, and like magic, my legs seemed to fall into just the right place. In the next moment, Lyric began to move, her walk big and swinging, so much more mature than when we last came together. Both of us had changed over the years, hips broadening, bodies more purposefully athletic than simply blessed with the energy and flexibility of youth. But what had not changed was the absolute feeling of homecoming.

Tears came again, and I let them fall down my temples as I looked up into the purely blue sky. Sun caressed my face as my body loosened, releasing all the mental tension that had built up. "*Retrouvailles*," I whispered, over and over, using the word to soften the lump in my throat, fear melting away with every iteration.

But as this is no Hallmark movie, I must tell the full tale rather than end on that beautiful moment. Not three strides after the tears ceased, Lyric tripped. Over what, no one knows, but as my hips dropped to follow her motion, adrenaline speared me with heartless cruelty. My hands clawed for the pommel of the saddle and her mane, curling me into a ball of panic. My spine arched painfully, shoulders dropping toward Lyric's even as my legs went rigid and clutching. In response, she threw herself up into the next stride as if to catch me, before coming to a halt with her neck raised high.

Her actions should have been enough to pull me out of the fear. Few would have a horse so determined to keep their rider on in the midst of so much overwhelming panic. Many might have dumped me and fled. Instead, I buckled further, arms wrapping around her neck as shame lanced through me with the burn of lightning. The joyful tears now scalded; my lungs bruised by the heart galloping away with my emotions.

I hated myself for the weakness. For the inability to overcome the fear, to be what Lyric needed me to be. After all, had I not done so during our actual wreck? I did not hesitate then, thinking first of her injuries, ignoring my own. But no, I could not find my way out of the blackness closing in on my vision as beads of sweat soaked into my shirt.

Jo's cool fingers wrapping around my elbow shocked me back to awareness. Suddenly, I felt Lyric's heaving ribs, as if she were the one caught in my panic. I sat up too quickly, head swimming as I shoved my feet back into the stirrups.

"I am sorry! So sorry! I am an idiot. Forgive me?" I asked Jo, though my hands were stroking the same apology into Lyric's neck. "I promise you, I am not inept. Thank you for stopping her."

My friend released her grip on my arm only when I met her eyes. "I didn't stop her. She stopped of her own accord. I told you, she wants you up there."

I dashed tears away on the back of my gloves for the second time as I smiled down at Lyric. "Oh, *fille merveilleuse*, I do not deserve your heart." Then I looked to Jo, my smile cracking, sure she would regret her offer to help me. "Nor do I deserve yours, my friend. Forgive me?"

Jaw out thrust, Jo went from soft with sympathy to warrior hard. "I'm not going to forgive you for fighting through your fear, Jaque. I may challenge you, push you, and even wait you out when it gets hard, but don't you dare apologize for fighting."

Taken aback at the snarl in her words, I straightened in the saddle. "But…"

She held up a hand to stop me, then fixed me with a stare I recognized from Aaron. One that called on the warrior in me. "No. There will be no apologies. You're having to dig out old wounds, and the scars aren't going to give up easily. My whole life, I've been more afraid to not try than to actually fall, because the rewards have always been the greater on the other side of that fear. And somehow you decided, despite your valid fear, that this would be worth the risk. That you wanted it badly enough to try. That is the bravest thing I can possibly imagine, Jaque, and you won't cheapen your efforts with needless apologies."

I sat there for who knows how long, feeling her words hit like a hundred needles. Some of them found their mark in my old wounds, draining away the infection that had lingered far too long. Others lanced my recent panic, pulling out the poison of my self-doubts. But a few sun bright lancets hit me deep in the heart, pointing right at my courage. Rousing it from where it slumbered, as if a great beast were waking with a stretch and reclaiming its territory with a growl.

"Yes," I agreed, purposefully letting go of the tension that hummed through every tendon and ligament with primal fear. "Yes, I want this." Pushing out a determined breath, I pet Lyric's neck with both hands, no longer apologizing. Only thanking. "She is worth the risk of falling."

Swatting my knee with a bit more force than necessary, Jo grinned. "I think she'd say the same thing about you, my friend."

Then we went back to work as if nothing occurred. Jo put me through my paces at the walk at first, having me stretch toward Lyric's ears, swiveling toward her tail, touching my toes. Twice more, Lyric tripped, and the storm of fear threatened. But each time, I pushed it back, grounding out the blackening burn in the deepest anchor I could claim. Love.

Love for Lyric, most certainly. But I had so much more love in my life now. Sisters in my friends, a lover in Aaron, a family in Gallant Company. Nor could I discount my own self-love. Much as I did this for Lyric, I did this for myself. As much as the rest of them meant the world to me, I myself was worth the risk of falling.

When we moved into the trot, all the years of training in the carriage, and all the hours we put into Lyric's fitness, reminded me of another joy. The thrill of burning muscles as our bodies rose and fell in counterpoint, her power fueling mine. There, she tripped just once. When I responded by closing my leg to send her forward, the tripping disappeared entirely. Our resolve now united, I laughed in bliss. We were flying!

We ended shortly thereafter, as the jousters came through the gate for their practice. Two by two, they came, Aaron and Bart on the spare horses, then Alex and John on their regular mounts. Jo invited me to stay, if I felt comfortable, and unwilling to part from my lovely mare just yet, I agreed. She unwound my reins and offered them back to me with all due solemnity.

"These reins are not what connects the two of you, Jaque. Don't forget that."

I nodded and smiled, feeling the years of love between Lyric and I that steered us through every obstacle. "Thank you for reminding us, sister."

With a pleased grin, she unclipped the long line and walked away, winding it up as she went. Lyric's weight shifted as if she meant to follow. "Stand." Immediately, she settled, tentatively stretching her neck until she felt my hands. I kept them soft, following, maintaining our connection without asking for a thing. Then she sighed, and I felt my body come into even closer sync with hers.

"*Retrouvailles.*" I whispered one last time, my eyes falling closed to better enjoy this refinding of ourselves. We were reunited, whole but for a few stubborn splinters I would need to work to remove before I healed completely. But I knew with every bit of my soul that we would get there. I wanted it more than anything else, even more than our competing. No ribbon, no accomplishment would ever compare to this reunion of souls.

So we sat and watched our new family go to their own work. Lyric only worried over the armour sounds for the first few passes, but as I studied the riders with fascination, she relaxed. Still taking her cue from me, even after the upheaval of the last hour. I cherished that realization as much as any that Jo helped us find, for we found it on our own.

Aaron and Bart did not joust, merely rode about in their armour and made trotting passes at the quintain to accustom General and Ivan to the sounds and concussion. The white grey gelding, General, carried himself in a perpetual state of disgruntlement, neck flat, ears canted outward, and head tilted away from the blow of the lance. Aaron stopped and patted him after every run, Jo stepping in to give the gelding a cookie in reward. Before long, the wrinkles of worry over his eye faded, and his steps grew jaunty, as if he were proud of his work.

Ivan required a more deft hand. He did not want to trot, and fought Bart every step of the way, rooting at the bit and gapping his mouth at the contact. Bart used his leg to push the gelding into circles, spending the momentum without breaking into a canter. When no longer fighting, Bart would straighten him out and let the big freight train chug down the lane. He smacked the quintain with his hand instead, which hardly got a rise out of the gelding. After my own experiences with Ivan, Bart had my sympathies. While Ivan did not fear much, he was strong willed. Whoever rode him needed an equally strong will, but a soft hand, else he would fight all the harder.

The actual jousting passes seemed a little anticlimactic after the ups and downs of my morning. Alex recovered from every blow with an amazing flexibility, as if his spine were made of springs. And John rode so relaxed, it looked as though the hits traveled through him without resistance. Both men doted on their mounts, a sight that never failed to warm my heart. While neither were lifetime horsemen, like their Captains, they were unfailingly kind. Kindness could cover a multitude of other sins.

Speaking of kind, Aaron approached as his knights went to the block to have their helmets removed. While he smiled at me, his eyes were on Lyric, who studied him closely. "Ladies, may we approach?"

I smiled in return, her pricked ears of no worry to me as long as her spine remained relaxed. "You may, good sirs."

"How was your lesson?" he asked as he swung General in beside me. Sweat had his hair plastered down in some places, and standing up in others, so I lifted the reins and cued Lyric with my leg to step her closer. While she took a moment to gather herself, she answered readily, stopping as soon as I asked. As simply as that, I felt another of the splinters dissolve with the proof of our connection.

 This made my smile radiant when I finally turned it on my knight in shining armour, his smile intensifying as I plucked off a glove and finger-combed his hair into some sort of obedience. "It was exactly what we needed, thank you."

Further conversation halted as the rest of the knights approached, making a circle of horses and riders. Aaron spoke candidly, offering suggestions to help with their hits while Bart gave pointers to improve their riding. The men soaked up every word, Alex asking serious questions for clarification, while John poked fun at his shortcomings in order to lighten the mood. When Bart threw him a stern look, he finished with a promise to work on his leg position in the next few weeks.

"Speaking of the next few weeks," Aaron took up the reins of the conversation again, steering them back on track. "While we are out in Pennsylvania, I need you two to cover the pub gathering at Auld Warhorse. Think you can handle a night of looking pretty and chatting up the public?"

Alex's expression twisted in on itself, moustache lifting in a sneer. "Can I? Certainly. Will I enjoy it? Unlikely."

Shoving at his rigid friend, John laughed. "Oh, come now, the ladies will fawn over you. Stop being so dramatic. You might just enjoy yourself." Then the red-head looked at Aaron, a rare expression of determination overtaking his general good humor. "Caroline will be there as part of the royal court, so you can count on me. And I'll drag the stick-in-the-mud along, whether he likes it or not." Then he bumped his rotund Belgian with both heels to wake up the sleepy sorrel gelding, before turning away with a parting taunt. "Come on, Alex. Caroline is making stuffed shells for dinner, and I don't want to be late. If you're lucky, maybe she'll let you organize the Tupperware afterward."

Alex barked a reluctant laugh, turning his black Clydesdale, J.T., to follow in the Belgian's substantial wake. But he caught

Aaron's eye on the way out. "I'll be there. You know the Company can always count on me."

"We do." Aaron answered, watching them go with a shake of his head. "I swear, I've never seen two such different people be such good friends."

"Sometimes, we need our opposite to balance us out," Jo interjected even as she patted Ivan's neck, then looked up at Bart with the kind of love I wished everyone in the world were lucky enough to find. "Sometimes, we need our mirror." Then she turned for the gate, Bart on her heels without a single word being said.

"And sometimes, we need our navigator," Aaron murmured, holding his hand out for mine. I took it, reveling in how he always reached for me. "What do you say, my lady? Shall we ride together and see where the road takes us?"

Heart full of so many good emotions that they flooded out every ounce of old doubt, I nodded my agreement. We carefully turned as one, our hands remaining linked even when the path challenged us. But as we rode back down to the barn, I knew that our linked hands were not what coupled us together like a pair in harness, any more than the reins connected me to Lyric.

Love alone made the bonds that would see us all through, no matter what came before or next.

Fini

⟨Coming Next⟩

Sir Alex Black is an enigma, and he likes it that way. He can go from the boardroom to the lyst field without breaking a sweat, but he keeps a part of himself in the dark, hidden even from those he cares for most. Though he plays the villain in Gallant Company the rigid aloofness he has maintained for so many years is beginning to soften within the confines of his found family.

A chance brush with a fiery dancer threatens to burn away the boundaries he has spent his whole life constructing. The icy cool he is known for is threatened with every encounter.

Will he flee or will he fall in this tale of
JUXTAPOSED HEARTS

Connect on **Facebook**
to get series updates and teasers on all the upcoming books!
Just search for **Gallant Hearts Gather Here** & join the fun.
I'll see you there!

Check us out online at
www.gallanthearts.com

🕯Appendix🕯

French

épater - to wow, to stun, to amaze

faire des pirouettes sur le nombril- Literally means "making pirouettes around the belly button" and is a nice sounding idiom for sex

fais de beaux rêves- sweet dreams

garçons, soyez poli- boys, be polite

je te verrai dans mes rêves- I'll see you in my dreams

je vous prie- You're welcome

merveilleuse- marvelous

mon amant- my lover

mon canard- my duck

mon coeur- my heart

mon tresor- my treasure

mon coquin- my rascal

ma fille- my girl

ma petit (chou)- my little (cabbage)

oui, c'est bon- yes, it's good

retrouvailles- meaning something like "refindings", this word refers to the reunion you would have with someone you care deeply for but whom you have not seen in a long time.

Sainte mère, Sacre, Cris- sacres, or sacraments, are swear words in the Quebecois culture

son coeur est bon- his heart is good

sucre- sugar

voler sur- fly on

vous êtes belle- you are beautiful

Glossary

JOUSTING

Buffe- bolts on beneath the grand guard, deflecting blows that skip up toward the neck and head

Cuirass- refers to both the breastplate and backplate that sandwiches together to protect the jousters torso

Cuisse- section that covers the thigh

Gorget- protects the throat

Grand Guard- A target bolted to the jousters left shoulder to receive blows, often gridded to catch and break the lance more effectively

Grapper- metal back plate on the lance that supports it against the torso

Helm- essential protection for the head, with several hinged sections to allow it to fit closely to the skull and jaw.

Lyst- the roped off lanes in which the jousters make their passes

Manfair- a gauntlet that covers the jousters left hand, just in case a blow goes awry

Pauldron- covers the shoulder

Realgestech- full contact style of jousting in which the goal is to break your lance or unhorse your opponent

Vamplate- metal front plate on the lance that protects the hand

Brayette- chainmail and leather skirt meant to protect the front of the pelvic region without sacrificing movement

Want to see full contact jousting near you? Here are a few companies to check out!

Knights of Valour
http://www.knightsofvalour.ca

Knights of the Rose
http://theknightsoftherose.com

New Riders of the Golden Age
http://www.warhorse.com

Knights of Mayhem
http://www.knightsofmayhem.com

For the excitement of combined driving, please visit

https://americandrivingsociety.org

for a listing of competitions near you!

And because I was once a commercial carriage driver, like our Jaque, I humbly request that you visit your nearest town and take a carriage ride for yourself.

Don't forget to tip your driver and thank your horse!

Acknowledgements

To my Alpha-Beta, Jessica Post. The original. I hope you are still enjoying the ride!

To my Bravo-Beta, Laura Hargis. Can't wait to beta YOUR books. Get on it!

To my Charlie-Beta, Tonya Smith. Living the dream is better than reading about it. So happy for you!

To my Dirty-Beta, Kat Moran, I hope you are ready for more glitter! It's coming soon!

To my Ego Beta, Amy Hawes Coger. Seriously, without your encouragement, this would have taken so much longer. Welcome to the Company!

J.A. Campbell, thanks for stepping into the role of editor. Your heart shows in the work.

Also, Nancy Kay Clark, proofer extraordinaire! (All remaining errors are my fault alone!)

All the Kickstarter contributors, who made this book possible: Julie, Andrea, Kimberly, Kali, Susie, Pat, Katherine, Tasha, Jen, Sherry, Sharyl, Rich, Nancy, Synthia, Carrin, Kirsten, Vivian, Mindy, Sue, Erin, Jessica, Kristin, Megan, Laurie, Melissa, Tonya, Shannon, Auburn, Laura, Amy, Hanah, and Diana.

To my husband, Nog.
Thank you. Forever. I'd be lost without you.